An Unconventional Officer

Book 1 of the Peninsular War Saga

By

Lynn Bryant

This book is dedicated to my family.
To George William Bryant and Iris Bryant, parents who
always believed in me.
To my kids, Jon and Anya, who have had to share their lives
with Lord Wellington.
And to Richard, without whom literally none of this would
have been possible.
Thank you all.

About the Author

Lynn Bryant was born and raised in London's East End. She studied History at University and had dreams of being a writer from a young age. Since this was clearly not something a working-class-girl-made-good could aspire to, she had a variety of careers including a librarian, NHS administrator, relationship counsellor, manager of an art gallery and owner of an Irish dance school before realising that most of these were just as unlikely as being a writer and took the step of publishing her first book.

She now lives in the Isle of Man and is married to a man who understands technology, which saves her a job, and has two grown children and a Labrador. History is still a passion, with a particular enthusiasm for the Napoleonic era and the sixteenth century. When not writing she walks her dog, reads anything that's put in front of her and makes periodic and unsuccessful attempts to keep a tidy house.

Acknowledgments

There have been many people who have helped me since I rashly embarked on a career as a writer. Some of them, I did not even know when the first edition of this book was published in 2017 but since then I've received so much help and advice, and what I've learned has gone into the new edition of this book.

Research is a huge part of the writing I do, and I'd like to thank various historians and writers who have helped me with the maddest questions, especially Jacqueline Reiter, Rob Griffith, Rory Muir, Andrew Bamford, Charles Esdaile, Zack White and many others on social media and in person. There will be some I've missed out and I'm sorry but thank you all.

As always, I'd like to thank Mel Logue, Jacqueline Reiter and Kristine Hughes Patrone for reading sections of the work and making helpful suggestions.

Thanks to Richard Dawson, my husband, for his amazing cover, for technical help and for endless support and patience during the writing of this book.

Thanks to my son, Jon and his girlfriend Rachael, for sharing my study during lockdown and completely ignoring my historical mutterings and to my daughter, Anya, for helping to keep me on track when I was really struggling to motivate myself.

The re-editing of this and all the other books would never have happened in the way it has without the intervention of Heather Paisley, my editor, proof-reader and partner-in-crime for more than thirty years. I've always known she was an amazing friend but I'd no idea she was such a good editor. I'm looking forward to working with her on many more books.

Finally, thanks to Oscar, the star of *Writing with Labradors* for sharing my study and bringing me joy.

And in loving memory of Toby and Joey, my old Labradors who have died since I first wrote this book and broke my heart. You will both always be with me in spirit.

Chapter One

It had rained for a week solid. Drill and training were conducted in sodden misery, and after two hours of desperately bad bayonet training with the twenty new recruits to the light company, Sergeant Michael O'Reilly was looking forward to a drink, a meal and dry clothing. He was squelching towards his barracks, when the voice of his officer made him swear under his breath.

"Sergeant, a word."

O'Reilly turned and stomped back to the long two-storey building where the officers' mess was situated. Lieutenant Wheeler was standing in the doorway, looking pleasantly warm and dry. He stood back to let O'Reilly pass him, a grin on his face, and then led the way into the office at the back, which actually belonged to the commander of the 110th. Colonel Dixon was seldom in barracks, and when he was, he tended to conduct most of his business from the comfort of an armchair in the officers' mess, while Major Johnstone, who commanded the first battalion and did most of the work, was currently in London. Lieutenant Wheeler seated himself behind the desk and the sergeant stood to attention, dripping on the floor, and saluted.

"Sir."

"At ease, Sergeant. You're a little wet."

"I am, sir. Had a good afternoon yourself, have you?"

Wheeler laughed. "Sorry," he said. "It's foul, isn't it? Be nice to get back to India, get some sunshine, eh, Sergeant?"

"Apart from the monsoon season, of course, sir," the Irishman said. He liked Johnny Wheeler better than any of the other officers of the 110th. Wheeler was in his late twenties, old for a lieutenant, with no money to purchase a promotion. O'Reilly had served under him in both Europe and India and knew that he was a steady man in a fight and had a good working relationship with his men.

"I've been introducing myself to our two new officers," Wheeler said.

"Oh bloody hell," Michael said gloomily. "Not more of them."

Wheeler grinned. "Now, now, Sergeant, be an optimist. I know we've not had much luck..."

"Sir, what worries me is that one of these baby-faced twats...sorry, I mean young gentlemen... is actually going to stick around long enough to get shipped out to India with us. We've had four of them in six months and every bloody one has been about as much use as a eunuch in a whorehouse and has either sold out or transferred out in a matter of weeks." Michael thought about it. "In fact, I'm fairly convinced that Ensign Rogers actually was a eunuch."

Wheeler was shaking his head, but it was a mild reproof. Michael would not have spoken so frankly to any other officer, but the hard work of managing a company with a chronic shortage of officers for almost eight months had created a bond between them which overrode the usual gulf between officers and NCOs. Michael had been doing the job of an officer and he knew that Wheeler recognised it.

"Sergeant, the light company isn't the easiest command, and the fact that our captain is still stuck in India ill and our major is struggling to staff the rest of his companies doesn't help. And I admit, a lot of them just want to wear a red coat and impress the ladies, so they're not keen to be told the regiment they just bought into is about to go to India and will probably be expected to fight there."

"Well, they should join the bloody militia then," Michael said grimly. "Have these two been told that yet?"

"They have. They're both twenty-one, purchased directly on to lieutenants' commissions, which is fair enough given their age. And they've both been to Oxford..."

"That's useful," Michael said with heavy irony. "Why have we got two of them, we're only one lieutenant short?"

"Because Major Johnstone thinks we need an extra officer given the state of poor Captain Mason's health," Wheeler said. "So we've an extra lieutenant instead of another ensign. If he can't march, we can share the workload."

Michael nodded, appreciating Wheeler's willingness to share information which, as an NCO he really had no right to ask. Some of the other officers of the 110th would have damned his impudence for asking questions, but Wheeler was unfailingly polite. "Fair point, sir."

"They're old friends from childhood, which might work in our favour because if one stays they'll probably both stay. Both have just done around eight weeks basic training with Sir John Moore down at Shorncliffe, which is much better than any of the others have managed, so they can run drills and training. I don't know much about their background yet, although I've a feeling they're local. Both are going to live in barracks, their choice. They're up there now, unpacking; neither has brought a valet."

"Probably means they've spent all their money on their commissions then. What do you want me to do, sir?"

"Get yourself cleaned up and go and introduce yourself. Give them the tour and answer any questions and then let them get settled and I'll see them in the mess for dinner with the rest of the officers. We'll start them on drills tomorrow." Wheeler grinned. "And they can take the early drill. I've earned a lie in."

Michael laughed. "Yes, sir."

"And Sergeant – try not to frighten them off, will you? I'm getting bored with going through this process."

"Do they seem easy to frighten?" Michael asked.

To his surprise, the lieutenant gave the matter serious thought. "Swanson is really pleasant. Interested, keen to learn and I think I could get to like him."

"And the other one?"

"Paul van Daan. He says his father was Dutch, and his mother English. I can't make him out yet." Wheeler shrugged. "There's something about him."

After two days, Michael O'Reilly, who had seen officers come and go, agreed with Lieutenant Wheeler. He found Lieutenant Carl Swanson a pleasant, easy-going young man, with a taste for hard work and an ability to ask intelligent questions, which the sergeant found refreshing in a new officer. It was clear that their training at Shorncliffe had not been wasted. Both seemed competent and reasonably confident with the men. They were on the parade ground each morning for early drill and neither seemed to resent taking advice and instruction from a non-commissioned officer, so it was hard for Michael to pinpoint what he found irritating about Paul van Daan.

Van Daan was a good-looking young man, clean-shaven with fair hair cut shorter than was fashionable, and a pair of penetrating deep blue eyes. The 110th was a relatively new regiment and commissions were inexpensive, so Michael had assumed that both the new officers were short of money, but he revised that opinion quickly. Mr Swanson might have needed to watch his finances, but Paul van Daan had something of the natural arrogance of the very well-born or very wealthy. The fact that he did not trade on it, was almost more annoying. It was hard to fault his behaviour in barracks. He was taller than the average and very fit and strong. Michael's previous experience of young light infantry officers was that they found the long hours of physical training with the men very difficult to start with, but Paul van Daan took everything in his stride.

"What do you make of him, Sergeant?" Lieutenant Wheeler asked, at the end of the first week.

"Which one, sir?"

Wheeler looked at him sternly and Michael grinned. "I don't know, sir," he admitted. "He's certainly not much like any new officer I've come across before. There's something slightly different about him. I mean he seems just as pleasant and polite and eager to learn as his friend. With Mr Swanson I think it's real. With Mr van Daan – I don't know."

"I've got a feeling they're going to stay."

"So have I. And that's a good thing because we need officers. They're both grown men at least, not a couple of pasty-faced sixteen-year-olds." Michael hesitated but he was unable to put into words his sense of something

3

being slightly off about Paul van Daan. "I have a feeling I'm missing something with him," he said finally. "But it's not really my place."

Michael took himself out that evening and shared a meal and a few drinks in the convivial atmosphere of the Boat Inn down by the canal, a popular tavern with the regiment. His fellow NCOs moved on early, and O'Reilly thought about joining them. It was a while since he had wasted his money and a few enjoyable hours at Carrie Megson's house, and he was aware of a nagging sense of wanting a woman. On the other hand, it was money he could put to other uses. He sat on at the Boat trying to make up his mind, and suddenly realised that the two men who were seated at the table in front of him were his new officers.

Michael sighed and got up. Army regulations and traditions were rigid on the subject of NCOs and enlisted men socialising with officers, and he could not go and join them, although he was surprised to realise that he wished that he could. He was interested in the fair young man with the pleasant baritone and eyes which looked as though they were used to scanning bigger horizons, and he would have liked to have shared a drink and got to know him better, but it was time to leave. Michael heard laughter and realised that it was the first time he had heard Paul van Daan really laugh. It was surprisingly infectious. Michael stood watching him, smiling despite himself. He was resisting how much he could probably get to like the man, because the difference in their stations made actual friendship impossible, when Van Daan looked up and saw him and waved him over. Michael approached and saluted.

"Sergeant. All alone?"

"I was with some of the lads, sir, but they've deserted me in search of women."

"Not in the mood?"

"I could be. Not sure if I need a lassie or a new pair of boots more."

"A difficult choice," Van Daan said gravely. "You could join us."

"I can't, sir. Not the done thing."

"I know. It's a pity, though." Paul nodded towards the bar. "We were just admiring the girl behind the bar. Do you know her name?"

"Sally. Sally Crane. Yes, she's a pretty lass." O'Reilly was amused. Sally Crane had a complicated relationship with his friend and fellow sergeant, Rory Stewart. For two years they had shared a bed whenever Stewart was in barracks, although Michael knew very well that this did not stop Stewart finding other diversions when he was posted abroad, and he had heard rumours that Sally also kept herself well entertained. Rory was home at present, and Michael doubted that Sally would show an interest in this arrogant boy. "You could give it a try, sir."

"You sound sceptical."

"Sally's a law unto herself. Honestly, I'd take yourself off to Carrie Megson's, sir, if you've got the urge. Her girls are nice and clean and they like the officers. I can give you directions."

4

"I know the way," Van Daan said, and Michael had no doubt of it. "You seem very sure about this lass."

"You'll not get far with her, sir, most of us have tried at one time or another, but she's awful choosy."

"Married?"

Michael hesitated and then ignored the promptings of his better self. It would do Lieutenant van Daan no harm to receive a set down from Sergeant Stewart's strong-minded girlfriend. "No. I think she has an understanding, but she's her own woman."

"That's what I like to hear, Sergeant. I'll let you know how I get on."

His grin was infectious and Michael O'Reilly, cynical after four years of army life and a lot of young officers, could feel himself resisting the pull of the other man's charm. "She won't do it for money, sir," he said.

"If I paid her, it wouldn't be much of a challenge," Paul said. "Good night, Sergeant."

He got up and walked to the bar. O'Reilly stood by the door watching him for a while. He was leaning on it, talking to the girl. Sally continued to clean the glasses, throwing back an occasional remark. She did not seem overly impressed.

"Care for a wager, Sergeant?" Carl Swanson said quietly beside him. He too was watching his friend.

"I'd be fleecing you, sir."

"Then we'll make it a small one. Just for fun. A shilling says that when she goes up to bed she'll take him with her."

O'Reilly smiled. Lieutenant Swanson was easy to like and far more straightforward than his friend. "Not unless he's planning on holding her down, sir."

"Good God, don't say that to him, he takes a very poor view of rape, Sergeant."

"I'm glad to hear it, sir, I do myself. But I'm going to take your wager, even though I should know better than to gamble with an officer, because Sally Crane is not going to give it away to your lad, no matter how pretty he is. She eats pretty young officers for breakfast."

"I rather imagine Paul would enjoy that," Carl said placidly, and it was so unexpected that O'Reilly laughed out loud. He looked sideways at the younger man.

"I hope you stay, sir," he said. "I could work with you."

"I'm pleased to hear that, Sergeant. You off?"

"I am. Shouldn't be here drinking with the officers. But I'll make sure I get a report from Charlie as to how he gets on." Michael hesitated. "What makes you so sure? You don't know her."

"I don't need to," Carl Swanson said, amused eyes on the girl at the bar. "I've been watching him since he was around sixteen and you need to believe me, Sergeant, if he's made up his mind that she's going to bed with him, then she is. And don't ask me how he does it because I'd pay to know. I'd make it more than a shilling, but I'd be robbing you."

Michael shook his head and looked over at Paul van Daan again. He was still speaking to Sally, smiling at her and Michael watched him for a moment. "It would do him good to get a set down from her. Is he always this full of it?"

Michael could have bitten his tongue the moment he said it, but Lieutenant Swanson merely smiled.

"All his bloody life," he said. "And you're right, it would. But it's not happening tonight, Sergeant. I'm waiting to meet the girl who sends Mr van Daan about his business."

"Sorry, sir, forgot who I was talking to."

"Don't worry about it, you're going to pay me a shilling to make up for it. Goodnight, Sergeant."

Michael turned to go. Suddenly he heard a woman laugh. He turned back and looked across at the bar. Sally Crane had put down her cloth and was resting her chin on her hand, leaning forward to give Paul van Daan a clear uninterrupted view down the front of her dress. Paul was not looking in that direction. He was looking into her eyes and smiling, and she was smiling back as if he had just said something that pleased her enormously. After a moment she moved away, and then came back with a bottle and two cups. She placed them on the bar between her and the young officer and poured, then sat down and picked up her cup. Paul van Daan did the same. O'Reilly looked across at Carl Swanson. He was laughing and holding up a shilling, which he then slid back into his pocket.

"It's just a drink, sir," Michael said although he was suddenly less certain.

Carl reached for his glass and looked across at the couple sitting talking at the bar. "I give her less than an hour," he said. "'Night, Sergeant."

The moment stayed with Michael. He was happy in the regiment, although he had come to it as so many Irish did, in desperate times. His father was a schoolmaster of very respectable birth, and Michael had been a student of classics in Dublin when he became involved with the rebellion under Wolf Tone. As the uprising collapsed, Michael found himself at twenty, a hunted man, and slipped quietly over to England to find a recruiting party. He had never heard of the 110th and did not care but had signed up under a new surname. A commission had never been an option but despite the poor pay and conditions, Michael did not regret his decision.

Michael rose quickly to the rank of sergeant and learned to adapt his manners between the mostly uneducated and illiterate enlisted men and the commissioned officers, who made shameless use of his intelligence and education without ever wondering how he came to be serving in the ranks. There were many Irishmen in the ranks, which gave Michael an anonymity which suited him. After more than four years of service, he had developed the NCO's fine contempt for the incompetence of some of the officers who acquired their commissions and promotions by purchase. There were exceptions. He liked and respected the quiet effectiveness of Johnny Wheeler and thought it a shame that he was unlikely to rise much higher in the ranks, but he would not have considered Wheeler a friend. There was an unbridgeable gulf between officers and men and Michael O'Reilly had never before regretted it. Laughing with Paul van Daan in the inn on the previous evening he realised with some surprise that it bothered him that he was unable to sit and share a drink with the boy, only a few years his junior, who was beginning to look as though he was going to remain with the regiment.

Both officers were on the parade ground early the following morning, and Michael watched without interference as Paul van Daan took the lead and put the light company through a gruelling drill, moving them from line to square and back. He was unusually meticulous, taking them back through the manoeuvre long after most officers would have been satisfied. Michael watched the steady blue eyes as the men ran the drill yet again and felt an unexpected jolt of satisfaction. He realised that he very much wanted this man to stay and to go to India with them in two months. He would like to see what Paul van Daan could achieve on a battlefield. He would either get himself killed really quickly, or he would be an officer to be proud of, and Michael wanted to see which it would be.

Michael found no opportunity to ask about Van Daan's attempt to bed Sally Crane, although he was sure that she would have sent him away. The lad was good looking and definitely had a way with him, but Sally was too experienced to fall for his charm. He reminded himself to ask Charlie when he was next at the Boat, how the evening had ended, and then forgot about it, as three wagon loads of new uniforms and supplies came in and Lieutenant Wheeler kept him in the office for the next two days dealing with bookkeeping and paperwork.

He was checking off the last of the new bedding on a list when his lieutenant got up from the desk.

"Sergeant, what is going on out on the parade ground?"

Michael was vaguely aware of the rising noise. "Bayonet training, sir. Mr van Daan is supposed to be running it."

He got up to go to the door. The men had been paired off and were running through the basic movements using wooden bayonets. Michael had looked out earlier and it had been going smoothly. The young lieutenant had obviously paid good attention to his lessons on the south coast. He had paired up each new man with an experienced soldier and he, Lieutenant Swanson and Sergeant Stewart had been doing the rounds of the men, commenting and correcting. By now, O'Reilly was fairly sure that the light company had found its new officers. It was still early days, but they were workers. There had not been a single morning when he had arrived for early drill on the parade ground and found either of them absent or late.

Something had gone badly wrong now. Sergeant Stewart had been demonstrating a drill using a real weapon and the Van Daan lad was still holding the wooden replica he had been using earlier. What had happened, Michael had no idea, but Stewart was steadily advancing on the younger man, his face grim and set, and Van Daan was backing up, parrying quickly. Around them the men had all stopped to stare. Carl Swanson called out to Stewart to stop, and the Scot ignored him. Michael stared in horror for a moment, as Lieutenant Wheeler yelled an order to Stewart. The sergeant did not appear to hear him.

"What the bloody hell is he doing?" Wheeler demanded, spinning round in search of a weapon. "Has he gone stark staring mad?"

"Sally Crane," Michael whispered. He was temporarily frozen to the spot. "Oh dear Christ, this is my fault, Stewart is going to kill him."

"Not on my bloody parade ground he's not," Wheeler said. He had located his pistol and was loading it fast. Michael ran out onto the parade ground, shouting again at Stewart but the Scot did not even look round. He lunged suddenly and Michael was nowhere near close enough to reach him. The point thrust directly at the boy's throat and Michael closed his eyes in horror, then there was an agonised yell, and he opened them again because it had been the broad Scots of Stewart's voice that shouted.

Paul van Daan and the Scot were both on the ground. As O'Reilly watched, Paul got up. Stewart lay there, clutching both shins in agony. Van Daan tossed aside the wooden training tool and picked up Stewart's bayonet, which he had dropped. Astonished, O'Reilly realised that the young officer had waited until Stewart was close enough to reach him, and then dropped onto the ground and hit him across the legs with the wooden bayonet. He must have used considerable force, as Stewart seemed unable to get up. Paul van Daan stood over the Scot and pointed the bayonet directly at his throat and O'Reilly caught his breath at the expression on the younger man's face. Suddenly he looked nothing like the laughing young man from the tavern.

"Get up."

Paul's voice rang across the parade ground. Stewart did not move.

"Sergeant Stewart, I suggest you get to your feet double quick and shift your fucking arse into the gaol before I use this bayonet on you. That was attempted murder. You've got a count of three, and please don't think I'll hesitate. When you were farting around barracks in India, I was fighting the French on a man o'war under Nelson, and if I put you down, you'll stay down."

Stewart scrambled to his feet. Paul van Daan jerked his head and the Scot limped towards the gaol block. Behind him, Michael heard Lieutenant Wheeler let out a long breath.

"What in God's name just happened?" he asked.

Michael did not reply. Carl Swanson was giving orders to the men to stand down, in a pleasant unemotional tone. Wheeler lowered the pistol and stood watching as training ended and the men dispersed to other duties. Carl walked over to the two men.

"Well, that was unexpected," he said mildly.

Wheeler lifted his eyebrows. "Very. I have the oddest feeling I've been taken for something of a fool, Mr Swanson."

"Not deliberately," Carl said. "It's a somewhat difficult story and he's a very private person. You've not told us much about your background either yet, Johnny, these things take time. None of us were expecting this, let's face it."

There was something about the younger man's immovable calm that made Michael want to laugh, despite his shock. He wondered how much of his young life Carl Swanson had spent pulling Paul van Daan out of trouble and smoothing the storms he created.

"I suppose not. Is he all right?" Wheeler said.

"Well, he's pissed off, that's for sure." Carl looked around. Paul was stalking back across the empty parade ground, his expression stormy.

"Sergeant O'Reilly, a word," he said peremptorily, and jerked his head towards the office. Wheeler looked as though he would have liked to intervene, and then stopped himself. Michael did not blame him. The new lieutenant might be very young, but he was giving the impression of a man who knew exactly what he was doing. Michael, still puzzling over what he had heard, followed Paul through. Paul sat down at the desk and Michael stood to attention in front of him and saluted. There was a long silence. Then Paul said:

"What the hell was that about?"

"I don't know, sir. Didn't see how it started."

"It started with a perfectly normal training exercise and ended with one of my sergeants trying to put a bayonet in me. And he's bloody drunk, I could smell it on him. Don't piss me about, O'Reilly, I'm not in the mood. I've been here for two weeks now, and Stewart hasn't shown any signs of being a homicidal maniac before. And when I just looked across at your face on that parade ground, you looked bloody horrified. You know what that was about."

Michael wondered at what point Paul van Daan had found time to study his facial expressions. "Sir – Rory's a good man. I know he's in serious trouble. But..."

Lieutenant Wheeler had entered the room behind him. He gave a snort of derision. "Sergeant, he's due a hanging. He just got drunk and tried to murder an officer in front of the entire light company. You don't seriously think any other verdict is possible here?"

"No, sir."

"He'll have to go for trial, but Christ, there are over a hundred witnesses."

"What was it about, Sergeant?" Paul van Daan said with dangerous quiet. Michael studied his expression and decided that this was no time for prevarication.

"Sally Crane," he said.

Paul looked at him blankly. "Excuse me?"

"I'm guessing," Michael said, aware that both Wheeler and Carl Swanson were staring at him, "that two nights ago down at the Boat Inn, you had more success than I expected, with Sally Crane."

Paul van Daan looked as though he wanted to explode and was restraining himself with an effort.

"Under normal circumstances, I would tell you at this point to mind your own bloody business, Sergeant, because who I go to bed with in my off-duty hours is nobody's business but my own, and hers. But yes, I remember laughing with you about it. And yes, I spent the night with her. In fact, I spent two nights with her."

Michael watched the blue eyes. Realisation came suddenly and Paul van Daan stood up. "Are you telling me," he said, and the tone of his voice had changed completely, "that you stood in that tavern two nights ago and laughed with me about that girl and it didn't occur to you to mention that she was involved with one of my sergeants?"

"Sir, I'm sorry. It didn't occur to me, that you stood a cat in hell's chance of her saying yes," Michael said candidly.

"How the hell would you know? And what possible reason could you have...oh!" Paul's tone was icy. "It was intended to take me down a peg or two, wasn't it?"

"Yes, sir." There was nothing else Michael could think of to say.

Nobody spoke for a moment. Then Paul van Daan turned away. "Piss off, Sergeant, and stay away from me for the rest of the day. I want to punch you and I'm aware that you can't punch me back, so you really shouldn't put temptation in my way."

"What are you going to do, sir?"

"I'm going to speak to Stewart."

"What happened out there, Paul?" Carl asked.

"We were demonstrating increasing speed. He was holding back, being bloody awkward to tell you the truth. I didn't realise at that point that he'd been drinking. I made an off-colour remark about his manhood to get him moving. Completely harmless, but not coming from a man who had just spent two nights in bed with his girl, especially one of his officers. Christ, he must have thought I knew and had said it deliberately, because he couldn't do a bloody thing about it. I feel like a complete shit." Paul looked again at O'Reilly, then turned and walked to the door. Michael could not resist asking.

"Sir?"

"What?" There was nothing encouraging about Van Daan's tone.

"When I was watching you out on that training ground the other day, I had a sudden thought that this wasn't your first time in the army. Or in command. What was it you just said to Stewart?"

"Not army, navy. Two and a half years. I was a petty officer when I left."

"You were a common seaman, sir?" O'Reilly said in disbelief.

"Lower than that, Sergeant, I started as a pressed man. After that experience, there's nothing that your light company is going to throw at me that is going to cause me to turn a single hair. What you are going to do is piss me off, and you should know that I'm an officer who likes to share the pain."

He stalked out, closing the door firmly behind him.

Lieutenant Wheeler sat down. He gave Michael the impression of a man who had had enough. "I don't see how we can avoid a charge," he said. "Whatever the reason..."

10

"You can't charge him if Lieutenant van Daan won't give evidence," Carl said quietly. "And he won't. You were an arsehole, Sergeant. Especially since Stewart is supposed to be a friend of yours."

"I was," Michael said. He was feeling sick, but with an undercurrent of desperate hope. "Sir, do you really think...?"

"I really think he's likely to punch you, he's bloody furious. Do I think he'll let Stewart hang because of your stupidity? No, although the mood he's in right now I don't think much of your chances, Sergeant."

Michael felt slightly better. He glanced uncomfortably at Johnny Wheeler's grim expression. "Mr Wheeler, if Mr van Daan doesn't want to press charges..."

Unexpectedly, Wheeler gave a weary sigh and shook his head. "Oh, give it a rest, Sergeant, that over-hopeful expression is extremely unconvincing, you know he's going to get away with this. I must say that if this is life in barracks, I can't wait to get to India with you lot."

"I'm sorry, Mr Wheeler, I really am," Carl said.

"So am I. My life was relatively peaceful. There's brandy in the cupboard behind you, get it out, will you? Sit down, Sergeant. It's completely inappropriate, but you look as though you need it. And will somebody for the love of God tell me how I've ended up with Paul van Daan in my light company? To think I was worried at what they sent me before. What's the story, Mr Swanson?"

"Have you heard of the Van Daan shipping line?"

"Of course, I have. They provide a lot of ships to the board of transport. Troops and military supplies to South Africa, India and the West Indies. We'll probably sail on one of their transports to India..." Wheeler broke off and Michael could see him making the connection. "I can't believe I missed that. He has to be swimming in lard, what the hell is he doing in this regiment living in barracks?"

Carl Swanson set three cups on the table and poured. "His choice. Admittedly he's good with his mess bills, and the uniform and horses are of the best," he said. "His father is Dutch, started off as a clerk with the East India Company and ended making a fortune in trade and marrying a viscount's daughter. He had two sons and a girl who died. Paul is the younger, I've known him all my life. They've a country estate not that far from here, and my father is the local parson, so we grew up together.

"His mother died with his sister when he was ten. Smallpox. He'd been her favourite and his father thought she'd spoiled him. He was clever, bookish according to his father. He was also bloody difficult. At fourteen he got kicked out of school and his father decided that he needed discipline, so he apprenticed him to one of their ships for the voyage to the East."

Carl picked up his cup and drank and Wheeler did the same. Michael hesitated. In the years he had served with the lieutenant, he had never before sat like this with him, drinking as if he were one of the officers and it felt wrong. He glanced at Wheeler and realised that his lieutenant was also aware of the strangeness. There was a brief pause and then Wheeler pushed the cup towards Michael. Michael picked it up and drank.

"A tough life for a well-bred lad. And did it make a man of him?"

"More than they planned. The ship was wrecked and one boat made it out. The survivors were picked up and dropped off in Antigua. All of them were hauled in twenty minutes later by the press gang, and he spent two and a half years in the Royal Navy before his father even realised he was still alive. We all thought he'd gone down with the ship and a pressed man doesn't get shore leave or access to writing materials."

"God Almighty," Wheeler breathed.

"His father finally got a letter from him in Egypt. For a pressed man he did surprisingly well. Rose to be a petty officer, fought under Nelson at the Nile, and in several other skirmishes and finally got the opportunity to let his family know he'd survived. It was a shock to Franz van Daan, but he secured Paul's release double quick. It hadn't done much to improve their relationship and Paul didn't want to share a house with him. I was bound for Oxford, my father wanted to make a parson of me, so Franz suggested Paul join me, he hoped he'd go into the law."

"The law?" Wheeler said doubtfully.

"It was never going to work, but I think Oxford was good for him. He'd rather lost most of his youth...anyway, he was never going to go home to work with his father. Hence the army. I joined with him." Carl shrugged and drank. "Unlike Paul I need to earn a living."

"There was a moment out there on that parade ground when I thought he was going to use that bayonet on Sergeant Stewart," Wheeler said quietly.

"If he'd needed to, he would have." Carl glanced at Michael. "Don't be fooled by the boyish charm, he's been killing men since he was fourteen."

"That's probably longer than I have."

"Very possibly, Sergeant." Carl looked at Wheeler. "I'm sorry. I think he should have told you from the start, but it takes him a while to open up to people. He's not one to get drunk in the mess on the first evening and tell you his life story. He likes you. He'd have told you when he was ready."

"I'm beginning to think I could get to like him too," Wheeler said. "But with his money he could have bought into the best cavalry regiment in the army, what the hell is he doing with us?"

"His choice, Johnny. He wanted light infantry."

"He could have gone for the rifles. Or the 43rd or 52nd."

"He could, but they're beyond my purse."

"I see. Loyalty like that is rare."

"It is."

"I thought he was dead earlier," Wheeler said candidly. "He was bloody quick."

"He takes some killing. Let's hope you show similar resilience, Sergeant, because until he calms down, you're in trouble." Suddenly he grinned. "And by the way, you owe me a shilling."

Paul van Daan walked into the gaol block and paused to take a deep breath before going down the row to the cell where Rory Stewart was confined. He was furious with O'Reilly for putting him in this position, the more so because he was aware that he liked the man and had begun to let his guard down with him. He was also irritated that Lieutenant Wheeler had found out about his chequered past in such a public manner. He supposed that Carl would explain, but Johnny ought to have heard it from him. It was a mess, and all over a girl in a tavern and Paul's impulsive decision to take up O'Reilly's challenge. He might not have known that she was involved with Rory Stewart, but he had known she was involved with somebody, and it hadn't stopped him talking his way into her bed. It was typical of Paul to act first and think later, when it came to a woman and it was not the first time it had got him into trouble.

Stewart was lying on his back on the wooden bench, which was the only furniture in the cell. He looked round at Paul's approach but did not move. Paul nodded to the guard who hesitated and then unlocked the cell.

"Thank you. Wait outside, will you?" Paul said.

"Sir – I should stay."

"He's not going to attack me, Private."

The guard left, closing the door behind him and Paul walked into the cell.

"Sergeant Stewart."

"I'm guessing it should be Private Stewart now, sir," the Scot said.

"Sergeant Stewart. Get to your feet, there's an officer in the room."

Stewart regarded him for a long moment then hauled himself to his feet in a display of dumb insolence which Paul silently applauded. He saluted and stood to attention. Paul studied him then sighed.

"Sergeant Stewart, I owe you an apology. If I'd had even the faintest idea that she was your girl I wouldn't have gone within a mile of her, I swear to you. Although that probably doesn't help that much right now."

Stewart's startled expression almost made Paul laugh aloud. "Apology? Sir, I just tried to gut you with a bayonet on the training ground in front of the entire light company and you're in here apologising to me?"

"For Sally. Not for almost breaking your legs, you had that coming."

"Who told you?"

"Sergeant O'Reilly."

Stewart shook his head miserably. "I'm sorry, sir. Can't believe I was that bloody stupid, I just went mad. But whatever you did, she let you, so it's not you I should be angry with."

"No, but I was there, being a smart arse as usual, and you can hardly go after her with a bayonet. At least, I'd rather you didn't, we actually would have to hang you for that."

"I canna see how you can get away with not hanging me anyway, sir. When Major Johnstone gets back he's going to hear about this..."

"He's going to hear that you got drunk on duty and made an arse of yourself and that I gave you a thump as a result and put you on latrine duties for a month. Which I'm afraid I'm going to. I'll argue against demotion, but if he insists, you'll have to put up with it and earn those stripes back in India. And you do need to learn to control your temper better."

Stewart stood quietly for a moment. Finally, he said:

"Thank you, sir."

"Stewart – this bit is actually none of my business. But if she's got you so worked up you're trying to kill people, you need to have a conversation with her about it. Because you two need to agree the rules here; I doubt I've been the only one."

"When I'm away we both do what we like," Stewart said. "But when I'm home, she never...when Charlie told me, to start with I thought you'd forced her."

"No wonder you were pissed off."

"No, I knew you'd not, when he said you'd been with her last night as well. But Christ, sir..."

"Has it occurred to you that this might be more to do with you than me?" Paul said gently. Stewart's taut misery was making him feel appallingly guilty. "She's a lovely lass, Stewart. Have you talked about making this official?"

"Didn't think it worthwhile, with me being away so much."

"Well, she let me pick her up in a bar full of men who were going to tell you about it, so I'd say she's trying to tell you something, Sergeant. Better get yourself over there and find out what. Make it official or end it, it makes no difference to me. But you can't go around killing every man she decides to go to bed with. As far as I'm concerned this is done with, but if you ever point a bayonet at me again, you'd better be prepared to use it a bit faster than you did, because next time I'm not pissing about with counting."

Stewart saluted. "Yes, sir. Thank you. I'm not sure most officers would have taken it this way."

"No." Unexpectedly, Paul's sense of humour revived. "Mind, most officers would probably have been a bit more careful whose girl they went after in a tavern. Let's call it even, Sergeant. Now get out of here and go and see her. I'll write you a leave pass and leave it in the office. Get moving, I want my dinner and a drink."

Paul watched Stewart leave. Into the darkness he said:

"You can come out now, Michael."

The Irishman stepped out of the shadows. "Sir. I notice there were a few things you missed out there."

"He's your friend, Michael. If you want to tell him you encouraged me to fuck his girl for a bet, that's your business."

"Would you?"

"If I'd done that to Carl? Christ, no. I'd chalk it up to a moment of stupidity and leave it alone. He's been hurt once, why make it worse?"

"Good advice, sir."

14

"I'm full of it today." Paul studied the thin dark face thoughtfully. "You were bloody lucky, Michael. I suspect a fair few officers would have sent him for trial whatever the cause of that."

The Irishman looked steadily back. "I know that, sir."

"And what were you going to do then?"

There was a very long silence and then Michael O'Reilly took a deep breath. "Open that door and get him out of here, tell him to run. That's why I was listening, sir."

Paul was silent for a moment. He was still angry, but he also wanted to laugh. "You've got bloody balls, Sergeant, you know that?"

"Sir."

"Don't 'sir' me. If you ever put me in a position like that again, I'm going to cut yours off, are we clear?"

"Yes, sir. I am sorry."

Paul eyed him thoughtfully. "Is this how you normally deal with new officers, Sergeant?"

"New officers aren't normally much like you, sir."

"I'll just bet they're not. I wonder how many poor little bastards you've seen off, because you didn't like the look of them. Are we done here because I actually do want that drink?"

"I had you completely wrong, sir."

"You were looking for a stuck-up little twat, Michael, so that's what you saw. I'm sure that by now Lieutenant Swanson has told you the rest."

"Yes, sir. It explains a few things that have been puzzling me. You should probably have told Mr Wheeler before."

Paul turned to look directly at him. He had intended to leave this until later, but he was still angry enough with the Irishman not to care. "Are we sharing secrets, Michael? Because I'm very sure that you're not the amiable Irish bog-trotter you're pretending to be and I'm wondering how much of that you've shared with Mr Wheeler or Major Johnstone?"

O'Reilly laughed softly. "And if I were to tell you that I'd been mixed up in Wolf Tone's rebellion a few years back, sir, and needed a new name and a new career, would that send you to make a report to the major before we sail for India?"

Paul looked him over. "It might if I wanted to lose my best sergeant. Now let me get changed and then you can buy me that bloody drink. I have decided to ignore the rules about not drinking with the enlisted men, now that I have embarked on a career of sleeping with their women. And not at the Boat Inn, I think. Let's leave Stewart to sort out his own love life, shall we?"

O'Reilly fell into step beside him. "They are not going to like this, sir," he said.

"They'll get used to me, Sergeant. Where are we going?"

"We can go to the Red Lion, sir, you won't find any of the other officers in there. Although it can get a bit rough at times."

"That's all right, Michael. Giving someone other than you a punch might make me feel better and keep you a lot safer."

O'Reilly looked at him. Paul could see that he was wondering, trying to assess how far he might go with a new officer who was clearly not like any other officer he had come across. Almost, Paul could see him weighing up the risk. Then the Irishman said:

"Paul?"

Paul could not decide whether to laugh or punch him. "Sergeant?"

"Welcome to the light company. I've a horrible feeling that all of my past sins against young officers are about to come back and bite me in the arse."

"Cheer up, Sergeant, at least I've not killed anybody yet. Although if you call me that in front of anybody else, I will rip your fucking head off. Lead on."

Chapter Two

Carl Swanson was surprised at how quickly the officers of the light company adapted to shipboard life, although Paul, only four years out of the navy, seemed at home from the first. Carl was allotted a small cabin shared with Paul, Johnny Wheeler and Peter Denny, a very young ensign. In addition to the crew there were over a hundred men aboard, living in cramped conditions below decks and Carl wondered about discipline during the long months of the voyage to India.

Denny and one or two of the other officers suffered badly in the first days from seasickness, and many of the men below were similarly afflicted. The 110th first battalion was led by Major Johnstone, a borderer with an impressive set of military whiskers and a booming laugh, who informed Paul and Carl that he always puked like a pregnant woman for three days.

"I'm told you're an experienced sailor, though," he said to Paul. "You both seem comfortable with the men, you've settled in quickly. That's good, because if the news from India is correct, you'll see action soon. Learn from Wheeler."

"Yes, sir," Paul said. "I was wondering if we could get the men on deck for some of the day, weather permitting. The more time in the air, the less sickness."

"I'd say yes, but there's often trouble with the seamen."

"I know, sir, but we could rope off an area and keep our men within it and the NCOs can keep things under control. They spend their time gambling and arguing below. Up here we might be able to do some limited training in small groups. I'd be happy to supervise it."

"I don't know how the captain will see it."

"May I speak to him about it?"

Carl concealed a smile at Johnston's puzzled expression. "Aye, if you like. If he says yes, give it a try. But you don't have to spend all your time with the men, Van Daan. We don't see enough of you in the officers' quarters."

"You will, sir, I promise you. But it's an opportunity to get to know the men and to let them get to know me."

17

"As you wish. We'll dock at Cape Town for a week and the officers will get shore leave, although not the men. Can't risk desertions, of course, especially among the criminal element."

"I know Cape Town well, I've family there. You must come and meet them, sir. Thank you, I'll talk to the captain later, if I may?"

He saluted and walked off, and Johnstone looked at Carl. "He's going to make a damned good officer. Both of you, you're settling in very well. I wish him luck with the captain though, he's an awkward old bastard."

"I doubt he'll give Paul much trouble, sir, his father owns the ship."

The major grinned and strolled off and Carl joined O'Reilly at the rail. Paul was in the centre of a group of soldiers, teaching two of the younger ones to use a sword. The men were watching him with a kind of fascination and Carl wondered if they had ever come across an officer this willing to engage with them. Paul looked like a man thoroughly enjoying himself and Carl watched his friend, smiling. He felt a touch on his arm, and the Irish sergeant passed him a well-worn pewter flask, which contained rum. Carl drank and felt the raw spirit warm him. He passed it back and Michael took a pull and stoppered the flask, his eyes on Paul.

"He's the strangest officer I've ever served under."

"You could do worse."

"Believe me, sir, I have. The seventh company is commanded by a complete arsehole who flogs the men just for a laugh."

"Tut, tut, Sergeant, that's no way to speak about Captain Longford. We've met. Has he flogged you?"

"More than once when I first joined. Wonder what your laddie would make of him? Could be good entertainment. I don't think Mr van Daan gives a shit about seniority somehow." Michael glanced sideways at Carl. "Or about any other rules."

Carl shook his head. "Mr van Daan knows every rule in this army, Sergeant, he's read the training manuals which is more than I have. How closely he'll stick to them is another matter."

"He'll get himself into trouble sooner or later, if he doesn't, sir."

"I'm confidently expecting it, Sergeant."

Michael was still watching the swordplay. The deck was wet in places, and as Paul lunged, his foot slipped badly. The infantryman reached instinctively and caught his arm before he hit the deck, hauling him upright again. Paul started to laugh, steadying himself with a hand on Private Cooper's shoulder and after a surprised minute, the other man laughed as well. Paul clapped him on the back in thanks.

"Be a shame if he gets himself cashiered," Michael said dispassionately. "They like him."

"I'm hoping we can avoid that, with a bit of effort," Carl said.

***

18

To relieve the boredom, Paul befriended some of the naval officers, and spent time with them during the long hours of the night watch, taking turns with the instruments, refreshing knowledge he had not used in a long time. He was on deck one evening when Johnny Wheeler approached him. Paul nodded amiably and they stood for a while, watching the darkening skies, the white flecked waves and the billowing sails overhead.

"We're making good time," Paul said, throwing his head back to observe the moon peeping out from behind a cloud. "Mr Clinton says at this rate we'll make the Cape in four or five days."

"It'll be good to get ashore, even briefly."

"Yes, I hate long voyages. Bloody tedious."

"Not so much, this time. Watching you work has been a revelation."

Paul slanted an amused glance at his companion. "Really? I'm flattered."

"You should be. I've seen officers come and go but you're something else. I can't wait to see you on a battlefield."

"If you put a bullet in me, I bleed just as much as anybody else, Johnny."

The older man's grey eyes narrowed in amusement. "Don't try it with me, Paul, you don't need to, I'm already a convert. You're very good. You've a way with the men, and old Johnstone loves you, which is a compliment because he's one of the better ones. If you've got the money, you'll have your company within the year."

"Why don't you?" Paul asked. "Money?"

"What else? The best I can hope for is a field promotion and they're few and far between."

Paul studied him thoughtfully. "Best stick close to me on the battlefield then, Johnny, and get noticed."

Wheeler burst into laughter and clapped him on the shoulder. "You're an arrogant bastard, Van Daan. If you manage to stay alive for long enough, I look forward to your future career. But by then you'll have left me far behind, trust me."

Paul joined in his laughter but shook his head. "No, I won't, Johnny, I promise."

"We'll see. I'm going below. Enjoy."

Paul watched him go and turned back to watch the galloping waves, wishing he had been more tactful. It had been meant as a joke, but it was probably not funny to a man of Johnny's calibre who had been passed over for years due to lack of money. After a while, he was distracted by a sound and he looked around, then went to investigate. Close by, were two boats, shrouded in canvas and lashed to their frames, and the sound seemed to be coming from behind them.

The girl was huddled with her back against the boat. In the darkness it was hard to see anything about her, other than a mass of fair hair and a pale face. At Paul's approach, she seemed to shrink back against the boat as if trying to make herself invisible. The crying had stopped.

Paul looked around, then crossed to where a ship's lantern hung from one of the beams, lighting the way to the companionway. He lifted it down and

19

returned to the girl, setting the lantern down close by, then he seated himself on the deck beside the girl and looked sideways at her.

"Aren't you cold?"

She stared back at him with wide blue eyes, damp with tears. She was a slight creature, probably not as old as he was, her pale face dusted with freckles, and without her distress, Paul suspected she would be very pretty. She was shivering in a thin muslin dress, with bare feet and a worn and faded woollen shawl. Paul took off his coat and draped it about her shoulders.

As he touched her left arm Paul saw her wince and he looked more closely at her face. The right eye was darkened and slightly bloodshot, beginning to swell. Paul reached for the shawl and drew it away from her arm. In the lamplight, the bruises were shaped like the fingers of a man.

"What's your name?" Paul asked gently.

"Nell, sir." She was looking at him warily.

"And your husband? Army or navy?"

"Army. Not the 110th though, he's with the engineers."

There was a small contingent of engineers aboard, but Paul did not know them well. They tended to keep themselves separate from his men, and he had not taken the time to get to know their names.

"Does he do this often?"

"When he's been drinking," Nell said, and something in her tone suggested that it was a frequent event.

"Have you been to India before?"

The girl shook her head. "I travelled to Ireland with him, but then he lost the draw to bring his wife, so I stayed with my mother. This time he won the draw again." There was despair in her voice and Paul thought that she must have dreaded this.

"How old are you?"

"I'm nineteen, sir. Wed three years. He wasn't like this at first, but his drinking got worse."

"Where else are you hurt?"

Her hand rested on her side. "Just a bruise or two, he punched me. But…"

"Sit up," Paul said, turning towards her. "And keep still."

She allowed him to probe her ribs until he found the source of her pain and then she gave a little scream, quickly silenced by her own hands over her mouth.

"At best you've a badly bruised rib. It could be broken."

"It hurts when I breathe."

Paul got to his feet. "Come with me. I want the surgeon to have a look at you."

Nell shook her head. "No, sir, I need to get back. He'll wake up soon and see I'm gone, and he'll be that mad."

She slipped out of his coat and handed it to him, then walked quickly away, her head bowed. Paul stopped himself from calling her back. His instinct was to insist, but he realised that he would only frighten the girl, and he would prefer to direct his sudden fury at the right person.

20

On deck the following day, when some of the men were practising bayonet drill in small groups, Paul sought out O'Reilly and drew the Irishman away from the group to the ship's rail. "Sergeant, do you know the engineers at all? One of them has a woman travelling with him, his wife. She's called Nell."

"Oh aye, that'll be Billy Kemp. Surly devil sitting whittling a piece of wood on that box over there. He drinks like a fish, and that's impressive coming from me."

"I'd like a word with him in private, can you arrange that?"

O'Reilly gave him a surprised look. "Yes, sir. But he's not really our responsibility."

"He's beating her. She's half his size and terrified. That makes it my responsibility, Sergeant."

O'Reilly said nothing for a moment, then saluted. "Yes, sir. Shall we say fifteen minutes on the orlop deck? It'll be nice and empty at the moment; you won't be interrupted."

Paul nodded. He waited for a few minutes then strolled below and was waiting in the shadows when O'Reilly appeared with a bewildered and slightly belligerent Kemp.

"In you go then, Billy, the officer would like a word with you."

Kemp stepped forward, glancing behind him at O'Reilly who had taken up a stance with his arms folded. Kemp looked at Paul, and apparently remembering his rank, staged a sketchy salute. "Sir."

"Kemp. We've not had a chance to talk so far."

"No, sir, you're always so busy making friends with the light company. And you're not my commanding officer."

The man's tone was openly insolent, but Paul kept his tone even. "I wasn't aware you had a wife with you."

"I tell the bitch to keep below out of sight, out of the way of the officers, sir. No sense in putting temptation in her way. Or theirs."

"I met her yesterday evening nursing a black eye and a broken rib. Was that because she'd forgotten your instructions by any chance?"

"Well, it's nothing to what I'm going to do to her for blabbing to you. What happens between a man and his wife has nothing to do with you." Kemp was swaying slightly and for the first time Paul realised how drunk he was. "Keep yourself away from her, boy, or you'll find yourself in a dark corner of this ship with my dagger in your ribs."

There was a long silence. Paul looked past Kemp towards O'Reilly. "Is he drunk or stupid?" he asked, conversationally.

"A bit of both, I think, sir. He's an engineer, so he is, and all they do is move shit around all day with their little shovels. But he's had a skinful, to speak to an officer that way."

Paul looked back at Kemp and thought about the girl's bruised, swollen face, then stepped forward and threw a fast combination of four punches and stood looking down at the man who lay clutching a bloody face on the deck. O'Reilly came to stand beside Paul. Kemp tried to get up and Paul kicked him

21

hard in the ribs. Kemp screamed. O'Reilly put a hand on Paul's arm. Paul resisted the urge to shake it off.

"Move again, and I'll do the same to your balls, you bullying arsehole."

Kemp did not move and Paul crouched down and took a handful of his hair, forcing his head back. "Now then, let's start this whole conversation again. I don't have any right whatsoever to intervene in your marital affairs, apart from the fact that I hate men who hit women. Fortunately, you've made this very easy for me because you've threatened to murder an officer in front of my sergeant here, which means you're going to spend the rest of this voyage in irons chatting with the rats, with the prospect of a flogging or a rope around your neck when we get to India. Stupid. Just as I said." Paul stood up. "Lock him up, Sergeant, I'll report to Major Johnstone."

Paul waited outside, absently wiping his hands on his handkerchief, when the Irishman joined him. "All secure, Sergeant?"

"Aye, sir. Nice and safe. That was a pretty combination you threw; I can tell you're a boxer."

"Thank you. I used to go to Jackson's when I was in London. Do you box, Michael?"

"I did so, sir, a long time ago, before I joined up. Although the kick in the ribs was awful dirty."

"Wasn't it?" Paul said. "D'you know what, Sergeant? I doubt his wife enjoyed it much when he did it to her either. He can sit in that damp hole and think about that for a month or two, the spiteful bastard. I'll go and speak to Major Johnstone. Will you find Nell Kemp for me and let her know that she's safe for the remainder of the voyage? From her husband at least. Will she have any trouble from any of the men?"

"No sir. I'll make sure the lads know where they stand regarding Mrs Kemp. She'll stick with the other wives, there's four of them, as you probably know."

"There are eight of them to my certain knowledge, Michael, and probably a few more that I've not discovered yet."

The sergeant grinned. "That can't be right, sir, given that only four men drew the right to bring their wives with them. You're seeing things."

"I must be. You don't have a wife of your own stashed away down there, do you?"

"Me? Oh no, sir. Footloose and fancy free, that's me."

"Just making sure. I'm careful with my sergeants' girlfriends, as you know."

The Irishman gave a choke of laughter and saluted, and Paul went to find Johnstone.

***

Michael found Lieutenant Swanson on deck, supervising some of the men organising impromptu wrestling matches. Paul's scheme of getting the men on deck every day was going well, and Michael was aware that both morale

22

and discipline were better than usual on a long voyage, although he wondered if Paul realised that the amount of time he spent with his men was causing raised eyebrows among the other officers on board.

Carl glanced enquiringly at him. "What's up, Sergeant?"

"Mr van Daan has been having a bit of a chat with Billy Kemp from the engineers."

"Why, what's he done?"

"Using his wife as a punch bag, it seems."

Carl winced. "That won't have gone down well."

"I doubt he'll be doing it again any time soon."

"I imagine not, the lieutenant's not fond of bullies."

"Especially if the victim is a pretty girl."

Carl grinned. "It doesn't take long to work out that if Mr van Daan has a weakness, Sergeant, it is that he is constitutionally incapable of listening to his brain over his dick. If he ever gets himself cashiered it will be because he's slept with the wrong man's wife."

"At least we can be fairly sure that she'd have been willing," Michael said with a grimace. "I'm never accepting a wager on that again."

"If she wasn't, he wouldn't do it."

Michael eyed him thoughtfully. "Rape is a crime in the army, sir, and none of the officers encourage it, but we all know it happens. Most of these are good lads but there was a girl or two at Seringapatam a few years back who probably got more than she asked for when they broke through. If I'd caught them, they'd have been sorry, but..."

"If he catches them, they'll be dead, Sergeant, so probably best make sure they know that." Carl studied him and Michael could see him weighing his words carefully. Finally, he said:

"Paul doesn't make friends quickly, Michael. He's very pleasant, but actual friendship takes time with him. But he liked you from day one. He sees you as a friend, not just an NCO."

Michael was conscious of an irrational sense of pleasure at the thought. "Aye, he's not much like an officer for that, sir." He studied Carl thoughtfully. "But then neither are you."

"No. But then you're not much like a typical NCO are you, Michael? It's a mystery to me why you didn't join as a gentleman volunteer and wait for a commission without purchase, but Paul informs me that it's better not to ask that question. So I'm going to trust you with the part of the story I didn't tell Johnny Wheeler. You probably won't hear this from Paul. As far as I'm aware, he's never told anybody but me, and he was drunk when he did that. But it bothered me that nobody knew anything about him when we joined up. And I realise it's bothering me that I'm still the only one who knows exactly what he's capable of."

"I'll keep it to myself," Michael said quietly.

"I hope you do. Can you imagine what it was like for an attractive fourteen-year-old lad dumped below decks by a press gang, Michael? There was an older seaman who saw the younger boys as his personal playground.

They'd all suffered at his hands. Paul must have looked like a gift from the gods to him. There was an incident. An assault. I don't know the details, and I doubt I ever will. What I do know is that two nights later the man was found in his hammock with his throat slashed from ear to ear. His balls had been cut off and stuffed in his mouth."

O'Reilly prided himself on being difficult to shock, but he gasped. "Oh Jesus Christ, at fourteen? Sir, you're not serious?"

"I really am. Paul was suspected, but there was no evidence. They thrashed his back raw, but he told them nothing and eventually they had to let him go. Nobody else bothered Paul or any of the other lads during their time at sea and by the time his father found him two years later, he'd earned his promotion to petty officer."

"Christ Almighty."

"He's a good man, Sergeant, and he'll be a bloody good officer. And I suspect that in a year's time, the light company will follow him to hell and back for a smile and a word. But when he loses his temper, he needs somebody around to step in, before he kills somebody. And I might not always be there, so you need to know that. Also, like I said, he is a little touchy about rape, so best make sure the lads know that they should be very sure a local girl is willing before they indulge."

"I'll remember that, sir."

***

Paul did not see Nell Kemp again until the evening before the ship arrived in Cape Town, when she appeared beside him as he took his customary stroll around the deck in the evening.

"Nell – how are you?"

"I'm well, sir. I wanted to find you. To thank you."

"There's no need. Although I've no idea what will happen to him when we get to India."

"I won't go back to him. Not now." Paul approved the determination in the girl's voice. "I'm going to look for work with one of the other regiments. Perhaps find myself a better man. I'll tell them I'm a widow."

"Good girl. I'll keep an eye on you until you've found something, make sure you're not in need. But I'm glad you've decided to leave him, there's no reason for you to put up with that." Paul studied her and smiled. "Trust me, India is not full of girls as pretty as you, Nell, somebody is going to snap you up. Just make sure you're choosy, you can afford to be."

"Did he really threaten to kill you?"

"Surprisingly, yes. I didn't think he'd be so stupid, with Sergeant O'Reilly there as a witness, but it made things a lot easier. Are they taking care of you below?"

She nodded. "The other wives understand, and Sergeant O'Reilly has been kind. But I wanted to thank you."

"It was nothing."

"It was something. Everybody knew, even the officers. In Dublin I was black and blue some days, but nobody stepped in until you did. I won't forget it, sir."

She stepped forward suddenly into the shadow of the boat where Paul had first seen her, took his hand and drew him to her. Paul was startled, and then touched at the feeling of her mouth on his and the warmth of her body pressing into him, arousing him to immediate consciousness that he had not been near a woman in months.

"Nell…lass, there's no need."

"I want to," she whispered, and Paul bent his head and kissed her, holding her lightly, waiting to see some sign of doubt or hesitation in her. There was none. Taking her hand he drew her into the depths of the shadows under the boat and settled her down on the deck, stripping off his coat to pillow her head. Her mouth was warm and sweet on his, and he opened her bodice enjoying the curves under his hand, the eagerness with which she reached for him.

"Are you sure, Nell? Because this isn't the price of my help, now or in the future."

"I know it isn't. And I'll never forget that either, sir."

He ran his hand up her leg to the soft skin of her thighs. "Paul," he whispered softly against her lips. "My name is Paul."

"Paul."

She welcomed him with pleasure, which seemed a surprise to her. Perhaps it had never mattered to the brute she had married, but Paul wanted her to enjoy him, as he was enjoying her. When they were done, he lay holding her against him, looking up at the deep blue of the sky, spangled with stars, and waited for his breathing to settle. After a moment, he turned to look at Nell.

"Are you all right?"

"Oh – yes, of course." The question seemed to surprise her. "That was…nice. You're so gentle."

"You're so lovely."

She tilted her head to look up at him. "Sir…"

"Paul. You cannot call me sir, after what we have just done."

"Paul, then. May I ask a question?"

"Of course you may."

"How old are you?"

Paul laughed. "I wasn't expecting that. I'm twenty-one."

"They all wonder, the men. Because you seem much older."

"I've had a varied and interesting life. Thank you for this, beautiful Nell. You are as lovely as you are generous."

The girl looked up at him from wide eyes. "And you're as gentle as you are kind," she said. "I didn't know men could be like you. I should go, before somebody comes."

Paul helped her to her feet and restored her clothing, watching her as she walked towards the hatch. At the top of the ladder she turned.

"Do you always walk up here late at night?"

"I do."

"Then I'll see you again some night, Lieutenant van Daan."

When she had gone Paul moved to the rail, savouring the sense of release that her body had given him. He did not feel guilty about Nell Kemp, and he would not refuse her if she offered herself again one dark night. Sometimes a simple exchange of pleasure and goodwill was enough.

"Was that the lovely Mrs Kemp I saw whisking her pretty ankles down the ladder there?" a voice said at his elbow, and he turned to find Carl beside him.

"It was. She came to thank me."

"I know very well what she came for, my lad, it's a good thing it was me who wandered past and heard you, and not the major."

"Ah. We shall be more careful next time."

His friend was studying him from amused green eyes. "What is it about you?" he asked. "I look at you sometimes, but I just can't see it."

"Thank God for that. Yours is not the type of beauty I admire."

"God help the woman you marry, Paul."

"Carl, it wasn't my idea, I promise you, she made a very direct offer and I accepted."

"I'm not judging you, Paul. Really, I admire your technique."

Paul looked out over the darkness of the ocean. "I didn't stop her husband from beating her half to death so that I could fuck her, Carl," he said, suddenly angry.

His friend put his hand on his shoulder. "I know you didn't, you'd have done it for any woman, you're bloody soft. Ignore me, I'm just envious. At least it will be a break from the monotony of this bloody voyage. I'll be ready to kill the Maratha or anybody else by the time I get there."

Paul looked around at him, his anger dying as quickly as it had flared. It usually did with Carl. He could not remember a time when his friend had not been there, his calm presence anchoring him when his temper got the better of him as it frequently did. "Sorry," he said. "This much inactivity isn't good for me."

"It's not good for any of us," Carl said. "She's a pretty lass."

"She's very sweet. Look, don't mention it to Sergeant O'Reilly, will you, I don't want the men to know. They might think it makes her generally available and I'd hate to have to throw one of them overboard to make a point, I'm just getting to like them."

"It's nobody else's business. But since I don't suppose this will be the last time, don't get caught. I'm pretty sure there's something in the rules about sleeping with the wives of the enlisted men."

"There isn't," Paul said seriously. "I checked."

In Calcutta, the light company was reunited with the rest of the first battalion and Paul was introduced to Captain Mason who commanded the light company, a seasoned but world-weary officer of many years' service in India who suffered from recurring fever. Although he claimed to be well enough to march, Mason's yellow skin and shadowed eyes suggested a history of poor health. He received his new officers with tired civility, and what Paul suspected was considerable relief.

There were seven companies of the first battalion already settled in the cantonments, and at dinner in the mess, Paul and Carl were introduced to their fellow officers. The meal was rich and heavily spiced and seemed to go on forever. As the afternoon wore on into evening, Paul was faintly astonished at the quantity of wine and brandy being consumed. He excused himself fairly early, leaving Carl and the others, and made his way back up to the lines where his tent had been erected. His men either sat or lay around in their bedrolls drinking, talking or gambling and they greeted him cheerfully as he passed. Paul went in search of O'Reilly.

"Jesus, sir, what are you doing back so early?" the Irishman said in surprise. "Generally they'd be going until midnight."

"They'll be going for longer than that I suspect, but I'd had enough, it's as stuffy as hell in there." Paul motioned him to follow. Outside his tent he pulled out two camp chairs, leaned back and looked up at the stars, brilliant in a clear black sky. "I prefer it out here. I did, however, manage to liberate this." Paul pulled a bottle of brandy from his coat and saw Michael's dark eyes light up with amusement.

"You're a marvel, sir. Anyone would think you'd been doing this for years."

"If you can purloin rum off a ship's purser, Michael, this is child's play."

Paul rummaged for cups and they sat in silence for a while, listening to the sounds of the camp. Eventually Paul stirred.

"The major says we'll have a few days to rest before marching. I feel as though I've done nothing but sit around for weeks."

"Aye, a long sea voyage will do that to you. Unless, presumably, you're a petty officer, in which case I imagine you're busy enough."

"Not busy enough for me, Sergeant, which is why I joined the army and not the navy. Too many hours doing bugger all aboard a ship."

The Irishman grinned. "I'd rather guessed that. It's good that we've a bit of a march, it'll get the men used to the climate and make sure they're fit enough to fight when needed."

"I shouldn't think the officers will be fit to stagger in the morning, let alone fight."

"I've never seen you drunk," Michael said, studying him.

"You won't often. I like a drink but I'm not so keen on the hangover."

"Or the loss of control," Michael said quietly and Paul looked sharply at him and laughed.

"Very likely." He leaned back in his chair. "Jesus, look at those stars. Why in God's name would you want to sit in that dining room all evening when you can be out here looking at this?"

The Irishman reached for the brandy, his eyes on Paul's face. "I can remember when you walked into the barracks at Melton, thinking that I just couldn't make you out," he said. "And I'm not sure I'm much closer now.

What are you doing, Mr van Daan, sitting out here under the stars with an enlisted man when you should be socialising with your own kind?"

Paul looked across at him. "I thought I was," he said.

"Sooner or later somebody is going to ask questions about that, sir, you do know that don't you? They don't like people who flout army traditions, and for all your cockiness you're still only a bloody lieutenant."

"I know, Michael. But I won't always be."

The Irishman studied him as though he suddenly understood. "No," he said. "And that's your aim, isn't it? You want to be where Wellesley is."

"Yes," Paul said. He realised that he had sounded unusually serious, thought about it, and decided that he did not mind admitting his ambition to Michael. He drank again and grinned. "But there are other ways to achieve it, than kissing arses, Sergeant, although half the army doesn't know that yet. Are you coming with me?"

It was a casual remark, but it felt oddly significant, and Paul watched the Irishman's face and realised that Michael felt it too, although he answered lightly.

"It looks that way, sir. I might even be looking forward to it if I weren't worried you're going to get me killed on the way."

"I'll try not to, Sergeant." Paul leaned forward and picked up the bottle. "Have some more brandy. You might need it."

***

By the time the 110th joined up with General Arthur Wellesley's army at Poona the following year, Michael O'Reilly had come to the conclusion that the light company had struck pure gold with its new officers. Within the regiment, the light company was seen as the elite, but they were not easy to command. With Captain Mason so often absent, the three lieutenants shared the responsibility between them, but increasingly Michael was aware that even Johnny Wheeler whose length of service gave him seniority, was beginning to implement Paul van Daan's ideas about training and discipline. Lieutenant Swanson was happy to follow, but Michael found him a steady and intelligent officer with a tactful approach, which was invaluable given Paul's rather more abrasive manner. There were times, at the end of a long day, when Michael felt an urge to punch Lieutenant van Daan for his insistence on perfection in every drill and manoeuvre, but as the light company grew accustomed his level of expectation, they responded in a way that Michael had not seen before and he was conscious of a pride in his men that he had never known.

English territory in India was governed by the East India Company, which faced the difficulties of managing vast territories while trying to turn a profit. The English occupied three areas and in between, lay huge areas governed by local rulers, including the Maratha Confederacy, which consisted of five separate principalities, currently at war with each other, with the British intervening on behalf of the deposed Peshawar. When negotiations failed, the

Governor-General decided to invade the Confederacy from both north and south. Major-General Arthur Wellesley was commanding the troops from the South, and had recently moved his force into the Confederacy, and restored the deposed Peshawar to his principality at Poona It was there that Major Johnstone and his seven companies joined him.

They found a sprawling army camp of some six thousand men, a mixture of English and Indian troops. With war imminent, Wellesley was keen to maintain regular drills and training and organised a series of parades to keep the various troops under his control up to scratch while he gathered both supplies and intelligence and waited for the monsoon season to begin.

The inactivity made discipline a challenge, and officers and NCOs tried to keep a tight rein on the light company, although Michael was aware of the tendency of some of them to disappear into the local towns and villages for arrack and women more frequently than they should. He was not wholly surprised one evening walking back up from bathing in the river with Lieutenant van Daan to see several of his men lined up before a captain and two lieutenants from one of the East India regiments.

Paul paused. "What's going on?"

"I'll find out, sir."

Michael made his way over to the lines and Paul followed him. There were four of the light company men lined up. One of them, Private Dawson, had a thin cut across his face.

The captain turned and stared at the new arrivals. "Lieutenant. Are these your men?"

"Yes, sir."

"Well, they are going to be flogged, sir, all four of them, tomorrow."

"Why, sir?"

"Because they were caught out of camp, sir, with no permission. And they were bloody insubordinate with it. I won't have it."

"What did they say, sir?" Paul enquired, turning to look at the four men.

"That they were hunting for their supper. Rations not good enough for them, apparently. They were probably looting or after women. Well, I'll have the skin off their backs, by God, I'm reporting them. Fifty each at least, and another twenty-five for that one for his cheek. Speak to me that way..."

"Sir, they had permission."

The captain paused. "What did you say?"

"They had permission. They came and asked me earlier. I didn't give them a ticket, I forgot, sir, my fault." Paul's expression was apologetic. "New to the job, sir."

Michael looked across at the four men. Their faces were completely blank. During his time with the 110th, Michael had not known Paul van Daan to forget any aspect of training or rules. He was absolutely certain not one of the men had asked for permission to leave the camp.

"Who the devil are you, sir? Don't recognise you from the mess."

"Lieutenant van Daan, sir, 110th light company, under Captain Mason."

29

"Ah." The captain turned to his two companions. "This is the boy Colonel Andrews was talking about the other evening, gentlemen. Spends his time down in the lines with the men instead of in the mess with his own kind and yet he seems to think himself a cut above the rest of us. You've been spending a lot of time training and drilling the light company, haven't you, Mr van Daan?"

"Yes, sir."

"They're looking very impressive."

"Thank you, sir."

"And you want me to let these men off a flogging that they richly deserve because you made a mistake."

"It was my mistake, sir, not theirs."

"And what about this fellow's insubordination?"

Paul looked at the bleeding weal across Dawson's face. The riding crop had just missed his eye. Paul often wanted to hit Dawson, but the sight of the mark infuriated him.

"It rather looks as though you've already dealt with that, sir," he said, trying to keep the edge from his voice.

"Well, you can't be flogged for your error, can you, Mr van Daan?"

"No, sir. But they probably shouldn't be."

Paul stopped himself from saying more. He was longing to tell the captain that it was not his job to be disciplining another regiment's men, along with a few other things about hitting enlisted men with a riding crop, but he could sense that would only make the situation worse.

Finally, the captain said:

"All right, let's come to an agreement. Tomorrow afternoon, when you've finished your drills, Mr van Daan, you can get your arse down to my lads and take them through the same thing. For one week. My officers and I could do with a rest."

Paul looked across at his four men, struggling to decide if he wanted to hit them or the officer more. Drills and training began early, so that they were over before the hottest part of the day. To come from his own company and work with another through the afternoon would be the act of a madman. Neither Wheeler nor Johnstone would approve of his intervention. All four men were experienced soldiers and knew the penalty for what they had done, and there was no reason for him to interfere.

Michael glanced at Paul. "Sir..."

"Did I ask you to speak, Sergeant?" Paul enquired frostily.

"No, sir."

Paul could almost feel the scars on his back tingling. He had been fourteen and the pain and humiliation had never left him. He looked at the three officers. None of them would ever know what a flogging felt like. Paul glanced at his men again and could see resignation in their faces. They expected nothing from him and were probably surprised that he had even made the attempt. His entire company was going to assume that he had gone completely mad.

"Sergeant O'Reilly, march them back to the lines." Paul looked at the captain. "I'm sorry, sir, I don't know your name."

"Captain Gregson, East India Company, 17th Bengal Infantry. You'll find the local boys do better than your lads at working in the hottest part of the day. Don't know how you'll do, mind, especially after working all morning with your men. But you won't mind that, in the name of justice, will you?" Gregson's voice was mocking. "Or you could just let them be flogged, of course."

"No, problem, sir. I'll get things settled and be up to the mess later to buy you a drink. By way of an apology for Dawson's lip."

Gregson looked completely nonplussed which Paul found satisfying. "Really? Good of you. I'll see you then."

As the three officers walked away, Paul could hear their laughter floating back and he turned to glare at O'Reilly and the other men, who had not moved. "Did I not tell you to march them out, Sergeant?"

"Yes, sir."

Nobody spoke during the short walk and Paul disappeared into his tent. He had no particular desire to explain himself to Carl or Johnny, and he was fairly sure he could rely on his sergeant to do it for him. O'Reilly looked as though he could barely contain himself. Sitting on his camp bed, Paul picked up a letter which sat unopened on his brass bound chest. It was from Joshua and had been sitting there for two days. Paul sighed, put it down and got up to get the brandy bottle. He sat with a glass in his hand and opened the letter, wondering who would be the first through the tent flap to tell him he was being an idiot.

***

Michael watched Paul go into his tent and looked around to see Lieutenants Swanson and Wheeler sitting over a card game. Carl waved Michael over.

"Is he all right, Sergeant?"

"Not that I can see, sir. He's gone bloody mad."

Wheeler gave a theatrical groan. "Oh what now, Sergeant? He needs a full-time keeper, for God's sake."

Michael explained briefly and Wheeler glanced at Carl.

"He can't do that. Gregson is an arsehole; he must know Paul can't keep that up in this weather. You need to talk to Paul."

"It won't do a blind bit of good, Johnny, but I will if you like."

"Permission to find those four twats and find out exactly what happened, sir?" Michael said grimly.

"By all means, Sergeant."

Michael headed down the lines to find Dawson, Cooper, Bryant and Smith with Sergeant Stewart, who had clearly been getting the story.

"Am I hearing this right?" Stewart demanded.

31

"I don't know." Michael surveyed the four men. "Get to attention you useless bastards! What the bloody hell were you doing out there?"

"Sarge – going for grog, Sarge. There's an arrack shop in the village."

"Without permission, Cooper?"

"Yes, Sarge."

"And what particular lie did you tell Captain Gregson?"

"That we were hunting for rabbits, Sarge. Didn't matter what we told him, he was going to flog us anyway. He lost a bet last week during the parade, thought his lads could beat us. Made him look stupid."

"Sergeant, Mr van Daan's not really going to do this, is he?" Smith said. "We'll take the flogging; he's going to kill himself out in that heat all afternoon."

"If it were me, Smithy, you'd be flogged, you bloody deserve it. This lad? If he says he's going to get you off this, I think he will. But I'm going to make sure your week is every bit as bad as his, believe me."

***

Word had got around by the following afternoon and there was an audience up on the hillside as Paul approached the sergeant of the first company of the 17th Bengal. The man saluted.

"Sir."

"At ease, Sergeant. What's your name?"

"Thomas, sir. Formerly Welsh guards."

"Well, you've got me for the next seven days, Sergeant, and it's bloody hot out here. I'm guessing you heard the story?"

"Yes, sir. Looks like half the army has heard it."

"Doesn't it? Cheer up, Thomas, it's hot on that hillside as well, and they'll get bored before I do. Get the lads round for me, I want to explain what we're doing before we start. How's their English?"

"Good, sir, most of them have served for years."

"Excellent. We'll start with standard close order drilling and move to musket training when they can't run any more. By the end of the week, they'll all be on three rounds a minute and be able to run the basic drills without thinking about it."

"As good as your lads, sir?"

Paul studied him with interest. "Is that what this is about, Sergeant?"

"Captain Gregson likes to win, sir."

It confirmed Paul's suspicions. "Well, Captain Gregson can have this one. He's up there, having a good laugh and I'm down here doing his job for him. I can't punch him, he's a senior officer, but I do intend to show him what his company can do with two grown-ups in charge, so are you ready?"

There was a gleam of amusement in the Welshman's eyes. "Yes, sir."

As Paul arrived back at his tent, hot and tired, he found Private Dawson awaiting him. Paul paused and lifted his eyebrows. Dawson stood to attention.

32

"Sir – we'll take the flogging."

"Not your choice, Dawson." Paul turned to go into his tent.

"I've served out here before, sir, I know what the heat can do to you. You shouldn't be out there in it all day."

"Jesus Christ, I'm amazed at how delicate you all think I am. I can survive it for a week. Dismissed, Dawson."

"Sir..."

Paul sighed and turned. "Did Sergeant O'Reilly thump you, Dawson?"

"Yes, sir. And we're mucking out the pack animals all week."

"Good. I hope those bloody bullocks have raging diarrhoea. Now go away. And if I ever catch any one of you four sneaking off without coming to me for permission again, you are going to find yourself head first and face down in the biggest pile of dung that I can come up with; believe me, you'll wish I'd flogged you. Have I made myself clear?"

"Yes, sir." Dawson saluted. "Thank you, sir."

"You aren't going to be thanking me after this week's drill with me, Dawson, because trust me, if I'm feeling bad, you'll be feeling bad. Now get lost, I need a drink and a lie down."

On the third day, Paul was in his tent lying on his camp bed as his commanding officer ducked in. Wearily Paul moved to get up and Johnstone waved him back.

"This has gone far enough, Lieutenant."

"I'm fine, sir."

"You're not fine, laddie, you're exhausted. You've made your point, now give in. The lads would rather take the flogging than see you..."

"Are you ordering me, sir?"

Johnstone glared at him. "I'm trying to get you to see reason."

"I'd rather finish this, sir. With your permission."

Johnstone shook his head. "You are a stubborn young bastard, Mr van Daan."

"I know, sir."

When he had gone, Paul lay back again. "I know you're there, Michael, stop lurking and come in."

The Irishman emerged from behind the tent flap. "You've got the hearing of a bat, sir. Are you all right?"

"I'm tired, but that isn't going to kill me, although it appears my entire battalion, from the major downwards, thinks it is."

"Why the hell are you doing this, sir? Those bastards had it coming."

"They had something coming. Having the skin taken off your back for sneaking off for a drink seems a bit much to me. Besides, I don't like flogging."

"The army likes flogging."

"Just because I'm in the army doesn't mean I agree with all its rules and traditions, Michael. If I did, you wouldn't be in here talking to me like this. I can't change everything, but I can bloody well stop my men from being flogged, if I get the chance. If they need discipline, I can deal with them, I don't need an arsehole like Captain Gregson interfering. It doesn't work anyway."

"I can tell it didn't work on you, sir, you've remained a pig-headed bugger."

Paul regarded him with amusement. "Carl, I presume?"

"Yes, but I'd noticed when we were swimming anyway. Some nasty scars. They beat you bloody, didn't they?"

"They did. I survived. But it's left me in a fairly unusual position for an officer, I know how bad it feels. I also know it doesn't work. I like your solution better; I was going to suggest the latrines, but bullock shit feels about right for that lot. And when this is done I'm going to have a little chat with those four, which will guarantee they don't wander off for quite some time. Now piss off and let me sleep, Sergeant. I don't know what it is about my tent, it's like the bloody market square on Mayday."

By the fifth day, Paul realised he was probably suffering from sunstroke. The back of his neck was burned raw and he had a permanently pounding headache. Apart from drill and training, which he attended without fail, he saw little of his men or the other officers, preferring to spend his free time resting. Carl, who knew him better than the others, was quiet on the subject, steadfastly ensuring that he was well supplied with food and drink, and not allowing the others to bother him unnecessarily, and Paul blessed him for it. Carl had found a girl in the regimental cook's tent, who made juice, a concoction of local fruits pressed together, and Carl arranged for her to take some to Paul on a daily basis. It was cool and soothing, and after a few days, she brought a salve made from aloe, which she silently applied to Paul's burned skin. He smiled appreciatively, wondering if she had any idea what he was doing or why. She smiled back and left him to his restless sleep.

The audience had tailed off over the week, although Paul was aware that most of the light company came out to watch him every day. On the final day, however, the slopes were crowded again, and Paul turned the last hour into a mini parade, taking the sepoys through the drills and training they had worked on through the week. Standing beside Sergeant Thomas Paul watched them and felt a sense of satisfaction which more than made up for the misery of the past seven days. They had improved out of all recognition.

"Not bad, Sergeant. Want me to come back next week and get five minutes off that for you?" he said softly, and the Welshman began to laugh.

"Excuse me for saying this, sir, but you're a bloody madman," he said. "Captain Gregson's approaching."

Paul turned and saluted. "All done, sir."

"Yes." Gregson was watching his men. "You coming up to the mess tonight, Van Daan? I'll buy you a drink." He laughed suddenly. "I can't believe you stuck this out."

Paul thought of a number of replies he would have liked to make. He bit all of them back. "Thank you, sir," he said cheerfully. "I'll be there when I've cleaned up."

"Gentlemen."

34

Paul turned. He was startled to see Major Johnstone approaching with the tall spare figure of General Wellesley. He saluted. Wellesley was watching the end of the drill as Sergeant Thomas began to call the men into line.

"Very impressive. Your work, I understand, Mr van Daan."

"Yes, sir."

"I imagine you won't forget to give your men a ticket again when they go off after...what was it, rabbits?"

"I believe so, sir. No, I don't think we'll have a repeat of this." Paul risked a glance at Wellesley and was surprised to see a gleam of laughter in the hooded blue eyes.

"I imagine you'll need a rest this evening but come up to my office tomorrow at ten. I've a job for you."

"Yes, sir."

"Try not to get drunk in the mess tonight. Although some of my officers have complained that you prefer drinking with your men."

Paul froze for a moment, not sure if he was being reprimanded or not. "Have they, sir? I'm sorry to hear that."

"Carry on then, Lieutenant."

Paul turned and gave Thomas the order to dismiss the men. As he was walking back up the hill towards the lines, he was surprised to hear cheering, and glanced around to see the light company on the hillside yelling. After a moment the noise intensified as the sepoys of the 17th joined in. Paul laughed, saluted and went wearily up to his tent. He found the girl waiting for him with salve and a drink and he smiled and shook his head.

"Can you leave it? I'm going down to bathe in the river; I'll have it later. Thank you."

She nodded. "This is the last day?"

"Yes, thank God. You've been a big help. I'm sorry; I don't know your name. I forgot my manners this week."

"My name is Manjira, sahib."

"Manjira – thank you."

Paul would have preferred to stay with his men, but he still had a point to make, so he bathed and changed and joined the others at the mess where Captain Gregson became offensively cheerful after the second bottle, drinking toasts to Paul, while Paul smiled pleasantly, accepted the jokes and thought how much he would enjoy punching the smile off Gregson's face. He excused himself when he decently could and went back to his tent. The girl was there, sitting demurely on the edge of his bed with her bare feet crossed. He had been hoping she would be. Paul smiled and held out his hand.

"It's too damned hot in here," he said. "Would you like to come down to the river with me?"

She went with him down to the soft sandy banks and went into his arms. They undressed, and she giggled a little over his struggles with the unfamiliar fastenings of her sari, then she led him into the cool water. Paul wondered fleetingly if the sounds of their lovemaking could be heard up at the lines and decided that he did not care.

Chapter Three

Paul arrived in Wellesley's office the following day to find the general with Major Johnstone. Wellesley looked Paul over thoughtfully and Paul returned his regard with some interest. As a very junior officer he had been introduced to Wellesley briefly but had never had a conversation with him until yesterday and had no idea why he was here.

Major-General Arthur Wellesley was probably in his mid-thirties, a little more than medium height, lean and dark-haired with a hooked nose, a determined chin and a pair of intelligent hooded blue eyes. Wellesley had been in India for several years, and his older brother was currently serving as Governor-General. With no personal knowledge of the general, Paul had formed an impression of a highly self-contained man who made no attempt to ingratiate himself with either officers or men.

"An interesting week, Mr van Daan," Wellesley said finally. "You're nothing if not persistent. I've had very mixed reports of you, sir, but I'm inclined to give you a chance. Will the men follow you?"

"Yes, sir."

"We'll see. We are having trouble with supply wagons getting through. Three days ago we lost two wagons of valuable food and medical supplies to roving bands of Maratha cavalry. We also lost eight men and a dozen horses. It won't do, Mr van Daan. I'm about to go further into Maratha territory to try to bring them to a pitched battle and I need my supplies secured."

"Yes, sir."

"I am expecting a convoy of bullock carts bearing two more guns and a quantity of ammunition from the south and they need to reach me. Major Johnstone is needed here, I am putting him in charge of two battalions of sepoy infantry along with his own infantry companies and he'll need some time to work with them. I'm sending his light company to meet the convoy and escort it back here. Are you up to the job, boy?"

Paul felt a little jolt of excitement. It was an opportunity, and he knew it. "Yes, sir."

"Excellent. I've sent a messenger asking the convoy to await your arrival at the village of Pular. I'll show you here, on the map, there's a small escort of native light cavalry with it. You have temporary command of the light company, Mr van Daan."

Paul was puzzled. "Yes, sir." He glanced at Johnstone. "But sir…"

"Captain Mason is too ill to march and I've asked that Lieutenant Wheeler remain with me," Johnstone said. "I need an old hand to help me whip these battalions into shape. Do you think you can manage without him, Mr van Daan?"

"I think so, sir," Paul said appreciatively. He could sense that both Wellesley and Johnstone were testing out a new and possibly promising officer, but he could not have taken command of the company on his first time against the enemy ahead of Johnny Wheeler, who should have been promoted long ago. Being chosen as effective second-in-command to Johnstone, even for a short time, was a good opportunity for Wheeler and Paul knew he would seize the chance.

"You'll march tomorrow," Wellesley said. "Carry on, Mr van Daan."

The journey from Poona to Pular was tedious but without incident and Paul gave orders for a rest day in the village before setting out on the long march back. The convoy travelled cautiously north, each man spending much of his time looking over his shoulder as their route took them through scrubby hills and rocky valleys. The coming of the monsoon brought rain most days, and the light company trudged through torrential downpours, which turned the dirt tracks to mud and made it hard for the bullocks to drag the heavy wagons. The twenty Bengal light cavalry, under a young Scottish subaltern, who had formed the original escort, seemed relieved at the addition of the light company but by the time they by-passed Wai and crossed the river, Paul was beginning to wonder if the general had been mistaken about the likelihood of an ambush.

The convoy of twelve wagons, each drawn by four bullocks, was an impressive sight streaming across the ford. His horse up to its knees in water, Paul paused to watch it pass. They were making good time.

"No sign of trouble yet," Carl said. They had spent the journey down to Pular assessing the countryside and knew exactly where they were most likely to be ambushed. Paul's favourite was a sloping valley winding for around five miles between barren hills, littered with scrub bushes and cacti. The hills were shallow enough for a skilled horseman to ride easily over the top, and it was the place he would have chosen to make an attack.

There was no hope of keeping their route a secret. There could have been Maratha scouts behind any thicket or bush and Paul was sure their progress had been observed and reported. Once the convoy was through the ford, Paul rode up and down the long snaking train, putting his men on the alert. He had already shared his plan in case of attack, but for it to work, his men needed to trust him and follow orders.

As they marched down into the valley, Paul motioned to O'Reilly and the sergeant ran forward, leading the small band of riflemen selected as the advance party of skirmishers. They were fast and agile, carrying their rifles easily, eyes scanning the slopes. There was no sign of horsemen as Paul led his men into the valley, but Paul was not reassured. It was warm and muggy, with the ground faintly steaming from recent rain, and the atmosphere felt heavy, but the weather did not account for Paul's discomfort. Something was bothering him, although he could not have said what it was.

A bird rose, high above the hillside, circling lazily against grey clouds. It looked like some kind of huge crane, and Paul watched it for a moment, wishing that he had its view of the hills. There was no other movement apart from the dull green of the riflemen's jackets, and the vivid splash of red indicating the presence of Sergeant O'Reilly among them.

There were eight riflemen attached to the light company, led by Corporal Grogan, and their presence baffled Paul. It was not unusual for men from the 95th to be used for detached duties but generally once the particular mission was completed, they would be returned to their own battalion. Paul had made repeated enquiries about Grogan and his men and received a variety of answers, none of which made any sense. As far as he could tell, they had joined the 110th during a previous campaign and simply never left. Sergeant O'Reilly seemed to have adopted them as his own, and their presence was never questioned. At times like this, they were invaluable.

Paul looked up at the crane again, as it made yet another wide, graceful circle above the hills. As he watched, the sky below it filled with more birds, smaller and white, possibly doves, a whole flock of them starting up from the reverse slope of the hillside above the convoy as though something had disturbed them. Paul felt his stomach lurch.

"Attack! Form up, defensive square! Move!"

Paul heard Michael's yell, simultaneous to his own and the bugler took up the call. The wagons lurched to a halt and the men were moving before the first Maratha horsemen came over the hill. To Paul, his men seemed painfully slow, but he knew from past experience that time stood still in battle, and they were moving well and remembering their orders as the Maratha swooped down towards them. O'Reilly and his men raced for cover among rocks at the foot of the slope, and Paul yelled at his sergeant to bring them in, but he saw immediately why Michael did not. There were more horsemen coming from the opposite direction, and if the riflemen sprinted towards the wagons they would be cut down in mid-flight. The huge boulders were a natural fortress and Paul silently thanked God for his sergeant's eye for terrain.

Paul's stomach was tight with fear. He was not new to battle although this was different to the churning terror of the dim lower decks of a man o'war with guns crashing and deadly splinters flying around him, where there was no room for inventiveness and very little choice but to fire the guns and keep pounding at the enemy. All the skill involved in a naval battle came with the chase and manoeuvring into position, and it was why Paul was here, where he could fight on his own terms. He had worked for this and trained for this and chosen this, and he took a deep steadying breath.

"Backs to the wagons. Remember your training and don't panic. They're not expecting this, and they won't have a fucking clue how to deal with it."

38

Paul's voice carried in the still air, even over the thundering hooves growing closer, and those men close enough to hear him properly, shot him a startled glance. One or two of them even managed a grin. It was the effect Paul had intended, although even he was surprised at how confident he sounded. As the Maratha drew closer, he rode to the square which opened to let him inside.

It was not, in fact a square at all. The most effective defence against a cavalry attack was the traditional infantry square, and Paul had toiled for long hours with these men over the past months, keeping them out on the training ground long after the rest of the battalion was at rest, drilling into them the importance of being able to move quickly and smoothly. But an infantry square generally consisted of at least a battalion, and Paul had not enough men. Nor did he have enough cavalry to send them out against the Maratha. The twenty men of the escort would be slaughtered within minutes.

Instead he had instructed the drivers to draw up the wagons into two rows, side by side, forming a solid rectangle and shortening the length of the convoy. Each evening on the journey, before allowing the men to make camp, he had made them practice forming a thin square around the outside, their backs to the wagons, with the cavalry mounted inside as a second line of defence should the enemy break through. The square would have been too fragile to stand by itself, but the wagons would prevent the cavalry sweeping through as they could with infantry caught in line and would enable the muskets of the infantry to mow down the approaching horsemen. If the light company broke, it would be possible for them to fall back between the wagons or even to take refuge inside them for a final stand.

The Maratha horsemen came fast, armed with the long spear and savage curved tulwar, riding in from two directions. The first group split into two as they approached, and Paul saw some twenty of them bearing down fast on the rocky ground where Michael waited with his small group of rifles. A spear flew through the air and Paul felt sick, but it bounced off the rock behind which Corporal Grogan had vanished, and there was the crack of a rifle, then another, and two horsemen fell.

There was no time to worry about the skirmishers, as the main body of horsemen approached the wagons. Paul yelled an order, and it was taken up by Sergeant Stewart. As the Maratha galloped in, several spears flew, one of them embedding itself in a wagon, the others clattering harmlessly to the ground.

"Number one, fire!"

The muskets crashed with an explosion of sound which made Paul's ears ring, and there was a squeal of horses and cries of agony as the first line of horsemen were blown away by the volley.

"Number two, fire!" Stewart roared again, and the second volley thundered out. With no possibility of the standard double ranks, Paul had allocated numbers to every man in the line, so that three volleys could be fired, giving time to reload. Musket drill had been going well, and Paul could see no sign of panic.

Beyond his men, the Bengal cavalry were restless on their horses, and one or two of them were pointing carbines. Paul touched his horse and moved forward.

"Mr Fraser get your bloody troopers under control before they hit my men, they've no call to be shooting yet. Mr Denny, close up that gap."

Two men were down and being dragged back into the shelter of the wagons by some of the ox boys. The bullocks were restless with the noise of the shooting, and Paul shouted an order to the drivers to keep them calm. His worst fear was that the cattle would panic and bolt, breaking his fragile defences wide open and leaving his men to be slaughtered.

Muskets crashed again and the acrid smell of smoke caught Paul's throat and invaded his nostrils. Up and down the rows of wagons his men stood solid, cutting down the attacking horsemen with steady fire, and the Maratha were beginning to hang back. There were many of them on the ground, along with several horses, forming an extra barrier in front of the light company. Paul looked over his troops, watching the concentration on every face as they loaded and fired, loaded and fired, while Stewart and his corporals called time, again and again and again. The air filled with smoke, the Maratha seemed to howl with fury, but Paul could sense that they were wavering. They had expected an easy kill, a small escort and a triumphant lifting of the supply convoy and Paul thought that they did not have the stomach for a long fight.

"Number one, fire!"

There was a yell of panic and an answering cry of triumph in a language Paul did not understand, and he wheeled his horse, and saw to his horror, that a man was down at the far end of the wagons and his companions were trying desperately to close the gap. The main body of the horsemen had pulled back under shouted orders, ready for another pass, but four of them remained, forcing their horses forward, their curved tulwars swinging while Paul's men fought for their lives with bayonets. One of the horsemen was sliding from the saddle, blood pumping from a wound in his thigh, and two of the light company were on him in seconds, stabbing down savagely. A third pricked his horse in the rear, sending it thundering out onto the hillside again, but three Maratha remained, and the gap was widening. In minutes, the Maratha commander would see his opportunity and bring his horsemen thundering in and the square would be broken.

Paul urged his horse forward and rode into the fray swinging his sword. He had not been trained to fight from horseback, but he was a very skilled rider, and he controlled his horse with his knees, moving in on the horsemen, wielding his sword to cut them down, while trying to dodge their tulwars. In this fight, their spears were useless, as coming close enough for an effective throw made them vulnerable to a musket volley, or the accurate rifle fire which was still coming from Michael's rocky fortress.

One horseman was down, his mount galloping away, and Paul fought a furious duel with another, relying on his strength, length of reach and speed. He was gaining ground, with the Maratha parrying frantically and backing his horse away from the line and out of reach, when he felt a sharp pain across the top of his arm, and he swore and wheeled around to slash at the final horseman who had cut him. For one terrifying moment he felt trapped between the two Maratha, but there was a yelled order and suddenly more horses bore down from inside the defences and half a dozen of the Bengal cavalry drove off the remaining horsemen leaving Paul breathless, in pain and bloody, but alive. He yelled at his rescuers to come back and his infantry closed the gap smoothly and waited.

Paul looked out over the heads of his men and saw the enemy wheeling about. There were dead and wounded on the ground, both men and horses, and he could sense that the remaining cavalry had probably had enough and that left to themselves, they would have fled. Their commander had other ideas. Scanning the ridge, Paul could see him astride a large grey horse, part way up the slope, shouting orders and pointing, giving directions for another pass. Paul hesitated for a moment, knowing that it was a gamble. The loss of their commander might galvanise the horsemen into a final and more savage attack or it might send them on their way. As his men reloaded muskets, gulped mouthfuls of water from their bottles and waited for the next attack, Paul trotted to the other end of the defences and raised his voice in a shout that echoed through the valley and bounced off the hills, startling several of the Bengal cavalry horses into restlessness and making one of the bullocks bellow aggressively as if in response.

"Sergeant, your three best shots! Take him down!"

The Maratha commander heard it clearly and turned his head to stare down at Paul. Even at this distance, he had a face of distinctive beauty and Paul looked back steadily, wondering if the man had understood the order he had just given. Almost certainly he understood the meaning of Paul's pointing finger, and he turned his horse quickly, as if to gallop down to join his men, but Michael's voice was already echoing Paul's.

"Carter! Grogan! Thompson! Take down the bastard on the hill! Mr van Daan doesn't like him and neither do I."

Three men ran forward, dropping into cover with the expertise of long practice. Rifles lifted and steadied, and three shots rang out. The Maratha commander fell, almost lifted out of the saddle by the shot.

There was a long silence, punctuated only by the muted sound of hooves on the soft earth of the valley floor and the jingling of harness and weapons as the Maratha realised that their commander was dead. Paul held his breath and around him, his men were silent, waiting.

Another order was called, in a different voice, and suddenly the horsemen were riding, heading off at a gallop along the track. Several of them wheeled in towards the wagons, and Paul realised they were shouting to their wounded on the ground. A musket fired one shot, and Paul shouted a furious order to hold, and watched with surprised admiration as a number of the more mobile wounded staggered forward and were swung up onto their comrades' horses. A cloud of dust followed the horsemen as they crested the rise, and then disappeared over it and down the other side, out of sight of the light company.

For a moment, the silence was absolute, and then somebody raised a slightly wavering cheer, and it was taken up by others. Paul let it go on for a moment, his eyes scanning the hillside, but there was no tell-tale cloud of dust and he thought that the Maratha had probably gone. He felt an enormous sense of relief and with it, a wave of nausea which he forced down.

"Mr Fraser stand guard with your troopers. Sergeant Stewart, check for prisoners, disarm them and get their dead piled up over there. Sergeant O'Reilly do a roll call, if you please. And keep an eye out. I doubt they'll be back but let's not get sloppy."

Paul slid from his horse and patted the sweating animal on his neck. "Good lad. Hold steady and we'll get you a drink in a minute."

"I'll take him, sir," one of his men said, and Paul handed over the reins with a smile.

"Thanks, Samson. All right?"

"Right as rain, sir." Samson lifted the wicked looking tulwar he had taken from a fallen Maratha. "Had my eye on one of these for a while now."

"When we've time, I'll teach you how to use it," Paul said. He walked along the column, checking his men for injury. There were a number of minor wounds, and already their comrades were busy with emergency treatment, but he found no dead until he reached the position where he had fought to close the square. One man was on the ground, and two of his friends were kneeling beside him. Paul joined them.

"Ralston, sir. Tulwar across the head. Bloody bastards."

The man was dead and brain matter spilled out into the dust. Paul felt his stomach churn again. He reached out and gently closed the man's eyes. "I'm sorry," he said simply. "Was he married?"

"No sir. Third service overseas, twice in India. He liked the life."

"Let's get him buried, Private."

"Yes, sir."

There were no other serious casualties among the light company although one of Fraser's cavalry was dead and another seriously injured, both victims of accurately thrown spears. The men moved among the dead Maratha, looting the bodies and lining up the few survivors as prisoners. Paul walked up the slope to where O'Reilly stood with his three sharp shooters, all dressed in the distinctive green jackets of the rifles.

"Who got him?" Paul asked.

"Carter, sir."

"Well done, Carter. Your prize, take what you like."

Paul turned to look back down at the wagons. The graves for Private Ralston and the cavalry trooper were underway, the wounded were being tended and some of the men were filling their canteens from the river. There was still no sign of another attack, and Paul called out to Fraser to allow his men to water their horses in small groups, while still keeping a watchful eye on the hillside.

The men were comparing plunder, swords, the occasional pistol and a variety of exotic garments. Paul watched them affectionately. He felt slightly shaky and enormously proud of them. Their performance was a vindication of the work that he, Johnny and Carl had put in over the past months, but their courage under fire was a credit to them. Watching the burial party, Paul wondered if burial was the right thing for the Indian cavalryman. He had a feeling that cremation would have been more appropriate, but it was not an option here. He must find out his name and ask one of his friends to speak at the burial.

"Mr van Daan."

Paul turned. Carter, the youngest of the riflemen, was holding out a sword balanced carefully across two hands. Paul took it. It was a tulwar, encased in a beautifully worked sheath, studded with semi-precious stones. Paul drew the blade. It was delicately wrought with engravings and wickedly sharp. He tried a pass and the balance was perfect.

"You've struck lucky with this, Carter, it's beautiful."

Carter touched his belt. "Already got one, sir, from one of the other bastards. This one's for you."

It was probably the most valuable piece of plunder from the battle. Paul felt his throat constrict.

"I can't take this from you, Carter. You earned it."

"I want you to have it, sir. All the lads will agree. Officer's sword, sir. Should be yours."

Paul looked past the man. Michael O'Reilly looked serious, but his dark eyes were smiling. "Take it, sir," he said quietly. "Your victory. Your prize."

"Thank you," Paul said. "Not really a prize, since I didn't win it, but I'll accept it as a gift. Come on, let's get poor Ralston buried."

They had dug the grave deep and laid Private Ralston and Trooper Das in it, bringing rocks to protect the bodies from scavengers. Paul said a short prayer, then allowed the men time to speak their brief tributes to their fallen comrades. When the graves were filled in, Paul turned to address his men.

"We'll get out of this death trap and make camp in the open by the river. Double sentries and a short night, and we'll march at quick time to get back to Poona. This lot will be missed and I've no wish to encounter their pissed-off cousins before we've time to recover. Let's go."

Paul reached up to check the flesh wound at the top of his arm. O'Reilly had fashioned a bandage from a Maratha silk sash about it and the bleeding seemed to have stopped, although it was sore. Paul went to his horse with a nod of thanks to the trooper who had watered it and took the reins.

"Sir."

Paul turned. The eight riflemen were lined up at the front of the light company. The oldest of them, Corporal Grogan, a grizzled veteran from Dorset, took his hand from his pocket and tossed something to Paul, who caught it instinctively. He looked down at it. It was a white armband made out of some kind of cord. Paul recognised it as the single stripe allotted to a chosen man. Three of his green-jacketed riflemen wore it, including Carter.

"Chosen man, sir," Carter said. They were all grinning, and the laughter spread through the ranks as the other men realised what it was. Chosen man was an informal award for a common soldier, an acknowledgement of courage and skill and leadership, and was usually a step on the way to promotion to NCO. It was not an award for an officer and most officers would not have dreamed of wearing it, but Paul suspected that it was an acknowledgement of more than just his leadership in the skirmish.

Paul handed the reins back to the trooper and pulled the armband over the sleeve of his jacket, pulling it into place as the others wore it. He gave an appreciative grin and nodded to Carter, then turned to his men, who seemed to be waiting for him to speak. Paul raised his voice so that they could all hear it.

"Thank you, I'll try not to disgrace it. I told you they wouldn't have a bloody idea what to do against that, but what I really meant is they'd have no idea what to do against men like you. I'm proud of every one of you, and I'm proud to command you, even for this short while. Well done."

He saluted and as he turned to his horse, the men raised a cheer and O'Reilly came forward to hold the horse steady for him to mount.

"First time I've seen that done," he said.

"I'm not sure if it's a compliment or not."

"It's a compliment, trust me."

"I hope so. With any luck, they'll promote me to corporal in a year or so."

"Don't push your luck, sir."

Paul grinned. "Line them up, Sergeant. Let's get these guns back to Wellesley and have a drink."

"With the men, sir?" his sergeant said, wide-eyed. Paul laughed. He had told Carl about Wellesley's remarks and by now he imagined the whole of the light company knew that he had been reported for drinking with the men.

"I prefer drinking with men to maggots, Michael," he said, and wheeled his mount around. "Fall in."

They marched into Poona to a good deal of interest. As Paul dismounted at the armoury, a young ensign came running up and saluted him. "Compliments of General Wellesley, sir. He wants to see you at headquarters."

Paul glanced back at Carl. "Your company, Mr Swanson. See the stores safe and get the men back to camp."

"Yes, sir."

As he followed the ensign, Paul heard a murmur of laughter rippling through the ranks. "See you later for a drink, sir," Private Cooper said, and Paul masked a grin.

"If you're buying, Cooper," he said softly and heard the shout of laughter as he moved away.

Paul walked up to the headquarters building and was shown into Wellesley's office. Major Johnstone was present and surprisingly, so was Captain Gregson.

"Mr van Daan. Let's have it." Wellesley said.

44

Paul saluted. "Yes, sir. Convoy safely delivered; my men are supervising the unloading under the guidance of the quartermaster."

"Trouble?"

"We were attacked about thirty miles out of Poona, in the valley. Loss of two men, one of the escort and one of mine, Private Ralston. Some wounded."

Wellesley came around the desk. With eyes that missed nothing he studied Paul from head to toe. "How many Maratha?"

"Hard to say. We took down around twenty, killed and wounded. They got some of their wounded off, but we took four prisoners, you may want to talk to them. My sharpshooters killed their commander."

"I see." The general reached out and touched the white armband. "Nice touch, Mr van Daan. These aren't easy to come by."

"No, sir."

"A gift?"

"Yes, sir."

"I've never been offered one of these," Wellesley said.

Paul met his eyes. "Sorry sir," he said. "But you can't have mine."

The general unexpectedly laughed. "You're an impudent young dog, Van Daan, but you did damned well. I do wonder if you'd have found them quite so easy to lead if you'd not taken their punishment for seven days, but I rather expect you already thought of that, didn't you, boy?"

"Oddly enough, sir, that isn't why I did that," Paul said. "I just don't like flogging."

Wellesley snorted. "You seem to be doing all right without it so far, but don't allow your squeamishness to affect discipline, Lieutenant. Major Johnstone, it seems you were right about him." Wellesley glanced across at Gregson then looked back at Paul, and Paul could see a gleam of amusement in his eyes. "I'd offer you a drink, Lieutenant, but I imagine you'll want to get cleaned up. Get yourself back to your men. No drill tomorrow, and I've ordered a bottle or two to be sent down to your tent. You have my permission to share it with your men, as it's a special occasion."

Paul met Wellesley's eyes, keeping a straight face with an immense effort, and indicated his dirty clothing. "Of course, sir, I'm in no fit state to be drinking with gentlemen."

"No, you're not. By God, you're not, sir." Wellesley was openly laughing now. "Back to your ruffians, then, and look after them. I'll be needing them again."

"Thank you, sir."

Paul felt a combination of satisfaction, relief and sheer exhaustion as he made his way through the town and up towards the camp. It was busy at this hour of the day, and he nodded a greeting to other officers he knew. One or two of them called out congratulations. Gossip spread like wildfire in an army camp, and Paul knew that success in his first command was important. Not knowing his chequered past, his fellow officers would assume that he had no previous experience of combat.

Wellesley's promised brandy awaited him in his tent. Paul called Michael, and had it distributed among the men. They sat around the cooking fires and the company women served them hot food and listened to accounts of the skirmish. Paul sipped his drink and watched them, admitting with rueful self-knowledge that this, rather than down in the officers' mess, was where he would always be happiest. As darkness fell, Manjira arrived, her working day done, and Paul drew her to sit beside him. She noticed his wound and would have fussed over it, but Paul shook his head, and kissed her instead. He sat quietly in the darkness, listening to the laughter and chatter around him, and thought how pleasant it was to feel her sitting peacefully beside him.

"I'm glad you're here, Manjira."

He felt her lips brush his jawline very softly. "I also," she said, and Paul put his arm about her, drawing comfort from her nearness.

***

Within days Wellesley had broken camp and marched towards the north-east, further into Maratha territory. Wellesley kept the light company busy, using them as scouts, regularly sending them out ahead of the main army to report back on any troop movements. It was evident that he had taken a liking to their colourful young lieutenant, and although Johnny Wheeler had returned to their ranks, Major Johnstone remained in command of the sepoy infantry regiments and Captain Mason was seldom well enough for active duty which meant that Paul retained effective control of the light company. Paul wondered if Wheeler would feel resentful of his sudden informal promotion, but Johnny seemed surprisingly accepting of the change, stepping up to act as Paul's second-in-command on those occasions when Captain Mason was not there. There was something very reassuring about Wheeler's steady competence beside him and Paul felt a passionate gratitude for the older man's attitude.

By the middle of August, Wellesley and his army had taken the city and fortress of Ahmednaggur. Too impatient for a lengthy siege, he used artillery to blow breaches in the walls and sent his men over by escalade. It was Paul's first experience of storming a fortress, and his first experience too, of the suddenness with which an army could run wild in a captured town. The Maratha forces, led by their French officers, had fled the town by the time Wellesley's men entered the city, and there was an orgy of looting and pillage by many of the sepoy troops and their camp followers. Wellesley was furious when the European sentries he had posted to prevent rioting, joined in the looting, and sent a troop of cavalry to chase off the looters and restore order, summarily hanging two sepoys caught in the act as a warning. The 110th light company had no opportunity to join the looting, having been removed from the city at speed, the moment the fighting was over. Michael O'Reilly had described how these same men had run wild in Seringapatam several years earlier and Paul was determined it should not happen again.

After several weeks replenishing supplies, Wellesley led his army on in pursuit of the Maratha forces, seeming determined to force a battle as soon as possible. Some of the more cynical officers in the mess pointed out that a young and relatively inexperienced general needed a big success to cement his reputation, but Paul felt that there was good military sense behind Wellesley's urgency. If he could catch the Maratha during the monsoon season while the rivers were flooding and the roads were poor it would severely hamper their cavalry, which was the pick of their forces.

Reports of a small force of Maratha cavalry in the vicinity of Nalni, sent the light company out again towards the middle of September, under the command of Captain Mason who seemed to have recovered a little. Mason rode at the head of the company in quiet conversation with Ensign Denny and Paul dropped back to ride alongside Carl and Johnny. He was uncomfortably aware that the men had developed a tendency to refer every order back to him as if he was still in command. Johnny was inclined to make a joke of it, but Paul wondered if Mason had noticed, and if it bothered him.

There was no immediate sign of the reported cavalry. Moving cautiously northwards, they explored a series of small hills in the otherwise flat river basin and Paul instructed the men to keep their voices low. The Maratha were reported to be about twelve miles away, but they would have outposts and patrols, and in country like this it was possible to be ambushed very quickly.

They were two miles out of the village of Assaye when Captain Mason suddenly reined in and held up a hand. Paul heard it at the same moment. He glanced at Mason who looked back at him and nodded. Paul slid from his horse and beckoned to O'Reilly and Private Carter. The three of them jogged forward past the small hillock and up a sloping ridge to look down over the village and Paul caught his breath.

"Christ aid us," O'Reilly whispered. Below them, spread across the land between the Kaitna and the Juah Rivers was the Maratha army, encamped over several miles of ground. They appeared to be wholly oblivious of the light company's proximity.

"We need to get back to Wellesley," Paul said. He was running his eyes over the thousands of Maratha infantry and horsemen milling about below him, trying to commit as much as he could to memory. They were about four miles from Wellesley's camp and Paul wondered if one of the officers should ride on ahead of the company to inform Wellesley.

There was a high-pitched scream, quickly cut off, and then further cries and the sound of horsemen. A rifle cracked, followed by another one, and there was a yell of agony.

"Move!" Paul shouted, and took off at speed over the rise, with O'Reilly and Carter in hot pursuit. Both were loading their rifles on the run, which slowed them down a little, so Paul reached the battle first, his sword drawn. A Maratha cavalryman swooped down on him, and then a rifle cracked from behind him and the man fell from his horse. Paul cut and thrust at a second, parried a third and swung around to see several of his men on the ground.

"Light company, to me!" he roared. "Form square!"

They scrambled to obey, and under his bellowed directions managed to form a small square, bayonets fixed. The six riflemen and O'Reilly had fallen back to the scrubland at the foot of the hill where they could give themselves time and space to reload and aim. The only officer left on horseback was Ensign Denny, and he was slashing about him with his sword as the Maratha tried to bring him down.

"Rifles – give Denny cover!" Paul yelled. He had no idea where his captain was and did not have time to look. He stabbed another horseman. "Denny – ride for your life, man, and tell Wellesley! The Maratha army is here – all of it! Not where he thinks them!"

Paul fell back with an oath as a horseman; taking advantage of his temporary distraction slashed him across his chest. It hurt like hell, but it was a superficial wound and Paul stabbed upwards and brought the Maratha down. The riflemen turned their attention to the horsemen surrounding Denny, and the moment he was free he touched spurs to his horse and set off back in the direction of camp. Paul sent up a brief prayer that he had understood his message but could do nothing more. The light company was fighting for its life.

Without the expertise of O'Reilly and the riflemen they would not have survived. Time and again the rifles cracked, and a horseman fell. Back-to-back in the square, the company fought, every moment of the hours of training Paul had pushed them through coming into play. A square consisting of one company was far too small to be effective, but it was still the best way to combat a cavalry attack and Paul's men had practised the manoeuvres so many times that it was second nature to them. The remaining officers stood not in the centre, as was usual, but in line with the men, and the sound of the muskets reverberated through Paul's brain.

Time stood still. Paul's arm ached and his chest hurt. Sweat ran down into his eyes, but he barely had time to wipe them on his sleeve. The battle seemed to go on longer than he could bear, and he bore down on his exhaustion and concentrated his attention solely on each Maratha who rode at him, stabbing at horses and legs and stomachs, dragging them from their horses when possible, cutting and thrusting and parrying over and over again until he began to feel that it would never end and that sooner or later, he would not be able to lift his sword arm. Around him, his men fired muskets whenever they could, and slashed up with bayonets when they could not. Paul had no idea how many men had attacked them, but it was a small troop and they seemed leaderless and poorly organised, possibly a foraging party.

It was over as quickly as it had begun. Suddenly there was nobody to fight, and Paul took a gasp of air and swung around to see four horsemen riding back towards the Maratha lines.

"Bring them down!"

The rifles cracked again, and one by one the four horsemen fell. Paul stood, sword by his side, took air painfully into his lungs and had time finally to look around him.

His men stood dazed and bleeding, as he was. Few of them had escaped entirely unscathed and some lay on the ground. Paul sheathed his weapon and ran towards the prone body of his captain. Mason lay still and silent, his open eyes staring at the sky. His entrails spilled from a gaping cut through his abdomen and four of his men lay dead around him, brought down in the first shock of the attack. They had gone for the officer first, Paul realised. If he had been there with Mason, he might have died as well.

Both Carl and Wheeler were on their feet and O'Reilly and the riflemen were running from the scrubland to help their comrades. Paul had not really had time to think about them during the fight but their survival seemed miraculous.

Paul knelt by Mason and reached out to close the open eyes. His stomach was churning, and he realised despairingly that this time he was not going to make it. Michael O'Reilly put a hand on his shoulder and Paul got up.

"Michael, I'm going to be sick. I don't want them to see."

"Let them see, sir," O'Reilly said quietly. Paul ran to the edge of the scrub and was sick, briefly and violently, and the Irishman stood beside him. When he was done, he straightened, and Michael offered him his canteen. Paul rinsed his mouth and spat, and then drank.

"Here, sir," Private Carter was beside him, handing him a small flask. Paul drank, and the rum burned its way down into his stomach.

"Thanks, Carter. You all right?"

"Yes, sir." The young rifleman was eyeing him with an expression bordering on awe. "Do you know how many you killed there, sir?"

Paul did not. Now that the madness of battle had passed, he stared at the heap of Maratha dead with something like bewilderment. Carl was staunching blood from a flesh wound on his shoulder. "How many did we lose, Carl?"

"Eight, plus the captain."

"It would have been a lot more if you'd not rallied them so quickly," Wheeler said quietly.

Paul looked around him at the dead. He could see Carl regarding him questioningly, but he shook his head.

"We don't have time to bury them. I hate to leave them, but at any moment we might be spotted from the lines."

"You're right, sir," O'Reilly said.

The horses had long gone and Paul hoped they would find their way back to camp in their panic. "Light company, fall in. Pair up with anybody wounded. We don't leave any man behind, but we need to move. Quick time."

Paul went back to the captain, and briefly went through his pockets, retrieving a pocket watch, a miniature portrait of a pretty fair-haired girl, and a locket containing a lock of hair. He knew nothing about the captain's personal life, but these might be of value to somebody in the coming weeks. Glancing around he saw that some of his men were going through the pockets of their comrades. Before he could say anything, he heard O'Reilly's voice.

"Dawson - Jackson has a wife. What you just found is hers."

"I know, Sarge."

Their arrival back in camp caused a considerable stir. Through his miserable exhaustion, Paul could sense that his tired men were enjoying the sensation they were causing. It was clear that the rumour of the extinction of the light company had spread.

As the weary and bloody men began to unload their gear at the lines, Paul called Carl and Michael over. "I'm riding up to the village to see Wellesley, he needs to know what happened. Send over to the quartermasters for extra grog for them, Carl, tell them to charge it to me, Christ knows they've earned it. And Michael, see if you can rustle up a sheep or a goat to roast. I want them to celebrate tonight."

"Aye, sir, I'll do that, one of the locals will have meat to sell, for sure." The Irishman turned to go.

"Michael."

"Sir?"

"Well done," Paul said. "Your sharpshooters saved us today."

"No, sir. You saved us today."

Paul collected one of his spare mounts and rode wearily up the slope to the large white house which Wellesley had chosen for his headquarters. He dismounted, handed the reins to a groom, and walked through into the cool stone hall. He was met by Lieutenant Drydon, who came forward with hand outstretched. "It's good to see you, Paul, we thought you lost when your horses came in without you."

"To tell you the truth, Chris, so did I," Paul said. Now that it was over and there was no further need to remain constantly alert, he found that he was bone tired.

"Come through. He's got Major Johnstone with him and Captain Murray."

Paul followed him into the long room, which Wellesley was using as his command centre. As he entered, Johnstone came forward. "I can't believe you're alive," he said. "Denny told us he saw you cut down."

"It was a glancing blow, it bled a lot but nothing serious. But I'm sorry sir, Captain Mason wasn't so lucky. We lost nine, including the captain and both corporals." Paul met Johnstone's eyes, feeling perilously close to tears. "There was nothing I could do for him."

"Come and sit down, Mr van Daan."

Paul obeyed. Wellesley studied him down the long, hooked nose. "You look all in," he said, with surprising humanity. "Get him a drink, Murray, there's brandy on the side. We'll all have one."

When the drinks were poured, Wellesley looked at Paul. "What happened?"

"We were ambushed. Totally wrong information. Their forces are on this side of the ridge, camped between the two rivers. It's hard to estimate numbers but I'd guess it's the whole army. We were attacked by a small cavalry troop."

"Without warning? How did you survive that?" Murray asked.

"A bit of luck and sheer bloody-mindedness. They're a tough lot, my lads, and they don't like being shoved around, or seeing their captain with his guts in the dust. They fought like demons, but I honestly didn't think we were going to make it. Denny managed to get clear and back here to tell you."

"You fought your way out of that?" Wellesley said neutrally.

"Yes, sir. It was a close-run thing."

"And their army didn't see you?"

"I don't think so, sir. We left nobody alive, and we weren't pursued. Although sooner or later they'll find the bodies, we didn't stop to bury them, I'm afraid."

"Just so, Lieutenant. Where are these troops? Can you show me on the map?"

He got up and walked over to the large table on the far side of the room, which was spread with maps and drawings. Paul got up and followed him, studied the map to orient himself and then pointed.

"Here and here. There are encampments as far down as the river here. This is where we were hit."

"Damn our informants! I thought them much further away than this."

"I know, sir."

"I'll need time to consider this. Very well, get yourself back to your tent and cleaned up, and off to the mess for dinner. After that, according to your reputation, I imagine you'll be celebrating in camp with your men."

"Yes, sir." Paul was too tired and upset to be bothered with pretence. "Is that a problem?"

"Not if this is how you lead them," Wellesley said briefly. "Well done, sir, and congratulations. With Major Johnstone's approval, you are promoted to captain, effective immediately, and the light company is now yours to command. Are you happy with your current officers?"

"Yes, sir. Carl Swanson came with me from England, and Johnny Wheeler is a good man." Paul hesitated his thoughts in a whirl. "He is also my senior in both years and experience."

"Lieutenant Wheeler did not bring eighty men back from certain destruction with valuable intelligence, Captain van Daan."

"He can't pay for it anyway, laddie," Johnstone said gently, and Paul knew it was true.

"Do you think he will find it difficult to serve under you?" Wellesley asked. "We could look for a transfer…"

"No – Christ, no. Johnny is a friend, there are few men I'd trust more."

"Then you shall have him. Nominally you will continue under the command of Major Johnstone with the first battalion, but I am detaching your company to operate under my personal command, and you will report directly to me. There will be a briefing at ten tomorrow in this office once I have had the opportunity to consider this new information. Be there, please, I may have more questions. Anything further?"

"No, sir. Thank you."

"Then you are dismissed. Eat and rest, and ensure that your men do the same, I expect to engage very soon."

Paul went to search for his horse and rode back down the lines to his tent. Private Olson, who acted as his valet, was awaiting him with hot water and Paul washed, shaved, and changed his clothes with relief. He examined the cut on his chest and found that it was no longer bleeding, so he went in search of Carl.

"Carl, do you know where Johnny is?"

"I think he went down to the river to bathe. Let me just finish here and change and we'll go up to the mess. How was Hookey?"

"Surprised to see me. They'd thought us all dead." Paul hesitated. "He's given me command of the company, Carl."

"Congratulations. I was wondering why you wanted Johnny. Don't worry, he'll be fine."

"I hope so, but I need to tell him myself."

Paul walked down to the riverbank and found Wheeler just pulling on his shirt. "I needed that."

"I'd have joined you if duty hadn't intervened. I've just come from Wellesley, Johnny."

Wheeler met his eyes. "Congratulations, sir," he said steadily, and Paul realised that he had known it was coming.

"Thank you. I wanted to tell you myself. I feel awful about it, Johnny. I couldn't have done this without you."

"And without you we would quite certainly all be dead," Wheeler said. He came forward and put his hand on Paul's shoulder. "Paul for ten years, I've watched idiots and incompetents promoted over me because they can pay for it. I think this will be the first time I can actually celebrate a promotion. You earned it. You've worked your arse off with this company this past year, I've never seen anything like it."

"And for how long have you been working your arse off in this army, Johnny?"

"Stop it. This is your day, Paul. We both know you got this on sheer merit, but you'd have got it anyway because you can afford it and I can't. That is not your fault. But you know what? I don't feel the way I normally do about this; I'm feeling optimistic. If you don't get me killed, sooner or later my promotion is likely to be in your gift. Now come and get a drink, Captain, and then get some rest. You look like you need it."

Paul put his hand over Johnny's on his shoulder. "I will never forget how you were over this," he said.

"Just make sure you remember it when they ask you who is next in line for promotion, Captain."

Reaction set in part way through the evening, and Paul excused himself early and went back to his camp, leaving Carl and Johnny getting happily drunk with Colonel Patrick Maxwell of the cavalry. He shared a drink with his men, finding that they also were surprisingly sober. Sitting by the fireside he found himself thinking about Captain Mason, a man he had hardly known, a man he would never know now.

"Feel like company?"

Paul glanced up to see his Irish sergeant lowering himself into Carl's camp chair beside him. He passed Paul a bottle and Paul drank gratefully. He looked at his sergeant and drank again. "This is not local grog, Michael."

"No, sir, that is best French brandy. It fell into my hands, so to speak, while we were in Ahmednaggur. A reward for going over that bloody ladder."

"How the fuck did you manage that, I was watching you all like a hawk? Never mind, it's bloody good."

"Thinking about Mason?"

"Yes. And about myself. I think I almost died out there today, Michael."

"You did. We all did, but you were in the thick of it. I thought you down a couple of times, was trying to keep some of the bastards off you. You're a crazy bugger in a fight, sir, you know that don't you?"

"All I could think about at the time was not letting any of them get back to the lines."

"Well, you certainly made sure of that. You've the luck of the devil."

"Oddly enough that was what my lieutenant used to tell me aboard the Hera."

"There's nothing odd about that, your childhood nurse probably observed it."

Paul made an attempt at a smile. "I'm not feeling so devilish this evening, to be honest. I'm feeling sick and a bit shaky. Is that normal?"

"Very. There's a reason men drink after a battle."

"Yes, Maxwell said something of the sort earlier on."

"Maxwell hasn't even been in a fight today, and he's so drunk he can't walk. Don't worry about it, sir. There are officers who can watch men die around them and feel very little. You're never going to be one of those, you care too much. It makes you a damned good officer, but it has its downsides."

"Thanks, Michael. God, I'm tired. I'm going to bed."

The Irishman stood up and clapped him on the shoulder. "Get some sleep," he said quietly. "We've a fight coming up."

Chapter Four

In the dim light of Wellesley's briefing room, the following morning, Paul was the youngest and by far the least experienced of the officers present, but he knew that the previous day's action had earned him his place there. His chief called on him, and Paul stood up and walked to the front where Wellesley's aide had pinned a sketch map of the area. Briefly Paul outlined the events of the previous day and pointed out the troop locations he had seen.

"Thank you, Captain van Daan. Gentlemen, we're going to make a fight of it," General Wellesley said calmly. "Here, on the edge of Assaye."

There was a stunned silence around the briefing room. "Sir, what about Colonel Stevenson?" Maxwell said. There was no sign of the raging hangover he deserved. "Shouldn't we wait for him? Our force is split in two."

Wellesley fixed Colonel Maxwell with an arctic gaze. "Surprisingly, Colonel, I am aware of that," he snapped. "Two of our scouts went out last night. They report that it is possible that the Maratha army may be pulling out. I don't want to lose this opportunity; we have the element of surprise. I'd intended to join up with Colonel Stevenson at Borkadan but I'm not waiting for him, he'll join us when he is able, I've sent a message." Wellesley motioned to his aide who picked up another sketch map and pinned it to the wall. "Gentlemen, my plan of battle."

"It's suicide," Johnny Wheeler said later, as Paul outlined the general's orders to his officers in his tent.

"Not necessarily," Paul said. "Wellesley is ambitious but he's not stupid. If we wait for Stevenson, this campaign could drag on for months. Wellesley is fairly sure that the irregular forces won't stand for long. Scindia's infantry probably will, but with good discipline we can take them."

"Where does he want us?" Carl asked.

"At the rear initially, with the 19th and the Madras cavalry. He's leaving half a battalion of sepoys here to guard the baggage and the camp. The other half will fight under us, while Johnstone takes the rest of the 110th. Wellesley wants fast manoeuvrable troops, ready to move in and plug any gaps. He's going ahead with a cavalry escort to reconnoitre the Maratha position, the rest of us will follow. We have about two hours, gentlemen, get them ready."

The Maratha commanders had positioned their army in a strong defensive position along a tongue of land stretching east from Borkadan between the Kailna River and its tributary the Juah. Their army was commanded by a Hanoverian mercenary by the name of Anthony Pohlmann, apparently a former East India Company sergeant, who had positioned his infantry to the east of the Maratha camp in the plains around Assaye on the southern bank of the Juah. As Wellesley approached with his cavalry escort in the late morning, it was evident that he was facing the entire combined army.

The weather was clear. It had rained during the night, and the day was cooler than average, although out on the river plain with his men, watching the Maratha and Wellesley easing their troops into position, Paul was already too hot. Mosquitoes, the permanent irritation of India, were particularly prevalent towards the end of the monsoon season and up and down the line, Paul could see his men swatting irritably at the creatures.

Pohlmann was deploying his infantry battalions in a line facing southwards behind the steep banks of the Kailna with his cannon arrayed directly in front. The great mass of Maratha cavalry was kept on the right flank, leaving the irregular infantry to garrison the village of Assaye to the rear. The only obvious crossing point over the river was a small ford directly ahead of the Maratha position, and Paul thought that Pohlmann was hoping to funnel the British and Madras troops across the ford into the path of his artillery, and then on to the massed infantry and cavalry behind. Wellesley's local guides had assured him that no other ford existed nearby, but any frontal assault would have been suicide. While reconnoitring, Wellesley had noticed two unguarded villages on each bank of the Kailna beyond the Maratha left, and it became obvious that there was a second ford. Wellesley led his army east to the crossing in an attempt to launch an attack on Pohlmann's left flank.

It was three o'clock when Wellesley's men crossed to the northern bank of the Kailna, unopposed apart from some distant cannon fire. Once across, Wellesley ordered his six infantry battalions including most of the 110th to form into two lines, placing his cavalry in a third line along with Paul's light company and the sepoy infantry. Wellesley's Mysore cavalry were left to the south of the Kailna to keep an eye on a hovering group of Maratha cavalry.

"Pohlmann is not going to let us get away with that," Carl commented, studying the distant Maratha troops through a small telescope. "He's already swinging around to create a new line."

He was right, Paul saw. Pohlmann moved his infantry and guns through 90 degrees to establish a new line spread across the isthmus with his right flank on the Kailna and the left on Assaye. Paul thought that it was a good defensive move, which would protect his flanks, but it negated some of the advantage of his superior numbers. "They're moving fast," Paul said, his own telescope to his eye. "Hookey needs to get a move on or we'll be outflanked."

The same thought had obviously occurred to the general who immediately extended his front to avoid the danger. A battalion of pickets and the 74th

Highlanders were ordered to move to the right. This allowed the 78th to cover the left flank and the four Madras infantry battalions plus the rest of the 110th to form the centre of Wellesley's line.

The Maratha cannonade was beginning to do some damage. Initially Wellesley ordered his own artillery forward to counter the attack, but it was not powerful enough to be effective. The guns were turned onto the infantry, pounding them relentlessly with canister, grape and round shot and Paul moved his horse forward restlessly, feeling powerless as the guns punched into the British lines. It was infuriating to be so far back with no part to play in the battle.

It was impossible from the rear to see everything that was going on. Wellesley was a commander who liked to move freely around the battlefield in person, relaying orders to his various commanders, but no orders came to the reserve. Paul seethed with impatience and lack of information and it was a relief when a young ensign from the 78th rode up, sent back out of harm's way with a badly wounded arm. He slid from his horse, blood dripping, and Paul and Carl both ran forward to assist him. Carl eased him out of his coat and Paul did his best to staunch the flow of blood and sent O'Reilly in search of a temporary dressing.

"What's happening?"

"The infantry is advancing. We've taken heavy fire, but we're holding our own and moving forward. I got this when we charged the gunners. It's going well but we're taking losses. The sepoys are a bit wild; two of the Madras battalions took off in pursuit but we got them back. I want to get back there."

"Well, you can't, sir, not when you can't hold a sword," O'Reilly said, winding a towel carefully around the wound. "Sit down, drink some water and take a breath, and then you need to find the surgeon. I'm told they've set up a temporary field hospital about half a mile back. You've done your share."

Paul had been concentrating on the injured man, but he suddenly became aware of sounds of battle from a different direction.

"Sergeant, what's that?"

Michael paused, listening. "I don't know, sir. It sounds like there's action to the right."

Paul ran back to his horse and swung himself into the saddle, reaching for his telescope. The other officers and some of the men began to cluster around him.

"What's going on, sir?"

"I don't know. The pickets are advancing ahead of the 74th, but...oh Christ, that can't be right. They've taken the wrong line."

"Paul?"

"The guns. They're marching directly into the path of the guns. Who the fuck is in charge of those pickets, he needs to get them back?"

"I think it's Colonel Orrock, sir," the young ensign said. "He's a good officer."

"He's a bloody imbecile if he can't see what's happening. Why in God's name doesn't he retreat?"

"It looks different on the ground, sir, you know it does."

Both Carl and Johnny had mounted their horses to get a better view, and they sat in shocked silence, watching disaster unfold. Eventually, Paul lowered his glass, partly because his eye was aching and partly because he could not bear to watch any more. Even without the telescope it was possible to see that the pickets and the following Highlanders were being slaughtered by the Maratha guns in and around the village of Assaye.

"I can't stand to watch it," Johnny said softly, echoing Paul's thought. "The pickets have been almost completely wiped out."

"The Highlanders are going to be wiped out as well if Wellesley doesn't do something, can't he fucking see?" Paul said. He knew that he was being unfair, and that Johnny was right. No commander could see every part of the field unless he was on a substantial hill, and even then, features of the landscape could easily obscure parts of the action. Even so, Paul could not understand how at least one of the officers of the 74th had not realised they were marching into disaster.

"Why hasn't one of them ordered a retreat?" he said, almost in a whisper.

"Because they're following orders, sir," Johnny said gently.

Paul turned to look at him, then turned back and raised his telescope once more. Even from this distance he could see bloody bodies piled up, with the Highlanders scrambling over them to advance. Despite horrific casualties, with iron and lead cutting into them they had reached as far as a low cactus hedge about a hundred yards out from the village, but they could go no further. The guns continued to fire, a low monotonous boom, interspersed with screams of pain as men were killed and maimed. Through the glass, Paul could see that the earth was stained with blood.

A man lay sprawled, immobile on the ground, and his leg, a bloody pulp, lay four feet away from him. Paul hoped that he was already dead. Others were still moving, trying to crawl towards some kind of safety despite their savage injuries, but there was no safety on that field. The guns crashed again, and the bodies disappeared in a cloud of black smoke. When it cleared a little, the dead or dying Highlander was no longer there, his remains blown apart. Paul wondered if he was going to be sick.

He looked back at Johnny. He had never seen anything this bad, even below decks on a man o' war, and he knew that he needed to do something.

Wheeling his horse, Paul cantered down the line to where the cavalry waited for orders under their Irish commander. Maxwell saw him coming and rode forward to meet him.

"Van Daan?"

"Can you see what's happening?"

"Aye. Waiting for orders."

"We need to go in, they're being slaughtered over there."

Maxwell shook his head. "I'm waiting for orders from Wellesley, Captain," he said, and his voice betrayed his anxiety. "They'll come."

"Of course they'll come, he's got no-one else to send in, but it's going to be too late," Paul's voice was rising, but he was too enraged to consider the proprieties of rank. "We need to go in now before they're all dead."

"Is this your first big battle?"

"Yes."

"Well, you need to learn that it's not our decision, laddie, we wait for orders. That's how it works."

Paul turned and looked out over the field. The 74th could go no further. They were rallying around their colours now, forming a square, and Paul could see them pulling the bodies of their dead comrades to form a rough rampart around them. For a moment, Paul wondered what the hell they were doing, forming square while under artillery fire, and then he heard a yell, and a distant thundering of hooves and he understood.

"Cavalry," he whispered. "Their cavalry is charging. They're going to die, every one of them."

"Mary, mother of God," Maxwell said.

The cavalry crashed into the square. There were so many of them, that Paul could no longer see the Highlanders, could only see the bright square of the colours fluttering overhead. They were hugely outnumbered, but the square had not broken, and for a short time, they were probably safer since the punishing fire of the guns had stopped to allow the cavalry to make their charge. Looking at the massed dead in that corner of the field, Paul thought that it must be a small square, with the remaining Highlanders fighting with bayonet for their lives and for a moment he was back in the tiny square of the previous day, remembering his terror as Maratha horsemen rode down on his men. That had been a small patrol, but the 74th were facing a massed cavalry charge and they would not stand for long without help. Paul felt very sick. He turned to look at Maxwell.

"I'm going in."

"You're not going in. You've no orders."

"The orders will come, you said it yourself, I'm just anticipating them. I'm going in before they get completely annihilated."

"You've got one light company and half a battalion of native infantry. You'll be slaughtered alongside them. I'm ordering you to wait, Captain. What the hell are you going to do?"

Paul's brain was working furiously. "I'm going to draw them off. We'll form a second square, and I'll send a runner to find Wellesley, he can't have seen what's happening over there."

"You need cavalry, man."

"I don't have cavalry, sir, so I'll need to work with what I've got." Paul raised his voice. "Light company, to me! Form line! Native third battalion, fall in behind!"

The men had been waiting for the order. Paul dismounted, handed the reins of his horse to a groom and drew his sword. The light company fell into rank with the precision of a clockwork toy, with the sepoys lined up behind them. As Paul gave the order to march, he heard a furious oath from Maxwell to his rear and he said a brief, passionate prayer that he had not misjudged the man.

Paul let his men across the field at a steady pace and he scanned the battle, picking out the crumbling lines of the highlanders. What he did next, would depend on Maxwell. Even as he had the thought, Paul heard the Irish colonel bellowing orders and he felt his body flood with relief. Within two minutes the colonel was riding up beside him.

"If Wellesley sends me to a court martial for this, I'm taking you down with me, you arrogant young bastard," he told Paul, and gave the order to charge, his men overtaking the light company on both sides and thundering down towards the enemy.

The cavalry smashed into the rear of the Maratha lines and Paul turned to his officers. "Right, change of plan. We're going to cut across and plug the gap left between the 74th and the 10th. Don't let them split our line any further, we'll let the cavalry do the slaughter, it's our job to stand firm. Watch those bloody gunners in case they turn on us, get through to the Highlanders and protect their left."

Covering the ground quickly, they caught up with Maxwell's men who were engaged in fierce fighting with the Maratha light cavalry. The remains of the Highlanders were barely on their feet, and Paul could see none of their officers. Through the thick of the fighting the light company slashed their way with sword and bayonet, and under orders bellowed by the NCOs they formed square to create a barrier between the cavalry and the beleaguered 74th. Paul was appalled at the number of casualties. The dead lay piled up, impeding their advance. The guns were deafening, and a thick layer of smoke hung over the battlefield, making it hard to distinguish friend from foe.

Paul took up his position in the middle of the square, yelling orders and watching for any sign that his men might break, but there was none. He was impressed with the Indian infantry, who were clearly experienced fighters and stood firm against the cavalry passes. There were fewer of these as Maxwell's savage attack began to take effect, but as the Maratha cavalry were drawn off by the dragoons, it left the squares vulnerable to artillery fire again. Even as Paul thought it, the guns crashed again and there were screams of agony which told Paul that his right flank was hit. The officers scrambled to drag dead and wounded into the square and plug the gap, but Paul knew that like the Highlanders, they were a sitting target for the guns. He swung around to locate Johnny and Carl.

"We need to shut these bastards up and let the cavalry do their job. Sergeant O'Reilly, ten men and with me. Johnny, hold the square for as long as you can, but if we don't make it through, get them out of here, don't let them get slaughtered like the Highlanders. I…"

"What are you going to do?"

"I'm going to take out the gunners."

"Are you bloody mad?" Johnny said furiously. "You won't stand a chance, they'll cut you down before you ever get close. It's suicide."

"No it isn't if I take the right line. I've got a clear run, and Maxwell's men are keeping them busy. Stop arguing, Mr Wheeler, you have command."

"Probably permanently if you do this, you bloody idiot."

"Well, if I don't make it, look after them for me. It should have been yours anyway." Paul clapped him on the shoulder, threw an ironic salute to Carl, and ran to join Michael who had assembled his small band. "Right, listen to me, I don't have time to repeat this."

Paul gave his orders quickly, then led his men towards the guns at a cautious run. The gunners on the far right had no need to aim any more as the packed mass of advancing British presented an easy target. They were concentrating their fire on the 110th and the remains of the Highlanders, ignoring the battle raging between the cavalry to avoid hitting their own men. Paul could see three guns. He crouched low behind a small clump of cacti, assessing the distance, and felt O'Reilly's hand on his arm.

"Easy, sir. Wait until they're reloading. The timing is as reliable as our own men shooting a volley, I'll count you in."

Paul glanced over his shoulder at his men. "Ready? We'll go for the gunners on the right first, then work across to the left. On my mark."

"Make sure every one of the bastards is dead," Michael added. "They're the devil for playing dead, and before you know it, they're shooting you in the arse. Watch for them hiding under the bodies. Here we go. One, two three…"

The gunners were quick and efficient at loading, but Paul and his men were on them before they were halfway through the process. Each gun had a small group of infantrymen defending it, but they were no match for the men of the light company, and the gun was silenced within five bloody minutes. Paul stood for a moment catching his breath, looking around him. The ground was saturated with blood and eight gunners and their guards lay dead.

"Well done, sir," his sergeant said. He was wiping blood from his hands down his tunic.

"Bryant, Smith, stay to guard it until the lads come up. Kill anything you don't like the look of."

Smith gave a yellow toothed grin. He was a fearsome sight, covered in blood, his bayonet held in steady hands. "Does that include Bryant, sir, he's an ugly bastard?"

"Later. Come on, Sergeant, let's find ourselves another gun."

To reach the next gun, Paul's men found themselves cutting through the remains of some Maratha infantry, but they seemed leaderless and quickly backed off from the savage assault of the light company bayonets. The second set of guns was in sight when Paul felt a sharp pain slicing through his left thigh. He stumbled and fell, rolled over onto his back and slashed up at a Maratha who was lunging down at him with fixed bayonet. The man screamed and fell back, blood spurting. Paul sat up and felt cautiously at his leg.

"You all right, sir?" Private Carter pulled up in his headlong run and offered his hand to Paul, helping him to his feet.

"Musket ball, I think," Paul said, probing and wincing. "Thanks, Carter."

The light company reached the second set of guns and swarmed over the gunners in seconds. There was less noise now, although across to the left he could hear that the guns he had thought silenced by the advance of the 78th had started up again. He glanced at Michael, who shrugged.

"I told you so. They play dead and then they're up again, shooting you from the rear. I saw it the last time I was in India. Clever tactic."

"Well this lot aren't getting up again. Ready?"

"Aye, and it'll get easier now, the heart is out of them, and I'm not seeing many officers about either. Perhaps it was getting too dirty for their pretty French uniforms. Smithy, what the bloody hell are you doing here, you were told to secure that gun."

"Bryant's down. Some bastard cavalryman came through running scared and slashed him on the way."

"Dead?" O'Reilly asked.

"Didn't look good, Sarge." Smith glanced at Paul. "Compliments of Mr Swanson, sir, the enemy is in full flight and General Wellesley has ordered him up to protect the guns."

Paul was trying not to think about Bryant's laughing face only fifteen minutes earlier. "Thank you, Private. Tell him we'll join him when we've spiked the rest of these guns."

"Are you all right, sir?" Michael said, indicating Paul's leg.

"I think so." Paul tested it. It hurt badly, but he had not lost strength and it was bleeding sluggishly. He had no idea of what damage had been done, but he did not need to stop now. Paul began to run and found it bearable. He was conscious of the Irishman keeping pace with him, making sure he did not fall, and shot an appreciative glance his way. O'Reilly's thin face was grimly amused.

"You're a hard young bastard, sir."

"You've the navy to thank for that, Sergeant."

They overran the guns with no further casualties. Two of them had already been abandoned, their gunners either dead or fleeing across the field, and Paul found himself facing the straggling ranks of the 78th. A major whom Paul knew slightly saluted him, pulling out a canteen and gulping down water.

"Captain van Daan, things seem a lot quieter over on the right. Would your ruffians have something to do with that?"

"Along with the dragoons, sir, we came in to support the 74th, then some of us came up to silence the guns."

"Lose many?"

"I don't know yet, sir. One man went down defending the first gun, but we took some heavy shooting to our right. We'll not get out of it unscathed."

"None of us will, laddie, but they're on the run now. Their French officers took off, and they've no discipline left. Eyes right, the general is approaching."

Wellesley reined in. He looked exhausted and the horse he was riding was not the one he had set out on that morning.

"Major McTavish, Captain van Daan."

Paul saluted, and Wellesley surveyed him.

"You're hurt, Captain van Daan."

"Not serious, sir."

"I hope not. I sent a man over to send you into battle, but he was unable to find you."

Paul glanced up at him warily. "I was around, sir," he said.

"But invisible, it seems." Wellesley studied him with thoughtful blue grey eyes. Finally, to Paul's relief, his lips twitched slightly. "You anticipated correctly, Captain. You may not always be right, however. I prefer my officers to await orders."

"Yes, sir."

"Did Colonel Maxwell..."

"No, sir," Paul said definitely. We went in ahead of him, he waited for your orders, sir."

"You're a bloody liar, Captain. I've sent Wallace to rally the remains of the 74th and get them out of the range of those guns, but I see that I need have no concern from this side. They have started up again on the left and I have given orders for Colonel Harness to take the 78th in while I will lead the remains of the native cavalry personally from the east. Captain van Daan, retrieve the rest of your men, if you please, and join the 78th. Try to remember that Colonel Harness outranks you and is therefore supposed to be in charge.

"Yes, sir." Paul nodded to his sergeant who took off at a run to summon the rest of the light company and the Madras infantry. Wellesley was looking over towards the Juah through his telescope and gave an irritated snort.

"What in God's name is Colonel Maxwell doing on that side of the river, I gave no orders for him to cross?"

Paul turned to follow his gaze. Even without the increased height of being on horseback, he could see Maxwell's troopers milling about on the far bank. He suspected that having done their work, Maxwell's troopers had gone out of control and crossed the Juah, and that Maxwell had followed to bring them back. It was not unusual for it to happen with cavalry. "He'll get them back, sir."

"I sincerely hope so, I need them over here. Why do officers of the cavalry seem incapable of following a simple order?"

"I might not be the best person to answer that today, sir."

Paul had spoken without thinking, and he flinched internally, wishing he could take it back. Wellesley turned his head very slowly, staring at him as though he could not believe he had heard correctly. Paul stood instinctively to attention, his eyes straight ahead, but as the silence lengthened, he could not resist turning to look at the general.

Wellesley was laughing silently, his shoulders actually shaking. Something about the unlikeliness of laughter on a blood-soaked battlefield made Paul start to laugh as well, even though he knew it was probably a reaction caused by pain and exhaustion.

"Sorry, sir. Sometimes, I just speak without thinking."

"I imagine that will get you into a good deal of trouble in the future, Captain. I find I rather like it. Get your men, this is not a social occasion."

He was gone, his horse cantering eastwards, avoiding corpses and injured men on the ground. Paul turned to find the light company approaching, with the remains of the Bengal infantry marching in good order behind them. There were a lot fewer of them, and Paul felt his gut clench as he ran his eyes over his men and realised how many familiar faces were missing. There was no sign of Sergeant Stewart, and the light company was led by Carl Swanson, his face black with smoke, his green eyes shadowed with exhaustion and misery. Paul went forward.

"Johnny?"

"Wounded. I don't know how bad."

Paul nodded, knowing it was not the time for a barrage of questions that Carl would not be able to answer. "We're supporting the 78th to re-take those guns. Please God, that will see the end of this."

The attack was short and brutal. The Maratha army was bloody and weary and many of their officers had already fled the field, but they put up a spirited defence, trapped between the infantry and Wellesley who was leading the 7th Native Cavalry. The battle was beginning to seem endless to Paul, fighting in a blur of pain and exhaustion. His men launched into the attack with bayonets, and Paul went with them, yelling encouragement as they drove the Maratha infantry back. Wave after wave of enemy troops hurled themselves against the ranks of the 78th and Paul's depleted men. Paul kept himself on his feet through sheer determination. His sword arm felt too tired to lift the weapon, but he lifted it nonetheless. His men were still on their feet and still fighting and while they stood, so must he.

The end came suddenly, and it was almost a shock to Paul as he realised that the waves were receding, and the Maratha were running. The 78th charged in pursuit, but Paul yelled for his officers and NCOs to call his men back. He had lost too many already and without a direct order from Wellesley, he had no intention of pushing them further.

Paul leaned against one of the recovered guns and let his eyes wander over the carnage around him. He had a very clear memory of the bloody boards of the surgeon's room in the aftermath of battle at sea, but he had never seen anything like this, and the sheer scale of the slaughter was more than his exhausted brain could bear, so he closed his eyes. It was slightly better, although it made him more aware of the smell of blood and the sounds of dead and dying men and horses.

"Time to go, sir. Back to the village. It's over."

Paul opened his eyes and pushed himself up wearily. He gave the order, and the remains of his men fell in behind him. Paul began to walk but stumbled immediately as the injured leg gave way. He realised in some surprise that he was in a lot of pain. Beside him, Michael caught his arm to stop him falling.

"Lean on me, sir," he said quietly. "Be easy now, your job is done, and you did it bloody well."

Paul glanced sideways at him. "Thanks, Michael."

"Ah, you're welcome, sir."

The rest of the 110th were resting just outside the village, near the river. A sepoy was drawing up water, and the men were sitting or lying around. At the sight of the remains of their light company they raised a ragged cheer and Paul waved in acknowledgement.

"Sit down before you fall down," Carl said. "Christ, that looks like a mess."

Paul was surprised that he was pointing not at the injured leg, but at his neck. He raised a hand and realised that he had a large gash across the top of his shoulder and onto his neck, which was bleeding heavily. He laughed, feeling suddenly shaky. "I didn't realise I'd done it," he said. "What casualties, Carl?"

"Later, sir."

"Now, Mr Swanson."

Carl sighed and led him over to two rows of bodies neatly laid out and covered mostly with their own coats. Beside them were five or six wounded men, among them Sergeant Stewart, his side laid open by a sabre cut. Paul knelt beside him with difficulty.

"Rory, it's a relief to see someone looking worse than I do," he said.

"Did you bring O'Reilly back, sir?"

"I did. Nothing but a bruise on his toe to show for it."

"We won, sir."

"We did. Hold on, Rory, I'll get you up to the surgeon."

"You'd better, sir. I promised my girl we'd get married next time I'm home. If I don't make it, she'll be after you."

"Christ, I'm glad you told me. If you don't make it; I'm not going back, she's probably already pissed off with me." Paul got up and went to survey the dead. He counted eighteen bodies. He had started the day with eighty-five men.

"Bryant?" he asked.

Carl shook his head. "I'm sorry," he said, indicating the body at the end. "The 74th lost all their officers to death or injury except Grant, their quartermaster, who ran from the supply wagons and led them at the end. Huge losses. It could have been worse, we lost most of these in that first volley. I know it's no consolation, but if your party hadn't stopped those guns we'd have been wiped out like the Highlanders."

"That doesn't help right now. Did you get these men off the field, Mr Swanson?"

"Yes, sir. The general has ordered the bodies to be cleared and burned, we can't leave them out in this heat. But these are our lads."

Paul felt a fierce gratitude. "Thank you, Carl, we bury our own. Sergeant…"

"I'll get the lads digging and I'll set a guard on them until we're ready. Now for the love of God, sir, will you sit down before I knock you over?"

Paul allowed his sergeant to help him to sit down. As he did so, he suddenly remembered. "What about Johnny, Carl? You said he was wounded. Where is he?"

There was a silence and Paul felt very sick. "Is he dead?"

"Sir, I don't know how he is, he took a tulwar right across the midriff. I sent him by stretcher straight to the surgeon. There's no hospital yet – nothing until the baggage gets here from Nalni – but some of the surgeons have managed to set up a field station in the village and are dealing with emergencies."

Paul held out his hand. "Get me up, O'Reilly. Where are my horses?"

"Paul," Carl began, sounding exasperated.

To Paul's relief, the sergeant hauled him up.

"Over at the back, sir. Come on, we'll get you down to see him."

"Sergeant, he needs to rest, he's injured himself," Carl said shortly.

Paul ignored him and Michael gave an exaggerated sigh. "No point in trying to stop him, Mr Swanson, if I don't help him, he'll bloody walk it, you know him. I'll send the stretcher-bearers back for Stewart and the others. Be easy, I'll go with him and make sure he gets those wounds looked at as well. We'll be sleeping in Assaye tonight, the baggage and the tents won't be here until tomorrow, so best get the men down and find a nice dry shed or barn. I know he should rest, but to be honest, if we get there and find that Lieutenant Wheeler is lying in the hot sun unattended at the end of a long queue, wouldn't you say that the captain is just the man to make sure he gets to the front of the line nice and quick, now?"

No hospital had been set up yet, but the surgeons had arranged for tents to be erected at the edge of the village, and the wounded lay scattered around them waiting to be seen. Paul needed his sergeant to help him down from the horse and stood stiffly surveying the carnage. The smell was appalling, and overhead he could see the ominous shadows of vultures circling. There were Indian bearers moving among the wounded, armed with clubs to beat off the birds if they came too close, but there would be plenty of food for them on the battlefield.

"Over here, sir," O'Reilly called, and Paul limped between supine bodies to where his lieutenant lay on the bare ground under a thin blanket. He was drenched in his own blood. For a moment Paul wondered if he was already too late, then Wheeler stirred.

Paul went down onto one knee with difficulty. "Johnny," he said softly.

Grey eyes opened in the white drawn face. Wheeler attempted a smile. "Paul, you made it. Christ, that's a mess."

"You look worse than I do, lad," Paul said. He was trying not to look at the blood-soaked blanket. "Just hold on, I'll get you seen."

65

"Private Jenson is before me," Wheeler said faintly, and Paul realised that the man next to Wheeler was one of his. Jenson was unconscious, lying on a threadbare blanket and the lower part of his right leg was in ruins.

Paul reached across and checked the man's pulse. It was still beating surprisingly strongly, but the wound was horrific, and Paul suspected that the surgeon would have to amputate. Jenson was twenty, a good-looking lad, popular with the women and he had recently begun a liaison with a local girl.

Paul reached out his hand and O'Reilly pulled him up. The pain of his own wounds was getting worse and he was feeling light headed with hunger, thirst and exhaustion. Determinedly he limped over to the surgeon's tent.

It was like walking into a level of hell. The stench of blood and excrement was overpowering. Four tables were set up and three surgeons were working furiously. A man lay waiting on the fourth. One man was being held down by three orderlies while the surgeon worked furiously to amputate his arm. He was screaming through the piece of leather in his mouth.

Paul walked over to the youngest of the surgeons. He was probably in his thirties, of middle height with a pleasant face, although he was currently scowling fiercely, intent on his work. He was quick and effective and after a few minutes observation, Paul decided this was the man he wanted. At the same moment, the surgeon became aware of his presence.

"What the devil do you want?" he demanded.

"Two of my men are lying outside, I'm having them brought in. If they're not treated soon, they won't live."

"There are many who won't live to be treated," the surgeon snapped.

"Not in my company."

The surgeon paused at Paul's tone and turned to look at him with some surprise. "And you are?"

"Captain van Daan, 110th light company."

"Really? I've heard of you. Bit of a rising man, I'm told." The surgeon returned to his work. "Now that I look at you, you could do with some attention yourself."

"I can wait, my men can't."

"I'm the junior surgeon here, Captain."

"You're the quickest surgeon here, doctor, I've been watching."

Unexpectedly the doctor grinned. "I've almost done here," he said. "Crellin, Dunlop, go with the captain and bring his men here."

"Thank you," Paul said.

"You're after them," the surgeon said.

The orderlies lifted Wheeler and Jenson into the tent, where the doctor was just finishing with his patient. He motioned for them to carry him away, and Michael helped to lift Jenson onto the table. The doctor did not flinch at the horror of his leg.

"It'll have to come off just below the knee. He's very weak, but I'll do my best." He motioned to one of the orderlies. "Hold him down. He may stay out but hold on to him just in case."

66

As he began to cut, Jenson bucked against the orderlies and screamed. The surgeon clamped his leg hard with one hand and looked around for help. Paul felt sick, but he stepped forward. The surgeon looked up at him in some surprise and then nodded. "Hold him here," he said pointing to the thigh. Paul obeyed, trying to close his mind to the boy's agony, and the sickening sound of the saw cutting through the bone. It seemed to take forever, and his hands were soaked in Jenson's blood. Mercifully, the man had lost consciousness. Paul released his grip slightly but kept his hands in place. Eventually it was over, and the surgeon was closing the wounds. He looked up at Paul.

"Well done. It's in God's hands now, he'll be very weak." The surgeon glanced at Paul. "There's no hospital yet and we're the only surgeons. If you leave him here, there's nobody to tend him."

"We'll take him back to the village," Paul said. "Thank you, Doctor."

Paul watched while the orderlies returned Jenson to his makeshift stretcher, and Johnny Wheeler was lifted onto the table. He groaned as the surgeon probed the wound delicately, picking out shreds of cloth. Johnny lay rigid, clenching his teeth.

"It's a surprisingly clean wound," the surgeon said. "Tulwar, but not as deep as I'd feared, it's not touched any of the internal organs as far as I can see, although it's bled a lot. I can close it and dress it and I'll bleed him against infection."

Paul watched the surgeon stitching the wound with quick efficiency. His stomach was churning, and he was feeling lightheaded with pain.

"That will do. Sergeant, will you go and find some men to carry these two back to the village, and if there are any more of your men who need treatment send them up to me."

"Yes, sir. Thank you, sir."

"Carry on." The surgeon pointed at Paul. "You. Up on the table before you fall over."

Paul complied. He sat in silence as the surgeon dressed the savage cut across his neck and shoulder.

"What's this?" he asked, indicating the wound on Paul's chest.

"That? Oh – yesterday. There was a skirmish, we lost our captain."

"You almost lost more than that," the doctor said. "You ought to have seen a surgeon then. It's opened up today, I'm going to put a few stitches in. So you've been in charge of that company for how long?"

"About twenty-four hours I think, and I've already lost about a third of them. Not a good start."

The surgeon turned his attention to the leg wound.

"I'll have to dig the ball out. Lie back."

Paul obeyed. He felt very sick and light headed and wished that O'Reilly had stayed. There was something reassuring about the Irishman's presence.

"Paul van Daan. You've made a bit of a name for yourself."

"I wasn't aware of it."

"I had a major of the 74th in here earlier. I think he'll live although I'm not sure he'll use his left arm much again. He told me you led a small party through the lines and removed four of the guns from action, probably saving the lives of the remainder of his regiment."

"The major is generous," Paul said, trying not to yell with the pain. "There were many men out there today who saved lives."

"I've spent hours putting together what those guns blew apart, Captain van Daan. I appreciate the extra work you may have spared me." The surgeon dug deep, and Paul gasped and bit his lip. Agony sliced through his leg and he closed his eyes, wishing he would lose consciousness. It did not happen. Minutes passed as the man cut and dug and Paul tried to visualise home, the smooth green lawns of his father's house near Melton, and the fresh cool breeze of a spring day. The agony mounted. He tried again and thought of Oxford and the quiet halls of his undergraduate years, the echoing peace of the quad and Agnes, the daughter of the landlord of the Bell Inn, her golden curly hair tickling him as she snuggled against him.

Paul revived and realised that he must have passed out. His doctor gave a satisfied grunt.

"Got the bugger. That was in deep and no mistake. Here you are, Captain van Daan – the source of that pain."

He was holding up a long pair of forceps with a bloody musket ball. Paul grimaced. "I can live without a souvenir, Doctor. Thank you."

"It will hurt like hell for a while, it grazed the bone. You're lucky it didn't smash it; we'd be looking at an amputation. You'll need to rest it. Don't be stupid about it."

"I won't."

Michael O'Reilly appeared beside Paul. "I've brought Stewart and the others up to the doctor, sir. Let's get this dressed and then we'll get you back to Assaye. I've rounded up a few bearers to help."

"Where did you find those?" the doctor asked. "They're like gold dust, they've been deserting all week."

"I'm a persuasive man, sir."

Paul lay still as the wound was dressed. "You've been nothing but helpful today, Doctor, and I realise I've neglected even to ask your name."

"Adam Norris."

"Doctor Norris, thank you. I'm sorry to have been such trouble."

"Oh you've been a refreshing change, I hope your men appreciate you, Captain. Keep off that leg, you may find it takes a while before you regain your strength. Is this your sergeant? Don't worry, I'll see to him now and the bearers can bring him over to the village." Dr Norris helped Paul to sit up. "The men I've treated should be kept quiet and under cover if possible. There'll be a hospital set up eventually, but Wellesley was so quick to get into battle he neglected to plan for the aftermath. I know you have no tents tonight..."

68

"Don't worry, sir," O'Reilly said. "Mr Swanson and Mr Denny have found a nice little house with space for us all out of the cold. When the baggage comes up tomorrow, we'll get them comfortable."

The treatment of his wounds had tried Paul more than he had realised. With his men settled in piles of straw in a clay-built farm building, he grudgingly agreed to rest, and slept immediately and deeply, waking from restless dreams of gunfire and dying horses to see Carl resting peacefully on the floor across from him. As he stirred, his friend rose and came across.

"It's all right, Paul."

"Johnny…"

"All the wounded are safely here and being tended. As soon as the baggage arrives, we'll have plenty of tents. They're going to set up a hospital for the wounded about ten miles out, but I've told them we'll keep our men here."

Paul nodded. He was surprised at how exhausted he felt. "What about burials?"

"Early tomorrow. Wellesley has ordered mass cremations for most of them, but I've said we'll bury our own, the graves are almost dug. There have been losses in the rest of the battalion as well, but Major Johnstone is fine. I'd tell you to stay here and rest, but I know there's not a chance of it, so I'll get you some crutches and we'll get you out there. Bad enough for us, but Christ knows how the 74th feel, their regiment has been destroyed. They're still bringing them in off the field."

"How's young Jenson doing?"

"Still alive, which is surprising. Paul – Colonel Maxwell is dead."

Paul stared at his friend, appalled. "Oh Christ, no. What happened?"

"Canister shot; it was instant. I'm sorry, I know you liked him. I did myself."

Paul lay back wearily, thinking about Patrick Maxwell's booming laugh and merry dark eyes. Logically, he knew that his own rash decision to go in ahead of orders had had nothing to do with Maxwell's death. Wellesley had admitted that he had been on his way to give that order. It did not change Paul's heavy sense of guilt that he had survived, and Maxwell had died.

Paul received a visit from his commanding officer some days later. The baggage had been moved up and Paul was resting in his tent when Johnstone arrived.

"Came to see how you're doing, Captain. Mr Swanson tells me you're up and about on crutches. Are you coming up to the mess to eat? They've set up in a house in the village so there's a good chance of an edible dinner tonight."

Paul summoned a smile. "I'd rather not, but I've a feeling that you're going to tell me that I should, aren't you sir?"

"If you're strong enough," Johnstone said. "How are you, Captain?"

"Mending, sir. I still can't walk far."

"Aye, it takes time. We lost good men. I've come with news from Wellesley, laddie. The light company is going home. You'll need to take some leave to recover, and so will the other wounded. When you're established in barracks, you've leave to send out a recruiting party and replenish your numbers."

"Yes, sir."

"Get yourself fit, Van Daan, that's an order. And listen to me. I'll be writing to Colonel Dixon. When you get back to barracks, I want you to take over responsibility for training. There are two companies of the first battalion and the whole of the second in barracks just now, and very few of them have been in combat. You've done remarkable things with that company this year, to say nothing of the 17th Bengal infantry. I'd like the rest of my regiment up to that standard."

"Yes, sir."

"I'm not sure how much news you've heard from Europe but it's war again against France."

"I'd a letter from my father," Paul said. "Nobody's surprised, sir. The idea of peace might have got people very excited, but it was never going to last. The City is pissed off, they were hoping for at least a spell of peaceful trade, but Bonaparte wasn't going to rest for long, he's just used it as an excuse for a break. He'll have been recruiting and training and we should have been doing the same."

Johnstone got up. "Well, that's why I need you," he said. "I know you're finding it difficult. We all do, but you're still very young. This week you led men to their deaths, and you've lost people who matter to you. Just remember that your actions saved lives."

Paul indicated his leg. "I'd do better if I wasn't just lying here."

"Exactly, so get yourself up to the mess. You'll be welcomed, I promise you. We're bloody proud of you, Van Daan."

When he had gone Paul hauled himself up onto his crutches and made his way up the lines to the low house, which the 110th had turned into a temporary regimental hospital. Paul had been out to one of the hospitals set up by the medical board, and after a brief look at the overcrowded, filthy conditions, he had made the decision not to move his wounded men. The sheer volume of sick and injured men was overwhelming, and Johnny and the others would be better off tended by their comrades and the regimental servants and bearers. They were joined by the wounded from the rest of the 110th, and Adam Norris had co-operated against the wishes of his superiors and made regular calls to check on Paul's men. Surprisingly even young Jenson seemed to be growing stronger.

Paul toured the hospital and spent some time with Johnny, then limped painfully back to camp. There was nothing to do until the wagons arrived to transport the remains of the light company back to the coast and Paul was finding the waiting difficult. As he approached, he found Michael O'Reilly outside his tent in heated conversation with a woman dressed in shabby muslin and a well-worn shawl, carrying a child in her arms.

"I can't keep her," she was saying as Paul approached. "I lost my man in the battle, going to marry again but I've three of my own, I can't ask him to take this one as well."

"I've not the least idea why you think it should be our problem," the sergeant said shortly. "Captain, give me five minutes and I'll get rid of her."

Paul grinned and went into his tent. He could hear his sergeant arguing with the woman and smiled as he lowered himself to sit on the edge of his bed. He had no idea why the woman believed the child was Michael's responsibility, but he had every faith in his sergeant's ability to deal with her.

Paul's enforced immobility had given him leisure time, and he had borrowed a couple of books from Wellesley who had an impressive collection brought from England. To his surprise the general had been in to see him several times, and despite his abrupt manner which bordered on rudeness at times, Paul looked forward to the visits. There had been an odd moment of kinship out on the battlefield, and Paul suspected that Wellesley recognised it as well.

Putting his feet up with some relief, Paul began to read. He became aware of being watched and looked up to see the child standing just inside the tent looking at him. She was very young, Paul guessed, probably not yet two, a fair-haired scrap in a dirty frock and apron. One finger was in her mouth. Paul smiled.

"She's too busy arguing to notice you've wandered off, isn't she?" he said. The child regarded him steadily and Paul set down his book.

"Come here," he said gently, and to his surprise the child toddled over to him and put one hand on his knee. Despite her grubby appearance she looked healthy and well-fed. Paul wondered what had happened to her parents. Probably the father had died in the battle. Paul had no experience of children, but he felt a tug of sympathy for the orphan.

"Poor brat. You're too young to be left alone, and far too cute to be unwanted."

Suddenly the child's face broke into a grin, a wide gappy smile. Using him as a ladder she scrambled up onto the camp bed next to him and reached for the book. Paul laughed and removed it.

"No, I don't think the general wants your mucky hands all over his book, lass. Here."

He passed her instead the pewter cup from the box beside his bed and she examined it with considerable interest. There was an engraved design on it and the child ran her finger over it, then looked up at him and held out the cup for him to see. There was something about her, which looked suddenly familiar. Puzzled, Paul reached out and lifted her onto his lap, studying her. She made no objection, reaching up to touch the dressing on the side of his neck. Paul shifted her into the crook of his arm, reached for the book and opened it at one of the illustrations, and the child bent to look. She pointed to a horse and looked up at him and he felt, once again, that sense of familiarity.

"Horse," he said.

"Horse," the child agreed.

"Clever girl." Paul pointed again, his eyes on her face. "Castle."

"Castle." She struggled more with the word but managed it. Still watching her face, Paul pointed to himself.

71

"Paul," he said.

The child pointed to herself. "Grace," she said, very clearly.

"Good to meet you, Grace." Amused, Paul took her chubby hand and bent to kiss it and the child gave a gurgle of laughter, scrambled up and planted a kiss on his face. Paul looked into the child's blue eyes which were regarding him trustingly and with a sudden shock he understood. He swung his legs off the bed, ignoring the knifing pain in his thigh, and got up, scooping the child up onto his hip and reaching for one of his crutches. Outside he found that the woman and his sergeant had abandoned their argument and were frantically searching for the child.

"Thank God," Michael said. "What the devil are you doing with her, sir?"

"She came to visit me." Paul looked over at the woman who was holding out her arms for the child. He did not move. "What was her name? The mother?"

"Fraser, sir. Married to Sergeant Jamie Fraser. He died in the battle and she died a couple of days afterwards of fever. She'd been ill a few weeks, but I think his loss killed her, they were devoted."

"How long had they been married?"

"Not long, sir, this one was from her first marriage."

"Her name?"

"Nell. I think her first husband must have been one of yours, sir. I nursed her, she told me right before she died to bring her up to the 110th light company. I can't remember the name, if I ever heard it."

"Would it have been Kemp?"

The woman looked relieved. "It was. Billy, now that I think of it. Was he one of yours, sir?"

"We'll take her," Paul said quietly. "The women can take care of her on the voyage. Thank you for bringing her."

His sergeant stared at him in complete astonishment as the woman moved away. "Billy Kemp's brat?" he said incredulously. "Christ, sir, I know you helped his wife out, but this is taking it a bit far. What the hell are you going to do with her?"

Paul was looking at the child, who was playing with the braiding on his jacket. She seemed completely comfortable in his arms. He supposed that her life had already been turned upside down by the loss of her mother and the only father she had known, but her adaptability amused him. "She isn't Kemp's," he said quietly.

"What?"

"The age is all wrong. Kemp never made it out of gaol, he was awaiting court martial in Calcutta and died of dysentery in the prison there. I knew Nell had remarried but not that she was already pregnant. But she must have been, this lassie is too old to belong to Fraser. And Kemp never got near her again."

"One of our lads?"

"Don't be so bloody dense, Michael."

72

"Oh." Michael stared at the child and started to laugh. "Oh bloody hell, sir. Look at her."

"Yes." Paul studied the child with rueful amusement. Grace stared back at him thoughtfully.

"I didn't realise you'd..."

"On the voyage. Nell was lonely and grateful, and I was not going to say no to a girl as pretty as that. She was married to that bastard at sixteen, no experience of anything apart from his brutality. We had a good time for a couple of months, and I got very fond of her to be honest, she was really sweet. When we first arrived, I kept an eye on her for a few weeks, but she met Fraser within the first week, and he was not stupid, knew a good thing when he found one. I was glad for her, he'd a good reputation, I thought she'd done very well for herself. I told her to come to me if she was ever in need. She didn't tell me she was pregnant. Looking at this lass, she's well fed and cared for, I think Fraser treated her as his. But she can't be, she's at least eighteen months."

Michael was regarding the child. She looked back with interest and Paul saw his lips quirk into a smile. "Not much doubt, looking at her, she's the image of you. I'll get one of the women to come up, you'll need help with her. What are you going to do with her?"

"Take her back to Southwinds." Paul realised he could not stop looking at Grace. "I've another daughter," he said. "I've never seen her, never will, although I pay for her keep. I was very young, still at Oxford. I've often wondered about her."

"Have you never wanted to find out? Who was her mother?"

"Her name was Catherine...she was a pretty girl, respectable family."

"No temptation to make an honest woman of her?"

"I was fairly sure that I wasn't the only one," Paul said. "No doubt the child could have been mine, but I knew what Cat was like. I wasn't the only possible father, just the wealthiest."

Michael studied him. "And yet you paid."

"It's hardly the child's fault. Whoever fathered her, I can afford to give her a start in life. But I think that's why I never wanted to see her; I wasn't really sure she was mine."

"Were you fond of her? The mother?"

Grace was examining the shiny buttons on Paul's coat. He watched her, fascinated to see his own features so clearly on another face.

"Cat? She looked very good with her clothes off, Michael, and I had a good time, but if I was the first man she'd done that with, I'd be very surprised although she said I was. Nell Kemp had less experience than Cat did. I've always rather wondered if she already suspected she was pregnant and took up with me because I was a new undergraduate and she had every right to assume I was very naive."

"She has my sympathy, sir, we've all been fooled by that butter wouldn't melt look you have. Did she push for marriage?"

"I think she'd have liked to, but she took what I offered. If I got that wrong I was a bit of a shit to her, but I don't think I did. They're all right, her lawyer keeps me informed."

"I'd say even at that age your instincts were fairly good, sir." Michael was watching him with the child, shaking his head in amusement. "But Christ, you really need to get it under control. Sooner or later you're going to get yourself into so much shit over a woman that you are not going to find your way out again."

Chapter Five

By the time Paul reached the final stage of the long months of his journey home, he was exhausted. Unable to ride long distances with his leg still painful, he had hired a carriage and had arranged for wagons to transport his men to the barracks at Melton Mowbray in Leicestershire. The barracks were seven miles from his childhood home, but Paul was determined to see his men safe and settled before going there. He found the elderly Colonel Dixon in residence, visibly shocked at the condition of his officers and men.

Escaping gratefully after an hour of pleasantries, Paul found Carl in the yard about to mount. "Going home?" he asked.

"Yes. I'm granted a month's furlough, but I'll be over to see you as soon as the charm of my family reunion wears off."

"I'll see you in the morning then," Paul said, and Carl laughed.

"Very likely," he said. "Where's Grace?"

"Asleep in the carriage with Jenson, I didn't want to disturb her." Paul clapped his friend on the shoulder and went over to the hired post chaise. He climbed in awkwardly. Private Jenson was sitting with Grace's sleeping head pillowed on his knee. He had spent the long months of the voyage learning painfully to hobble around on the wooden leg that an Indian carpenter had made for him. Paul had taken the opportunity to employ him as temporary valet, and the arrangement seemed to suit both of them, so he had suggested that the young man accompany him to Southwinds during his furlough.

It was dark by the time they turned into the long winding drive of Paul's family estate. He was almost too exhausted to speak, but he smiled at his orderly. "All right, Jenson?"

"Yes, sir. But you look knackered."

"That's a fair estimate," Paul said. The carriage pulled up onto the circular drive, in front of the graceful house, and the post boy jumped down to lower the carriage steps. Paul leaned forward and peered out. "Oh Christ, my father's here. I'd rather face a troop of Maratha cavalry just now."

Jenson gave a choke of laughter. The door opened and Paul eased himself wearily out of the carriage. It felt like a huge effort to speak, but he could see his father approaching followed by his brother and sister-in-law. He glanced back into the carriage. The child was sleeping still.

"Paul." Joshua reached him first, hesitated, and then embraced him. Paul tried not to flinch. His brother stepped back, scanning his face with concerned eyes. "Christ, man, you look exhausted."

"I've been better," Paul said. "Father."

Franz took his hand. "A bad business. A famous victory I'm told, but many deaths."

"I lost almost half my company over two days."

"We heard that Carl was safe."

"Came out of it without a scratch, would you believe, he's like a cat with nine lives for he was in the thick of the fighting."

"And you're hurt," Patience said. "You look as if you can hardly stand. Come inside, Paul. For how long are you with us?"

"A few weeks, certainly. And I'll be nearby after that, in barracks. Don't look so worried, Patience, I'll be all right. I just need rest; this leg wound has taken longer than I would have expected. No, wait, there's somebody else you need to meet. Jenson, pass her out to me."

Paul turned and reached inside the carriage, scooping up the child in her blankets. She stirred and murmured but did not wake. Paul walked towards the house, followed by his shocked family, and Patience scuttled ahead of him. "Bring her into the drawing room, Paul, and lay her on the sofa."

Paul paused by the butler who was holding the door open. "Bartlett, my man Jenson is here. He doesn't walk that fast as he lost half a leg at Assaye. Will you look after him and get him settled, please?"

"Of course, Captain van Daan. Welcome home, sir."

Paul went through into the drawing room where a fire burned brightly, and a tray was set out with glasses and decanter. Gently he lay Grace onto the sofa, rearranged the blankets and brushed the fair hair back from the child's sleeping face, then lowered himself to sit beside her. His father went to the sideboard and poured brandy. Paul sipped and savoured the warmth. There was something unreal about the luxury around him, as though he no longer belonged in a place like this. He glanced down at his sleeping daughter.

"Who is she, Paul?"

"My daughter," Paul said quietly. "Her name is Grace, and she is not quite two years old. She has nobody else."

His sister-in-law studied the sleeping child. "She has your nose and the shape of your chin. Does she have your eyes?"

"Yes," Paul said.

"One of your officers' wives, Paul?"

"I don't sleep with my officers' wives, father. Grace's nominal father died shortly after arriving in India in a prison cell. He was a brute and no loss to Nell. We were friends. She was grateful and I think lonely and I…. I was myself, as usual. It's a long voyage to India." Paul shrugged. "I didn't know about Grace until Nell died. I couldn't leave her to strangers."

"No, I suppose not." Franz went to stand beside his daughter-in-law to look down at the sleeping child. "Who looked after her on the journey?"

"Some of my men have wives with them. They helped." Paul did not elaborate further. For the long months of the voyage his daughter had slept in his bunk curled in his arms, eaten meals sitting in his lap and brought him more joy than he had believed possible. He knew his conventional family would be horrified to realise how much of the care of Grace he had taken to himself. She had made the voyage and his grief and the pain of his wounds bearable for him. He glanced at Patience. "I know this is going to become your responsibility, Patience. Hire all the nursemaids and governesses you need, but…"

"Hush, Paul, don't be silly. She'll be a joy to have."

"I hope so, I've become very fond of her these past months." Paul sipped his brandy. "I'm sorry. I seem to be very tired."

"Go to bed, Paul. Patience can take the child up and get her settled. Nurse is still with us, although officially she has retired, but she would love to have a little one to fuss over."

"She'll be just what Grace needs while she settles in, but I warn you, once she has found her feet she'll need somebody younger and stronger and much firmer, because she's a little hellcat. God knows where she gets it from. I think I will go up; I'll make a lot more sense in the morning."

Paul found Jenson in his room unpacking. "What the devil are you doing?" he demanded. "Aren't you tired? You need to rest that leg."

"In case you haven't noticed, sir, I've been sitting on my arse on a wagon, a ship, another wagon and a post chaise for around six months. It's rested."

Paul gave a choke of laughter. "Thank God you're here," he said. "You remind me of real life. Are you settled?"

"Yes, sir. Got a bigger room here than our whole company billet in Assaye."

"How the hell would you know, you slept for weeks, you idle bastard?"

"I was just resting, sir, like you recommended."

Paul laughed aloud, and his valet grinned back at him. "Need anything else, sir?"

"You can help me haul off these boots if you would?"

Jenson complied. As he rose, Paul stood up and walked over to the table. He poured two brandies and passed one to his valet. Jenson laughed and took it. "Your family would have a fit."

"They've been having a fit about me for years, they should be over it by now. Good health, Jenson." Paul looked around. "This feels strange."

"Too much comfort for you, sir?"

"Exactly. But you know what? I think I'll manage."

"You bloody should, sir. You've spent the past months worrying about me, Sergeant Stewart, Mr Wheeler, your daughter and every other man of the light company and you look completely exhausted. And now you're pouring me drinks and I'm supposed to be waiting on you. Go to bed and get some sleep, sir. And if it will make you feel better, I'll do the same."

"Thanks, Jenson. Good night."

"'Night, sir. And if you wake me up at dawn because you think you're on early drill, I'm going to forget that you're an officer and punch you."

***

Paul found his month at home easier than he had expected. He had not expected any problems with his brother or sister-in-law. Joshua, five years his senior, had dominated his childhood, seeming to negotiate the river of life with an ease that Paul had never felt. He had been ready, on Paul's return from the navy, to offer support and help with easing his delicate younger brother back into the world. Upon finding instead, a tough, self-contained young man who did not require his assistance, he had adapted to this surprising new sibling remarkably well. As a child, Paul had envied Joshua, and often hated him. As an adult, he found his brother a rock, who never wavered or failed him.

He was very fond, too, of his gentle sister-in-law. Patience lived up to her name, never seeming to be irritated or exasperated with the towering personalities of her father-in-law and his sons. She was a devoted wife and an affectionate sister-in-law. Paul realised, to his surprise and pleasure, that he had given her an unexpected gift in bringing Grace home to her. Patience had not managed to carry a child to full term, which was the only sorrow in her marriage. Paul had thought only of the extra work he was bringing to her but realised now that her niece filled a gap he had not known existed for her.

Paul had not spent so much time around his father since boyhood. Their relationship had always been difficult, and after he had returned from the navy he had not voluntarily been in the same room as Franz. His time in the army seemed to have mellowed his anger, or perhaps it was simply that he had grown up in the past two years, and their shared experience of India created an unexpected bond. They spent hours riding together or walking through the coverts with their guns and a couple of spaniels, often talking little, but building, by small steps, a new relationship.

They rode out the day before Paul's return to barracks. Franz was unusually silent, and Paul followed his lead. As they began the steady climb up past the old Bradgate house, Franz said:

"I'm going back to London next week. The business doesn't run itself and I've been away long enough. God knows what mistakes the fools have made in my absence."

"I feel rather the same," Paul said.

His father shot him a sideways smile. "Many officers in your position, would choose to live at home. It isn't far, and you've junior officers and NCOs to supervise training and drill and recruitment."

"That is true. But if they didn't do it the way I wanted them to, I could hardly blame them if I found myself attacking the guns on some muddy field in France with a bunch of unfit layabouts who take ten minutes to load a musket."

Franz gave a crack of laughter. "Undoubtedly you have a point. But come often to Southwinds, Paul, while you have the opportunity. It is good for Joshua, and I rather suspect it is good for you."

"It is," Paul admitted. "One of the benefits of living in tents and in flea ridden hovels for months on end, is that it gives one a new appreciation for the comforts of home." He glanced across at his father. "And for the company of one's family."

Franz returned his look, a smile curving his austere lips. "I have decided to accept that as a compliment," he said dryly. "Consider it returned. You may not know that I have, since you joined up, made a point of cultivating one or two acquaintances at Horse Guards. I had dinner with one of them not long after the reports came in of Assaye. He was able to describe the battle to me, and also one or two smaller actions in which you had been involved prior to the battle, so I have some idea why you came home limping, with a rather horrific scar down the side of your neck."

"Because I command the company, it's my name that goes on the reports, Father, but every single man who fought that day was extraordinary."

"I know. But they are not my sons, so for them I do not feel such an immense sense of pride when another man tells me what they have achieved. Sitting at that dinner table listening to him telling me what you had done, I felt slightly ashamed that I have not always known what you were capable of. I realise now. This will not stop us arguing in the future, I have no doubt. Joshua is very easy to live and to work with. You and I are not. But just this once, I wanted to tell you that I do appreciate the courage and the talent you have brought to your chosen career. And I am proud."

"Thank you," Paul said. He could not have said more without a betraying crack in his voice.

Returning to barracks, the officers of the light company quickly fell into a familiar routine of training and drilling the men. In addition to Paul's light company there were the final two companies of the first battalion currently in barracks, along with eight companies of the second battalion, each commanded by their own captain. All of them were older and longer serving than Paul and he was immediately aware of their resentment. Despite recent reforms most officers still obtained their commissions by purchase, as he had, but promotions were less easy to buy and for regiments not in combat, there were rules being introduced about length of service and seniority before a promotion could be purchased. Paul had already by-passed these with his field commission. Moreover he had come with letters from Major Johnstone, readily endorsed by the amiable Colonel Dixon, authorising him to take charge of the training and drilling of all companies currently in barracks, which effectively placed him in charge of the other officers although he was the same rank as them and more recently promoted. During the first weeks he trod as carefully as he could, trying not to offend his fellow officers. Tact was a new skill for him, and he found it considerably harder than leading men into battle.

After an especially gruelling day working the men's musket skills, Paul arrived in the officers' mess to find Carl and Johnny already there. He sank down tiredly, and the mess sergeant brought him a drink.

"Thanks, Joe."

"You eating in tonight, sir?"

"Not sure, Joe. I've an errand in town, I might get something out."

Carl raised his eyebrows. "Aren't you coming to the Carletons' reception?"

"No, will you give my apologies? I can't face being social tonight."

Johnny laughed. "You persist in behaving as if we're still living in tents on the plains of Assaye, Paul. You need to relax a bit more, come out and enjoy yourself."

Paul glanced at him, considered an excuse and discarded it. "I don't enjoy it much," he admitted. "Too many witless conversations about Assaye and the glory of war."

Johnny nodded. Both his friends were aware that Paul still struggled at times with his memories of India.

"Give it time," Carl said gently. "In the meantime you need to grit your teeth and resume your place in society as an officer and a gentleman."

"Shouldn't think he knows how, do you old boy?"

Three officers of the seventh company had wandered in and sat down at the next table. Captain Longford was looking over at Paul with a thin lipped smile.

"I'll work on it," Paul said amiably, refusing to be drawn. "Drink, Longford?" He signalled for Joe, who took bottle and glasses to the other table. Carl looked away, hiding a smile. Longford was looking furious. Lieutenant Zouch was grinning broadly. Carl caught his eye and shook his head warningly. They were all becoming tired of Longford's unrelenting hostility, especially Zouch who had to listen to his constant complaints, but Paul was determined not to rise to the bait. It surprised Carl who knew his friend's quick temper, and there had been occasions when both of Paul's lieutenants had longed to punch Longford's supercilious face.

"What's your errand?" Carl asked.

"I'm going to see Miss Mason. Major Johnstone asked me to take the captain's personal effects to her, but she's been away in Scotland with her aunt for several months. I wrote to her and she has written to tell me that she is home. I need to get this out of the way."

"Want company?"

Paul shook his head. "No, go and enjoy yourselves. You can safely do so, Lady Carleton is after money for those girls, so you can flirt as much as you like without fear that she'll latch onto you. I'll see you in the morning."

Paul drained his glass and stood up. Longford laughed unpleasantly. "Going to have a try at the pretty orphan, Captain?" he said. "Don't blame you. She's young and probably not up to snuff with only the spinster aunt to protect her. I've heard about your reputation with women."

A number of other officers had entered the room by now and Longford's remark caused a shocked silence. For the first time since he had arrived, Paul looked directly at Longford.

"She's seventeen and just lost her father, who was my captain, by the way. Vent your spleen some other way, Longford."

Paul continued towards the door. Carl let out his breath slowly, but Longford had obviously worked himself into a rage. The other officers were watching and listening with considerable interest.

"Let's not be coy about this, Van Daan. Remember I've family locally, and rumour has it that you screwed your way around the county before you joined the army and weren't always picky if they were willing or not. To say nothing of the blue eyed by-blow you've foisted onto your family as your ward."

Paul turned abruptly. "Did you just call me a rapist?" he demanded incredulously.

"Oh shit," Carl murmured, getting up.

"Well, you'd know better than I would, Captain," Longford drawled insultingly, and Carl closed his eyes briefly.

Paul shook his head in disbelief. "Jesus, Longford, the list of things I know better than you is so long it isn't even worth getting started. Do you seriously expect me to start a brawl with you in the middle of the mess over an accusation that you made up five minutes ago? I'd sooner attend this bloody party than waste my time wiping the floor with your arse. What are you hoping to do, provoke a duel? In the first place I don't care enough about you or your opinion to be bothered to challenge you, and if you could somehow induce me to do so, I promise you I can put a bullet through any part of your anatomy that I choose before you've managed to work out which end of the pistol to point at me. And don't get me started on your swordplay, my youngest recruit could disarm you in less than three minutes. Now if you'll excuse me, I've things to attend to. Please feel free to continue getting drunk at my expense." Paul looked across at Carl and Johnny, neither of whom was attempting to hide their laughter. "Gentlemen, when he falls over, get him back to his quarters before you leave, will you?"

Paul turned and walked out to a barrage of laughter and whoops of encouragement from everybody else in the mess. Outside he stood still for a moment, taking in a deep breath. Across the yard stood four men, three privates stood to attention, and a sergeant who had his back to Paul and who was addressing them on their shortcomings in training in melodious Irish tones. Paul strolled across and waited until his sergeant had finished and dismissed the men. Behind him he heard the door to the mess bang. Turning he saw Longford storming towards his quarters without looking at Paul or Michael.

"Would you look at him, now?" O'Reilly said wonderingly. "What's got his goat, I wonder?"

"I did," Paul admitted.

"Oh, thank God it's nothing serious, then," Michael said, relieved. "I was thinking that they'd burned the Irish stew again."

Paul laughed aloud. His sergeant grinned at him. "Feel better?"

"Yes," Paul admitted. "I lost my patience and had a few words with him. I'm annoyed with myself, though, I was determined not to let him rile me and I thought I was doing well."

"Oh don't worry about it, sir, he's never going to let up until you deal with him. The others are all coming round gradually, and you've done a fine job of being nice to them, it's been making me want to vomit for weeks. But he's a nasty bastard and always has been. Sooner or later you're going to have to kick him."

Paul eyed him thoughtfully. "Have you had any trouble with him, Michael?"

"Oh Lord love you, sir, nothing I can't handle. He's hoping he can push me into administering the kicking myself because he knows if he has me arrested, you'll intervene. But I've served under Captain Longford before, I've got his measure. Where are you off to?"

"Going to see Captain Mason's daughter. And avoiding the Carletons' reception."

"Ungrateful bastard. You'd rather be down at the Boat drinking with us, wouldn't you?"

"By far. In fact I'll probably be down later on. Although Carl is right, I should try a bit harder to socialise with my own kind. The trouble is half of them are idiots."

"Good practice for dealing with Captain Longford, sir. I'll see you later, then."

Paul walked the fifteen minutes to the address given to him in Caroline Mason's letter. She was a pretty fair girl of seventeen and Paul found her dignified grief touching. He gave her the small collection of items and answered her questions about her father's death as frankly as he could, without causing unnecessary pain. She seemed grateful for the truth and he left with a sense that he would have liked to know Caroline Mason better, but he would not call again. She was very young and very vulnerable, and Paul knew how easy it would be for him to take advantage of that, without ever meaning to.

It was half an hour's walk to the Boat, which was near the canal, and it was still fairly light and pleasantly warm. Paul was in no particular hurry and took his time. He wondered if he should have made the effort to accompany his friends. At some point he was going to need to move past Assaye and resume his place in local society, although flirting with a series of well brought up girls, whose mothers were trying to find a wealthy husband for them had no appeal for Paul, and he was not sure that time would improve that.

Paul had almost reached the inn when he heard a sound from the bushes, which lined the towpath. Some instinct of danger made him spin around quickly. There was a blur of movement and then a hard body cannoned into him, a knife slashing up towards his neck. Paul was saved by the speed of his reactions and his height, which made it harder for an average man to stab upwards, but the knife caught him a glancing blow across the scar at the side of his neck before he grasped the man's wrist and twisted hard. His attacker screamed and dropped the blade onto the towpath. Paul twisted again and his assailant gave a sob of pain and dropped to his knees in an attempt to release some of the pressure on his arm.

"My arm..." he said, and Paul twisted harder.

"You'll be lucky to get out of this with a broken arm, you stupid bastard! Stop struggling or I'll kick you into the bloody canal!"

The door of the tavern opened, and three men came out, all in uniform, peering through the fading light.

"Is that you, sir?" Private Carter's unmistakable cockney tones sounded. "You all right?"

"Yes. Dodgy area this, mind." Paul hauled his assailant to his feet and shoved him forward. "He must be the most stupid footpad in Leicestershire to try his luck down here."

As he came closer Carter noticed the blood on his neck. "Bloody hell, sir, can't you even come out for a quiet drink without getting yourself into trouble? Bring him in here – grab him, Dawson, will you? I'll get you something to put on that."

Paul relinquished his prisoner and allowed Carter to lead him to a table. The tavern was full of his men and as he sat down, Rory Stewart got up and came over. "You all right, sir? Bloody footpads! They don't usually carry a blade, mind. Sally, bring a towel over, will you?"

Paul accepted the cloth and held it to the wound. Dawson shoved his attacker forward into the light of the lamps and Paul stared at him in some surprise.

"Don't I know you?" he said.

"You bloody do, sir," Carter said, staring at the man. "It's Venables, seventh company."

"Jesus, sir, what have you been doing now?" Sergeant O'Reilly said, coming through from the other bar. "Did he do this?"

"He did. It's fine, Sergeant, it's not deep. But I rather think he was intending to kill me."

"Why, for God's sake?" Michael said, turning his eyes to the terrified private.

"Probably couldn't face another early drill with you, sir," Carter said meditatively. "I've thought about it myself."

"Very funny, Carter. Christ knows why, I've never spoken to the man, I wouldn't even have known his name, let alone...oh."

"What is it, sir?" Michael said quietly. Paul stared at the frightened man. He thought he understood although it was almost impossible to believe.

"Captain Longford's company."

"What...Jesus, you don't think...?"

Paul was watching Venables frightened face and knew he was right. "Did he pay you or threaten you?" he said, and there was a hard edge of anger in his voice now that the shock was passing.

Venables did not reply. After a moment, the sergeant said:

"Venables. The officer asked you a question."

"Sir?" Venables was probably in his thirties, a stocky man with the soft burr of the West country and warm brown eyes which were wide with terror.

"Venables, I have just had the novel experience of almost getting my throat cut by a man from my own fucking regiment. Do I look like I'm in the mood for a laugh? Captain Longford sent you down to wait for me on my way back. Did he pay you or threaten you? You know as well as I do the penalty for striking an officer, so unless you want to spend your last few days in the gaol imagining what it's going to feel like when the rope snaps your bloody neck, I suggest you start talking to me right now."

"I'm a dead man either way," Venables said, his voice barely a whisper.

"Venables, you've been the biggest bloody idiot this side of the channel, don't make it any worse, just answer the officer's questions and don't make him angry." O'Reilly glanced at Paul's face. "More angry," he amended.

"Sir, he said if I didn't do it he'd make my life hell. Flog me for every offence, and some I didn't do, dock my pay. I've a family, sir. And I've seen what he can do."

Paul studied the man in silence for a moment. Carter said:

"Want me to throw him in the canal, sir? He doesn't look like he's the swimming kind, he'd be cleaner if he ever went near water."

"I am tempted, Carter," Paul admitted. "But I'm not Captain Longford. Venables, get to attention!"

Venables straightened and saluted. Paul studied him. Suddenly he felt a rush of compassion. "You bloody idiot, Venables, you should have come to me."

"I didn't think you'd believe me, sir."

"I suppose you don't know me, do you? All right, get back to barracks and get your kit moved. You're being transferred to the light company, we're short of men. See to it, Sergeant O'Reilly, I'll get the colonel's approval in the morning."

Venables looked completely bewildered and O'Reilly grinned. "Sir, for the love of God, are you sure you want this useless gobshite in the light company? I've seen his shooting and his bayonet work is worse."

"Give me a few months with him and he may at least be able to pull off a surprise attack against an unarmed man without getting his arse kicked. Either that or he'll be dead. Take him away, Sergeant, I need a drink."

"Yes, sir. Get some food into you as well, you're as white as a sheet. Carter..."

"I'll take him up, Sarge, you stay and see to the captain." Carter eyed Venables with a genial expression which Paul found frankly terrifying. "Welcome to the light company, Private Venables. Just so we're clear before we get started, you lay one fucking hand on our officer again, and we'll string you up by your balls 'til they can hear you screaming in Derbyshire, I don't care who the bloody hell paid you to do it. Now get your arse out that door."

Paul watched them go. "Poor bastard," he said, accepting a drink from Sally Stewart. "We'll have to watch him, Sergeant, Longford will go after him."

"I'll keep an eye on him, sir. Come on, let me clean that up and then we'll get some food into you." Michael eyed him severely. "And next time perhaps you'll have the sense to go to the reception with your own kind."

"And miss this? I thought you knew me better, Sergeant."

Chapter Six

Paul made no mention of the incident the following day when he rode over to his family home for dinner. His sister-in-law greeted him with a hug and his daughter climbed onto his lap the moment he sat down and gazed up at him wide-eyed ready for a story. During the long months of the voyage home, Paul had discovered an imagination he had not known he possessed when it came to weaving fantasy tales for Grace, and she had come to love it. He told her an improbable tale involving dragons and when he was done, she remained curled up in his arms ready for her afternoon nap with clearly no intention of returning to the nursery. Catching Nurse's eye, Paul smiled and shook his head and the woman retired.

"I thought you'd be at the Carletons' yesterday, Paul," Joshua said.

Paul grinned. "I was playing truant down at the Boat with Michael and a few of the lads," he admitted. "Did I miss anything?"

"You'll get cashiered for that one of these days. You didn't miss much. The eldest girl – Maria is it – is finally engaged, but she's still got three – or four if you count the little one - to dispose of. I don't blame you for giving it a miss, she'd be onto you like a hawk, brother, she's after money."

Grace had fallen asleep. Paul shifted her to a more comfortable position and dropped a kiss onto the fair head.

"Paul, do you want me to take her up to the nursery? She's getting heavy," Patience said looking around for Nurse.

"Are you mad? I'd pay for an hour like this," Paul said with a laugh, kissing his daughter's soft head again. "I remember the Carleton girls when we were young. Amiable enough but not that pretty. Did they improve?"

"Yes, I think so. The prettiest lass is the young cousin, but she's never invited to parties."

"Why not?" Paul asked.

"Poor relation. Lady Carleton's sister made an improvident match, and this girl was left an orphan. They left her at a charity school for years, but she's old enough to be useful now. I think she acts as unpaid governess to the youngest daughter who is only about eight. We see her at church, but she's seldom invited anywhere. Shy little thing, but very pretty. She's called Rowena."

"Pretty name."

"I feel sorry for the girl," his sister-in-law said. "I don't think she receives much kindness from Lady Carleton."

"I imagine not. I always liked Lord Carleton, but she's an unpleasant woman. I wonder what made him marry her?"

"Father assures me she was very lovely in her youth," Joshua said. He was watching his brother in some amusement. "I never expected to say this, but fatherhood suits you, Paul. Look at her."

Paul looked down at his daughter with a grin. "I get the best of it this way," he said. "All the games and stories and fun and then I ride off back to barracks just as she's ready to scream her way through bedtime."

"I would imagine most fathers are the same," Patience said with a laugh. "I'm going to ring for Nurse, however, because dinner will be served shortly, and unless you intend to eat with her on your lap..."

"I probably wouldn't mind," Paul said. "I've eaten in far more awkward circumstances, believe me."

"It astonishes me that you manage to feed yourselves at all in those conditions," Patience said, pulling the bell cord.

Paul watched Patience with affectionate understanding. He knew that she would not settle until Grace was safely back in the nursery although he would have been happy to keep his daughter on his lap for the rest of the afternoon. He had become very close to her during the long months of their journey home, and he knew that his conventional sister-in-law would have been horrified if she had known how much of her day-to-day care he had managed without help. He adored Grace with the most uncomplicated emotion he had ever felt.

"Hookey's soldiers never go hungry. He manages to combine being a brilliant tactician with a phenomenal organiser. He's revolutionised the way the supply lines work in India, which gives him so much more mobility than other generals."

Josh was smiling. "He's certainly made a convert of you," he said. "I'd say that's his most impressive achievement to date, I've never known you to speak with admiration of an authority figure before, Paul. Usually you're picking them apart after the shortest acquaintance."

"Am I that bad? It's true, the army has an interesting variety of commanders and a few of them shouldn't be there at all. The thing that horrified me the most in India was how many of them drink. I don't just mean the usual amount. I mean they are drunk for most of the day, I've seen some horrors. God help the men who serve under them."

When Grace had been removed, Josh went to the sideboard.

"Sherry, Paul? How are you getting on in barracks? Has the colonel started complaining yet about you drinking with the men?"

Paul shook his head, laughing. "I suppose Carl told you that story?"

"Carl is a wealth of good stories," Patience said. "All the ones you never tell us."

"He makes half of them up, I swear. I don't have any problems with Colonel Dixon. Major Johnstone told him to give me free rein and he's not a man to make waves if he doesn't have to. Not popular with everybody, but they're getting used to me, I think."

The butler arrived to announce dinner and Paul went to take his sister-in-law's arm. "Will you walk down to church with us after dinner, Paul, before you go back? Or you could stay tonight and ride back in the morning."

"I'll come to church and ride back afterwards. It's a fine evening and there'll be a moon. I quite like night riding."

After the meal Paul took himself off to walk through the grounds. Southwinds had been his boyhood home and he knew every inch of the woodland and coverts. He had run wild with Carl over these lands, swum in the lake and learned to fish and to shoot. He walked down to the lake now, its waters cool and still in the early evening light and stood for a while looking out across the water, then made his way over to the church. Paul seldom attended services of his own accord, but for his sister-in-law it was a familiar and much loved ritual and he always went with her when he was at home. Paul liked the local church, with its Norman tower and cool musty interior. He was early for the service and debated whether to call at the rectory to pay his respects to Carl's father first.

The church door was ajar, and Paul walked up the path through the lych-gate and went inside. The early evening sunlight was pouring through the stained glass windows, spilling rainbow patterns over the stone slabs on the floor in a glory of jewelled colour. Paul trod up the aisle, running his fingers over the dark wood of the high pews. The church was very well kept, more so than he remembered, and smelled of incense, beeswax polish and fresh flowers. There were two large arrangements at the front on either side, and Paul stopped to admire them, inhaling the scent of roses and stocks.

The door to the vestry opened and Paul looked up expecting to see Mr Swanson or his curate. Instead he saw a girl dressed in sprigged muslin with a simple straw bonnet. Seeing his tall figure looming up in the dim light, she jumped and gave a slight gasp.

"Don't be alarmed," Paul said quickly. "I didn't mean to startle you; I was early for church and came in for a look around. I was just admiring the flowers; did you do them?"

The girl came further into the light. "Please don't apologise, I just didn't realise anybody was here. Yes, I did these."

Now that she was in full light he could see her properly. She was slight and very fair with a pair of arresting green eyes. "I've not seen a church decorated like this before, but it's lovely," Paul said, studying her. "I don't think we've met. Captain Paul van Daan, 110th light company. You may know my brother and sister-in-law, though."

"I think I have met them. But you and I have not been introduced."

"No, I've been away, not back long. And I'm very sure I would have remembered you."

She coloured prettily. "Sir, I should not..."

"Let me make a guess since you are clearly a well brought up lass who cringes at the thought of conversing with a man she doesn't know. Would it be Miss Summers? You're not one of Lord Carleton's daughters, I'd recognise them, but you're new and my sister-in-law mentioned you. How do you do, Miss Summers?"

She bobbed an uncertain curtsey. "Sir. Are you...do you live at Southwinds?"

"I'm currently in barracks at Melton. I dined with my brother and said that I would attend service before I ride back. Is that why you are here?"

"Yes. I am invited for sherry at the rectory."

"Then I shall join you. I was just debating whether to call, but you have decided me."

Miss Summers looked up at him, unconsciously giving him an excellent view of her very charming countenance beneath the bonnet. "Do you know Mr Swanson?"

"Better than he would like. I grew up here, played dice in his confirmation classes and was thrown out of the choir for passing notes to the girls. His son is my lieutenant and an old friend." Paul offered her his arm and she took it shyly.

They were greeted at the rectory by a very young curate, who gazed worshipfully at Miss Summers and showed them into the parlour before disappearing to find the parson and his wife. Paul looked at the girl.

"I should have known," he said. "The curate. Has he proposed yet?"

She blushed a fiery red. "Captain van Daan, you cannot..."

"He will. And when you reject him he will be completely unable to fulfil his duties."

"Mr Edwards is very conscientious," the girl said reprovingly.

"Is he? Don't tell me that his passion is reciprocated?"

"This is not a proper conversation," the girl said. She could go no redder. The blush spread down the smooth column of her neck. Paul watched her with a slight smile. She was very pretty and very young and his direct flirtation was clearly new to her.

Reaching for her hand he raised it to his lips. "Don't worry, I promise to behave myself."

The door opened and Paul released her and turned to greet Carl's parents.

"Paul, how are you? We don't often see you here for services. I see that my son is not with you."

Paul shook the rector's hand. "How are you, sir? Ma'am. No, Carl is on duty this evening. I am playing truant visiting my brother and walked down ahead of them. I was in the church, admiring Miss Summers' handiwork."

"Yes, we are very fortunate that she gives us her time. My church has never been so well cared for," Mr Swanson said warmly, smiling at the girl. "I was not aware that you were acquainted with her, however."

"I met her by chance on her way here and having no company manners whatsoever I introduced myself. She will feel better now that you are here to do it properly, mind. Although it feels a little excessive to me. Perhaps we could skip the actual introductions and just pretend you have done so. How are you, sir?"

"Very well, Paul. I observe army life has not changed you at all. Miss Summers, as you probably know, this is Captain van Daan, recently returned from India. Captain, this is Miss Summers who has recently come to live with her aunt, Lady Carleton. Have some sherry."

Under the soothing parish chatter of the parson and his wife, Miss Summers regained her composure. Paul, who had known the Swansons since childhood, was able to maintain an easy conversation about local affairs, and after a few moments the girl was able to join in. When the time came to go over to the church, the rector went off in search of his sermon and his reading glasses, and his wife hesitated, torn between her urge to join the search and her social obligations.

"I shall escort Miss Summers to church and leave you, ma'am," Paul said, coming to her rescue. "My brother and Patience should be there by now."

"Thank you, Paul." Mrs Swanson came over and stood on tiptoe to kiss him on the cheek. "Tell my son to come and visit me, I see less of him than when he was in India."

"Gladly," Paul said. "He is a bad son but an excellent officer, ma'am."

Outside the rectory, he offered his arm to Miss Summers. "Let us go. I have done my duty and feel suitably virtuous now."

"I do not think that I expected you to be on such good terms with the Swansons," the girl said naively, and Paul laughed.

"Why? Because of my military exploits or my outrageous flirting? You will be surprised to hear, Miss Summers, that I was brought up as a proper English gentleman. The fact that I very seldom behave as one does not mean I don't know how."

She blushed again. "I would not have been so rude," she said.

"You should be as rude as you like, lass, it does me no harm at all."

The girl's voice was so quiet he had to stoop to hear her. "Captain, you should not be talking to me like this, I hardly know you."

There was a group of parishioners in the churchyard gossiping. Paul took her hand once again and lifted it to his lips. This time he held it there for far too long. "Miss Summers, I hope to learn to know you much better," he said gravely.

***

Paul met with Colonel Dixon the following morning and gave him an edited version of the events of the previous twenty-four hours. The colonel, who did not like problems, regarded Paul with a worried frown.

"Really, this is very difficult, Captain van Daan. Longford has been here for a long time. A good officer..."

90

"Good officers don't terrorise their men and try to murder their fellow officers, sir." Paul took a deep breath. "Do you approve Venables' transfer?"

"Captain, what I ought to do is insist on his immediate arrest!"

"That would please Longford and he'd be safe enough, Venables is too terrified to name him. But I'm not having it."

"If you choose not to pursue the matter, I will accept that."

"Thank you, sir. I would also be grateful if you would issue an order that men of a company can only be disciplined by their own officers. I don't want Longford to have control of punishments over my men. He'll use them to get at me."

Dixon regarded him soberly. "You really think he is that bad?"

"His men think he is that bad, sir, and I have learned to listen to them. They are, after all, the ones experiencing it."

"Major Johnstone warned me that you might be difficult. He didn't tell me the half of it." The colonel regarded Paul thoughtfully. "I will issue the order, with the proviso that if two officers disagree over a matter of discipline I am to be the arbiter."

"I am perfectly happy with that, sir."

"You flatter me," Dixon said ironically. "I may have an idea which will remove the problem for a while. I am going to send out a recruiting party, both battalions are very much under strength. I could put Captain Longford in charge of it."

Paul regarded him with a sense of relief. "I would be grateful, sir. I know it's not a permanent solution, but it would give us all time to calm down and rethink. Perhaps before he returns we will have another posting."

"That is what I am hoping. He won't object to it; he will enjoy the break from routine. In the meantime, Captain van Daan, you had better get my regiment up to scratch."

"I'll do my best, sir." Paul stood up. "Thank you, Colonel."

Captain Longford departed some four days later, at the head of a small recruiting party. He looked happy with the posting, and Paul, who had managed to stay out of his way, did not repeat his conversation with the colonel to anybody.

The following Sunday Paul rode over to Southwinds. His daughter had just taken possession of a new puppy and he spent two happy hours playing with them both on the back lawn. When Grace was finally tired he delivered her back to her nurse and then walked down to the church where, as he had hoped, he found Rowena Summers in the vestry industriously polishing a pair of candlesticks.

"Captain van Daan." She looked startled to see him.

"Miss Summers. Do you spend all your Sundays down here?"

"I am usually free on Sundays. I like to get out of the house and there are always things to be done here."

"Is it very dreary up at the house?" Paul asked gently.

The girl stood up and walked out of the vestry into the church. Paul followed her. "I am very grateful for everything my aunt and uncle have done for me," Rowena said evenly.

"And that tells me exactly how they treat you, Rowena."

"That is not fair, sir. You don't know everything about me."

"I don't, and I'd like to know more." Paul came towards her and lifted her hand to his lips. "I am sorry, Rowena, I'm out of the habit of polite society. Come for a walk with me and remind me how to behave. Come on, it's too lovely a day to shut yourself away in a dim church."

She hesitated, but then allowed him to lead her outside. "You should not be using my name," she said. "We don't know each other that well."

"We will. I should ask your permission, of course, but I'm not going to as you would feel obliged to say no. And you can hardly stop me calling you whatever I like. I love your name, it's one of the prettiest I've ever heard."

They walked up to the forest, and Rowena told him, under his easy questioning, about her life and her family. She spoke of the harsh years she had spent at the charity school and Paul reflected that it was not surprising that she was so shy, given how little experience she had of the world.

Within a few weeks, Paul's Sundays fell into a regular pattern. After visiting his family he would meet Rowena Summers, either in the church or up at the edge of the forest and they would walk together, talking, until it was time to go back down to sherry at the rectory and then service, after which he would ride back to barracks and Rowena would walk back up to the hall. Paul found himself enjoying Rowena's company immensely. Her naivety was unexpectedly charming, and her serenity was very restful. She was unlike any of the girls he met at society parties and although he was very aware that he should not be making assignations with a vulnerable unmarried girl, he knew he was finding excuses to continue to do so.

On leaving India Paul had said an affectionate farewell to Manjira, leaving her with a generous gift in the company of a delighted cavalry captain. Since his return he had spent the occasional evening at Carrie Megson's establishment, and after a visit to the theatre in Leicester he spent some time with one of the dancers who seemed more than willing to share her bed with him, but he had no regular woman in keeping and he missed the companionship. He had found that companionship with Rowena Summers and he was not ready to give it up although he felt some qualms about the damage he might do to her reputation if their friendship should be noticed.

Paul was also aware of how attractive he found her, and he was fairly certain that the attraction was mutual. Rowena had no experience of men, but his experience of women was considerable, and he could sense her response to his occasional touch. Up until now he had restrained himself. She was very young, and she appeared completely unprotected. Her guardians, such as they were, seemed to care nothing about how she spent her time when she was not acting as their unpaid servant and governess. Walking through the mellow summer afternoons at her side, Paul watched her and thought that sooner or later some man was bound to seduce a girl this pretty and this vulnerable. It was very tempting to think that it might as well be him.

***

Rowena Summers was a very practical girl. At no point did she delude herself that the attractive captain of the light company was falling in love with her. He clearly enjoyed her company, and she suspected that her shyness and her naïve reaction to his outrageous flirting amused him. Rowena imagined that he was bored with his routine at the barracks, and their stolen hours walking through the forest during the summer afternoons and early evenings or sitting by the lake while he told her stories of India and the Cape of Good Hope, were a diversion for him. Rowena was trying to take the same light-hearted attitude to their friendship, but she was finding it very difficult. She had not realised that anybody else had noticed their meetings until the Rector raised the matter while she was helping him tidy the vestry.

"Miss Summers, I know that you are in a somewhat unusual position at the hall. You have no parents, although I am sure Lord and Lady Carleton take their responsibilities very seriously...."

Rowena felt herself blush. "Sir?"

"I have noticed that Captain van Daan has become somewhat particular in his attentions."

"Oh – we have met a few times when I am out and about. But it means nothing, sir. I promise you, I have no idea of anything else." Rowena gave a small tight smile. "My position makes marriage an impossibility and I know he has no intentions."

"You are a sensible girl, I am glad to know that you understand."

"You don't like him?"

Mr Swanson laughed, and walked over to the shelf where he busied himself tidying a stack of bibles. "I do like him. I have known Paul van Daan since the day he was born, and he has always been my son's closest friend."

"But you don't trust him?"

"Child, I would trust him with many things, but not with a young and innocent girl. I agree that he has no matrimonial intentions, but forgive me, that does not mean he has no intentions at all. I know for a fact that there was a girl at Oxford, whose child he maintains. And although he refers to little Grace as his ward, few people believe it."

Rowena knew that her face was scarlet. "I will take care," she promised. "But I do not think that he will go beyond flirting, sir."

Rowena thought about the conversation as she walked up to the hall and decided that the rector was right. Her friendship with Paul van Daan, however much she valued it, was not wise for a young woman in her position, and it was probably time to make a graceful withdrawal.

He took her by surprise the following Sunday afternoon as she was pulling weeds from around her mother's gravestone. Rowena had not heard him approach and his voice made her jump.

"Charming," he said, looking her over appreciatively. "Only you could manage to look so lovely while weeding the graveyard."

Rowena tried not to meet his eyes, but she could not help it. They were smiling, as they always did when he looked at her.

"Captain. I am glad you have come because I need to speak to you."

"By all means. Let us walk up to the spinney and you may tell me anything you choose."

Paul held out his hand and Rowena took it, more aware than ever of the warmth and strength of his hand. He tucked her hand into his arm, and they began to stroll up the gentle rise away from the church towards the trees.

"What's troubling you, Rowena?"

"I spent some time with Mr Swanson during the week, and he has spoken to me about you."

"Ah – suddenly everything becomes clear. Has he warned you that I am not a fit person for you to be wandering in the woods with, little one?"

Rowena glanced up at him. "More or less," she admitted. "He is always very kind to me. But I have been thinking about it, sir, and I believe he is right."

"About my unsuitability?"

"No, that I should take care. I am...you must know that I am dependent on my aunt's goodwill for my support. She would be very angry if she knew that you and I had been spending time together. And I know that people would think the worst of me, however innocent this has been."

Rowena sensed rather than saw his mouth curve into a smile. "It has certainly been innocent on your part, Rowena. Best not look too closely at my motives."

They had reached the edge of the trees and he paused. Rowena walked a few feet away from him. A bramble hedge ran alongside the copse here, and she lifted her muslin skirts away from a trailing branch. Paul leaned back against the trunk of an elm tree. "Are you telling me to stay away from you, Rowena?"

Rowena took a deep breath. This was harder than she had expected. "Yes," she said, trying to sound firm. "Captain, I know that you are amusing yourself. But if Mr Swanson has noticed, how long will it be before somebody else does? I cannot afford that kind of attention."

"Mr Swanson has a naturally suspicious mind when it comes to me," Paul said with a laugh.

"Perhaps. But I need to be sensible, Captain. There are a lot of other girls out there..."

"I don't want a lot of other girls, Rowena, I want you. But I think you know that."

Rowena felt his hands on her shoulders. Panic flooded through her and she was not sure what to do. Apart from kissing her hand or taking her arm he had never touched her before.

"No!" she said.

"I'm not going to hurt you, I promise." His mouth was very close to her ear. Rowena could feel her heart hammering in her breast, the blood pounding in her head. Delicately, Paul pressed his mouth to the side of her neck, just below her ear, kissing her very gently. Rowena was shocked at the rush of pleasure that flooded through her body.

Very gently he slid his hands down her arms and around her waist and drew her back against him, his mouth moving down her neck to her shoulders. One hand cupped her breast and Rowena heard herself make a little sound. The pressure of his fingers through her gown felt wonderful and she could feel all her best intentions drifting away.

"You are so lovely," he whispered. "I've been wanting to do this for weeks."

"Captain, we must not."

"We definitely should not, but I can feel how much you want to, Rowena. And my name is Paul, I think we've moved beyond formality, don't you?"

"Paul..."

"Don't be afraid, Rowena. Just lean back and let me show you how good this can feel."

She complied, her body relaxing against him, her resistance slipping away under his stroking hands. Eventually he turned her towards him and kissed her and Rowena pressed close to him. She had never felt anything like this before, and she realised that she had no intention of stopping him.

Paul drew back eventually and looked down at her. "This is probably the point where I should ask if you're sure, Rowena."

"I want to."

"That's very clear, darling girl, but we're about to cross a line here, and I'm not doing it without having a conversation. I know I shouldn't be doing this. But sooner or later, someone is going to seduce you, you're too lovely, and I'd rather like it to be me. But I'm not making you any false promises here."

Rowena felt a little shock of reality. He was not touching her, and she understood that he wanted her to make her decision clear-headed. It was ridiculous, given that she was dizzy with longing, only wanting him to touch her again, whatever the consequences. The consequences would be hers, not his, but Rowena did not care. She wanted this, in a way that she had never allowed herself to want anything else.

"Paul, I know."

"You're sure?"

"Yes."

He reached for her again, lifting her into his arms and carrying her into the trees. They emerged, after several minutes, into a clearing warmed by sunlight dappling between the branches, the grass scattered with wildflowers in a glorious riot of colour, and he lay her down and removed his coat, folding it to form a pillow for her head. As he bent to kiss her, the last vestiges of Rowena's common sense and self-control drifted away, unregretted, although

95

as he whispered her name, she thought how typical it was of him to have found in advance, such a perfect place for seduction.

***

Paul was as gentle as he could be, enjoying her surprised pleasure in his arms. When it was over she lay shocked and breathless, her head pillowed on his shoulder, and Paul rested quietly as his breathing slowed. When he turned to look down at her he saw tears on her cheeks, and it wrung his heart.

"Did I hurt you, Rowena? I'm sorry, I tried hard not to."

"No...only for a moment. That's not why..."

"I know, love." Paul leaned over and kissed her tears very gently. "You are so beautiful, and that was just so lovely."

"Yes, it was."

Paul laughed at the wonder in her voice and leaned over to kiss her again. "You look like a painting entitled 'Girl in a Flower Meadow' although I've never seen a piece of art look quite as lovely. I brought you here on purpose."

"I realise that."

"Because I was hoping you would agree to do this...and because I wanted to see you lying here with your hair loose against the grass and flowers. It was such a good idea."

She gave a ripple of laughter, as he wiped her tears away. "Paul, you are such a flatterer."

"Only when it's called for."

"All the time," she said, reaching her hand up to cup his cheek. Paul kissed her again, thinking how very good it felt to be with her, and he hoped she felt the same way. He knew that Rowena had helped to ease him back into the world after the horror of Assaye, and she deserved better than some brief tawdry affair, but it was difficult to feel guilty at this moment, with her gentle eyes smiling up at him. Already she was more relaxed in his arms and he deliberately pushed his nagging sense of guilt to one side. With rueful self-knowledge, he admitted that he had probably been intending to do this ever since he had seen her that evening in the church. Their time together might be limited by a new posting and he had no intention of wasting it in regrets.

They lay finally in the golden light of approaching evening, entwined together, and Paul stirred reluctantly.

"I hate to say it, but I need to take you back, it's getting late. Are you all right, Rowena?"

"Yes," she said, sounding surprised to find it true.

Paul bent over to kiss her, feeling a rush of protective tenderness which caught him unawares. She reached up to caress the side of his face, and he turned his head and kissed the palm of her hand.

"I'm a bastard, and I know it," he said quietly. "But being with you is so good for me. You remind me of a swan – beautiful, pale and elegant, gliding gracefully across the water of life, disrupting nobody. Just looking at you soothes me, Rowena, and that's rare."

Rowena gave a soft laugh. "You're very poetic all of a sudden."

"The effect of you in my arms, it would seem. Let's do this again next Sunday, and I'll write a sonnet for you."

"Somehow I don't see you as a man of letters."

Paul eased away from her and sat up, reaching for their clothes. "And there you wrong me, my sweet. I studied classics at Oxford before I joined the regiment and can quote perfectly obscene Roman poetry with considerable aplomb."

Rowena struggled into her chemise. "You may safely do so to me, for I understand no Latin," she said.

Paul came to help her with her gown, fastening the tiny buttons at the back. "I will translate for you."

"Thank you." She stood still while he readjusted her clothing, picking off grass and specks of moss. "You are very good at this, aren't you?"

Paul smiled, watching as she twisted the golden cascade of her hair up into a simple knot and secured it with the pins he had retrieved for her. "I'm very good at a number of things," he said. "But I take it you are referring to my skill as a ladies' maid? Yes, I have had a fair amount of practice."

He reached out and smoothed one shoulder of the simple muslin gown into place. "You'll do. It's charming, but I'd love to see you in something other than your cousins' hand-me-downs, you're prettier than any of them."

"No!" Rowena said quickly, and Paul caught her meaning and was slightly appalled.

"Love, I wasn't trying to insult you," he said. "That's not what I meant."

"Just don't buy me gifts, Paul."

To his surprise Paul felt a twist of pain. "I won't, I promise."

"You probably don't understand."

"Yes, I do," Paul said, taking her hand and kissing it. "You think I'm trying to buy your favours."

"That's what the rest of the world will think. Either that, or they'd think I'm a light skirt."

"Well, they'd be wrong on both counts and I don't give a damn what the tabby cats have to say, you're worth a dozen of any one of them."

Rowena was studying him, her green eyes serious. "Thank you. What I just did…I did it because I wanted to."

Paul felt a weight of guilt. "So did I," he said. "But we both know who seduced whom there. And now that I have, I would rather like to do it again. Will you meet me here next Sunday, Rowena?"

"I will. But I may cry off sherry and church this evening, I think I need some time alone."

"Of course. But please do something for me. Don't spend the time castigating yourself for what we have just done, it's not a crime, whatever the world tells us." Paul bent and kissed her very gently. "I'll be here next Sunday. I hope you will too."

***

97

Carl was surprised to find that the absence of Captain Longford caused an immediate improvement in morale. Without his constant carping, the various officers who commanded the other companies seemed to relax, and the atmosphere in the officers' mess became more friendly and convivial.

The first draft of recruits was marched in within a month and there was amicable squabbling in the mess about their division between the various companies. During Captain Longford's absence his company was under the command of Lieutenant George Zouch who was Paul's favourite of the younger officers. He was young and enthusiastic and lapped up new skills like a well-trained gun dog. Paul had suggested that they combine their companies for training purposes. The seventh had the worst morale in barracks while the light company had the best, forged on the battlefields of India.

Paul did not enter into the competition for the best of the new recruits, and Flanagan called across to him as the men pored over the lists.

"Van Daan, if you don't take an interest, you're going to get left with the dregs. Longford is a lazy bastard, almost half of these are from the courts and the prisons."

"You go ahead," Paul said cheerfully. "I'm happy with what you allocate."

"I'm warning you, Van Daan," Cookson said, laughing. "We'll split the volunteers between us and you'll end up with a pack of vagrants, pickpockets and poachers."

"I like poachers, they're often good shots."

"Do you seriously not care?"

"It doesn't matter what you allocate to me," Paul said with infuriating smugness. "Give me eight weeks with them and they'll be better than any of yours." He got up. "I'm off to change, I am invited to a select evening party by Mrs Bennett and must not be late."

"She's after you for that eldest daughter of hers," Lieutenant Zouch said.

"She is. But I shall spend the evening lauding your virtues, dear George, and before long she will be after you." Paul sketched a wave and strolled out.

"He's in a good mood these days," Cookson said, pouring more wine into Carl's glass. "What's got into him? He used to be a serious fellow in the mess, but he's all amiability now. Longford's absence, do you think? I know they didn't get on."

"We're all in a better mood for Longford's absence," Flanagan said. "But you're right, he's a different man these days. I used to wonder what everybody saw in him, but I'm beginning to realise why that pack of hedge-birds he's trained will follow him into hell and back."

Carl grinned. He had his own opinion about his commanding officer's improved mood. Johnny Wheeler caught his expression and got up to collect another bottle of wine, lifting an enquiring eyebrow at Carl.

"I see you have the solution to the puzzle. Tell us, Carl."

"You wrong me, I know no more than you do. But from past experience, I would say that my esteemed captain has found himself a woman. Probably young, pretty and very willing."

"Ahh," Graham said with a grin. "And not with matrimony in mind, I take it?"

"Definitely not. You're right, he's very relaxed and permanently cheerful which I'm guessing means he's being very well satisfied. Paul's always happier when he has a woman in keeping, but there's no point in asking me more, because he's not the man to discuss his latest mistress over a brandy."

"I've not seen him down at Carrie's for a few months," Flanagan said.

"No, it's not one of her girls. I've honestly no idea, but whoever she is I would like to raise a glass to her." Carl lifted his glass. "To the lass who is currently sharing a bed with my captain, thereby making him easier to live with. God bless her, whoever she is."

As the summer drew to an end, news came that Paul's mentor was to be knighted for his services in India and Paul hosted a celebration dinner in the mess to toast Sir Arthur Wellesley and his future successes. He also hosted a far more riotous celebration at the Boat Inn for the men who had fought under Wellesley and survived Assaye. Carl observed that although there were women aplenty at the Boat, none of them appeared to be under Paul's protection. He was becoming very curious about the girl who was keeping his commander so well entertained.

At the end of September, Paul received a letter from Wellesley and took it to Carl. "Keep this to yourself for the present, but we may be going to Naples. Sir Arthur writes that General Craig is gathering an expeditionary force in Malta to join forces with the Russians. He's short on properly trained light infantry skirmishers, and Wellesley has recommended us."

"Are we ready?"

"I think so, training is going well. And I admit it would suit me to be out of here before Captain Longford returns to us. He's taking furlough over Christmas and will be back in the New Year and I'm no closer to knowing how to deal with him."

"It won't be so bad," Carl said. "The others are used to you and your methods by now, Paul. He'll be isolated."

"I know, but that's likely to make him even nastier. I'm not worried about us, but I am concerned for the men. Colonel Dixon's new rules mean that he can't discipline them for minor infractions, but if he manages to provoke one of them into punching him, there's nothing I can do to protect them."

"Are you worried about Michael?"

Paul shook his head. "Michael is too experienced for Longford. But if he manages to stir up the likes of Carter or Cooper or Dawson, they'll lay him out, especially after what happened with Venables. And I am worried about Venables. He's settled well now that Carter has stopped tormenting him, but Longford is going to be after him."

Carl stood up. "We'd better hope for Naples, then." Something caught his eye. He leaned forward and delicately removed a hair from Paul's coat. It was very long and very fair, almost white.

"So she's a blonde, is she?" Carl said, sounding amused. "Very pretty colour."

His friend laughed and swatted him away. "Have you been looking for evidence?"

"Only of hair colour. I didn't need any evidence to know she existed, she's done you the world of good. Are you going to break her heart when you sail off to Naples?"

"I hope not."

"And yet you know that you will. Poor lass, I hope she finds somebody else quickly who will treat her better."

"They usually do."

Carl laughed. "I'm going to visit my parents before they forget what I look like. Do you want to come?"

"No, I've got a pile of paperwork, and I want to reply to Wellesley's letter. Give them my best wishes."

"I will."

Reverend and Mrs Swanson greeted their son with muted enthusiasm. Carl was an infrequent visitor, not because he was not genuinely attached to his parents, but because he found his mother's incessant questions about his welfare, eating habits and possible romantic interests to be wearisome. He bore it patiently for a while, until his father rescued him on the pretext of showing him some repair work in the church.

As they went through the side door into the vestry, a woman came through carrying a pile of choir robes. She stopped at the sight of Carl and placed the robes on a chair.

"Mr Swanson, good afternoon. I was just returning these, I've been mending them. Some of the boys are so careless with them."

Carl smiled. "I was myself," he admitted. "It's Miss Summers, is it not? We met at the garden party, I think."

"Oh yes – I remember, of course," the girl said. She had coloured prettily but came forward to shake his hand. The autumn sunlight glinted through the high windows onto her fair hair, and Carl stared at her in shocked realisation.

"I was just showing my son the excellent work the stonemasons have done on the East wall," the rector said, leading the way. "You will know that the Van Daans provided the funds for it. Paul informed me that he was not having the place fall down upon his family's head during service."

Carl was watching the girl's face. She was not looking at him, but he was in no doubt now. The mention of Paul's name brought a subtle colour to her face. When she had walked into the vestry and caught sight of his uniform, had she initially thought it was Paul?

They watched her walking back up the hill towards Carleton Hall. "She's a lovely girl," Mr Swanson said. "We have grown very fond of her. In fact I

100

think your mother had ideas of attempting to match-make, but I have told her not to interfere. You will find your own wife when you are ready."

"Thank you for that," Carl said, his eyes still on the girl. "She is very lovely, but even if I was on the catch for a wife, I don't think there is the least possibility that Rowena Summers would look at me, do you?"

Mr Swanson started, and stared at his son. "Carl, is there something that you know?"

"No," his son said, returning his gaze. "But it's clear that it's not a new idea to you, is it?"

"I had hoped that I was imagining things," Mr Swanson said heavily. "He comes over most Sundays to see his family, and always comes to evening service with Mrs van Daan before going back to barracks. So he has met Rowena many times. Often he comes for sherry before the service and she is nearly always there. But once or twice I have seen them out walking earlier in the afternoon. I have spoken to her of it, because I was worried that if somebody else saw them it would not be good for her."

"I imagine not."

"Has he said anything to you of her?"

"No. But that means nothing, he would not. He has a very strict code of behaviour, which is completely baffling to me. He would not dream of boasting of his conquests in the mess and yet is apparently very willing to seduce an innocent – and I imagine largely unprotected – girl."

"Seduce? You think it has gone as far as...?"

"Yes," Carl said baldly. He saw his father's distressed face and smiled. "I'm sorry, Father. But if Paul is taking the trouble to come out here and meet her every week, you need to believe me when I tell you that he is getting a lot more than a chaste kiss for his pains. It will end soon because it looks likely that we will be off to Naples to fight the French before long. But I intend to speak to him about it because he needs to stop it immediately, for obvious reasons."

Paul was in his room writing letters when Carl returned. He looked up with a smile and motioned to the armchair. "You're back earlier than I expected. Just let me finish this and we'll go to the mess for dinner."

"I wanted to speak to you," Carl said.

"Is there a problem?"

"Somewhat," his friend said, and his tone made Paul raise his eyebrows. "I ran into Rowena Summers in the church this afternoon. She was looking particularly lovely – a real glow about her these days."

Paul put down his pen. "Ah."

"And I see I'm not wrong. You need to stop it, Paul. Now, before she really gets hurt."

There was a brief silence. Eventually Paul said:

"I am tempted to tell you to mind your own business, but you are of course quite right. I have been thinking so for several weeks."

"And yet you have continued."

"I was waiting for my conscience to speak up," Paul said lightly. "Thank you, Carl, what a good thing I have you."

Carl felt a rush of rare fury. "Don't be a supercilious arsehole," he said. "But satisfy my curiosity, will you? Was there not just one point, before you carried her into the shrubbery and removed her clothes where you thought about it and realised that it was not a good idea?"

"If there was, I don't remember it," Paul admitted. "You ought to know me by now. But I have been feeling guilty, and I will put a stop to it." He met his friend's stern gaze and gave a rueful smile. "Carl, nobody gives a damn about that girl. Sooner or later some dashing sportsman up for the hunting was always going to catch sight of her and work out that she's pretty much unprotected. I'm not making excuses for myself, but…"

"Yes, you bloody are," Carl said shortly. "Just because she has nobody to take care of her doesn't give you an excuse to take her maidenhead with no intention beyond a summer's entertainment. You think about what you've just done and you're going to feel like shit. And you should. Put a stop to it now. Write to her and I'll make sure she gets it. Or tell her next week if you prefer. But however you do it, do it now and leave the girl some dignity. She's worth twenty of you."

"I know," Paul said quietly. "I will."

"Good. I'm going to change."

***

When he had gone, Paul got up and went to the window and stood staring out over the parade ground. Part of him felt relief that Carl had made the decision for him. He had known for weeks that he needed to end it. He had been mad to begin it in the first place, and he knew she would be hurt, but it had proved more difficult than he had expected to say goodbye to her. With a sigh, Paul went back to his desk and picked up his pen. He sat staring at the blank sheet, wondering what to say to her. Best to keep it polite and civil and excuse himself on the grounds of his impending departure to Naples.

Paul wondered for a moment if he should speak to her in person, but he rejected the idea. For all her shyness, he sensed that Rowena had a good deal of pride, and if she were upset she would not want him to see it. She had never showed any sign of expecting more from him than he had offered, and Paul had a good deal of respect for her quiet dignity. He knew she would make no further attempt to contact him and writing the letter, he was angry with himself. Rowena's life was difficult enough and he had made it no easier for her. He had told himself that their light-hearted love affair would do her no harm but faced with the need to end it he admitted how selfishly he had used her. She had been very good for him and he had given her nothing in return.

The light company received their formal orders some two weeks later, to join General Craig in Malta immediately after Christmas and embark for Naples with his combined British and Russian forces. Busy with his preparations for departure, Paul heard nothing from Rowena Summers. He deliberately changed the day of his regular visits to his family to spare her the awkwardness of running into him by accident and determinedly put her from his mind until the final week in December, when he received a note from the rector asking him to call. Paul could think of no reason for the request other than Rowena and he rode over at the appointed time and found Carl's father in his cluttered study.

"Thank you for coming. Sit down, Paul."

Paul lowered himself into the chair and accepted the glass of wine his host handed him. He studied the rector's lined face. "Thank you, sir. I have a feeling that I am about to receive a dressing down that I richly deserve. Miss Summers?"

"Yes."

"Did Carl tell you? Have you seen her? Is she all right, I've been worried..."

"No, Paul, I am afraid she is not."

The words hung heavily in the room. Paul leaned forward and placed his glass on the desk carefully. He could think of only one meaning to the vicar's words.

"She's with child?"

"Yes. Some four months, I think. I assume there is no question..."

"No. Oh no, of course it's mine." Paul got up and walked across to the window staring out at the rain soaked garden. After a long moment he asked:

"Do they know? The Carletons?"

"Not yet but she cannot hide it for much longer. I have told her that she can come here for a while at least. Lady Carleton will not house her, I am sure of it, she is not a forgiving woman."

"No, I imagine not." Paul turned, frowning. "Why didn't she come to me?"

"You had already ended the connection."

"I was trying to do the right thing," Paul said. "A little late, I know. But I told her to come to me if she was in need. She must have known what I meant, Rowena isn't stupid."

"Rowena has too much pride, Paul," Mr Swanson said quietly. "She only told me because I found her in a dead faint in the church two days ago. I have talked about her various options with her. They are limited, given her circumstances. She could go away to have the child, but she has no money. There are orphan asylums, of course, who will take in indigent women, and care for their children..."

Paul was appalled. "Sir, you cannot think I am going to leave her to manage this on her own."

"That is what she thinks," Mr Swanson said. "The other alternative is that she marries, and I have made a suggestion to her, but she is unwilling to consider it. My curate, Mr Edwards, is..."

"I know. He is so infatuated with her that he can barely speak. But that is likely to change when he realises she carries another man's bastard child."

"Very likely. But Mr Edwards is young and poor and ambitious, and he might be induced to overlook her indiscretion if a good living could be found for him somewhere."

"You think a wealthy patron would sweeten the deal?" Paul said bitterly. "You're probably right, sir. And that leaves Rowena living with a man who may well despise her for the rest of her life because I bought him off."

"It may still be the best alternative."

"It isn't. Not for her. I need to talk to her, sir."

"She does not want to see you, Paul."

"Why would she, she thinks I'm about to sail off and leave her in this mess? Poor Rowena, she must be frantic. I can't believe she didn't come to me."

"What did you expect her to do, Paul, walk to the barracks or make her way to the back door at Southwinds like any other desperate girl when the young master gets her into trouble?"

Paul bit back a furious response. He was angry, not with Mr Swanson, but with himself. He had sincerely meant it when he had written to Rowena that he would take full responsibility if she should find herself in any kind of trouble, and he knew she would have understood. Rowena was an intelligent young woman. He also realised that he had not given much thought as to how she would do so, or whether pride might prevent her from arriving on his doorstep as a beggar. It was not how he would ever have seen her, but he had completely failed to put himself in Rowena's shoes, and he was bitterly ashamed.

"Paul – what were you thinking? You're not in love with the girl. Forgive my bluntness, but surely you could have found another woman? More suited to..."

"You mean why didn't I stick to chorus girls and opera dancers, or visit the local brothel?" Paul said sardonically. "You're right, of course, sir, it's what we're supposed to do. Although it occurs to me to wonder what those girls do, when a man like me pays up for the night and walks out the door leaving them pregnant."

There was a long silence. Then Mr Swanson said in flat tones:

"I have had some experience with charitable organisations, Paul, would you like me to tell you?"

Paul turned back to look at him. "No," he said. "I already know. I'm furious with myself, sir, and I'm also more ashamed than I've ever been in my life. I told myself that if it hadn't been me, it would have been somebody else, but Carl was right, that was just an excuse."

"I am glad to hear you say it, Paul. But despite your appalling lack of self-control, I knew that you would help her. Perhaps if you can settle some money on her she can go and have the child quietly somewhere."

"I know how it works, sir."

Paul thought about Rowena. For weeks, immersed in preparations for departure, he had tried to put her from his mind, but she was there now, her face tilted up to look at him, the gentleness of her voice, and the unexpected passion she had displayed in his arms. Paul had missed her more than he had admitted to himself, and the thought of what she must be going through horrified him.

"Sir, I need to talk to her, and I can't exactly go up to the hall to ask for her. I'm sorry to involve you further, but I'm going to need your help."

"That is why I have asked her to come to see me this afternoon. In fact, I rather think that I see her approaching."

Paul spun around and went out into the hallway. As he opened the front door to the rectory, Rowena was approaching the gate. She saw him and stopped. For a moment they looked at each other, then Rowena turned and walked away. Paul threw open the gate and caught up with her at the foot of the hill, catching her arm.

"Rowena, wait. We need to talk."

Rowena turned. "He has told you, hasn't he?"

"Of course he has, lass, as you should have. Why didn't you write to me?"

"It is not your concern, Paul, I shall manage."

"Oh, don't be daft, love, it's not your job to manage this on your own. How long have you known that you were carrying my child?"

Rowena blushed. "I have suspected for a few weeks. But Paul, you were very honest, I knew that for you it was..."

She broke off. "Entertainment?" Paul said with heavy sarcasm. "Sometimes, I make myself cringe, Rowena, but I will not leave you in this mess, I promise."

Rowena looked up at him. "Thank you," she said quietly. "I haven't known what to do. But if you could help me until the child is born, I can try to find work..."

Her quiet dignity was heartbreaking. Paul studied her for a long moment. She looked pale and tired, the green eyes shadowed as though she had not slept for weeks. He felt a desperate urge to take care of her, to smooth the worried frown from her brow. Suddenly he knew, with absolute certainty, what he wanted to do.

"No, lass," he said softly. "I think we can do better than that. Marry me."

Rowena stared at him uncomprehendingly. "Marriage? You cannot be serious."

Her incredulity made him laugh in spite of himself. "I can understand why you would think that, you've no reason to think that I have the least sense of responsibility. Rowena, I didn't intend to do this to you, but it's done now, and I am not letting you creep quietly away to manage this on your own."

"It wasn't just your fault, Paul."

"How old are you?"

"I'm eighteen."

"Eighteen and straight from a charity school. Trust me, it was my fault. Let me put it right."

"Your family cannot want you to marry a penniless nobody without morals," Rowena said bitterly.

"What the devil does it have to do with my family? Besides, I doubt there's much wrong with your morals although mine definitely need some work. I am serious about this. Marry me."

Rowena pressed her hands to her cheeks. "Paul – this is so generous. But..."

"It's not generous, Rowena. I knew what I was doing, and I knew the risk to you and I bloody well did it anyway. You have nothing to be ashamed of and neither does our child. You think I don't know how this works? You pretend to be a widow and keep your head down and try to feel grateful for the monthly allowance, and once again a child grows up thinking that his or her father doesn't give a damn. Well, not this time, lass, it's time I grew up."

"Oh Paul..."

"You realise Grace is mine?"

Rowena nodded. "And I think there is another...?"

Despite himself Paul grinned. "I'm glad you know the worst, love, it saves me making a confession. Cat recently married, I've no responsibility for her girl other than financial, but Grace's mother is dead, and I don't want her growing up feeling that she's unwanted. She isn't, I adore her. So if you marry me, you're not just taking on me and our child, you're taking on my daughter as well."

The green eyes were steady on his. "Paul, do you think I'd mind that?"

"Actually I rather like the idea," Paul said. He had a sudden vivid picture of her with Grace, and it occurred to him that they could easily be taken for mother and daughter. "Rowena, listen. It will take a week or two to get the licence, and make the arrangements, and then we can be married very quietly. My company is sailing to Naples within the month, which gives us an excellent excuse for a hasty wedding, and by the time you come back to Southwinds, the baby will have been born and there will be no cause for gossip."

"Paul, you don't have to do this."

"I want to."

"You're not in love with me."

"Lass, I'm not making a declaration here, you know how honest I am. I've never been in love, quite possibly never will be. Does that matter? How many people marry for love? We have liking and respect and mutual attraction, which is so much more than many people start with. I never planned to marry because to be honest I'm never going to stop being a soldier and I suspect that will make me the devil of a husband. But I will try, I promise you."

Paul could see tears in the green eyes, and he felt bitterly ashamed of himself. "Every man on that transport is going to know why I'm there," she said softly.

"Every man on that transport is going to treat you with the respect you deserve, Rowena, you have my word on it. And I swear to God that if you give me the chance, I will make this up to you. Let me take care of you, sweetheart, because that's what I want to do. I'm not standing here wishing my way out of this. I'm standing here asking you to be my wife. Please."

Slowly she nodded, and Paul drew her into his arms, holding her close.

Chapter Seven

For Michael O'Reilly, returning to Dublin after an absence of almost ten years was a strange experience. Since he left, his country had been absorbed into the Union with England, and the city in which he had studied had changed considerably. Dublin's Parliament House was converted into a bank, and several of the old Irish mansions were now hotels. Too many of the Irish landlords had removed themselves to England, increasing the problems of absenteeism and dishonest agents were causing poverty and suffering among the people. Michael had fought against similar abuses as a younger man, and it was disquieting to see that very little had improved.

There were a large number of Irishmen in the four companies of the 110th, which had been requested for duty in Ireland by the new Chief Secretary, many of whom had joined for similar reasons to Michael. He had always felt fortunate that he had not been posted back home before now and wondered how many of the Irish recruits felt the same sick feeling of dread arriving at the new barracks on the edge of Phoenix Park. As a child he could remember being taken to watch military parades in the park by his mother during visits to Dublin. These barracks had not existed then, and there was an irony to the knowledge that they had been built to accommodate the extra troops required to control the rebellion in which he had taken part.

The men of the 110th were left at ease in the barracks yard while the captain of the light company inspected the accommodation allocated to them. Michael refreshed himself from his flask and found himself grinning as he heard the rising tones of his captain's voice explaining why the accommodation was not adequate for his companies. Around the yard it was possible to pick out the new recruits, all of whom were staring in some surprise at the sound of Paul van Daan's voice. Those men who had accompanied him to India and Italy had not made any attempt to move or unload their goods, and none of the officers had moved either. Ensign Hardwick, who was new, was gently restrained by Lieutenant Swanson when he moved towards the officers' quarters.

"Men get settled first, Mr Hardwick."

"Yes, sir." Hardwick looked over towards the barracks building. "What's the hold up, sir?"

Johnny Wheeler grinned. "They're trying to put four companies into barracks big enough for two. Saves them clearing out the others, there's plenty of room here. Don't worry, Ensign, this won't take long."

The barrack master, a young lieutenant, emerged from the barracks. He was scarlet faced as he walked over to the administrative block. After a moment he returned with a burly Irish sergeant who had a belligerent expression and Michael grinned.

"Now he's about to have a really bad day," he commented. "Glad it's not raining. Do you think we'll be settled in time for dinner?"

Carl glanced at his watch. "Easily." He glanced across at Captain Ellison of the guards' company. "What do you think, Tony? Another ten minutes?"

Captain Ellison nodded. "I didn't like the look on that Sergeant's face, poor bugger, he's used to pushing the new officers around. He's definitely in for a shock. Why didn't Wellesley warn them?"

"He's got a funny sense of humour himself," Wheeler commented, just as Captain van Daan's voice raised another notch.

"Sergeant McLeod. It may be your idea of good military practice to place your men in overcrowded, unsanitary, inadequate accommodation, but it is most assuredly not mine, and since this is my regiment, we will be adopting my standards here, not yours. You will get those other huts unlocked and cleaned, and you will do it within the next half an hour without any further discussion, or you will be spending the next three weeks cleaning out the barracks latrines with a noticeable absence of sergeant's stripes on your coat. And if you don't think I'm capable of it, I suggest you send a message to Sir Arthur Wellesley to check his views on the subject. In the meantime, get your arse moving before I lose my temper and start kicking it."

Both the sergeant and the lieutenant emerged from the huts and disappeared from sight just as a carriage came through the gate. Carl approached the carriage as the post boy jumped down and moved to let down the steps and open the door. Carl offered his hand and his commander's wife stepped down from the carriage.

"Welcome to Dublin, ma'am," Carl said with a smile. "He won't be long, he's just having a chat with the barracks sergeant."

Rowena van Daan gave a tired smile. "Is he shouting yet?"

"I think the shouting is mostly over. Why don't you come into the mess and have some tea, they should be able to manage that. Is Francis asleep?"

Rowena nodded. "Yes, Sarah has him, I won't wake him."

"Otherwise there will be two yelling Van Daans in barracks," Carl agreed mildly as Paul emerged from the hut and came to greet his wife.

"Feeling better?" he asked, kissing her cheek. Rowena nodded, but Michael thought she still looked pale after her ordeal aboard ship and Paul studied her face in some concern.

"Carl, rather than unload everything here and then load it back up, I'm going to take Rowena straight to our lodgings, Sir Arthur tells me it's only ten minutes away. She needs to lie down."

"I'm fine, Paul, really."

"No, you're not," Paul said. "But you will be when you've had the opportunity to sleep for a bit on dry land and without your son jumping all over you. If we travel with him again I'm putting him on a different ship, preferably with a different destination. China, perhaps? Is Grace awake?"

"Yes, but she's being very good."

"That's a novelty. Why both of my children had to resemble me to such a degree, is a mystery. I was hoping that Francis would have just a little of your serenity, my angel. Ah, Johnny, there you are. I'm going to get Rowena settled and come back, will you...?"

"Don't worry, sir, I think they've got the point, we'll be settled in by the time you get back." Wheeler smiled at Rowena. "Get some rest, ma'am."

Rowena nodded tiredly. "I'll be better tomorrow," she said.

Michael, Carl and Johnny stood watching as the carriage left. "She does very well," Johnny said. "It can't be easy for a woman."

"Being an army wife or being married to Paul?"

"Both." Johnny was still staring after the carriage. "When I first heard he'd married her – and worked out why - I felt sorry for her. But actually he treats her very well. I never thought of our captain as a family man."

"Nor did I, but I think he's surprised himself," Carl said. "He's very fond of her, and she's good for him, she brings out his protective instincts."

"It hasn't kept him faithful, though, has it?" Johnny said.

"No. But with the exception of that dreadful Cartwright woman in Naples, he's been sensible about it. It looks as though the sergeant is coming back. Get them lined up, Sergeant O'Reilly, and get them settled. I am dying for a drink."

Sergeant O'Reilly, having unloaded his kit to his satisfaction, took himself on a tour of the barracks to ensure that the rest of the companies were adequately provided for. It was not officially his role as light company sergeant, any more than it was his captain's role to take command in barracks, but the custom had become so well established during the past two years that it was never called into question. There was a small room at the far end of each long hut for the NCOs, and when his inspection was complete, Michael went to find Sergeant McLeod.

"All settled, Sergeant. How are the mess arrangements here?"

"Good enough for most, but who knows with your officer?" McLeod said with a grunt. "Awkward bastard. I've had a few thousand men through here, never seen an officer make that kind of racket, and he's only a bloody captain. He got good connections or what?"

Michael laughed and withdrew a bottle and two cups from his pack. "Have a drink, it's the best solution after your first introduction to Captain van Daan."

"You're not joking. Arrogant little shit."

"You're not the first to call him that. But on the other hand we're now warm and dry and comfortable and not sleeping in dirty huts four to a bed, so I'm not complaining."

"You used to luxury in the 110th then?" the sergeant said with faint contempt.

"We fought at Assaye, laddie. He was just as arrogant then, when he was up at the surgeons' tents with a gash down his neck and a ball in his thigh, kicking up a rumpus to make sure a twenty-year-old lad got his leg amputated before he died of his wounds. Very luxurious, that was." Michael drank and regarded the sergeant steadily and after a moment McLeod looked away.

"Surprised to see light infantry here," he said. "We usually get the dregs."

"We've been in Italy. Sir Arthur Wellesley, the new Chief Secretary requested the 110th. Specifically, Captain van Daan. I suspect he wants us to hand in case of another posting abroad." Michael pulled a face. "It's a long time since I was in Dublin, Sergeant, but we serve where we're sent."

"Local?"

"Not really, though a few of my lads are. I'm from the South. I knew Dublin quite well as a boy, mind."

"Seen some changes."

"Aye, I can see that already."

"Good barracks, these. I'm guessing your laddie will have found himself somewhere comfortable in town."

"He's brought his wife and children, so they've rented a house. But don't get your hopes up, Sergeant, he'll be here more than he's there. I'm guessing there's not much to do other than training and drilling."

McLeod shook his head. "Escort and guard duty mostly. I'm told Wellesley is intending to take a tactful approach with the Catholics, so he'll not want a big show of force, but there's resentment so there's risk of assassination. And you must know that there's always talk of rebellion. Mostly it's just talk." McLeod shrugged. "There are a fair few regiments in and around Dublin, they're always worried something will blow up, but it's been quiet for a while. Most of the officers make the most of the social life and have a rest, but I'm told the new secretary likes to organise regular parades, so if your officers want to do a bit of drill practice...."

Sergeant O'Reilly gave a sardonic smile. "I expect they'll manage a bit," he said. "You might want to join us, Sergeant. Just to keep in practice."

***

Having seen his wife and children settled in the neat town house, which Wellesley had arranged to be rented for him, Paul took himself to Dublin Castle to call on the new Chief Secretary for Ireland. He found Wellesley in his office, dictating letters to a harassed looking secretary. He stood up as Paul entered and came forward.

"Captain van Daan. Welcome to Ireland."

"Good to see you, sir."

"Sit down. Hogan, will you get Captain van Daan a drink? All settled, Captain?"

"Should be by now. There was a bit of a conversation about the accommodation in barracks, but I think it's settled. I've left Rowena at the house, it's excellent, thank you, sir."

"Think nothing of it, it is being rented out by an old acquaintance. I understand you've brought the children this time."

"Yes, it seems a good opportunity to spend a little more time with them. We've brought their nurse, although personally I think a menagerie keeper would do better with both of them. I understand that I have to congratulate you as well, sir."

"Yes, thank you. A fine boy." His commander shook his head. "She worries a lot, though and I'm sure I'm the best at soothing her anxieties."

"I suspect that's common. Fortunately, my two are horribly robust. In fact, Francis could do with a dose of something to calm him down a bit." Paul accepted the drink with a smile of thanks.

"You have more experience of this than I have, Captain, which may be useful if I need advice."

"Sir, you never want advice, about anything at all. In fact you positively dislike it."

"Fortunately, Captain van Daan, you are one of the only men of my acquaintance who gives it anyway. I have no idea why I bear with you."

"Novelty, sir. Why am I here?"

"Why do you think, Captain?"

"I'm hoping it's because you're working like hell to get out of this office and back in the field and you're planning on taking us with you. I'm fearing it's because Major Johnstone wants me out of barracks because Captain Longford is back there."

Wellesley gave a snort of laughter. "Very perceptive of you, Captain. A little of both. There is talk of an expedition very soon, in which I hope to be involved. If I am, I want your companies with me. The packet is due in, so I may know more if there are letters tomorrow. And yes, I'm doing a favour for Johnstone. You can work your lads just as easily in Phoenix Park as you can in Melton Mowbray, and with less chance that you'll be cashiered for murder."

"Oh I can make it look like an accident, sir," Paul said pleasantly.

"I am well aware of that, Captain, I'm just afraid that you might, I am never completely sure what you'll do next. Will your wife have recovered enough to be social tomorrow evening? I'm hosting a reception to welcome your officers and to introduce you to Dublin society, it will give you the opportunity to meet the officers from some of the other regiments."

"She'll be delighted, sir," Paul said mendaciously.

It was a twenty minute walk back to barracks, and Paul took it at a leisurely pace, wondering if his wife was managing to get some sleep. He had left strict instructions with the children's nurse, Sarah, that she was to keep the children occupied and away from Rowena. His wife was a doting parent and much too inclined to give in to Francis' and Grace's demands for attention.

It had been a hectic two years since his December wedding in Reverend Swanson's crumbling church. He and Rowena had spent a chaotic year and a half in Italy, shunted between Naples and Sicily with sporadic fighting and a frustrating lack of direction, which had sorely tried Paul's temper. Their son had been born aboard ship, a big, determined child whose birth had exhausted Rowena so much that Paul had worried for her health for a long time afterwards.

Francis had been christened in the Southwinds church during a brief spell at Melton Mowbray before Paul was summoned to Ireland. Paul was grimly aware of his commanding officer's reluctance to place him and Captain Longford within reach of each other more than was absolutely necessary, and he supposed that Ireland was not such a bad place to await another posting. He had maintained a regular correspondence with Wellesley since India, and he knew that Sir Arthur was fretting to get back into the field as much as he was. In the meantime, he had accepted the position of Chief Secretary for Ireland and Paul wondered with some amusement if the Irish establishment knew what they had let themselves in for. Wellesley may have taken the post because he needed the money, but once in it, he was likely to take the job seriously.

Paul took Rowena to London for a spell before their departure for Ireland, leaving the children with Patience. Since their hasty wedding they had rarely had time to themselves, and Paul enjoyed showing her the sights, taking her to the theatre, and bullying her into replenishing her wardrobe in the shops of the West End. Their marriage, begun in such difficult circumstances, had developed over the two years they had been together into a bond of genuine affection. Rowena had not changed much from the slender, shy girl he had flirted with in the church. She still found social occasions difficult, and did not make friends easily, which made the frequent moves and changes of the life of an army wife hard for her, but she was an easy and undemanding companion. She never complained about the inconvenience and hardships of army life, and never argued or questioned his choices or decisions. Paul knew that the wives of his fellow officers regarded her with amused condescension for her shyness and her lack of social skills, but their husbands envied Paul his openly affectionate relationship with his wife.

Rowena was waiting for Paul at the house for a late meal when he was finally satisfied with the arrangements in barracks. She looked considerably better for some sleep and seemed pleased with the house and the staff arrangements.

"The housekeeper is very nice and seems well-organised," she said. "And there is plenty of space in the nursery."

"Good. We'll put up bars."

Rowena regarded him severely. "He is your son, not a wild animal."

"It's difficult to tell the difference sometimes." Paul surveyed her for a moment, then laughed. "I'm putting off breaking it to you that we are invited out tomorrow evening."

His wife pulled a face. "I suppose it was only to be expected," she said. "Sir Arthur Wellesley?"

"Yes, he's holding a reception to welcome us. A chance to show off your new clothes."

"I shall do my best."

"You are a very good wife, and I shall not have to beat you," Paul said gravely, and Rowena laughed and signalled for the servants to clear.

"You will be giving the footmen a very odd idea of you, Paul."

"It's best to get that over with early, in my experience. After a few weeks, nothing I say or do will surprise them any more. I think I gave the barracks sergeant a fairly odd idea of me today. It's a mystery to me why a simple request for proper accommodation is so difficult to manage." Paul got up and took his wife's hand.

"Did you shout at him?"

"I did. But at least I probably won't have to do it again any time soon." Paul put his arm about her. "I have just remembered that we have our room to ourselves again with the children in the nursery. Come to bed, Rowena, I've missed you."

Stretched out beside her in the big tester bed he kissed her gently. "You're looking better."

"I am aware that you consider me very feeble to be unable to endure even a short sea voyage without sickness," his wife said ruefully. "But only consider how irritating it is to me that you have no idea what it feels like."

Paul laughed. "I know, love, it must be infuriating."

"You're very patient," Rowena said softly.

Paul kissed her again. "A manifest untruth, I am not known for my patience anywhere except here. If I'm patient with you, you repay it a hundred fold, I'm the most exasperating husband in the army. As well as the most fortunate. By the way, did I mention you're looking very lovely tonight?"

"Paul, you are so transparent."

"I really am. But I swear to God I was sitting in Wellesley's office earlier thinking about...."

Rowena's mouth stopped his and Paul drew her closer.

She was still asleep when Paul left the following morning, and he kissed her gently and gave instructions that she should be allowed to sleep on. Riding through the chill early morning he savoured the feeling of content, which always followed a night spent in Rowena's arms. His decision to marry her had been completely impulsive and he was aware that both his family and friends had expected it to be a disaster, but there had been something about Rowena, which had made it completely impossible for Paul to abandon her. Paul had spoken the truth when he had said that he had never intended to marry, but he had found to his surprise that his young wife gave him a stability that he had not even realised he lacked.

Paul had never fallen in love with her. Sometimes he wondered if he was capable of that degree of passion, or if he was simply too absorbed in his career to ever be able to put a woman first. Rowena's gentle, loving companionship suited him, and watching the storms and difficulties of some of his fellow officers' marriages he considered himself a very lucky man.

Paul had not always been faithful to her. He was not sure if his restless nature would always seek something new, something different, but he had tried to be intelligent and discreet when he strayed. There had been an Italian girl or two, and a Sicilian innkeeper's daughter with the wild charms of a gypsy. During his time in Naples he had shared the bed of the bad tempered but lovely wife of another officer and afterwards he was disgusted with himself. He did not even like Arabella Cartwright, and felt sorry for her downtrodden husband, but her eagerness for his lovemaking was hard to resist and Paul did not try.

None of the other women had any impact on the steady affection Paul felt for his wife and he hoped that if she was aware of his lapses, she understood that. Certainly she never gave any hint of jealousy or possessiveness. On a morning like this, fresh from the memory of a very happy night, Paul wondered why he did it. None of his passing mistresses left him feeling the way Rowena often did.

The 110th were arriving on the parade ground as Paul rode in, and he dismounted and gave his horse to Jenson who led it to the stables. There were four other companies in the barracks, two from a local Irish regiment and two companies of the 117th foot. None of them appeared to be awake yet and Paul stood watching as his men fell into perfect formation, practicing close order drills. Sergeant O'Reilly rapped out an order and Paul glanced across as Johnny Wheeler emerged holding a cup of coffee.

"Morning, Johnny. It feels lonely out here."

Wheeler laughed. "I'm not sure they know about early drill."

"I hope we're not waking them up," Paul said with a grin.

"I think we are." Johnny nodded as a rumpled figure emerged from the officers' block and wandered over.

"Good morning, Lieutenant Corrigan," Paul said cheerfully. "Jenson, get Mr Corrigan some coffee."

His orderly grinned and disappeared into the mess. Corrigan regarded Paul with disfavour. "You have to be all about in your heads," he said. "You don't even have a senior officer with you, and you're out here freezing your arses off. And you're crazier than the rest of them, sir, don't you have a rather pretty wife tucked up in bed?"

Paul laughed. "I do. She's still asleep."

"Are we expecting to be invaded this morning?" the Irishman said, taking the coffee from Jenson. "Thank you, laddie. Jesus, you're making the rest of us look like idle dogs. Which is perfectly fine by me, for I am one, but you're going to upset those two stuck up little pricks from the 117th."

"Are we?" Paul enquired. "Who would they be, I've not met them yet?"

"Captain Tyler and Lieutenant Yelland. They spend a good deal of their time looking down on the locals – that would be me – and telling stories of the grand life they were leading in London before they came here. They like to tell us what we're doing wrong with our companies."

"Are they all like that?"

"No, the others are all right, but Tyler is the senior captain and thinks he should be a major." Corrigan regarded the four companies of the 110th moving across the parade ground. "Mary mother of God, I'm not putting my lot out here at the same time as these, even I'd be embarrassed. You've practiced this, haven't you, sir?"

"They tell me I'm a pernickety bastard, Mr Corrigan, but it pays off. Sorry we've disturbed you."

"It's all right, I'll get some wax for my ears while you're here. But I'm glad I saw this, sir, it's something to aspire to, although I doubt I could put the work in to achieve it." The Irishman glanced sideways at Paul. "Something tells me you've not perfected this for the joy of looking good on the parade ground. Where have you served?"

"India and Italy."

"Were you with Wellesley in India?"

Paul nodded. "I went home after Assaye."

"Jesus, was that the mess they said it was?"

"I've had better days."

"Wounded?"

"Musket ball in the leg. My orderly lost half of his."

"Did he? Christ, I'd noticed the limp but he's bloody good on it." Suddenly Corrigan began to laugh. "Oh Jesus, the good Lord sent you to me to give me a laugh. Look what's coming onto the parade ground, they've never been out here this early before."

Paul followed his gaze and grinned at the sight of two companies of the 117th emerging in bewildered resentment from their barracks, with their officers bellowing orders at them. Lieutenant Swanson handed command to Sergeant O'Reilly and came to join Paul. He was laughing.

"You've started something now," he said. "Morning, Corrigan, how's your head?"

"Well, yours ought to be just as bad, laddie," Corrigan said morosely glaring at Carl. "What's wrong with you lot, don't you get hangovers?"

"India cured me of them," Carl said with a grin. "Never seen drinkers like it in my life. Do you remember the state of Patrick Maxwell the night before Assaye, sir?"

"I do. Of course he did get himself killed the following day, but I don't think that was because of his hangover. What on earth are this lot doing?"

Johnny was watching in apparent fascination. "I think they're trying to push our lads off the parade ground," he said. "Is that supposed to be line or square, because I honestly can't tell?"

116

"I'm not sure I've seen this particular drill before," Paul said, beginning to laugh. "Do you think we can replicate it, Johnny?"

"Jesus, I hope not."

The officers of the 110th watched in disbelief at the chaos on the parade ground. After a bewildered few minutes of being shuffled across the ground by the newly arrived first and second companies of the 117th, the 110th were moving steadily in four companies. It was a complicated manoeuvre, used mainly for dress parades, but Paul had taught it because it was excellent for teaching the men to work as a unit and at speed. He watched in growing amusement. After a brief word with his fellow sergeants, O'Reilly shouted an order and the 110th set off. Compared to the other regiment they moved with the precision of a clock mechanism, and before the officers of the 117th had realised what was happening, the four companies of the 110th had moved around the men of the 117th neatly trapping them in a square in the centre of the parade ground. One of the sergeants of the 117th was bellowing like an enraged bull but without physically attacking them his men could make no headway at all against the solid lines of the 110th.

"What the bloody hell are your men doing?" Captain Tyler yelled, storming across to Paul, who regarded him in mock surprise.

"Early drill, Captain. Happens this time every day, doesn't it?"

"Get them off this parade ground, Captain!" Tyler spat, furiously. "We have seniority..."

"Oh for God's sake, Tyler, stop making an arse of yourself." Paul was shaking with laughter. "None of us have seniority here and there's plenty of space, your sergeant buggered up the turn and got himself stuck. Stop being so dramatic, it's a drill not a battlefield."

Tyler seemed too angry to speak for a moment, and Paul relented, although he was still laughing, and raised his voice.

"Stand them down, Sergeant O'Reilly, and get on with morning inspection and cleaning. We'll save musket drill for later. Well done, lads."

"You arrogant bastard," Tyler snarled. "You're trying to make a bloody laughing stock of me."

"I'm honestly not!" Paul protested although he was unable to stop laughing. "Although it was funny. My sergeant is showing off, that's all. Come and get some breakfast, Tyler, and we'll work out who is doing what and when, so that it doesn't happen again. There's really no need for so much drama over it."

"You haven't heard the last of this, sir," Tyler ground out, and turned to stamp away. Paul regarded his retreating back, shaking with laughter.

"He's forgotten his men," he croaked, and there were tears of mirth in his eyes. "Look, Yelland has gone after him and they've left the companies out on the parade ground. I don't think that the subalterns know what to do, and I can't even see the other company captain. Johnny, for God's sake get them stood down, I honestly can't do it for laughing."

117

Wheeler was shaking his head at his captain, although he too was laughing. "You have the diplomatic skills of a five year old, Paul. Go and get some breakfast, for God's sake."

He turned back to the parade ground, and the bewildered and sleepy companies of the 117th. "All right, Sergeant. Form line and let's get them stood down. Can't stay out here all day."

***

By the time the officers of the 110th arrived at the castle that evening, the story of the events on the parade ground had made its way through the entire officers' mess through Lieutenant Corrigan and was being gleefully repeated among the officers of the various other regiments stationed in and around Dublin. Paul was ruefully aware that he was going to need to mend bridges with the officers of the 117th at some point. He arrived separately with Rowena in the carriage he had hired, to find his fellow officers already there.

"Evening, Van Daan," Captain Withers said. "Missed you at afternoon drill. Were you worried it would be a bit crowded out there?"

Paul's lips twitched. "Do not set me off again, Charles," he said warningly. "Are Tyler and Yelland here?"

"Not yet. Perhaps they're taking advantage of the extra space to practice forming square."

Paul began to laugh. "Christ, it was funny," he admitted. "But I will need to apologise. I literally couldn't speak for laughing. That bastard O'Reilly. He didn't crack his face, which made it worse."

"You've made Corrigan's year. He and Fitzgerald and Moore aren't fond of the lads from the 117th," Captain Young said with a chuckle.

"Well, clearly the man is an arse, but I should have controlled myself better," Paul admitted. "And then he stormed off and left them on the parade ground. I wonder how long they'd have stood there for if Johnny hadn't intervened? His subalterns had no idea, God help them if they ever have to do that with cavalry bearing down on them."

"I've never been sorry that I wasn't on early drill before," Young said. "You couldn't have left your lot out there like that, O'Reilly would have told you where to get off."

"You're wrong about that, Kit. I once left them out there for a lot longer and I can promise you they didn't move a muscle. But they knew it wasn't an accident and they knew what it was for. Come and find Wellesley, Rowena," Paul said, and towed his wife through the throng to find his host and his wife.

"Captain van Daan. Mrs van Daan. Welcome." Wellesley bowed gallantly over Rowena's hand. She was looking charming in soft pink, with her fair hair in simple ringlets and was the focus of admiring glances from a number of the other men present. Paul was very proud of his wife, and wished she realised how lovely she looked. Rowena responded softly to Sir Arthur's enquiries about her journey and the house, then turned with relief to Lady

118

Wellesley whom she found easy to talk to. Paul joined the Chief Secretary who looked down his long nose forbiddingly.

"And what have you been doing?" he demanded.

"Laughing at the wrong moment, sir," Paul said. "Who told you?"

"It's general gossip thanks to bloody Corrigan," Wellesley said with grim amusement. "You're going to have to apologise."

"I will. Although strictly speaking, I didn't have anything to do with it, it was my sergeants, instigated by Michael O'Reilly. But I did laugh a lot."

"You are entirely responsible for training that pack of jackals, Captain, so the blame lies at your door. They take their lead from you and you know it. I wish I'd seen it, though. See if you can find an opportunity to speak to him this evening, will you?"

"I will, sir. Of course I notice nobody is asking the other captains of the 110th to apologise here."

"Nobody is under any illusion about who is in charge up there, Captain," Wellesley said dryly. "Even Captain Tyler can work that out."

The evening wore on and Paul found himself in demand with various local dignitaries and politicians. He kept a wary eye on his wife who was never comfortable in social situations and was grateful that Lady Wellesley seemed to have taken her under her wing. Several hours had passed when Carl appeared beside him.

"Paul, you're needed," he said quietly. Puzzled, Paul excused himself civilly to his companions and followed his lieutenant through the reception rooms.

"What is it, Carl?"

"Wait until we're outside."

They stepped out into the street and Paul saw his carriage drawn up. He looked at Carl.

"Where is Rowena?"

"She's in the carriage. She's a bit upset, and you need to take her home."

"What happened?" Paul asked, bewildered. He knew how much his wife hated social functions, and he was annoyed with himself for becoming distracted and not keeping a closer eye on her, but he could not imagine what had happened to cause her to leave so suddenly.

"Paul, Captain Tyler was rude to her," Carl said quietly. "Don't blow up."

"If you don't tell me exactly what that incompetent little shit has said to my wife, you'll see me blow up," Paul said precisely.

"You see, that's why I made you come outside."

"Is he still in there?"

"Paul for Christ's sake, you cannot go in there and make a scene at Wellesley's reception. Just listen to me and then take her home and calm down. You can speak to him tomorrow."

"What did he say?" Paul enunciated very slowly and clearly in tones of pure ice. His lieutenant took a deep breath.

119

"He tried to kiss her. He's drunk, he made a series of very personal remarks about her beauty and how he would like to teach her what it was like to go to bed with a real gentleman, only he didn't phrase it quite like that and you are not to question her about it because she'll die of embarrassment. He grabbed hold of her and tried to kiss her. She's not hurt, just upset and embarrassed. She'd gone to the retiring room – something about a torn flounce on her gown, but you know Rowena, she was probably just trying to escape for a bit. He caught her in the hallway. Lieutenant Moore heard part of it and chased him off before he came looking for you. Fortunately, he found Johnny first. He's in the carriage with her." Carl regarded his friend sternly. "You need to put her first, Paul."

Paul took a deep breath. He knew that Carl was right, although his instinct was to go back into the reception, find Captain Tyler and throw him through one of the long windows. He restrained himself with a huge effort.

"All right. Will you give my apologies to Wellesley, Carl? And grab Moore for me to pass on my thanks, I'll speak to him myself tomorrow. I'll take her home."

Carl looked visibly relieved. He saluted and Paul went to the carriage and opened the door. "Thanks, Johnny."

"You're welcome, sir." Johnny eyed him warily as he climbed out. Paul climbed in and took his sobbing wife into his arms. He held her as the carriage made its way back through the streets to the town house, led her gently through the house into their room, and closed the door.

"All right, lass, time to stop now before you drown us both," he said quietly, and Rowena looked up with tear drenched eyes.

"I'm sorry. I'll be all right in a moment."

"Come on, let's get you into bed." Paul seated her on the edge of the bed and went to the washstand for a cool cloth to bathe her hot, damp face, grateful that her maid had not waited up for her. Rowena had never become comfortable with being waited on, and although Paul insisted that she employ a personal maid he was ruefully aware that the woman probably had the easiest job in his household. He unbuttoned Rowena's gown and eased it down from her shoulders. She had stopped crying finally and sat in drowsy silence as he removed the pins from her fair hair. Reaching for her silver backed hairbrush Paul began to brush out the long silky waves. After a long time, she said:

"Do you think other men do this for their wives?"

Paul smiled. "I don't know, love. Most other men don't have wives as beautiful as mine."

Rowena looked up at him over her shoulder. "I am so lucky," she said softly.

"So am I, Rowena." Sensing that she was finally calm, Paul set the brush down. "Do you want to talk about it?"

"Not really. I think he was drunk, I shouldn't have let him upset me so much."

"You shouldn't have been placed in that position." Paul sat down on the bed beside her and drew her into his arms. "I'm sorry, Rowena, I should have been with you."

Rowena shook her head. "You shouldn't have to," she said. "I am so hopeless at being your wife. You ask so little of me, and I can't even manage to get through a reception..."

"Hush. You think I give a damn about that? I don't care if you never want to go to another of these things, but you are not going to be driven out by an arsehole like Tyler." Paul tilted her head back and kissed her. "And I know exactly what I ask of you, love. Other women are in their own homes with their family and friends about them, and I drag you from pillar to post after me, because I like having you with me. Do you want to go home, Rowena?"

Paul's hand had moved to the laces at the front of her stays and he could already hear the change in her breathing. "No," she said.

"I'm glad." Paul eased her back onto the bed. "Let me get out of these clothes, and I'll see if I can give you a reason to want to stay."

"I'm already convinced," his wife whispered, and Paul laughed and stood up, beginning to undress.

She slept finally in his arms and Paul lay awake listening to her regular breathing and admitted to himself that his wife had a point, although he would never tell her so. The social aspect of regimental life was more difficult with Rowena, and he suspected that she would never become comfortable with it. Her gentle nature was the reason he had first been attracted to her and he could hardly complain if it meant that he needed to take care of her more. He had known it when he had made that first impulsive decision to marry her. What he had not realised was how much her loving companionship would come to mean to him. Paul wished she had slapped Tyler's arrogant face for him but he knew that Rowena never would. She had aroused Paul's protective instincts from the first time he had seen her. Paul had never been faced with a situation where somebody had hurt her in any way, and he was not sure he had ever been quite so angry in his life.

Paul arrived on the parade ground in time for early drill and was interested to see that every one of the officers of the 110th were present. He wondered what they were expecting him to do, and what any of them imagined they could do to stop him. Carl approached him as the men marched out.

"How is Rowena?" he asked.

"She'll be all right. Of course it might take me another two years to get her to attend a social event again. Anybody seen Tyler yet?"

Carl shook his head. "Sleeping it off, I imagine. He made a complete arse of himself, Paul, and he'll need to apologise, but he was stupidly drunk."

Paul studied his friend. He was remembering Rowena as she had looked this morning, her fair hair tumbled across the pillow and her eyes still slightly swollen from crying so much. He had spent the remainder of the night watching his wife and visualising Tyler putting his hands on her, and his rage was white hot.

121

"I certainly think an apology is in order, Mr Swanson. I'll remember to mention that to him. Carry on with drill, would you?"

***

Carl stood watching with mounting concern as his friend walked across the yard to the barracks block. Johnny called an order to the NCOs then joined Carl. "I had a feeling this was going too well," he said.

"This is not looking good," Carl said. "What in God's name is he doing?"

Sergeant O'Reilly joined them. "I thought you said he looked fairly calm last night?"

"Sometimes I get things wrong, Sergeant."

Paul walked into the barracks occupied by his light company and emerged after a moment carrying a bucket. Carl recognised it immediately as a waste bucket, waiting to be emptied into the latrines, and it was full and reeking, Carl could smell it across the parade ground. The officers and men of the 110th watched in frozen horror as Paul approached the officers' block.

"Oh no," Carl said.

"Jesus, he isn't going to...?" Withers said in awe.

"Do you think Tyler locks his door?" Young asked.

"I don't think it matters whether he does or not," Johnny said. Paul had disappeared into the block and there was a sudden explosion of sound, echoing around the silent parade ground as Captain Tyler's door was kicked open, breaking the lock. After a long moment there was a bellow of horrified rage and disgust.

Captain van Daan reappeared carrying the empty waste bucket, which he dropped by the door. He walked over to the pump. A bucket, already full of icy well water, stood beside it. Paul picked up the bucket and disappeared back into the block, and a second outraged scream followed the first. Paul re-emerged and set the bucket down. Behind him Tyler exploded into the yard in his nightclothes, urine, excrement and cold water streaming off him. He was yelling profanities at Paul's uninterested back. Paul walked over to Johnny and spoke as though nothing at all had happened.

"Johnny, I'd a note this morning from Wellesley asking me to call, apparently he's had news from London. Will you finish drill and inspections? You might want to get a carpenter to fix Mr Tyler's door for him, tell them to send the bill to me, would you? And get four volunteers to clean up his room, it's a bit of a mess. Tell them there's a bottle or two in it for them, and a present for whichever lass has to do the laundry."

"Yes, sir," Johnny said without expression.

"Thank you."

"You are not getting away with this, you arrogant bastard!" Tyler yelled.

Paul turned and Carl tried not to audibly catch his breath. "You owe my wife an apology, Tyler. I suggest you put it in writing before the end of the day, I don't want her upset by the sight of you. And if you go anywhere near her again or say anything more personal than 'good day' to her; I will throw you through a window without bothering to open it first. Have I made myself perfectly clear?"

"By God, sir, I'm not letting you get away with this. I'll see you at dawn, sir."

"It is fucking dawn, Tyler, and it's not an hour that you see very often, but I'll be out here every day at this time, so if you want to go and find a sword or get a pistol and give me the opportunity to make you look like an even bigger twat than you already do, go right ahead, and I'll just wait here for you. I'm not here to prat around with you, I'm here because I'm ordered to be here, and actually I'm fairly pissed off about it because I'd rather be killing Frenchmen. But if you want to give me a bit of extra practice, you just let me know right now."

There was complete silence around the parade ground. Into it, Paul said:

"I thought not. Then if you'll excuse me, I need to go and see the Chief Secretary, and I suggest you get a bath, because I can smell you from here. And don't forget to write that letter to my wife, or you'll be woken up tomorrow morning with two buckets of that. Good morning."

Paul's fellow officers watched as he walked to the stables. "Bet it's a long time before Tyler manhandles another man's wife again," Young said.

"He was unlucky, mind," Carl said, fair-mindedly. "A normal husband would have just insisted on an apology. I hope Tyler remembers to write that letter."

"I can't believe it will slip his mind," Johnny said. "Personally I'm going to wait until after inspection and go for breakfast at O'Donnell's. I'm not eating in the mess until that smell has gone."

"It could have been worse," Michael said dispassionately, and the officers all turned to stare at him at once.

"I love an NCO with an optimistic outlook," Johnny said.

"No, you don't," Young argued. "It's unnatural, they're supposed to be permanently gloomy. You're an aberration, Sergeant. Go and get the cleaning crew organised and I'll send a message to the carpenter."

Michael grinned and saluted. "Yes, sir. I just meant that at least he didn't fight a duel or get court martialled."

"There's still time," Johnny said. "I doubt we've heard the last of this, Sergeant."

***

Paul found Sir Arthur at the breakfast table. Wellesley waved him to a seat and indicated for Paul to help himself. "Is Mrs van Daan fully recovered?" he enquired. "I understand she was upset by some idiot who had drunk too much."

"Who told you, sir?"

"One of my aides heard about it. I shall speak to Captain Tyler myself, believe me. Disgraceful behaviour in an officer." Wellesley studied Paul thoughtfully. "I am presuming that by now you have already had words with him?"

"I have, sir."

"I see. Perhaps you can tell me about it later. Or not at all. Whatever you've done to him, I'm sure I will hear about it soon enough. I am going to London, Captain. Parliamentary duties call, and I've an interview with the foreign secretary which I hope will end in a posting."

"Good news, sir."

"I want you to come with me. Better to give Captain Tyler a chance to recover from whatever appalling thing you have said or done to him."

"Yes, sir."

"I've some news for you," Wellesley said abruptly. "Letters from Horse Guards. It appears that Colonel Dixon is retiring from active service. Not that he has seen much actual activity for some years, but it's official now. Major Johnstone has been promoted to colonel-in-charge of the regiment. I know you'll be pleased."

"I am, sir. I get on well with him."

"Yes, he has always thought very highly of you." Wellesley studied Paul thoughtfully. "I have been somewhat surprised to find you still a captain," he said. "It's not lack of money, that's for sure. So I am presuming that it has been because you have not wanted to change regiment for a majority."

"Yes, sir. And I felt I needed more experience."

"Well, you have enough now. It appears to me that you've been effectively commanding the first battalion for two years, we may as well make it a reality."

Paul felt his pulse quicken. "Sir, I'm not even close to being next in line for this."

"No, you're not. It ought to be one of the older men. But you can afford it. A lot of them can't and Johnstone particularly wants you. It's his majority you're buying, and as regimental colonel he can effectively block anybody else."

Paul studied him uncertainly. "Would he?"

"You can talk to him about it when you see him, Major. I wasn't expecting you to turn this down."

"I'm not going to turn it down, any more than I turned down the command of the light company when he gave it to me over Johnny." Paul shrugged. "Money buys promotions, sir. The 110th is a new regiment and a lot of the officers can't afford to purchase up as easily as I can. They're all used to being passed over by wealthier officers."

"Most wealthy officers don't want the 110th, Major."

"No. And I know a lot of them wonder why I did. If Colonel Johnstone wants me, I'll make sure he doesn't regret it. And I'll work on the others, they'll come round. Thank you, sir. I suspect you may have had some influence on this."

"A little, perhaps. It does mean that you'll need a new captain for your light company."

124

"Yes, sir." Paul regarded him speculatively. "Do I get to make that appointment? I'm very happy to purchase my majority but do you think I can persuade them to give me a captaincy without purchase for one of my officers?" He paused. "Or at least make it look that way."

Wellesley did not smile although a hint of it lurked in the blue grey eyes. "There are a lot more shady transactions than that going on every week at Horse Guards, Major, as I'm sure you know."

"My majority being one of them."

"That is one way of looking at it. I had purchased my own majority by your age, it's not that unusual and the army is full of men stuck where they are for lack of money. Can I guess? Mr Wheeler?"

"Yes, sir."

"Well, you'll need another captain, and I don't think much of anybody's chances of purchasing in and taking over your light company from outside, they'd eat them alive. I'll talk to them for you, but I imagine they'll say yes. A captaincy is cheaper than a majority and he's a good officer. Don't mention it to him until we get back, though, will you?"

"No, I won't. Thank you, sir."

***

The visit to London took almost three weeks. Paul took the opportunity to see his family and to order some necessary supplies, and recognised with some appreciation, that Wellesley had been right. Once his temper had cooled he was able to see the incident with Tyler more objectively.

Paul returned to Dublin ahead of the Chief Secretary and went first to see his wife and children. Rowena had settled into a comfortable domestic routine and seemed untroubled by the events of the previous month. Paul took himself off to the barracks and found his men working with the two Irish companies at musket training. Carl came to greet him.

"Sir – when did you get back?"

Paul smiled at his friend. "Late last night. Bloody awful crossing, I'm glad Rowena wasn't with me. Is all well?" He ran his eyes over the companies. "Have we acquired some extra men?"

Carl laughed. "Corrigan asked us to help him out, I think he was feeling the pressure." He eyed Paul thoughtfully. "Am I seeing things, or do I need to salute a bit straighter?"

"Yes. And it looks as though we'll be off to Denmark for a spell. Wellesley is not in command but he's in charge of the reserves, and I'm happy to work with him again. They've agreed to a promotion for Johnny. Where is he?"

"That's really good news. He's probably in the barracks with Michael."

Paul turned to stare. "That was going to be my next question," he said. "I wondered where he was. Is something wrong, Carl?"

"Yes, I wasn't sure whether to write to you or not. There's been a bit of a problem with Michael."

"Is he ill?"

"He's injured." Carl took a deep breath. "You need to take a deep breath and not lose your temper, Paul."

"Whenever you say that Carl, I feel immediately enraged. What happened?"

"I wasn't there, at the start. None of us saw what happened, but Michael got into a bit of an altercation with Captain Tyler and came up before a regimental court martial. He's been demoted and flogged."

Paul felt his temper rise. He took a deep breath and clamped down on it hard. "All right," he said with an assumption of calm. "I'm going to go and see him. Where's Tyler?"

"Took a few days' furlough – family business, apparently. He should be back in a couple of days." Carl eyed him grimly. "Which will give you a chance to calm down."

"Yes. Thank you, Carl." Paul clapped his friend on the shoulder. "I'm sorry I sailed off and left you and Johnny in the middle of this, it was my bloody fault."

"Not entirely. He is a twat, sir."

"I know. But I could have avoided this."

Paul walked into the barracks. He could hear voices and followed them through to the light company bunks. His sergeant was lying face down on his bunk, shirtless, with a light blanket covering him. Johnny Wheeler was sitting on a low stool beside him. As Paul approached he stood up. Michael pushed himself up onto his elbows.

"Lie still, you dopey bastard, it's me," Paul said shortly.

"Welcome back, Captain," Michael said. Johnny was regarding Paul's coat with amused appreciation.

"No, no, Michael, you've got it wrong. We've a new major in the barracks. Very shiny, sir. Was that difficult to stitch on?"

"You'd need to ask my sister-in-law that question, you can't imagine I did it. I'm hoping you've kept in with the women, Johnny, because you've some sewing of your own to do." Paul slipped a hand into his pocket and drew out a captain's bar. "Congratulations, Captain Wheeler. There will be some paperwork to go over."

There was a stunned silence. Johnny took the stripe and looked down at it then looked up at Paul. "Did you...?"

"Promotion on merit, Johnny. Johnstone approved it and it's ratified at Horse Guards. A few years overdue, I'd say, but we got there in the end. I'm commanding the first battalion under Colonel Johnstone, Dixon has retired. You'll take over the light company. Although they're still my lads, Johnny, and don't you forget it."

"Christ, Paul, I don't know what to say."

"Well, we'll be celebrating later on, so save it for then. Get out of here and tell the others – Carl knows."

"I remember you joking about this on the way to India, but I didn't think you meant it."

126

"Then you're a bloody idiot and you don't know me as well as I thought you did."

"I should have. Thank you, sir." Johnny saluted. He glanced down at O'Reilly. "We've a problem with needing a new sergeant, mind."

"No, we just need to kick the arse of the one we already have. Get going, Johnny, I want to talk to Michael."

Johnny left and Paul sat down. He drew back the blanket and studied the bloody stripes. "How many?"

"Seventy-five. I'm still due another twenty-five when I'm fit for it."

"That isn't going to happen."

"Let it go, Paul," Michael said quietly.

"Michael there are some things I need to learn to let go, but watching my friend being strapped to a post and flogged isn't one of them. I'm senior officer in barracks and I'm commuting your punishment. I didn't bring stripes for you because I didn't know you'd need them but consider yourself reinstated. We're going to Denmark with Wellesley in a few weeks, and Captain Tyler will not be accompanying us. I'll need my best sergeant. What happened? Don't tell me you lost your temper with him, I watched you with Longford, you can't be baited."

"Turns out I can. He went after the men, sir. Couple of incidents, never with any of our officers around. I tried to ignore it, but then he'd collared young Blake from the second company. Reckoned he'd been disrespectful. Blake had no bloody idea what was going on, but when I came on them Tyler was kicking hell out of him."

"How old is Blake?"

"Sixteen. Joined as a drummer, but he's a bit of a favourite of mine, to be honest. He can read and write and he's bright, I'd like to train him up. Which I'm guessing is why Tyler went for him."

"Did you hit him?"

"Not really, but I shoved him out of the way and got between him and Blake, refused to stand down when he told me to. It might have been worse if Mr Swanson hadn't got there. He was pushing me to hit him and I really wanted to. I can't argue with the verdict, I did what he said I did."

"This is my bloody fault."

"He's an arsehole, sir."

"I know, but the army is full of them. I need to get better at dealing with that. If I'd not lost it so badly on the parade ground that morning...or even if I'd done what Wellesley told me to do and got hold of him at the reception to apologise, he'd probably never have gone after Rowena and I wouldn't have lost my temper. I honestly forgot about him that evening, but I shouldn't have." Paul shook his head. "The truth is that I thought it was a load of unnecessary bollocks and I couldn't be bothered with it and I was too arrogant to listen to anybody telling me otherwise. I'm sorry, Michael."

"Sir, it wasn't you trying to make a fool out of him at drill that morning, it was me and the other sergeants, I had this coming. But you need to let it go

127

now." Michael gave a painful smile. "It's a few years since I was last flogged, I'd forgotten how much this hurts."

"What was it last time?"

"Longford, not long after I joined. Accused me of stealing."

"Why?" Paul asked, astonished. His friend laughed.

"Sir, it is always a surprise to you that not all officers are like you. Actually it's you that's unusual. Someone had been on a pilfering spree and Longford used it to pay off a score. He didn't like me, probably because I thought he was an idiot and didn't bother to hide it. Taught me a valuable lesson about keeping my head down." Michael twisted his head to look at Paul. "The trouble is, since I've been with you I've forgotten a lot of what I learned back then. I expect to be treated like you treat me, so it's tougher to stand back and let a bastard like Tyler beat up a sixteen year old boy because he's bought his commission and he can."

"I'm sorry, Michael. I know I'm awkward."

"You are the most difficult bastard I've ever served under in terms of what you expect, but the difference is in how you go about achieving it. What you've done with this regiment...and you've done it without needing to flog anybody. Although they've called you a few names along the way."

"I know."

"Still, when I think of what you did to him. You tipped a brimming bucket of the light company's shit and piss all over his head before he was awake, and then followed it up with a bucket of the coldest well water this side of the Wicklow Mountains. Believe me, a flogging is nothing to that. I swear to God, I just get to the point where I think you can't shock me any more and then you come up with something like that."

Paul had started to laugh again. "I really did," he admitted. "Christ, I was angry. And honestly, I could do it again. I'm looking at your back, and I know that was meant for me, and I want to kick him so badly that it hurts. But you're right. He wrote to Rowena like I told him to, and I'm a senior officer now, so he can bloody back off and leave my men alone. I'll settle for your stripes back and no further punishment, and as long as he doesn't lift his head above the parapet again while I'm here, he's safe. Although I'm tempted to leave him a present of a shit bucket in his bed the morning we leave."

Michael began to laugh. "You'll get to be a general one day, sir, if you can learn to control that bloody temper," he said. "Leave him alone. Tell me about this posting instead. What the hell are we going to Denmark for?"

128

Chapter Eight

The winter of 1808 was horribly cold in Yorkshire, with snow lasting through Christmas well into January. The weather seemed to echo Major Paul van Daan's mood as he celebrated his return from Copenhagen by trying to set to rights the appalling problem of the 115th North Yorkshire Foot, a posting which after only two weeks looked set to outstrip the battle of Assaye in Paul's catalogue of unpleasant experiences.

Rowena was not with him. The short campaign in Denmark had achieved its aim, and the battalion returned to barracks while Wellesley fumed at his administrative tasks and waited for orders. Paul did not join his men in barracks, although he wished he could have. Copenhagen had been a difficult campaign which had placed a strain on Paul's usually good relationship with Wellesley. His chief had recommended him for the temporary posting in command of the 115th and Paul knew perfectly well that it was intended as a punishment.

Rowena was very settled at Southwinds with Patience, Francis and Grace, and Paul kissed her and told her that he would miss her. He thought that she deserved some time at home and took himself north with a faint sense of relief that whatever else he had to deal with in Yorkshire he would not have to worry about taking care of his wife.

Arriving in Yorkshire in the icy chill of January, Paul thanked God that he had not brought her, as the barracks were in an appalling state. The buildings were in disrepair, morale was non-existent, training was worse, and equipment and rations had fallen victim to peculation and dishonesty in the quartermasters' department. Surveying the enormity of the task ahead of him, Paul felt a reluctant admiration for the ingenuity of Sir Arthur Wellesley's punishment. He was well aware that some aspects of his behaviour in Copenhagen had caused Wellesley a serious headache and he had been left in no doubt that he was lucky to have retained his commission. The 115th North Yorkshire foot was Wellesley's revenge and if conditions had not been so miserable, Paul would have found it funny.

The colonel of the 115th had departed due to ill health and no replacement had been sent, which gave Paul effective temporary overall command of the regiment. There were four companies currently in barracks, all woefully under strength and the lack of food and pay and decent accommodation was causing not only desertions, but also bad behaviour in local taverns and inns.

None of the officers lived in barracks due to the appalling state of the accommodation. Like the men, the officers were under strength and demoralised. Paul found Lieutenant Robert Carlyon, a local man two years younger than him, to be the friendliest and most receptive to his ideas. Cynically he wondered if Mr Carlyon was ambitious for promotion, which made him keen to be on the right side of the new commander. Whatever his reasons, Paul welcomed his support, and was grateful for his offer of accommodation in his family home. Carlyon's father was the local MP and a small landowner, and their estate lay only a few miles from the draughty, run-down barracks. Beset by difficulties, it was a relief to Paul to return there, at the end of the day, to a hot meal and a comfortable bed.

Paul quickly realised that the tactful approach which he had used at the Melton barracks would not do for the 115th. With the exception of Carlyon, the officers were either indifferent or actively hostile to his intervention. Paul wrote immediately to Horse Guards regarding funds for the necessary improvements, but he decided that the situation required dramatic measures. By the end of the first two weeks, the regiment had come to loathe their energetic young commander with a passion. All normal training was suspended, and the men were set to scouring, painting and repairing all buildings. The training ground was levelled and cleared, and bedding and kit was laundered and scrubbed. The officers were summoned to account for the lack of training and drills and when the quartermaster became aggressive over the gaps in his financial records, Paul lost his temper and threw the man bodily into the street before appointing Robert Carlyon to replace him. The son of a mercantile family, Carlyon at least appeared to be honest and could add up a column of figures.

"It's a disgraceful affair," Benjamin Carlyon said at breakfast. He had been listening to his son's account of his new duties. "Public money gone to waste while we've troops in the field in need of pay and equipment." He eyed his guest thoughtfully. "You need to take some care, mind, Major. Some of your measures aren't popular with the men and they're used to running wild and doing as they like in the area. Watch your back."

"I will, sir. Will you excuse me, I should be going. My thanks, ma'am."

Paul smiled pleasantly at Mrs Carlyon and went out to retrieve his hat and riding whip from the hall. "Are you coming, Lieutenant Carlyon?" he enquired. "Ah, no, I have just remembered. The dentist."

Robert Carlyon pulled a face. "I'd rather be in barracks," he said.

"Even with that pile of accounts awaiting you? You must fear the worst. Good luck." Paul smiled and went out to his horse. He patted the animal's neck, and the big roan nuzzled his pockets in search of treats. Rufus was a new purchase. Paul had found him in Ireland just before going to Denmark but until now had spent little time with him. One of the few compensations of his new posting was the opportunity to try his new mount, although given the weather, he was cautious on the rutted road out to barracks, concerned for his horse's legs.

"Are you seriously going out in this, sir?" his orderly enquired.

"Yes, but you can stay here, Jenson, there's no need for both of us to freeze. If it gets worse, I'll stay in barracks tonight."

"You think the rest of your officers might not show up today?" Jenson said with a grin.

"They'll regret it if they don't. But after what I've said to them about it, I need to set an example. I'll take it slowly."

Jenson studied the weather. "You're bloody mad, sir, this is getting worse. Take care, it's a crap road at the best of times, I don't think you should be doing this."

"I'll be all right, Jenson."

It was snowing heavily again. Paul pulled up the collar of his greatcoat, adjusted his hat with a sigh and set off into the storm.

Three miles from the barracks Paul was ready to admit that he had made a bad decision, but it was closer to go on than to turn back. He would have to spend the night there as it was not fair on Rufus to risk his legs in snow this heavy, and the wind was picking up as well, causing great drifts to blow across his path and making visibility even worse. Afterwards it occurred to Paul that he might have noticed the man behind the trees if he had not been so focused on not allowing Rufus to slip in the rapidly drifting snow. The first he knew of it was a stunning blow to the side of his head, which knocked him sideways and toppled him from the saddle. He fell heavily and lay winded, hearing the thud of Rufus' hooves taking off in fright in the direction of the barracks.

Paul's first thought was for Rufus, but there was nothing he could do about it. The horse was sure-footed and would do better without the weight of a rider. Paul wondered what would happen when Rufus arrived in barracks riderless. Presumably his officers would realise that something was wrong and send out somebody to search, but Paul wondered ruefully how long it would take them. His unpopularity was such that his officers would probably enjoy the thought of him trudging through snowdrifts to reach the barracks, while they sat warming themselves at the mess fire and drinking hot punch.

Paul pushed himself up cautiously and swore as he got to his feet. As he tried to put weight on his left leg, an agonising pain shot through his knee, and Paul realised he must have twisted it as he landed. He stood very still, counting to ten in his head, since an outburst of rage would not help him here. He looked around and saw the instrument of his downfall lying on the snow close by. The rock was big and had sharp edges. Paul bent to pick it up and felt the side of his head. His hand came away red.

The snow was so heavy now that Paul could barely see, but he set off grimly in the direction of the barracks, limping heavily. Neither of his injuries was serious, but if he did not keep himself moving, the cold might prove more dangerous than either. His assailant, presumably some disgruntled man of the 115th, must be long gone.

Ahead of Paul there was nothing but white, and the snow blew into his eyes. He blinked it away and then blinked again as he realised that he was no longer alone. A slight figure in a long dark cloak was coming towards him along the track from the direction of the barracks.

"Are you all right?" a woman's voice called. "I saw a horse go past without a rider, was that yours? Do you need help?"

"I could ask the same of you," Paul said, in considerable surprise. "What the devil is a woman doing out in this, unaccompanied?"

The woman came up to him. He could see little of her face within the hood, but dark eyes looked up at him thoughtfully. "Unlike you, I know where my horse is," she said. "Come along. There's a shepherd's hut about half a mile up here, that's where I've left my horse. Best get out of this until it eases off a little, it's getting worse. You're limping, were you thrown? Lean on me, it's not far."

She took his arm and pulled it across her shoulders. With her support, walking became easier. Paul hobbled along, not speaking until the building loomed up through the blizzard. The woman stepped forward and lifted the latch and Paul followed her into the hut and closed the door. It was instantly warmer, with hay piled in the corner and a stone drinking trough. An elegant black mare was tethered to a wooden manger by the far wall, delicately nibbling at some hay. The woman went to her and greeted her, running her hand reassuringly down the smooth neck. Then she turned, pushed back her hood and looked at Paul. Paul looked back at her.

"Good God."

The girl was tall and slender, and much younger than he had expected, a slip of a girl to be out in this vile weather unescorted. She was also startlingly beautiful. Out in the snow he had thought her a farm girl, but the quality of her horse and her clothing told him that she was not. Her hair was black, worn up in a smooth arrangement of braids in defiance of the current fashion for curls, and she had a perfect oval face with almond shaped eyes, which were so dark they looked almost black in this light. Her mouth was well shaped and as she unclasped the heavy cloak, which was soaked, and tossed it over a bundle of hay, he could see that the dark green riding habit was fitted to show a slender body, sweetly curved. Paul had developed a habit of comparing attractive young women to his wife over the past few years and it had made him remarkably smug, but he admitted to himself that his wife, however pretty, could not hold a candle to this girl. The dark eyes were regarding him quizzically.

"What have you been doing to yourself?" she said.

"Falling off my horse," Paul said. "I am beginning to think it a blessing in disguise, mind. When I set off this morning, I was definitely not expecting to find myself shut up in a barn, in a blizzard, with a beautiful girl."

The girl gave a peal of laughter. "You're very impertinent, sir. I would point out that since I'm the one who still has a horse and can get out of here, it might behove you to mind your manners a little more."

Paul grinned. "I beg your pardon, ma'am, you're quite right, it wasn't a good start. May I introduce myself? Major Paul van Daan of the 110th first battalion. Currently I am…"

"Ah – now I do know who you are," the girl said. "Currently you are upsetting the stalwarts of the 115th in Cuddingham. Is it true that you threw the quartermaster through a window? No wonder they are throwing rocks at you."

Paul could not take his eyes from the fine boned, remarkable face. "How did you know it was a rock?" he asked.

"Well, you've a gash the size of a small boulder on the side of your head, Major, and you don't look like a man who falls off his horse easily. Sit down on the edge of the manger and let me look at that."

Paul felt slightly disoriented, although he was not sure if it was the result of his fall or the extraordinary behaviour of the girl. He obeyed and she came close, taking out a white handkerchief to carefully clean the blood from his wound. There seemed to be no shyness or awkwardness in her. She was as direct and open as a boy, but she was the most feminine woman he had ever seen.

"What else have you heard?"

"That you are a war hero, with a wife and children and that most of the officers at Cuddingham, and pretty much all of the men, would like to murder you." Suddenly the girl relented, smiled and held out her hand. "Anne Howard," she said. "Lieutenant Carlyon is visiting a lot at present. He is trying very hard to marry me for my money and he has talked of you."

"Ah," Paul said. He could remember Carlyon mentioning the girl in passing but had not taken a great deal of interest. He took her gloved hand, and instead of shaking it, raised it to his lips. "He did not mention how beautiful you were."

The black eyes danced with amusement. "I'm not sure he's noticed how I look, Major, he's too dazzled by the size of my dowry."

"Seriously? I need to rethink my opinion of Mr Carlyon if he looks at you and doesn't see what I see, lass."

"For a respectable married man you're an awful flirt, Major van Daan."

"I've been told that before. How old are you, Miss Howard?"

"I have a feeling that is an impertinent question," the girl said. "I'm seventeen, although I am told that I appear to be older. I believe you have been invited to my coming out ball."

"I believe I have. I'm not sure if I've replied yet, but I'll definitely be there."

"I think I should be a little on my guard."

"Don't be. I am known for having very few scruples when it comes to women, but I think even I baulk at seducing a seventeen-year-old lass who is potentially going to marry one of my junior officers."

It was an outrageous thing to say, and Paul knew it. He was surprised at himself but there was something about this girl's direct manner which touched an answering chord in him. Colour flooded her face but she was still laughing.

"You are definitely going to have to work on your company manners, Major," she said.

Paul studied her appreciatively. "I'm not the only one though, am I? I know I've spent a lot of time in the army, but surely you should have had the grace to look horrified or faint or something even slightly ladylike."

"Oh Lord, I should, shouldn't I?" the girl said. "I'm sorry, Major, have I shocked you?"

"I am remarkably hard to shock, but you're certainly surprising. Still, at least you're taking my mind off my headache."

"Does it hurt much?" She had cleaned the wound and was examining it thoughtfully. "It's quite deep, he'd a good aim."

"Yes. When I've worked out who it is, I should consider him for rifle training."

She gave a gurgle of laughter. "A flogging?"

"No, I don't use flogging. But he's definitely due a punch in the face."

"I don't blame you, I'd be furious." Her fingers brushed his face as she leaned forward to look at the wound again. "There's nothing in it now, it will be fine."

Her face was close to his and Paul gave in to his impulse. He raised his hand and cupped her face gently, turning her towards him, then leaned forward and kissed her very gently on the lips. "Thank you," he said. The dark eyes widened in surprise, but she neither screamed nor slapped him which was surprising. Intrigued, Paul stood up and took her very carefully into his arms, parting her mouth under his. Her response was immediate and instinctive, and he drew her closer, kissing her harder. They stood locked together for a long moment, and then she seemed to recollect herself and drew back.

Paul released her immediately and she stepped back and stood looking at him, her eyes wide and shocked. "Major van Daan…"

"Oh Lord – I am sorry, lass. Definitely not the behaviour expected of an officer and a gentleman. Are you all right?"

"Yes, of course I am." The black eyes met his again, and then, to his complete astonishment, she gave a rueful grin. "Really, my own experience is very limited in comparison to yours, but I can honestly say that is the first time a complete stranger has kissed me. Is that your usual greeting to a girl you don't know?"

Paul was enchanted. "No, I generally make do with a handshake. Although I admit I don't often find myself alone with a girl who looks like you, any sensible man coming within a foot of you must want to do that. But I should know better than to act on the impulse. You need to take a chaperone out with you, lass, preferably armed, looking the way you do. I am not going to be the last man to try that, although I rather suspect I was the first."

She flushed slightly. "You were."

"I'm surprised you didn't scream or slap me."

134

"Well, a scream is only likely to frighten Bella, and I'm not sure that I could hurt you very much if I hit you. I suspect you've been hit harder than I could manage."

"More than once. But just for future reference, if I do that again, hit me anyway. It will get your point across a lot better than kissing me back, that's only likely to get you into trouble with me."

The blush deepened. "I'll remember that," Anne said, and Paul smiled at her embarrassment.

"It's all right, lass, that was my fault, not yours. I'm old enough to know better."

The black eyes met his steadily. "So am I, Major," she said, and Paul realised in some surprise that she was not upset at all.

Walking to the door, Paul opened it and looked out. If anything, the blizzard had become thicker than ever. He glanced at the girl in some concern. "Lass, we shouldn't be here together like this. I think you need to wait here and I'm going to walk to Cuddingham and get help there for you."

Anne Howard walked to stand beside him and looked at the weather. "That's a mad idea, particularly since you're limping. I realise this isn't ideal, but I'm not letting you risk yourself just because propriety says we can't be alone together."

Paul studied her, surprised. "Your self-possession is remarkable, Miss Howard, but you're very young and you've a reputation to consider."

The girl reached out and pulled the door firmly closed. "It might surprise you, Major van Daan, but I'd put a man's safety ahead of my reputation."

"And what would your parents think about that, Miss Howard?"

"Mostly, they're fairly resigned by now," Anne said. "I don't think you're going to attack me, Major. In fact I'm probably safer here with you than being alone, if some vagrant wanders in looking for shelter."

Her calm practicality amused Paul. "Fair enough," he said. "Come on, let's sit down, we may as well be comfortable."

Paul settled himself against the wall with his legs stretched out in front of him while she seated herself on a pile of hay with the unselfconsciousness of a boy and regarded him with eyes bright with interest.

"Since we have time," Paul said, "will you satisfy my curiosity, Miss Howard? What in God's name are you doing out alone in this?"

"I was searching for a lost child," the girl said. "Molly Parsons, one of our tenants, had lost her Billy again. He's the most venturesome brat this side of Harrogate. Myself I think I'd chain him to something. He's eight and was out with one of the shepherds, bringing the sheep in. He must have wandered off. It's not the first time. Molly came up to the house in a panic, so I came out with three of the grooms to search."

"Did you find him?"

"Yes. Reynolds did, he came up to me about ten minutes before I saw you, to say they'd got him, and were heading back. I'd left Bella here, as I wasn't going to risk her knees for that snotty-nosed little brat, so I said I'd see him back at the house. To be fair I didn't realise how bad it would get, or how quickly, but I'd still have done the same."

"What of your parents?"

"My father is away until Tuesday. My stepmother will be at home raising a fit by now, she told me not to go, but there's little they can do in this. I wish I'd told Reynolds where I'd left Bella. He might guess, but to be honest I doubt he'll have made it back to the house. He and the other grooms will probably stay with Molly until it dies down. In which case my stepmother will assume that I'm with them, so she won't worry too much. And the lads won't worry about me, they know I've the sense to take shelter."

"Who is your father?" Paul asked.

"He is Sir Matthew Howard, of Helton Ridge. Manufacturer of woollen cloth. A very prominent – and may I say – a very wealthy businessman. I am his youngest child."

"Really? Are all the others like you? If so he has my sympathy."

Anne gave a gurgle of laughter. "No, how can you say so? We are a respectable family."

"They might be..."

"Implying that I am something else? I can hardly argue with that, can I? My eldest brother wishes to enter Parliament. My second brother is learning the business, and my sister is shortly to be engaged to a very dull man who has just been appointed to a position in the Treasury. She is away at the moment, staying with his family. My mother died when I was born, so I have a stepmother whom I love dearly although I think I am a trial to her."

"I should think you'd be the death of her," Paul said with a grin. "Do you usually career around the countryside without so much as a groom to escort you?"

"When I can get away with it," Anne said. She sighed. "It is going to be more difficult now that I am officially being brought 'out'. I am expected to be sensible and find a husband and settle down."

"Lieutenant Carlyon? I wouldn't have thought he would appeal to your father, there isn't much money."

"My father isn't looking for money, Major, he has plenty. What Mr Carlyon brings is a seat in Parliament for George. His father is going to retire and has control of the seat. He would sponsor George in return for my dowry and a substantial allowance. But Mr Carlyon is not the only option my father is considering, I can assure you. I have a number of suitors."

Paul was charmed by the openness of her manner. "And what do you want, Miss Howard?"

"To be left alone mostly, but there is very little chance of that." The black eyes met his. "My friends call me Nan."

"I like that. My name is Paul. We should not be on first name terms, of course, but let us ignore the conventions."

"To tell you the truth," Anne said, "I am not very good at the conventions."

"You astonish me," Paul said promptly, and Anne gave a choke of laughter.

"You are a fine one to talk," she said severely. "You are a married man and just kissed a girl you only just met merely because you felt like it."

"I did. I must say you have been remarkably forgiving about it. I was just thinking how much I wish my own regiment was stationed here, they'd have been out and searching by now. I rather think the officers at Cuddingham will get my poor Rufus settled in his stable, have a good laugh over my misfortune and go back to playing cards and drinking hot toddies, safe in the knowledge that I am unlikely to catch up with them for quite some hours. And the Carlyons won't worry because I told my orderly I would stay in barracks if it got worse."

Anne did not reply for a moment. Then she said:

"If that rock had knocked you out, you could have frozen to death out there in this."

Paul had already thought of it. "Yes."

"Do you have any idea who might have thrown it?"

"I could probably narrow it down to two or three. My former quartermaster would be on the list, but I believe he has left the area. But there are three men who were drunk on duty last week, I'd guess it's one of those."

"Did you flog them?" Anne asked.

"Good God, no. Removal of grog rations and a week shovelling out the stables. But I did give them a mouthful in front of the entire battalion, which they're not used to, they're a bit more sensitive than my lads. Are you all right? You're shivering." Paul stood up and went to retrieve the girl's cloak. It was still very wet. He felt his own great coat and found that it was much drier. "Here, put this around you."

She accepted it with a grateful smile. "Thank you."

Paul spread her cloak out to dry, then limped to the door and opened it. He could see nothing but snow. It was drifting up against the walls of the building, and he could barely see the trees on the other side of the road. Stepping out, he tested it and found that even on the road it came up almost to the top of his boots. He came back into the hut and glanced around. There was an ancient broom leaning against the wall by the feed trough. Paul picked it up and began to sweep, clearing an area of loose straw.

"Are you clearing an area for a fire?" Anne asked.

"Yes, I have a feeling we may be here for a while. I'm going to collect some wood from the copse across the road, it'll be fairly dry under the trees."

"Can you manage with that knee? I can go."

Paul tested the leg. "It will be fine, it's feeling better already. Just twisted it, I think." He looked at her amused. "You would, though, wouldn't you?"

"Of course I would."

"Nan, you'd be a rare hit in an army camp. I'm waiting to find out exactly what throws you into confusion."

"You did fairly well earlier, Major," the girl said dryly, and held out her hand for the broom. "Let me do that then. Here, you'll need your coat."

137

She shrugged out of his coat and gave it to him, and he put it on, handed her the broom and went out into the storm.

Paul returned three times, piling up the wood just inside the door. When he came back the third time, she had found a bucket and was scouring it out with clean snow, her elegant riding gloves ruined with her efforts. Paul stood watching her for a moment and had a sudden acute vision of this girl in an army camp. The discomfort and embarrassment of her situation did not seem to discompose her at all. He added his wood to the pile, came forward and took the bucket to fill it with snow. As he filled the trough so that it would melt for Bella to drink, he watched the girl carefully constructing a fire. To his immense surprise she was very good at it. He refilled the bucket and set it close to the fire to melt drinking water for them, and then found his tinderbox and struck a spark, using hay to help the fire to catch. The flame burned brightly, and he took off his coat and draped it over the hay to dry off. The snow was still falling steadily. Glancing at his watch Paul saw that it was already mid-afternoon. He wondered if it had dawned on her that they were unlikely to be able to get away from here before nightfall.

The girl looked around and met his eyes. She was achingly beautiful, and Paul felt his body stir in response. Then she smiled and he felt a sudden shock of pleasure. He felt a ridiculous sense of kinship with this odd, friendly girl. "Your hair's coming down," he said.

Anne lifted a hand to it. "It often does. Never mind, there's only you to see and I don't suppose you care."

She pulled out several remaining pins and shook her head and Paul caught his breath as it fell in a curtain of black silk about her shoulders. "You little flirt, you did that on purpose," he said softly.

Anne laughed with him, making no attempt to deny it. "I'm sorry," she said.

"No, you're not." Paul studied her with considerable appreciation. "I'm very tempted to come over there and pick up where I left off earlier, but I won't."

He watched her as she went to her horse and fussed her for a while, giving her water and talking softly to her. The horse nuzzled her with an affection that made him smile. Anne reached into one of the saddlebags and withdrew a brown package. She came to sit beside him and opened it to reveal some bread and cheese, and two apples.

"I brought it out with me in case I got stranded somewhere with that blasted brat," she said. "I wasn't expecting to need it, but here."

Anne broke the bread and Paul accepted his share with a smile of thanks. "This is a pleasant surprise. I was expecting to be very hungry before we are able to get out of here."

"You mean before morning," the girl said steadily.

"I was trying not to alarm you. We might be lucky."

"I doubt it. It's getting dark already and the snow isn't stopping yet." Anne gave him a determinedly cheerful smile. "I'm not alarmed, although I think I might be if I was stuck here on my own all night. It's a good thing you're a respectable married man, Major."

"Yes," Paul said, aware of a sense of irony. "Perhaps after all it is a good thing that we're a long way from Melton and my regiment, nobody knows me here."

"Would my reputation be in trouble, then?"

Paul felt a twinge of discomfort, but there was something about this girl that made it difficult to prevaricate. He decided to be honest. "Yes. That's why I was keen to try and walk out of here. But you were right, it's not worth killing myself or risking you. I just hope that your people get here before the officers of the 115th, since they're less likely to spread the story. I am sorry, Nan."

"From what you've said about the 115th that sounds likely," Anne said. She sounded unconcerned and Paul wondered if it was an act or if she genuinely did not care. "It is cold. I'm going to see if my cloak is any drier."

"It will dry quicker in front of the fire. Move it closer and then come over here, you'll be warmer next to me."

Anne hesitated, then spread the cloak out and walked over to him. For the first time she seemed uncertain. Paul held out his hand and she sat beside him cautiously. He concealed a smile, put his arm about her and scooped her close against him. "I just want to stop you shivering, lass, I promise."

Anne turned her head to look up at him with unconscious enchantment. "No, you're right. I already feel warmer, thank you," she said. "I'm sorry to be so missish, Major, you're being completely charming about this and I'm not helping. Tell me about the regiment."

"The 115th?"

"No, your own. How long have you been in the army? Infantry or cavalry?"

"Infantry. I joined five years ago. I was in India, then fought in Naples and Denmark. And I was in Ireland, which seemed to involve a lot of parties. At some point soon I'm expecting orders to go with Wellesley to South America."

"Tell me about India."

Anne relaxed against him and Paul was amused and a little touched at how quickly she had made herself comfortable. There was something endearingly trusting about her body resting against his. He leaned back and talked, speaking of his officers and men, telling her of his early days in the regiment, and the various campaigns in which he had fought. She asked questions when he paused, and it struck him how much she seemed to know about current affairs and the complex politics of Europe. She must have read everything she could get her hands on. Curious to learn more, he moved the conversation on to other topics, to books and music, to philosophy and religion. Anne was extraordinarily well-read for such a young girl, and the insights she offered suggested a formidable intelligence. Paul realised he had never had this kind of conversation with a woman before and he wondered if Anne realised how unusual she was.

They talked late into the night, getting up periodically to feed the fire or get some water. Anne pulled a face at the brackish taste of the melted snow but drank it philosophically, and Paul took out his silver flask, coaxing her to try the brandy he had brought with him. She accepted and passed the flask back to him. Paul drank, then shifted reluctantly.

"I'm going outside for more wood. See if your cloak and my coat are dry, will you? We're going to need them in the night, the temperature is dropping."

***

Anne Howard watched him go then went to test the garments and found them dry and smelling of wood smoke. She carried them over to the nest he had made for them in the hay and sat down, staring into the dying fire.

An intelligent girl, Anne was well aware of the difficulties of her situation. Whoever found her in the morning was going to wonder exactly how she and Major van Daan had spent the hours together and she supposed that people would be sceptical if she told them that they had discussed French philosophy.

Paul van Daan was the most well-read man she had ever met. From an early age, Anne had thirsted for knowledge and haunted her father's library. None of her governesses had ever kept up with her, and since none of them had ever been able to exercise the least control over her either, her stepmother Harriet had dismissed the last of them when Anne was fifteen, employing only a French master and a dancing master. Sir Matthew had always found his over-educated daughter an irritation. Certainly, neither he nor any other member of her family had ever been able to talk to her about her reading as the major had done. He spoke of his time at Oxford fondly and Anne wondered about the contradictions in his nature, which had taken him from the study of classics to killing men on a battlefield.

She wondered too about his marriage. He spoke little of his wife, but she supposed that he might well feel awkward given the evident spark of attraction between them. No doubt he was amusing himself with a harmless flirtation with a pretty girl before going back to his wife and his regiment. For Anne, who had never even kissed a man before, it was harder to dismiss the whole incident, but she could hardly expect him to remain outside and freeze to death to satisfy her sense of propriety, so she needed to be sensible and tell herself that the moment of madness had passed and would not occur again.

The door banged and Paul came back into the shed, dropping a pile of wood. "It's getting windy as well," he said. "I'm going to make a couple more trips in case it's hard to get out of here in the night. It's drifting badly now."

Anne watched him leave and thought that if she had to find herself trapped in a snowstorm with anybody, she was glad that it was Paul van Daan. He gave the impression of being immensely competent, calm and in complete control. Another man might have been panicking about their situation or raging at the callousness of his officers who should definitely have been out looking for him. Instead, he was practical and pleasant and seemed almost to be enjoying her company. Ruefully Anne admitted that despite the cold and discomfort she was enjoying his. It was a shame that none of her prospective husbands was as well-read and entertaining as Major van Daan.

She collected some of the wood he had left and rebuilt the fire. The door banged again, and she turned. Paul was brushing snow from his coat and hair, laughing, his face flushed from the wind. He seemed very young to be even in temporary charge of a regiment and Anne wondered how old he was.

"I should have put my greatcoat on," he said, taking off the regimental coat and shaking it. "Never mind, it'll dry." He stood for a moment, inspecting the fire. "You're very good at that. Something tells me you don't get up with the maids to build the fires in the morning. Who taught you?"

Anne laughed, slightly self-conscious. "I spent a lot of my childhood with the grooms and the farm children," she said. "My father was away a lot, and my governesses never had much control over me. I had a terrible taste for low company and was the despair of my stepmother; always climbing trees and fishing in the stream and stealing apples from the neighbours' orchards. I was a great trial to her."

"But you did acquire some very useful skills," Paul said, draping the red coat over the hay and coming forward. "It is bloody cold out there. I think if we'd tried to make it back we'd have been found frozen in a ditch by morning. I feel sorry for any poor souls caught out in this, it's foul."

He held out his hands to the fire and unthinkingly, Anne touched his hand and found it freezing. "Good God, didn't you have any gloves?" she said and enclosed his hand in both of hers to warm it.

Paul was looking at her, and suddenly the expression in his eyes caused a disturbing flutter in her stomach. "Yes, but they were too wet to be much use," he said. "Not a sign of my bloody regiment sending out search parties. I imagine they're tucked up in bed by now. God help them when I catch up with them."

"You sound as though you mean that."

Unexpectedly, Paul gathered her against him, and kissed her gently on the top of her head. "I do. Apart from the discomfort and inconvenience to me, it has put you in a damnably awkward position, Nan. If you'd not stopped to help me, you might have made it at least back to one of the cottages where you're known. Come and sit down again, we may as well be comfortable."

Anne settled back against him, looking up at him with a rueful smile. "I'm sorry, Major, if you end up having to give an account of yourself for this. None of this was your fault and I've made it worse by talking you half to death."

The blue eyes regarded her steadily. "Nan, I can honestly say I've enjoyed every minute of it, despite the cold. It's funny, isn't it? If this hadn't happened, we'd have met at your party and I'd have admired your beauty and probably flirted with you a bit and never known anything about you. That would have been a considerable loss on my part because you're extraordinary."

Anne felt herself blush. "Are you trying to flatter me, Paul?"

"I'm honestly not. I could become very poetic, if you like, about how lovely you are. And you are, no question. But there is so much more to you than that beautiful face."

Anne met his eyes. "Thank you," she said. "That's probably the best compliment I've ever received. And I can return it, you're a rarity, Paul. You don't treat me like an idiot or a child which is more than I can say for most of the men I meet. Are you like this with every woman?"

"I doubt most of them would appreciate it," Paul said. "I'm still hoping we can get you out of this without it becoming generally known, mind."

"Your reputation?"

"Yes. People tend to assume the worst with me when it comes to a lassie."

"And is it true?"

"Some of it. And before you ask the unsuitable question I just know you're dying to, no I have not always been entirely faithful to my wife. But I am fond of her and I try not to hurt her."

"At least you're honest which is more than you can say for most men who stray."

"Cynical, Nan. Although possibly true. Your parents seem keen for you to marry young, although you're very mature for a seventeen-year-old. Still…is it what you want?"

"Not to any of the men my father has chosen," Anne said honestly. "But I'll make the best of it. It's what girls do."

"Not at your age, lass. At this age most of them are starry-eyed, trust me."

"I've never thought of myself as starry-eyed, but perhaps I could be," Anne said softly. "But what would be the point? I already know my future, Paul. We both do."

There was a long and difficult silence, the atmosphere heavy between them, and Anne had no idea how to break it, or to lighten the mood. She had been enjoying their light-hearted flirtation, but it had shifted suddenly into something different, and far more dangerous. She was confused and fascinated, and curious, and desperate to explore further the stirring of her body that his nearness provoked.

Paul took a deep breath and gave a smile that looked like an effort. "That doesn't mean I can't want something else, Nan. And that, I think, is the point at which we should try to get some sleep. It's almost midnight, and we're not getting out of here now until morning. Come on, let's get you as comfortable as we can."

"Would you be better if I moved…?"

"No, you'll freeze. Lie down."

Anne did so, and Paul tucked her into the hay, with her cloak around her, then settled behind her. She could feel the warmth of his body through the cloak and she savoured it. Ridiculous to feel this way with a man she had only just met, but his presence made her feel safe and protected and cared for,

142

and since there would be only this short time, Anne lay very still, pretending to sleep, and concentrated on enjoying the moment.

***

Paul lay beside her, feeling very wide-awake. Anne did not speak again, and finally he heard her breathing settle and slow. The satin curtain of her hair had fallen over her face and he drew it back very gently and lay looking at her, his head and his leg both aching. The enormity of her composure fascinated him. He was trying hard not to compare her to his wife, but it was impossible. She was several years younger than Rowena, with a fraction of her life experience but she seemed years older.

Paul shifted uncomfortably and smiled to himself. He was not even close to sleeping, and he imagined how much his friends would laugh at the situation he found himself in. If he moved away, she would be cold, but lying this close to her was making it impossible for him to sleep, or even think straight. He was as aroused as he had ever been with no possibility of doing anything about it and he knew that Carl, at least, would have gleefully told him that he had deserved every moment of this discomfort to make up for the many times he had failed to employ any self-control at all.

"You're staring at me, Major," the girl said without opening her eyes, and the surprise of it made Paul laugh out loud.

"You caught me, Miss Howard. I thought you were asleep."

"I was pretending to be asleep," Anne said, turning over to look at him. "I thought it might make it easier."

"Nothing is going to make this easier, Nan, but I appreciate the thought. Don't worry about it. It's a seldom acknowledged fact that it doesn't do a man any harm not to get what he wants occasionally, and I am not going to do anything to frighten or embarrass you no matter how much I'd like to."

Her lips curved into a smile. "Paul, are you always this direct?"

"Not with a girl I barely know, bonny lass, but there is something about you that makes me want to break all the rules. And what fascinates me is you don't seem to care. I thought a gently bred girl was supposed to faint or scream if a man gets too close."

"Don't tell me you've not broken that rule before, Paul."

Paul could not help laughing. "I have. More than once. But not like this, Nan. Just at this moment I am reciting a list of all the reasons I can't touch you over and over in my head and it's not really helping much. All I can actually think about just now is how much I want to find out if you feel as good as you look."

Anne moved very deliberately, shifting her body closer to his. She reached up and placed the palm of her hand on his cheek. Paul turned his head and kissed her palm. He closed his eyes for a long moment, breathing deeply. When he opened them, she was still there, the heart-stopping perfection of her face close to his. Paul leaned forward and kissed her, gently at first and then harder as she responded immediately. She was unpractised but neither shy nor uncertain and Paul moved so that he was leaning over her.

"Nan Howard, do you have any idea how much trouble you're in just now?"

"I think I'll be all right, Major."

"You bloody won't if you don't stop looking at me like that, lass, I am not noted for my self-control. I don't want to frighten you..."

"Paul, I thought we agreed you're not dealing with a child here. I'm not afraid of you."

"Nan, you're extraordinarily mature in some ways, but you have no experience of a man like me, and we shouldn't be doing this."

The dark eyes met his. "No, I know. But sometime soon I'm going to be expected to do this with a man I barely know and probably won't like that much, and nobody is going to worry about my feelings then, are they?"

Her words cut into Paul. "Oh Christ, lass," he said softly. "Don't think of it that way."

"Don't tell me what to think, Paul. That's how it is for girls like me. And trust me, being starry-eyed isn't going to help much with that."

Paul studied her in silence for a long time, letting himself feel what he had been trying hard not to. He was conscious of desire, but also of a flood of confusing emotions which were completely unfamiliar to him. She looked back from those extraordinary dark eyes, and then suddenly, unexpectedly, she reached up, winding her arms about his neck, pulling him down to her.

Paul was lost. His hands were on her clothing, dealing with buttons and ties with the ease of long experience. He had half expected a furious protest and was ready to pull back with a laughing apology, but instead she lifted her body up to let him slide her clothing from under her.

"Dear God, you're so beautiful," Paul whispered, and moved his lips gently down her body in light kisses until he reached her thighs. He removed her stockings, his mouth tracing a line down her inner thigh and she murmured with pleasure, then reached for his shirt, lifting it over his head, running her hands over his bare chest. Paul kissed her again, losing himself in the richness of her, learning the lines of her body under his hands. His mouth moved down and found her breast and she gave a cry and arched towards him as he teased at her nipple with his tongue. He slid his hand over her and then down between her legs and she moved against him with an exclamation of surprised pleasure.

"How does that feel?" he whispered and laughed at her startled expression as he moved his hand insistently.

"Good," she managed. "It feels good. Paul..."

Paul shifted his weight onto her and felt her move instinctively under him, parting her legs, drawing him closer and he kissed her again, urgently, realising that she wanted him every bit as much as he wanted her, realising that she had no intention of stopping him.

Paul froze.

"Oh bloody hell, what am I doing?"

144

He rolled away from her and lay beside her in the hay taking deep breaths, horrified at his loss of control. Anne lay still and quiet next to him, and he knew she must be upset. Bad enough to have done what he did, but his abrupt withdrawal had been worse. When he was sure of himself, he turned towards her, bracing himself for her tears. She was not crying. The wide dark eyes were studying him, looking almost concerned.

"Paul, I'm so sorry, I pushed you to do that."

Paul was appalled. "Jesus Christ, Nan, that wasn't your fault, it was mine. I've no bloody self-control."

"It turns out you have, Major."

"Sweetheart, I'm sorry I've upset you…"

"I'm not upset."

"Love, I ought to have…"

"Look at me. Listen to me. I'm not upset."

Paul looked down into the dark eyes and realised, in some surprise that she was speaking the truth. "No, you're not, are you? I'm sorry, you've got me confused. Lass, I didn't mean to go that far."

She smiled and reached up to smooth his hair back from his face and he knew instinctively that he had said the right thing. "I know. But I wanted you to, Paul. I've been wanting this ever since you kissed me."

Paul kissed her very gently, and then eased her back, leaning over her again. "So have I," he admitted ruefully. "I ought to stop this right now but I'm not going to, although we need to agree a few rules here. I'm going to stop when I need to, which doesn't mean we're not going to enjoy ourselves. But if I do anything you're not comfortable with or if you think I'm going too far, you need to stop me. Yell at me if you have to, I'm not going to make you do anything you don't want to."

Anne's wide dark eyes studied him. "Paul, if you want to stop now…"

"I don't. I ought to, but I don't. Do you?"

"No."

"All right then. I won't lose control again, I give you my word. Come here, girl of my heart, you look very wide-eyed and very vulnerable and I'm appalled at how much I'm enjoying that. Kiss me again."

She had, Paul discovered, a natural sensuality and despite the strict limits he had set on himself she was a joy in his arms, quickly overcoming her shyness, wanting to learn how to give pleasure as well as to receive it. She seemed completely unembarrassed by her inexperience and unashamed in her enjoyment of her own body and his. Paul was enchanted by how easily she laughed, leaning over him so that her hair tickled his face, watching his expression as she stroked him into mindless bliss. He lay finally, relaxed and warm with her wrapped in his arms and sought for guilt or regret, finding only an immense content and a somewhat painful sense that he had just discovered something rare and special, which was out of his reach.

"Are you all right, Nan?"

The dark head shifted on his chest to look up at him. "Yes. Should I not be? I'm so hopeless at knowing the right thing to do, I'm not sure if I should be laughing or crying."

Paul stroked her hair gently. "Personally, I can't get the smile off my face. I wish I could have taken it further, but I'm not putting you at risk."

The expression in the dark eyes made him catch his breath. "Paul – just at this moment I'm not sure that I would care."

"I know you wouldn't, bonny lass, that much is very obvious. But trust me you would feel differently waking up in the cold light of day knowing that you could be bearing a bastard child to a married man." Paul leaned forward and kissed her with great tenderness. "I should tell you I'm sorry, and God knows I shouldn't have done even what we have, but I honestly can't find any genuine regret in me. What is more surprising is I don't see any signs of it in you either."

"I don't regret it," Anne said softly. "Being here like this with you feels so good. I had no idea I could feel like this."

"I've a feeling you're supposed to make that discovery with the man you marry, Nan."

The dark eyes slanted up at him. "I don't get to choose the man I marry, and I can't really imagine feeling this way with any of the men my father has in mind, Major. But what do I know, I've no experience to go on? None of this is new to you."

Paul felt a rush of tenderness. "Oh Nan, experience is one thing, but I've never come across a girl like you, and that has very little to do with the way you look. Although, looking at you just at this moment is no hardship whatsoever. But I imagine you hear that from a lot of men."

"I get complimented a lot. Girls do, you know. Growing up, George and Arthur were told how clever they were. I could run rings around them in any lesson we shared, I didn't even have to try. But I was only ever told that I was beautiful, as though that was something I should be proud of." Anne gave a little laugh. "I'm sorry, you've got me on my hobby horse. My stepmother tells me I'm ungracious. But I'm not sure half these men would even like me if they knew me. It doesn't matter. They take one long hard look and all they think about is…" She broke off.

"Darling girl, I can't condemn any man for that, I wanted to make love to you about a minute after I saw you."

"I know. But then you had a conversation with me, and you behaved as though what I said mattered."

"It does matter. I could spend whole days just talking to you and learning who you are. I hope you're all right after this, I can't stand the thought I might hurt you. I wish…"

Paul broke off, suddenly realising what he was about to say.

"Go on," she said.

"I wish I could have more," Paul said quietly.

"You're being very restrained, Major. Which, I suspect is a new experience for you."

"That's not what I meant. And I shouldn't be saying any of this to a chance-met girl in a barn when I have nothing to offer you."

Anne reached up to kiss him. "Say it anyway."

Paul studied her, realising with some surprise that his usual fluency with a woman had deserted him. "I'm not sure I can find the right words. Being with you is different. You're different. I've just spent around fifteen hours with you and I'm already trying to work out when I'll be able to see you again, although I know that's wrong. I think...damn it, I'm usually better at this, Nan."

"You're doing very well so far, Major."

Paul shifted and bent over her, kissing her very gently. "I'm nine years older than you, but I swear to God I'm not sure who is the older here. You make me feel uncertain in a way I've not felt for years."

"Is that good or bad?"

Her voice was suddenly husky, and desire flooded his body again. "Good," he said. "In more ways than you'd imagine. There's so much I'd like to know about you, I wish we had more time together."

Anne caressed his face, her eyes on his. "We have tonight," she said softly, and he kissed her again, his hands drifting over her body.

"We do. Come here and let's see if I can make it memorable for you, girl of my heart."

Anne gave a gurgle of laughter, and Paul thought, with a stab of pain, that it was a sound he wanted to hear for the rest of his life. "Is that what you call all your girls, Paul?"

Paul kissed her very gently on the tip of her nose. He had no idea where the phrase had come from, but he realised he had no desire to take it back. "No, I think that's a new one," he admitted. "I might save that one just for you."

Chapter Nine

Anne awoke to find a soft daylight bathing the hut and shivered without Paul beside her. He had tucked her into a nest of hay and placed her cloak and both his coats on top of her to keep her warm. Anne sat up and looked around her and saw that he had rebuilt the fire. Shivering, she slid out from under the covers and reached for her clothes. She had always been good at dressing without a maid, and by the time Paul reappeared she was dressed and was combing through her long dark hair with her fingers.

"Good morning," he said, and Anne turned to look at him. She was unsure this morning of how he would be and was prepared for awkwardness or embarrassment, but he came forward and scooped her against him for a long leisurely kiss as if it were the most natural thing in the world.

"Still all right?" he asked quietly, and Anne felt a rush of sheer irrational joy at being in his arms.

"Shamefully so. Is that sunlight I can see?"

Paul nodded, reaching for his coat. "And something else. Come and see who I've just found."

Anne walked to the door and found a tall roan gelding standing patiently at the edge of the road. "Oh poor thing, has he been out here all night?"

"Clearly he didn't make it back to barracks, as I thought. Which excuses them a little, although not much. He seems unhurt although he must be freezing. He wasn't here when I came out for wood, so he must have come back to where he last saw me once he'd stopped panicking." Paul ran his hand lovingly down the russet neck. "Clever boy."

Anne was touched by his obvious affection for the horse. "So you'll be heading for home."

"No, I'm going to carry on to the barracks, I need to have a little chat with a few people. But I want to see you safe first, how far is it to your home?"

"About five miles. But you could take me as far as Molly's and see if Reynolds and the other grooms are there."

"We'll try that first. It's probably better if they take you home rather than me. Are they discreet?"

"They'll do anything for me," Anne said, then felt herself blush slightly, wondering if he thought her arrogant. Paul merely grinned.

"That doesn't surprise me at all. Let me go and douse the fire properly, and we'll bring your Bella out and see how the road is. Most of the drifts are at the sides, I think, although it will be slow going. Come with me."

Paul towed her back inside the hut, threw water on the fire and kicked the hay around to conceal where they had lain. Anne watched him, feeling an immense sadness. The night had been too short, and there was so much more that she wanted to know about this extraordinary young man. He stood silently for a moment, as though thinking, and Anne's heart sank. She suspected that she knew what was coming and she had no wish to hear it. Eventually, he turned.

"Nan – I'm well aware that I ought to have a speech ready about last night..."

"Don't," Anne said quickly.

"Don't what?"

"Tell me you're sorry."

"I'm not going to, bonny lass, because it would be a lie. I can't possibly pretend to regret anything that felt that damned good. But I should know better."

"You didn't force me to do anything I didn't want to do, Paul."

"That's a remarkably mature statement for a girl of your age. But..."

"What did you say?" Anne demanded. She was suddenly furious. "Excuse me for mentioning it, Major, but if you were worried about my age you were remarkably quiet about it last night."

Paul looked so completely astonished, that Anne wondered if he was unaccustomed to a woman speaking to him that way. She did not care. Their time together had been magical for her, and it had seemed to mean something to him as well. She was angry that he should speak to her like a child now that it was over. She stood glaring at him, daring him to speak again. When he did, his response was unexpected.

"Christ, that really was patronising wasn't it?" he said.

"Yes."

"I am sorry. I was trying to take responsibility, not insult you. Should I start again?"

Anne's anger died as quickly as it had flared up, and she laughed at his stricken expression. "It's all right, Major, I understand. I have a lot less experience than you, and for all I know, you might do this with a different girl every week. I appreciate your honesty, but I am telling you that if I'd wanted to stop you last night I would have. You wouldn't have held me down."

"How the hell do you know that Nan?" Paul said with rueful tenderness which brought tears to Anne's eyes. She stepped forward and stood on tiptoe to brush her lips against his.

"Because that's not who you are, Major. I may be very young and very inexperienced, but I'm not stupid. If I'd let you, you'd have walked out of there yesterday into that blizzard rather than risk my reputation. You're not a man to deliberately hurt a woman."

"That doesn't mean that I can't," Paul said quietly, tracing the delicate curve of her face with his finger. "I surprised myself last night in more ways than one. But even though your virginity is surprisingly still intact, Nan, if anybody realised what we'd been doing it would ruin you, so don't hang a halo on me, I don't deserve it."

Anne smiled through her tears. "A halo? I don't think it would suit you, Paul."

"Nan, in all my twenty-six years I've never met a woman like you, but I don't have anything to give you except trouble. I'll be away from here in a few months, and the chances are we won't see each other again, although I'm never going to forget you. But what happens between now and then is up to you. If it will make this easier for you I will cry off your ball and stay away from any event you're likely to attend. That's not what I want to do. I'd like to dance with you and ride to hounds with you and pretend for a while that we can have more than we can. But not if it is going to cause you problems or upset you in any way. I don't know what you want, you'll have to tell me. And don't be polite about it, we've gone well beyond that. What do you want me to do, girl of my heart?"

Anne was unexpectedly touched by his direct sincerity. "I don't want you to walk away," she said quietly, reaching up to caress his face. "I don't understand how this happened, or why I feel the way I do, and I suppose it is hard for me to feel guilty about your wife when I don't know her. But I would like to spend time with you, for those few weeks. My family is going to push me into marriage very soon with a man that I may not even like that much, because they think it will settle me down, and I hate it. I certainly don't feel guilty about him, whoever he is."

"Good, you've nothing to feel guilty about. I'll be careful, I promise, I'm not going to damage your reputation. And I need to tell you, that at the end of this time, I will put my wife and children first, I'm not going to lie to you. If that makes a difference..."

"Is this a conversation you usually have?"

"I've never had this conversation before, because I've never needed to."

The stark admission froze Anne for a moment, and she wondered if she had misunderstood him, but the expression on his face told her that she had not. "I would never ask that of you," she said quietly. "My word on it."

"Thank you, I trust you. Now, kiss me again, bonny lass, and then let's get you home, after which, I intend to make the officers and men of the 115th foot wish that they had never been born."

As Paul moved to lift her into the saddle, he said suddenly:

"I don't, by the way." Anne looked at him enquiringly and he grinned. "Do this with a different girl every week. I'm very picky."

Anne laughed. "I believe you, Major. You'd have prepared that speech better if you did."

"That speech was going fine. It would have worked on most women, trust me."

"It sounds as though you would know," Anne said sweetly, and walked Bella forward into the white, sparkling snow.

***

Paul delivered Anne back to her grooms who accepted her return with an insouciance which told him that they had expected their young mistress to take care of herself and return in one piece. Presumably they were used to her, but Paul was not, and he wondered, riding cautiously away from her, if the husband they found for her would have any idea what he was taking on with this extraordinary young woman. He was fiercely envious of the man who would share his life with Anne Howard.

Paul arrived in barracks over an hour later, having given Rufus an easy ride, careful of his legs in the snow. The horse was surprisingly well for his night's ordeal and acting on instinct Paul followed his hoof prints in the snow to find out where he had been. The results were interesting. He rode into the stable and dismounted, handing the reins to a groom with a word of thanks. There was no sign of life out on the pure white snow of the parade ground. Paul walked over and tested the depth. It was a pleasing eight or nine inches, with an underlying layer of ice.

Paul walked over to the stores, nodded to the elderly sergeant who acted as store master, and walked through to the back. He was aware of the old man's puzzled regard as he lifted a rifle down from the rack, and checked it, then collected some ammunition. Standing in the doorway he loaded swiftly, observing the surprised expression on the store master's face at the speed, although Grogan or any one of his riflemen would have considered it slow. Nodding again, he walked out of the store and across to the mess. It was warm inside, and Paul leaned the rifle up against the inside of the door and surveyed his officers benignly.

There were currently seven of them. Paul had recently been informed that new officers had been commissioned to make up the full complement, but none had yet arrived. Lieutenant Carlyon was not present, presumably at home still suffering from the after-effects of having a tooth drawn, and Paul was glad, as it absolved him of any possible hint of favouritism. Captain Moore was lounging closest to the fire, with his boots on the fender. Beside him sat Lieutenants Bagnall, Walsh and Hendry, with a pack of cards strewn across the table before them. The three young ensigns were sitting further away from the fire. As Paul entered, all heads turned but nobody moved.

"Don't get up," Paul said gently, and every man scrambled hastily to his feet, saluting, Moore taking the longest. Paul returned the salute and indicated that they should sit. Ensign Franklin was staring at him, wide-eyed.

"What happened to your head, sir?"

"An accident on my way here yesterday."

"Were you caught in that storm?" Moore said, far too casually.

"In a manner of speaking. Somebody threw a rock at my head on my way here and I ended up on the road with a twisted knee and no horse. I thought Rufus would have made his way back here, but presume he didn't, or you'd have sent somebody out to look for me."

Walsh looked at the others. "No, sir. Was he…did you get him back?"

"Oh yes. He must have been running loose all night in that storm, and then made his way back to find me. Fortunately, I found a shepherd's hut to spend the night in, because I couldn't have walked far in that weather."

"Thank God for that, sir," Bagnall said heartily. Paul looked around at the seven men, noting the obvious discomfort of the three ensigns.

"No drill this morning?" he asked, still pleasantly.

"No, sir. Parade ground snowed under."

"Never mind, I don't suppose it will take long to clear."

Paul allowed his eyes to wander from one face to another, observing that young Franklin, who seemed more perceptive than the others, looked terrified.

Paul picked up the rifle.

"Can any of you load one of these?" he enquired.

"I know how, sir," Hendry said. "Not often had to do it, and of course our men use muskets."

"I've found it useful to learn both. I've half a dozen riflemen in the light company, and they'd laugh at how slow I am. Still, I think I can probably engage to reload fast enough to put a ball through every one of you fucking liars before any of you could get out of the room. Who wants to go first?"

He lifted the rifle and aimed it squarely at Walsh's knee. Walsh gave a nervous laugh.

"Shouldn't wave that thing around in here, sir. I mean I know it's not loaded, but…"

Paul lowered the rifle and fired. The shot hit the floor between Walsh's feet and the man yelled and leaped backwards, almost stumbling into the fire in his haste. Paul reloaded. Nobody else moved.

"Rufus' saddle and tack were bone dry this morning when he turned up looking for me," he said quietly. "So I followed his tracks. Of course, the ones he made yesterday would have been covered up. But this morning they led all the way from his stable. He turned up here yesterday, just as I thought, and you all decided to have a jolly good laugh about me getting thrown on the road and stuck out in that storm. And if I'd frozen to death in a ditch, you'd have shaken your heads and silently thanked God that there was nobody here to kick your lazy, useless arses into action any further. And you know what? That is not what has pissed me off. What has really made me fucking angry is that this morning, you saddled my horse and sent him off on his own, to God knows where, in weather likely to cause him to break his legs, just so that I wouldn't be able to work out what you'd done. You're bloody lucky that he's got more brain than you have and managed to get to me in one piece, because if I'd had to shoot him with a broken leg, I'd have shot you as well. If you want to come after me, you're welcome to try, I'm big enough to take care of myself. But when you turn on my animals, you've crossed a line and I intend to make your lives a bloody misery from now until they either post me somewhere else or you sell out."

Paul turned, opened the door, and roared:

"Sergeant-Major Holland. Where the fuck are you?"

There was a long, painful silence. Eventually the door to the nearest barrack block opened and Sergeant-Major Holland appeared, stuffing his feet into his boots and pulling up his trousers. "Sir?" he said, sounding incredulous.

"Battalion on the parade ground, Holland. Now!"

The sergeant stared out at the pure white expanse. "But sir…"

"You've got ten minutes, Sergeant-Major, and you ought to be able to do it in five, you're a bloody disgrace!"

Holland saluted. "Yes, sir."

He jogged off and Paul turned to find a private standing before him, obviously dressed for sentry duty. He saluted and handed Paul a letter. "This just came for you, sir."

"Thank you." Paul gave a brief smile and opened the letter. He scanned it and gave an appreciative grin. It was a very civil note from Lady Howard, thanking him for his assistance in getting her step-daughter to shelter during the storm and inviting him to dine before the ball on Thursday. Paul wondered exactly what Anne had told her. He looked up.

"Will you wait a moment, Private? I'd like to reply immediately, and you can send one of the grooms with it."

"Yes, sir."

Paul looked back at his officers. They were still rooted to the spot, staring at him. "I want that parade ground cleared," he said. "From barracks wall to barracks wall. And when you get to the bottom of the snow, I want the ice chipped away as well. It will be fit for use by tomorrow, and you'll all be nice and warm by then."

"Us, sir?" Bagnall stammered.

"You, Mr Bagnall. Each and every one of you. Set your men a good example for once in your lives. Go and get a spade each and get digging alongside them. If I see you stop for anything longer than a piss, I'm going to shoot you for mutiny. And before you open your mouth, Walsh, I know your father is high up at Horse Guards, and if he turns up here whining about it, I'll shoot him as well. I can make it look like a training accident, and nobody will ever know." Paul surveyed the seven men with merciless eyes. "The reason you've got four companies of lazy useless gobshites is because they're led by lazy useless gobshites. I intend to amend that, starting from now. Get moving!"

Paul walked through the mess room and into his office, motioning to the sentry to follow him. Reaching for a pen and a sheet of paper he seated himself at his desk and wrote a polite acceptance to Lady Howard. He folded and sealed it, then looked up at the sentry with a pleasant smile and caught what was undoubtedly a grin, hastily wiped. Paul, who was missing his men sorely, responded.

"Don't say it, Private," he said quietly, and the man laughed aloud.

"No, sir." He saluted and turned go, then turned back. "Sir?"

"Yes, Private?"

"It was Dobbins, sir. First company. He was boasting about it in barracks last night." He indicated Paul's head.

"Thank you, Private. Name?"

"Barforth, sir. Same company."

Paul studied him and made a guess. "Former NCO?"

"Yes, sir. Demoted over a year ago."

"Why?"

"Insubordination, sir. Demotion and thirty lashes."

"What did you do?" Paul asked, getting up.

"Called an officer a twat, sir."

Paul gave him a sharp glance. "Why?"

"Because he was a twat, sir," Barforth said placidly.

Paul laughed aloud. "You make me feel very homesick for my light company, Private. Take that and get it sent and then come out to the parade ground, will you?"

"Yes, sir."

Paul walked out. The men were assembled, after a fashion. Few of them were properly dressed or armed, and more than one was visibly drunk. None of them had expected him to be back today, officers or men. Paul looked at Sergeant-Major Holland.

"Pathetic." Paul stood in silence for a moment, his eyes moving over the parade ground. "I see that I wasn't expected back here today," he said in matter-of-fact tones, his voice carrying easily on the still, cold air. "Sorry to disappoint you, lads, but if the French, the Poles, the Maratha and Lord bloody Nelson can't kill me, I don't think you were in with much of a chance. Dobbins, get over here, now!"

A tall, thin faced private of around forty approached at something like a run. He was looking slightly sick and was unsteady on his feet. He stopped before Paul and gave a shaky salute.

"You're not looking well, Dobbins. Celebrating your success last night, were you?"

"Sir."

"You have my sympathy. I've got a headache, and you've got a stomach-ache. Or at least, you fucking will have."

Paul punched him hard in the midriff and the man doubled up with a groan. Paul caught hold of his hair and hauled his head up to look him in the face. "That was in place of the court martial that could have hanged you for assaulting an officer, Dobbins. Normally I'd think twice about hitting a man in your state, but it's a pleasure to make an exception in your case. If you ever throw another rock at me, or even look at me the wrong way, you'd better keep running because I promise you, I will beat the living shit out of you

154

before I put you on a charge. Now get to the stores, get spades and picks and start clearing this ground. And move fast because anybody left without a tool will be using their bloody bare hands."

He released Dobbins and turned to Private Barforth who had reappeared. "Private Barforth. You have just been promoted to battalion sergeant-major, don't let me down. I'll find you some stripes. In fact, you can take Holland's, he isn't going to be needing them any more. While this lot are working off their excesses, take a couple of men and go through the barracks, every block. Remove any illegal grog and get those women out of there, starting with the one I suspect you'll find in Private Holland's bed. Make sure they get home safely, don't just let them wander off in this weather."

Barforth saluted smartly. "Yes, sir."

"You'll be delighted to know that in the spirit of fostering good relations, your officers have decided to come out and help your men clear the ground. They're just putting their boots on. I'll go and hurry them along, then I'm going for breakfast. I'm bloody starving, which is probably why I'm in a particularly bad mood."

"Hadn't noticed, sir."

"You are going to be an excellent NCO, Sergeant-Major Barforth. Now piss off and let me eat."

***

Anne's stepmother received her favourite stepchild back from her night's ordeal with practical good sense, hot baths, and a vague sense that she had spent most of the night at Molly Parsons cottage, thanks to the new major of the 115th who had escorted her there. Anne knew that her stepmother had heard some of the stories of what was going on at the regiment from her daughters' former nurse, whose nephew was in barracks, and Lady Howard was grateful to the officer for his prompt and discreet assistance. She uttered a mild reproof to Anne for riding out in a snowstorm. Anne was not surprised. With her stepdaughter about to be formally launched into local society, and several wealthy or influential gentlemen lined up as possible husbands, the last thing Sir Matthew and his wife wanted was any whiff of scandal to touch the new debutante.

Anne had chosen her own gown for the ball, an elegant high waisted creation in pure white, threaded through with silver, which displayed her figure to advantage. She wore a simple string of pearls with matching earrings, and her hair was dressed high on her head. When she was younger, Anne had wept over the stubborn refusal of her smooth dark hair to remain in fashionable curls, but now she preferred her own style which highlighted the shape of her face and the elegant curve of her neck. Fully dressed, she turned to her stepmother. "Will I do?"

"You look beautiful. Far too beautiful, you are making me cry."

Anne gave her a hug. "What a ridiculous reason to cry," she said affectionately. "Never mind, before the end of the evening I will have said or done something highly unsuitable and you will be so cross with me that you will forget your lapse into sentimentality, dear Stepmamma."

"Almost certainly. And don't call me that."

They had invited a select number of people to dine before the ball, including Anne's principal suitors and their families. In the drawing room Anne stood beside her father and stepmother to greet the arrivals, most of whom she had known all her life. Julian Carew was the eldest son of the local squire, condescending to a daughter of the middle classes because of their debts and crumbling ancestral home. Samson Battersley, the cotton spinner and John Henshaw of the breweries both sought an alliance of local financial giants. Anne greeted them all pleasantly, and felt her pulse quicken at the sight of Robert Carlyon's red head, not because she was particularly interested in either his political connections or his person, but because he was accompanied by his commanding officer, tall and easy in his dress uniform, who bowed over Anne's hand with commendable aplomb.

"Miss Howard. I hope you are fully recovered?"

"I am, thank you, sir."

"I hope you will save a dance for me later."

"I should enjoy that."

Paul moved on into the room, and Harriet looked at Anne. "Why did I gain the impression that your gallant rescuer was fat and forty?" she enquired.

"Probably because most majors are. He's quite young for a major, I think."

"Plenty of money?"

"I think so, although I don't think that entirely explains his success. I think he killed a lot of Maratha in India, and then a number of Frenchmen in Naples."

"From what Moira tells me, he's working on killing the 115th," her stepmother said tartly, and Anne gave a choke of laughter. Her maid had enlivened a tedious morning of needlework by describing the scenes on the parade ground at the 115th, and Anne, who knew more about the events leading up to that day than she was prepared to share, thought that Paul van Daan had not improved his popularity in the regiment. If he cared, he gave no sign of it.

As a married man without a wife present, it was Major van Daan's duty to entertain whichever female was left without a partner, and Anne concealed a smile when she saw that he had been partnered with Miss Carew, an angular spinster of forty who kept house for her brother, Sir Giles. He was placed opposite Anne at table, and Anne watched him covertly during dinner and decided that his ability to charm was not limited to pretty young females in a snowstorm. Anne was seated between Robert Carlyon and John Henshaw, the two gentlemen most favoured as possible suitors by her father, and she divided her attention evenly between them, and wondered what on earth Paul van Daan was finding to discuss so pleasantly with the vinegary Miss Carew.

The ballroom at Helton Ridge was situated on the first floor, and at ten o'clock Lady Howard and her younger step-daughter stood at the top to receive their arriving guests. Anne, looking out on a sea of faces, had long since ceased to know what she was saying as she murmured pleasantries to everybody and was thankful when Harriet finally released her to go into the ballroom. There was no shortage of partners for a girl with her fortune and she danced with Robert Carlyon, Julian Carew, John Henshaw and then miserably with Samson Battersley, who was not a natural dancer and could not easily manage conversation during the set.

When Anne returned to her stepmother, she was greeted by two of her contemporaries, Hope Battersley and Lucy Grey.

"You look lovely, Nan. That dress!"

"Thank you," Anne said, surreptitiously checking that Mr Battersley had done no damage to her hem or her slippers.

"Lieutenant Carlyon seems very taken," Hope said archly. "My brother will be jealous."

"Mr Carlyon is all very well," Lucy said. "But my dear – have you noticed his friend?"

Hope giggled. "Lucy – he is married."

"More's the pity. Did you notice that he even managed to wring a smile out of old Miss Carew at dinner?"

"Look, he's coming over," Hope whispered, and Paul approached with a slight bow and smiled down at Anne.

"I believe you promised me a dance, Miss Howard."

He held out a hand and Anne allowed him to lead her onto the dance floor. Despite his height and military bearing, he danced with assurance, and Anne relaxed into the set and began to enjoy herself.

"How are you finding Yorkshire, Major van Daan?"

"Better now," he said with a smile. "How are you enjoying your party?"

Anne lowered her eyes demurely. "Better now," she said. "At least you do not tread on my feet."

He laughed aloud. "Poor Mr Battersley, I feared for his life, you looked very fierce. What a terrible flirt you are, Miss Howard, I've been watching you."

Anne raised her eyes to his face. "Major, how you can say that? I am a novice beside you."

"For a beginner you are doing remarkably well," Paul said. "Mr Henshaw was dazzled at dinner."

"Mr Henshaw almost dozed off at dinner, he would rather be back at the brewery. And you should not have been eavesdropping, sir, you should have been attending to your own dinner partner."

"I was, she is an interesting lady. I couldn't help looking at you, though." As the set brought them together, he said softly:

"You look beautiful. I would hardly have recognised you in this setting."

Anne looked up into his eyes. "I was probably not at my best the last time we met."

"On the contrary, I think I prefer you that way."

Anne felt a blush scorch her cheeks and she met his eyes. "That wasn't fair."

"It really wasn't, I'm sorry, I won't do it again in public. You're an excellent dancer, Miss Howard."

"Thank you, so are you. I don't know why, but I didn't expect you to enjoy dancing."

"It might surprise you to know that I was brought up as a very respectable English gentleman and learned all the necessary skills, I don't know what went wrong. But my enjoyment does depend on my partner."

Anne had regained her composure and her complexion. "Should I take that as a compliment, sir?"

"It is probably the best I can do in this setting." He lowered his voice. "If we were alone, I could be a lot more specific."

"I know you can, Major," Anne said ironically, and he laughed aloud at her effrontery as the set spun her away from him.

**

After a while, the charm of the evening began to pall. Paul danced with a variety of ladies and uttered too many platitudes to shy young ladies in their first season, or flirtatious young matrons missing the freedom of their youth. He made civil conversation with his officers, who had barely spoken about anything other than their duties since the previous week. They were stilted and awkward with him, and Paul thought ruefully that he would need to make an effort to be more human with them. He had lost his temper very thoroughly and it had achieved his immediate aim, but he could not lead men who were this terrified of him.

Making an excuse, Paul removed himself quietly from the ballroom and went out through a side door into the extensive gardens for a stroll. To his right the smooth lawns stretched either side of the drive. To his left was a brick archway lit by pale moonlight, and Paul went through it and found himself in a kitchen garden with neat beds intended for vegetables, salads and herbs. At this time of year, they looked bare, although the snow had cleared during the past week.

Paul had thought himself alone, and he had almost reached the far end of the walled garden when voices made him turn. Two people were standing further along the next path, and the glow of the girl's silver gauze skirts was the only thing he could see clearly, but her voice was immediately recognisable, and his pulse quickened a little.

"You've misunderstood, Mr Carew, I came out alone for some fresh air, but I'm going back inside now."

The man said something inaudible and Paul heard the sound of a scuffle. He sped up then heard a ringing slap. Paul winced and grinned. She had intended that to hurt.

"Let go of me, Julian," the girl said, and she had dropped any pretence at formality. "I'm fairly sure you're drunk, but I'm not impressed."

158

Paul reflected with some amusement that this was a girl who took a different approach to an over-familiar drunk than his wife and spent a brief, pleasurable moment imagining Anne Howard dealing with Captain Tyler. He stepped forward from the shadows. "Good evening, Miss Howard," he said pleasantly. "Were you leaving, Carew? You can trust me to escort Miss Howard back to her stepmother."

Carew hesitated. Paul could see him weighing the wisdom of holding his ground. He realised that Carew was still holding Anne's slender wrist and was surprised by a spurt of pure rage at the sight of his hands on her.

"Let her go. Now. I can see that you're considering whether it would impress her if you hit me, but I wouldn't if I were you. It's hard to be dignified when you're flat on your back in the cabbage patch. Get yourself back into the house and sober up before I throw you in the duck pond. I suggest you come back and apologise in the morning when you've realised what an arse you've made of yourself. Move."

Carew glared at him, then bowed stiffly to the girl and stalked off towards the house. Paul looked down at Anne Howard, who was rearranging her spangled scarf over her arms with alarming composure.

"Are you all right?"

"Yes, thank you. I suppose it was my own fault for slipping out here alone, he probably thought I wanted him to follow me."

"I rather think you should be entitled to walk in the gardens of your own home, Miss Howard. Why did you?"

"I had to get away for a moment, or I'd have screamed," Anne said frankly.

"A surfeit of suitors?" Paul asked gravely, and Anne laughed.

"I was losing track of names," she explained. "One has to make allowances for poor Julian. I expect his father told him to make sure of me if he could, and besides, I think he actually quite likes me."

"I can't blame him for that," Paul remarked, drawing her hand through his arm and beginning to stroll along the path again. "But he isn't particularly good at it. Perhaps he'd have done better if he were sober."

"Possibly. Although I doubt it. I'm a little on my guard this week."

Paul looked down at her, his eyes lingering on the curve of her throat as she tilted her head back to look up at him. It was a cold, clear night, with the moon spilling bright white light over the garden, and the silver dress had a soft glow all its own.

"That's a pity," he said. "I was just wondering if I could persuade you to spend half an hour with me in the rose arbour."

"It's very cold," Anne said. Paul's eyes flickered over her. The enormity of her self-possession amused him.

"You need to trust me, Miss Howard, that you wouldn't notice that after a very few minutes."

"Major – you are completely outrageous as you very well know."

They had reached the far end of the garden and Paul took her hand and pulled her into the darkness beside one of the brick outbuildings. "Stand still.

This is not the time to make a mess of your hair or your gown, which is a shame because I'd like to. But while I am considering how best to find an opportunity to get you alone properly again, this will have to do."

Paul kissed her hard, his desire suddenly fierce and urgent in a way that caught him completely unawares. He wanted to pick her up and carry her to some sheltered place and make love to her. He wanted her with a hunger that had no place in his ordered life.

He was married and this girl was seventeen and a virgin and the daughter of his host. Paul lifted his head and took a deep steadying breath, looking down into the liquid darkness of those extraordinary eyes.

"Anne Howard, what is it about you? God knows I've kissed some pretty girls in my time, but you have a very strange effect on my ability to think straight. They are going to be looking for you, and you absolutely cannot be found out here like this with me."

Anne reached up and placed her palm against his cheek in a gesture he found painfully natural. "No. I must go. Thank you for rescuing me, Paul."

Paul watched her walk away towards the house and wanted to call her back with an intense longing, which was completely new to him.

***

There was an air of frozen civility in barracks. Since the day the officers and men of the 115th had spent long hours clearing snow and ice from their parade ground, the atmosphere was quiet and strained although discipline had improved notably. There were no further incidents of drunkenness in barracks and the officers performed their duties reliably, albeit with no sense of enjoyment. The carpenters had arrived to start work on essential repairs, and Paul had set them to work first on the officers' quarters and the mess. He wanted his officers to have reason to remain in barracks, and he wanted to move there himself. He had found, with the help of Sergeant Barforth, two men of the second company who could cook, and installed them in charge of the mess. As soon as the repairs were finished, he hoped to establish a custom of his officers dining together each day. Discipline had improved, but morale was appalling.

Paul was surprised to receive an invitation to dine from an acquaintance he had met at the Howard ball. Captain Moore and Lieutenant Bagnall were also invited, and Paul accepted in the hope of thawing the atmosphere slightly. He was surprised and delighted, on arrival in the elegant drawing room, to find that the Howards were guests. Sir Matthew was friendly and welcoming, and his younger daughter offered him her hand with a charming lack of formality.

"Major van Daan, you're still with us. Isn't your wife missing you?"

"Probably not. She is being thoroughly spoiled by family and friends and is enjoying the comforts of home without the rigours of army life."

"Not so rigorous, eh, Major?" Bagnall said with a laugh. "Plenty of balls and pretty girls, what?"

160

"As you say," Paul said.

Anne Howard was watching his face. "And has that been true of your service overseas, Major?" she enquired.

"I've served in India, Naples and Copenhagen, Miss Howard, but all during campaigning, where the social life is limited."

"Aren't you due a rest, Major?"

"Perhaps that's why they sent me to the 115th."

"No, I think that was to give the 110th a rest," Anne said, and Paul laughed aloud at her impertinence.

"They say that Naples is very gay," Bagnall persisted. He appeared completely oblivious to Paul's distaste for his conversation although Paul thought that Anne was very aware of it. "All those Italian beauties. And in India, I hear that the officers live a life of luxury, although I believe the society is not of the best."

Paul met the girl's sparkling black eyes. "How did you find the society, sir?" she asked.

"It was definitely below standard, ma'am, but I was there in '03 and spent much of my time with Maratha cavalry trying to kill me," Paul said apologetically.

"Aye, so you did. Damned bad affair, from what I've heard. Excuse me, miss, soldiers' language. Were you with Wellesley there?"

"I was," Paul said, wishing he could think of a way to change the subject.

"I've not seen any action myself. Hope to soon, though. Can't wait to get a crack at the French." Bagnall laughed. He had a particularly irritating laugh, which reminded Paul unaccountably of a donkey. "Mind you, Major, would have thought you'd be better off fighting the French than throwing your weight around in barracks. Men don't like it. Officers don't like it. Bad for morale." The braying laugh came again. "Reckon you spent too much time in India. Gone native and forgotten how English officers behave."

The sudden rush of anger surprised Paul. For the first time in more than two years he was back in India with the heat and the dust and the metallic smell of blood as he knelt beside Johnny Wheeler outside the medical tent. He could remember the piles of dead Highlanders, the endless burials and the soft crying of some of the women who had lost their men. He remembered the mangled corpse of Private Bryant and the lifeless face of Captain Mason, and he wanted very badly to hit Bagnall, who had never seen a friend cut down beside him, never felt the pain of loss as his men were lowered into largely unmarked graves.

The dark-haired girl beside him said quietly:

"Mr Bagnall – please go away."

Bagnall muttered what might have been an apology and moved out of Paul's view. The girl stopped a servant and took two glasses of champagne from his tray. She handed one to Paul and then she stepped deliberately between him and the rest of the room.

"It's all right," she said quietly. "Think about something else for a moment. He is a very stupid man and not worth your attention."

161

Paul drank, and did so. He thought about the taste of her lips in the moonlit garden and the feeling of her body under his hands in the shepherd's hut. Gradually his pulse returned to normal and he was calm again. Anne watched him with steady dark eyes, and he had the sense that she was protecting him, until he recovered.

"Are you all right?" she asked softly.

Paul nodded, his eyes on her face. "Yes, I am now. Thank you. How in God's name did you know?"

Anne shrugged her shoulders. "I don't know," she said. "I just knew you were hating the conversation. It's all right, you don't need to talk about it."

Paul's breathing was back to normal again. "It happened after Assaye," he said. He owed her an explanation. "I lost so many men. But I usually have it very well under control. I've fought in other actions since, so it didn't occur to me that this could still happen. I suppose it was Bagnall, braying like a donkey about going to war. I'd like to have him under my command in the field for a week or two. Although I'd be worried about the men under him..."

"Yes, it would hardly be fair on them. Lieutenant Carlyon tells me that you have a very distinguished career for one so young. I don't imagine you achieve that without seeing death."

"I saw death from a very young age. But Assaye was different. I suppose it was because I had a command by then. They were my men. I gave the orders to send them into action. I sent them to their deaths."

"That must be incredibly hard. Far harder, I would think, than flinging oneself into the breach, which really when you think about it, any idiot can do. Even Lieutenant Bagnall."

Paul gave a splutter of laughter. "You are actually as rude as I am," he said. "Nan – thank you."

His hostess stopped beside them. "I see you are already acquainted with Miss Howard, Major. Will you take her into dinner?"

"I should be delighted, ma'am."

Paul took Anne's arm to lead her in. As he held her chair, the silk scarf slipped from her shoulders and he caught it and restored it, his fingers brushing her bare skin. Anne turned her head to look up at him with a quick smile and Paul felt a sudden shock of emotion, which was completely unfamiliar to him. He sat down and looked at her and the black eyes looked back at him steadily.

"Major?"

"I'm staring, aren't I? I am sorry. I was just thinking that I hope you choose the right one. Whoever he is will be the luckiest bastard in the world. And now we need to think of a suitably entertaining topic of conversation before I give in to temptation and kiss you right now. Can you come up with anything because I'm struggling?"

Anne gave a gurgle of laughter. "I shall try," she said. "How are the 115th doing now? Other than the unpleasant Mr Bagnall, since it is clear that he still needs some work. Did you really threaten to shoot your officers that day?"

Paul's lips twitched. "Did Carlyon tell you that?"

162

"No. My old nurse, Moira, has a nephew in the regiment." The girl's black eyes were sparkling with amusement. "You have certainly been providing the neighbourhood with food for gossip, sir."

"It was not my aim. There has been dishonesty and incompetence on a grand scale, and the conditions the men were expected to live in...."

"I don't think any of the other officers much cared about how their men lived, Major."

"Probably not, but if they were expecting those men to stand beside them on a battlefield they might think again."

Anne sipped her wine. "So, did you?" she asked.

"Threaten to shoot my officers?" Paul grinned. "I'm afraid I did. When I realised what they'd done with Rufus I lost my temper quite thoroughly. It's usually the job of my sergeant and my officers to prevent that, but I'd nobody to intervene. It's a shame you weren't there, lass. You did a very good job yourself just now."

"No, after what they did, I'd have handed you the gun."

"They have been better behaved since," Paul said. "But they're not happy. To be honest, I came tonight in an attempt to lighten the atmosphere in barracks. They're all walking around on tiptoe and they flinch every time I speak to them. My cursed temper. I keep telling myself I'm not going to do it again..."

"Is this a recurring problem?" Anne enquired gently, and he smiled ruefully.

"It is. And there's usually a good reason for it, but it's not necessarily the best way of handling things and I recently found myself in a fair bit of trouble because of it. I am trying."

"You have my sympathy, I've a horrible temper."

Paul stared at her for a moment and then smiled. "Yes, I think I caught a glimpse of it."

"You did. You retrieved your position beautifully, Major, it must be that military training."

"I know when to retreat, lass." Paul sighed. "Captain Moore wants to arrange a series of parades, and I suppose I shall have to give in."

"What's the objection?" Anne enquired, smiling at the footman as he set a plate before her.

"Well, first of all, I shall have to be pleasant to people, of course," Paul said, and enjoyed her laughter. "Secondly, I would be personally embarrassed to put this sorry bunch on show in the condition that they're in at the moment. It takes them so long to form square that I frequently doze off, and I swear half of them don't know their right from their left. If they had to do that under fire or with cavalry bearing down on them, they'd be dead in ten minutes. And what bothers me is they don't realise it."

"Have you had to do that under fire?"

Paul caught a note of concern in her tone and tried not to be pleased about it. "More than once. And you need to believe me when I say that is when those hours on the training ground actually matter. I don't give a damn how

163

good they look on parade." Paul thought about it. "Unless it will annoy my fellow officers," he amended.

"There's a story there, Major."

Paul told her about Dublin and Captain Tyler, and Anne laughed so much that he became aware that it was attracting attention. He realised that he would not have told that story to any other female of his acquaintance, but he had suspected that this girl would enjoy it and he had clearly been right.

"Oh dear, I'm making them stare," Anne said finally, wiping her eyes discreetly with a lacy handkerchief. "It is not ladylike to laugh like that in public, I shall get a scolding."

"I'm sorry."

"No, it was worth it. I do hope you have a parade. I don't usually attend such things, but I would like to see you about your work."

"I'll do it, if you'll attend."

"I will, I promise. And you must know that most of Thorndale will not know that they are doing it wrong as long as their coats are red and their buttons shiny. Do you hunt, Major?"

"I grew up in Leicestershire, so yes. I'd like to see you on horseback, without the snow."

"Then you shall have the opportunity on Tuesday, I shall speak to the Master and ensure you're invited."

"I look forward to it, Miss Howard."

***

After the miserable winter, spring came early in Yorkshire that year. Anne had not looked forward to her debut into society, knowing that her affectionate but traditional father saw it purely as a means to find a husband for his wayward daughter. Anne was not ready for the stifling confines of marriage, and until meeting Paul van Daan she had dreaded the idea of the marriage bed. While not revising her views on allowing Mr Battersley or Mr Henshaw to make love to her, she concluded that in this matter, the choice of partner made a great deal of difference.

Anne saw a good deal of Paul in public. She knew that he had reluctantly decided that socialising with his officers was going to be a necessary part of improving their morale. In the narrow confines of Thorndale society, the regimental officers were invited everywhere, and more often than not, Paul and Anne were guests at the same functions. Anne watched with amused admiration, as having compelled his officers' obedience, Paul set himself deliberately to earn their loyalty.

Anne quickly realised that socially Paul van Daan came from a different world. She had only been to London once, when she was fifteen, to see the sights. She remembered walking in the park, watching the upper echelons of London society riding or driving in the Row, and she had wondered in passing if the ladies and gentlemen of the aristocracy and the Ton were so very different to the squires and mill owners of her own small town. Since then, Anne had spread her wings a little at assemblies in York and Harrogate, where she had the opportunity to dance and converse with gentlemen far above her socially. Anne was cynically aware that her beauty was a passport to acceptance in the ballroom and she never felt overwhelmed or particularly impressed by her company, but she knew none of the elegant young men who flirted with her on the dance floor would consider her a suitable wife.

Anne suspected that the Thorndale social season would generally have bored Paul, but he appeared to be enjoying himself immensely. Local ladies, writing for gossip to their London friends and family, quickly discovered that Paul's mother had been a viscount's daughter, his sister-in-law was a cousin of the Cravens and his father was considered one of the wealthiest men in the City. Nothing more was needed to ensure that Major van Daan was a guest at every ball and reception, and Thorndale approved his easy manners and noted that he never behaved as though he considered himself above his company.

Anne was popular with the officers which made it easy to spend time with Paul. While her stepmother kept a careful eye on her suitors to ensure that they kept well within the bounds of propriety, it would not occur to her that Anne was in danger from a married man. Paul and Anne took shameless advantage of the fact, meeting regularly on her early morning, solitary rides up on the moor, and finding opportunities to be alone whenever they could. Anne was touched and at times exasperated at his insistence on keeping strictly within the boundaries he had set for them during that first night. When she was in his arms, she wished his scruples to the devil. When she was alone again, she was grateful and a little guilty at how hard she sometimes pushed him to break his promise. Within his self-imposed limits, they were lovers, and Anne had never been so happy in her life.

Anne had always been sceptical about falling in love. From childhood, she had known that, like her sister, she would be expected to marry the man her father chose for her, and although her independent nature rebelled at the idea, she had thought herself resigned to making the best of it. All her careful common sense seemed to have been swept away as she tumbled into love with a man completely out of her reach. Anne sleepwalked through the time they were apart and treasured every moment they were together. Paul van Daan made her laugh, made her think and made her feel in a way she had never thought possible.

Anne wondered sometimes how it was for him. He was nine years her senior with a wealth of experience that she lacked, yet it seemed at times as he rode beside her through the morning mist, or met her eyes across the dinner table, that this was more to him than just a pleasant interlude to relieve a boring assignment. Anne did not ask. It would not be fair to ask questions that he could not possibly answer. Whatever his feelings for her, he was an honourable man, and he would put his family first. There was no place for her in his future and when he left Anne would make the marriage expected of her, and try to make a success of it, although she suspected that the memory of his eyes and his smile and the sound of his voice would stay with her for the rest of her life.

Chapter Ten

The Howards attended the parade at the barracks in May and Anne graciously allowed Lieutenant Carlyon to be her escort for the occasion. Around her, the cream of Thorndale society murmured its surprise at the neat parade ground and freshly painted and repaired buildings. Drill was carried out in a manner which impressed everybody, and afterwards the men were rewarded with their own celebration in barracks, while the officers dined in state at the Assembly Rooms nearby and accepted the compliments of Thorndale's grandees at the improvement in the 115th.

Anne was standing beside Harriet on the balcony overlooking the crowded hall when Major van Daan appeared beside her. "Lady Howard. Miss Howard. I hope you're enjoying the evening."

"I am impressed, Major van Daan," Harriet said. "I suspect that this is all the result of a lot more hard work than one would imagine, and you have not had much support."

"I have, ma'am. It has just taken them some time to come around. If you will excuse me, I am deserting you for a while to see how the rest of the regiment is doing."

He smiled and bowed, and Anne said impulsively:

"May we come?"

Paul glanced quickly at her stepmother. "You may. I warn you they've been drinking, and I can't answer for the language you may hear. But if you would like to...?"

Anne looked at her stepmother. "Please?" she said.

"Very well. Just for a short time."

Paul led them through the back door and along to a side door of the barracks, then took them through into the officers' mess. They stood at the door watching. There was music here too, not the stately airs of the assembly rooms, but a fiddle playing dance tunes. They stood in the dark, watching the men of the regiment and their women dancing in the lamplight of the parade ground, and heard their raucous laughter and Anne found it suddenly and surprisingly infectious. She glanced at Paul's face and saw, with abrupt understanding, that this meant more to him than the champagne and compliments of the Assembly Rooms.

"Dobbins!" he called suddenly.

A man dancing past paused and looked up, surprised. "Sir?" He snapped to attention and saluted and Paul grinned.

"Is there a reason I'm dying of thirst over here?"

Dobbins hesitated. "There's only grog, sir. Or rum."

"What makes you think that's a problem? Get moving before I punch you again."

The man grinned and ran, returning with a brimming mug. Paul took it and raised it in salute, then drank. "Who's the lassie, Dobbins?"

"My girl, sir. Mary."

"Very pretty." Paul was smiling, watching as the man ran back to the plump fair-haired girl.

"You're not going to drink that, are you, sir?" a voice said beside him, and Paul looked around. His orderly removed the mug smoothly and offered a tray. Paul took two glasses of champagne and handed them to Lady Howard and Anne, then took a third.

"You have your uses, Jenson."

"I'm glad to hear that, sir. Aren't you supposed to be at the Assembly Rooms pretending to be a gentleman?"

"We have guests, Jenson, watch your mouth."

"So I see, sir. Welcome to the 115th, ma'am. Miss." Jenson glanced at Paul and grinned. "Although I think it's fair to say that the person here most likely to say the wrong thing..."

"If I say the wrong thing it'll be because you've driven me to it. Lady Howard, Miss Howard, this is my orderly, Private Freddie Jenson. He's from my own regiment, the 110th which is why he has no sense of propriety and a mouth on him. Going smoothly, Jenson?"

"Yes, sir. Barforth's a good lad, knows his work, he'll keep them in order. Which is why you could safely return to the Assembly Rooms if you wanted."

"Are you trying to get rid of me?"

"Just reminding you of where you're supposed to be, sir, I know how you forget." Jenson glanced at Anne. "You could do with your wife here to keep you in order."

Anne managed not to laugh at the pointed reminder. She had seen the young, lame private several times from a distance, in attendance on Paul, and had asked about his disability, but she was intrigued by this glimpse of Paul's relationship with his own men, and Jenson's freedom of manner suggested an informality which she found very endearing.

"Jenson, we both know that if my wife was here, she would have sneaked off by now carefully avoiding both social occasions." Paul smiled at Anne. "Rowena hates parties of all kinds."

167

"Does she? I wonder if it is because she spends her time wondering what you are likely to say or do next, it must be a worry for her. Have you been with him a long time, Private Jenson?"

"Yes, miss, since Assaye. We were both wounded, and we practised walking together. The major is better at it than I am now, mind."

Anne smiled at him. "You do very well, Private. It must take an incredible amount of patience and courage to learn to walk all over again, I'm not sure I could do it."

Jenson looked startled. "It wasn't that easy, miss," he admitted. "But well worth it. And the major taught me to ride, which turned out to be surprisingly easy."

"Did you grow up on a farm?"

"No, miss. I was a town boy, from Liverpool. I'd no experience with horses but it turned out I'd a knack with them."

"I hope he's good to you, then, or you'll be running off to the cavalry. Tell me about Liverpool, I've never been there."

***

Paul watched as they talked, enjoying the slightly dazzled expression on his orderly's face. Sir Matthew Howard's younger daughter had a gift for putting people at their ease and she did not seem to mind using it with her social inferiors. Paul looked at Lady Howard and saw that she was watching her step-daughter with resigned affection, which suggested that it was not unusual for Anne to strike up a conversation with a groom or coach driver.

Eventually, Jenson appeared to remember his duty, and collected the empty champagne glasses. They watched the dancers for a while longer and Paul tried hard not to spend the time gazing at Anne in case something in his face betrayed his thoughts. Finally, her stepmother touched her arm. "We should go, Nan."

"Yes. Thank you for bringing us, Major. It's good to see the other side of the regiment." Anne smiled at Private Jenson, who was waiting respectfully by the door. "It's nice to have met you, Private Jenson. Take care of him."

"I will, miss."

Paul bowed and took Lady Howard's arm, his eyes still on the girl walking beside them. He realised that he had been living in a bubble of happiness, removed from his own world and the responsibilities of his wife and family. Jenson's pointed reminder had pricked the bubble but standing outside it did not change the way Paul felt about Anne Howard. He had fallen in love with her without ever intending to, and while it changed nothing about his future, he felt a desperate longing to tell her so.

Anne was not like any other woman Paul had met. She was unconventional and outspoken and so different to his lovely, conformable wife that it made comparisons impossible. Paul knew that he was never going to wholly recover from the pain of leaving her behind. He suspected that she felt the same way and he wished he could do something to ease her unhappiness.

Delivering them back to the Assembly Rooms, he found a moment to speak to her.

"Can you get away tomorrow? I'm away for a few days after that, but I was wondering if we could meet up at the shepherd's hut."

***

Paul was waiting for Anne when she arrived, and he lifted her down and took care of Bella while she stood watching him, then he removed his coat and spread it in the hay. "Come and join me, Miss Howard."

Paul took her into his arms, kissing her for a long time, savouring the feeling of her slender body against his and the joy of holding her without any fear of interruption.

"Are you all right?" he asked softly, and she nodded, reaching up to caress his face.

"Yes. Just making the most of this."

"Me too, girl of my heart. Although not as much as I'd like to."

"Are you always this scrupulous, Major?"

Paul gave a short laugh. "In my head I hear the howls of laughter of my friends at the word 'scrupulous'. I know how badly I'm behaving, Nan, to both you and Rowena. I've never wanted anything in my life as much as I want you, but I'm trying hard here."

"You're doing better than I am, Major," Anne said, and her honesty made Paul smile.

"Trust me, I'm not. It's bloody difficult, but I've realised that I care too much to put you at risk."

Anne settled her dark head on his shoulder and snuggled close to him. "I wish I could have just one night with you, without feeling I'm doing something wrong."

The words cut into him. "So do I," he said quietly. "More than I can tell you, lass."

Anne turned her head to look up at him. "You look younger without the uniform. Like a boy."

"I'm not sure if that's a compliment or not."

"How did you get so far, so young, Major? It can't all have been about money."

"Money definitely helps in the army. But I've been lucky. I'm also very good at what I do, and I suspect I've the sort of personality it's hard to overlook."

"I'd say so. You married young too. Are you going to see your wife for a few days?"

Paul nodded. "I should have gone before, I keep putting it off. It's as if seeing Rowena puts some kind of barrier between you and I, and I'm not ready for that." He waited for a moment, watching her face. "Any other

169

woman in the world would have a dozen questions. Ask, Nan, you have the right."

"What is she like? Should I like her?"

"I hope to God you never meet her, for I can't imagine how that would feel." Paul's arms tightened about her. "It would be easy to tell you that I didn't want to marry Rowena and that I don't love her. But things are never that simple, and I am very fond of her."

"Was it an arranged marriage?"

Paul hesitated. For a moment he was ashamed to tell her the truth, then he realised he could say anything to this girl.

"No. It was a necessary marriage because Rowena was carrying my child."

He saw Anne's eyes widen in surprise. "Oh. Oh, my goodness, I see. No wonder you've been so determined not to put me in that position."

"I'm embarrassed to admit it. I was such a young idiot."

She gave a peal of laughter and kissed him. "You sound like a grandfather. What are you now, twenty-six?"

"I know, love. And looking at where I am now, you'd be hard put to believe that I've grown up at all, but I think I have. When I was in Copenhagen, I made myself a promise that I'd try to be a better husband, and I thought I was doing well until..."

"Until you met me, and I threw myself at you."

"Nan, none of this is your fault."

"I'm not sure either of us is to blame for this, Paul. Are you in love with her?"

Anne had never asked him anything like this before. Paul studied her, taking in the perfection of her face and the expression in her dark eyes and suddenly he wanted to tell her the truth.

"No. Not in the way that you mean. Not like this."

"This?"

"Rowena is so easy to love, I've never known why I held back. We're close, we do better than most couples. But I feel as though I was waiting for you, Nan Howard, only God help me, I didn't know it. I love you, girl of my heart. I hope you know that."

Anne lay still and quiet against him, seeming to absorb the sense of his words. Finally, she tilted her head back to look at him. "I love you too, Paul." She gave an impish smile. "Not a word about me being too young to know what that means?"

"Nan, you may be very young but you're more mature than some of the young ensigns we send out against the French." Paul kissed her again very gently. "My friends would take one look at you and they would see that beautiful face and that very lovely body and they'd think they understood this, but they'd be wrong this time. I didn't fall in love with the way you look, I fell in love with the woman you are. Although I'm not sure it helps much to hear me say it."

170

"Oh Paul, it helps, trust me. Whoever they make me marry, at least I'll know how it felt, once, to be with somebody who..."

"Nan, don't. I can't bear it just now."

"I can. Tell me about Rowena."

"Nan, no."

"Please, Paul. She's part of your life, the most important part. I want to understand."

Paul held her close and told her about Rowena and Nell and Catherine. Anne was a good listener, and the telling became easier. He spoke for longer than he had intended and when he had done, she leaned over and kissed him gently.

"So you've a daughter as well?"

"I have. Possibly two, although I'll never be sure about Cat's lass. I'm told Cat married recently. I hope it goes well for her. As for Grace...I wish you could see her, Nan. And Francis. I never thought I'd be such a besotted father, but I am."

"I'm glad you told me."

"I find myself wondering if one day you'll be telling the story of me, while lying in the arms of the man you love."

"I'm already in the arms of the man I love, Paul. I don't expect that to change. But I will have to marry."

"I know, and I bloody hate it, which makes me a hypocrite. Every time I see you dancing with Julian Carew and see the expression on his face as he looks at you, I want to punch him, and I have absolutely no right to feel that way. I'd no idea what this felt like. My marriage is so safe and secure and causes me no pain. This hurts and it's going to hurt even more when I ride away from here, leaving you behind."

"I know. But it's been worth it, at least now I know what this feels like. I wouldn't change that. Is this how we're ending this, Paul?"

Anne's voice was steady, but Paul could hear the sadness and he tightened his arms about her and told the truth.

"It's certainly the last time we're doing this, bonny lass. I don't trust myself anymore. Sooner or later I'm just going to do it and I'm not convinced you'd stop me."

Anne rested her dark head on his chest. "I wouldn't," she admitted. "Really, I've shocked myself at how little I seem to care about my virtue, it's as if I can't believe that this is wrong. But I know what everybody else would think of me."

Paul shifted to lean over her and kissed her very gently. "Nothing can make me believe that what we have is wrong. I wish you could be mine, Nan, but since you can't I'd like to think you could find someone who can give you what Rowena has given me. It might not be this, but it's worth having, trust me." Paul studied her, trying to read her expression. "Was that patronising?"

Anne reached up and caressed his face, smiling. "No, that was rather lovely. Does she know how lucky she is?"

"She says she does," Paul said. "But I'm lucky too. I'm sorry, Nan, we shouldn't be talking about this."

"It's all right. Somehow it helps to know you're going back to somebody who will be good to you. I know I should do something extremely noble, and tell you that we should end this now, Paul."

"Don't. Let's wait. The army is going to make this decision for us, no question about it. Let me enjoy what I can of you until then."

***

Orders came in early July.

Paul received the letter in his office, to tell him that Sir Arthur Wellesley was going to South America and wanted Paul and the first battalion of the 110th to join him. Colonel Kincaid, invalided out of India, would be taking over command of the 115th, and Major van Daan, his work there done, was to re-join his regiment at Melton.

Paul re-read the letter three times, then he put it down on the desk and stared out of the window at the immaculate parade ground, where Lieutenant Walsh and Sergeant Barforth were putting the third company through drill. It was going well. During the past month relations with his officers had finally begun to thaw. All the officers were now living in barracks, and repairs and renovations were complete. Robert Carlyon had proved an excellent quartermaster with a genuine talent for administration and finance and had been appointed, Paul understood, to a permanent position in the south on the strength of his achievements in Yorkshire.

His time with Anne Howard was over. They had both known that this must end, now he needed to see her and tell her so. And then he must pack his bags and get himself away from her, to allow her to choose between her various suitors.

Paul was due to see Anne that evening at her father's house. Miss Katherine Howard had returned from her extended visit wearing a betrothal ring and the Howards had arranged a party to celebrate her official engagement to Mr Gisbourne. Paul had been waiting daily for orders to arrive, expecting it and dreading the moment of saying goodbye.

He took Anne, once the party was in full swing and nobody would notice her brief absence, into the shadowy bowers of the ornamental garden and held her gently in the bright moonlight. After a moment Anne said:

"You're going, aren't you?"

"Yes. Orders came this morning. I've a week or so to set everything in order."

"Where?"

"South America. Not my ideal posting, but we'll be under Wellesley which is what I wanted."

Anne smiled. "You really like him, don't you? I wish I could meet him."

"I'm not so sure about that, girl of my heart, he has a very good eye for a pretty woman himself and I know you like clever men. Best keep you two apart, I think. They're going to expect you to make a choice, soon, Nan."

"They are already pressing me. Once Katie is married, I rather imagine that will get more insistent."

"I want so badly to give you advice, Nan, but I can't. I wish they'd let you wait."

"Because I'm too young?"

"Christ no, how can I say that, if I wasn't married, I'd have offered for you by now. No, I just don't think any of the men they've chosen are good enough for you. But I know how the world works, they're not going to leave you alone until you're safely wed. I'm going to remember this when it comes to Grace, nobody is bullying her into an early marriage unless she wants it."

"She's lucky. I'll be all right, Paul, I promise you."

The pain in her eyes was like a knife in his heart. "I've been telling myself for weeks that I could cope with this," he said. "Now that it's come, I can't believe how much it hurts. Nan, I don't think we should see each other again after tonight. There has to come a point where we say goodbye, and I don't know that I can get through the next week seeing you and touching you and knowing that it is almost the last time. I think I need to end it now."

"Of course," Anne said, and her voice was suddenly not steady. "I think I had better develop a headache and go to bed early, because I don't think I can go through the rest of this evening..."

"Neither can I," Paul said ruefully.

"Then kiss me goodbye, Paul, and leave. I love you. I'll never forget you."

Paul took her into his arms and kissed her very gently. Impossible to believe that this was the last time he would ever hold her. He could taste the salt of tears and did not know if they were hers or his. He pulled her closer and felt the length of her body against his.

"Paul," she whispered, and he kissed her harder, more insistently, his hands sliding down her body. Faced with her loss he wondered despairingly if it would really matter if just once, he made love to her as they both wanted.

"Love, I need to let you go," he said softly.

"I don't want you to, Paul. Can't I just make this one decision for myself before they barter me off to a man I may not even like?"

Paul breathed in the scent of her. "Girl of my heart, I'm trying so bloody hard to do the right thing here."

"Are you so sure it's the right thing?"

He kissed her again, very gently. "Yes. Because I can't be here to take care of you if this goes wrong and you end up carrying my child. And do you know what I think? I don't even think you'd tell them it was mine. I think you'd carry it alone rather than damage me. I am the biggest bastard in the known world for doing what I've done to you, Nan, but at least you still have a limited choice. If I make love to you now and you end up in three months' time with your belly swelling with my child, I'll be somewhere in South America and I won't even know about it. They'll make you marry quickly,

173

and it might not be the man you choose, it'll be the man who will take damaged goods. And I will not – I absolutely will not – do that to you. Please, love, turn around, go back into the house and don't make this more difficult for us than it already is. I love you, and it's over. Go."

Anne turned and began to run, and Paul stood watching her take his heart with her. Not calling her back was the hardest thing he had ever done.

***

Sergeant O'Reilly arrived six days later in a post chaise, his amused black eyes assessing the immaculate state of the 115th North Yorkshire Foot regimental barracks. His commander greeted him with obvious pleasure and led him through into his office.

"Thank God you're here," he said, opening a cupboard and removing a brandy bottle and two cups. "I was beginning to think they were going to leave me here for the rest of the war."

"Apparently not. Do I hear that they've promoted some poor bastard back from India to take over here?" O'Reilly glanced around him, observing the freshly painted walls and the neat row of ledgers on the shelf. "Although I can see you've been having fun here. Killed anybody?"

"No, although it's been a close-run thing at times. But what in God's name are you doing here, Michael, don't they trust me to find my way back to Melton?"

"They do. But you need to know there's been a slight change of plan. We're not going to South America, sir. We're going with Wellesley to Portugal."

"Portugal?" Paul paused, the brandy bottle in his hand.

"Aye. He means to take Lisbon back. I've letters for you here."

Paul poured the drinks and sat down to read. His first thought was that he wished he could share the news with Anne. He would have liked to hear her opinion and he wondered painfully, for how long she would be the first person he wanted to share things with. With an effort he pulled his attention back to the letters.

When he had finished reading, he picked up his cup. "Interesting. I've an idea that Wellesley's plan for Portugal and Spain and London's might be very different. It certainly makes more sense than South America. How is Captain Longford?"

"Buggered off to Ireland, thank God, with the second battalion. There was a bit of an incident with young Dawson, I'm afraid. Johnstone was away and there was nobody to intervene."

"Is Dawson all right?"

"He had to sleep on his front for a week or two, but we've all been there. Thank God he didn't actually hit Longford, the bastard would have tried to have him hanged, and then I think Mr Swanson would have killed him. I don't often see Carl get really mad, it was a privilege."

"What did Dawson do to get flogged?"

"Extreme insubordination on the training ground. I missed it, but Rory Stewart tells me it was well worth hearing. He's got a mouth on him, that lad, you should be proud. Apparently, Longford gave one of our new recruits a bit of a kicking for no good reason and Dawson got pissed off. It's all right, it all settled down again, and nobody got cashiered or hanged, which with the light company is the best we can hope for."

"I wish I'd been there. Is the man all right?"

"Broke his hand. Stamped on it. Bloody unnecessary, whatever the lad had done."

"Bastard. Good thing he's gone."

"Probably a good thing you weren't there, sir. You never know what you'll come up with next. I'm still recovering from Copenhagen."

Paul shot his sergeant a look. "We do not speak of Copenhagen," he said. "Why has Longford gone with the second battalion, he's in charge of my seventh company, isn't he? Or has he transferred?"

"No, he's still there. I think Colonel Johnstone got rid of him before you got back. He's spent three years trying to keep you two apart. Shouldn't be so hard now that we're going back to Europe. I wish he'd sell out, mind. Must be a pain for Johnstone having to keep the seventh separate from the rest of the battalion."

"When I finally catch up with him, he's going to wish he'd sold out. Bullying my bloody men is my prerogative, not his. I hope they put him in barracks with the 117th, he and Tyler should have a lot to talk about."

"Tyler isn't there. Mr Swanson told me, he had a letter from Corrigan, you know they've stayed friendly. Captain Tyler's company has been sent to the West Indies."

"Christ. Poor bastards. I'm not sure I'd wish that even on Tyler What about Corrigan?"

"Believe it or not he's coming to Portugal with us."

"Good thing he did that extra training then. He'll have to wake his ideas up under Wellesley or he'll get a rocket up his Irish arse. Jenson is seeing to my packing. There are one or two letters I should write, the locals have been very welcoming, but I can do those from Melton. And I'll invite the officers to a celebration dinner this evening. They probably feel like celebrating too, seeing the back of me."

His sergeant laughed. "Sir, I've served with you now for six years. You've been here for what – five or six months? By now I'd pretty much guarantee that every single one of these bastards is secretly wishing that he could go with you. I'll see if Jenson needs a hand and then I'll take myself off to town while you wine and dine the officers. Best not upset them on the last evening by getting drunk with your sergeant."

"You should get drunk with my sergeant here. I'll introduce you, he's a local man called Barforth. You'll like him. I wish I could get him transferred over to Melton, they could do with somebody good to keep them in line while we're overseas."

Paul's sergeant eyed him thoughtfully and said nothing. He was surprised that the major looked heavy eyed as though he had not slept well for a week or two. He was behaving completely normally, but Michael had been with him for a long time and he had a strong sense that something was wrong, although he could not imagine what. It was clear that Paul had done what he had come to do with the 115th, and whatever the officers and men might have said about him during the past six months, they would probably be drinking toasts to him and reminiscing about the highlights of his time with them for years to come.

He went to Paul's quarters to find Jenson packing boxes. Michael watched for a while. "Is he all right?" he asked.

Paul's orderly glanced at him. "I think so."

"Looks tired."

"Yes. Only the past week or so since orders came. I don't think he's sleeping much, and the brandy has been disappearing faster than normal for him."

"I'd have thought he'd be glad to get back, we all know this posting was his punishment for Copenhagen." Michael studied him. "Freddie, you know him as well as I do, anything I should know?"

Jenson strapped a box and turned with a sigh. "Sarge – I don't know. It's been difficult, but he's been all right. In a really good mood for most of the time."

"How good?" Michael said with deep foreboding.

"Too good."

"Oh Christ. Do we know her name?"

"I don't know if her name matters all that much. I don't know anything for sure, Sarge, except that he's been socialising more than normal. He wanted to get the officers on his side, so that makes sense, but normally he'd have got sick of that very quickly and been a bad-tempered bastard. And he hasn't."

"Well, we need to get him away from here fast, before husband or father works out what he's been doing with some poor lassie."

"Father, I'd say, Sarge."

Michael studied him. "You know who it is."

"Just a guess. I only saw her briefly and she had her mother with her. Lovely girl, but I'd say she's a handful. His lassies are usually very sweet and very accommodating, but this one looks like she'd take your eye out if you said the wrong thing. I liked her, though. Hope she's all right, it's not like him to go after a girl like that."

With the assistance of his sergeant, Paul was ready to leave early the following morning. His boxes were strapped onto the post chaise and Paul said his civil farewells to those officers whose hangovers had permitted them to rise early to see him off. He had spoken to all of them the previous evening, and he admitted to Michael he would miss some of them. One or two in particular had come a long way since that freezing day when they had shovelled snow for long backbreaking hours on the parade ground.

176

Michael and Jenson waited outside in the yard for him to finish his farewells. There was a woman hovering by the gate to the barracks and Michael wondered if she was waiting for her sweetheart. He could not see her face as she wore a blue cloak with a wide hood.

Major van Daan emerged from the barracks alone and his sergeant walked with him to the waiting carriage. He glanced across at the girl and saw that she had put back her hood. Michael stopped. He could not help himself. She was beautiful, with shining black hair and huge dark eyes. She was looking towards Michael, but not at him, and he turned to look at his commander and realised that Paul had seen the girl.

"Wait here," Paul said, and his voice was suddenly unsteady.

"Oh, Jesus bloody Christ, not again."

"Michael, will you for the love of God get in the carriage, and keep your eyes and your mouth firmly shut. I will be with you in five minutes."

"Sure, and that's a bit quick even for you," Michael snapped.

"Take a bloody order for once in your life, Sergeant."

"Keep your bloody hands off a woman for once in yours," Michael retorted. He watched as Paul walked towards the girl, making no attempt to hide the fact that he was listening, because it was clear to him that neither of them was going to notice that he was there. He saw Paul catch the girl by the hand and pull her into the concealment of the unoccupied gatehouse, and then he reached to cup her face in his hands and his mouth came down onto hers with desperate passion.

They remained locked together for a long moment, then Paul raised his head:

"I'm sorry, Nan. Christ, I'm sorry."

The girl reached up to caress his face. "I know, it's why I came. I'm all right. I wanted you to know that. I love you, and I don't regret anything. Take care of yourself, Paul, promise me."

Paul turned his head and kissed the palm of her hand. "I promise, love. I am never going to forget you," he whispered. "I love you too. Now get out of here before somebody sees you. Go on."

He turned and ran back to the carriage. Michael held the door open for him and Paul got in. Michael followed and a moment later they were moving forward through the gates. Michael saw that the girl was still there, watching them leave, and for all the stricken expression in her eyes she was not crying. There was something extraordinarily gallant about the slim figure. Unexpectedly she saw Michael watching her and met his eyes as the coach slowed to turn out of the gates. He expected her to look away, embarrassed, but to his surprise the girl smiled suddenly, and lifted her hand in acknowledgement. Then they were past, and Michael leaned back against the squabs and looked at his commander. Beside him Jenson was deliberately looking out of the window. Paul had his eyes closed.

"What the bloody hell have you been doing, sir?" Michael demanded. Something about the dark girl had touched him unexpectedly. He felt as

177

though her haunted face was engraved on his memory and he was suddenly furious.

"Nothing. It was nothing. A flirtation with a pretty girl, Michael. You know how prone I am to those."

"What I know," O'Reilly said in measured tones, "is that your last summer flirtation ended up giving birth on a ship in Naples. Is it bigamy you're hoping will solve this one? That's not some tavern girl, sir, do you think I couldn't see that in two minutes?"

Paul took a deep breath. "It is none of your business, Sergeant. But since you make it so, you are right. She is not a tavern girl. There is no possibility of her being pregnant, there is nothing to be concerned about, and I really don't want to talk about it."

Michael sat in silence for a long time, as the coach bounced over the rutted road out of Thorndale. Finally, he said:

"I could see why you'd be tempted. Lovely looking girl."

His commander opened his eyes, and Michael was shocked to see that there was a sheen of tears. "Michael, just let it drop," he said wearily, then turned his head away and closed his eyes again.

***

Behind them Anne stood for a long time in the shadow of the gatehouse. She was glad she had come, although it had involved a number of small deceptions to evade a chaperone. Leaving Paul as she had done a week ago had been unbearable, and she was willing to risk a scolding to reassure him that she would be all right. She was exasperated by his conviction that her unhappiness was his responsibility, given that neither of them had chosen to fall in love so unsuitably, but she hoped that the sight of her, whole and capable as ever, would soothe some of his anxiety about her.

Anne had left her horse in an unoccupied stall in the regimental stables next door and she drew her hood up around her face again and slipped back along the street and in through the stable door.

"Miss Howard, what a pleasant surprise."

Anne jumped and turned. Behind her in the stall was Lieutenant Carlyon. He was smiling in a way that made her feel uncomfortable. Could he have seen her with Paul? Anne did not think so, but she could feel her face growing warm. The best she could think of to do was to feign complete ignorance, so keeping her voice pleasant and friendly, she said:

"I was just leaving, Mr Carlyon. Shall we see you on Sunday at the hunt supper?"

"I have not yet decided," Carlyon said. There was something different about him, an expression in his eyes, which was unfamiliar. Anne had spent a good deal of time around Robert Carlyon and she had always found him pleasant, if not especially interesting, but she was suddenly very uneasy. She turned towards her horse, and heard him move, so looked back. He was walking towards her, too quickly, and Anne stepped back in alarm and tried to walk past him. Carlyon took her by the arm and twisted and Anne gave a cry of pain. With her arm twisted up her back at an unnatural angle, he pushed her into the empty stall next to Bella. Anne opened her mouth to scream and his hand covered it, muffling the sound and bruising her mouth.

"We're going to be married, Miss Howard." Anne hardly recognised the flat, hard voice as his. His eyes were watching her without a trace of compassion as he forced her arm up her back and pushed her down to the ground. She saw to her horror that he was fumbling with the front of his breeches and she knew with sick certainty what he intended to do. "Very quickly as well, in case there's a bastard brat to show for it. I've not the least idea if it will be mine or his, and to be honest, I don't care."

Anne was on her back in the straw and he twisted his scarf into a ball and thrust it into her mouth. It tasted foul and smelled of sweat and leather. Roughly he pinned her arms above her head. Anne tried to work the gag out of her mouth using her tongue, but she could feel him dragging up her skirts and pulling her legs apart. She tried to kick him, but she was hampered by her own heavy riding habit. For a moment, she managed to get one hand free and scrabbled for his face, trying to reach his eyes, but he avoided her clawing fingers and forced her arm down, pinning it painfully between his body and hers. Anne was shocked and terrified at how strong he was, and none of her desperate struggles were making the slightest difference.

She felt his weight lowered onto her then there was a tearing pain and he thrust into her hard and brutal, slamming her into the floor. Initially Anne continued to struggle, sobbing into the gag with the pain of it and then she realised that it was pointless, and she lay still, turning her face away from him, feeling tears on her cheeks, wanting it to be over.

Eventually, Carlyon shuddered with a muffled groan and was still. His weight lifted from her and Anne curled away from him, waiting for the pain to stop. She felt torn and humiliated and her whole body was shaking as if from cold. Anne heard him getting up and she lay still, curled into a ball, wishing he would just leave, but she knew he was not going to, knew that her ordeal was not yet over. Nothing in her young and sheltered life had prepared her for this. Carlyon still did not speak, and Anne could not bear to lie there, so she moved cautiously, pulled the gag from her mouth and pushed her skirts down to cover herself.

"Well, well, well," her attacker drawled. He sounded amused. "Of all the things I was expecting, it wasn't a virgin bride, my dear."

Comprehension flooded through Anne and she rolled over and pushed herself into a sitting position. He was casually adjusting his clothing. The white handkerchief, which he had used to wipe himself, was stained with flecks of blood. Her blood. Carlyon looked at it then tossed it to her. Anne let it fall to the straw and looked up at Carlyon.

"You knew," she said.

"About your regular little trysts with my dashing commander? Of course I knew, I'm surprised half of Yorkshire didn't know. Didn't you realise how you looked at each other? You are my golden future, Miss Howard, the girl who is going to go to her father – or perhaps your step-mamma would be best – and confess that our mutual passion overcame us and that we need to be married damned quickly because you're very likely going to be bearing a little Carlyon shortly." Carlyon reached down, grasped her wrist and pulled her to her feet. "I enjoyed that more than I expected," he said quietly.

"You unspeakable bastard," Anne said. She was shocked and shaking, but she was also aware of a small flame of anger, and she seized it, fanning it, recognising that it was a healthy sign. "I hope you did, because it will be the last time."

"Defiant as well as lovely, although you've the language of a guttersnipe. I look forward to taking my time with you, sweetheart. What do you think your father would say if you admitted that you did not come here to meet me, but to meet Major van Daan, a married man? You know, of course, that he has a wife and children, but that didn't stop you, did it, Anne? All those quiet moments when suddenly neither of you were anywhere to be found!" Carlyon laughed. "Did you know, I wonder, that he has the reputation of lifting the skirts of half the regimental wives? He must have thought you easy sport."

Anne looked at him, and then indicated the blood-stained rag on the floor. "Clearly he did not," she said.

"No, by God. And that's a bonus, since if there is a brat, it will actually be mine. What stopped him, I wonder, was he worried he'd get you pregnant with no cuckolded husband to take the responsibility?"

Anne did not reply. She could feel the walls of the trap closing in on her and it was difficult to think straight. "I can simply tell my father the truth," she said.

"And I can bring at least two witnesses who saw you locked in a passionate embrace with your lover in the yard out there about half an hour ago," Carlyon said quietly. "Both officers, and neither with cause to love our major. Within two weeks, everyone in Thorndale will know that you gave yourself to a married man then tried to blame his bastard onto me."

"My parents…"

"Don't be naive. Once your father hears that story, your family will think about it and they'll remember all the times you danced with him and sat next to him at dinner and rode beside him. Don't tell me your stepmother didn't notice those long silent looks, she watches you like a hawk. Your father will write to his commanding officer about his behaviour, and believe me, he'll remember all the bad things he has ever heard about Major van Daan's reputation with women. And all the time, you'll be a pariah. You'll be the girl who spread her legs for a married man who drove off leaving her to face the consequences."

Anne turned away from him, pressing her cold hands to her face. Inexorably his voice went on:

"I imagine that will be the end of your sister's engagement. Gisbourne is a rising young man in the government; he won't ally himself to a scandal this big. Likewise, your brother's parliamentary ambitions. My father won't support the brother of a girl with your morals. It probably won't affect your

180

father's business much, although his friends will be laughing behind their hands in the Red Lion I expect at what his daughter has been getting up to in the local barracks. And it will put a very big brake on the impressive career of Major van Daan. The army establishment doesn't take kindly to married men who seduce well-born virgins, too many of these old farts have pretty daughters themselves. They won't want a man like Van Daan in charge of barracks after this. He could probably get a commission in the Indian army, mind, I'm told he can fight like a demon and they're not so particular there."

"I despise you," Anne whispered. Unusually for her she could not find the words to express her hatred.

"And yet you'll marry me. Quick and quiet. I've a posting to the quartermaster's office in Southampton, which will suit me very nicely. I realise your father is not going to hand over your share of the money all at once, but I'll settle for my debts being paid and a comfortable allowance so that I no longer dread the mess bills. And when the old man is gone, I can sell out and live in comfort on your money, dear wife."

Anne turned and looked at him and he laughed softly. "You look like a cornered fox," he said. "And you're trying so hard not to show that you're afraid. But you are. You're afraid of what will happen if you say no. To you and your family and your lover. And that's why you're going to say yes. Aren't you, Miss Howard?"

Anne looked away again. Her mind felt frozen, locked still in that terrible moment when she had felt his body invading hers. "I need time to think about it."

"You can have until the day after tomorrow. After that, rumours will begin to spread. I reckon they'll reach Melton before he goes to Portugal." Carlyon laughed. "The best bit is that even his own friends won't believe him. That Irish bog-trotter he's so friendly with was watching you this morning and nobody could call that a chaste kiss goodbye."

He was right, Anne knew it with a feeling of cold certainty. Her relationship with Paul had given him the opportunity to do this. She was going to be condemned as a girl who had lost her virtue, either to Paul or to this man. If she were pregnant, there would be no way to convince her parents that the child was a result of rape once they knew about her relationship with Paul. The very fact that she had sneaked out of the house to see him this morning would work against her.

Anne turned back to look at Robert Carlyon, feeling as though she had never really seen him before.

"I thought you were his friend," she said.

"So did he," Carlyon said. "I wonder just how pissed off he'd be if he knew that I just enjoyed what he's been denied all these months. But it doesn't really matter who had you first, Anne, you need to be married now, and I'm the only one offering. He's gone, and he's married anyway."

"If he knew what you'd just done to me, I think he'd kill you."

"You'd better make sure he doesn't find out then, because what would happen to him then?"

Anne felt the trap snap closed. "Get out of my way, Robert," she said quietly. "I'm going home."

"I will escort you..."

"You bloody won't! If I find I have to put up with you for the rest of my life, I'm taking this time to make the decision on my own. You can come to the house tomorrow morning. If I agree to see you, you'll know the answer is yes."

Carlyon seemed surprised at the sudden authority in her voice, but he nodded and stepped back. Anne could feel his eyes on her as she worked to restore herself to something like respectability with shaking hands.

Anne lay awake through the long hours of the night, thinking once again about Paul van Daan. The ache of losing him had not diminished beside the horror of the rape, but she could no longer allow herself the luxury of mourning, since tomorrow she must decide. She imagined telling the truth to her shocked parents. There would be no point in telling them she and Paul had never fully made love. They would not believe her once Robert had spun his lies, and if she turned out to be pregnant, they would assume it was his. There would be consequences for her family, she was sure Robert was right about that. There would be consequences for Paul too.

Paul would know that no child of hers could be his, but nobody would believe him given his frank admissions about his history with women. There would be pressure on him to sell out or take a commission in another, less prestigious regiment. His family would be embarrassed and the young wife he clearly cared about would be hurt and humiliated. And what would Anne gain from it? The life she had resented so much, of choosing between wealthy and eligible suitors, was over whatever decision she made now. She could be blamed for an affair with Paul, and damage people she loved. Or she could admit an affair with Robert Carlyon and limit the damage to herself. If she married him, he would have the right to use her body as often as he chose, and the thought sickened Anne. But she could not go back, could not save herself from ruin. She could save other people. She could save Paul van Daan and let him go on his way with warm memories of her in his heart and his reputation, his marriage and his career intact.

Anne lay watching the dawn light filter through the curtains of her bedroom and thought about Paul and found that she could still smile. In the end she supposed she would always choose to protect the people she loved. She knew he would have done the same for her, but this was her fight, not his. Anne could hear his voice in her head, as clearly as though he was in the room with her.

"That's a remarkably mature statement for a girl of your age."

"Shut up, Major," Anne said softly, but aloud. "Go away and just let me do this, will you?"

Chapter Eleven

The news that Anne Howard had married Robert Carlyon came to Paul through an unexpected source. It had been an infuriating, and in many ways, a disastrous year for the British forces, and the fact that Paul and his light company had missed the worst of it was due solely to an unexpected outbreak of camp fever at a crucial time.

They had started off with high hopes, with most of the first battalion of the 110th sailing to Portugal with Wellesley in the July of 1808. Wellesley was not in command of the British army in Portugal, that honour being shared somewhat confusingly between Sir Harry Burrard and Sir Hugh Dalrymple. Neither of them was present, however, when Wellesley marched towards Lisbon and defeated the French, firstly at Rolica and then at Vimeiro. It was a comprehensive defeat which left the French reeling, having sustained huge losses of both men and supplies.

In the aftermath of battle, Paul hoped it would be the end of the French in Portugal. He was relieved to be back in the field in command of the whole of the first battalion except for the seventh company, which was on duty in Ireland. It was Paul's largest command so far and he found it immensely satisfying to be in a position to make decisions that mattered. His men fought well, making the most of their training and new equipment, and morale was high. Two of Wellesley's brigades did not even make it into action, so efficient was his use of the rest.

Marshal Junot offered complete surrender and at that point matters began to go wrong. Under the terms of the Convention of Cintra, Dalrymple offered the French unbelievably generous terms. Their defeated army was transported back to France by the British navy, complete with all guns and equipment along with chests of treasure and artworks looted from Portugal. Paul was incredulous, Wellesley maintained a tight-lipped silence and in Britain there was an outcry in the Press and in Parliament, which led to the recall of all three generals to answer for their actions, leaving Sir John Moore to command the British forces and lead them into Spain.

By then most of Paul's battalion was in no fit state to accompany him. Camp fever, which he had previously avoided, swept through their lines, resulting in deaths and lingering illness. Rowena van Daan sickened with them. Racked with guilt at ever putting her at risk, Paul remained by her bedside and prayed for her recovery. His feelings for the girl he had met in Yorkshire had in no way diminished the genuine affection he felt for his wife, and Rowena's slow return to health felt like a second chance.

By the time Colonel Johnstone arrived in Lisbon, he found his first battalion severely depleted by illness. Johnstone himself did not look well, after a fever picked up on campaign in Alexandria, but he assured Paul that he was well enough to take command of those companies fit to march. He left to join Sir John Moore in Spain, leaving Paul and the four companies worst affected to form part of the Lisbon garrison. Since there was very little chance of a French attack, Paul had nothing to do but nurse his convalescent wife and wait for news from London and from the front. It was hard to be left so far from the action but for once Paul made no push to accompany the army. He felt very protective of Rowena, whose fragile appearance terrified him, and he did not wish to leave her.

News from Spain filtered through slowly and it was some time before the full horror of what had occurred was clear. Finding the Spanish forces in disarray and completely unable to offer him the support he had expected, and with news that Bonaparte himself was on his way with reinforcements to join Soult, Moore made the decision to retreat towards Corunna on the coast, as he was now cut off from Portugal. Moore's army marched for two hundred and fifty miles over mountains in snow and ice, with men, women and children dropping dead from starvation and cold. He made his final stand on the coast and his men, although almost dead from exhaustion and lack of food, put up a heroic fight at Corunna and won the day They left Moore dead on the field and boarded the transports to England in horrific condition.

Paul had rented a villa in Lisbon from a grandee who had fled to Brazil until Napoleon should be defeated, and he sat numbly reading accounts of the suffering. His own men were recovering fast and raging at the plight of their comrades. There was nothing for them to do except training and drilling and waiting. In January, they were summoned back to England for a brief period in barracks. Paul left Rowena at Southwinds to complete her recovery while he turned his attention to the rest of the first battalion which was ravaged by hunger, sickness and battle wounds. Johnstone was on sick leave and Paul sent out recruitment parties and set his quartermaster to organise new kit and uniforms for the survivors of Moore's disastrous campaign.

Paul had been home for a month when he received a welcome summons to London. He met Sir Arthur Wellesley for dinner at his club to find that his general had good news about the Cintra inquiry which had been occupying all his attention.

"Exonerated," Wellesley said exultantly. "By God, it would have been hard for them to prove anything else, but this delay has been a waste of time."

Paul lifted his glass in a toast. "Congratulations, sir, I'm very glad. Will we be going back to Portugal?"

"As soon as I can arrange it. This time, I shall be in command."

"That's even better news."

"Not that it has been a universally popular choice. There was some talk of Chatham, who is senior to me, but I believe he turned it down. Still, there are politicians who are waiting for me to fail. I loathe politicians, Major."

"I thought you were a politician, sir."

"I loathe politicians who are not me. How are your men, Major? Got over their ague?"

"Yes," Paul said. "Although I wonder if their ague might have been a better option than that God-awful retreat. Colonel Johnstone still isn't well, and we still have too many on the sick list."

"I don't want Johnstone, I want you," Wellesley said bluntly. What can you pull together for me?"

"We can put together five or six companies, I think, including my light company. I've started recruiting for both battalions again immediately, and those men who recover can join us later. Will that be enough?"

"It's a start."

"I was sorry about Sir John."

"Very sad," Wellesley said. "Moore was a great man, one of the best."

Paul concealed a smile. Wellesley had not always been as complimentary about Sir John Moore, but it would have been tactless to remind him of the fact. "I spent the first six weeks of my army career under him at Shorncliffe. I learned a lot from him that I've used in training my own men."

"Yes, he was a genius with light infantry. Bloody waste, Major. But we'll see about Bonaparte now, by God." Wellesley eyed Paul over his wine glass. "I ran into a fellow the other day who knew you, by the way. He's quartermaster down near Southampton. Carlyon. He said he knew you in Yorkshire."

"Robert Carlyon? Yes, he acted as my quartermaster for a time. I threw the previous one through a window. Carlyon was the only one there I trusted to do anything, to be honest."

Wellesley fixed him with an arctic gaze. "You threw him through a window? You were supposed to be learning to control your temper better, Major," he said frostily.

"You sent me there, sir, and you must have known what I was walking into," Paul said placidly. "Let's be honest, that's why you did it, it was a very neat solution. I was punished for upsetting the navy in Denmark and the 115th was put to rights. The man was a thief and a scoundrel, and he was lucky I let him sell out; he ought to have been cashiered."

Wellesley gave a reluctant smile. "You did very well," he admitted. "Kicked up a rare dust, by all accounts, but Kincaid is in charge up there now and he's been singing your praises. Young Carlyon has got married since you saw him last. I met him at some dreadful army dinner. I didn't meet the girl, but I saw her from a distance waiting in the carriage. She's a beauty, lucky dog."

Paul put down his wine glass. "There was a girl he was courting in Yorkshire," he said slowly. Ice had settled around his heart. "Quite young, very dark, I knew her. It's a small social circle up there. But to be honest I rather thought there was somebody else that she'd choose over Robert."

"Perhaps the red coat convinced her, because this was a dark girl, and very beautiful. He tells me they're off to the Cape."

"Are they?" Paul felt sick. "I've family there, I should write to them to watch out for Robert. I'm not sure how he'd be on the battlefield, but he was a good administrator."

"Make a good staff man at headquarters, eh? I'll remember that, Major."

Paul walked back to his father's house afterwards through the cold winter streets and mocked himself for being a fool. He had known she must marry somebody, and perhaps with him out of the way she and Robert Carlyon had formed a genuine connection. Anne did not owe anything to him. She would sail to the Cape and perhaps meet his family, and he wondered how she would like his cousin Christina, who was fair and pretty and of a practical turn of mind herself. He had always thought that Anne would be good at army life, but that might just have been part of his impossible dream of what could never be. She had been in his heart and his mind every day since he left her but all he could do was try his best to wish her happy in the choice that she had made.

It was April before the 110th was ready to set sail with Sir Arthur Wellesley on the transports to Lisbon. As always the days before embarkation were a logistical nightmare, and Paul had no time to think of anything until the ships sailed away from Southampton dock. The first night aboard was always the worst, with more than half his men seasick, and Rowena crying in her bunk because she felt so ill and because she was missing the children. Paul divided his time between the hold and his wife and wondered if it might have been easier to succumb to sickness himself than to deal with other people's.

Paul slept briefly when his wife finally dozed off and then awoke early to the ships bell and realised that he would sleep no more. Getting up, he dressed quietly and slipped out onto deck in the grey half-light between night and day, when only the ship's crew would be about. He loved this time of day aboard ship, and he stood still, breathing in the crisp morning air. It was a relief to be underway. His men were settled in their cramped quarters below, under the strict supervision of their NCOs, and until they arrived in Lisbon there was little for him to do. As always, he felt nostalgic at the sound of the sails flapping, the smell of brine and the faint spray in the air. At this hour there were only sailors about. Wellesley would no doubt be at work already, poring over maps and charts and supply lists. Soon he would go in search of food then join his commander. In the meantime, he stood and watched the glory of the sunrise falling across the deck.

As Paul approached the ship's rail, he realised he was not the only early riser. There was a woman standing there, leaning on the rail with her back to him. She was dressed in a plain dark gown with a woollen shawl about her shoulders. Clearly, she had not expected to encounter anybody this early either, because her hair was loose down her back. It was black and reached almost to her waist. The wind caught it and blew the black silk strands across her face and she lifted her hand and pushed it back in a gesture, which was painfully familiar. Paul stopped in his tracks. He must have made some sound because the woman turned.

***

Anne Carlyon woke early in the grey half-light and slipped silently out of the narrow bunk she shared with her husband. The past few days, since Robert had received the completely unexpected summons to join Wellesley's staff going to Lisbon, had been a whirl of packing and shopping and preparation. Now that she was awake, she was unwilling to lie beside Robert longer than she needed. As quietly as she could, she dressed and pulled a brush through the long dark curtain of her hair. There would be nobody on deck at this hour and Anne needed fresh air.

"Where are you going?" Robert said from the bunk. He had pushed himself up onto one elbow to look at her.

"On deck. I need some air."

"You should do up your hair, you look like a tavern slut."

"How singularly appropriate, dear Robert, since that is how you treat me."

Robert got up and came towards her. Anne stood still trying to force herself not to flinch away from him. His moods were unpredictable, and after more than six months of marriage she could still not always tell when he was going to hit her. Anne had learned in those months the bitter lesson of pretending not to care. He could rape her and hit her, and on one occasion when she had mistakenly given free rein to her scalding contempt, he had beaten her bloody with a riding crop, but it was a matter of pride that he should never know how much her body cringed when he came close to her.

Robert pushed Anne back against the wooden partition, hard enough to hurt her. He took her hair in his hands and pulled it until she felt tears behind her eyes. "Remember how thin these cabin walls are, Robert," she said softly. "I know you don't like other people to know how you treat me."

"When I get you alone, you'll regret that. As it is, by all means take the air, dear Nan. I've no use for you, I had what I wanted last night."

Robert shoved her away so suddenly that Anne stumbled. He returned to the bunk and Anne climbed the narrow steps onto the deck and went to stand at the ship's rail. She had never been a girl who cried much but since marrying Robert, she seemed to have lost the capacity for tears.

The weeks leading up to Anne's wedding had been strained and difficult. She had felt the weight of her father and stepmother's disappointment in her. They had done their best to still gossip, with the tale of Robert's posting to Southampton as the reason for such haste, but Anne had seen the knowing grins of many of Carlyon's fellow officers and she knew that he had told them that his bride was already secured, already enjoyed. He had enjoyed her ever since, and Anne was shocked by his unexpected desire for her body. She passed her days in barely civil silence with him, and her nights rigid and unresponsive or aching from his violence when she could bear it no more and fought back. Somehow Anne had assumed that once he had the money, he would quickly lose interest in her, but he came to her bed frequently, almost angrily, as though somehow he was seeking something that he had still not found. She had not yet become pregnant and the irony of that was almost unbearable.

Anne had received news of her sister's wedding and subsequent move to London, and her brother's successful election to Parliament and tried to be glad for them. These family triumphs had been bought with her body, although they would never know it. Somewhere out there was Paul van Daan, no doubt heading for greater glory in his chosen field, and he too never needed to know the bargain she had made to preserve his reputation and his future career. Since Anne had made her choice, she would live with it with as much dignity as she could manage.

In her darkest moments, Anne wondered if she should write to her father and tell him how badly the husband he had chosen was treating her. She knew that Sir Matthew would have intervened and would have come in person to bring her home. Anne also knew, with complete certainty, that Robert was a vindictive man who could still do both her family and Paul a good deal of damage. Katie was safely married to the eligible Mr Gisbourne, but George's political career was in its infancy and he would be vulnerable to scandal. So, she imagined, would Paul van Daan be if her husband chose to spread his rumours. She had come this far in order to protect those she loved, and she would not falter now.

Anne had been shaken by the news that they had been diverted to Portugal. She knew that Paul had joined Wellesley and had felt a stupid lift of pride when she had seen his name mentioned in one of Wellesley's published dispatches after the battle at Vimeiro. She wondered if Paul knew of her marriage and wished she could have warned him. She had read the lists of dead and wounded officers after Corunna and he was not mentioned, although his regiment was, but with Robert on Wellesley's staff it was looking increasingly likely that she and Paul might meet.

The first light of dawn was beginning to appear in the sky. It washed deck and sea in a rosy glow, highlighting white crested waves and the outline of a seabird following the ship. A faint light crept slowly across the sky, like the first flickering of fire touched to paper, and then thin slivers of pink and gold light streaked across the horizon as the sun began to make its first majestic appearance of the day. Around Anne, the deck appeared bathed in pale pink and the beauty soothed and calmed her. There was a sound behind her and she turned, expecting one of the crew. Instead, she found herself looking into the startled blue eyes of Paul van Daan.

They regarded each other in silence. It had been almost a year since Anne had last seen him, but it felt now as though it had been only a few days since he had driven off from the barracks while she stood watching him.

"Nan," he said.

"Paul. I didn't know you were aboard."

"Or I you."

Anne forced a smile. "We weren't supposed to be. Robert had an appointment to a post at the Cape of Good Hope, but one of Sir Arthur Wellesley's assistant quartermasters was taken ill, so he asked for a replacement and they sent him Robert."

"Oh dear God, that may have been my fault," Paul said. "Wellesley mentioned that he'd met him, and I praised his administrative skills. I'm sorry, Nan."

"You couldn't have known, Paul. You knew then? That we had married?"

"Wellesley told me. I had dinner in London with him and he mentioned he'd met Robert and seen you at a distance. His description was unmistakable."

"Is your wife with you?"

Anne saw his eyes widen in something like panic. "Yes, she's below, Rowena never does well with sea voyages. The social circle in Lisbon is very small, Nan, you're going to meet her."

Anne had to bite back a smile at his anxious expression. "Paul, we're on the same transport. Unless you intend to lock the poor girl in the cabin, I'm going to meet her before Lisbon. You're not worried I'll cause a problem, are you? I thought you knew me better than that."

His face softened into a smile, and Anne's heart melted. "Oh love, I do. Are you all right? This can't have been easy."

"I don't suppose it's been easy for either of us, Paul." Anne tried to keep her voice steady and pleasant, but she suspected she was not doing well.

"I'm going to have to get better at this, because just at the moment, it seems insane to me that I can't just put my arms around you and kiss you."

Anne turned her head to look at him. "I thought it was just me," she said. "But this is real life, Paul, and we are both married to other people. Nothing has changed for me, but I won't wreck your marriage because we have no self-control."

"I notice you aren't worrying about your own marriage, Nan."

"That isn't fair."

"I don't want to be fair. Why did you marry him?"

"Because he asked, and I had to marry somebody."

"It was too soon. What are you, eighteen? They shouldn't have pushed you. They should have let you wait, to choose for yourself." Paul closed his eyes for a long moment, then opened them again and returned her gaze. "I'm sorry. I can't stand to think of you with him, but that's not your fault. I'm jealous, and it's killing me. I'll do my best, Nan, although self-control around you has never been my strong point. And you're right, I don't want to hurt Rowena. But love, I need to know you're all right, I've been worrying about you ever since I left. And even more so since I knew you'd married. Hard enough for me, and I'm fond of Rowena. I hope he's good to you, because if I see one single sign that he's not I will bloody kill him and drop him off this transport without a second thought."

"Oh Paul..."

Anne was laughing despite herself, as the sound of his voice washed over her, and she closed her eyes for a moment. He had been with her in spirit every day since he left her, but she had wondered from time to time if the girl who had endured six months of Robert's brutality would ever be capable of feeling desire again. She had the answer now. Paul seemed to sense it, because she felt him suddenly much closer to her and then his arms were about her and his mouth was on hers and her heart, which had been broken, was whole and strong again.

Paul released her in a moment and Anne stepped back and turned away from him to look out over the sea. "Not a good start," she said, striving to keep her voice steady.

"No. I did say I'd struggle."

Anne looked around at him. "I've wondered, over this past year, if you'd forgotten me. If everything that happened..."

"I wondered the same thing myself when I heard you'd married Robert." Paul studied her as though he could not take his eyes from her face. "I don't think a day goes by when I don't think of you."

"Paul, you've been more real to me than he has."

"Oh Christ, lass," he said softly. "You know how I feel about you. One year or ten, that's not going to change."

Anne heard footsteps and turned to see another officer approaching them, a man of around Paul's age, slightly above medium height with soft brown hair and a pair of merry green eyes.

"Paul, your friend Carlyon is aboard. Hookey has poached him from the Cape garrison at the last minute."

"I know. Carl, meet his wife, Anne, I knew her in Yorkshire. Nan, this is my oldest friend, Lieutenant Carl Swanson."

Carl took her hand and bowed over it. "A pleasure, Mrs Carlyon. I hope Lisbon won't be too much of a shock for you."

"It's very good to meet you, Mr Swanson."

Carl glanced at Paul. "Where is Rowena?"

Paul's lips quirked into a smile. "You'll notice that is his first question when he finds me on deck in conversation with a beautiful woman, Nan. He's a suspicious minded bastard."

Carl Swanson shot his friend a startled glance. "Paul, watch your language, will you?"

Anne laughed. "It's all right, Lieutenant, he isn't going to offend me."

"I'm more likely to offend him, Nan, his father is a parson. Rowena is below, Carl, you know how sick she gets. Don't worry, I'm not about to seduce Mrs Carlyon. Although I can't wait to see her at a headquarters reception, there's going to be a riot."

"I'd be surprised if there's anything I can do to shock them if they're accustomed to you," Anne said. "I was wondering if perhaps I could go to see your wife, Major. There seems to be very little for me to do, and perhaps I could make myself useful."

190

"She would probably appreciate it," Paul said after a moment's hesitation. "If you're sure..."

"I'm sure," Anne said quietly.

Paul led her to the ladder. Away from his friend, he said:

"Nan..."

"Stop worrying. Better to do this now than wait until we are in a crowded reception room. I'm guessing she knows nothing?"

"No."

"Then there is nothing to worry about."

Anne followed Paul down the ladder and along the narrow passage. He paused and glanced at her. "You can have no possible idea how uncomfortable this makes me feel."

"If you are under the impression that this is easy for me, Major, allow me to disabuse you of that idea."

Suddenly Paul began to laugh. "Oh Jesus, Nan, I have dreamed about hearing you call me that again," he said. "Nobody else in the world says that word quite the way you do. Come on, let's get this over with."

He tapped at a door and opened it.

"Rowena, you have a visitor. Mrs Carlyon has come to see how you are."

"Paul, I'm not well enough...."

Anne could hear the distress in Rowena's voice, and she looked at Paul's expression and saw guilt, realising that he was forcing this meeting in order to get past the awkward moment. Unexpectedly, Anne felt the older and wiser of the two and she placed her hands on his shoulders, moving him gently to one side.

"Go away, Major, you're not helping here," she said, and she could see the tumult of emotion across his expressive face, anxiety and confusion and sheer happiness at the touch of her hands. Anne smiled at him, trying to tell him that she felt the same way. When he had gone, she entered the cabin as Rowena van Daan pushed herself cautiously into a sitting position.

"I'm sorry," she said weakly. "I wasn't expecting visitors."

Anne regarded Paul's wife with interest. The girl was probably in her early twenties with tumbled fair curls and wide green eyes. There were dark circles under her eyes and her face was very pale. She looked ill and extremely nervous, and Anne felt unexpectedly protective.

"Don't apologise, it was my idea. Paul said how ill you were feeling, and I wondered if I could help in some way. Seasickness must be horrible. I've never travelled before, but it doesn't seem to have affected me."

"I get it every time," Rowena said with feeling. "The worst was the Irish Sea, I thought I was going to die."

"Is he helpful?" Anne enquired, nodding towards the closed door where Paul had gone. "Don't you have a maid with you?"

"She's worse than I am," Rowena said. "Paul is very kind, but he doesn't understand."

"I can imagine."

"It's worse when we have the children with us."

"Do they suffer as well?" Anne asked.

"No," Rowena said. "They are exactly like him, it doesn't seem to affect them at all."

"That must be awful, I think I'd want to murder all of them. Doesn't it help to be outside? It's very stuffy in here."

"I can't bear the thought of anybody seeing me looking this bad," Rowena confessed.

Anne studied her with her head on one side. She was beginning to understand a number of things, one of which was that Paul van Daan had not fallen in love with her because she reminded him of his wife. She could also see, with painful understanding, how easy it must have been for him to find comfort with this girl on his difficult return from Assaye. Even in her illness there was an aura of appealing gentleness about Rowena van Daan, which Anne was ruefully aware she would never possess.

"Well, you'll need to get over that," she said briskly. "You need fresh air. Come on, up you get, and we'll get you dressed. You'll make yourself really ill staying in here the whole time."

She coaxed the other girl into her clothes and hunted under the bunk for her shoes, then reached for a hairbrush and ran it through the long fair hair. Rowena van Daan was looking slightly stunned.

"Is your husband with the regiment?" she asked.

"He's with the quartermaster's department seconded onto Sir Arthur Wellesley's staff. We've only been married six months."

"And you knew Paul in Yorkshire?"

"I did. Robert was his quartermaster. Paul threw the previous one through the window."

"Oh no."

"Didn't he tell you?"

Rowena shook her head. "No. He often doesn't, I think he worries about upsetting me."

"I think it would upset me more not knowing," Anne said.

"It does," Rowena said and Anne met her eyes in the mirror and recognised a shared moment of sheer exasperation. It made her like this girl more than she had expected to.

Rowena sat still while Anne twisted her hair up into a simple knot and pinned it neatly. "You're very good at this."

"Not that you'd know it looking at me," Anne said, indicating her own loose hair. "I must look like a gypsy."

"You look beautiful," Rowena said quietly, studying her. "Arabella Cartwright is going to have a fit."

"Who?"

"She is one of the officers' wives and the toast of Lisbon. Very lovely. But I don't think she's as beautiful as you are. And she's certainly not as pleasant."

Something in Rowena's tone made Anne wonder. Paul had made no mention of Mrs Cartwright, but he had been very frank about his occasional infidelities. Looking at the fair girl sitting on the bed, Anne thought ruefully that the woman married to Paul would need to develop a sharp set of claws, and it was clear that Rowena had none.

"Is she unpleasant to you?" she asked quietly.

Rowena looked startled. "Sometimes," she admitted. "I am not good at parties. Paul is very patient about it."

"Paul needs to stop being patient and start throwing his weight around a little more. I'd wager that she'd shut up fairly fast if she thought it might affect her husband's career."

The green eyes widened in horror. "Mrs Carlyon, Paul would never do that!"

Anne could not help smiling. "Rowena – if it suited him Paul would do pretty much anything. Don't worry. If she starts around me you won't need Paul, trust me." She glanced in Rowena's mirror. "Oh dear. I should, of course, go back to my cabin and do up my hair, but I'm not going to. Sooner or later, I'm going to shock the officers, I may as well start now. There, you look lovely. Come along."

Anne towed the girl up onto the deck. There were more people about now, as some of the officers had finished their breakfast and were taking the air. Anne drew Rowena over to the ship's rail and they stood breathing in the cool, damp air, looking out across the gunmetal waves to the masts and sails of the other transports. Gradually Anne noticed some colour coming back into Rowena's face.

"Better?" she asked.

"Much," Rowena admitted, glancing sideways at Anne. "Thank you, Mrs Carlyon. You've been very kind."

"Not in the least, I've an ulterior motive. I know nothing of Lisbon or of military life and will need a friend to guide me through it. And you should call me Nan, I am not good at formality. You may have noticed that."

Unexpectedly Rowena van Daan began to laugh. "Are you always like this?"

"Sometimes I'm worse," Anne admitted. "Good morning, Major, I've brought your wife up for some fresh air."

"Good God, Rowena. What on earth are you doing up here? Are you all right?"

Paul and Robert were accompanied by an older man, possibly in his late thirties, with dark hair and a prominent hooked nose. Rowena bobbed a polite curtsy to him.

"How do you do, sir," she said softly.

"Very well, ma'am. Good to see you're feeling better."

Paul was looking at his wife with affectionate amusement. "You look like a new woman," he said.

"I do feel better." Rowena shot Anne an unexpectedly mischievous glance. "Mrs Carlyon proved to be an excellent remedy. Bracing, but effective."

Paul laughed aloud, took his wife's hand and kissed it. Anne thought with a sharp pain, that they looked very natural together. She probed at the pain cautiously and was relieved to find that it was manageable. Alongside her envy of Rowena van Daan was liking and a strong wish to get to know the other girl better, and it seemed to help.

"How on earth did you achieve this, Nan?"

"I bullied her. I'm surprised you hadn't thought of it yourself."

Paul's eyes lit up with amusement. "I never bully my wife."

"No, you saved that for the poor souls of the 115th North Yorkshire," Anne said. Seeing Paul standing beside Robert was making her feel slightly sick. She had a sudden acute vision of Paul's reaction if he ever found out what Robert Carlyon had done to make her marry him, and she pushed the thought aside. More than ever now she needed to hide the truth.

***

As he stood on the deck beside Wellesley, Paul regarded his wife in some surprise. Rowena was genuinely looking much better, and far from resenting the bracing directness of Anne Carlyon's manner, she seemed to be enjoying it. He watched them standing together at the rail and thought that two women could not have been more different. His wife was angelically fair, neat and ladylike from head to toe. Anne Carlyon was half a head taller, her hair falling around her shoulders in a curtain of black silk and her eyes bright and amused, resting with some curiosity on the austere countenance of Sir Arthur Wellesley. She looked achingly beautiful and not at all ladylike. Paul glanced at his chief to see his reaction and the expression on his face made it all too clear what was on the general's mind.

"Won't you introduce me, Lieutenant Carlyon?" Wellesley said.

"This is my wife, Sir Arthur," Robert said quickly. "We were married last year."

"Almost newly-weds, eh? Devil of a way to spend your honeymoon, m'dear," Wellesley said, and Paul wanted to laugh at his genial tone, given that three minutes earlier he had been speaking of the Ordnance department in London in tones of biting scorn. "Thought you were on your way to the Cape, didn't you?"

"We did, sir, but Robert is happy to serve where he is needed. It's an honour to meet you."

"Likewise, ma'am. Shall you like Lisbon, do you think?"

"I don't know very much about it," Anne said, frankly. "I read a great deal about the Cape of Good Hope, though, so if you require any information about that, I am the woman to ask."

The commander gave a bark of laughter. "I shall remember that if I'm posted there next, by God I shall," he said. "Carlyon, you impudent young devil, you should have introduced me before. I shall return the favour, my dear, and if you will take a turn about the deck with me, I shall tell you all about Lisbon. With your permission of course, Carlyon."

"Of course, sir."

Wellesley held out his arm, and Anne accepted it. She glanced across at Paul and he winked at her shamelessly. Anne looked away, and Paul admired her demure expression.

Sir Arthur Wellesley was an accomplished flirt, and it was clear to Paul that his opinion of the voyage to Lisbon was markedly improved by the presence of a beautiful girl. During dinner he insisted on sitting beside Anne, talking freely of the coming campaign. Anne seemed inclined to be amused at first, but before long she became visibly more interested. Paul watched her become involved in the discussion about supplies and transport and could see his chief responding to her questions with growing enthusiasm.

"Carlyon, you need to watch the general with your wife," Carl said softly. "I've seen him flirting before, but I've never seen him quite so taken with a lady. She's lovely, you're a lucky man."

Paul watched Anne's husband during the meal trying to decide if Robert was jealous of Wellesley's attentions to Anne. He did not seem like a particularly affectionate husband. There was none of the laughing banter that Paul knew Anne to be capable of, and he realised that apart from essential communication, the couple hardly spoke to each other or looked at each other.

Anne was leaning one elbow on the table informally, her attention wholly on his chief. Wellesley, who had a marked talent for dividing his attention, was talking about bullock carts and pack animals and looking at the girl's shoulders and breasts, amber in the candlelight. Rowena had excused herself early and gone to bed and Anne was the only woman at the table. Paul glanced around him and hid a smile. His newest officer, Ensign Aldous, was only eighteen, and he had not spoken or taken his eyes from Anne for most of the meal. Carl and Johnny were talking quietly about the new rifles which Paul had managed to obtain for the light company, but Paul was amused to notice that even the staid Wheeler glanced across at the girl every now and then with a kind of exasperated amusement at his own response to her. Every other man around the table was spending at least half his time looking at her. The general's attention was temporarily claimed by his other neighbour and Anne looked at Paul and smiled. She looked remarkably at home. Paul reached for the wine bottle and refilled her glass.

"I knew it was a mistake to let him anywhere near you, bonny lass," he said very softly, and Anne gave a choke of laughter.

"I do like him," she said, equally softly.

"I can see you do," Paul said dryly.

***

On arrival in Lisbon, the Carlyons had arranged to stay temporarily in barracks. Most officers with wives found other billets as quickly as they could, because few women enjoyed the experience of being under the gaze of so many enlisted men as they went about their day-to-day business. Paul

195

wondered if the Carlyons would do the same. They were not expecting to be in Lisbon more than a week or two as Wellesley was determined to move against the French as quickly as possible. He had a point to prove to London, and he was also keen to raise the morale of the dispirited troops in Lisbon. Many of the officers were negative about the chances of the English holding on to Portugal. Privately, Paul felt that they did not yet know much about their energetic, determined commander-in-chief. Whatever bleatings were coming out of London about defensive moves only, Wellesley intended to fight a battle and win.

Robert had taken up his duties at headquarters, and Paul had barely spoken to him. He had liked Robert well enough during his stay in Yorkshire, but their relationship did not seem to have stood the test of time, and Paul felt no particular urge to seek out his company. Already Robert seemed to have found several convivial drinking partners and played cards each evening in the mess for high stakes. Paul, who knew that the money had come as part of Anne's dowry and who could not imagine why a man married to Anne would choose to spend his time away from her, was slightly contemptuous. Whatever the story of this marriage, it was clearly not a love match and Paul was torn between being sad for Anne's sake and being fiercely glad that she had not moved easily from his arms to another.

Riding down from the villa, Paul arrived through the arched gate of the barracks. The place was teeming with men. A battalion was executing a tight drill in square on the parade ground, and Paul reined in to admire their work. They were almost as good as his men, and he nodded approval to a grinning captain as he rode on past. In the distance, he could hear the clicks of muskets as a company of infantry practiced dry firing out at the range. And ahead of him there was a tangle of wagons as two Portuguese carters delivering food and bedding locked wheels and began to shout loudly at each other, gesticulating wildly.

An English voice bellowed at the two men and Paul grinned, recognising the dulcet cockney tones of Private Danny Carter, formerly of the rifles, who had recently been made part of his light company. Like Paul's other skirmishers from the rifles Carter flatly refused to change uniform and Paul did not try to make them. He still wore the white armband that Carter's men had given him after his first battle, and he retained an immense fondness for the independent, obstreperous riflemen.

Carter's voice rose above the two Portuguese.

"Jesus bloody Christ if ever I saw such a pig's ear! Stop whipping the horses you silly bugger and hold still or you'll have the winter feed for the officers' horses used as carpet for the bloody Connaught rangers to dance on!" Carter was yelling as he ran to the centre to try to disentangle the two locked wheels.

Paul stopped to admire the chaos, but before he could ride forward to intervene there was a peal of laughter and a woman's voice called out to Carter. "You're making a worse mull of it than they are. Hold still and I'll come down and help."

She had called from an upstairs window of the officer's block and Paul would have recognised her voice anywhere. In a moment she had arrived through the door and went quickly to the head of one of the frightened horses.

"Here, ma'am, you're going to get hurt!" Carter said in a panic, worried, Paul knew, about whether he could somehow be held responsible for the injury to some officer's mad wife. But the girl took the bridle of the frightened beast and spoke quietly to him. The driver lifted his whip and Anne held up an imperious hand to stop him.

"Stop that! It will frighten him. Stop and wait."

The sense of her words, if not the content, was clear and the driver lowered his whip. Anne beckoned to Carter. "Come here and hold him. Gently, now."

"Yes, ma'am." Carter had clearly just seen the girl properly for the first time, and Paul did not blame him for the expression on his face. She wore a white shirt, like a man's, open at the throat, and a dark riding skirt, which emphasised the small waist and gentle curve of her hips. She had obviously run down without finishing her toilette because her hair was still loose about her shoulders and Paul remembered the feel of it under his hands and felt a stab of longing.

Carter took the bridle and Anne went to the other horse. Talking soothingly to him, she carefully backed him up, and Carter led the other horse to one side, separating the carts. The two drivers both burst into voluble thanks in Portuguese and Anne smiled at them impartially. One of them, the younger of the two, took a flower from the buttonhole of his dark jacket and leaned down to give it to Anne.

"Obrigada, señor," Anne said, and the driver, who had the benefit of knowing that he would be gone before the lady's husband reappeared, placed his fingers to his lips and blew her a dramatic kiss before driving off.

Anne stood twirling the flower between long, elegant fingers. The other driver moved away and Private Carter came forward uncertainly.

"Thank you, ma'am."

Anne turned to look at him. Then she pointed at the retreating driver. "It's all very well scattering flowers around to passing females," she said, "but if he doesn't improve his driving skills the next person he comes across is likely to be a fat choleric colonel with a riding crop and a bad attitude." She tapped the flower onto Carter's chest to emphasise her point and turned at the sound of an approaching horse. Shading her eyes against the sun she looked up at Paul. "And I notice that you kept well out of reach until the work was done."

Paul was conscious of poor Carter, unable to take his eyes from the vivid laughing face. He swung down from Rufus. "I was admiring your technique," he said.

"With the horses or the drivers?" Anne enquired, going to Rufus' head. "Good morning, boy, how are you again?"

"Both," Paul said. "Rufus is pleased to see you. He knows a woman who keeps carrot tops in her pocket."

"He's out of luck, I left my jacket upstairs," Anne said. "How are you, Paul?"

"You know I do think we may have to find you a billet out of the barracks," Paul said. "Now that I have seen you in action, I realise that it is a matter of keeping my men safe. Close your mouth, Carter."

"Yes, sir," Carter said. "You know the lady, sir?"

"To my cost. This is Mrs Anne Carlyon. Lieutenant Carlyon is on Sir Arthur Wellesley's staff. I met Mrs Carlyon on my trip to Yorkshire last year. At the time she was still choosing between her many suitors."

"Welcome to Portugal, ma'am."

"Thank you, Private Carter. You have much better manners than your commanding officer."

"We've tried to teach him, ma'am."

Anne shot him a startled glance, visibly taken aback by Carter's straight-faced impudence, and then burst out laughing.

"Keep trying, Carter, he may improve," she said.

"I have come with messages from Rowena," Paul said. "Is it possible that you could stop flirting with the enlisted men and invite me in for a drink?"

"Unchaperoned?" Anne looked up at him from under long lashes. "Is that the right thing to do here? I need Rowena to tell me how to behave."

"You actually do," Paul said, laughing. "Robert has all my sympathy, he is never going to be able to control you."

"And what makes you think you'd do any better?" Anne said lightly.

"I'd never make the attempt; I know my limitations." Paul was very aware of Carter's interested regard.

"Excuse me, sir, but this has just come for you."

Paul turned at the melodious Irish tones of his newly promoted sergeant-major. "Good morning, Sergeant-Major O'Reilly. Thank you. Carter, would you take Rufus to the stables and deliver him to the groom, who should have been here to take him if he were not probably flirting with the cook's daughter."

"How do you know the cook has a pretty daughter, sir?"

"I notice these things," Paul said, scanning the message quickly. "This is an invitation to something that I have no intention of attending. Lose it, Sergeant-Major."

"Just as you say, sir." Sergeant-Major O'Reilly said woodenly.

"Excellent," Paul said cheerfully. "I feel that my day is starting well."

***

Michael noticed Anne from a distance as he walked up to find Paul. It was difficult not to, there were very few well-dressed women in barracks, let alone one who had not even troubled to put up her hair. Michael studied her as he approached. For a moment, he could not believe what he was seeing, but as he got closer, he was very sure. Carter had moved away with the horse, still watching Anne, and Paul glanced from one to another.

"I think perhaps introductions are in order," he said. "Sergeant-Major…"

"Sir, the lady may not wish to be introduced to an NCO," Michael said warningly. At times he found himself wondering if his commanding officer had ever been taught the rules of society, but the girl with the lovely dark eyes was smiling. Paul smiled back at her and continued as though Michael had not spoken.

"Sergeant-Major O'Reilly, this is Mrs Anne Carlyon, who is married to Lieutenant Robert Carlyon on Sir Arthur's staff. Nan, this is Michael O'Reilly, my sergeant-major without whom the battalion would not function. Michael is here to remind me of my duty, and Nan is here to flirt with Danny Carter and two Portuguese drivers."

Michael was looking at the girl's face. He remembered her as he had last seen her, a gallant little figure in a blue cloak who refused to cry. He wondered if she had any idea who he was, then she smiled again, a smile of warmth and recognition and genuine interest and to his complete astonishment held out her hand. "I remember you," she said. "I saw you in the carriage that morning in Thorndale."

Michael felt a jolt of surprise, not at her recollection but at her willingness to acknowledge it. He was not used to shaking hands with an officer's wife, but he could hardly ignore her outstretched hand, so he shook it.

"You've a good memory for a passing face, ma'am."

Paul looked at her. "I didn't know you'd seen him," he said quietly. "Nan…"

"Don't look so worried, Paul. If you trust him, then so do I. I am glad to have met you properly, though, Sergeant-Major, I've heard a lot about you."

Michael was studying her. He was very aware of her startling beauty, but there was something more about this girl that he found immensely appealing. Her frank acknowledgment of her relationship with his commanding officer was both surprising and impressive and he glanced at Paul and was shocked at the unguarded expression on his face. It was clear that the passage of time and her marriage had not affected Major van Daan's feelings about Anne Carlyon.

"It's good to meet you too, ma'am," he said gently. "I should be getting on." Michael looked at his commanding officer. "Are you coming, sir?"

"Yes, I'll be with you in a moment." Paul turned back to Anne. "Are you attending this ghastly reception this evening?"

Anne nodded. "Yes. Was that the invitation that you were just trying to get your sergeant-major to lose?"

"It was. But if you'll be there, I'll come. We're only going to be here for a week or so, Wellesley wants to take Oporto back and he's in a hurry. I don't know if he'll want Robert with us or if he'll leave him here, but I'm concerned about you living in barracks without him."

"You mean without you," Anne said.

"Yes, I do." Paul ran his eyes over her with a rueful smile. "Look at you. Poor Carter nearly passed out when he got a good eyeful, and he won't be the only one. I don't know how much your husband cares, I only know how much I do. I'll talk to you later, I have to go."

He lifted her hand to his lips and ran to catch up with his sergeant-major. Neither of them spoke for a while. They walked up towards the training field. Finally Paul said:

"If you've anything to say, Michael, better get it over with now."

"Yes, sir. Something of a surprise, and that's for sure. Did you know she was coming?"

"No. They were on their way to the Cape and Hookey intercepted them. He needed a good administrator. And Carlyon is one, whatever else he is."

"And what about your wife, sir?"

"She's met my wife already, Sergeant-Major," Paul said with grim humour. "They like each other."

"God love you, sir, only you could get yourself into this one. Does anybody but me...?"

"No. I've told nobody and I won't. She was a lass I met in Yorkshire and now she's Carlyon's wife and Rowena's friend. That's all."

"Well, you'd better get bloody better at it than that, then, sir, because you just looked at her as though she's a gift you never expected to get."

"She is," Paul said quietly.

Michael turned to study his commander's face. Paul had an unusually expressive countenance and Michael had learned to read him very well. It made for an effective working relationship and an easy friendship which his sergeant-major had come to take for granted, but he had never seen his friend like this.

"Jesus Christ, sir, how in God's name, after sleeping with half the women in England, did you come to fall in love with a girl that young and that out of reach?" he said softly. "I swear to God I thought you immune."

"So did I," Paul said. He glanced sideways at his sergeant-major. "I never intended it, Michael, but I've never met a woman remotely like her. I know what you see, lad, and that's what the rest of the army are going to see as they trip over their own feet every time she walks past. But I'm telling you, there's a lot more to this girl than the way she looks."

Michael could not help smiling. "I get that, sir. But you need to be careful, not just for your wife's sake but for hers too. She's newly married and very young and you know what the headquarters gossips are like with a reputation."

"Michael, she's here, when I never expected to see her again. I will get better at it, and I'm not going to hurt Rowena. But don't ask me to lie to you and pretend that I'm not bloody happy. Because I am. And next week I'm going to fight the French, which believe it or not is what I came here for."

Chapter Twelve

The citizens of Lisbon welcomed the arrival of Sir Arthur Wellesley with joyous relief. General Cradock, the man he was replacing, was seen as a gentlemanly but ineffectual commander and Wellesley, with his triumph at Vimeiro fresh in the public memory, was a hero. The streets of the town were lit up for three nights in a row, and the wealthier citizens of Lisbon vied with each other to entertain their general and his officers.

The reception was held in one of the large, elegant mansions higher up above the narrow filthy streets, which led down to the port. Major van Daan had offered to collect Anne and Robert in the carriage he had hired for his wife's use while they were in Lisbon. The Carlyons had been allocated two rooms in barracks, a sitting room and a bedroom, and Anne was sitting before her mirror in her petticoats twisting her long hair into a plaited coronet when her husband came into the room.

Robert ran his eyes over her without smiling. "I spoke to Van Daan today," he said. "He was up at headquarters for some meeting with Wellesley and Beresford. He was wondering if the general will want me to accompany the army north."

"Do you want to?" Anne asked.

Robert nodded. "I won't get promotion sitting behind a desk at headquarters. I need experience in field administration. It occurs to me that Van Daan's close relationship with the general could be useful."

Anne met his eyes in the mirror. "Perhaps you should try to be civil to him then," she said. "Since we've arrived you've barely spoken."

"I'm sure you've more than made up for it, dear wife. Although that could be useful. I've seen the way he still looks at you. And Wellesley is almost as bad. Perhaps you could be useful for something other than your father's money and to save me going to the brothel."

"Feel very free to go back to the brothel, Robert."

"You speak to me like that again and you'll wish you hadn't."

Anne got up. She was suddenly angry. "If you hit me anywhere it shows you'll wish you hadn't," she snapped. "You could have done what the hell you liked to me at the Cape, but you need to be a bit more careful here,

201

because if Paul van Daan gets the slightest hint of what you're doing to me, he'll kill you, Robert. I may have married you in part to save his career but believe me when I tell you that he won't give a damn about it."

Robert lifted a hand and Anne steeled herself not to flinch away, but he lowered it again. "And I see it's still mutual," he said. "Feel free to flirt as much as you like, Nan. Just remember, when they're whispering sweet words in your ear on the terrace, to mention just how much you would appreciate a chance for your dear husband."

"Certainly, dear Robert. Just how far would you like me to go to further your career? I seem to remember on the day you first raped me that you didn't seem much interested in who fathered my children, but before I offer to sleep with the general or Paul van Daan to pay for your promotion I should just check that you approve."

Anne saw in his eyes that she had gone too far. He wrenched her towards him, dragged her over to the bed and threw her forwards onto it. Anne rolled over onto her back and watched him open his clothing, dreading it, wishing that she had not lost her temper.

"Robert, no. Please, no. Not now."

"You should have thought of that before opening that mouth of yours, I can hurt you without bruises that show, Nan."

"I've reason to know that," Anne said bitterly. His weight was above her and he took her wrists and pinned her arms to the bed. Anne tried to detach her mind as she often did, but this time it was not working.

"Robert, no. Why do you do this?"

"I wouldn't need to if you weren't such a bitch, Nan."

Anne felt his hands dragging up her petticoat and suddenly she knew that she could not bear it. "Robert, wait. Wait."

The change in her tone surprised him and he paused. Anne could feel her heart hammering in her chest. For six months she had scratched and bitten and fought him and she was exhausted. This could go on for the rest of her life. Anne closed her eyes for a long moment and then opened them and made herself meet her husband's eyes.

"Wait," she said, making her voice softer. "I'm not going anywhere. Just let me go for one minute."

He was so surprised that he released her. Anne sat up cautiously, studying him.

"What do you want from me, Robert?"

The question seemed to surprise him. Finally, he said:

"You despise me, don't you?"

"It's hard not to, given what you've done to me these past months. But I'm tired of being hurt. So, I want to see if there's an easier way." Ruefully Anne shook her head. "I thought once you had the money it would be enough."

Her husband regarded her steadily for a long time. Then unexpectedly he said:

"So did I. It isn't."

"All right. We're married. You have the money, and you have me. I've nowhere else to go, so please, just stop hurting me, you don't need to."

Anne reached up and pulled the pins from her hair, shaking her head so that it fell about her shoulders. Sitting up she reached for the laces of her stays and undid them very slowly, her eyes on his face. The abrupt change in her behaviour appeared to have frozen Robert. In silence she slid out of her petticoats and chemise and reached for his clothing. He allowed her to undress him, apparently mesmerised, as though he had never been with a woman before. Anne lay back, her heart beating so hard that she was feeling sick, and drew him down to kiss her, pressing her body against his.

His mouth covered hers and Anne parted her lips and slid her tongue into his mouth. She had never once kissed Robert like this and to her surprise she felt his immediate, urgent response. Very lightly she drew her nails down his back and he gasped in pleasure and moved above her. He hesitated, looking down at her, suddenly uncertain, as if he had never really seen her before. Anne felt almost ill with nerves, but she shifted again, very deliberately keeping her body as relaxed as she could.

"Nan?"

Anne reached up to caress his face. "It's all right," she said.

She was surprised at how quickly he seemed to respond to the change in her attitude and she wondered suddenly if this compliance was what he had been wanting from her. He was almost tender with her body, and Anne moved against him, her eyes on his, letting him enjoy her without fighting him or pulling back. It was not easy, and she suspected it never would be, but it was bearable, better than the violence she had become used to. Somehow being close to Paul again had given her courage. When it was over, she heard him whisper her name.

"Nan – dear God."

Robert lay beside her and Anne did not move, frightened to do anything to antagonise him. After a long moment he pushed himself up and leaned over her.

"Kiss me again," he said, and Anne felt overwhelming relief. She reached up obediently, and he ran his hands very gently down her body.

"That was good," he whispered.

"Better?"

"Yes." Robert studied her. "You're very beautiful. I don't think I really thought about that before I married you, but they all see it, even Wellesley." He paused. "I didn't expect to want you this much."

"I'm here. You don't need to hold me down every time."

Robert shifted reluctantly away from her. "I'm going to change next door. Don't be late."

In the carriage to the reception, Anne made easy conversation with Rowena who was girlishly pretty in a soft rose-coloured dress. Seated close beside her husband, Anne could sense that Robert was tense and uncomfortable and realised with some surprise that she was the cause. It was as if he had never allowed himself to admit his desire for her. She

203

acknowledged ruefully that the girl who had reluctantly agreed to marry him six months earlier would have rebelled angrily at the idea of using her body to keep his violence at bay, but Anne had grown up during that time. She was conscious of a sense of self-disgust, but she had left his bed whole and unbruised for the first time ever. Given that she had to live her life with him, Anne decided that she needed to set her distaste to one side and keep herself safe.

"Robert, have you thought about billeting arrangements?" Paul said.

Robert shook his head. "There's not much decent accommodation in the town."

"Has Hookey spoken to you about coming north with the army?"

"Not yet."

"I think it's likely, he needs effective quartermasters. And if you are, you shouldn't leave your wife in barracks unprotected." Paul glanced across at Anne and she saw a flicker of a smile. "Rowena has suggested that you two take the top floor of our villa. We have the first two floors, and there are rooms on the second, which Carl and Dr Norris are using, but the top floor is virtually unused. She'll be company for Rowena while I'm away and it's more comfortable than the barracks."

Robert looked startled. "Are you sure? It would be ideal, sir, but…"

"Do I get a say?" Anne asked sweetly.

"No," Paul said. "Not when it comes to this. If Robert is with the army, he needs to know you're safe."

Anne met his eyes and despite herself she smiled. "That's thoughtful of you, Major."

"You should also find yourself a maid since you didn't bring one with you."

Anne shot a glance at Robert and was relieved that he did not seem to be angry. Paul's concern for her welfare was in sharp contrast to her husband's indifference and Anne loved it, but she did not want it to jeopardise her new and very fragile peace with Robert. She looked back at Paul, shaking her head.

"Paul, there is a limit to the interference I am prepared to accept with my domestic arrangements."

Paul grinned. "You don't take a particle of notice of anything I say, Nan."

The reception rooms were brilliantly lit, chandeliers glittering with the light of a thousand candles. The orchestra played a series of light introductory airs as Anne gave her hand to Sir Arthur Wellesley and saw a reflection of her husband's desire in his hooded eyes.

"You look beautiful, ma'am. You shall save me a dance if you please. More than one."

"Sir Arthur, you are commander-in-chief. I should not dare refuse."

He gave his short, barking laugh. "By God, I wish all my officers were as ready to obey, ma'am. Where's your husband? Carlyon, my compliments on your wife, sir. Most beautiful woman in Portugal, I swear it."

"Thank you, sir."

Wellesley looked back at Anne. He was still holding her hand. She was conscious of Paul, who had stopped with Rowena to talk to Marshal Beresford. He was struggling with an expression of unholy amusement.

"I am thinking of stealing your husband to come north with me, ma'am. We'll need experienced quartermasters. What do you think?"

"I think he would be honoured to go with you, sir."

Paul joined them. "Mrs Carlyon is going to be moving into the spare rooms in our villa, sir. If you've need of her husband, she can keep my wife company."

"Excellent notion. Can't have a lady this lovely alone in army barracks, can we, Major?"

Paul looked at Anne and smiled as though he could not help himself. "No, sir. I was there this morning and you need to trust me when I say that she's a menace to the peace of mind of my battalion. I need her out of there if they're going to be capable of fighting at all."

Wellesley lifted her hand to his lips again. "I believe you," he said. "I shall come and find you for my dance, ma'am." He glanced around to see that Robert's attention had been claimed by Colonel Murray. "Take care of her, Major."

Paul took her hand with a grin. "Yes, sir." He drew Anne into the ballroom. "What the devil have you done to Robert tonight, he took off like a scalded cat. Have you quarrelled?"

"Not at all. Although Sir Arthur seems jumpy too."

Paul turned and gave her a long steady appraisal.

"I'm not surprised. You're making me jumpy, and I ought to be used to you. I need to go and have an intelligent conversation about supplies with Señor Ronaldo, but like my commander, I expect more than one dance with you this evening and am prepared to fight for the privilege. Let me introduce you to an old friend of mine whom I think you will like. And will you keep an eye out for Rowena for me? She's all right with Beresford, he has a soft spot for her, but she hates these affairs."

Anne laughed. "I will. But honestly, Paul..."

"I know. I have a nerve asking you, don't I? But you're good for her, lass." Paul lifted her hand to his lips, his eyes on her face. "You're going to spend the evening listening to men telling you how beautiful you look, Nan, there's nothing new I can say to you."

"There probably is, Paul, you can be very imaginative with your compliments as I recall."

He smiled down at her, still holding her hand. "I'd probably better not say that here, bonny lass, people are going to notice you blush. Come and meet Kate."

He led her across the room to a group of women, one of whom was an older woman, possibly in her late fifties, dressed in an old-fashioned gown of dark blue. Her iron-grey hair was pinned up neatly under a white lace cap and her weathered face bore a pair of shrewd dark eyes which surveyed Anne thoughtfully as Paul made his introductions.

"Kate, this is Mrs Carlyon who is new to Portugal and will be billeted with us. Her husband is at headquarters. Nan, this is Mrs Kate Barry. Colonel Barry commands the 120th and her youngest son, whom you have met, is one of my ensigns."

He bowed and moved away, and Kate Barry surveyed Anne with thoughtful eyes. "Mrs Carlyon, welcome to Lisbon. May I introduce Mrs Cavendish and Mrs Denholm, both married to lieutenants in the 120th. They have been in Lisbon for a little while."

"How do you do?" Anne said, aware that both women, who were a few years older than her, were studying every detail of her gown, her hair and her appearance.

"So you are new to army life, my dear?" said Mrs Denholm. "And you are to be billeted with the Van Daans I hear?"

"Lucky you," Mrs Cavendish said with a giggle. "So much more luxurious than most of our accommodation."

"To say nothing of the pleasure of dining with Major van Daan several times a week," Mrs Denholm said, rolling her eyes expressively. "I wonder if Rowena van Daan has any idea how lucky she is."

Anne smiled. "I have been fortunate. Robert and I both knew Paul from England and Rowena and I became friends aboard ship."

"Poor dear Rowena," Mrs Cavendish sighed. "We all feel for her."

Anne felt an edge of irritation. "Do you?" she said, lifting her eyebrows in what she knew to be her most supercilious manner. "I can't imagine why."

"I should not gossip. Although perhaps you should be placed a little on your guard if you are living under his roof." Mrs Cavendish studied her. "You are, after all, very young, ma'am, and possibly innocent concerning men like Paul van Daan. Let us say he is not the most faithful of husbands. I shall say no more but no doubt you will hear all about it when you have been here longer. Oh look, Lady Sinclair has arrived. My dears, what a quiz of a gown! But I must say 'how do you do' to her. Please excuse me, Mrs Carlyon."

The two women flitted away. Anne took a sip of champagne and looked at Mrs Barry. There was a glint of amusement in the older woman's gimlet eyes.

"I can see I have a lot to learn," Anne said. "Should I ask you to enlighten me, ma'am? I am sure you know everything there is to know. I am beginning to realise why Rowena dislikes parties."

"I am sure that before the end of the evening Mrs Cavendish or Mrs Denholm could easily be persuaded to enlighten you, despite their dislike of gossip."

"I have no doubts," Anne said. "Will you forgive my impertinence if I said that I feel your version might be a little more reliable and a little less sensational?"

Kate Barry gave a crack of laughter. "Very impertinent indeed, for a newcomer. But I am inclined to think that your intentions are good."

They had reached the long windows at the end of the room, open to allow a breeze through. Kate stepped out onto the wide stone terrace. She took up a position at the stone balustrade. Anne leaned on it and looked out over the lights of Lisbon.

"Beautiful," she said. "From here there is no sign of the dirt or the squalor, only the charm."

"The smells are further away as well," Kate said, and Anne laughed.

"We are lucky to be up here."

"Paul insists on the best for his wife. He is very good to her in other ways too. But those silly women are not wrong, of course."

Anne turned to look at her. "Is that why you brought me out here?"

"I have decided that I can trust you not to gossip unduly, although most of this is common knowledge. But you seem to have a kindness for Rowena, and she does not have friends among the officers' wives."

"She seems very shy."

"She is. I have always thought her a surprising choice for Paul. I've known him since he first arrived in India back in '02. He has always been a disgraceful womaniser, but he does try to be discreet now that he is married. Some of his liaisons are more scandalous than others. You will, at some point, be introduced to Mrs Arabella Cartwright, a rather lovely redhead who is married to my husband's quartermaster. It is common knowledge that her relations with Paul have gone well beyond flirting. She is not a pleasant woman, and she will be jealous of you, so be warned."

"Heavens, why?"

"Because you are younger than she is and very beautiful and living under Paul's roof, something she would love to have achieved. Her reputation is not good, but people feel sorry for her husband, so she is tolerated. I think Paul probably broke it off a while ago, but she would be happy to rekindle the affair if he would let her."

"Is that what Mrs Denholm was referring to?"

"Partly. Gossip has also linked him to a pretty brunette who is the widow of an elderly major in the Highlanders. Major McBride was killed at Corunna. She was years younger than him and has set herself up in a charming apartment in Lisbon where she entertains the officers. Rumour has it that Paul van Daan was her lover even before her husband died."

"Rumour?"

Kate shrugged. "It may not be true. After all, who is likely to ask him?"

"Does Rowena know?"

"I have no idea, but I imagine so. She does what most women do, pretends to notice nothing."

"That's a pity. I think it would probably work better if she slapped his face occasionally, but she's too nice for that."

Mrs Barry regarded her in some amusement. "Is that what you would do, ma'am?"

"Quite probably, I don't have Rowena's tolerance." Anne turned as the curtains moved and the subject of their conversation appeared before them.

"Here you are. I've been looking for you, Wellesley is about to send out search parties. There is to be dancing, and he wants you to open the proceedings with him."

"Does he? I hope I don't step on his toes, then."

Paul laughed. "You dance better than he does," he said. "Aren't you cold out here? This thing is designed for the ballroom, not a stroll in the night air." He reached out with both hands and adjusted her silk scarf about her shoulders. Anne felt his fingers brush her back, lingering in a deliberate caress and she felt her heart skip a beat. Colour scorched into her face and she was glad that it was too dark for Kate Barry to notice.

"I'll go and find him," she said.

***

Paul stood with his friends and his wife, watching Anne dancing with Wellesley. Robert had disappeared into the card room.

"Well, this has put a smile on Wellesley's face for once," Carl said. "She is a lovely woman, mind."

"She is," Wheeler said. "Although I'm not sure I'd want to be married to her. She seems to be on first name terms with half the officers in the army and she's only been here a few days. Didn't you know her in England, sir? What's her background?"

"Her father is a wealthy manufacturer. Plenty of money. Very respectable."

"Maybe so, but she's quickly establishing herself as the worst flirt in Lisbon. Do you think it bothers Carlyon?"

"I doubt it. He got what he wanted, which was her money. Her brother got a seat in Parliament in return. A very simple sales transaction." Paul could hear the distaste in his own voice. "I don't suppose either party really cared much about what happened to the merchandise. Rowena, would you like to dance?"

He led his wife onto the floor, and Carl glanced at Johnny. "What's he pissed off about?" he enquired.

"God knows. I think he has a liking for the girl."

"I don't blame him, I like her myself. She's kind to Rowena, too, which is nice to see. Most of these women are bitches to her. Jealous, probably."

"Yes. I'm just being a stickler for propriety. But be honest, Carl – doesn't it affect you when that girl looks up from those big dark eyes and calls you by your given name and leans forward just a little too much giving you an excellent view..."

"Oh yes."

Johnny laughed aloud. "I'm glad it's not just me. Thank God she's become so friendly with Rowena. It'll keep Paul's hands off her. But I imagine he's thought about it."

"I imagine he thought about it two minutes after meeting her. It'll do him good, for once, lusting after a woman he really can't have."

Paul took his wife home early. Rowena seemed to enjoy herself and Paul had noticed Anne Carlyon's protective attitude to her. He was unaccustomed to his wife making friends, but she had spent much of the evening with Anne and he had watched them talking and laughing together and was surprised to find that it pleased him. Leaving Rowena with her maid, he walked up through the town to return to the reception. He was too restless to sleep and thought that Carl and Johnny might feel like going on for a drink at the tavern frequented by the NCOs and men of the 110th. Michael and Rory would almost certainly be there. The crowd was thinner by now, with most of the ladies having left, and he was surprised to see Anne Carlyon talking to Carl and Johnny near the door.

"I thought you'd be long gone," Paul said, joining them. "Weren't you going back in the carriage with Clevedon and Withers? Where the devil is Robert?"

"Card room," Johnny said succinctly. "He's looking very settled, so we have been making the most of it." He smiled at Anne and she laughed.

"Captain Wheeler means that he is dying to get home to his bed but is too gallant to desert a lady," she said, and Paul saw with rueful amusement the expression in Johnny's grey eyes as they rested on her face. It seemed to have taken her only a few hours to bring his censorious friend under her spell.

"That would be true in the case of most of the ladies I've met tonight, ma'am, but you are definitely the exception," Johnny said. "I was privileged to witness that set down you gave to Arabella Cartwright earlier, and after that I will wait with you all night if necessary."

"Arabella Cartwright?" Paul said, suddenly alert. "What the devil does she have to say about anything?"

"More than she should," Anne said. "Although I suspect she'll be quieter for a while."

Paul was regarding her. "I'm taking you home," he said. "You can tell me on the way exactly how you come to be having words with Arabella Cartwright at your first headquarters party."

"Only if you'll tell me exactly why Mrs Cartwright is any of your business, Paul."

There was a stunned silence. Paul was well aware that his two friends were staring in complete astonishment at the dark-haired girl. She was looking at him with steady black eyes and he took a very deep breath.

"You've been here five minutes and already you're seducing my men, flirting with my general and frightening the ladies of headquarters. Christ knows what you'll manage in a month." Paul looked at Carl. "Before you leave, Carl, will you give my compliments to Lieutenant Carlyon and tell him I have taken his wife home – as he should have done."

"Paul, for God's sake! You can't take her home in a closed carriage."

"You wrong me, Carl. I don't have the carriage, we're going to walk." Paul looked at Anne's evening slippers. "If Mrs Carlyon can manage that. It isn't far."

"Mrs Carlyon will manage. If my shoes hurt, I'll take them off."

"And walk through town in bare feet?" Paul enquired.

"What makes you think I wouldn't, Major?"

"I know you would, you have the decorum of an alley cat. Carl, if you don't want to deliver my message, I will do it myself."

"No, you won't. I'll tell him she left with you and Rowena. Ma'am are you sure...?"

"It's all right, Lieutenant. I promise to keep my shoes on and stay in well-lit places. And if he tries anything improper, he'll be sorry. Thank you both for taking such good care of me. Good night. I'll fetch my cloak, Paul."

Johnny Wheeler watched her go and glanced at Carl. "Do you want me to speak to Carlyon, Carl?"

"No, it's all right. Carlyon looks set for the night, I doubt he'll care what his wife is doing." Carl shot a look at Paul. "Which is probably just as well if she's wandering around in the dark with Major van Daan."

"Are you being disrespectful to a senior officer, Lieutenant Swanson?"

"I think he's just being honest, sir," Johnny said.

"Cheeky bastard. Don't worry, Johnny, I'm just escorting her home."

"I'm not worried, sir, I think Mrs Carlyon can take care of herself. She won me over the moment she called you out over the Cartwright woman, we've all been dancing around that subject for two years. I've never heard a woman speak to you like that before."

"Neither have I. Do you think it will be good for me?"

"I do hope so, sir. I think the lady is ready."

The streets of Lisbon were partly lit, with lanterns hung outside some of the houses. Paul gave Anne his arm and they walked in silence for a while. Eventually he said:

"Are your shoes hurting?"

"If I can dance in them, I can walk in them, Paul."

"I could carry you."

Anne laughed. "I know you could, Major, but we both know where that is likely to lead, don't we?"

"What happened with Mrs Cartwright?"

"Seriously, Paul? She was a bitch to your wife, and I took exception to it."

"Rowena has never said a word to me about having trouble with Bella."

"No. That's how it works with you two, isn't it?" Anne said and Paul could hear the anger in her voice.

"She's not like you, Nan."

"Clearly not. Because if I were married to you and found out you'd been sleeping with Arabella Cartwright, you'd both wish you hadn't."

"I already wish I hadn't, Nan. It was a long time ago and I'm still ashamed of myself. But if she's being unpleasant to Rowena, I can put a stop to it very quickly, and I will."

"That's what I told Rowena."

Paul was torn between concern and amusement. "Oh God, I don't even want to think about the conversations you might be having with my wife."

210

"None of them need worry you, Paul. She's so lonely; it makes me want to cry. She needs someone to talk to."

Paul gave her a sideways glance. "You really like her, don't you?"

"Yes. Why should that surprise you? I like you as well."

"Well, I don't like your husband that much, Nan. And I've a strong suspicion that you don't, either."

Anne did not reply but there was something about the expression in the dark eyes which unexpectedly broke Paul's heart. "They bloody made you marry him, didn't they?" he asked quietly.

He could see her considering a lie, but after a long pause, she nodded.

"Jesus Christ, I could kill them! I hope your bloody brother enjoys being an MP, because he's sitting on the most expensive seat in Parliament." Paul studied her. "Is he good to you, Nan? Because if there is anything..."

"Paul, no. We can't have this conversation. It's too painful. And it isn't fair to ask it of me." Anne looked up at him. "Robert married me for money. I married him because I had no choice. Of course it has not been easy, but it will get better. I will find a way to make it better."

Paul could hear a mixture of determination and desperation in her voice. He wanted to ask more, but he knew that he had no right.

"Well if you don't, bonny lass, and he needs killing, you just let me know."

Anne laughed. "Paul, the worst thing about that is that I know you are only half joking."

Paul gave her a small grim smile. "If I thought he'd put a foot out of place with you, love, it wouldn't be a joke. But I'm not going to make your life difficult, don't worry. And, by the way, if I were married to you and you found out I'd been sleeping with Arabella Cartwright or anybody else, I'd be halfway to South America by now."

Anne gave him an amused sideways glance. "I'm not sure where I stand in terms of being jealous of who you sleep with, Paul, it's confusing."

Paul gave a soft laugh. "Christ, Nan, I can't even describe how confused I feel. Watching you with Rowena...I used to think that would be about the worst thing that could happen to me. But honestly, despite everything I'm just so bloody glad to see you again. I can't pretend anything else."

Anne looked up at him. "Nor can I," she said warmly. "I like your friends."

"They like you too, girl of my heart. You've melted Johnny Wheeler, he was all set to disapprove of you. I'd give a lot to know what you said to Bella."

"Why don't you ask her?"

"We're not on those terms these days."

"Your taste has got better then."

"It really has, love." Ahead of them the low walls of the barracks loomed. "Kiss me," Paul said quietly, and Anne turned and went into his arms for one long desperate kiss. Then it was done, and he stood watching her until she was safe inside her quarters and out of his sight.

211

With the help of several of Paul's men, Anne and Robert's possessions were moved to the villa before Wellesley led his army north to Coimbra towards the end of the month. Anne was at the barracks to watch the 110th leave. Robert had ridden out earlier with the other quartermasters, and Anne had checked the bare rooms to make sure that she had left nothing behind before walking down the stairs to watch the departure. Already Paul was mounted, riding up and down the lines of his companies, stopping for the occasional word. He looked business-like and remote and Anne studied him, knowing that he was unaware of her presence, glad to be able to observe him unseen. She had heard him speak many times, during their months together in Yorkshire, of battle and death and the work that he did. Now she was seeing it first-hand, and she allowed herself to wonder if he would come back alive.

"Do you have an escort back to the villa, ma'am?" a voice said at her elbow and she turned and saw Paul's Irish sergeant-major regarding her. Anne smiled and nodded.

"Yes. Pedro is waiting with my horse. Good luck, Sergeant-Major."

"Thank you, ma'am. Take care of yourself."

"I'm not in any danger," Anne said. Her eyes were on Paul.

"Do you want to speak to him, ma'am, before he leaves?" Michael asked quietly.

Anne turned to look at him. "No," she said. "I don't think there's anything that I could say that would be helpful to him just now, do you? I'm sure that Rowena said all that she should this morning."

"Yes, ma'am." Michael seemed to hesitate. "Try not to fret about the major. You'll have heard all sorts of stories about him being reckless in battle. And he's a brave man, no question. But he doesn't risk the lives of his men without a good cause, so he's not as mad as you'd think."

Anne smiled at him. "Thank you, Michael," she said. "Is this the speech you give to his wife as well?"

The Irishman looked startled. Then his face broke into a smile. "Mrs Carlyon, you're being awful familiar with an NCO," he said.

"Does it bother you?"

Michael looked at her steadily for a long moment and then said:

"My commanding officer has done a very large number of things in his life that I've not understood at all, girl dear. But falling in love with you is beginning to make a fair bit of sense to me. I'll keep an eye on him for you, as well as I can. Keep yourself busy and we'll see you again soon."

Anne stepped towards him, stood on tiptoe and kissed him lightly on the corner of his mouth, then turned and walked towards the stables. Michael went to join his company. They were out of the gate and well along the road when his commanding officer reined in beside him.

"Sergeant-Major, was I seeing things back there, or were you just kissing an officer's wife?"

"I think you'll find she kissed me, sir."

"I wasn't aware you were on kissing terms."

"Nor was I, sir, but she's a girl who knows her own mind. Although to be fair I'm not sure it was me she wanted to be kissing. I wasn't sure you'd seen her there. You could have said goodbye to her."

Paul shook his head. "No, I couldn't. Not in front of the entire battalion. I'm not all that good at saying goodbye to Nan, I made a complete mull of it last time."

"Did you, sir? I'd say she's forgiven you."

"Yes. That's why I thought I'd better not chance it again." Paul touched his horse with his heels and cantered up to join Carl and Johnny Wheeler at the head of the battalion.

***

With Paul and Robert both absent, Anne settled quickly into life in the villa with Rowena. She became firm friends with Mario, who acted as butler and general factotum, and found that within a week he had begun to consult with her about household affairs rather than Rowena who was shy with the staff. At Anne's request, he found her a tutor to help her to learn Portuguese. Rowena seemed both amused and impressed at Anne's determination to learn the language.

"I am hopeless at languages," Rowena admitted, as they sat down to supper one evening. "I learned French at school, but I can only remember a few words, I was a terrible governess. Paul is fluent, he spent some time in France as a boy."

"I'm good at languages," Anne said. "I learned French and I used to sit in on my brothers' Greek and Latin lessons until my stepmother banned me because she said I distracted the tutor."

Her friend laughed. "I'm sure you did."

The door opened and Anne looked round in surprise. The newcomer, a pleasant-faced man of medium height, bowed politely and joined them at the table. Rowena gave him a warm smile.

"Adam, what a pleasant surprise. Nan, this is our other house guest, you've not met him yet, he's hardly here. Dr Adam Norris is in charge of the Eastern hospital. Adam, this is my friend Mrs Anne Carlyon. Her husband is with the army in the quartermaster's department."

Anne shook hands. Adam Norris appeared to be in his mid-thirties. He applied himself to his food with enthusiasm and Anne suspected that he rarely sat down to a proper meal. She had not met anybody from the medical corps so far. Anne was interested and found Norris very willing to talk about his work. He admitted laughingly that he spent too much time at the hospital.

"I'm married to my work, ma'am. And it's probably just as well, because there are too few qualified surgeons, and the trainees and hospital mates they send us from England are often of no use."

"That's true," Rowena said. "The 110th lost its regimental surgeon to fever last year, and we still don't have a replacement."

"What about nurses?" Anne asked curiously.

"We employ some of the women; wives and girlfriends, but it isn't always a success. And we use walking wounded as orderlies, but they often don't want to do the job and they're uncaring. We lack staff and supplies and time, so I don't often make it back here to eat properly and spend time with two lovely ladies. It's a treat."

Anne refilled his wine glass. "Do any of the officers' wives help?" she asked.

"Rarely. The work is hard and dirty, and no man wants his wife thrown together with the enlisted men. It's not work for a lady."

Anne was aware of an immense curiosity. "I've never tried my hand at nursing," she said. "I've no idea if I'd be any good. But I'm interested, Dr Norris. I've nothing to do here apart from talk to Rowena, study Portuguese and listen to gossip. Mario runs the place, we're of no use. I might be completely hopeless, but if you genuinely need help, perhaps I could try."

Norris studied her in some surprise. "Come down and I'll give you the tour. Although I don't know what your husband might say."

"Why don't we see how I get on and then I'll ask him."

Norris regarded her from shrewd blue eyes. "Is that how you usually do things, ma'am?"

"I've not been married long, Doctor, but it's certainly how I managed things as a daughter at home, I've never been very good at rules."

The following day, escorted by Paul's head groom, Anne took herself down to the hospital, which was situated in an abandoned monastery. She followed Norris around the wards on his rounds, trying not to be appalled at the smell and the dirt and the cries of pain of sick and wounded men. She was surprised at how many wounded there were.

"They're coming in steadily, from skirmishes as the army converges on Oporto," Norris said. "It's manageable at the moment, but given a battle, things very quickly get out of control and we have them lying outside the hospital, dying before we can get to them."

"How long have you been doing this?"

"Ten years. I trained in London, but good hospital posts are short and I wanted experience, so I took a position with the army medical board and went to India. I met Paul van Daan at Assaye. It was a mess, Wellesley made a sudden decision to give battle and they'd no hospital set up so a few of us operated out of tents at the edge of the village by the battlefield."

"That battle was bloody, wasn't it?"

Norris nodded. "The worst I've seen so far. Paul was a young, newly promoted captain and he distinguished himself on the field. I'd heard his name over and over, treating the remains of the highlanders that day. He took his men through ahead of orders and took out the guns that were decimating them. I'm told that they hold a dinner each year to commemorate what happened that day, and his name is among those toasted. Although if you mention that to him, he'll tell you that if you get a Scotsman drunk, he'll end up toasting the bedpost."

Anne thought back to the dinner party in Thorndale, and Paul's sudden and surprising loss of control. "Assaye was difficult for him, he talked of it in Yorkshire when we first met."

Norris shot her a surprised look. "Did he? You surprise me, he doesn't often talk about it, but you're extremely easy to talk to. I've often thought that Wellesley pushed for Paul's promotion too young. He obviously recognised his capabilities but didn't give much thought to how he'd cope afterwards. But he recovered very well. I've seen young officers who are never quite the same after a battle like Assaye. Some of them sell out and others turn to drink."

The door flew open, interrupting them. "Doctor, we need your help."

Norris turned. Two guardsmen were lifting a man down from a bullock cart, which had just driven in. Norris excused himself to Anne and went to look, and after a moment Anne followed.

He was a big man, probably in his forties, balding and sunburned with yellowing teeth and a determined jaw, which was clenched with pain. His uniform was filthy and flies hovered about him. His lower leg was a mangled ruin. Anne stared at it, feeling her stomach clench. The smell was overpowering.

"What happened?" Norris asked.

"Small party got cut off. Went looting, I think. Surprised by a French scouting party. All dead but these two, and I doubt they'll make it. They've no field hospital set up yet, so the officer got a local farmer to bring these two back."

Norris glanced into the cart. The second man was younger, soaked in blood and unconscious. "We need to get up there and get set up, it's ridiculous transporting them all this way, no wonder we're losing so many. Bring them through, Garrett, this leg is going to have to come off. The farmer..."

"It's all right, I'll deal with him, he should at least have something to eat and drink for his trouble." Anne stepped forward and spoke to the driver in her halting Portuguese. Norris stared at her in some surprise and then moved back into the hospital.

Anne joined him once the driver had been settled, standing well back as Norris directed two young hospital mates and a grizzled orderly to lift the man onto the operating table. The orderly held a wineskin for the man to drink. He was very pale under his tan but surprisingly calm. Norris was preparing his instruments.

At the first cut into the leg the man bucked against the hospital mates, and blood spurted high. Norris swore.

"Hold him still, for God's sake," he snapped. One of the boys stepped forward and grasped the soldier but the other backed away and Anne saw his face.

"I can't," he whispered, and Anne stepped forward.

"You can't be sick in here, go outside," she ordered, and he glanced at her and then ran, his hand over his mouth. The patient was sobbing quietly, trying to control himself, and Norris was bending over him again, cutting into his leg. Once again, the man's body twisted convulsively, and the knife slipped.

"If you can't keep him still, he's going to lose more than half a bloody leg!" Norris snapped, and Anne came fully forward. She was mesmerised by the sight of the wound, but to her surprise she found that with a job to do, her churning stomach had settled. She moved to the soldier's left side and took his arm and shoulder.

"Hold his leg still," she said to the orderly. "And you – what's your name – Garrett? Take his other arm and look away if you need to. I'll hold this side."

Norris was visibly appalled. "Ma'am, you cannot..."

"Or perhaps I can," Anne said quietly. "Let's see, shall we?" She studied the man's face and gave him a warm smile. "Try not to hit me, I bruise easily, Private."

Anne saw his eyes focus through a haze of pain and widen in surprise. She took his hand and leaned on his arm and shoulder to keep him steady. "Look at me and don't think about it, he'll be quick," she said, and Norris bent to his work. The man went rigid, but remained still, studying Anne's face as though he could not believe he was seeing her.

The room was full of the metallic smell of blood and Anne knew her pelisse would be splashed and stained but she did not move, concentrating all her attention on the patient. "You're doing very well, Private," she said softly, and he nodded, not taking his eyes from her.

"That's it. Let's tie it off, Garrett," Norris said, his voice brisk. Anne turned her head to watch in fascination as he ligated the blood vessels and the flow slowed and stopped. Garrett handed over a dressing and Norris looked up at Anne.

"Why don't you do this bit?" he said suddenly, and Anne moved closer. Norris passed her the dressing and gave instructions. Anne obeyed, her eyes on her work and her hands steady although there was a part of her brain that wanted to scream at the horror and the smell. When she had done, she stepped back and turned back to the patient who was still staring at her.

"Well done," she said. "I think you've earned a tot of rum after that, Private."

The man's face cracked into a yellow toothed smile. "I think you have too, ma'am," he said, and Anne laughed.

"Let's get you cleaned up and onto the ward, Private, and we might have a tot of rum together."

She turned to where the three men were staring at her. Norris said quietly:

"Mrs Carlyon, this wasn't exactly what I had in mind."

"Or me," Anne said. "But Doctor, I think I might be able to help you."

"And what is your husband going to make of that, ma'am?"

"Well, perhaps now is the time I should write to ask him," Anne said calmly. "Will somebody get me some water, this man needs cleaning up before we put him on the ward."

"We don't generally bother, ma'am. They're not that clean to begin with."

Anne studied the patient thoughtfully then smiled. "He won't mind, Doctor, and it'll make me feel a lot better. I can't believe this much dirt is good for healing. Humour me, I'm a volunteer."

"I suppose you are," Norris said with a grin. "All right, Garrett, get Mrs Carlyon what she asks for, since you seem incapable of doing the job yourself and we'll see how this goes."

Chapter Thirteen

Anne rode down to the hospital each morning, escorted by Pedro. Her presence beside Adam Norris as he worked was greeted with astonishment and disapproval by most of the surgeons and hospital mates working at the general hospital, and many of them made no attempt to hide it. Anne endured their snubs and rudeness philosophically. The nature of the work proved so unexpectedly fascinating that she was prepared to put up with considerable inconvenience to continue with it.

After the first ten days Norris abandoned any attempt to shield her from the horrors of the job. Anne realised that when they were working, he had ceased to think of her as an officer's wife at all and treated her as one of his trainees. He taught her, as casualties and sick men were brought in, to stitch up wounds and apply dressings and dig for musket balls. She held men down as he amputated and tied-off blood vessels and learned more about pain and death and sickness than she had ever expected to know.

Anne knew that Norris was worried about the reaction of her husband when he learned what she was doing. She had been working with him for more than two weeks when he escorted her out to her waiting horse one afternoon and asked her:

"Have you heard from Lieutenant Carlyon yet?"

Anne nodded. "I had a letter yesterday. He's approved me helping you although I doubt he's really aware of what I'm doing. His only concern appears to be one of propriety, to be honest."

Norris laughed aloud. "He can't know you that well if he thinks that would bother you, Nan. But I've a suggestion to make. I know you've no personal maid yet, I heard Rowena say so. There is a young woman who works here in the laundry, a Spanish girl by the name of Teresa Cortez, she's probably a year or two older than you."

"Yes, I've seen her about. She doesn't speak much."

"She won't, she's very wary. I let her sleep in the kitchen, she has no home. She was a very young novice in a convent in the north when the French came through. You can probably guess the rest."

"Poor girl."

"I found her on the streets of Lisbon about six months ago. She'd travelled in with the remains of the Portuguese army and I'm not sure she did much better with them than the French. It's not ideal, her living here, but she'd rather that than make a living out of prostitution. I'm wondering if you might be willing to give her a try." Norris gave a sardonic smile. "I wouldn't advertise her background to your husband or the other ladies of headquarters. But she's hardworking and honest, and she'd have no trouble accompanying you to the hospital if you intend to carry on doing this."

"I do," Anne said. "Adam - Robert has asked me to join him with the army. Are you going...?"

"Yes, I finally have orders to move up to Oporto as soon as possible to set up a field hospital, so we can escort you. But I'm surprised he's asking you to go, Nan, most men with wives out here don't want them so close to the fighting. I suppose you've not been married long."

"No. Rowena tells me that Paul won't allow her to join him."

"Paul needs to be able to concentrate on what he does without worrying about his wife. To be honest, I think I would feel the same way. But if you're going to be there, Nan, you'll be a Godsend to me. I honestly don't know when I've come across somebody with such a feel for this work." Norris grinned. "I've got to be the only man in the army who would say this, looking at you, but it's a shame you're a woman."

Anne laughed. She would be glad of the opportunity to continue to work with Adam Norris, and she admitted to herself that she was genuinely curious about how she would cope with life in the field, but she was dreading being with her husband again.

Anne met with Teresa Cortez, finding her a thin-faced silent girl who might have been very pretty under different circumstances. She seemed astonished at Anne's suggestion of work but agreed to give the post a try, and it was quickly clear that it was going to be a success. Anne found her new maid very restful. Teresa was discreet and seemed to make no judgements about her new mistress's unconventional behaviour, adapting with quiet effectiveness to Anne's routines.

Wellesley split his Anglo-Portuguese army into three. Mackenzie was left to protect Lisbon with twelve thousand men while Beresford's forces were positioned to ensure that Marshal Soult was unable to pull back to join Victor. The remaining eighteen thousand men, including the first battalion of the 110th marched under Wellesley to attempt to bring Soult to battle. Soult seemed reluctant to take the bait and retreated towards the city of Oporto, pulling back completely across the River Douro and blowing up the bridge of boats behind him.

Wellesley took up residence in the convent Mosteiro da Nossa serra do Pilar which gave him an excellent view of the French dispositions. As his army marched into the town of Vila Nova de Gaia on the south bank of the Douro, Wellington sent out scouts to survey the surrounding area. The 110th bivouacked on the river bank and Paul gave permission to eat what rations they carried while they waited for orders. He sat with his officers eating a makeshift meal of tack biscuit and cured beef, his eyes on the town on the opposite bank, wondering about Wellesley's plans.

"Major van Daan."

Paul stood up and turned to see one of Wellesley's young ADCs walking his horse carefully between the men of the 110th sprawled on the dry grassy bank.

"Captain Gordon, any news? We're falling asleep down here."

Gordon saluted and grinned. "I don't believe you, sir, you never let them sleep. He's spent the entire morning taking intelligence reports from anybody who has anything to tell him, including the priest's granny, most like. He's spent the rest of the time staring at the French pickets through his telescope."

"And?"

"And ten minutes ago, he closed the telescope and told me to get you up there and to ensure that you have your men at the ready, specifically your light company. He also sent for Colonel Waters. The intelligence officer."

"I know Colonel Waters." Paul felt his heart give a little flip at the prospect of action. "Jenson..."

"Here, sir." His orderly was already moving towards the horses.

Johnny and Carl came to join him. "Orders, sir?"

"I think so. He's found a way across, somehow, I'm going up there." Paul looked at his sergeant-major who was approaching. "Sergeant-Major, I want them ready to move at a moment's notice."

"Yes, sir."

Paul found Wellesley in the grounds of the convent with General Hill and Lieutenant-General Edward Paget. A third man present grinned at Paul as he saluted.

"Major van Daan. Why am I not surprised to see you here?"

"Colonel Waters. I'm guessing I'm here for the same reason you are." Paul looked at his chief. "We're going over?"

"We are. The French are looking the wrong way, I've been watching them all morning. They're deployed to the west of the city and they can't see any way of us crossing here. Waters, on the other hand, has found us some transport." Wellesley pointed up towards a large, isolated stone building that stood on the heights above the opposite bank of the river outside of the eastern suburbs of the city. "The Bishop's Seminary. It's deserted, Waters has had a couple of his scouts over to check. Do you think we can defend it, Paget, if we can get you over there?"

"Yes, sir," Paget said. "But how?"

"We've found a ferry about three miles upstream at Avintes. It's damaged, but it's being repaired as we speak. I'm sending a detachment under Murray to cross up there. Meanwhile Colonel Waters has been behaving like an intelligence officer and has found me four wine barges, unguarded and undamaged on the north shore, east of the city. They'll be over here in an hour, we've found local crews. You'll command, General Paget. We need to get men over there, quickly and quietly and begin to fortify that building. By the time they realise, we'll be in."

"How many can cross at a time?"

"Thirty in each barge. It's not many, and we need those men to be effective from the moment they hit the bank in case the French wake up. Which is where you come in, Major van Daan. I want you in the first boats with your light company, will they be ready?"

"Yes, sir."

"How long?"

"Now, sir."

Wellesley permitted himself a slight smile. "As I expected, Major."

"What other troops, sir?" Paget asked.

"The Buffs, the 66th and 48th and the rest of the 110th. We'll have the artillery batteries from the gardens here trained on the roads coming up to the seminary, but I'm relying on the fact that the first two crossings will get Major van Daan's light company over in case they work out what we're doing more quickly than I hope. You'll need to be able to hold them off, Major."

"We will, sir. I'll leave Captain Wheeler to bring the rest of the battalion across."

"Good. Get moving, I want you down there when those barges arrive."

By mid-morning, the first half of the light company was climbing silently into the barges. Paul nodded at General Paget who was waiting on the shore to follow with the second crossing. Up in the grounds of the convent, the artillery was waiting, and Paul knew that Wellesley would be back with his telescope watching the French.

"How long do you think we have?" Carl asked quietly.

Paul was studying the approaching bank, his eyes watchful. "God knows. They're looking the wrong way, but even so, it's broad daylight, you'd think some sentry would wander off to take a piss and notice that the enemy is out for a sail. I reckon we'll get all our lads across, and if that place is as defensible as it looks, that's all I need. Waters has got agents in place on the other side. Once the French start attacking us, he's hoping they'll be distracted and give the locals a chance to get more boats over to Hookey."

"What about Murray?"

"It's his job to cut them off if they run." As the boat reached the bank, Paul looked behind him. "Sergeant-Major?"

"Ready, sir."

As the crew began hauling in the barge, Paul was off and splashing through the shallows towards the scrub and grass covered slope which led up to the long, white buildings of the seminary. Once inside the walls Paul paused, looking around the gardens.

"Sergeant-Major O'Reilly secure the gates. Mr Swanson, upstairs, rifles at every window you can find. I'm going to scout through the buildings and assess what we need to do to make this place secure. Stewart, get down to wait for the next arrivals and get them up here as fast as you can."

Paul made his way through the seminary, making mental notes as he went. The wall surrounding the seminary was around eight or nine feet high, which would mean a firing step would be required, and he summoned O'Reilly and told him to start working on it. The roof of the building was flat with a strong parapet and there were numerous windows for rifles and muskets to fire through. It could hardly have been better designed. There was still no sign of activity from the French and Paul paused at one of the windows to watch Paget on his way over with the rest of the light company and the first men of the Buffs. Paul's men were in place at the windows and walls, watchful and ready, and Paul ran down and out to meet General Paget as he began the climb up to the seminary.

"No trouble, Major?"

"Not a squeak, sir, Soult has dozed off and no mistake. I've concentrated my lads on this side as their rifles are more accurate, but once the French come, if you need skirmishers, we can get them down." Paul led the colonel through the hall and up the stairs, pointing out the defences in place and making further suggestions. Paget listened intently then began to issue his orders.

"Will you remain up here, Major, with your men and deploy the others as I send them up. I don't know how much longer we have, but once they notice us, they'll move fast."

"Yes, sir."

Paget gave a smile. "Good to be working with you finally, Major. I've heard a good deal about you."

"You shouldn't believe everything you hear, sir."

Paget laughed. "The general seems to think highly of you."

"The general thinks I'm very useful as long as he keeps a close eye on me, sir. I'm surprised he let me across that river without him to be honest, he must have faith in you."

As more and more infantry reached the building, the seminary was gradually turned into a fortress. Paul took out his watch and glanced at it. It was almost an hour since the crossings had begun, and he would estimate that

222

there were around six hundred men deployed around the buildings now. He could hear Paget, up on the roof now, calling out orders as he organised his men around the parapet.

"Sir!"

The urgency in Carter's voice made Paul turn quickly and run to the window. The rifleman pointed. "Got company," he said, and at the same time Paul heard Paget's voice calling him. On the crest of the hill above the seminary a line of tirailleurs appeared. Paul ran up to find Paget.

"It looks as though they've woken up, sir."

"Indeed, Major. Was that one of your lads I heard yell?"

"The one with a voice like a bloody foghorn? That was Private Carter, sir."

"You should make him an NCO, you wouldn't need a bugle."

Paul could hear the drums now, steady and ominous as the French advanced. Low behind the parapet he studied them. "Three columns by the look of it," he said. "Do you think they know there's only 600 of us?"

"No, but they'll work out how we're getting over here fairly quickly. Hill is joining us soon, I hope they don't start shooting at the boats before then."

"My lads can give them cover if they do, and Sir Arthur is ready with the artillery."

"Back to your men, then, Major. I'm not going to be shouting orders down to you. From what I've heard you'll do what you feel like anyway."

Paul grinned. "You've been listening to Sir Arthur, I swear I obey orders more often than not, he's just sore about Assaye. Good luck, sir. Keep down, this parapet isn't that high."

"I'm not as tall as you are," Paget said. "But I will."

Paul joined his men on the floor below. "Nice and steady," he said to Carl and Michael. "Fire at will once they're in range and cover our transports as much as you can. Pick them off, the muskets will do the heavy work."

The drums were closer, a thunderous roll, and Paul stood behind Carter watching as the French came on. "Carter, get those tirailleurs down, they'll do some damage in a minute," he said, and Carter nodded, his eyes on the advancing skirmishers. There was an enormous crash as the first of Wellesley's guns fired, and almost immediately Carter shifted his position slightly and fired, and a blue-coated skirmisher fell.

Throughout the seminary there was the roar of musket and rifle fire as Paget loosed his men. The French columns came on steadily, firing at the seminary, but they were making little headway against the steady rolling fire from rifles and muskets on four levels, plus the guns from across the river. Paul moved from room to room checking on his men. They were covering the targets fast and easily, firing as if in practice and in the cover of the seminary walls, few of them missed their man.

"They're bringing up artillery, sir," Carl called, and Paul ran to join him. Already Carl had shifted half a dozen men to overlook the approaching guns.

"They're joking, surely?" Paul said, watching as the draft animals hauled the first of the guns forward. He could not imagine how the French thought that they would get time to set up artillery. "Carter, don't let them unlimber it, there's a good lad."

As he spoke there was an enormous crash, and a shell from one of the British howitzers across the river burst in front of the French gun. As the smoke cleared, Paul observed that the gun was dismounted and the gunners and pack animals were either dead or wounded, one man desperately crawling away from the lethal fire coming from the roof. "Don't bother, Carter, I think Wellesley has this covered."

"Major! Major van Daan, General Paget's down."

"Shit." Paul wheeled and headed for the stairs up to the roof. The area was thick with grey smoke which almost completely obscured the parapets, and the noise of the muskets was deafening. Paul felt the smoke catch in his throat and coughed.

"Over here, sir."

Paul ran to his commander and knelt. Paget had been hit in the right arm and the shot had shattered it. He lay in a pool of blood, his head pillowed on a coat, one of his lieutenants kneeling beside him desperately trying to stem the bleeding. Paul took a deep breath and reached for the thin scarf he always carried inside his coat. Assaye had taught him its usefulness. He wound it hard around Paget's arm, over and above the appalling wound. Paget was conscious, breathing hard, his eyes wide on Paul's.

"All right, sir. Let's get you below where you're less likely to get your head blown off as well." Paul kept his voice deliberately calm. "What's your name, Lieutenant?"

"Bridge, sir."

"Get him below, Mr Bridge, into one of the internal rooms. Is Major-General Hill over yet, I've not seen him?"

"No, sir."

"Right." Paul stood up and peered through the smoke. There were some gaps in the defenders now, as men had been wounded or killed, although the French were getting the worst of it. Paul ran to the top of the stairs. "Sergeant-Major O'Reilly, up here with ten men, fill the gaps. Mr Swanson, take over on that floor."

"Sir."

Paul went to the parapet and looked over, peering through the clouds of smoke down below as O'Reilly deployed his men. "Keep them steady, Sergeant-Major and watch to make sure no silly bugger lifts his head too high and gets it blown off. No need for anybody to die up here."

"Yes, sir."

Paul ran lightly down and went below, checking on the other floors to see where gaps had occurred. Outside he toured the walls and then went to meet the next contingent of troops coming up from the boats, under a young lieutenant he recognised from Hill's brigade.

"Mr Egremont get your men up to the first floor to reinforce. Any losses on the boats?"

"None, sir, whoever is covering isn't letting them get near."

224

"Is General Hill on his way?"

"Will be. Where's the general, sir?"

"Down. Get a dozen of yours down to that wall as well, over to the left there. I'm going up to see how he's doing."

He ran up the stairs to find Paget laid out on a narrow bed in a windowless room with a wounded private in attendance. Paul sat beside him. "Sir."

Paget opened his eyes. "Major, how is it going?"

"No problems. Most of the Buffs are over now, General Hill will be here soon." Paul examined the wound. It was still bleeding steadily but not with the flow of earlier. "We'll get you to the surgeon as soon as we can, sir. Here."

He took his flask from inside his coat and helped Paget to drink. Paget managed a weak grin. "Good brandy, Major, that's not army grog."

"Medicinal, sir. Try and get some rest and don't worry, it's going well."

"Glad you were here," Paget said. "I'm going to lose this."

Paul studied the arm. Paget was right and it would be insulting to lie to him. "Probably, sir."

"Are they all right up there? Only a couple of young officers..."

"My sergeant-major is up there, sir, if anybody lifts his head too high, he'll thump it."

Paget attempted another smile. He was obviously in agony and Paul wanted to tell him that there was no need to be stoic about it, but he did not. In the circumstances, he would probably do the same no matter how bad the pain. It was expected of an officer, and to some extent of any British soldier. Paul wondered if it helped.

"Thank you, Major. You've got command until Hill gets here."

"Yes, sir."

Paul went back down, aware that the sound of the battle had died away. Outside in the garden he realised that the French had broken and were fleeing back towards the town. He went to speak to the officer commanding there and then moved around the walls, checking on wounded men and getting the dead removed and laid out. There were surprisingly few of them.

"Sir, General Hill is coming up."

Paul turned and went to meet the general, saluting. "Sir."

"They've gone quiet, Major, what have you done to them?"

"We had a bit of help from those guns, sir. But General Paget is down, bad arm wound."

"Oh no. Where is he?"

"I'll show you." Paul led Hill up the stairs and left him with Paget, going back down to supervise the deployment of the latest arrivals. Hill joined him shortly.

"Looks nasty. I doubt he'll keep that arm."

"No, sir. How's it going?"

"Soult is retreating, I got the message just before I embarked. He'd like to get away with supplies and guns which means he'd like us out of here."

"That's not going to happen, we're doing fine."

"I agree. They'll have another go, but Wellesley thinks they've brought up the troops who were guarding the boats."

"Lets go up and have a look."

They went up to where Carl was already at the window, drinking from his canteen and looking out. He saluted. "We're about to get a bit more help," he said, and stood back so that Hill and Paul could see. With the boats left unguarded, the Portuguese citizens had taken to the water in a wide variety of craft of all shapes and sizes and were crossing the river to ferry the rest of Wellesley's troops over to the town.

"Sir, they're coming again."

Hill smiled grimly. "Let them come. We've got an ample garrison now, we can hold, and I've a feeling that in a short time they're going to be hit in the backside by the Brigade of Guards."

The short lull was over and three French battalions were thrown into a desperate final attack on the seminary. In their position, Paul would not have wasted the men. With the help of the Portuguese boatmen, the men of the 29th Foot and the Brigade of Guards were swarming up the steep streets into the heart of the city towards the French flank. Within a short time the French were fighting on two fronts, making a frantic running retreat as Soult abandoned the assault on the seminary and ordered a general retreat from Oporto along the road to Valongo. Paul stood at the window watching them go and thought that if Murray did his job properly, Soult's troubles were not yet over.

***

The hospital had been set up in a convent. Arriving in Oporto, Anne found her husband busy managing the transport of guns and supplies captured from the retreating French. Robert had been allocated a billet in a small house near the centre, and Anne settled herself in quickly then went to join Adam as the first wounded were being brought in by wagon. They were both French and English and had travelled in unsprung wagons along rutted and unpaved streets, caked in their own blood with only rudimentary dressings.

Under Adam Norris's watchful eye, Anne cleaned, dressed and stitched wounds. She had become surprisingly immune to filth and blood and the smell of human waste and infected wounds, and she remained busy at the hospital long after many of the surgeons and their assistants had left. Dr Norris, ignoring the disapproval of his fellow surgeons and physicians, had begun to give his unorthodox assistant more and more responsibility as he realised incredulously, that this slip of a girl had the makings of a fearless and talented doctor. On the journey he had lent her some of his own medical books and papers and Anne devoured them and returned with endless questions. During the many hours she had spent in her father's library, Anne had studied for her own amusement, but now she worked with a purpose on a new subject which she found both challenging and absorbing.

226

Going forward as the orderlies lifted down the wounded, Anne went through to where Adam was working. He looked round at her in relief.

"I see I've lost Henley and Gerrard again. They're bloody useless."

"What do you need?"

"I need somebody to hold him still, I can't work like this. Watch he doesn't hit you."

"Get on with it, Adam, there are dozens of them waiting."

Norris grimaced and Anne positioned herself beside the French tirailleur and held him still as Norris began to dig for the ball. The man gave a scream of pain, and almost threw her off, and Anne clamped down hard.

"Try and keep still, it will be over sooner," she said, switching to French. "Teresa, bring him some rum."

Norris shot her a glance. "I didn't know you were that fluent in French. It could be useful today, there are a lot more of them than of our lads."

Anne worked steadily beside him. After weeks of working together daily, she was beginning to anticipate his requests and choices, so that it was often unnecessary for them to talk much. It was late in the afternoon when he called a halt and instructed her to go back to her billet.

"You've been here for six hours, Nan, it's enough. I'm going to take a break as well. Let some of the others take over for a while. You have to be tired and hungry, and your husband will be wondering where you are."

"He's probably still working. I am tired, Adam. But I'll be back in the morning."

Norris hesitated, regarding her thoughtfully. "Nan, how confident are you? I know we've been working together, and you need to believe me when I say that you are worth ten of these inexperienced lads they send me from London. But I'm getting a lot of complaints from the other surgeons."

Anne studied him. "Are you telling me you want me to stop?"

"No." Norris took a deep breath, then seemed to come to a decision. "Come with me a moment."

He led her through to a room where he had set up a rest area for the surgeons and went to his pack. After a moment he turned and handed her a bag. Anne took it, looking down at it. Finally, she opened it. It was a surgical kit, neatly laid out. Anne closed it and looked up at him.

"Adam?"

"I've been watching you for these past few weeks, you're more interested and you've learned more than any of the hospital mates. I know what it's going to be like in the months to come, when they're being carried in by the dozen and there's nobody to help them. Young Felton, my junior surgeon, died in the Lisbon fever ward last week. You're already better than he was. You can't be official and you'll never get pay or recognition, and you'll be up to your elbows in blood and filth, working with men your father wouldn't even have let you speak to. But if you want to do this, and your husband will allow it, I'm willing to train you until somebody orders me not to. It's up to you, Nan."

Anne studied him for a moment. Then she said:

"Can we set up another table tomorrow? I know what I can handle and what I can't, I'll pass over to you."

Anne worked with him through the following day, and then into the night, sending a message to Robert so that he would not worry. A lot of her work consisted of washing and dressing the wounds. It was by no means usual to thoroughly clean either patient or wound, but Anne felt an instinctive distaste for dirt around open wounds. If she had cut her own finger, the first thing she would have done would have been to wash it. So she ignored the open scorn of the orderlies and hospital mates and continued to clean each wound meticulously before stitching or dressing. Since she was unqualified and unpaid, they could hardly complain.

General Edward Paget was brought in part way through the second day, and Norris called her over as he was laid out on the table.

"Nan, are you busy? Come and help me with this."

Anne obeyed, stopping to wash her hands in the basin that Teresa provided. Her maid had begun to join her at the hospital, acting as her nurse and assistant. In the past weeks she had developed a surprisingly close relationship with the Spanish girl. They did not talk a great deal, but Anne found her an easy companion who asked no difficult questions and seemed to think nothing of spending hours in the hot, dirty hospital amidst blood and excrement and the smell of infected wounds.

Paget was conscious and clearly in considerable pain. Anne sent Teresa for laudanum and watched while Norris examined the wound. After a long moment he straightened and looked at her enquiringly and Anne shook her head. Norris nodded.

"General, I'm going to have to amputate."

"I know, Doctor, I've been expecting it. Hurts like hell." Paget glanced at Anne. Clearly he was confused by her status. "Sorry, ma'am."

"General, when you are brought in with a wound like that, you are allowed to swear as much as you like," Anne said with a smile, and she was pleased at the lightening of Paget's face.

"I've never had such a beautiful nurse, ma'am. Almost worth it."

Norris was collecting his instruments. "I'm going to get a couple of orderlies to hold on to you, sir," he said.

"I can help," Anne said quietly. The strained dignity of the general had touched her.

"So can I."

Both Norris and Anne looked up startled as Paul van Daan walked into the room. "I brought him up," he said.

"I'd like him to stay, Doctor," Paget said.

"Of course, General. Major van Daan has done this before, the first time I met him," Norris said encouragingly. "You'd better hope he's a good luck charm, because the lad did very well and is still with him."

Anne studied Paul. He looked tired but seemed perfectly well. "Are you all right?" she asked.

"I'm fine. We took no losses. When we're done here, I'd like to have a conversation about what the hell you are doing here, but we'll save that."

Paget gave a startled look. "This is not your wife, Major...?"

"No, sir, you'll find my wife is safely in Lisbon where she should be," Paul said grimly.

Anne bit back the extremely vulgar response she would have liked to have made in the face of this high-handedness. Instead, she said very sweetly:

"Yes, she's very well behaved. And I am right here, close to my husband, Major, which presumably is where I should be."

Adam Norris gave her a surprised look. Paul met her eyes and his face softened into a smile. "As if your husband had any choice in the matter, Mrs Carlyon," he said.

"It was his idea. Although I didn't argue, I wanted to come to help Adam. Where do you want me, Adam?"

"Take his other arm, Nan, he'd probably rather look at you than Paul. General Paget, drink some of this. I'll be as quick as I can. Teresa, have you got everything ready?"

"Yes, Doctor."

"Let's do this then."

Paget endured the ordeal with a rigid dignity, which broke Anne's heart. She talked to him quietly, knowing that he could not answer but wanting to distract him from the pain. Occasionally, she shot a glance at Paul, who was watching her as if he could not believe what he was seeing.

When it was done, Adam stepped back. He looked exhausted and his hands were slippery with blood.

"Nan..."

"Let me." Anne took the first thread from Teresa and began to tie off the blood vessels. Already she was quick and accurate although she was acutely aware of Paul's white, appalled face as he watched her. He said nothing, however, and Anne took the dressing from Teresa and bound up the wound under Norris's careful eye. Mercifully, Paget had lost consciousness, and Anne looked at Paul.

"Where is he going?"

"Wellesley has a room for him up at headquarters, he'll see that he's taken care of. There's a wagon outside and his orderly is here."

"I will find him," Teresa said quietly and left. Anne went to wash her hands, acutely aware of her rumpled and bloody appearance.

"Thank you, Nan," Norris said. "Rest for a little, now. Paul..."

"I'll take her outside for a bit. Adam, thank you."

Anne went to the door, removing her apron and hanging it up as she went past the hooks. It was late afternoon, with the skies already growing darker. Outside Paul led her silently through the courtyard, still crowded with men waiting to be seen by the surgeons. There was a small garden on the far side, and he led her through into the quiet cool shade of olive trees, then turned to look at her.

"Paul..."

229

"Jesus, Nan." Without hesitation Paul took her into his arms and bent to kiss her. She felt him pulling the kerchief from her hair, running his fingers through its silky length. Anne closed her eyes and parted her mouth under his, sensation flooding through her tired body. He drew her closer, cupping her face with his hands, kissing her harder and Anne leaned into him and allowed herself to enjoy the feel of his body against hers.

Eventually he raised his head. Anne looked up into his eyes. "I'm glad you're safe, Paul."

"So I gathered." She heard the slight unsteadiness in his voice with a little rush of happiness, knew that her touch affected him just as it always had. "Lass, what are you doing here?"

"Robert wanted me to join him. And I wanted to come, to help Adam. Paul, is everybody..."

"Yes, they are all fine. A few minor injuries only, Paget was bloody unlucky. Thank you for what you did in there, you were amazing with him."

"Were you there when it happened?"

"I was in the seminary, although I didn't see him hit. My light company were the first across."

"Why doesn't that surprise me?"

"We're marching towards the Spanish border. Nan, I know Robert is coming..."

"So am I, Paul."

Paul was suddenly very still. "No," he said.

"Paul, I will be fine. I'm bringing Teresa, my new maid, and Robert tells me that the hospital and the quartermaster's billets will be close together."

"I don't give a damn, both Robert and Norris should know better. Why the hell has he sent for you?"

"Because he wants me here," Anne said quietly, and she saw him flinch. "Paul..."

"No – don't tell me any more, Nan. You can't come with us. You're going back to Lisbon and..."

"No, Paul, I'm not, and you don't have the ordering of my life." Anne tilted her head and looked up at him. "I can be useful, Paul. Ask Adam. Even some of the other surgeons and physicians have begun to accept my help, although they persist in complaining about it. And if there is to be a battle, you know how short of medical staff the army is."

"Nan, I've just stood and watched you sew up a man I'd consider a friend, I'm not questioning your competence."

"Then what?"

"I'm questioning the wisdom of you being within a few miles of a battlefield. Apart from the filth and the sickness and the danger, what happens if we don't win, and the French overrun the lines? They've a tradition of being good with our wounded when they're captured, but they don't have a good record with women. I've marched through villages in Portugal where they've raped every young woman they come across and their officers, unlike most of ours, do nothing to stop them. And frankly there is a man or two in

230

our army who might not be much better if he catches you on your way back to your billet one dark night." Paul scanned her face with anxious eyes. "None of what I'm saying is having any impact on you whatsoever, is it?"

"Yes. It tells me you care."

"It doesn't tell you how much, girl of my heart. If I had my way, I'd take you back to the villa and lock you up until I come back to you, but you're right, I don't have the authority to order you around." He studied her for a long moment. "Come with me," he said finally.

Anne took his hand and allowed him to lead her out of the garden and across to the stable where his horse was being fed and watered. A pair of saddlebags hung over the rail. Paul nodded to the orderly who was dealing with Rufus and rummaged through one of the bags. He withdrew something, and led Anne back out into the yard.

"Here."

She took it. It was a leather sheath attached to a narrow strap, containing a thin bladed wicked looking knife. Anne examined it. She looked up at Paul and he grinned and took it from her.

"Hold out your left arm – you're right-handed, aren't you? It fastens this way, under your sleeve. That's right. Now take it out with your right. That's right, good. Try again." He watched her critically. "When we get a chance, I'll show you how to use it properly. It was given to me in Naples by an Italian partisan I'd done a favour for. If you're set on this madness, Nan, I want you to promise me that you'll wear this. You're not going to hold off a French scouting party with it, but you might give yourself a chance to run or scream for help if there's any to be had. Promise me."

Anne nodded. "I promise."

She looked down at the knife again and touched it and suddenly his hand covered hers. "I wish I were in a position to give you diamonds, Nan. Ironic to think this might be the only gift I ever give to you."

Anne looked up at him quickly, picking up on the wistfulness in his voice. "Do you know how common it is for a man to give a woman jewellery, Paul?" she said teasingly. "Now this...this, I'll remember all my life."

He gave a choke of laughter then said suddenly:

"Has he ever given you jewellery? Apart from a wedding ring."

"No. And I wouldn't want him to. But I will treasure this. Thank you, Paul."

"Is Rowena all right?"

"She is. Missing you. Worried about you."

"At least she's safe," Paul said pointedly. He took her hand and led her across the yard and back into the garden. She knew before he touched her what he intended, and she was ready for him, her body at home in his arms as he kissed her. They remained locked together for a long time. Finally, reluctantly, Paul lifted his head.

"The worst of it is that even knowing the danger and the discomfort and the fact that you'll be with your bloody husband, I'm still happy that you're going to be there. What does that say about me?"

"I'm glad too," Anne said. "I've been worrying about you, every day."

"And that makes me feel happier than it ought to. We need to get back. Kiss me again, love. It will be the last chance for a while, and I need to remember what you feel like in my arms when I'm freezing my arse off in some ditch waiting for the cannons to start."

Anne obeyed, and then they walked back up to the hospital, not loosing hands until they came within sight of the buildings.

Chapter Fourteen

Several days after the battle, Robert Carlyon appeared at the hospital unexpectedly, and Anne greeted him warily. She introduced him to Adam Norris, who heaped praise on the work she was doing, while carefully failing to mention exactly what that work entailed. Anne could see by his expression that Robert was not entirely happy, and she could feel fear resurfacing. Robert had seemed genuinely glad to see her on her arrival and had not so far questioned the hours she was spending at the hospital.

"Are you the only woman working here?" he asked, looking around one of the wards.

"I always have Teresa with me, Robert." Anne could feel her heart beating slightly faster. "I know it's unusual, but I would like to continue. It keeps me busy, with you so often on duty. Unless you want me to return to Lisbon?"

"Is that what you want?" Robert asked, and Anne could hear the edge in his voice. She took a deep breath.

"No," she said. "But I'll go if you want me to."

"I don't. I want...I'd like you to stay." Her husband reached out and took her hand, his eyes fixed on her face. Adam moved away tactfully. "You seem happier. Since Lisbon. Since that night, the reception...it's been better, hasn't it? You and I."

"It has," Anne said, trying to infuse some warmth into her voice. She supposed that it was true. She had returned to his bed with furious resentment, but she had pushed it to one side and tried hard to please him. It was not difficult. Robert seemed surprisingly responsive to even the smallest gesture and Anne been rewarded by a level of kindness she had not known from him before, but she was not deceived. It would take only a small act of perceived defiance to set off the violence again. Anne did not want to put herself in danger, but she desperately wanted to continue working with Adam.

"Lieutenant Carlyon. Come down to see what your wife is up to, have you?"

The genial tone startled both of them and they turned to see Sir Arthur Wellesley approaching, escorted by a junior ADC and Major Paul van Daan. Robert saluted smartly and Anne gave a slight bow.

"My husband gave permission for me to help with the wounded, sir," she said. "But he wanted to see for himself what I have been doing."

Wellesley took her hand and raised it to his lips. "If I have understood correctly, ma'am, you have been helping to save the life of my very good friend General Paget."

Anne's eyes flew to Paul's face. His expression was guarded but as she met his eyes, she saw a little smile flicker and she wondered suddenly if he had known of Robert's intention to come down today and timed this visit to coincide.

"Dr Norris operated, sir, I simply helped."

"And have been up every day since to dress the wound. Paget tells me it is the first time he has ever looked forward to being visited by a doctor."

"I'm happy to help, sir."

Wellesley looked over at Robert. "Carlyon, I owe you my thanks for letting your wife assist. We're permanently short of medical staff and I'm told she's saved lives. Ma'am - the army and I are in your debt. Major van Daan tells me you're coming to Spain with us."

"With my husband's permission, sir - and yours."

Wellesley looked at Robert with a gleam of amusement. "Well, I don't think we'll have to ask him twice, ma'am, I'm very sure he'd rather be sharing a tent with you than a fellow officer. As for me, I'm aware I have the reputation of not approving of ladies accompanying the army, but I am prepared to make an exception for a lady who does what you do." He kissed her hand again. "To say nothing of a lady as lovely as you. Bring her with you, Carlyon, if you wish. We can always send her back if things get too difficult."

"If things get difficult, I hope she'll stay," Norris said, coming forward. "She's more use than most of my trainees already. But it is up to Lieutenant Carlyon."

"Naturally, I would like my wife with me," Robert said. "Although Major van Daan does not approve, I understand."

"No, I don't," Paul said bluntly. "I don't think we know enough about what we're marching into, to take a vulnerable woman into a country at war, especially one as lovely as your wife. But Mrs Carlyon has already told me exactly what I can do with my opinion, and if she's made up her mind, I shouldn't think that half Victor's army is likely to stop her. Just make sure you keep an eye on her, Robert."

"I'm not a child, Paul," Anne said, irritated. "And I'm not stupid."

"Neither are the French, ma'am, and they're going to know exactly what to do about you if they catch you too far out of camp on a sunny afternoon. Sir, will you excuse me, I've things to attend to."

Anne watched him go with a mixture of exasperation at his protective attitude and warmth at his obvious concern. She was grateful, however, for what she was sure was his deliberate intervention to push Robert into giving his consent both to her medical work and her march with the army.

Wellesley gave up his pursuit of Soult's depleted and demoralised troops after only a few days, and the French made a scrambling retreat over the mountains, leaving their artillery, their heavy baggage and their sick and wounded beside the road. The weather was appalling and the roads, which were already poor, quickly became impassable with the constant rainfall. With the next stage of the campaign in mind, Wellesley chose to give his victorious army time to recover rather than continue the chase in difficult conditions. Anne found herself dealing with a stream of injured Frenchmen, as well as a collection of minor ailments among Wellesley's men, including boils, stomach disorders and a condition which Norris called foot-rot.

"I thought you needed hooves to suffer from foot-rot," Anne said, as Norris explained his treatment.

"You do, you won't hear the term at medical school. It's my name for what happens to a man's feet when he's expected to march hundreds of miles in soaking wet shoes which are not fit for purpose. Or in some cases, with no shoes at all."

"I'm told that several consignments of shoes are on their way from London," Anne said, gingerly beginning to clean the foul-smelling blister on a soldier of the 110th."

"Major van Daan says he'd like to shove a pair of these shoes up the arse of the idiot who ordered them. They're bloody useless."

"Watch your language, Cooper," Norris said sharply, but Anne laughed aloud.

"It's all right, Private Cooper, I've been learning the most astonishing collection of French swear words all week, and I suspect you've censored Major van Daan's language for my benefit."

Cooper grinned. "A fair bit, yes, ma'am. He sent a party out to get boots off the French dead, but there weren't that many."

"He has my sympathy," Anne said, picking up Cooper's discarded shoe and studying it. "This has rotted away. How long have you had these, Private?"

"A few months. They don't last. French ones are much better, we need another battle."

"I wondered why we were fighting this war," Norris said conversationally. "You'll need to keep this dressing on, Private, and get it checked if it opens up again. Off you go."

During the last week of May, Wellesley's army set off from Oporto and marched south. With no previous experience of life on campaign, Anne had wondered how she would cope, but within a week she felt as though she had been part of the army for years. Some nights were spent billeted in local farmhouses or villages, while others were spent under canvas. Anne quickly became used to the routines of an army on the move and was beginning to learn a lot more about how Wellesley's army worked.

Robert was mostly absent during the march, as it was the duty of the quartermasters to move ahead of the army to find billeting or a suitable campsite for the night. The army marched from dawn until mid-afternoon, and then made camp or settled into billets, and prepared their main meal. The officers of each regiment managed an officers' mess of some kind, even under the most difficult of circumstances, while the men were mostly divided into small groups who cooked and ate together.

There were a number of wives, or local women marching with the army, and some of them took care of laundry, cooking and mending, and occasionally acted as nurses. Others set up as sutlers, the pedlars of the army, selling tobacco, food and drink to the soldiers and running semi-official grog tents whenever they were able, where the men could congregate to drink, socialise and find women. They were a rowdy bunch, with a reputation for looting and stealing which surpassed that of their menfolk. Wives and camp followers were subject to army discipline along with their men. Courts martial were held on a regular basis with officers sitting on the bench on a rotational basis, to deal with disciplinary matters and desertions. Anne treated her first flogging victim during the march, a German convicted of looting. She wondered, as she bathed the torn, damaged skin of the man's back, how Paul dealt with such infractions among his battalion. He had once told her that he found flogging ineffective, but he must have some means of dealing with discipline because she discovered that the 110th had the reputation of being among the best disciplined battalions in the army. Not all regiments did as well, and Wellesley was reputedly furious over several incidents of looting and plundering of the local population, sending out a general order to his officers giving strict instructions on how to improve things.

The nights were cold, and officers and men congregated around their separate campfires drinking and talking and speculating as to when they would encounter the French. There were no other officers' wives present, and Anne was extremely popular. She and Robert received numerous invitations to dine informally with other regiments, including several from Sir Arthur Wellesley. Paul and his officers were never there, and Anne mentioned their absence casually to Major Mackay during supper with the 74th.

"Aye, you won't see the 110th mixing much with the other officers on the march, ma'am. He keeps them on a tight rein, claims that's why the rest of us are losing control of our men, because the officers think they're on the strut in Mayfair. Arrogant fellow, but he's Wellesley's pet." Mackay drained his glass and grinned. "Those lads can fight, mind. I was at Assaye with Paul van Daan when he was newly promoted to captain. He saved the remains of my regiment that day, so I don't care how eccentric he is."

***

Paul quickly became aware that during the day, Anne rode alone or with the medical staff. It had not occurred to him that Robert could not be with her, and he could not resist the opportunity. Dropping back, he fell in beside her.

236

"Come and join us, you look lonely back here."

"Thank you, Major."

Anne spurred forward, and they trotted up the long, snaking column to catch up with the 110th. Paul reined in beside the light company and caught his sergeant-major's quizzical expression.

"Welcome to the 110th, ma'am. Don't let him take any liberties, now."

Behind Michael, Private Carter grinned. "Not sure what liberties he's going to take in front of the entire army, Sergeant-Major, but the major does like a challenge."

"The major is going to kick your arse if you don't keep your mouth shut, Carter," Paul said amiably.

"I'm not sure that's fair, it was the sergeant-major that started it. And you should watch your language in front of a lady, sir."

Anne was laughing. "Thank you, Carter, I'm glad somebody tells him."

"You would be shocked to hear Mrs Carlyon's language when she's angry, Carter, it is straight from the stables." Paul touched his heel to Rufus and drew ahead, out of earshot of his men, studying Anne with some interest. "How are you coping? You look as if you were born to it."

"I've surprised myself," Anne admitted. "Didn't you want Rowena to come?"

"She's close enough," Paul said. "I don't want her within sight or sound of that battlefield." He smiled grimly. "I don't want you there either, girl of my heart, but it seems that's not my decision. And I'm not sure it would be even if I were your husband, you've a mind of your own."

Anne smiled and said nothing. They rode in companionable silence for a while. Anne looked around her at the wide, open countryside. It was a glorious day, with tiny white clouds drifting lazily across a dazzling blue sky. Paul spent his time watching Anne. She wore a dark blue riding habit, her hair dressed in a trim chignon under a simple riding hat. The fresh air brought colour to her cheeks and she looked very beautiful.

"You're staring, Major."

"My apologies, Mrs Carlyon, but my entire battalion is staring, and I don't blame them. I wonder if your husband would notice if I forgot to deliver you back at the end of the march."

"Eventually he would."

"Round about bedtime I imagine," Paul said, and Anne glanced sharply at him. Paul had not intended to make his jealousy so obvious, but he could not stop himself. "Lieutenant Carlyon's very obvious desire for his wife is becoming something of an ongoing joke in the headquarters mess. It's one of the many reasons I don't go there much."

"Paul..."

"Love, I can't bear it," Paul said quietly, and Anne reached out and touched his arm with quick understanding.

"I know it's difficult, Paul. But at least we have this."

Paul smiled somewhat painfully. "Given that I thought I'd never see you again, this feels pretty damned good to me just now. How are things with Robert? I'm surprised he hasn't objected to you working with the surgeons."

"I think Sir Arthur Wellesley's approval helped. Did you arrange that visit?"

Paul grinned. "Yes," he admitted. "Robert is after promotion, he'll do anything to curry favour with Wellesley."

"I'm surprised. I thought you disapproved of what I'm doing."

"No. Not after seeing what you did with Paget. But Christ, Nan, you frighten the life out of me. I never know where I'm likely to find you next or what you'll be doing. I'm used to Rowena who is very conformable and never gives me a moment's anxiety. I'd feel sorry for Robert if I didn't want to murder him half the time."

Anne laughed aloud. "Poor Paul. You really aren't used to not being in control, are you?"

Paul studied her with a rueful smile. "No, it's new to me. But I've a feeling I could get used to it, Nan, you're like a breath of fresh air in my well-ordered life. Disruptive, but healthy."

"I am happy to be of service, Major."

"I'm just glad you're here. You should ride with us when Robert isn't around. Unless you think he'd object?"

"I don't know, Paul. He may not even notice."

Knowing how quickly gossip spread within the army, Paul doubted it. He met Robert outside Wellesley's billet the following morning, and nodded pleasantly to him, and he was not surprised when Carlyon paused and saluted punctiliously.

"Major Van Daan, I hear you've been escorting my wife."

Paul managed not to grin. "News travels fast in the army," he said. "Yes, I asked her to ride up with us yesterday. Is that a problem?"

"You don't have the best reputation with other men's wives, Major."

"Army gossip, Robert, you should know better than to listen. She was riding alone, and I know you can't be with her, so I thought she'd be safer up with us. I'm not sure that a girl who looks like your wife should be on her own in the middle of twenty-thousand men. I'm sorry, perhaps I should have asked you first."

The struggle was visible on Carlyon's face. "No. You're probably right, but I hope you're careful with her reputation, Major."

"I give you my word, Robert," Paul said gravely. He watched as Carlyon made his way to his horse. Paul had noticed a change in Carlyon's attitude to Anne since they came to Portugal. Aboard ship he had seemed completely uninterested in her, but now there was an edge of possessive belligerence to his voice, as if he had suddenly woken up to his young wife's extraordinary qualities. Paul wondered what had changed in their relationship and then closed his mind quickly to speculation which was too painful.

With Carlyon's grudging permission, Paul did not scruple to make the most of his time with Anne. The army marched in easy stages southwards

238

towards Abrantes. Each morning, Paul sent one of his officers to escort Anne to join the 110th and for two weeks, she rode beside him until Robert came to reclaim her when his duty was done. Often, it was very late, and Anne remained with him through dinner and well into the evening. Paul watched her getting to know his officers and some of his men and thought how well she seemed to manage the inconveniences of army life.

The town of Abrantes commanded the road along the Tagus and occupied the crest of a hill covered with olive woods, gardens and vines. An impressive medieval castle towered over the cobbled streets and pleasant squares of the town and there were spectacular views over the spreading river plain. Wellesley and the headquarters staff were billeted in the town along with many of his senior officers, while the army settled into a huge, sprawling encampment just outside the town walls.

Most of the walls had been rebuilt during the seventeenth century, and several bastions had recently been added by both the Portuguese and the French, during their occupation. While Wellesley organised his troops, awaited supplies and reinforcements and wrote increasingly irritated letters to his Spanish allies, Paul found a local guide and invited Robert and Anne to join a group of his officers in touring the town. They visited the castle and several beautiful churches and stood high on the battlements, admiring the view, before returning to camp to a small feast prepared by Sergeant George Kelly, Paul's cook and mess sergeant. Paul was deliberately friendly towards Robert and enjoyed watching his officers falling over themselves to supply Anne with food, wine and elaborate compliments.

Sir Arthur Wellesley was in a foul temper during his stay in Abrantes, and Paul found himself regularly summoned to headquarters. He could not decide if it was because Wellesley wanted advice, sympathy or simply somebody to yell at, but by the end of a week, Paul could feel his own temper beginning to fray. Some of Wellesley's irritability was caused by the poor behaviour of some of the troops during the march but much of it was the result of a delay in the arrival of money from London to pay his army and purchase supplies for the next stage of the campaign. Wellesley was also awaiting reinforcements and medical and uniform supplies and spent his time snapping at his staff, shouting at Paul and writing endless letters of complaint.

Wellesley used the delay to reorganise his army into four divisions, led by Generals Sherbrooke, Hill, Mackenzie and Campbell, with a separate cavalry division under General Payne and he placed the 110thth under Hill in the second division.

"I have informed General Hill that I may well decide to keep your men under my direct command," he told Paul. "It is useful for me to have a battalion that I can use in support at a moment's notice. We shall see when battle is joined. If it is ever joined, for if I do not get some sense out of General Cuesta soon, I shall abandon the whole thing and go back to Lisbon."

Paul grinned but did not reply. After a moment, Wellesley permitted himself a small, tight smile. "No. As you very wisely did not say, I am committed to this one engagement at the very least. But I have told General

Cuesta and the Junta that I will not remain in Spain after that, unless they are able to come up with the transport and supplies that I was promised. At any rate, we are ready, and will march the day after tomorrow."

From Abrantes, the army made its way along the River Tagus towards Plasencia, crossing the Spanish border on 3rd July and stopping at various towns and villages along the way. Supplies remained a problem, and Paul knew that Wellesley was considering placing his men on half rations. Paul had already done so, but he was also sending out his mess sergeant and his acting quartermaster to try to buy supplies from local farms. It was not easy, as it seemed both food and transport were scarce in this part of Spain, possibly due to the depredations of the French, but Paul knew that it was difficult to prevent hungry troops from looting.

With supply problems throughout the army, the various quartermasters and commissariat officers were constantly busy trying to source food and forage for the horses, and Robert Carlyon was seldom seen. Anne resumed her daily rides with the 110th and Paul was able to set his anxiety to one side in the pleasure of her company.

A message arrived for her as they rode into Plascencia, a beautiful medieval town on the banks of the River Jerte, which had been the centre of fierce fighting between the French and the Spanish during recent years. There were signs of destruction in the graceful streets and Paul knew that French reprisals in the town had been brutal.

"It seems I have a billet," Anne said, looking up from her note. "I should go and find it. Thank you, Major, for taking such good care of me again."

"I need to get my men settled, but Ensign Collins shall escort you, and make sure your baggage and servants find their way there. I believe we'll be here for a couple of days now, but if Robert is busy, I'm afraid Carl will have to take care of you tomorrow. I'm riding with Wellesley to meet with the Spanish, we have been invited to dinner."

"Oh, I shall be there," Anne said calmly. "General Wellesley has asked Robert and I to join his party."

"He's done what? What possible use can Robert be to…oh." Paul surveyed her with grim amusement. "It isn't Robert he wants, is it? Is my commander-in-chief trying to persuade you into his bed, Nan? Because if he is…"

"If he is, it's for me to deal with and not you, Major. Sir Arthur has never been anything other than respectful."

Paul was shocked at his own sudden anger. "He'd better be. I was in India with Wellesley and his tendency to sleep with his officers' wives was very well known, but if puts a foot out of line with you, bonny lass…"

"I am not even going to mention the name Arabella Cartwright at this point," Anne said frostily. "I am not going to engage in an affair with your commander or anybody else, so be reassured. I like him. He talks to me and doesn't treat me like an idiot."

Her tone made Paul flinch. He studied her. "Do I?"

"Not usually. You're having a bad day."

Despite himself, Paul began to laugh, his sudden anger dissipating. "I'm sorry, Nan. I have absolutely no right to feel jealous either of Wellesley or your husband. I'm behaving like an arsehole. Forgive me."

Anne shot him a sideways glance and then smiled. "Apology accepted, Major. I thought you'd be glad I'm going."

"I am, bonny lass, and you know it. Come on, let's find Collins before I dig myself any deeper into this hole."

Paul joined Wellesley and his senior officers the following afternoon as they met with a dozen of the Spanish commanders. General Cuesta, who had overall command of the Spanish forces was not there, although Wellesley had hoped he would be. He was assured by Cuesta's officers that he was awaiting the English commander at Casa de Miravete near Almaraz. Wellesley was evidently not pleased at the delay but managed to appear civil to the Spanish officers.

Paul was one of the more junior officers present, along with Wellesley's ADCs and Lieutenant Robert Carlyon who appeared slightly overawed by his company. The Spanish had set up their temporary headquarters in a large house just outside Plasencia and dinner was served in a massive, tiled hall. Anne was the only lady present and Paul wondered if she, like her husband, would be overpowered in this environment.

He realised within half an hour that she was not. Seated between two very senior Spanish officers, Anne appeared completely at her ease. Both the men spoke a little English and it was clear that Anne had been trying to learn some Spanish. She turned the meal into an impromptu language class, teaching them the words for the various dishes and then repeating them in Spanish, laughing freely at her own mistakes. As Wellesley did his best to impress upon the commanders the importance of keeping their promises concerning supplies and transport, the attention of most of the men in the room shifted gradually towards Anne. She was dressed in a simple gown of dark green with black trimming. Another girl of her age, faced with so many male eyes on her, might have become shy and awkward, or overly flirtatious. Sir Matthew Howard's young daughter managed the situation with the skill of a much older woman and Paul watched her through the afternoon and felt an ache of inappropriate pride at how well she was handling herself.

After dinner, their hosts invited them out into the garden and champagne was served in the warm evening air. Paul moved towards the Carlyons and was quickly joined by his commander.

"Mrs Carlyon, thank you for coming. I had not realised you were to be the only lady present, I hope you have not minded."

Anne smiled. "How could I mind when I have been so well entertained, sir? Thank you, it has been such a pleasure, Robert and I have enjoyed it very much. I hope it has been useful."

"It would have been more so if General Cuesta had managed to join us, but I am riding on ahead tomorrow and hope to meet with him then. Major van Daan, you will accompany me."

"Gladly, sir."

241

"I cannot believe that we are still no closer to receiving the supplies and wagons they promised us," Wellesley said. "I have asked them, but they behave as though it is of no importance."

"It will be if we can't keep the troops fed," Anne said. "I remember you talking aboard ship, sir, about the improvements in the Indian army with the introduction of bullocks as pack animals. Have we nothing similar that we can use here?"

Wellesley shot her a look of pure astonishment, but to his credit he did not hesitate to reply. "We could have, given time. To tell you the truth, my dear, I am beginning to wonder if I should have waited until we could bring up our own supply wagons. The problem is not only food for the men and horses, but the type of pack animal suited to the terrain."

It was one of his favourite subjects and Paul listened as he explained in detail his views on the importance of an independently supplied army. The girl was listening, her head on one side, with the appearance of genuine interest. She asked the occasional question, and they were sensible questions. For the moment, Wellesley had forgotten he was talking to a beautiful girl and was speaking to her as if she had been one of his more intelligent officers. Paul glanced at Carlyon who was watching his wife as though he could not take his eyes from her lovely face.

They rode back in darkness, Carlyon beside Anne and Paul on her other side. He was conscious of her every move, of the ease with which she sat her horse and of the faint smell of her perfume on the air. Ahead of them, Wellesley was deep in conversation with his quartermaster-general. Abruptly he called back.

"Mr Carlyon, up here a moment, if you please. Colonel Murray tells me you have some interesting ideas about grain supplies."

Carlyon spurred his horse forward and Paul fell in closer to Anne. "Are you all right, girl of my heart? You're quiet."

Anne glanced at him. "Yes. Sorry, I'm tired."

"It's more than that."

Anne smiled through the darkness and shook her head. She had been thinking about Robert, aware of his tense presence beside her, knowing with weary dread what it meant. Nothing had reconciled her to having to endure his presence in her bed, but she had grown surprisingly good at understanding how to please him and he had not hit her since they first came to Portugal. Anne felt, if she allowed herself to think about it, like a prostitute, offering her body and her compliance to pay for her safety. She hated it, but there was a hard-headed practicality in her which reminded her that it was the best option and she found herself wondering how many other young girls whose marriages were arranged by their well-meaning families found themselves in a similar position. But she could tell none of this to Paul, who would unhesitatingly have murdered her husband if he knew how badly she had been treated.

Beside her, Paul said softly:

"Nan?"

242

"Yes?"

"I've been watching you today. Charming the Spanish and flirting with my commander-in-chief who is in a surprisingly good mood, thanks to you."

Anne laughed softly. "Are you about to tell me off again, Paul?"

"No, girl of my heart. I'm about to tell you how much I love you. You are, without doubt, the most extraordinary female I have ever encountered. Never change that."

Anne turned her head, scanning him through the darkness. "Oh Paul, you know, don't you, that I feel the same?"

"I know, bonny lass, but I never get tired of hearing it, no matter how unsuitable it is. I'm going up to ride with Wellesley. Your bloody husband isn't that keen on us being friends and I am trying hard not to make your life difficult. You look beautiful in green."

Paul moved ahead without waiting for a reply.

***

Sir Arthur Wellesley finally met with General Cuesta two days later. After four hours of strained discussion through a translator, since Wellesley spoke little Spanish and Cuesta could not speak English, and would not speak French, a plan was agreed. It was clear to Paul, present only as an observer, that relations between the two commanders were not good and did not look likely to get better. Wellesley found the Spanish troops poorly equipped and trained and their commander suspicious and unwilling to cooperate. Nevertheless, a plan was grudgingly formed, and Paul rode back to his battalion with the awareness that battle was very likely within a few days.

They were an immensely frustrating few days. With supplies and transport still not forthcoming from the Spanish, Wellesley's army engaged in an infuriating game of cat and mouse with the French and the Spaniards. Paul knew that his general was desperate to bring the French to battle before the various elements of their army could converge on Talavera, but he was thwarted by Cuesta's reluctance to cooperate and his inability to mobilise his troops quickly. Twice an attack was agreed upon and then aborted when it became clear that the Spaniards were not ready to fight in support and Wellesley's temper was stretched to breaking point, making his staff jumpy and nervous and the commanders of his newly formed divisions reluctant to spend time with him. The 110th remained under the command of General Hill in the second division but Paul saw little of his battalion for several days as Wellesley kept him in attendance while he inspected his troops, surveyed the potential battlefield and visited some of the provision for wounded set up in and around the town of Talavera.

Paul found Anne in one of the smaller convents, organising the setting up of a ward in what had previously been the convent refectory. Already her Spanish was improving. Paul stood in the doorway watching and listening, completely fascinated both by her ability to pick up languages so quickly and by the confidence with which she was giving orders to half a dozen sullen orderlies who seemed slightly stunned by the experience. Wellesley was outside speaking to Dr Norris and Anne saw Paul watching and came forward, a pile of bedding in her hands, smiling.

"Major van Daan. What brings you here? Not injured yet, I hope?"

"No, ma'am. I'm dancing attendance on the general, trying to keep him from murdering our Spanish allies. Where's Robert?"

"Negotiating with some very obstreperous farmers about goat meat. I offered to go with him; my Spanish is better than his, but he didn't seem keen."

"A mistake in my opinion, they'd have given in within minutes. You're looking very lovely. I'd kiss you, but..."

"Don't you dare!"

"But it's a bit public here. Are you all right, lass? Where are you billeted?"

"Right here in the convent, there are a number of guest rooms. I'm amazed at how useful religious houses can be, there's so much space."

"Bonaparte feels the same, he converts most of them into barracks. I've only got a few minutes, we're off back to the lines. He's had a message that the French are on the move, we might finally see some action tonight or tomorrow. I hope so or he's going to die of frustration. Either that or I'm going to kill him. Even I'm getting bored with being yelled at."

"Is it true that the last attempt at battle was thwarted because the Spanish were asleep?" Anne asked. Paul grinned and nodded.

"Yes, who told you?"

"Adam."

"General Cuesta informed us that his men were too tired to fight on Sunday. He was sound asleep in his carriage, I actually thought Wellesley was going to explode. I wanted to laugh but I didn't dare, he's completely lost his sense of humour at the moment. But I've got a feeling that this is finally going to happen. Look, lass, I'm not likely to see you again until this is over. So..."

"I know. Paul, take care, will you?"

"I'll try. I was about to tell you the same thing. I honestly can't believe that irresponsible bastard you married has you this close to a battlefield completely unprotected and has buggered off to talk about goats!"

"It's his job, Paul."

"So is taking care of his wife. He should at least have employed a groom or an orderly to keep an eye on you. When I've got time, I'm going to find somebody..."

"Paul, I know I'm unconventional but even I can see that Robert would have a right to object to you providing a bodyguard for his wife."

"Well, I'll talk to him about doing so. Or I'll get Wellesley to do it."

"I'm safe. I have Teresa with me, and Adam Norris will keep an eye on me."

"I know. It should be fine, but if it's not...if something goes badly wrong and the French break through, it's going to mean a retreat which will be fast and unpredictable. If that happens, I'm going to come back for you on the way and I don't give a damn about propriety or your bloody husband, I'm not leaving you in the path of a victorious French army, I've seen what they can do."

Unexpectedly he saw a shimmer of tears in the dark eyes. Anne blinked them back. "Thank you for caring," she said softly, and Paul shook his head, his own throat tight.

"You'll never know how much. I need to go, I can hear him yelling. In fact, I imagine Soult can probably hear him yelling, the racket he's making."

"Where are you fighting?"

"He's put us under Hill, in the second division although he's not allocated us to a brigade which means he's keeping us under his direct command. He likes to do that; we're fast and well trained and it gives him manoeuvrability."

"And puts you into the firing line."

"It's where I do best, bonny lass."

"I know. Well, Rowena isn't here to do this, so I'm going to brave the scandal and do it for her."

Anne stood on tiptoe to kiss him very lightly on the mouth. Paul felt a rush of pleasure. He leaned forward, parting her lips very gently under his, prolonging the kiss. Anne drew back reluctantly. "Come back to us, Paul. She needs you and so do your children."

"And you?"

"I need you too."

Paul took a deep steadying breath. "I need you as well, girl of my heart. As much as I hate that you're this close to danger, it feels very good having you here. Stay safe."

Paul looked back as he reached the door. She stood watching him, a slender girl still holding the pile of sheets, a smile on her face and tears clouding her dark eyes. As he went to find his general and his horse to return to the lines, he could still see her gallant little figure and her image warmed him through the darkness.

Finally back with his men, Paul toured the lines, checking on equipment and on morale. The men were hungry. What limited rations they had managed to carry with them had been consumed and the commissariat wagons were empty. Paul wondered grimly how long an army could fight with empty stomachs and how successful they would be.

They had settled around fires, lit more for comfort than necessity in the warm evening, when there was a hail from the road. Sergeant-Major O'Reilly got up and went forward to meet his pickets and reappeared some minutes later. "Sir, I need a word," he said quietly.

Paul rose, lifting his eyebrows and went forward. "What is it, Michael?"

"We've a delivery."

Paul stared. The gig was driven by a thin faced Spaniard with a ragged boy sitting beside him and seemed to contain piled hay. "Fodder for the horses? We've plenty, Michael, are you sure..."

O'Reilly shook his head and beckoned. Paul came closer. Michael moved the hay to one side and Paul saw rush baskets hidden beneath. "What the bloody hell is this?" Paul asked.

"Food. There's bread in this one and some spiced sausages and what looks like a basket of cheeses."

Paul lifted a fourth lid and felt his empty stomach growl at a surprisingly appetising smell. "Cold mutton," he said in matter-of-fact tones. "Michael, where the bloody hell has this come from, the army hasn't had supplies for days. Has Wellington…?"

"I don't know, sir, he doesn't speak English, but he asked for us specifically."

Paul studied the driver and summoned his limited Spanish. "For us? This battalion? How much?"

"Paid, Señor."

"Who paid?"

The man grinned. "The lady, sir. Pretty lady. Very pretty. Your wife?"

Paul stared at him in complete astonishment. "At the convent?"

"Si, Señor."

"Where did she find all this?"

"People are hiding food, Señor. When the armies leave, we have to live."

"Jesus Christ, we're here fighting for their fucking country!" Michael said savagely. "Sir, can we accept this?"

"If it's bought and paid for, we're bloody going to, Michael. But very quietly. Get it unloaded but keep it buried under the hay. Over by the trees where it's sheltered. Get the light company to guard it and I'll send the mess orderlies over in ones and twos to collect a share for their men. Tell them they need to make it last for several days."

O'Reilly was studying him. "Mrs Carlyon?"

"Yes, she's working down at the hospital. She was laughing with me earlier about her bloody husband searching out supplies and she said that she'd offered to help him. I thought she was joking."

"Well, if she's this good at it, Wellesley should be employing her rather than him."

When the food was distributed, Paul moved again amongst his men. They were livelier now, warmed both by the food and the sense of privilege it gave them. Private Carter handed him the remains of a sausage and Paul ate it, smiling. "I hope you've saved some, Carter, you can't expect a windfall like this every week."

"Don't need it, sir, but it was bloody welcome tonight. How did you manage it, we were told there was no food to be had?"

Paul smiled slightly. "Between us?"

"Yes, sir."

"Mrs Carlyon sent it up from the hospital. I am not even going to ask how she did it, I'm just going to be grateful."

Carter laughed aloud. "She is a bloody strange officer's wife, sir. What the hell is she doing out here, she looks like she belongs in a palace not an army camp."

"Don't even get me started on that. Just be..."

There was a furious sound of firing, muskets exploding into the warm evening air. Paul spun around and his battalion around him dropped food into their packs and reached for arms with a speed which impressed even Paul. He held up his hand.

"Wait. Let's find out what that was, before we start shooting each other, Sergeant-Major."

Johnny Wheeler joined him. "That came from our right, over by the olive groves where the Spanish are."

"Yes. Might be a surprise attack, might be just skirmishing. Keep them ready, Johnny, we'll know shortly."

The 110th remained at arms, waiting for news. It came some thirty minutes later as a messenger rode in and Paul recognised one of Wellesley's aides. He dismounted and saluted.

"What's going on, Ensign?"

"Nothing to worry about, sir. Some of the Spanish infantry got spooked by some French dragoons and let off a volley which scared the rest into running."

"Oh Jesus, you couldn't make it up."

"The general has just set off to find General Cuesta, sir. It seems they ran into some of our supply wagons en route and have pillaged them."

Paul glanced across to his own supply wagons, safely under guard. "How many?"

"Four battalions. The general wants them stopped before they cause havoc in Talavera, he's afraid they'll loot the town and the civilians."

Paul felt his stomach lurch. "Have they made it down there?"

"Don't know, sir."

"Thank you, Ensign."

He turned as the young man remounted. "Jenson bring up Rufus. I'm going to ride down into town and find out what's going on."

"Without orders?" Wheeler said in some surprise.

"I won't be long, don't worry. I'll find Wellesley on my way back up."

Paul met Wellesley en route and his general waited for him, eyebrows lifted in some surprise. "Why are you away from your battalion, Major?"

"Just checking if you needed any help in the town, sir, I had your message."

"No, it is fine. General Cuesta has managed to stop the firing and has sent his cavalry in to round up the deserters. I have instructed him to search them for loot before he arrests them."

Fairly caught, Paul fell in beside him. "Sir, if this goes wrong, they're not going to stand. They're green troops, they've no experience of this."

"Too many of our own men are green troops as well, Major."

"I know, but at least they've the training and the equipment. Do you think they'll attack tomorrow?"

"We're lucky they didn't come tonight, they don't seem to have realised there was a sudden gap in our lines. But I think we'll see action tomorrow, and we'll be ready."

Paul glanced at him. "They're all right down in the town, then?"

"They are, Major, although your concern for the locals does you credit. Back to your men, we have no idea when they'll come."

Paul nodded and saluted. He watched as his commander rode on back to his staff and then sat looking out over the lights of the town.

"She'll be fine, sir, she's with the medical staff and the quartermasters, she'll be well guarded."

Paul turned, startled, to find that Michael had walked up from the lines. "I know. But I needed to be sure."

"Jesus, sir, you've got it bad."

Paul swung down from Rufus and fell into step beside his sergeant-major, leading his horse. "She shouldn't be here, Michael."

"I know, sir, but she is, and you need to trust that the men around her know what they're doing."

"Well, I don't. But you're right, I can't be in two places at once. Come on, let's see if we can get some sleep in this bloody chaos."

"What with the French, the Spanish and your girlfriend running her own personal commissariat service, sir, I'm not optimistic," Michael said. "But you can't say the lass isn't useful. You'd think she'd been doing this for years."

Paul had been thinking the same thing. He grinned. "Wellington would have a fit if he knew," he said. "What a bloody nerve she's got, Michael. Who'd have thought it?"

248

Chapter Fifteen

Anne and Robert had been allocated a room in one of the guest houses attached to the convent. On the night before the battle, Anne lay awake into the early hours, listening to her husband's breathing. Their evening had been disturbed by the fiasco of the Spanish panic, but the town was quiet now.

Anne had not told Robert what she had done regarding supplies for the 110th. It had been an impulse. The farmer had been brought in injured, ridden down on his way home by a French cavalry squadron. He had been charmed at having his injuries treated by a very pretty Englishwoman who knew basic Spanish and was able to converse sympathetically with him about his farm, his desire to be paid for his goods and his determination not to allow either army to plunder him. Robert was away and Anne knew that she ought to have told him about the farmer. Instead, she had accompanied the man back to his farm, been pleasant to his wife and admired his sturdy young son before spending a portion of her personal allowance on a wagon load of food for Paul's battalion. She wondered if it had reached him successfully.

Beside her, Robert stirred. "You're not sleeping."

"No, I'm sorry, did I disturb you?"

"No, I heard something."

Anne could hear it too now, muskets firing out in the darkness. Something told her that this was not another false alarm. Robert sat up.

"I think it's started," he said.

"Yes. Do you have to go?"

"I should get over to Headquarters, see what's needed."

"I'd like to go down to the hospital. Do you mind?"

Her husband studied her for a moment. "No," he said. "But Nan…"

Anne turned to look at him and he looked at her for a long time. Unexpectedly, almost angrily, he said:

"Dress sensibly. There will be all sorts going through that place. Don't give them reason to be disrespectful."

"I won't, Robert." Anne hesitated. Despite her enduring dislike of him, she could sense that he was genuinely concerned. "It means a good deal to me that I am able to do this. Thank you."

Her husband shook his head, his eyes on hers. "I never thought I'd give a damn what happened to you," he said. "But I do. So take some care, I'll send to you if I need you."

Anne nodded and slid from the bed to dress. The firing was louder now and more consistent. Impossible to know where it was coming from, through the darkness which lay over Wellesley's lines, but Anne's thoughts were all of Paul. She reached for the plain gown which she had set aside for hospital wear and felt Robert's hands on her shoulders.

"Kiss me," he said harshly, and she turned obediently and reached up. He kissed her hungrily for a long time and she could sense that he would have liked more, but he was conscious of his duty. Eventually he released her, and Anne finished dressing, then walked through several courtyards to the main convent building to join Adam Norris.

"What's happening, Adam?"

"Not sure, yet. They've made a night attack, somebody said it's up on the hill, the Cerro de Medellin."

"Who is up there?"

"I think it's mostly Kings German Legion. We've had none in yet, it may be too dark to bring them down. You could go back to bed and I'll call you."

"I can't sleep, it's too noisy," Anne said. "And I'm too much on edge."

"We'll get word soon," Norris said understandingly. "I'll get Teresa to make some tea. Have you managed to eat? There's not much, but…"

"I'm fine, Adam. I just want to get on with it." Anne shivered. "I wonder if they feel like that out there?"

"Probably. Come and sit for a while. You'll be on your feet long enough later on." Norris studied her. "You sure you're all right to do this?"

"Yes. But it's hard, not knowing what's going on. There are people I know out there now, Adam. Paul, Carl, Johnny…"

"I know, lass. At least Robert isn't engaged in fighting. I suppose this is why Paul never wants Rowena around close to the fighting, it must be hard. But we'll know soon enough. It's as dark as Hades out there, I can't imagine how anybody can see to fight in this."

***

From his position in the centre of Wellesley's lines with Hill's division, Paul was peering through the impenetrable darkness. None of them had slept, disturbed by the occasional musket shots of skirmishers, by men making their way down to the brook to drink and by the sounds of hammering as the French continued work on their artillery batteries, but the sounds floating down now from the summit of the Cerro de Medellin were more than that. Paul was on his feet, listening intently.

"They're attacking," he said. "Sergeant-Major, get the men to arms."

"Yes, sir."

The 110th scrambled into line, bumping into one another in the dark. Wheeler came to join Paul. "We've no orders, sir."

"Not yet. But something's going on, I want them ready."

Horses sounded close by and then a voice called. "Major van Daan, are your men awake?"

"Yes, sir."

General Rowland Hill rode in closer. "I'm not sure what's going on," he said. "I've sent the 48th up to have a look. Probably a false alarm, it'll be the Buffs doing something stupid, most likely. But General Wellesley is over with the Spanish so best not take chances. I'm going to follow them up."

"Do you want us to come with you, sir?"

Hill surveyed the roused men. "Do you ever let them sleep, Van Daan?"

"Occasionally, sir."

Hill grinned, his teeth showing faintly. "All right, follow me up. I've told Stewart's brigade to get to arms, but we may not need them."

Paul watched him ride on and turned, signalling to O'Reilly. The sergeant-major called out an order and the battalion moved forward cautiously to ascend the lower slopes of the hill.

The Cerro de Medellin was deceptive, and higher than it looked from below. It was clear as Paul led his men up the steep slopes that the French had attempted a night attack although in this light it was impossible to tell how serious it was and how many troops were involved. Ahead, they could hear Hill's horse cautiously making its way up though Paul could not see him. The gunfire was shockingly loud, and they could hear the shouts and cries of fighting men floating down to them through the still night.

"I wish there was more of a moon, this is a bloody nightmare," Wheeler said, and Paul grinned though he knew his friend could not see him.

"We need a cat here. Mr Swanson? Take the lead, would you?"

"Very funny," Carl's voice replied, moving ahead. Carl had always had phenomenal night vision. Behind him Paul heard Sergeant-Major O'Reilly swear as he stumbled into a rabbit hole and reflected that they would be lucky to reach the fighting without sprained ankles, but it would be useful to have a guide who could see his way reasonably well.

There was a sudden flash of light, a musket shot surprisingly close at hand, and Carl swore. "Christ, we're on top of them," he called. "I think Hill's been hit."

Paul raised his sword with a yell. "110th, to me. General Hill, are you there? Are you all right?"

He ran forward and realised as he did that Hill was still mounted, but that his horse was rearing up, with a French infantryman holding the bridle, trying to pull the general down. Paul gave a bellow and launched himself forward into the fray hearing his men on both sides of him as they raced to engage the enemy. Hill broke free as Paul cut down the Frenchman holding the bridle.

"Van Daan? Get up there and support the 48th, the Germans are under attack, I'm going back for Stewart's brigade."

"Yes, sir." Hill galloped off at terrifying speed given the appalling visibility and Paul went to join his men, swearing as he became entangled in a particularly vicious thorn bush.

It was hard to tell friend from foe. The skirmishers of Paul's light company pulled ahead in twos, aiming carefully at their opponents, finding them in the darkness only by the flash of musket fire. They called out sometimes to try to get shapes in the darkness to identify themselves, careful not to shoot their own troops who were already fighting on the hillside. It was a painful and tortuous advance. Behind them, General Hill brought up three battalions of Stewart's brigade, leading the 29th himself and managing to advance in line in circumstances which would have daunted a lesser man.

The sounds of battle were oddly muted in the inky blackness. An erratic burst of action would be followed by silence, with an occasional bugle call or a shouted order in French or English, as the two sides searched blindly for each other, while avoiding firing on their own troops. At one point there was an undignified scramble out on the right of Paul's line, as Young's company discovered that they had mistaken a cluster of French infantrymen for the King's German Legion in the darkness and were under attack at close range before they realised it. Two companies of the 29th stumbled over the skirmish just as Paul reached it with his light company, and the French fled in disarray down the hill as they realised they were about to be trapped between two English battalions.

"Major, is that you?"

"Captain Wheeler?"

Johnny appeared like a ghost beside Paul. He seemed to have lost his hat and Paul understood why he had not bothered to look for it. "Sir, General Hill is wounded."

"He's down?" Paul asked, appalled.

"No, he's still up, that's the damned problem, but he's bleeding badly from a head wound, and he's ignoring his officers' advice."

"Oh bloody hell, we're not losing Hill. Where is he?"

"Over to our left, I can hear him."

Paul listened and could hear Hill's voice calling orders somewhere over to the right. "Sir? General Hill?"

"Is that you, Van Daan? We're making progress, well done. Let's get them..."

In the faint glow of a sliver of moon, Paul could see the dark blood running down from the man's head. "Sir, we're fine, but you're hurt, you need to get out of here."

"I'm perfectly well. I can..."

"Get that looked at, sir, we can't lose you," Paul said sharply. He saw Hill's head turn in surprise at his tone and lowered his voice. "He can't lose you, he's going to need you before we're done here. Please, sir."

General Hill fell silent, listening to his men fighting around him. "All right," he said finally. "Where is Tilson, he'll take command."

"I'll find him, sir."

"Until you do, you have the field, Major."

"Yes, sir. Get yourself down to Dr Norris, he's in the small convent, it's the closest."

Paul strained his eyes to watch as Hill rode cautiously back down the slope. He was aware that the noise of battle seemed to be less, and he turned, straining his eyes through the darkness to find his own men. "Johnny?"

"Here, sir. They're falling back, we've got them on the run."

"Thank God for that. This is a fucking nightmare, I feel as if I'm going blind."

Wheeler was right. The French were retreating fast, realising that Wellesley's men outnumbered them on the hill, and Paul observed that the 29th had planted their colours firmly at the summit. He grinned, wondering where his own colours were. They were probably back with Private Jenson and the bandsmen. They would have known better than to follow him up a hill with such poor visibility, he would have been furious at the unnecessary risk.

"Sergeant-Major, get this ridge secured and make sure there are proper pickets this time. When it's light and we've time, somebody is going to have to explain to Sir Arthur Wellesley why half the Germans appeared to be asleep with no sentries and no warning when the French attacked, and I'm hoping to be somewhere else for that. I'm going to look for General Tilson, although he could be three feet away from me in this bloody darkness and I wouldn't know. Christ, I'm hoping tomorrow is better organised."

Paul stomped away, then spoiled the effect by tripping over the body of a French tirailleur in the darkness and uttering an appallingly vulgar oath. He could hear Carl and Johnny laughing softly and turned back.

"Go and find him, Mr Swanson, tell him General Hill is wounded and he commands the field."

"Yes, sir."

"There are a fair few wounded up here," Johnny said.

"Ours?"

"Not sure, yet. Sergeant-Major O'Reilly…"

"I'll get the NCOs to do a roll call once we're sure the French aren't coming back, sir. Impossible to see who's here and who isn't, but the lads up here have a good few down."

"We can't get them down until daylight. Get our lads settled until we get orders from Wellesley at daylight, Johnny. Once they're in position along this ridge, we can get some of them out searching for the wounded. We can't do much for them apart from give them water and note where they are but we'll get them shifted first thing."

***

Casualties began to arrive at the convent at daylight, as news of the night attack spread among the medical staff. Many of the men had been lying out for most of the night, as it had been impossible to convey men off the field in

253

the darkness without giving the British position away fully. They were cold and dirty and weak from lack of care and loss of blood. Anne positioned herself at a table close to Norris, and the orderlies and hospital mates bringing in the wounded men set them down in no particular order, leaving the surgeons to decide who should be treated first.

As Anne set to work, she was very conscious of the disapproval of most of the surgeons at the hospital. Several of them had spoken to Adam Norris about her presence, and Anne left it to him to explain, and justify and argue. None of them had the nerve to approach her directly to tell her to leave, and as the hours passed and the wounded men poured in, there was no longer time to squabble about who treated whom. Anne commandeered two of the inexperienced hospital mates who worked under Norris, and Teresa who acted as her silent and unruffled nurse and set about dealing with the horrors before her. As calmly as she could she stitched wounds and applied dressings and probed for musket balls and shot. For some of these men it was already too late.

Several times Anne recognised, with a lurch of fear, the silver-grey facings of the 110th, although none of them were officers and casualties did not appear to be heavy from Paul's regiment. Listening to the soldiers' tales, Anne gathered that Paul's men had constituted part of a rescue party, but it sounded as though he had survived the night.

As the last of the casualties were treated and moved onto the wards, Anne stepped outside in the cold early morning air, listening to the thundering of the French guns firing onto the British infantry on the Cerro de Medellin. Somewhere out on the slopes, Paul waited with his men. The thought of those destructive shells crashing into the lines of the 110th sickened Anne. She took a deep breath, inhaling the fresh morning air although she was conscious that it held a whiff of the decay of the hospital and the grave pits already being dug.

"Nan, are you all right?" Adam Norris asked behind her, and Anne turned.

"Yes. Just taking a break. What's next, Adam?"

"Now we wait. For Wellesley to make his move and for the French to respond. And then, God help us, they'll start carrying them in by the hundred."

***

Wellesley arrived on the Cerro de Medellin with his staff early the following morning to observe the field. The French guns had opened up from the Cascajal hill at dawn, causing some initial losses among the British infantry on the Medellin. Paul had pulled his own men back quickly into cover and got them to lie down, knowing how destructive French artillery could be and he observed that along the lines the other commanders were doing the same. He walked to meet Wellesley and saluted.

"Morning, sir. Good sleep?"

"Not at all, Major. There was a good deal of noise, it was very disruptive. Did you lose many?"

"Two dead and about eight wounded. Not counting bruises and twisted ankles from falling over each other in the dark. It was a bloody farce, sir. What happened, do we even know?"

Wellesley pulled an expressive face. He looked tired and drawn already. "A lot of confusion about which troops were supposed to be where. I think our staff work needs some attention, Major. It appears that the KGL from Lowe's brigade were under the impression that they were the second line troops, so they just settled down and went to sleep without proper pickets or sentries."

"Oh dear God."

"Just so. We've lost about 300 to death, injury and capture - about a hundred of the KGL were taken prisoner in their sleep. But I think the French lost more."

"How's General Hill?"

"He's had a fright, that's for sure - a bullet grazed his head. But the wound is not serious, he'll be back to take command up here shortly. He tells me you were invaluable last night."

There was an enormous crash as a shell fell close at hand, spraying them with earth. Wellesley appeared unconcerned although his ADC looked worried. Paul grinned.

"Sir, you need to shift out of range or else get off that horse and lie down with the rest of the men. Any orders?"

"I'm going to speak to Tilson and the others, I have observed movement in Ruffin's division. I think they're trying to soften us up before making another assault."

"If they come up this hill this morning, they are going to bloody regret it, I've had a bad night," Paul said grimly. "I wish we had better artillery, mind, we can't compete with this."

"No, we're going to lose an artillery battle. But they can't shift us off this hill like that, they're going to have to come up and get us. And as you say, I suspect they'll regret it when they do. Ah Dryden, is that Lieutenant Carlyon I can see approaching? Bring him up, will you, I wish to speak to him about our baggage train."

Paul looked down the hill, catching a glimpse of Robert Carlyon's bright red head. "I'm guessing you've had no more luck with supplies from the Spanish, sir? A lot of the men have completely run out of food."

"I know, Major, it's appalling. No, we've had nothing and I'm not sure we will. This is no way to fight a war. Are your men all right?"

"Better than some." Paul thought with warmth of the baskets of food, carefully distributed, and wondered how Anne Carlyon was coping down in the hospital.

"I have to go. Good luck today, Major."

"You too, sir."

Paul stood watching as Wellesley moved away in search of his divisional commanders and then turned as Jenson approached holding a steaming tin cup. Paul accepted the tea. "When did you arrive?" he asked.

"When I could see well enough not to break my good leg in the dark, sir."

"You've not brought the horses up?"

"No, sir I've left them at the rear with the grooms. They're close enough if they're needed. Drink that, you look freezing."

Paul drank. "Thanks, Jenson. You managed to eat anything?"

"A bit. We're doing better than most of the division, that's for sure."

Paul nodded and stood drinking his tea, looking out over the armies. It was an impressive sight in the pale pink light of early dawn. There must have been at least 100,000 fighting men from France, England and Spain with their associated camp followers, servants, grooms and other staff taking care of the cavalry horses, baggage trains and medical facilities. Around the various divisions, colours blew in the light morning breeze. Paul surveyed the Anglo-Spanish lines thoughtfully. Although they had a numerical advantage at around 52,000 men, only 20,000 of them were English and he placed no reliance on the battle performance of the untried Spanish troops. He was also somewhat cautious about some of the English troops. His own men were experienced fighters, veterans of Rolica, Vimeiro and Porto. Some had fought with him all the way back in India and many had been at Corunna with Colonel Johnstone and Sir John Moore. But there were boys out on this field who had never faced the French or anybody else in battle and Paul knew how terrified they must be and how much more terrified they were going to be when the drums began, and the columns were marching towards them.

Another shell crashed close by and Paul heard screams from some of the infantry who had been hit. He gulped down the remainder of his tea and ran over to where his own battalion had found limited shelter behind some low rocks. They were intact. Smoke was starting to cover the field and Paul could hear orders being shouted from other commanders as they tried to shift their men into less vulnerable positions. He handed his cup to Jenson.

"All right lad, get yourself off this hill and get all non-combatants back out of range. And make sure my horses are safe."

"Yes, sir. They coming?"

"Yes, there's movement in Ruffin's lines, this artillery will stop in a minute."

Paul settled down behind a large boulder. Within three quarters of an hour the French battery stopped firing and he heard, faint on the morning air, the steady ominous sound of the drums. Glancing across at his men Paul could see hands tightening on rifles.

"They're coming, lads, voltigeurs will be up first. Mr Swanson get the light company out, skirmish formation, they won't see you in this smoke, be a nice surprise for them. Johnny, keep the men in, don't let them drift backwards. They'll be shooting again but it should go over our heads, they won't want to hit their own men."

"Yes, sir."

The bugles sounded, the high clear notes drifting over the field, easy to hear over the sound of the French advance. Paul could hear the French drums rolling steadily and the shouts of "Vive l'Empereur" amidst the roar of the cannon. Closer, he could hear the sound of marching feet on the hard earth and the columns could be glimpsed through the haze of smoke. Along the English lines, officers and NCOs called out encouragement and reassurance to their men. Paul walked to a small hillock and stood looking out over his lines.

The forward skirmishers from the 60th rifles and the 110th light company retreated back to the main line. The French were making good progress up the slopes of the Cerro de Medellin with only a few of them brought down by the skirmishers and cannon shots from the Allied batteries. Lying flat at the top of the hill, Paul wondered what Ruffin's men could see and if they had any idea how many British now manned the top. He glanced over and saw General Hill, newly returned to his division, his head bandaged under his hat, his eyes steady and watchful with his sword in his hand, waiting.

As the French column drew closer, Paul saw Hill move, his sword arm raising and then falling in a signal. The seven British battalions on the summit rose to their feet in one fluid movement, appearing over the top of the hill with rifles and muskets trained on the solid block of the French column.

"Fire!" Paul yelled, and his officers and NCOs took up the call. The sound of bugles cut through the noise of battle and then the French screamed, their chanting silenced in three bloody minutes as the musketry volleys wiped out entire ranks of French infantrymen. Paul reflected, shouting orders down his lines, that in Ruffin's position he would have moved from column to line as he reached the top of the hill. There was something terrifying about the solid columns in which the French advanced, and he knew that Napoleon's armies had used this formation throughout Europe to sweep aside their opponents who fled in disarray before the noise and the sheer power of the marching blocks of men. But the English had not fled. Hill's men, frightened but determined, were standing, and they were standing well. Given that the columns had not achieved their purpose of intimidating the English, Paul thought that Ruffin's men would have done better to move into line where more of them could use their firepower and they would have presented a less compact target for the British muskets and rifles.

It was too late now. To do them credit, the French were trying to return fire, but those initial savage volleys had done their work and the columns were disorderly, with men unable to find their places. Those in the middle and at the rear were in no position to fire as another lethal volley swept aside the front ranks and the columns shifted and wavered. Paul took a step forward, then another, silently pleading with Hill to give the order. He could sense his men's eagerness to attack, seeing the chaos of the French columns.

Even as he thought it, the order came, and Paul yelled it back to his buglers. His men dropped into position, bayonets at the ready.

"Charge!"

The British swept forward, some of the men roaring savagely as they raced towards the French columns. Paul ran with them, swinging his sword as the first line of his battalion crashed into the French. They were not going to stand, he could see by the sheer terror on the faces of the first rank. He slashed at a man who fell, stepped over him and cut down a second. The third man was already turning and beginning to run and then the French were racing back down the hill, falling over the piled bodies of their own men and those of the English who had been cut down during the earlier artillery bombardment. Paul and his men followed, cutting down the French infantrymen in swathes as they fled.

There was blood on Paul's sword, and some must have splashed onto his face, as he could smell the sharp metallic odour. A Frenchman stumbled and fell ahead of him and was bayonetted before he could rise. Paul's men were running faster now, carried on by the downwards momentum, and none of the French were stopping to fight. With no immediate threat, Paul slowed down to survey the field as well as he could and realised that danger lay ahead. Another French battalion was heading up the hill to provide cover for their fleeing comrades.

"Sergeant-Major, call the halt," he bellowed. O'Reilly, ten feet ahead of him, came to an abrupt stop, turned then followed Paul's pointing hand. Seeing the danger, he began shouting orders, and the buglers took up the call. Across the line, the 110th pulled up sharply and Paul took out his telescope and kept a wary eye on the newcomers, not willing to risk being cut off.

There was the sound of battle from the south as General Sherbrooke sent his King's German Legion crashing into the exposed flank of the French. Steel clashed on steel and there were cries of pain, then a yell of sheer panic as the French realised they were fighting on two fronts. A thick blanket of smoke covered the battlefield, and Paul lowered his glass. He could see little through the haze, but it was clear that more English troops had descended the hill in pursuit of the French.

"Major Van Daan."

Paul turned to see General Hill approaching, trailed by two staff members. "Wait here for further orders. Sir Arthur has sent Stewart's brigade in a bayonet charge to finish them off."

"Yes, sir."

Paul unstoppered his water bottle and drank, trying to peer through the smoke. He could see nothing but could hear the sound of Stewart's men advancing. Stoppering his bottle, he went to find Sergeant-Major O'Reilly who was with Johnny Wheeler.

"Losses, Sergeant-Major?"

"We've lost a few to cannon fire, sir, mostly from the third company. Not bad apart from that. Orders?"

"We're waiting for Stewart's brigade to see them off and then we'll see what Wellesley wants. Get the wounded up to the back, Sergeant-Major, there are wagons taking them down to Talavera. Adam Norris is working at the small convent on the western side and I'd like our wounded taken there, if possible. He's got Mrs Carlyon helping him down there."

"Lucky man," Carl said with a grin, wiping sweat from his dirty face. "Could think of worse nurses."

"Just so. They're digging grave trenches down beyond those trees, Sergeant Stewart. Once you've got all the wounded out, get the bandsmen up and half a dozen of the second company to carry the dead men to the back."

"Aye, sir."

"Sir? What's happening with Stewart's brigade? Doesn't sound right, down there."

"No idea, Captain Young." Paul listened, and was not reassured. "All right, Sergeant, leave the dead for now, just get the wounded out of here then keep the men at arms, just in case."

An hour passed before the remains of General Stewart's brigade made their way back to the lines. They had chased the routed French infantry down as far as the Portina River where some of them had had the sense to stop. Others had continued across the river towards the Cerro de Cascajal where they were ruthlessly cut down by the guns from the French batteries and musket fire from Villatte's division. The remainder staggered back to their lines with the French guns still raking them. Paul pulled his men back into shelter and awaited orders, but no further attacks came and eventually the guns fell silent again.

Wellesley approached after about half an hour, his face blackened with smoke, and Paul came forward to salute him. "Are you all right, sir?"

"Yes. We've agreed an informal truce for both sides to collect their dead and wounded. God knows I don't want our men lying out here in this heat, injured or dead."

"No." Paul turned to survey the hillside, covered with dead and dying men of both sides. "I'll get the lads out there, sir. I see the French are taking the opportunity to cook their rations. Must be nice."

Wellesley looked over towards the French lines where the men were beginning to light fires, then turned back to Paul. "Of course, they will have stolen their food from the locals, Major. I am curious where your battalion got theirs from."

Paul shot him a startled look and then grinned. "It was paid for, I promise you, sir. It's not much and they'll be hungry enough in a day or so. But some of the other battalions have had nothing but a couple of tack biscuits for days."

"I am aware of the problem, Major. Best get your men moving."

The informal truce lasted several hours as both sides collected their wounded and dead and grave trenches were dug at the back of the lines and quickly filled in because of the hot weather. Down by the stream both French and English went to drink, fill water bottles, and to study each other curiously over the narrow river.

Paul stood watching as some of his light company stood smoking clay pipes eyeing half a dozen French tirailleurs who had limped down to the brook and were studying the water in dismay. Several bodies had just been lifted from the river in that part and the water was dark with blood. Private Dawson suddenly stepped forward and gestured. Taking out his own bottle he waved to the French and made his way further upstream to an area where the water had not stagnated and flowed down fast from the hills, still fresh and clean on the British side. Dawson filled his bottle and then reached out. After a long moment of hesitation one of the Frenchman passed his canteen and Dawson bent to fill it for him. Suddenly the others were there, wading into the cool water, laughing and passing the water bottles over. Carter and Cooper and one or two of the others went to join them, and then Paul saw the French sergeant reach into his pack and take out what looked like some cheese.

"Looks like a party," Carl Swanson said, coming to stand beside him, watching the men.

"Doesn't it? Do you ever wonder what the hell we're doing, Carl?"

"I do just now. I didn't when I marched through that village outside Oporto last month and saw that row of crucified villagers, including five children because they decided not to hand over everything they had to Soult's army. I wonder where that cheese they're sharing so charmingly with Private Cooper came from? Mrs Carlyon treated me to my breakfast this morning, but I'm not convinced they paid for theirs."

Paul surveyed his friend with a slight smile. "I am glad I've got you lad, it means I never need to develop a conscience of my own."

"You've got one, Paul. That's half your trouble. Come on, I'm going to fill my bottle and cool off a bit, it is bloody hot up here."

While the French generals apparently discussed their options, Wellesley took the opportunity to adjust his position in order to stop the French outflanking the Cerro de Medellin and taking the northern plain. He sent cavalry out to the north, along with a number of Spanish troops and some artillery and Paul, watching his chief make his preparations was not surprised when the French were abruptly called back to their lines.

By noon it was clear that the French were preparing a new attack, closing up their reserves from the rear and massing troops in front of Wellesley's centre. Two large columns pointed to the valley on the left of the hill, and a body of light troops were seen moving to gain the distant range of hills on the other side of the valley.

"They're going to try and turn us on the left," Paul said, studying the enemy movements through his telescope. "And hit the centre at the same time. Yes, sir?"

Hill had ridden along the line and reined in. "General Wellesley's orders, Major. He wants you to move your battalion down the hill to the left of his centre. He's concerned we're not strong enough there."

"Yes, sir." Paul turned and shouted an order and his men fell in ready to march. Glancing across towards the French, he could see movement. "Speed it up, Sergeant-Major," he said, suddenly anxious. "I don't think we've much time here."

The 110th had barely reached its new position when the French columns slammed into them, speeding over the flatter ground, giving Paul no time to send out his skirmishers and no time to formulate any kind of plan. General Sebastiani threw his men against the English with a single-minded ferocity which spoke of sheer desperation, and Paul had no idea what was happening elsewhere on the field. The fighting on all sides now was bitter and bloody and close at hand, with muskets and bayonets replacing the long-distance volleys of the morning's battle. Despite the speed of the engagement, Paul's skirmishers excelled at close range fighting, dodging between the lines, covering one another in pairs, firing and reloading when they could and then slipping back between the line infantry as it prepared to charge.

Bloodied and exhausted, Paul's men, alongside the 7th and the 53rd, pushed back Sebastiani's left column in savage hand to hand fighting with bayonet and sword. The ground was thick with dead and wounded from both sides, and Paul knew that he was losing too many men. There was no time, during the fierce fighting, to assess his losses or search for men he knew, but the French were falling back fast now, and there was a momentary lull. Paul rallied his men, calling them back into companies, keeping a wary eye on the French while running his gaze over the weary ranks of his men to see how many were missing. It did not look good. His first company had taken the worst punishing and Paul had no way of knowing how many were dead and how many lay wounded on the field, but more than half of them were missing including all of the officers. The light company was battered and depleted and there were faces he searched for and could not find.

"Sergeant-Major, where's Grogan?"

O'Reilly shook his head exhaustedly. He was sporting a bloody arm where it had been grazed by a musket ball. "Down, sir," he said quietly.

"Wounded?"

"Dead. No doubt."

Paul felt sick, remembering Grogan on the hillside in India, giving him the armband of a chosen man. Instinctively he felt his sleeve, where he still wore it, although it was grey and tattered now.

"Poor bastard. Isn't his wife expecting again?"

Michael nodded. "Any day now."

"I fucking hate this, Michael."

"I know, sir. D'you think they'll..."

"Sir, rider coming up, from the general!"

Paul turned, his bloodied sword in his hand and recognised one of Wellesley's aides. "Gordon?"

"General's orders, sir, you're needed on the right. The general is bringing the 48th over, but you're closer, the guards have crumbled under heavy fire and the French are breaking through."

"Shit, they're going to split our line. Get them moving, Sergeant-Major."

"Yes, sir." O'Reilly took off, bellowing orders, the buglers called and the remains of the 110th fell into line and set off grimly across the field.

261

They arrived into chaos. Sebastiani's right column had been successfully driven back by the guards, who had allowed success to go to their heads, and had pursued the French remorselessly, risking their lives in front of the French artillery and creating a gap in the English line, which the French moved quickly to exploit. Paul drew his men into a solid line, bellowing at them to stand firm, and they stood, buffeted by the triumphant rush of the French who believed they had found a way through.

"Three ranks! Sergeant-Major, call it!"

"Load, you sluggish bastards!" O'Reilly bellowed.

The musket volleys crashed out, deafening Paul, and the new English line, dangerously thin, wavered and then held. Muskets thundered again and the first rank of the French fell back. Paul dropped his sword arm with another yell and the second rank fired and once again the French fell. There were sounds to his right and Paul risked a glance and to his immense relief, saw Sir Arthur Wellesley coming up with the 48th.

"Keep them steady, Major, Mackenzie's Brigade is on its way. We can hold this until they arrive."

Wellesley's voice, reaching Paul through the smoke and haze of the battle, was as calm and steady as if he had been sitting behind his desk discussing plans and as always, it steadied Paul who felt a sudden rush of appreciation for his unemotional chief. With the support of the 48th they could hold until the reserves arrived, although Paul was agonisingly aware of how close it had been and how many men he might have lost in that first devastating charge. There was no time to wonder. He raised his voice to a bellow.

"110th, hold the line. Where are my bloody buglers, do I need to make myself heard all over the bloody battlefield?"

The French came on. Volley after volley crashed into them. Around Paul, men fell. He lost sight of his other officers, although he could still hear the voice of Michael O'Reilly shouting orders through the smoke and the ominous beat of the drummers as the French marched in column. Mackenzie's Brigade arrived to reinforce, and the line was strengthened and steadied. Paul's arm ached from the weight of his sword, and he cut and thrust and drove back each French infantryman who came close. As always in battle his mind was abnormally clear, and his vision, though blurred with sweat and the sting of the acrid smoke seemed to operate faster than usual. His mouth was dry but there was no time to stop and drink.

"Well done, gentlemen. They're falling back. The guards are reforming," Wellesley called. "Let them do their job now!"

"Let the grenadiers through, lads!" Paul shouted. "They've had a fucking rest, now they can take the brunt. But give them directions, they're so bloody stupid they'll start shooting at us!"

Captain Ellison of the 110th company of guards was passing, bellowing at his men to follow. "Piss off, Major!" he called, with an exhausted grin. "Fucking light infantry, you think you piss best brandy, don't you?"

"Good enough so that your lads wouldn't know the difference, Tony. Get on with it, will you, I need a drink. Steady, lads. Give them cover, we're almost there."

A horseman reined in beside him and Paul looked up at the commander-in-chief. "Sir."

"Well done, Major van Daan, they're slowing down, by God. Hold steady, I'm going over to see what's happening on the Cerro de Medellin. They're attacking again, but I doubt they've the stomach for it now that this assault has failed."

Wellesley rode off and Paul turned back and surveyed his lines. They were holding steady, with the guards fighting at the front now. Here and there, he could see movement as the men of his light company ran between the fighters, taking down individual Frenchmen. Paul knew a sudden instinct to call them back, they had lost so many today. But they were doing valuable work and he left them alone and turned to check on the remains of the first company and saw that a section of the French column had managed to charge through the guards and reach his first rank. He lifted his sword, bellowing orders, and those of the light company who heard him ran to their beleaguered first company and reached the French column just as he did, firing and slashing with bayonets and swords until the Frenchmen fell back.

The last of them was a thin dark man, probably of about Paul's own age. Occasionally in battle a face would leap out at him in the blur of death and injury and survival, and Paul would remember the expression on a man's face as he died. He saw the Frenchman look around as the three men around him fell under the rifle fire of the light company. Paul looked at him and met his gaze and saw the fury and the anguish and the killing madness in the dark eyes. A blue coat came close to Paul's left and he turned and swung his sword and the man fell with a scream. And then something slammed into him and lifted him back off his feet and he felt himself crash to the ground. Paul looked back as he fell, and he saw the thin dark man with his musket at his shoulder and then he was lying on the dry churned up ground. He knew it was bad, but he felt nothing for a moment, then his body exploded with the pain.

***

The French were falling back fast and the guards and the 110th pursued them cautiously, following Paul's orders not to allow the men to run out of control. Michael O'Reilly found himself with time to reload, so he did so, took careful aim and brought down a French officer. There was more space around him now as the enemy retreated, and Michael ran an experienced eye over the retiring troops and decided that the French had probably had enough, although it was not entirely over yet.

Catching his breath, he looked back across the line. Lieutenant Swanson was lowering his sword arm, also taking a breather, and Captain Wheeler was ahead, wiping sweat from his face with his sleeve. Michael could hear the clear tones of Gervase Clevedon from the second company calling his men into line. There was something missing, and Michael suddenly realised what it was. He could neither see nor hear Paul, and that was unusual, as his major was very vocal during a battle, even when smoke hid him from view.

Michael swung around. "Sergeant Stewart, where's the major?" he bellowed.

Through the noise of battle something stilled, and then there was movement as men from the light company began to run back, bending over fallen men, searching frantically. A cry came from further back and Michael ran, his heart beating unevenly. He dropped to his knees beside the body of his commander. There was so much blood on Paul's coat that it was impossible to see exactly where it was coming from, but he lay immobile and Michael could not see his chest rise.

"Oh no," he whispered. "Oh God, no!"

Carl Swanson dropped beside him. He reached out and felt for a pulse in the neck. "He's still alive," he said. "But he's been hit in the chest. Christ, it's bad."

"Get him back up to the surgeon," Captain Wheeler yelled. "Sergeant-Major, go with him. We're over the worst here now, get him out of here." He looked at Carl's white face. "Go with him, Carl."

"He'd tell me to stay here."

"He'd tell us to put him down and get on with shifting the wounded men off the field first," Johnny said grimly. "Luckily, for once in his bloody life he can't yell at us, so take an order and get him out of here. We need somebody to make sure he sees a surgeon quickly, the bandsmen don't have the authority. We need an officer."

Michael helped Carl and three of the bandsmen to carry Paul up through the piles of dead and wounded, to the dressing station at the back of the lines. They laid him down and the assistant surgeon, who was very young, knelt beside him and probed at the wound. Paul stirred and groaned.

"It's a bullet and a big wound. I can try to dig it out here…." The young man looked up and something about the expression on Carl's face seemed to cause him to lose his nerve. "I'm frightened to touch it," he blurted out. "It's bleeding so much, and it's close to his heart, it must be. If I make a mistake…"

"Lieutenant!"

Carl and Michael both turned. Michael recognised a captain from the King's German Legion.

"Captain Gruber," Carl said.

"There is a wagon going up to Talavera with some wounded and we can fit him on although there is no space for you."

Carl glanced at Michael. "Take him, Captain. We'll get the horses and follow you up. Try to leave him with Dr Norris if you can."

"He will be lucky to get seen at all, it is terrible up there. But still better than out here."

Carl and Michael ran back through the lines to where Private Jenson and the grooms waited with the officers' horses. Carl grasped his own bridle, and Michael took that of Rufus.

"The major is down, on his way up to the surgeons," Michael said.

"Oh shit, no." Jenson's face was horrified. "How bad?"

"Doesn't look good, lad."

"Get him seen, Sarge."

"We're on our way." Michael wheeled the horse and set off behind Carl. They walked cautiously between dead and wounded and when they were back out on the road began to canter south, back towards Talavera.

The town was settled along the banks of the River Tagus and was surrounded by two ranges of mountains. On the north bank was the larger and more populated area of the city, and the two areas were connected by three bridges. It was a richly fertile area with quiet, cobbled streets lined with elms, olive trees and cork oak trees, and graceful medieval houses and churches soaring into the hot blue of the sky. Michael and Carl rode through the town, which was crowded with army personnel and wounded men and over towards the small convent which housed one of the army hospitals. There were several other hospitals set up around the town, including the big convent on the eastern edge, which housed the general hospital for the area, but Michael knew that Adam Norris would be working here.

Michael walked into hell. The heat and noise and smell hit him like walking into a solid wall. Michael was hardened to death and injury, but he found his stomach churning at the sights and sounds that met him. Men lay scattered about, some wearing temporary or field dressings, others bleeding where they lay. Screams tore through the air and across the room, an open doorway led to the surgery where Norris and his two assistants worked on the injured men in a welter of blood and agony. Michael stood at the door and watched as Norris sawed through an injured man's thigh, and then he backed out and went to search for Paul.

He found him lying outside in the courtyard, one of a dozen men who had just been brought in. Michael thought he was paler and closer to death for his agonising journey in the wagon, but it had brought him back to consciousness and he opened his eyes as they knelt either side of him. Carl took his hand, and Paul tried to smile.

"Carl. Glad you're here." He looked across at the Irishman. "You too, Michael."

"Norris is in the middle of an amputation, Paul. I'm going to get you in there..."

"No. Don't bother." His friend coughed, and the agony of it seemed to freeze him for a moment. "Michael..."

"Don't try to talk, sir."

"Don't be stupid, Michael," his commander said gently. "I'm dying. Please - would you get Nan for me?"

Michael looked at him. Then he nodded. "Yes, sir."

He stood up and Carl stood with him, an expression of complete bewilderment on his face. "Nan? Is he talking about Nan Carlyon? What in God's name…?"

Michael ignored him. He grabbed a passing orderly. "Mrs Carlyon?" he said. "The lady who helps…"

"She'll be in with the surgeons, sir," the man said, and Michael nodded.

"Stay with him," he said to Carl. "Keep him talking. Don't, for Christ's sake, let him die until he's seen her."

"God, Michael, is there something I've missed?"

"There is, but it hardly matters now, does it? I'm going to find his girl for him."

Michael made his way over to the surgeons' room again and went in, past the table where Norris was still grimly operating on the sobbing man. At the far end of the room he saw her, a slender figure in a dark gown and white apron soaked with blood. Her hair was bundled up under a kerchief and she was bending over an officer of the cavalry, stitching a savage wound on his lower arm. Her Spanish maid stood beside her ready to hand her what she needed, and there was a look of total concentration on her face which made Michael stop in his tracks.

The officer sucked in his breath sharply. The girl looked up and gave him a reassuring smile. "Almost there," she said quietly. "Is there someone with you to help you?"

The man nodded. His eyes were on the drawn perfection of the girl's face and even in his distress, Michael felt a spurt of amusement at his expression. "Yes, ma'am. One of my men can see me back to my billet."

"Good. Try and get back up in a day or so to have this looked at. If we're still here, find me and I'll do it for you. Keep it as still as you can, drink plenty – water as well as rum, mind you – and I think you'll be lucky and keep that arm." There was something surprisingly soothing about her voice, amid the noise and heat and horror of the surgery, and Michael was not surprised that the officer could not take his eyes from her.

"Yes, ma'am."

Anne finished her work and reached for her scissors. When she had cut the thread, Teresa passed her a dressing and bandage.

"Girl dear," Michael said softly.

Anne looked up startled and seemed to read his news in his eyes. He saw what was left of the colour drain from her face, but she just nodded and looked back down at her work. When she had done, she straightened and gave the officer her arm. He eased himself off the table.

"Thank you, ma'am."

"You're welcome. Take care."

He caught her hand with his uninjured one and lifted it to his lips, kissing it with a familiarity which irritated Michael, but Anne did not seem bothered, simply smiled and watched him go then turned to Michael. "Paul?" she said with quiet dread.

"He's outside, girl dear, and he's asking for you. I wanted Norris to see him, but he's busy and I'm not sure it will help."

"Will you bring him through, Michael?"

"Lass, it might be kinder to go to him."

Anne Carlyon looked at him for a long, silent moment. "Michael." She spoke very patiently. "I am not a doctor with ten years training behind me. But I've a little practice now, and if you're asking me to go and sit beside the man I love and watch him die, while holding his hand like some heroine in a gothic romance, you are talking to the wrong girl. Now go and get him and bring him in here and if he argues with you, tell him that I am prepared to stab him with this scalpel if he is difficult. Move!"

There was something about her fierce determination that unexpectedly gave Michael hope. He turned and ran, weaving his way through rows of injured men back to where Carl knelt beside his friend. "Get him up, she wants him through there."

"What? Michael for God's sake…"

"Carl – what do any of us have to lose at this point? Take his feet. At worst he'll die with her there, which is what he wants. And at best…at best she might be able to do something."

They carried him through and laid him on the trestle table, and Anne reached for the edge of his coat and peeled it back. She took the scissors from Teresa and cut the shirt away from the wound and then examined it. Teresa brought a bowl with clean water and a cloth, and Anne swabbed blood and dirt and gunpowder from around the wound and then took the long forceps and delicately parted the torn flesh. Paul groaned and opened his eyes.

"Nan."

"Paul, love. Lie still for me." The girl's voice was gentle and soothing, and Michael watched with horrified fascination. "You've a ball in your chest and it's not an improvement, let me tell you."

"It hurts."

"It would. Were you not watching where you were going?"

"Apparently not. I wanted to see you. I didn't expect you to be operating on me."

"Well, it's your lucky day, love." Anne glanced over at her nurse. "Teresa, I need several threads. When I take this out, he's going to bleed fast and I'll need to get everything tied up quickly."

The Spanish girl nodded and set to work. Anne took Paul's hand. She raised it lovingly to her lips and he smiled.

"I'm glad you ignored everything I told you to do and came up," he said.

"You will be," Anne said.

"Girl of my heart, I love you."

"I love you too, Major. Try not to die on me, I'd miss you."

Michael saw his friend's lips curve in a smile. "We're shocking Carl."

"He'll get over it." Anne glanced at Teresa. "Can you get him some rum, Teresa?"

The Spanish girl came forward with a flask. Paul drank and pulled a face. "I hate rum."

"You're not drinking it because it tastes good, Major," the girl said. "We'll save the best brandy until you can appreciate it. Get this down you, I'm about to hurt you."

Paul nodded, his eyes on her face, and drank more. Anne took a long deep breath and turned to Carl and Michael. "Come over here and hold him. I need him still. If I get this wrong, it's going to kill him."

They came to stand either side. Carl was looking at her soberly. "Nan, do you have any idea what you're doing? A musket ball in the chest...is it even possible to survive that?"

"There's not a whole ball in there, but there are several pieces of metal." Anne said. "I think a ball would have killed him outright if it had hit him there. Something has deflected it - I've no idea what and I don't care. But the damage is less than you'd imagine, and I think I can do this. But if you think you can get him seen quicker..."

"Let her do it, Carl," Paul said, and his voice was so weak it shocked Michael. "I saw her with Paget. I trust her."

Michael took hold of his arm and shoulder. He saw his commander look up into the girl's dark eyes. "If this goes wrong," he said quietly, "make sure you remember that being here with you at the end is where I want to be."

"Close your eyes," Anne said gently. "Think about something else."

"That's hard with you here."

She bent over the wound, looking closer. "Then think about somewhere else."

"A snowy barn on the Cuddingham road, perhaps?" Astonishingly, through his agony, Michael could hear laughter in his voice. "Just do it, bonny lass."

"All right, love. There's more than one piece in there and I need to tie off the blood vessels as I go along because as I pull this out it's going to bleed a lot faster. Which means it's going to take some time and I can't rush it so it's going to hurt for a while. I love you. Try to think about that as we go along."

Anne probed swiftly and Michael clamped down hard as his commander's body bucked against his restraining hands. The girl did not hesitate or look up. She withdrew a piece of shot, dropped it on the ground and probed again. Something like a sob escaped Paul's lips as she drew out a second piece of metal. Anne reached for a thread as blood filled the wound and tied off two blood vessels carefully and neatly, then sluiced the wound again with cold water and examined it. He was still conscious, his body tense with agony against Michael's hands, and Michael was aware that his own body was rigid with stress as if he could feel Paul's pain through him.

"Almost there now, love. I'd like to get my hands on the Frenchman who did this to you, I'd geld the bastard." Once again, Anne's voice was level and soothing and she bent and probed and Paul sobbed in agony, her name on his lips. Michael looked at her face and wanted to look away at what he saw there but she did not hesitate or flinch. She withdrew the forceps and a third piece emerged, and suddenly blood filled the wound. Anne took the catgut thread that Teresa held out and began to tie off the blood vessels, her hands slippery with his blood. Michael could not take his eyes from her. It seemed to take forever, and he felt as though he was watching his friend undergoing torture, fighting to remain still and calm under her hands. Anne sluiced the wound again with water and stood watching.

"Another thread, Teresa, that one isn't going to hold." She took the thread, tied it off and then began carefully to draw the flesh together to close up the wound. Michael watched her face, and he felt a fierce gratitude for her courage. He was not sure he could have done the same given the obvious attachment she felt for his commander. She was sewing carefully, her eyes on her work and Paul finally seemed to have lost consciousness.

"Nan, are you all right?"

Anne did not look up at the sound of Dr Norris' voice. "I think so," she said. "It's all out and I've stopped the bleeding."

"You should have called me," Norris said, glancing at Carl's white face.

"You were busy and there wasn't time," Michael said. His eyes were on the girl's quick neat hands and he felt almost angry on her behalf. He could not believe what she had just done, a slip of a girl who barely looked old enough to be married. "Is there something you'd have done differently, sir?"

"No, nothing." Norris was watching Anne in some pride. "She's bloody good," he admitted.

"Thank you, doctor," Anne said with pleasant irony.

"Have you somewhere to take him?" Norris said. Generally, officers were not kept in the hospital but housed in their own billets. Michael glanced at Carl. They did not even know if the battle was over and there was no camp set up.

"He can stay in our room," Anne said.

"Will Robert mind?" Carl asked. Michael suspected that his mind was still reeling from wondering what else Robert might have reason to object to, but this was not the time to ask.

"Robert is on his way back to Lisbon," Anne said quietly. "I'll explain later. There, that's done it. Pass me a dressing, Teresa. Can you find a stretcher, Michael? It's only across the yard, and he'll be better close to here in case he needs help."

The room was a plain square box furnished only by a chair, a table, two chests and a mattress on the floor in the corner. They laid Paul carefully on the mattress and Anne disappeared to return with extra blankets. She tucked them around him with considerable care, checked the dressing to make sure that it had not slipped and then stood up.

"Go," she said quietly. "I know you've other wounded to find, and deal with, and you'll be wanting to tell Captain Wheeler and the others how he is. I'm going to stay with him, I could do with a rest for a few hours anyway, I've been working since last night without a break. Perhaps you can bring his kit back here when you've time. And I've no food, which he'll need. Robert seems to have taken my baggage along with our rations and what was left of my money when he left. I presume he thought the medical staff would make sure I didn't starve. But..."

"We'll see to it, girl dear," Michael said quickly. "Stay with him until we get back." He caught her hand and raised it to his lips. "We'll look after you, all you need to do for us is keep him alive."

"Call me when you start bringing your other wounded in," Anne said.

"I will."

***

When they had gone, Anne reached for the wooden chair. Now that the immediate crisis had passed, her legs felt shaky and she wanted very much to cry, but there were still things to do. She went to fetch water and collected a supply of brandy and laudanum from the hospital. Teresa had taken up position to assist Adam Norris.

"Is he all right, Señora?"

"I hope so, Teresa."

Back in the room, Anne sat down on the chair, watching Paul. His face was white and drawn with pain, still filthy from the smoke and blood of the battlefield. Anne felt an irrational urge to wash it, but she did not want to disturb him.

"Why did he leave?" Paul asked.

Anne jumped. "Dear God, I thought you were unconscious."

"It hurts too much for that."

Anne got up. "I've brought some laudanum."

"No, it's all right, I hate the stuff."

"Don't be so bloody difficult, Paul. I've just spent half an hour doing needlework in your chest, it's going to hurt. Take one dose."

Paul grinned tiredly and let her administer the drug. Afterwards he said:

"This is a good-sized mattress. Plenty of space for two."

"Even you cannot be thinking..."

"No. Don't make me laugh; I think it might kill me. But you said you'd been working since last night. You must be exhausted."

The temptation was irresistible. Anne kicked off her shoes and pulled off the kerchief, shaking out her hair. "I am," she admitted. Tiredly she lowered herself to the edge of the mattress and lay down beside him. Paul pushed a blanket towards her, and she covered herself and took hold of his hand. "Try to sleep, Paul. The laudanum will help."

"Tell me about Robert."

"It's nothing. The general is worried that we'll have to make a quick retreat. He's got scouts out trying to find out what the French are doing, and in what numbers. He doesn't want to lose all his stores and equipment so Robert and some of the other quartermasters are on their way back with a supply convoy and any unnecessary baggage. Including most of mine, it appears."

"And he left you here."

270

"I've been busy at the hospital, I didn't get his message in time."

"I'm too exhausted to call him all the names I want to. Don't worry, lass. Whatever happens to me, they'll see you safe back to Lisbon."

"I know, Paul. Now will you stop talking and try to sleep?"

"Only if you'll stay with me."

Anne pushed herself up and leaned over him, careful not to touch him. Her mouth brushed his gently, and to her horror he lifted one arm and held her head closer, kissing her back in a way that was anything but gentle. "Paul, for God's sake be careful!"

"Stop fussing and just kiss me, Nan."

Anne complied willingly. After a few moments she eased herself back to lie beside him.

"Nan…"

"What is it?"

"Am I going to die?"

Anne sat up again and looked down at him, meeting his eyes. She could hear, for the first time ever, fear in his voice. "Are you listening to me, Paul van Daan?"

"Yes."

"You're not going to die. I'm going to make sure that you don't. If necessary, I will spend every minute nursing you, but you are not going to die."

"You sound very sure, bonny lass."

"I am. I am very stubborn, and like you, I am very good at what I do."

Paul was smiling, and she could see that he appeared more relaxed, less tense with pain as the laudanum began to take effect.

"Why is it that I actually believe you?"

"Because you know how much I love you."

"I love you too, Nan," he said drowsily. "So glad you're here with me. Don't leave."

"I won't."

Anne took his hand again and lay still, and she did not remember drifting into sleep.

Chapter Sixteen

By nightfall, the battle was over. Casualties were high on both sides, and gradually the French assault petered out. During the night, Joseph's army slipped away leaving several guns in British and Spanish possession.

The battle ended without further participation from the 110th. Captain Wheeler received orders to leave the reinvigorated guards to protect the line and brought his men back to take stock and seek treatment for their wounds. Across the battlefield his men scoured the piles of dead and wounded looking for their own, and they had barely loaded up the final wagon when the flicker of fire was visible, and to the horror of the watching men, flames began to sweep across the dry grass. Lieutenant Clevedon looked over at Johnny.

"There are still men alive out there."

"Not our men," Wheeler said quietly. He glanced across at Private Jenson who had supervised the last injured man being lifted into the wagon and was swinging himself awkwardly up onto his horse. "Jenson, get them back to the hospital, then find Lieutenant Swanson and Sergeant-Major O'Reilly and find out what's happened to the major." He raised his voice. "Sergeant Stewart. All walking wounded to follow the wagons back. The rest of you can go with them. Make your way back up to the lines."

"What about you, sir?" Stewart asked.

Johnny paused. He had never been more exhausted in his life, and the weight of command along with anxiety about Paul was unbearable, but he knew that he could not leave.

"I'll hang on here for a bit, see if I can get any more men out of there. When the wagons are unloaded, will you send them back up?"

"What about burials, sir?"

"If they're still out there, they're staying there," Wheeler said. "They won't know the difference, it's the men still alive out there that I'm worried about."

"Yes, sir." Stewart turned back to the column. "Jenson lead the wounded up. All able-bodied, back to the rear and help the captain get men off this field."

The regiment broke away and moved back towards Johnny and he gave a tired smile. It occurred to him with a stab of pain that Paul would have been immensely proud of them and he hoped passionately that his commander lived to hear him describe their willingness to set aside their exhaustion and hunger to save as many of the remaining wounded as they could. There were isolated groups of men out there trying to help, but most of the troops had made their way back in search of rest and what little food they had.

"All right, Sergeant. We take those we can, from this edge of the field. Get them over to the other side of the stream, it'll act as a firebreak. No time for treatment, and don't discriminate between English, French or Spanish. Nobody deserves to burn to death after the day we've had. We're not going to get all of them out, the way this is spreading. Just live with that, do what you can, and don't be a bloody hero, we've had enough of those today. Carry on."

It was well after midnight when the last wagon dropped Wheeler off at the hospital. He was black with smoke and completely exhausted and it seemed that he could still hear the screams of wounded men they had not been able to reach ringing in his ears. In the courtyard outside the convent, he made his way through hundreds of injured men.

"Johnny."

Wheeler looked up and saw Carl Swanson beckoning from one of the buildings on the far side of the courtyard. He made his way over. "Carl, how is he?"

"He's alive. Sleeping upstairs. The bleeding has been stopped and the ball is out. God knows if he'll make it, I'd have sworn not earlier in the day. But he's bloody tough."

"Has he been conscious?"

"More than you'd expect."

"Did Norris operate?"

Carl shook his head. He led Wheeler through into a back room where he and the other officers had dumped their kit. On the window ledge was a brandy bottle, and Carl poured two drinks and handed one to his exhausted captain.

"Norris was busy amputating some poor bastard's leg. We ended up taking him through to Robert Carlyon's wife. It seems she's been learning surgical skills. It looks as though the shot was deflected before it hit him, possibly off another musket or rifle. She dug the bits out and got him stitched up."

"Jesus Christ, Carl, I'm surprised you allowed that."

"So am I. But I think he was dying, and I was desperate." Carl drank some brandy. "Are you aware that there's something going on between them, Johnny?"

Wheeler stared at him in some astonishment. "Paul and Carlyon's wife? Tell me you're joking, Carl."

"No. Although I'm glad to know I'm not the only one in the dark, because Sergeant-Major O'Reilly seems very aware of it."

273

"How long has that been going on? I can't see when they'd have had time."

"Or me. Whenever I've seen them together, Rowena has been there. Or her husband. But you know our bloody commander. If he wants a woman, the fact that she's his wife's best friend and the wife of a fellow officer isn't likely to stop him. If he weren't half dead, I'd be inclined to punch him."

Wheeler sat down with an exhausted sigh on the nearest bedroll. "He is such an arsehole when it comes to a woman." he said. "How long has she been married?"

"About a year. And don't get me wrong, Johnny, I don't think it was a love match. Paul has said from the start that Carlyon wanted her for her money."

"That's no bloody excuse. We all know what Paul wants her for, and it's not the pleasure of her conversation."

"What makes you think that?" a voice said from the doorway, and they both turned as Michael O'Reilly strolled in.

"This is the officers' quarters, O'Reilly, such as it is. Piss off and find your own," Johnny said irritably.

"Ah shut up and give me the brandy, you miserable bastard. He's alive and he's awake. Is there any food yet?"

Wheeler gave the sergeant-major a look. "Sometimes I dream of the days when I could have had you flogged for speaking to me like that, O'Reilly."

"Regulations say you still can if you like, sir. Although I'd rather you didn't."

Johnny gave a tired smile. "He'd kill me," he said. "Anyway, we're a bit past that. I can't flog a man I've got drunk with."

"That's why you're not supposed to drink with me, sir. Sorry I was arsey, I'm too tired to think straight."

"We all are, Michael. And it's not you I'm angry with. As for food, there will be soon. I sent the lads up to bring their kit down here, they can camp in the fields at the back. We're going to send the baggage off with as many wounded as we can load up, so we'll be travelling light when we march. Hookey is talking about having to leave the wounded in the care of the Spanish, and I wouldn't trust them to look after my grandmother's sick cat. Kelly is out back lighting the cooking fires and we've had the rifles out after game. Stew with turnips - looted, I suspect - and tack biscuits. Plus whatever is left of Mrs Carlyon's delivery. We're all going to be on half rations, the Spanish haven't come up with the supplies they promised and something tells me they're not going to, but we can keep them fed although we might have to fight off the rest of the army, the men are starving. Why, is he up to eating yet?"

"Mrs Carlyon thinks he should have something. He's a bit feverish, but she tells me it's to be expected."

Wheeler raised his eyebrows. "Is she up there with him?"

"She is."

"She has been since we brought him back," Carl said. "I went in earlier and she was curled up asleep next to him holding his hand. Very touching."

"Carl..."

"Why the hell didn't you tell me about this, Michael, and I'd have got him to put a stop to it?" Carl demanded angrily. "You clearly know all about it. Did it occur to you how Rowena would feel about this? Apart from Paul being an arse again, the girl is her friend. I can't believe he moved his bloody mistress in with his wife, that's beyond even him. Christ, she's so young, she can't possibly know what he's like. I could kill him."

"She's not his mistress."

"I know what I saw and heard in there, Michael."

"And just what is it you think you saw and heard, Lieutenant?" Michael said. He sounded suddenly furiously angry.

"It's bloody obvious that something is going on..."

"There's nothing going on. He hasn't been sleeping with her."

Carl looked at him hard and lifted an eyebrow pointedly. "Really? Because what I saw and heard earlier..."

"You heard him trying to say goodbye to the girl he loves. If you want to go up there and talk to him about that, go right ahead, but I wouldn't advise you to do it in front of her, because she's likely to slap you, and you'd deserve it."

There was a frozen silence in the small room. Then Wheeler turned, went to collect a cup and poured brandy. He passed it to the sergeant-major. "We've all had a bad day, Michael."

"Not as bad as he's having," Michael said shortly, tossing back the cup.

"Fair point," Wheeler said quietly. "Stop yelling at each other for God's sake. He's still alive and if it's thanks to the girl then I'm nothing but grateful to her. And in the end his marriage – and any other relationships – are his own affair."

"You know, I had a bad feeling about this from the minute I saw him with her on the transport. I'm assuming this started before she married?" Carl said more quietly.

Michael nodded. "In Yorkshire. I'd have been as much in the dark as you were if I'd not seen her. She came to say goodbye to him on the morning he left. It took all of two minutes and it told me all I needed to know about how they feel about each other. And I know no more than that, except that she's a girl in a million and as much as I like his wife, this is the lass he should be with. And he can't. They both know that. He thought he was dying, for Christ's sake. Of course he asked for her. And thank God she was here because I think she might have saved his life."

"I know, Michael. But Christ, how old is she?"

"I believe she's nineteen which is older than his wife was when they married. But she's not a child, sir. Far from it."

Carl sighed. "I agree, she's nothing like any of his previous women. But Michael, this has to end."

"It hasn't started, sir. Leave it alone, we've other things to worry about just now."

The door opened and Lieutenant Clevedon came in. "Is that brandy? Great. Food's almost ready. How is he doing?"

Carl looked at Johnny. "Do you need me? I'd like to go and see."

"Go," Johnny said. "As for you Sergeant-Major O'Reilly..."

"I know, sir. I'm going back to the men, they'll be dying for news of him."

"I'll come down and speak to them afterwards, Sergeant-Major," Carl said. "Save me some food or I'll shoot you."

***

Carl crossed the yard and climbed the stairs. Hesitantly he tapped on the door.

"Come in."

Carl entered. Anne was sitting on the edge of the mattress bathing Paul's face with a cloth. His commander opened his eyes and gave a weary smile.

"Carl. Come in. I've not died yet, so make the most of it."

To Carl's surprise he was propped up. Carl came forward. "I thought you'd be flat on your back."

"I was, but my medical advisor tells me that in cases of chest injury it helps to sit up as soon as possible. I'm not sure if that is the accepted treatment, since she also tells me that we will not be following the usual practice of bleeding me for fever, as she feels that the French have taken more than enough blood already. But it is certainly the treatment we will be adopting because she just kicked the surgeon out of here. Besides, she sounds very certain. Pull up a chair and tell me what is going on. I can smell food – is that supper or breakfast?"

Carl obeyed. "It could be either," he said. He was watching the girl. She stood up and removed the bowl then went to wash her hands. Paul was observing her with a grin.

"She also has a mania about cleanliness," he said.

"If you don't shut up, I'm dosing your food with laudanum," Anne said. "I'm going up to the hospital to find out how the rest of your wounded are getting on, and when I come back, I might bring you something to eat, if you're behaving."

Paul smiled tiredly. "Try to find time to eat yourself, will you, love? I have the oddest feeling that if anybody can keep me alive, it's you."

Anne smiled back, then looked at Carl. "May I have a word first?"

Carl nodded and followed her out of the room, closing the door. She looked at him from steady dark eyes and he thought with a stab of compassion that she looked completely exhausted.

"Try not to tire him too much. He's not as well as he thinks he is. A normal person would be sleeping at this point but there's something wrong with him." She smiled tiredly. "Carl – this is not as bad as it looks, honestly.

276

Whatever you want to say to him about me, just don't let him lose his temper. It's not worth killing him over."

"Nan, you saved his life. Right now, that's all I care about."

Anne smiled and Carl thought irrelevantly that despite her obvious exhaustion she was still a very beautiful woman. "No, it isn't. You're probably furious with both of us for Rowena's sake. But whatever I feel about him, I will never hurt her, I swear it. Just remember that he almost died, and he still could. I'm terrified that there's damage to the heart or lungs that I can't see and couldn't do anything about even if I could see it, and I know there's a very good chance that we'll have to move him long before we should. One of the reasons I'm staying with him is that if I'm here talking to him, he's more likely to keep still and relax. I need him to rest, and he won't do that if he's in a towering rage with you over something you've said about me."

Despite himself, Carl began to laugh. "I think you know him better than his wife does. It's all right. I might feel like punching him, but I'd like him to be in a fit state to punch me back when I do it. And I've nothing to say about you. I've known him all my life and believe me I know where the blame belongs."

Unexpectedly Anne smiled, reached up and kissed him gently. "You're a good man, Carl, and he's lucky to have you to pull him out of the mire on a regular basis. But you're not always right. Go on, go and see him."

Carl went back into the room and sat back down on the wooden chair. "I'm going to give you all the news I have," he said. "And then I'd like you to do me the courtesy of explaining what I've missed."

He gave a concise account of the remainder of the battle and the subsequent events, and Paul listened in silence. "Did we get all our wounded off the field?" he asked.

Carl nodded. "All those left alive. But losses have been heavy, Paul. They'll run into thousands dead and wounded. We've lost more than half of our first company, and that includes Captain Young, Lieutenant Andrews and Ensigns Bartlett and Carson. And all the officers from the fourth are wounded."

"Kit Young? Oh shit, no!" Paul lay quietly for a moment, thinking about Young, laughing with him at Wellesley's reception in Ireland. "What about the others?"

"Six dead from the light company, another dozen injured but none of them seem too serious. They're hard to kill. Dead and wounded, about a dozen from the second, about twenty from the third, and the same from the fourth." Carl shook his head grimly. "And I bloody well thought I'd lost you as well."

His friend gave a painful smile. "So did I," he said quietly. "Which is why I was a little less discreet than I might have been earlier."

"I was pissed off," Carl admitted. "She's Rowena's friend and another officer's wife."

Paul shifted slightly and winced. "All right, Carl, I owe you this I suppose. But it isn't for general discussion. I knew Nan in Yorkshire when

Carlyon was trying to court her. We met in a blizzard, got stuck in a barn together for almost twenty-four hours. I was more restrained than you'd expect although it almost killed me. She's the woman I never believed existed for me. I was married and you know I'd never desert Rowena. And Nan wouldn't ask me to. When I left Yorkshire, I didn't expect to see her again. It was a shock finding her on that transport. But I swear to God, Carl, we've not..."

"No. There's hardly been time, has there? Paul, Michael is right, this isn't my business. I don't really know the girl, but I like what I've seen of her and I'm unbelievably grateful for what she did for you yesterday. If you survive this, it will be because of her. But think about what you're doing with her, will you? Rowena really likes Nan, it would hurt her twice as much. And you need to think of the girl as well. Robert Carlyon's obsession with her has become a talking point in the mess, and I doubt he'd like to hear that she's spending her nights curled up next to you however innocent it might be." Carl stood up. "I'm going in search of food. Try to get some rest. If we have to get out of here in a hurry, you're going to need it."

"Yes. Thank you. Carl – about Nan Carlyon. Whatever you think, the truth is that she's been abandoned by her shit of a husband in the middle of a battlefield. Will you talk to the men about her? Make sure that everybody knows that until we get her back to safety, she and her maid are to be considered as under our protection? I don't like retreats, they tend to degenerate into chaos fairly quickly, and in case anything should happen to me, I don't want there to be any confusion about her status."

"There won't be Paul. Whatever happens we'll take care of her." Carl gave a tired smile. "She's over there now with our wounded. I've a strong suspicion that you probably don't need to tell any of them to look after her. Michael O'Reilly seems to be devoted to her."

"Yes, I'm keeping a close eye on him." Paul closed his eyes exhaustedly. "This really hurts and I'm as weak as a kitten. I hope to God we can pull together enough wagons to get our wounded back because I'm not leaving them here."

"We're already working on it, Paul. Try to sleep. Let the rest of us worry about it for a while."

***

Paul's prediction about the need for a hasty retreat was quickly borne out. The following morning, Brigadier-General Craufurd's light brigade marched into camp with bugle horns playing, having marched forty-two miles in twenty-six hours in an attempt to reach the army in time for the battle. They were given little time to rest. Scouts rode in with the news that Marshal Soult was advancing south, threatening to cut Wellesley off from Portugal. Wellesley's initial intention was to block him, and he moved swiftly east with those troops still in a condition to fight, leaving more than a thousand wounded in the care of the Spanish. Having just arrived, the Light Brigade

278

had to march for another fifteen hours to secure the Almaraz Bridge before Soult could take it, to protect Wellesley's links with Lisbon.

Anne set up a makeshift regimental hospital for the men of the 110th in the outbuildings of the convent. Paul was aware of the anxiety of the doctors about their position with regard to the advancing French, and he was quietly determined to find enough wagons to get himself and his wounded away. The French had the reputation of treating captured wounded well, but he had no intention of spending any time in a French prison camp and was not prepared to abandon his men. Transport was scarce in this part of Spain as was food for both horses and men, but Paul was in the fortunate position of having private means and he was prepared to use his own money if necessary, to ensure that his regiment made it away from Talavera before the French came.

Paul was desperately anxious about Anne. In an army camp of thousands of men, she was one of only a few officer's wives and she was not his wife, which gave her no official protection. Unable to be up and about, he lay helpless, sweating restlessly with fever and with pain knifing through him at every breath. He worried about what might happen to Anne as she made her way between the wards and the 110th's makeshift camp. She looked exhausted but surprisingly cheerful and dealt with the difficult conditions and sparse food without complaint or apparent ill-effect.

Anne spent each night with Paul, sleeping exhaustedly on the mattress beside him. When pain kept him awake, he watched her sleep and wondered if she had any idea how much she had come to mean to him. He could not bring himself to care about the proprieties, although he knew that her constant presence beside him worried his other officers. She seemed supremely indifferent to the difficulties of her situation and Paul looked forward to the time when they were alone together at the end of the day and she would curl up beside him and tell him about her day, and the gossip of his battalion, making him laugh so much that it hurt. The lack of provisions had brought out the scavengers in his men and they proved adept at finding sources of food which seemed to elude the rest of the army. Paul hoped his officers were making sure that the food was paid for.

Adam Norris came to visit him late one afternoon. He checked Paul's wound without comment, merely smiling and replacing the immaculate dressing. "Much pain?"

"Hurts like hell. But I'm in better condition than I'd have expected. I thought I was going to die."

"You probably were," Norris said. "How you survived without damage to either your heart or your lungs is a mystery, although I think myself it has a lot to do with how quickly she got that damned shot out before it could shift and do more harm."

"Yes, I'm still reeling a bit from that. How the hell did she move from holding their hands and giving them water to operating on them, Adam?"

Norris grimaced. "A lot of the army surgeons are asking the same question," he said ruefully. "Although I notice it doesn't stop them yelling for her help when they've a difficult wound to deal with and her hands are smaller than theirs. Paul – she wanted to learn. It started just because she was there, and she was interested. More so than any of the trainees they sent me. After Oporto, when the casualties came in, she was a Godsend. I lent her some of my old medical books and she must have stayed up half the night reading them then pelted me with questions. When young Felton died of fever, I gave her his surgical kit. I don't know why, it was a mad thing to do. But she's so good. She's more use with it than half my bloody doctors. But you don't have to tell me that it's causing some consternation. I'm surprised I've not had her husband after me." He shook his head. "If she was a man, she'd be a surgeon. And a bloody good one. As it is..."

"I understand. And you're hardly going to hear me complain since she undoubtedly saved my life. But she shouldn't have been there to do it. Why didn't she go with Carlyon?"

"I don't know. Apparently, he sent her a message when Wellesley told him to get the baggage train moving, which she didn't get until after he'd gone. It was a rush to get the convoy away and he did his duty. But I still can't believe he left her behind without a word. Most men with a young wife would have come in person to find her."

"Let alone cleaning out the food and money she had left and taking her baggage. It's a good thing it's likely to be a while before I see the bastard, I'll have simmered down by then."

"It's why I'm here, in part. I'm staying with the wounded. In theory the Spanish are guarding the hospitals, but I think when Soult gets here they'll run, so it's conceivable that I'll be spending a while as a guest of the French. I'm not worried; they usually release medical staff very quickly because they want us to do the same. Likewise, they're good with the wounded. But Nan..."

"You think you might have trouble convincing some randy French cavalryman that she's a member of your medical staff? Yes, I can see that. It's all right, Adam, I've every intention of taking her with us. I'm not risking her. If it had been up to me she wouldn't have been here in the first place."

"And then you'd be dead."

"Exactly. And I'm going to hear about that every bloody time I try to stop her doing something mad in the future."

"Shouldn't that be her husband's job, Paul?" Adam said dryly, and Paul grinned.

"I don't see him here to do it, Adam."

Wellesley's plans changed significantly after Spanish guerrillas intercepted a message from Soult to Joseph which revealed that Soult had considerably more men than he had originally thought. Realising that his line of retreat was about to be cut by a larger French force, Wellesley ordered an immediate retreat, with any unnecessary baggage to be abandoned.

Paul van Daan and the wounded men of the 110th were loaded onto three unsprung wagons which his officers had managed to acquire and set off towards the Tagus at speed, over rutted roads and escorted by the regiment's walking wounded and the men of his light company. Paul had sent the rest of his battalion on ahead with the main army under Johnny Wheeler. If the convoy were to be attacked by the advancing French, he would trust the light company to be able to get themselves away to safety.

Paul had given strict instructions that they were to prioritise the safety of Anne Carlyon over protecting the wounded. It was unlikely that the French would harm wounded soldiers, but watching his love riding beside the wagons on Bella, Paul was in no way prepared to risk her falling into the hands of French soldiers. The ordinary men of Napoleon's army had a poor reputation with local women, and although in theory Anne's status as the wife of an officer ought to protect her, he was not convinced that an isolated French patrol could be trusted with Anne and Teresa.

Paul watched her as the convoy lined up to set off, supervising the loading of the wounded men into the wagons. Sergeant-Major O'Reilly and Private Carter had taken it upon themselves to act as her assistants and Paul rested on the hard boards of the wagon and listened with considerable amusement as the young Mrs Carlyon gave her instructions. It did not seem to occur to any of the men not to obey her. They had become used to her during these past weeks and behaved as if she were any other member of the medical staff.

The journey tried Paul and the wounded of the 110th severely. Not one of them was left behind, and Anne spent exhausting evenings trying to patch up opened wounds and prepare the injured men for the next day. Wellesley moved his army fast and gave them little rest. Food was very short, and now that he was determined not to engage in cooperative action with the Spanish again, Wellesley wanted to be away. Back in Portugal there would be time to recuperate.

They were well behind the main bulk of the army, and it made it difficult to find food and provisions for the horses since the areas, already deprived, had been cleared by the passing forces. At the same time, away from the strict discipline of the general, Paul was happy to give the light company men their head. They proved surprisingly adept at shooting game and fishing in the river and streams, and with only a few horses and the mules which pulled the wagons to need feeding, they wheedled supplies out of local farms which might have appeared to have none. Paul permitted no theft and supplies were paid for, but he knew that the locals were under considerable pressure to share what they had. The army's case was too desperate to be entirely scrupulous.

They carried no tents and Anne spent the nights on the hard ground, her head pillowed on a borrowed coat, and slept the sleep of exhaustion, waking up sometimes to go to an injured man who seemed in pain or distressed. Paul, who slept little at the beginning, watched her move among his men as if she had always lived this life and wished passionately that this unexpected interlude could somehow continue. Despite his pain and discomfort, he was happy in a way that he would have found it hard to describe.

Paul was aware of Carl's anxiety about the girl. Riding beside the wagon, watching her as she rode beside Michael, bending to talk to him, Carl said suddenly:

"Is she going to be all right?"

"Why don't you ask her that, Carl?"

"Paul, she shouldn't bloody be here like this. She's a gently bred girl, she's not used to this. If this were Rowena..."

"Carl – Rowena isn't here, she's safe and comfortable back in Lisbon, thank God. I didn't want Nan to come, that was down to her bloody husband because now that he's finally noticed what he's got, he can't bear to let her out of his sight. Unless of course the French are coming, in which case he'll apparently dump her in the middle of an army camp without food, money or baggage."

"I know, Paul. This isn't your doing. I'm just worried about her."

Paul's eyes were on Anne, laughing down at his sergeant-major. "I'm not," he said softly. "She looks like she's doing fine, Carl. We're all so quick to protect our women, aren't we? We wrap them up in tissue paper against the world and then tell them they're not strong enough to cope. I have literally no idea why none of that worked with Nan, it was a conventional enough upbringing. But since I met her, I'm beginning to rethink my views on women. You can't look at her and tell me she's too delicate to be out here doing this, she's doing better than I am right now."

Gradually, against all the odds, in the bumpy and uncomfortable wagon Paul's wound began to heal. Anne regularly checked and changed the dressing, and when she had run out of dressings, he saw her scrubbing out the used ones down at the stream each morning with a panache that made his heart ache. After twelve days she removed the remainder of the stitching and Paul began, tentatively, to move about more to stretch his cramped limbs and to realise, with considerable amusement, that his life had been saved by an untrained nineteen-year-old with less than six months of surgical experience, who could never qualify as a doctor because she was a woman. He was probably not the only one among his men who owed his life to her care.

They lost one man, his amputated leg having become infected. They buried him beside the road, and moved on the same day, with no time to stay and mourn. Anne rode quietly beside the wagon. Paul watched her without speaking for a while, then said:

"Nan, do you think I can try riding tomorrow?"

Anne looked down at him, surprised. "Well, I'd normally have said no," she said with a grin. "But then normally you'd barely have been allowed out of bed by now. As to the difference between sitting on Rufus and being thrown around in that wagon, I'm not sure. Why don't you give it a try? If it's too much, you'll soon know."

It was harder than Paul had expected, but he was immediately happier on horseback, and despite the ache in his healing chest muscles he began to spend part of each day in the saddle. Anne rode beside him at an easy walk, and he was conscious of her protective manner as she watched him, quick to notice signs of tiredness or pain. It was easier to talk to her now. She asked him questions about his family and his home and his time at Oxford and in the navy. He asked her about her family and her growing years. They shared mutual interests in books read and ideas assimilated, and she questioned him more about his regiment.

"It's a question I've never asked. What is the difference between the light company and the rest of the infantry? I've heard you talk of it, but never known."

"It's in the job they do. Light infantry are skirmishers, it's their job to fight ahead of the main infantry, causing problems and delaying the enemy advance. Each regiment of foot usually has two battalions, each with a light company, a company of guards and eight to ten infantry companies. I've got most of the first battalion out here with me. Guards are the front-line troops. They'll stand – usually. Traditionally they're big and tough and we all take the piss out of them for not being very bright. The light company is at the opposite end. Fast, highly trained, a lot of capacity to act independently."

"I can see why that would suit you. Yours have rifles."

"That's recent. I've been working on it for a while. I've always had a contingent of rifles – Carter and his lads – attached to me, and they've become part of the company, although I can't get them out of those bloody green jackets." Paul smiled. "I finally wore Wellesley down to equipping the whole company with rifles. And up at Talavera he saw what they can do with them."

"And the rest of your battalion? Do you train them very differently?"

Paul grinned. "Ah. And there you have the reason why I'm considered bloody mad by pretty much every officer in the army. Because I expect the same out of every one of my lads. One of these days I'm going to get the whole regiment designated as light infantry." He glanced at her and laughed. "But you're eccentric yourself, aren't you, Nan? A lass doing surgery? Where the hell did that come from?"

"It was an accident," Anne said. "I wanted to help, and it turned out I got a bit more involved than I intended." She glanced up at him. "I'm fascinated by it. Adam has been amazing. He treats me like one of his trainees, although I could never do formal training or qualify. But out here they're so short of doctors that even the stuffiest of them are willing to turn a blind eye when the wounded start coming in and they can't cope."

Paul was amazed by the wealth of medical knowledge Anne seemed to have acquired in the short time that she had been working with Norris. She had read everything that Norris had given her and was quick to question Paul about his own experiences of the medical services, of what worked and what did not. He was entertained by her open questioning of some of the accepted medical practices of the day.

"This is what happens when you let a lass with no formal training try her hand at doctoring," he teased, after she had spent half an hour explaining her instinctive dislike of the practice of bleeding a patient. "Haven't they been using this technique since ancient Greece?"

"I could tell you a few other things they used to do in ancient Greece which might make you question their so-called wisdom," Anne retorted, laughing.

"You see my studies were more classical than medical." Paul gave her a grin. "And I could come up with a few things they used to do in ancient Greece that I'd dearly like to try with you."

"I can tell you're feeling better, Major." Anne gave him a sidelong glance, which sent his pulses racing.

"You'd best hope that we catch up with the rest of the army before I improve much more, lass, if you're going to look at me like that," he said softly, and Anne laughed aloud at his impertinence.

***

Anne walked down to the river that evening with a bundle of stained and dirty bandages and dressings. Many of the men were able to manage without by now, but there were still some who needed them, and she knelt by the water and scrubbed at the worn cloth to get out the worst of the blood and pus. It was still warm, and she felt pleasantly tired. They had crossed the Portuguese border that morning and for the first time this evening they had camped at a farm where there was food for sale, and she could smell roast pork as Sergeant Kelly prepared dinner. The evening sun was warm enough to dry the cloths, so she spread them out over the bushes, and then stopped as she heard a sound close by as though somebody was splashing in the water.

Anne finished hanging up the bandages and then moved cautiously to look through the trees. A pile of clothing lay on the bank, and the tousled fair head of Major van Daan moved across the centre of the river as he swam out. Already she could see that he had more movement in his chest and arms. As he stood, waist high, to sluice water over his face and hair to wash, Anne could see the angry scar across his chest, but it was healing well. Anne watched, smiling as he dived under the water, and then she walked forward, pulling her stained green gown over her head and dropping it beside his clothes. Paul came up for air, running his hands over his face and then he opened his eyes as she dropped her chemise and walked forward into the water to meet him.

Neither of them spoke as their bodies met. The cold of the water made Anne gasp, and then his hands and mouth were on her and she was no longer cold at all. He took her into his arms and kissed her, and then laughingly ducked both of them under and ran his fingers through her long dark hair to wash it, kissing her all the while. The feeling of his body against hers was like heaven.

"Bonny lass," he whispered, and Anne laughed and kissed him gently on the angry scar, sliding her hands down to find that his weakness had affected nothing of his desire for her. He caught his breath at the feeling of her hands on him and reached for her again, lifting her with the help of the water so that she was wrapped around him and he captured her breast with his mouth and explored lower with his hand, laughing at how quickly she was aroused, her eyes on his as he moved his hand steadily on her and felt her immediate response.

284

"You're right," he whispered. "I am feeling better."

Anne gave a little cry suddenly, and her legs wrapped harder around him as she let the sensation take over, burying her face into his shoulder to stifle the sounds of her pleasure until she shuddered finally against him. Paul lowered her gently back into the water and kissed her again with leisurely enjoyment feeling her heart pounding against him.

"Are you all right?" he asked softly, his mouth against her ear.

"You know I am, Major," Anne whispered. "How do you do that to me, I'd forgotten how good that feels."

Anne realised almost immediately what she had said, and she lifted her eyes to his face, slightly anxiously. She could see him thinking, assimilating the understanding that in all the essentials she still belonged to him. Suddenly, Anne wanted to know the truth.

"So why the hell won't you, Paul? Is it because of Rowena?"

"No," Paul said. "I think we'd both hate to hurt her but seeing us as we are right now would do that. But I want you so badly that wouldn't stop me. My reasons are very much the same as they always were. You're married to a cowardly shit, who rode away and left you to the mercies of the French. Yes – he did, Nan. Because if I'd not been wounded, we'd never have known you were still there, and they overran that hospital about three days after we moved out. I'd like to think that you'd be properly treated and handed back in one piece, but you might equally have been passed around like a prize of war because you're young and beautiful and unprotected. And he doesn't deserve to get you back after that. There's nothing I'd like more than to spend the next couple of hours on this riverbank doing everything with you that I've never let myself and I wouldn't feel the slightest twinge of guilt about Robert Carlyon. And believe me, I could do it. But then we pack up and ride on and nine months later you're giving birth, and with my bloodline it is highly likely to be a fair-haired, blue-eyed brat with a bad attitude, and where does that leave your situation with your husband?"

Anne laughed despite herself. "You're so damned sure of yourself, Paul. I've been married to Robert for over a year now, and just because I said what I just did, doesn't mean that he doesn't...." She broke off. "And there's not been a hint of pregnancy."

"No. And perhaps there would not be with me. Perhaps you can't conceive, Nan. Or perhaps you can and he can't. But he's not that stupid – whatever else he can or can't do, he can add up dates. If you get pregnant, he'll work out where you might have been, and with whom. And I'm not putting you at risk of that, girl of my heart. I'm just not."

Anne reached up and caressed his face, her smile ruefully tender. "Why couldn't I have fallen in love with a man with fewer scruples?"

He laughed aloud at that. "That would make my friends laugh given that I never had any until I met you," he said.

Anne ran her hands over his body. "Thank you for that. I think. Well, this, I suppose, will just have to do, then."

He gasped at her touch and then held her closer and she felt him relax as she caressed him, enjoying the sense of her hands on him. Anne realised that she had gained confidence during her miserable marriage, and he shuddered into climax against her feeling both pleasure and pain as his damaged muscles protested and then she was kissing him again, and he ran his hands down her wet, cool body.

"Oh Christ, Nan," he whispered.

"Are you all right?"

Paul laughed softly against her ear. "That hurt," he admitted. "But it was worth it. I'm not as strong as I thought I was."

"Strong enough," Anne said quietly, and he drew her, floating weightless in the water, to where he could reach her again, his eyes on hers.

***

Paul and Anne parted finally, reluctantly. They dressed and walked back up to the camp hand in hand. There was a moment as they approached when Paul thought of letting go, and then he smiled inwardly. Given their damp hair and clothing and the air of quiet bliss which hung about her, he was very sure that not one man of his company would believe that they had been doing anything other than making love on the riverbank, and clearly she did not care. He sat down beside her, their bodies touching, with his back leaning against one of the wagons, and accepted food from Sergeant Kelly. The farmer had provided fruit and bread along with the pork and it was a feast to men who had subsisted for almost three weeks on hard biscuits and the occasional hare or trout. He had also brought two small barrels of wine from his cellars, and Paul deduced that Carl had been generous with his payment. There was almost a party atmosphere. Within days they would be back in Lisbon and back with the rest of their regiment. Given the huge death toll of Talavera, every one of them felt like a survivor. Some of the men had produced pewter drinking cups from their packs and they passed the wine around freely. Michael O'Reilly had seated himself next to Anne's maid and was flirting cheerfully with her, and even the wary Teresa seemed to have relaxed and was laughing up at him. Paul glanced down at his love and saw that she had noticed it too.

"It's good to see Teresa laughing," he said.

"It's good to see Michael laughing. But if he lays one finger on her I'm going to break his legs," Anne said pleasantly, and Paul gave a splutter of laughter.

"Nan, you claim to be the daughter of a respectable manufacturer, but deep down in your soul you are a girl of the light company. Don't worry, you won't need to. He knows about Teresa."

Anne lifted enquiring eyebrows at him. "And how does he? More to the point, how do you?"

"I asked about her at the hospital. She seemed an unusual choice as a maid for a delicately bred lady. I was a little concerned that she'd rob you."

"You should have been concerned that I'd slap you," Anne said. "What business of yours is it whom I employ? Especially since you actively choose most of the men of your light company from the courts and the prisons."

"I know. But I didn't know you as well then as I do now. I was wrong. Forgive me and don't hurt me, I'm still not well."

Anne began to laugh. "You're going to live, Major," she said, and Paul gave in to his impulse and leaned forward to kiss her laughing mouth.

"Thanks to you, lass."

Paul watched Anne as the evening wore on. She seemed completely at home here and he was struck anew at the contrast between the girl brought up in luxury wearing a silver gown to her birthday dance, and this vibrant young woman. She wore the same green gown she had been wearing for a month and her hair was combed loosely with her fingers, drying like a sable cloak over her shoulders. She was surrounded by his enlisted men; foul mouthed and dirty and he observed that they had long since stopped taking care what they said around her. One or two of them, particularly Danny Carter, even went so far as to flirt with her and far from being shocked, she seemed very happy to flirt back. Nothing seemed to discompose her in this very masculine environment. She looked as though she had been brought up in the army's tail, although he knew her childhood had been more sheltered than Rowena's.

"How the hell are you so good at this?" he asked quietly.

Anne looked round at him. "I don't know," she said. "Did you find it hard, Paul?"

"Me? No. But don't forget I'd had three years at sea as a boy, I was used to living rough. But I've seen very few officers' wives who have made themselves so completely at home here. And you didn't grow up this way."

"I grew up feeling out of place," Anne said. "As though everything I did or wanted to do was forbidden. I felt restricted and confined and trapped by all the rules and the strictures. Harriet used to say she'd never make a lady out of me. And I think she was right."

Paul smiled and shifted slightly, drawing her back to lean against him. Anne rested her head back, moving to accommodate his injured chest, and he laughed and stilled her with his hands. "Stay there, it doesn't hurt. You're so light."

Paul slipped his arms about her and rested them under her breasts. They sat quietly, listening to the talk and the laughter around them, and he felt the moment when she relaxed fully against him.

"She asleep, sir?" Carter said quietly. Paul nodded.

"You all right with her? She can take my coat and lie down."

"Thanks, Danny, but she's fine for now." Paul glanced at the rifleman and smiled. "I'm making the most of this while I can."

Carter looked at him and nodded. "Yes, sir, I get that. We're all going to miss her, she's like a member of the company. She must be knackered. Four weeks of this and she gives half her rations away to the injured men. Not really come across an officer's wife like her before. Is she going to be all right, going back to him?"

"Christ, I hope so, Carter, because we don't really have much choice here, do we?"

"No, sir. Don't worry about her. The lads won't spread this around. They like a gossip as much as the next man, but nobody here would do anything that might hurt her."

"There's not that much to gossip about. I wish there was. But thank you."

It was late when the company broke up and Anne barely awoke when Paul helped her to lie down properly. He could see Teresa lying close by, her face peaceful in sleep, the wary tension gone for once, and Paul thought that they should give the girl more opportunities to enjoy herself. For all her hard exterior she was still young, and tonight, laughing and flushed in the firelight she had looked very pretty.

Paul slid his arm across Anne and eased her back against his body, and Anne repressed a shriek and giggled instead. "You made me jump," she whispered.

"Sorry. I thought you might be cold."

"Not now," Anne said softly.

Paul kissed her head gently. "If they gossip about this all round Lisbon, I am going to regret my restraint," he said.

"But you don't think they will."

"No. I'm counting on it. Still, if they do, I'll come and find you and we'll pick up where we left off. I'll be fitter by then as well."

Anne laughed softly. "Paul, you are outrageous. And I love you."

Paul drew her close into his arms savouring the feeling, conscious that his time with her was ending. He did not want to sleep, did not want to waste a moment of feeling her lying warm and loving against him. "There's so much I want to say to you, and we have so little time," he whispered, and Anne shifted and turned to face him, reaching to kiss him.

"Love, you don't need to say it all. I know it already."

Paul smoothed the dark hair off her face. "I've never felt anything like this in my life. Never felt this sure of anything. Nan, if we never have this opportunity again, just remember how much I love you. More than anything. I know I have to let you go back to him, and I've Rowena and the children to care for. But whatever I have to do because it's right...because it's my duty – I'm yours. Always. Don't forget that love."

"Am I likely to?" Anne said softly, teasingly. "Just hold me, Paul. I just want to enjoy how that feels."

He smiled, knowing she could barely see it through the darkness. "With no pillow and no blankets and nothing to make you comfortable...love, you're crazy."

Anne pushed herself up onto one elbow and leaned over him to kiss him. He returned her kiss feeling the leap of response in his body. Gently he eased her away from him and drew her down. "If we weren't surrounded by my light company, lass, I think I might have just forgotten all my good resolutions," he said. "Go to sleep, girl of my heart, I'm here."

The camp broke late in the day. Paul and Anne rode in rapt silence until Wellesley's lines were sighted. They reined in beside each other, as if by prior agreement, and looked out over the camp.

After a moment Anne turned to look at him, and Paul reached out and took her hand and raised it to his lips. "Always and forever," he said softly.

"For me also, Paul." Anne moved her horse away and back down the lines, as Carl came up to join him at the front.

"Are you all right?" Carl asked.

Paul nodded. "I'll go and find Wellesley, Carl. I'm going to tell him that we're heading back to Lisbon. I'm not fit enough yet to fight, and we all need a few weeks. He can send to me and tell me what he wants me to do next. In the meantime, I think Nan needs to get back to her husband."

"Yes. Don't worry, Paul, I'll see to it. He's probably at the villa but if not, I'll find out where and take her there."

"Thank you." Paul was still watching Anne riding away from him. "It hurts to look at her," he said.

"Christ, Paul, I know."

Paul glanced at him. "You're being remarkably quiet about this."

"Paul, I don't know how far this has gone, but I'm not judging you. I've known you all my life and I've never seen you like this. You're both in pain and I wish there were something I could do to ease it." Carl glanced sideways at Paul. "You're in love with her, aren't you?"

"I have been from the first," Paul said quietly. "Thank you, Carl."

Anne came to find him about an hour later. "Robert is in Lisbon and I'm going back now. Shall I tell Rowena...?"

"I'll be with her as soon as I can, Wellesley wants me to stay for a day or two. Carl will take care of you."

"I know. He's being very kind."

"Nan..."

"I know."

"No regrets," Paul said evenly. "Not one. For four weeks you've been as close to being mine as you'll ever be. Nothing will ever make me regret that. Nothing will ever make me forget how that felt. If I have to live with this pain, for that memory, it was worth it."

***

Rowena came running to meet her as Anne walked through the doors of the villa. Anne hugged her close, and told her reassuringly about Paul, about the battle and about their journey. Beyond Rowena she could see Robert, watching and listening, and his expression chilled her.

It was hours later when he came to their room and Anne stood waiting, wanting nothing more than to get it over with. He walked towards her and she could feel her heart hammering in her chest. He threw her down face forward onto the bed, and she heard the swish of the riding crop and felt the sharp pain, again and again across her shoulders and she buried her face into the

289

pillow and stifled her cries until he dropped the whip and pulled her over onto her back.

"Did you fuck him?" he asked.

"No," Anne said.

Robert slapped her hard across the face. "Did you fuck him?"

Anne shook her head. "No," she said.

He looked at her and Anne saw both rage and pain in his eyes. "I hate you," he whispered. "I hate you. You were the thing I used to get what I wanted, and I didn't give a damn about what you did with him. And now it's all I can think about."

His hand was at her throat, and Anne felt his fingers tighten. There were tears heavy behind her eyes, for Paul and for the time that they had and the time that they would never have. And then she reached up and drew Robert's head down to hers, ignoring the pain in her back.

"Robert, nothing happened. I got left behind, and they brought me back. Nothing happened, I swear. Kiss me."

There was a moment, as his lips covered hers that Anne was not sure she was going to be able to bear it. The memory of Paul holding her close was too recent and her mind rebelled. But she knew that it had to be done. Gently she eased her sore, aching body against Robert's and felt his immediate response, and then it was done and she lay still, feeling the loneliness engulf her.

As he slept finally, she lay silently weeping in the darkness.

Chapter Seventeen

Sir Arthur Wellesley was rewarded for his hard-fought victory at Talavera by elevation to the peerage as Viscount Wellington of Talavera and Wellington. Through the autumn and winter of 1809 his troops settled into barracks and billets in northern Portugal and endured the after-effects of the Talavera campaign. Sickness ran like wildfire through the troops and the under-staffed and badly equipped hospitals struggled to cope with the number of men afflicted. Many died, and those who lived were too weak to rejoin their regiments for months.

Lord Wellington had chosen the pretty village of Viseu in the mountains to the north of Lisbon as his headquarters, and Paul's regiment was quartered in a large farm just on the edge of the town. After the vicissitudes of the retreat from Talavera it was a relief to be warm and dry and well supplied with food. A number of Paul's men were showing signs of illness but Paul himself was recovering well from the effects of his wound.

Señor Ferreira, the farm owner, had been less than enthusiastic upon being informed that a battalion was being billeted on him, but after only a few weeks, relations improved considerably. The men were given several large barns for their accommodation, and the officers were housed in the big, rambling farmhouse. Paul managed to negotiate the use of a field at the back for training purposes, and as soon as he was able, he resumed regular drilling and training, keeping his men as busy as possible. The farmer quickly realised that the youthful major was both willing and able to pay for food and drink for his men, which precluded the need for looting or theft. Discipline was strictly enforced in the 110th and after one or two minor incidents, which were dealt with ruthlessly by their commander, the men settled well into their routine.

For the officers of Wellington's army, it was a time of rest and recuperation. Some of them welcomed the opportunity to hunt and ride and fish and attend the endless balls and receptions which the local Portuguese grandees held to celebrate the English presence. Others were bored and irritable. There were concerts given in local churches and convents, and some of the officers set up an amateur dramatics club which gave regular performances. To the bulk of his officers, it seemed that Wellington was happy to give himself up to socialising and relaxing and flirting with a number of Portuguese beauties, and with the lovely young wife of Lieutenant Robert Carlyon who had moved from Lisbon to be with her husband.

Paul knew better. Behind the calm there was frantic activity. The new Viscount Wellington was dealing not only with the fluctuating fortunes of government in England, but a sense of hopelessness throughout the army at the stalemate of the Portuguese campaign. Most of the officers believed that Portugal could not and should not be held, and news of Napoleon's success in Austria and other European theatres of war added to the despondency. The men were bored and restless, and sickness took its toll on both officers and men.

There were few men whom Wellington trusted freely with his opinions, but Major van Daan was one of them. He invited Paul to Lisbon with him to meet with the Regent, and to spend some time with his chief of engineers, Lieutenant-Colonel Sir Richard Fletcher.

"We need to be able to defend Portugal," he told Paul bluntly. "Can't plan any kind of campaign into Spain without knowing we can fall back in safety, and we can't rely on the Spanish for supplies and support or we'll end up like Moore. They have more men than we do and it is easier for them to bring in reinforcements. But I have a surprise in store for them. Come and talk to Fletcher with me. You'll like him."

Paul had not met Richard Fletcher before, although he was aware that the other man had a distinguished career behind him in the Indies and Africa. He was a dark-haired man of around forty, of medium height with bright, intelligent dark eyes and a ready smile and Paul took to him immediately. It was clear that he enjoyed an easy relationship with Wellington, and he greeted Paul with friendly interest.

"Major van Daan. I'm glad to meet you at last, I've heard a good deal about you. Come and sit down, sir. I hear that you had a difficult time at Talavera."

"I wasn't alone in that," Paul said with a smile, seating himself as requested opposite Wellington and accepting a drink. "I'm glad to meet you too, sir, although I'm not sure why I'm here."

Fletcher shot an amused glance at Wellington. "A man who gets straight to the point, sir. You were right." He looked back at Paul. "You are here because Lord Wellington tells me that you are an intelligent man who can be trusted. There are few enough of those around. We have a plan, his Lordship and I, and we would like your opinion. There are a few other selected officers who have been consulted on this."

"This is a matter of the utmost secrecy, Major," Wellington said. "I do not wish this to reach anybody, even your own officers. Before we proceed, I need your word on that."

Paul was puzzled. "You have it, sir."

"Good. Because Sir Richard has some drawings to show me, and I would like to know what you think. Come over to the table."

Paul got up and followed his chief to a long table at the other end of the room. There were several maps and drawings laid out upon it. Fletcher drew one towards him and pointed. It was a map of Portugal, with drawings and notations over it. Paul studied it for a moment. Then he set down his glass, leaned on the table and looked closer. Nobody spoke for some minutes. After a while, Paul looked up at his chief.

"Bloody hell!" he said. "Is this how you're spending the winter?"

"Did you think I was spending it going to parties, Major?" Wellington said, sounding amused.

"I know you're going to parties, sir, I keep meeting you there. Who is going to build this?"

"We're drafting in local labour. Sir Richard and his officers will supervise. But we wish, as far as possible, to keep this work secret. The fewer people who realise exactly what we are working on, the less likely it is that intelligence will reach the French."

"The men will know you're building defences," Paul said, looking again at the map. "But unless they go on a deliberate tour, there's no reason for them to know it is anything this extensive."

He studied Fletcher's drawings again. He had sketched a system of fortifications, which seemed to include blockhouses and redoubts with cuts of natural relief working within the features of the landscape. There were three lines of defence. It would be an enormous undertaking, but if it could be done, it was likely to stop the French dead if they decided to invade Portugal once again.

"Fletcher and I are about to take a small tour of the area so that it can be properly surveyed," Wellington said. "I will be taking a staff with me, and a small force of cavalry, but I would like you to accompany me, if your battalion can spare you."

"Captain Wheeler is more than capable," Paul said. "Thank you. I admit I'm fascinated."

"I don't anticipate any trouble, but there are still deserters and brigands to consider. Will your wife be furious with me if I steal you away again so soon?"

"She's used to it," Paul said. "She's very comfortable where we are, and since Mrs Carlyon's arrival she won't be lonely."

"Yes, it has been good to see how well they get on. I always felt your wife struggled a little with the social side of army life, Major, but since Mrs Carlyon came, she has gained confidence. It must be easier for you."

"It is, they see a good deal of each other. Robert is busy as you know, replenishing supplies after the retreat."

"Yes." Wellington looked at Fletcher. "Have you come across Lieutenant Carlyon? He is with the quartermaster's department now."

"No, sir."

"He's a useful man, I'll be involving him in sourcing labour and supplies for this project, and he also has a young wife who helps the surgeons. She did very good work at Talavera. Major van Daan claims she saved his life."

293

Wellington smiled. "She is also, Colonel Fletcher, the most beautiful woman in Portugal. Worth getting wounded for."

***

While Paul was touring the proposed site of the defences with Lord Wellington, Anne was immersed in her work at the hospital, which had been set up in a convent on the edge of Viseu. The doctors were still awaiting supplies of all kinds from England, and Anne felt intense frustration at the lack of blankets, mattresses and medicines of all kinds. There were still men recovering from the horrific wounds they received at Talavera, and as those were gradually repatriated on transports to England, they were replaced by fever victims. These were harder to treat. There was no effective cure, although in some cases Peruvian bark could alleviate the symptoms. Once fever took hold in the hospital it quickly spread, and men who had looked set to recover from their wounds took ill and died.

The Carlyons were billeted in a graceful house owned by a silk merchant in the old quarter of the town. Set on a plateau high in the hills of Beira Alta, the town had a medieval feel to it, with the remains of a walled centre and crumbling remains of walls built long ago by the Romans. It was a busy little town full of beautiful houses, historic churches and elaborate public buildings. The cobbled streets were cleaner than those of Lisbon, and the presence of the army headquarters drew many of the officers' wives and families out from the capital.

The town was surrounded by rich agricultural land. Wine and cheesemaking were the local industries, along with beautiful lace and a range of black pottery. With little else to do, the officers and their ladies explored the steep, winding streets of the town. Accompanied by Rowena and Carl Swanson, Anne visited the fortified Cathedral with its two towers. It was situated at the highest point of the town and dominated the skyline. It had been built in the thirteenth century but refurbished many times since and it was Anne's favourite of the many elaborate churches in the town.

When she was not occupied with her work at the hospital or with sight-seeing and shopping with Rowena, Anne persuaded Carl and Johnny Wheeler to go riding with her up into the mountains and hills surrounding the town. There were breathtaking views over lakes, gorges and streams with tiny remote villages, which felt unconnected to the chaos of the war, which raged around them. Wolves inhabited the hills and although they stayed well clear of the town, Wellington's officers were warned to go armed and alert if travelling at night outside the populated areas.

Anne enjoyed being with Rowena again. Her feelings for Paul did not seem to affect her fondness for his wife. It was as if she had found a way to separate the two completely, so that when the lovely Mrs Cartwright arrived in Viseu with her husband who had been transferred to work alongside Robert, Anne could feel only anger at the woman's deliberate baiting of her friend.

"Is Paul away again?" she asked Rowena sweetly one evening at a reception given by Dom Ricardo Alvera to entertain the English officers. "How you must miss him, dear Rowena. Do you not worry about what he might be up to? All those Portuguese beauties…"

Rowena gave a small tight smile and said nothing. Arabella and her acolytes tittered inanely, making Anne's palm itch to deliver a slap.

"Oh, Arabella, as if he would," Mrs Barclay said. "Although I am sure it will be a different matter when he gets back and realises that you are here. You two were so close in Naples…"

Anne felt Rowena flinch. She glanced at Carl and observed by the expression on his face that he was regretting the constraints of good manners.

"Lieutenant Swanson, why don't you take Rowena to show her the view," she said pleasantly. "I'll come and find you."

Carl met her eyes in some amusement. Since Talavera, Anne had become conscious of a significant change in her relationship with Paul's oldest friend. He had begun to treat her with the same affectionate informality which he displayed to Rowena and Anne enjoyed it.

Carl took his commander's wife by the arm with a grin. "Ma'am."

When they had moved away Anne turned to Arabella and took her arm. "Let us take a turn about the room. Are you an admirer of sculpture, ma'am? I believe these to be exceptionally fine examples."

"Oh – yes." Arabella appeared startled as Anne towed her gently away. "Ma'am…"

"I am not all that interested in art," Anne confessed. "I just wanted an opportunity to speak to you privately, Mrs Cartwright. I am very aware of your previous relationship with Paul. So is Rowena, but I think she has heard enough about it for now. Best stick to other topics when you're around her."

"My dear Mrs Carlyon, what has it to do with you?"

"She's my friend and I'm tired of watching you upset her."

Arabella glared at her. "It is none of your business, ma'am. I wonder that you should be so concerned for her given the many opportunities you had yourself to get to know Major van Daan on the retreat from Talavera."

It was the first time anybody had spoken openly of the impropriety of Anne's journey without her husband. Anne regarded Arabella calmly.

"Yes, it was educational, believe me. What I learned after a few weeks in Paul van Daan's company, is that if he finds out you've been deliberately baiting his wife, he could do your reputation an awful lot of damage in one evening in the mess. And he would. He might not be a particularly faithful husband but he's an awfully fond one. She'll never tell him, she has too much pride. But if I hear you doing that to her one more time, I promise I will."

The red-haired woman caught her breath. "What makes you think he'd believe you?" she asked.

"Trust me, Mrs Cartwright, he would. And is it worth the risk of finding yourself shunned by Lisbon society because he's regaled the entire mess with the story of exactly what you two did in Naples? They'll enjoy it, he's a good storyteller."

"You wouldn't dare."

"I promise you, I would. I know how jealous you are of her, but you're just going to have to get over it. I'm going to find her. Excuse me."

Anne found Carl on the terrace. "She's with Kate Barry." He handed Anne a glass of champagne. "What did you just say to Mrs Cartwright, ma'am? She doesn't look happy."

"I imagine she is reconsidering her behaviour around Rowena," Anne said, sipping the wine. "Thank you, Lieutenant."

Carl regarded her with some amusement. "You're a good friend, Nan. Just be careful. If Arabella Cartwright were to have the least idea..."

"If she knew, it would be all round headquarters by now. There's a lot less to tell than you probably think, Carl. The circumstances were unusual, but I care too much about Rowena to hurt her and so does he."

"Paul? He definitely cares, but it hasn't always stopped him in the past. I've immense faith in you, Nan, you'd never do that to her. But Christ, it must be difficult for you. He's not easy at the best of times and it worries me that he makes your life harder."

"I don't need looking after, Lieutenant."

Green eyes studied her and for one moment Anne had the oddest sense that this gentle, perceptive man saw more than anybody else. "Yes, you do, Nan," he said quietly. "Probably more than most people realise. Look, I think I understand why you might not want to talk to Paul. But if you need to, you can come to me."

Anne summoned a reassuring smile. "I'm all right, Carl, I promise."

***

It was several weeks before Anne saw Paul again and the meeting was completely unexpected. She had been visiting the fever ward at the hospital and was on her way back to her billet when she turned a corner and found herself face to face with him.

"Paul. I didn't know you were back."

Paul met her eyes, and she saw the smile come into his. "Nan," he said softly, and Anne realised she was smiling too. "How are you?"

"I'm very well. I've just come from the hospital."

"And I'm very sure you shouldn't be wandering around unescorted."

"In broad daylight? I don't think you need to worry about me, Paul."

"Well, somebody ought to and it's plain your bloody husband doesn't. I'll walk you home. Carl tells me you have been taking very good care of Rowena for me. Thank you."

"She has been taking care of me too, she stops me spending all my time at the hospital. When did you get back?"

"Late last night." He took her hand and drew it through his arm, and she glanced up at him feeling herself flush slightly. His eyes told her that he was well aware of the effect of his touch. "I arrived back at our billet to find two of my men trying to murder each other with Carl intervening. Very entertaining."

"That is what comes of living on a farm where wine is so freely available. What did you do?"

"Doused both of them with cold water and locked them in the stables overnight to sober up. This morning they are running around the training field in full kit until their hangover subsides. Or until they fall over. I am not very much interested in which comes first."

Anne laughed. "They'd have been flogged for that by anybody else," she said. "Do you ever use flogging, Paul?"

"No, I don't believe in it. It teaches a man nothing useful, especially not to respect an officer. I will occasionally thump one of them, but I prefer to do it man to man."

"So how do you maintain such good discipline?"

"Well, I've a bit of a mouth on me at times," Paul said with an admirably straight face. Anne gave a choke of laughter.

"I am shocked to hear you say so, Major,"

"You'd be surprised at how effective it is. I use hated tasks a lot as punishment. If you're cleaning out the latrines there's a fair chance you've pissed me off that week. Dock pay, although that's not especially effective when they've not been paid for six months anyway. Extra drill and training. They might as well get benefit out of a punishment. But mostly I find that after a while they just seem to fit in. The problem is not with the men, it's with the officers who can't be bothered to supervise them properly. If there's trouble in my battalion, it's when they're drunk. Those two will be on nice fresh well water for a few days and nothing else. They'll also be separated from the others when they're not training which they hate." Paul grinned. "They'd probably rather be flogged."

"It seems to work," Anne said. "I hate flogging. I've treated a few men whose backs will be scarred for life with it. It's brutal and it's humiliating, and I suspect that one or two of the officers use it without good reason. I'd like to strap them to the whipping post for fifty of the best and see how they like it."

"The idea has occurred to me more than once," Paul assured her gravely and they both laughed, arriving at her billet to find that Arabella Cartwright was emerging from the door. She stopped and stared in astonishment.

"Mrs Carlyon. And Major van Daan. What a surprise."

"Not especially," Anne said briskly. "I do live here, Mrs Cartwright."

She saw the other woman's lips tighten. "Yes. I was passing and Colonel Barry asked if I would drop in an invitation to his regimental ball on Thursday. You must know that my husband has just been appointed as quartermaster to the 120th. I believe Lord Wellington is going to attend." She looked at Paul. "Will you be there, Major?"

"I expect so." Paul glanced down at Anne. "Will you save me a dance, ma'am?"

"I will," Anne said. "Thank you for escorting me, Major."

"My pleasure, ma'am." Paul bowed slightly and Anne went into the house. She could hear Arabella requesting his escort back into town and smiled as she went through into the sitting room. It served him right that the woman was so determinedly trying to win her way back into his good graces.

Anne found that Paul had not managed to shake her off when she arrived at the ball the following Thursday. He was at the centre of a group of officers and their wives on the far side of the room. Rowena was with him, looking charming in a simple blue muslin gown, which suited her. Her fair hair was dressed high on her head with ringlets framing her face, and Anne thought, regarding her with affection, that she was worth twenty of Arabella Cartwright who was dazzling beside her in her favourite green.

Robert took Anne's arm and guided her to where Lord Wellington was talking to some of his senior officers. He broke off at the sight of Anne and bowed over her hand. "Mrs Carlyon, good to see you, ma'am. I have been hearing from Mr Guthrie of the wonders you have been performing with the fever patients. He tells me you are at the hospital most days."

"I enjoy the work, sir."

"It does you credit, ma'am." Wellington looked at Robert. "And you too, sir, for allowing your wife to be of service. Many men wouldn't, I applaud you for it. I shall expect the first dance with you this evening, ma'am, you are the best dancer in the army."

Anne laughed. "Thank you, sir. I shall look forward to it."

She bowed and moved on, glancing up at Robert apprehensively. Her husband seemed in an unusually mellow mood this evening, even going so far as to compliment her appearance, but he had become increasingly unpredictable when other men paid attention to her.

"Lord Wellington likes you," Robert said unexpectedly.

"I think so," Anne admitted cautiously.

"I mean, he actually likes you. Not just because..." Robert waved his hand to indicate her appearance. He paused. "It's a good thing. Gives him a good impression of me."

Startled, Anne realised that he was trying to thank her. "I hope so," she said neutrally.

Her husband looked down at her. "Nan...things are better again, aren't they? After...what happened. You know I didn't mean it."

Anne stared at Robert. She wanted to ask him how he had managed to beat her with a riding whip without meaning it, but she stopped herself in time. Robert had a breathtaking ability to justify his brutality by claiming that it was her fault. Anne was surprised he had raised the matter at all.

"Robert are you trying to apologise?" she said softly.

He looked uncomfortable. "Perhaps. Not really the time."

"No, not really."

"I've an engagement to play piquet with Cavendish," he said abruptly. "You'll be well enough entertained."

"Yes, I'll join Rowena. Paul is busy flirting with Mrs Cartwright."

Robert looked across the room and gave a slightly grim smile. "Yes. But we both know he is about to stop doing that, Nan," he said, and left her with a bow.

***

Carl Swanson watched Anne's arrival from across the room. She was dressed in a flowing gown of white silk threaded through with gold, which sparkled under the myriad candles and as she made her way around the room, pausing to speak to various acquaintances, male heads turned to watch her progress. She looked very different to the girl in the filthy green gown who had ridden back from Talavera. Carl looked at his commander and realised that Paul had stopped speaking to Arabella, probably in mid-sentence and was looking at Anne as if she were the only person in the room.

"I see that we are back to where we were," Johnny Wheeler said quietly beside him.

Carl shook his head. "I honestly don't think they can help it, Johnny, he said. "But people must notice."

"People are noticing. There is gossip at headquarters, Carl, which he would know if he ever bothered to listen."

"Is Carlyon aware?"

Johnny shrugged. "I don't know. You lived with them in Lisbon. How was he when she got back?"

"Paul wasn't there for a few weeks. Which was a good thing because I don't think her husband let her out of his bed much that week," Carl said in flat tones. Wheeler winced.

"Christ, that must have been difficult for her."

"Surprisingly, it was quite difficult for me," Carl said. "I don't like Carlyon, Johnny, I never have. There's something about him that sets me on edge, and I'd never say this to Paul because I think it might push him right over the edge, but I'm not sure he's not rough with her at times. But I've no proof, and she's not talking about it. I've tried to ask but she shuts me down very pleasantly."

"I can see why you wouldn't want Paul to suspect that. It would end in murder. Wouldn't Paul realise?"

"I've a feeling she'd work very hard to make sure he didn't," Carl said, watching Anne. "She's as protective of him as he is of her. And they're both protective of Rowena."

"Yes, she seems completely unaware." Johnny shook his head. "Ironically, he's probably more faithful to Rowena now than he's ever been. I've not seen him look at another woman since Anne Carlyon came to Portugal." He broke off at Anne's approach, and took her hand, bowing over it. "Ma'am, how are you?"

"I'm very well, Captain Wheeler, thank you. Mr Swanson, have your drunken men been released from the stables yet?"

"Did he tell you about that? I'm surprised he didn't put me in there with them," Carl said with a grin. "He got back late and with no sense of humour."

"He was probably hungry," Anne said, and both Carl and Johnny laughed aloud. Paul's tendency to become irritable when he had not eaten was a standing joke among his close friends, but Carl had not realised that Anne knew it. He thought again how well she seemed to understand his friend, and it saddened him. Paul was approaching and Carl watched Anne's expression as she greeted him. She was better than Paul was at concealing her feelings, but to Carl, who knew, her heart was in her eyes.

"Nan, you look lovely. Is that new?"

"No, but I've not worn it since I got to Portugal so it may as well be. There's not much occasion for ball gowns in the hospital. Rowena, I love your hair."

"Thank you." Rowena joined the group. "Although I am well aware that now that you have arrived, the rest of us may just as well have come in our walking dresses, dear Nan. But you do look beautiful."

Carl gave her a sharp glance. It was unusual for Paul's wife to express even the slightest hint of envy of another woman. With his conversation with Johnny in mind, he found himself watching Rowena and Anne through the evening. Their affection for each other was obvious and genuine, and Carl wondered if Paul felt any discomfort at seeing them together. He gave no sign of it. Watching his friend laughing with his wife at a story that Anne was telling, Carl thought that he looked relaxed and happy and hoped that it would last.

***

As they drove back to the farm later that evening, Paul listened to his fellow officers laughing and talking and watched his wife. It had occurred to him that evening, that he allowed the madness of his feelings for Anne to cloud the fact that Rowena was a very pretty woman in her own right. She was as gentle and serene now as he had thought her six years ago, when he had first made love to her in the woods of Southwinds, and Paul knew that he took her for granted every day. His feelings for Anne were completely different to those he had for Rowena but watching her back in their room as she draped her shawl over a chair and reached up to unpin her hair, Paul remembered how much he had once desired her, and how her soothing presence had helped him through those first difficult months at Melton. Paul felt suddenly an immense sense of gratitude and affection for her. She had been a rock in the storms of the past few years, and he wondered if she had any idea how much she meant to him. Walking forward, he put his arms about her.

"Keep still," he said softly against her ear, and he felt a shiver of surprise run through her. It had been a long time since he had touched Rowena like this, and as he slid his hand up to cup her breast, he heard her give a little gasp.

300

Suddenly Paul wanted her urgently, and he moved his hands to the buttons at the back of her gown while bending to kiss her neck. Rowena stood still under his touch, but he could hear her breathing quicken, and he tugged hard at the last few buttons and slid the flowing muslin to a heap at her feet. He was less gentle with the soft linen of her chemise and then his hands were on her body and she leaned back against him with a little murmur of pleasure.

"Paul." Her voice was husky. Paul turned her towards him and kissed her hard, not the gentle salute he gave her daily, then he picked her up and carried her to the bed, laying her on top of the counterpane.

"Don't move. I want to look at you." He finished undressing, his eyes on her body, and he could see by her heightened colour that she was very aware of his scrutiny. And then he reached for her and moved above her. "I've been wanting to do this for hours," he said, and his mouth came down hard on hers. Rowena gave a cry and arched against him and he laughed softly.

"Not yet, angel. I'm in no hurry tonight. Let's take our time, shall we, we've got all night."

Paul was aware of an enormous content when finally they lay still and he drew Rowena close, so that she lay with her tumbled fair hair spread across his chest. She was breathless and wide-eyed, looking up at him.

"Paul, whatever was that about?" she asked, laughing.

"Is that a complaint?"

"No. Definitely not."

Paul studied her with amused appreciation. "I suddenly looked at you this evening and realised that I am married to one of the most beautiful women in Portugal, and I just take that for granted. I'd forgotten the days when I used to wait all week to do this with you, and time would crawl past."

Rowena laughed aloud. "Paul, what has got into you? You've never told me that before, did you honestly?"

"Honestly. I would sit in the mess being bored to death trying to be nice to my fellow officers and think about how you looked with that hair like spun gold falling around your shoulders, and how your skin looked like honey in the sunlight."

Rowena was still laughing, and he could sense how much he had pleased her. "And I'd forgotten that I married a poet."

"I never did write you that sonnet. I wonder if I can still remember how it should scan? It's been a while since poetry featured much in my life."

"You shall make me a present of it for my birthday."

"That's a good idea, it'll give me something to do during the evenings when we're invading Spain."

They lay listening to the soft sound of an owl hunting through the trees, Rowena's head on his shoulder and her leg thrown across him. Paul had thought she was asleep, but then she said:

"Thank you for what you said earlier."

"Which part?" Paul said, lazily content. "I seem to have been spouting nonsense all evening."

"The part where you said I was beautiful."

"You are beautiful, Rowena."

"Sometimes I feel very plain," his wife said quietly.

Paul understood her meaning, and his heart ached for her. It would have been easy to turn her remark off with a joke and she would have accepted it, but she deserved better.

"You're not, Rowena but it occurs to me that every woman in the room feels plain standing next to Anne Carlyon. Don't let it bother you, lass. You're my wife and I'll always think you're beautiful."

Paul felt her snuggle into him and although he could not see her well, he sensed her smile in the darkness.

"That is probably why so few of them like her."

"Yes, she doesn't make female friends easily, does she?"

"Nor do I. Perhaps that is why we are so fond of each other."

Paul laughed. "Fellow feeling? You may be right. I'm glad you have Nan, Rowena, I don't worry about you so much."

"I know. Because now when you are not there you know that she will take care of me."

"I suppose I do take that for granted," Paul admitted. It felt strange to be lying here with Rowena talking about Anne.

"Do you think she is happy with Robert?" Rowena asked.

Paul was silent for a moment, the pain of thinking about it knifing through him. But Rowena was his wife and years of loyalty, patience and devotion had earned her the right to question him. "No," he said. "I don't. I can't imagine them lying here like this, talking and laughing."

"Nor can I. Although he does..." Rowena broke off and he knew, although he could not see, that she was blushing.

"The word you are looking for, my adorable little prude, is desire," Paul said, amused at her shyness. "He looks at her sometimes as though he can't keep his hands off her for another minute, but I've never seen the least sign of affection in him."

"No. Sometimes he looks at her as if he hates her."

Paul glanced sharply at her, surprised at her perception. "He married her for money, Rowena, very openly. I don't think he ever intended to feel the way he obviously does about her. I suppose it makes him feel vulnerable."

"Given how she flirts with every officer in the army, I'm not surprised," his wife said without malice. "She's not a wife to make a man feel secure."

"Unlike mine," Paul said quietly. Rowena looked up at him and he leaned over and kissed her again. "Don't think I don't appreciate all the things you never say to me, Rowena. I know I'm a bastard at times, but never think I don't care. You are a wife that I couldn't even begin to deserve, and I will undoubtedly hurt you all over again in the future. But despite everything, the best part of me knows that seducing you in that churchyard was the most intelligent thing I have ever done."

Rowena slept finally and Paul lay holding her and thought about his wife and about Anne and about his tangled feelings for both of them. Lying beside Anne on the hard ground on that last night of the retreat from Talavera he had dreaded coming back to his wife, dreaded that his feelings for her might have changed and that she would somehow realise it. He need not have worried. He felt the same steady affection for Rowena that he always had, and it had been easy and enjoyable to come back to her bed. Instinctively Paul knew that it had not been so easy for Anne and the unhappiness that she bore so stoically was a weight on his heart. He did not deserve Rowena, and he did not deserve that Anne should make it so easy for him. Paul wished there were something he could do for her in return.

***

Conditions in the army improved in time to give an air of festivity to Christmas. Transports had arrived at the beginning of December bringing supplies, horses and reinforcements as well as the money which London had been promising Wellington. Having finally been paid, the men of his army settled down to celebrate.

Paul had been dividing his time between his regiment, Wellington's endless meetings with the Portuguese, and Fletcher's engineering works. He had never taken much interest in military engineering before, having the soldier's vague contempt for this lesser branch of the forces, but he and Fletcher had struck up a real friendship during his surveying tour, and he found the engineer's enthusiasm for the project infectious. Fletcher was a soldier as well as an engineer and could swap tales of his service in the Indies and Africa for Paul's stories of India and Copenhagen.

Paul watched as Anne Carlyon danced her way through the headquarters festivities over Christmas, and the sight of her tried his resolve almost to breaking point. It was impossible to keep his distance. Her popularity with Lord Wellington made her a guaranteed guest at every party and Paul watched her laughing and flirting with an ache in his heart. Her husband trod behind her, his eyes following her around every room. Paul, who had come to loathe Carlyon, could almost pity him. He could remember the days when Robert had spent all his time and money at cards and had seemed indifferent to the whereabouts of his lovely young wife. Two years later he seemed unable to take his eyes from her but was no more comfortable in her presence than he had ever been. His fellow officers spoke behind his back with open amusement about Robert's obsession with his wife and her flirtatiousness with other men. Paul had heard that on one occasion Johnny Wheeler had intervened to some purpose when he overheard two junior officers speculating on Anne's relationship with Paul.

Anne's close friendship with Rowena made it impossible for Paul to avoid spending time around her even if he had wished to, but he did not. He tried hard not to make life difficult for her with her husband, although he was aware of Carlyon's simmering resentment. It threatened to spill over at the ball hosted by the Highlanders during Christmas. Paul danced with Anne and they remained beside each other when it ended, watching the Highlanders demonstrate a complicated reel. Paul was watching Anne's laughing face, the long, graceful line of neck and shoulders and the swell of her breasts above the silver gauze of her gown. At moments like this, despite all the complications of their relationship, Paul could not help feeling a surge of simple happiness that she was beside him, their arms touching. He did not notice Carlyon's presence until he spoke.

"Move away from my wife, Major."

Paul turned, startled. He was not sure if Carlyon was drunk, but he was looking belligerent. Anne turned too. "I am just watching the dancing, Robert," she said quietly and something in her voice told Paul that she spent a good deal of her time soothing her husband's jealousy.

"You may have been, but that's not where Major van Daan was looking."

Paul unexpectedly lost his temper. "I'm surprised you noticed from the card room, Mr Carlyon. Run through her monthly allowance yet, have you? Don't worry, she can come and eat with us if she finds herself short again."

"Paul, for God's sake!" Anne sounded horrified, but Paul was beyond discretion.

"How he spends your money is not one of the best kept secrets of the army, Nan. But keep at it, Rob, we all know that's what you married her for."

"It's none of your bloody business, Major!" Robert said harshly. "Get away from him, Anne, now!"

"Stay where you are, Nan," Paul said softly, his eyes on Robert's face. "I think he's drunk, and I'd rather you weren't around him in this state, I'm not sure he's in control of himself and I don't want you hurt." He placed his hand very deliberately on Anne's shoulder and Carlyon's face flushed scarlet.

"Get away from my bloody wife, Major..."

"That will do!"

***

Lord Wellington's voice was like the crack of a whip, and Anne turned towards him in relief. People had begun to stare, and she had no idea how to stop either Paul or Robert. Anne could not imagine what had suddenly made Paul so angry, he usually tried hard to be pleasant to Robert, but she was terrified that the angry words were escalating towards a demand for satisfaction.

Wellington looked at Carlyon and then at Paul and the expression on his face was not encouraging.

"I have no idea if either of you are drunk, but you will separate now and remain apart. Major van Daan, you have a wife, kindly join her. Mr Carlyon, remove yourself until you are calm. Ma'am, will you join me for a stroll?"

Both Paul and Robert saluted. Paul's eyes met Anne's, and she managed a slight shake of her head as she took Lord Wellington's arm. "Gladly, sir," she said, and allowed him to lead her away. Neither of them spoke as he drew her through the crowd, and out onto the broad terrace at the end. It was deserted and Wellington took her to the stone balustrade, which looked out over the town.

"Take a moment, ma'am. I think you are upset."

Anne looked at him with real gratitude. "Thank you for intervening, my Lord. I suspect by now they are both feeling rather stupid."

"Certainly, I imagine Major van Daan is. While his feelings are moderately obvious, he usually manages to keep them under better control. As for your husband, we are all aware that he finds it increasingly hard to control himself. I am sorry. It must be exceedingly difficult for you."

Anne was startled. "Does everybody at headquarters know, sir?"

"Everybody speculates, ma'am. Your husband's level of jealousy is unusual and attracts comment. As for Major van Daan, there is always gossip about him, much of it nonsense, but since you came to Portugal it has become very obvious that he has no interest in any other woman."

Anne shook her head. "Lord Wellington..."

"Ma'am, I don't judge you. You must be very lonely at times, I think," he said quietly. "I am too. Neither of us is happy in our marriage. It cannot be a surprise to you when I tell you how very attractive I have always found you, and if circumstances were different, I think I would be suggesting rather more than a stroll on the terrace, so I can hardly pass judgement on Major van Daan."

"Sir..."

"I am not going to embarrass you, my dear. Our situations are not the same, and while I do not think I would have any scruples about Mr Carlyon's wife, I could not reconcile my conscience with trying to seduce Major van Daan's mistress. I consider him a friend."

"I'm not his mistress, sir."

"No, but he would very much like you to be."

"He cares too much about Rowena, my Lord. And so do I."

"I know." Wellington gave a little smile, took her hand and raised it to his lips. "I don't always find it easy to make idle conversation, ma'am, but I find you very easy to talk to. I hope that nothing I have said this evening means that you..."

"No." Anne said quickly. "Oh no. I am honestly flattered. And you are right, sometimes I am lonely." She smiled suddenly. "I can understand why Paul likes you so much."

Wellington laughed aloud. "I am honoured," he said dryly. "He often has little patience with his senior officers, but he and I have been through a good deal together. We should go in, Mrs Carlyon, before somebody notices that either of us is missing. But before we do, would you be very offended...?"

Anne met his eyes steadily. His unexpected understanding had touched a chord in her. "No," she said, shocking herself.

Wellington placed one hand under her chin, tilting her head back. Gently his lips met hers. Anne closed her eyes and let him kiss her, and then she was conscious of his arm about her, drawing her closer. His body was hard, and she reached up and placed her hand on the back of his neck. Very delicately he parted her lips and suddenly his kiss was no longer tentative, and Anne was conscious of a surprising shiver of pleasure. He held her against him, and she was kissing him back without restraint.

It lasted a long time. Almost Anne wanted it to continue. She was slightly shocked to realise that if it were not for Paul she would possibly have been interested in the commander-in-chief's tentative offer. She had never felt this way with any man other than Paul and she was in love with him, but there was something attractively straightforward about Wellington's kiss and she rather imagined he would demonstrate the same direct enjoyment in bed.

Eventually Anne drew back, and looked up at him, smiling. "I don't think we had better do that again, my Lord," she said quietly.

The hooded eyes were amused. "Neither do I," he said. "I don't know which of them would be more likely to murder me. But I am glad that I did. It suddenly makes the exasperating behaviour of two of my officers much easier to understand. I just hope they don't end by killing each other."

"I'll try to make sure that they don't."

"Thank you, my dear. I feel obscurely flattered. Although I think I must allow you to go back inside without me. I am going to need a few moments alone, where it is dark."

Colour scorched Anne's face, but she was laughing. "I am sorry, sir."

"Don't be. I spend a good deal of my time doing things I don't enjoy. It is very pleasant now and again to do something I do."

There was a movement at the door and Anne turned quickly. Paul came out onto the terrace and she felt herself blush again, thankful of the darkness. He came forward, his eyes on her face, taking her hands in his. "Are you all right?"

"Major van Daan, you are beginning to try my patience," Wellington said sharply, and Paul saluted.

"I just came to apologise, sir, to you and to Nan. I'm going to take Rowena home, she's tired. I've apologised to Carlyon and he has accepted. Stupid of me. Perhaps I've drunk more than I realised."

"I doubt it, Major, but that is certainly the excuse we will be accepting," Wellington said. He came forward and Anne looked up at him and saw her own amusement mirrored in his blue eyes. "Your apology is accepted. Please don't let it happen again."

Paul lifted Anne's hand to his lips then released her. "I won't, sir." He turned to go, but at the door he looked back. "Mind, I'm not sure he'll be all that happy about you kissing her on the terrace either, sir," he said, and met Anne's eyes. She was momentarily appalled and then saw that he was laughing.

"Paul..."

"Christ, lass, I don't blame you. Between the two of us I'm surprised you're not driven mad. It would serve both of us right if you did find somebody else." Paul glanced at his chief and smiled slightly. "But don't make a habit of it, sir. I don't know how he'd feel about it, but just at the moment I'd like to punch you. Good night."

Through that winter, Paul had the sense that his marriage had steadied again. After the storm of Anne's presence in his life he had come to terms, in a strange way, with the feelings he had for both Anne and Rowena. He acknowledged that he was in love with Anne in a way that he had never been with Rowena, but he had found a way to reconcile those feelings with the very different emotions he felt for his wife, and when Rowena told him on the first day of the new year that she was with child again, it seemed fitting, given his new sense of commitment to her. It was also hardly surprising, given the amount of time he had recently spent making love to her.

The new year brought new challenges for Paul. Reinforcements had arrived, including the fifth and sixth companies of the 110th along with over a hundred men from the second battalion whom Colonel Johnstone had sent to fill the gaps left by Talavera in the first battalion. Many of these had taken part in the ill-conceived Walcheren expedition in the summer, and they brought with them to Portugal the deadly Walcheren fever, almost doubling the number on the sick roll in Wellington's army.

With over a thousand men now under his command, and too many of them sick, Paul went to Wellington to argue for funds and then to Robert Carlyon to ask for the services of his wife. It was not a conversation he relished, especially after their quarrel, but he knew that he could not speak to Anne before talking to her husband.

"I've taken over the neighbouring farm for billets for the extra men," he said, pouring wine for Carlyon at a table in the headquarters mess. "There's a big open barn that we're going to repair for a regimental hospital. We need to be able to isolate the sick from the wounded. Adam Norris is still a prisoner of the French or I'd ask him to take charge of this, and we're sending for a new regimental doctor and a couple of trainees from England. But Robert, if you would be prepared to let your wife help set this up, it would undoubtedly save lives. I've spoken to Wellington and he'll authorise the money, but I need your permission to speak to her."

"That's a novelty, Major. You don't normally ask what you can do with my wife."

Paul took a deep breath. "That's army gossip, Rob, and you know it. I've a wife who is going to bear me a second child and I'd never do anything to jeopardise that."

"You weren't so careful of her feelings in Naples, I hear, with Davy Cartwright's wife."

"No. But I'm older and wiser now. And you can hardly compare your wife to the Cartwright woman."

"In the mess after a few drinks I believe they do."

Paul grinned in spite of himself. "Well, I hope they're joking for their sakes. Any one of them could probably get into bed with Arabella, but if they tried the same thing with your wife, she'd break their jaw. It's a big step from flirting to adultery and Nan is very clear about that. I hope you realise it."

He realised suddenly that he had inadvertently said the right thing. Carlyon seemed to relax slightly, and Paul pressed his advantage.

"I'm not trying to seduce your wife, I promise. I know I've flirted with her, but I've done that with half the women at headquarters. I just want her help. She's so good at this, Robert. She'll have that maid of hers with her and I'm away a lot anyway. Rowena is here and you know how close they are..."

"I know." Carlyon took a sip of wine. "I'll be away a fair bit myself. Wellington wants me to take over organising the supplies for this building project of his. He's offered me a promotion."

"Congratulations, Rob, you've earned it. You're bloody good at what you do."

"Yes. It hardly carries the same cachet as leading the famous 110th though, does it?"

"No. But if you weren't doing what you are, the famous 110th would be marching barefoot and starving. And I for one appreciate that."

"Speak to her. She'll say yes."

"Thank you, Robert. I really do..."

Carlyon set down his glass and got up. "I'm not doing it for you, Major."

Paul studied him. "No," he said suddenly seeing the truth. "You're doing it for her, aren't you?"

"Make sure you're careful with her reputation."

"I will be," Paul said quietly. For the first time ever, he felt a tug of genuine sympathy for Anne's husband. It had never occurred to him that Carlyon felt anything other than lust for her, but he recognised that Carlyon had agreed to this purely to please her. Paul watched as Carlyon walked away and wondered if Anne had any idea. It was definitely not a conversation he was going to have with her.

Chapter Eighteen

Anne was surprised that Robert agreed so readily to her involvement in setting up the regimental hospital for the 110th. With his promotion, Wellington had allocated her husband a host of new duties with regard to the supplying of materials and labour for his engineering works. Whatever else he was, Anne realised that Robert must be a genuinely talented administrator, and she saw less and less of him. When he was not in endless meetings with suppliers and engineers, he was touring the works or off visiting new sites, and he was often away for weeks at a time. It was a relief to be spared his attentions in her bed and his brooding presence at her side, and Anne threw herself with enthusiasm into her new project.

The 110th took over a deserted farm about a mile and a half from Paul's billet, and with the help of local labourers, Anne supervised the repair of buildings and the preparation of a rough road between the two sites. The losses at Talavera had left Paul short of officers, and he sought and obtained permission to promote Carl Swanson to captain in charge of the light company, moving Johnny over to the fourth. When the new site was ready, Paul split his battalion between the two sites, with the officers remaining in their billets at the Ferriera farm. The fifth and sixth companies were under Captain Elliott and Captain March who were new to the regiment, transferred in after promotion, and both would need time to become accustomed to Paul's way of doing things. In addition, he had six new and very young officers arrived from England, at least three of whom seemed to Paul to spend more time gazing at Anne Carlyon than learning their duties.

The hospital was constructed from an old hay barn at the second site, and Anne supervised the building of stout wooden walls and the construction of rows of rough bunks, raised slightly off the floor to avoid damp. There was a shortage of blankets and medical equipment and still no sign of the new staff that Paul had arranged to be sent out, but Anne managed as best she could with what she had. Paul arrived unexpectedly one afternoon after dealing with a disciplinary matter and found her in the process of extracting shot from the foot of a red faced private from the second company. He was accompanied by a companion, who was showing signs of unseemly mirth. Paul hovered by the door watching. The wounds were not deep, and Anne was quick and confident.

"One more. This is the worst one, so grit your teeth and try not to yell, or you'll give your friend over there something to tell the lads over supper."

The man flinched as the forceps probed and issued a groan. Anne pulled out the final piece of shot and held it up. "That's it. Sit still while I clean that out and bind it up." She regarded his companion severely. "And you can wipe the smile off your face as well, Private. Wait until you end up in here with a shot in your backside because you walked across the line of fire." She looked up and smiled at Paul, and he felt the familiar rush of emotion. "Good afternoon, Major."

Both men turned, surprised, and the one standing, jumped to attention and saluted. Anne prevented the other from rising with a hand firmly on his chest. "I told you to sit still," she said. "What can I do for you, Major? Have you shot yourself in the foot as well?"

"I was just trying to decide if that was a yell or not." Paul said, strolling into the room. "At ease, Private."

"Not nearly as loud as you made when I extracted that ball after Talavera," Anne said. Paul was amused at the avid curiosity on the faces of the two infantrymen.

"My memories of that day are a bit hazy, so I'll take your word for it," he said. More than anything, he wanted to walk forward and take her into his arms, in front of the two goggling soldiers. He restrained himself with an effort.

"Mine too. It was a long day. There, that should do it. It's clean and not deep and it should heal quickly but no running around for a few days. I'll speak to Sergeant Grange about putting you on light duties and I'll look at it in a few days. Take him back to his billet, Private, and give him a tot of rum. Which doesn't mean that you need one as well."

"Yes, ma'am. Thank you, ma'am. Feels much better." The man slid off the board and saluted. Paul nodded.

"Carry on, Private." He waited until the two men reached the door. "Oh, Private?"

The men looked around. "For future reference, the French will be wearing blue coats. Try not to get confused again," Paul said, gently. Red-faced, the man hobbled out. Anne was laughing.

"You're a horrible man. Are you here in need of medical attention?"

"I definitely need something. Probably a large brandy. I'm about to send off another order for supplies and I came by to see if there was anything else you needed."

"No, I think I gave you the list. But isn't that a job for your clerk?"

"It would be, if my clerk were not stretched out in your fever ward sweating like a pig. I hope you don't spend too much time in there, Nan. I worry about you."

"I'm very healthy, Paul. So have you found a new quartermaster? Or even a clerk?"

310

Paul shook his head. "No. Hookey has them all frantically copying letters and drawings for the engineers or writing to London. I can manage."

Anne regarded him thoughtfully. "Let me come and see if I can help," she said unexpectedly. "There's nothing much for me to do here. I've co-opted some of the walking sick to do the basic care on the wards along with the women whom I've employed as nurses."

Paul grinned. "I bet the malingerers pray they don't end up on your wards, bonny lass, you probably work them harder than the army."

"If they do, they recover pretty quickly," Anne agreed. "Although Sergeant Campbell is a fairly permanent fixture. I actually think he likes the work, and he's extremely useful, he'd be wasted on the battlefield."

Paul took her hand and drew it through his arm. "I don't think I can reasonably ask you to act as my clerk as well as my doctor, Nan, especially since I don't pay you for either, but come and look over this list anyway before I send you home."

They strolled across to the former stable block where Paul had set up his office. Anne smiled as she entered. His desk was covered in papers and the long table down one side of the room was strewn with boxes and ledgers. Another pile of ledgers and a file of letters stood on the floor beside his desk.

"How on earth can you work like this? You're worse than my father."

Paul grinned. "Is he an untidy worker? I'm not usually quite this bad but I seem to be stupidly busy, running from this to the training ground, to Hookey's endless meetings, and if I have to sit through another dinner with half a dozen overweight Portuguese grandees, I think I shall lose my temper and shoot a few of them. My wife is no help at all, being too ill with this blighted brat to support me at these ghastly events. I know she plays on it."

"Your wife is a saint, and you don't deserve her," Anne said. "Every other officer in Portugal is complaining about being bored and not having enough to do. You and Robert are the only two who seem rushed off their feet. The penalty of being in Lord Wellington's confidence, I suppose." She had her back to him and was running her eyes down a column of figures. "Is this what you're paying for sheets and blankets, Paul?"

Paul came to stand behind her and slipped his arms about her waist, resting his chin on the top of her head. "Yes. They were the cheapest supplier I could find."

"Well, you were cheated," Anne said bluntly. It was wonderful, finally, to feel his arms about her again. Anne knew that she should protest and move away but she did not. Instead, she stood very still and leaned back against him with a sigh of pleasure as his hand slid up to her breast.

"I'll stop in a moment and we'll talk about blankets and opiates," he said with a laugh against her ear.

"Don't stop. That feels like heaven."

"You feel like heaven," Paul said softly, his hand moving insistently. "And I like the new gown. Eminently practical."

Anne had ordered the gown to make it possible for her to manage without a maid on campaign if necessary. Paul was unbuttoning the bodice and she

311

leaned back and gave herself up to the mindless pleasure of his caresses. Turning her round, he lifted her up so that she was sitting on the high table and kissed her waiting mouth, opening the gown fully.

"Oh Paul, no. We promised ourselves."

"I know, love." His mouth was urgent, and Anne gave up. Pointless to pretend that she had not wanted him to do this. Her body had missed him, had been aching for him.

"I just wish I could do this without feeling so bloody guilty," Paul said suddenly.

"I know, Paul, but you can't. And neither can I."

Paul kissed her for another long moment, and then gave a groan of frustration and stepped back. Anne drew her gown together and fastened it quickly. She slid off the table and Paul took her hand and kissed it very formally.

"All right, girl of my heart, if I can't make love to you, tell me instead what I am doing wrong with my quartermaster's duties."

Anne stood on tiptoe to kiss him gently. "It's called delegation. You need to stop dismissing all your quartermasters. Or throwing them through windows," she said. "You don't have time to do everything, Paul."

"I could find time for a long leisurely afternoon in bed with you," Paul said ruefully.

Anne looked at him severely and turned back to the ledgers. "Do you have to order through these agents? They're using long term army suppliers and they get greedy, they've had these contracts for years. Why don't you let me write to my father? He can supply sheets and blankets at half this cost and will probably help sourcing some of the other items, textiles are his business. And if you think anybody will try to cheat Matthew Howard out of a shilling, you're seriously mistaken. Especially if I ask him."

Paul stood looking at her in considerable surprise. She had moved from melting in his arms to dissecting his regiment's finances in an instant and he found the transformation slightly bewildering and unexpectedly attractive although he had no idea how to deal with it. Gathering his wits he said:

"Will you?"

"Yes. Show me where your clerk had got to with the ordering."

Paul passed her a half-written letter. Anne read it through quickly, snorted, crossed through two mis-spelt words and added some punctuation. Paul watched her, amused. He crossed the room and cleared the smaller table by the simple expedient of scooping the paperwork into a pile and dumping it on the floor.

"Your desk, Mrs Carlyon."

"Thank you. Tomorrow I shall look into your filing system, it leaves a lot to be desired. Pass me that knife. How on earth can anybody work with a pen this bad?"

Anne trimmed the pen quickly and neatly and reached for the ink. Paul watched her for a moment as she began to write in an elegant, legible copperplate hand. After a moment he sat down and reached for one of the ledgers.

They worked steadily through the afternoon. Occasionally Anne asked a question or got up to check something. Her presence was curiously soothing, her concentration making it easier for Paul to stick to his work. When she had finished a letter, she would pass it to him to read and sign. She was quick and accurate, and Paul was amused at this side of her which he had not seen before. Like both he and Robert, she came from a mercantile background and was comfortable around tradesmen and accounts. He wondered what Wellington would think if he realised that in addition to acting as regimental doctor, she was acting as his quartermaster. It occurred to him that if she had been a man she would have been a formidable success in her chosen field. As a woman her opportunities were extremely limited, and it was only the eccentricities of army life that had given her the opportunity to stretch her wings.

Eventually Anne sat back with a sigh and set down her pen. "I think that will have to do for today, it's getting too dark to see properly."

Paul gave a surprised glance at the window. "It is. Christ, I'd no idea it was that time, Nan. I should get you home."

"Don't worry, a solitary supper awaits me, Robert is away again. Although you'll be missed in the mess, Major, if you don't get a move on."

"The mess is right outside this door, my angel, which is why I need to get you out of here fairly soon before people start wondering what we're doing in here in the dark alone. It would be ironic if we start a scandal because of an afternoon of bookkeeping, given some of the other things we've been known to do. Why don't you stay to dine? Rowena would like to see you."

"I'd love to if nobody would mind. It's tedious eating alone."

"Never tell me you're not inundated with invitations, Nan."

"They've dried up a little since it was discovered how much of my time I'm spending with fever patients. Don't look so severe, I don't miss dining with Arabella Cartwright, believe me."

"I doubt she misses you that much either. She doesn't seem fond of you, love."

"I wonder why?" Anne said. "Really, Paul, I was surprised at you with her."

Paul gave a rueful grin. "Not one of my finer moments," he admitted. "I am usually fairly well-behaved with other men's wives. With one other notable exception. And even then, I tried."

"What about Mrs McBride?" Anne asked, carrying a ledger to the shelf and putting it away.

"How on earth did you know about her?"

"Mrs Barry."

"Damn and blast her for an interfering old woman. McBride was thoroughly in his grave before I even met his wife. I helped her with his pension, and I flirted with her a bit. I did not sleep with her, whatever the gossips said, although a number of officers did."

"Including Robert, I believe," Anne said, shelving another ledger.

Paul raised his eyebrows. "I wasn't sure if you knew about that."

"People do like to ensure that a wife knows when her husband strays."

"I'll bear that in mind." Paul hesitated. He was on uncertain ground and was not sure how she would respond. "I know we never talk about this, Nan, but for what it's worth I don't think Robert would go anywhere near another woman now."

Anne turned, a third book in her hands. "I don't care if he does," she said quietly. "I think it would bother me a lot more if I knew you were."

"Oh Nan," Paul said softly. He walked towards her, took the ledger from her hands and placed it on her desk then took her into his arms and kissed her. "Love, how the hell do you think I feel every time he takes you home to his bed?"

"Oh Paul, don't," she whispered. "My dear..."

"Nan, sometimes I lie awake at night and try really hard not to imagine you like this with him. I can't bear the thought of you in his arms and I can't stand the thought of him making you feel the way I make you feel. And given that I make very pleasurable love to my wife, that makes me probably the most selfish bastard in Europe."

Anne wrapped her arms tightly about him and kissed him long and passionately. It was almost completely dark in the room. "It hurts me too," she said. "But I am glad that you have Rowena. And there has never been one single moment when I have felt any of this with him. Now for God's sake get me out of here before your officers come trooping through the door and find us like this."

Anne sat beside Paul at dinner, with Rowena on his other side, and listened to the laughter and comradeship around her. After only a few weeks the new officers of the 110th were beginning to relax into the charmed atmosphere that Paul created. He was an extraordinarily good manager of people, Anne thought, with exactly the right mixture of banter and discipline and it seemed to come easily to him. On her other side Captain March asked her friendly questions about her work in the hospital and Robert's absence, and flirted with her a little. She responded readily, aware of Paul's amused appreciation.

When the meal was over, Rowena excused herself and Anne accompanied her upstairs and settled her into bed. Already there were visible signs of her pregnancy. Anne wondered as she walked back down the stairs, how it must feel to know that a new life was growing within. In her two years of marriage with Robert she had never shown any signs of conceiving. It did not seem to bother him and Anne suspected he would hate to share her attention and her body with a demanding baby. For months it had troubled Anne and she felt an immense sadness that she might never know how it felt to hold her own child, but she suspected that given the difficulties of her relationship with Robert, it might well be for the best.

"I'll walk you home," Paul said. He spoke a few words to his officers, and then fetched her shawl and set out beside her through the quiet streets of

Viseu. They spoke little during the walk. Finally, two streets from her billet he said:

"Thank you for your help today, Nan. I feel as though all you do is help me, and all I do is cause you pain."

"You also bring me great joy, Paul."

Paul drew her quickly into the shadows beside an arched porch and kissed her. "You are my joy," he said softly. "I know I shouldn't be glad about what you told me earlier, but how can I help it? It's harder for you, love, because in addition to caring about me I know you care about Rowena."

"I do. But that doesn't stop me wanting to be where she is," Anne said, and she knew that he had heard the pain in her voice.

"Oh, love..."

"I'm sorry. Sometimes I just need to say it, I've given up trying to pretend that this is ever going to go away." Anne looked up at him. "Do you mind if I ask you something very personal, Paul?"

"Anything."

Anne smiled. "You used to be a lot more cautious than that."

"Like you, I've given up."

"Are you still...do you still have other women?"

Paul was silent for a long moment. "Apart from you, girl of my heart? No. Since I met you, I believe the only woman I have made love to, is my wife. And you, to some degree. It hasn't been a conscious decision. I can't decide if it is simply that I've grown up, or if it would just complicate my life more than I could stand. I look, I can't imagine a time when I won't. But every lass that I look at now has to stand comparison with you, and no matter how pretty she is, she can't give me what you can, even though you're not mine. The maddest thing about this whole situation is that since I met you, I'm actually happier with Rowena than I used to be. Somehow, I see her through your eyes, and going to bed with some girl I barely know for a few hours pleasure doesn't have the appeal it used to." Paul laughed softly. "And although you've no more rights over me than I have over you, I've a strong suspicion that if you came across me kissing Arabella Cartwright on the terrace you wouldn't be as restrained as I was."

"Oh Paul, don't. I am so..."

"Love, it's all right. I was an arsehole that evening, and if he gave you comfort, you're welcome to it, although I'm entertained to see how quickly he took advantage of it. I'm only glad it was me and not your bloody husband who saw it."

"So am I. I should go in. I'll be up at the hospital in the morning, but I'm free in the afternoon if you want..."

"Best not ask me what I want to do with you, love. But if you're offering your help to sort out that bloody mess in my office, the answer is yes."

"I'll be there, Major. Good night."

***

Throughout the winter and spring of 1810 Wellington remained steadfastly within Portugal and worked with frantic speed on the lines of Torres Vedras. His army rested and recovered and trained and the French prowled backwards and forwards over the Spanish border like some restless giant cat batting at the English mouse.

There were increasing numbers of lightning attacks and skirmishes. None of them reached as far as the ever-expanding defence works, but in the north of Portugal there was an uneasy sense that Massena was on his way. Increasingly Paul found himself summoned to deal with incursions by French troops. His battalion was being used as it had been in India as a fast and mobile unit, which could move up and down the lines at speed with very little notice. Out on the border General Craufurd was in action with increasing regularity as well, and Paul had regular contact with the irascible commander of the light division. He worked well with Craufurd, who was disliked by many of his officers and adored by most of his men.

Robert Carlyon returned to his wife for several weeks during the early spring and Anne reluctantly curtailed her visits to the 110th. Paul had installed the new, young regimental doctor, Oliver Daniels, and two nervous and inexperienced hospital mates, which gave Anne more free time. Dr Daniels initially baulked at the idea of taking instructions from an unqualified female and Anne needed to call in Paul to speak to him, but he appeared to be settling well and learning his trade as increasing skirmishes brought in casualties. His working relationship with Anne improved steadily.

With the hospital and barracks well stocked from Anne's efforts, Paul grudgingly employed a new quartermaster and assistant, and Anne spent several afternoons taking Lieutenant Breakspear and Sergeant Fallon through the system she had helped to set up. Breakspear seemed willing and competent and faintly bewildered at Anne's involvement although he was far too polite to say so.

Robert asked nothing about Anne's activities in his absence and told her little of his. He continued to work long hours and when he arrived back at their billet, he would often speak no more than a few words to her until she was in his arms. She slept little during those nights, lying awake long after he had drifted into an exhausted slumber.

With Paul away so much and the hospital running smoothly with minimal supervision, Anne spent as much time as she could with Rowena van Daan who was suffering badly through her second pregnancy. She was tearful and exhausted and easily upset. It did not help that Paul was seldom at home and when he was, he was tired and in need of a bath and food and sleep with little energy to comfort his wife. Anne watched him with some sympathy as he tried hard to be patient. During one of Robert's brief absences, she had dinner with the 110th, listening to the officers talking about their recent encounters with the French. Abruptly Rowena got up and left the table. She was crying when Anne went to find her, and there seemed to be nothing Anne could do for her friend other than sit and hold her.

Eventually Rowena fell into a deep exhausted sleep and Anne got up stiffly and went down the stairs. She found that the company had broken up and Paul was waiting to take her home.

"I'll go to her when I get back," he said, as they walked through the quiet streets.

"Was she like this last time?" Anne asked.

Paul nodded ruefully. "Yes. Naples was chaos, we were shunted from place to place and she ended up giving birth on board ship, which was horrendous. I'd hoped that was just because it was her first baby and everything was so new, but I suspect Rowena just doesn't do well with pregnancy. I feel so sorry for her." He glanced sideways at Anne. "And at times so bloody exasperated with her."

"You're doing very well," Anne said. "I could have screamed at her myself this evening. But it must be hard, feeling so unsettled. When do you think we're going to have to retreat?"

Paul looked at her. "I observe you say when, and not if. Yes, Massena is coming, and he'll probably overrun Viseu and then try to take Lisbon. That isn't going to happen, but once we're in the thick of the fighting I can't keep Rowena here. I think perhaps she should go sooner rather than later."

"She might be better in the villa. If she needs to go, I'll go with her."

Paul looked at her steadily. "Nan, it isn't your job to make my life easier," he said quietly.

Anne shot him a mischievous glance. "I thought it was my job to make your life harder," she said. Paul gave a shout of laughter, put his arm about her and pulled her close.

"When you look at me like that, love, it definitely has that effect," he said.

They walked on in silence for a few minutes. Then he said quietly:

"Sometimes when I can't sleep, I lie there and think about you, and I try to imagine what it would be like just to have the right to be with you, without worrying about other people all the time. Just to be able to hold you and kiss you and touch you..."

Anne felt tears stinging her eyes and realised she was not going to be able to stop them falling. She bent her head, but Paul had already seen them.

"Oh Nan, love, I've upset you. I'm sorry."

Paul stopped and drew her into his arms and Anne buried her face against him. It felt so good. "Only because it's my dream too," she whispered. "But keep having it, Paul. Somehow it makes me feel better knowing that is what you would want."

"You know what I want, girl of my heart. Is Robert all right? He barely speaks to me these days, and I worry for you."

"No, it's fine. He is..." Anne shook her head, unable to find the words.

"I know what he is, bonny lass," Paul said. "His obsession with you is visible for the entire army to see. But I'm grateful that you keep the details to yourself, I don't think I could bear to hear just how much of your time you spend in his arms."

317

"I don't think I could bear to tell you," Anne said, beginning to walk on. Paul slipped his arm about her and they walked linked together.

"I got the better part of this bargain, didn't I, love?"

"I don't know, Paul. Given your imagination, you might as well be in the room with us and that can't be much fun."

Paul began to laugh, and after a moment Anne joined him, shaking her head. "I'm sorry, that sounded terrible, didn't it?"

They laughed less and less in the coming weeks, as French attacks kept Paul increasingly busy. He returned at the beginning of July looking tired and low with a bandage around his arm and having lost half a dozen men of his third company.

"I made a mistake," he told Anne over dinner that evening. "Almost got half my bloody battalion killed."

"What happened?"

"I made an assumption. We've dealt with so many of these raiding parties, I thought it was just one more, but it wasn't. They came in force and they had cavalry. I lost six men and it could have been a lot worse." Paul shook his head. "I'm furious with myself, I should have known better."

"You're not perfect, Paul."

"No. It's probably good for me to remember that, although tough on those lads. You should have heard Craufurd on the subject. In fact, I'm surprised you didn't hear him from here."

Anne studied him sympathetically. He was supremely indifferent to the opinions of most of the senior officers of Wellington's army, secure in his belief that he knew what was best for his regiment, but Craufurd's opinion mattered to him and she was aware that he must have loathed being given a dressing down, especially when his mistake had cost men their lives. "How did you get out of it?"

He grinned. "Sheer bloody-mindedness. In the end they got more of a shock than we did. But we were lucky. And we picked up information. Ney is at Ciudad Rodrigo. He's going to take it and then Massena will come."

Anne understood. "Robert is away at the moment," she said. "Do we need to leave immediately?"

"We're not in immediate danger here, but Rowena isn't well. She has another six weeks to go, we think, and I'd like her to be in Lisbon for the birth if she can. Certainly, I don't want her to leave it much longer in case we need to retreat faster than I'm expecting, these things are bloody unpredictable. We've a carriage we can borrow, and I can send an escort. I thought Michael O'Reilly could lead them." Paul gave Anne a steady look. "You don't have to do this, Nan."

"I offered, Paul. Does she want me to?"

"Yes, she's always better when you're around." Paul gave an ironic laugh. "Aren't we all? I'm going to talk to her this evening."

"I can leave a letter for Robert. He can follow me, or wait for me to come back, depending on the military situation. Don't worry, Paul, I'll take care of her."

"I know you will. Nan, thank you. If you don't make it back here before the invasion, I'll make sure your hospital is properly packed up and evacuated." Tiredly, Paul shook his head. "I wish he'd bloody come," he said shortly. "I'm sick of these skirmishes."

"You'll be better when you don't have Rowena to worry about," Anne said. "Paul, I'm going to leave Teresa here to pack everything up for me and to help with the hospital if need be. Can you…"

"Of course. I'll make sure she's taken care of. Like you, she's become part of the regiment. Can Carl take you home tonight?"

"Of course. I'll even engage not to kiss him in the moonlight."

"Thank you, I'd appreciate it. I have enough trouble keeping my bloody commander-in-chief's hands off you."

"My life is complicated enough, Paul."

"You have my sympathy. It's all right, I trust Carl with you."

***

Anne was aware that she had glossed over the issue of her husband's feelings about her going to Lisbon without him. She knew that Robert would be furious, and had he not been away, he probably would have refused to allow her to go. Anne's memories of the beating he had inflicted after Talavera were recent and painful, but she was concerned enough about Rowena to be willing to take the chance, and she was hoping that Robert would be reassured by the fact that Paul was not travelling with them.

The escort consisted of Sergeant-Major O'Reilly and six men of the light company, including Private Carter of the rifles. Paul had borrowed the carriage from the wife of one of his fellow officers. After so many months of being on foot or on horseback it felt strange to Anne to be seated beside Rowena against the padded seat of the carriage. It would take them five days or so to reach Lisbon, and Paul had worked with O'Reilly to map out a route of suitable overnight stops.

They spent the first night at a convent, on hard clean beds within the cool stone walls. Anne lay awake listening to her friend toss restlessly from side to side and prayed that once they were in Lisbon the baby would come quickly. Anne had regretted her own childlessness many times, but she was beginning to realise that there were advantages.

There was a small clean inn on their second night, with the men sleeping in the tap room below to guard the two women. Rowena slept better but Anne could not sleep, and lay thinking about Robert. She had taken pains over the letter she left for him, but Anne did not delude herself that he would take it well. She had undertaken the journey for Rowena's sake and also for Paul's, but the price was likely to be a beating, and Anne dreaded it.

They set off early the following morning, and already Anne was tired of the bouncing of the carriage over the deeply rutted roads. Next to her, Rowena was quiet and pale, and Anne wondered if she was feeling sick. They had brought food with them from the inn, but Rowena could eat nothing, although when they stopped at midday for a break and to water the horses, she drank from the stream and then sat in weary exhaustion on the bank.

The pains began almost as soon as they set off again. To begin with Anne thought that Rowena was simply feeling sick, but after a while, she realised it was more than that. She sat holding the other girl's hand in anxious silence for a long time. Eventually she said:

"Rowena, are you quite well?"

Her friend looked at her and shook her head. "I think the child is coming," she said, and there was an edge of panic in her voice. "Nan, what am I going to do, we're miles from anywhere."

Anne clamped down hard on her own anxiety. Despite her extensive experience of battle injuries and fever she had no experience of managing childbirth. Still, it was not Rowena's first baby and they would probably be able to find some help in one of the villages.

"Don't worry, love. We'll find somewhere to stop, and we'll get you some help. How typical of Paul's child to turn up at an awkward moment. Weren't you on a ship last time?"

Rowena nodded with an attempt at a smile. Anne's cheerful tone seemed to have calmed her a little.

Anne leaned out of the carriage door and shouted ahead to Michael who walked back immediately. "What is it, girl dear?"

"Michael, Rowena is in labour," Anne said quietly, glancing back at the other girl.

"Oh Lord!" Michael looked over at the other men. "All right, ma'am, we'll stop at the next village, see if we can find a woman to help. We should probably send a message back to the major, we're closer to Viseu than Lisbon still, I suspect he'll want her back there for a bit to recover." Michael leaned into the carriage and smiled reassuringly at his commander's wife. "Don't worry, ma'am, we'll get you settled as soon as we can."

It took half an hour to reach the village, a mere hamlet with a straggle of stone houses and one large farm. Rowena was quiet, lying back with her eyes closed, breathing hard every time a pain struck her. Anne held her hand, talking soothingly to her. She felt very helpless but there was nothing she could do for her friend.

It had begun to rain, a steady drizzle. The lumbering carriage drove slowly into the empty farmyard and Anne looked out. Michael was staring around.

"It's very quiet, I'm wondering if they've already packed up and gone towards Lisbon. Lord Wellington has sent out messages telling the locals to head south, he's going to scorch this area to make sure...."

There was a sudden flurry of sound. Horses hooves thundered on the packed earth and a shot rang out. One of Paul's men fell to the ground and the others were swinging around, reaching for weapons.

"Jesus Christ, it's a French cavalry patrol! Carter, get the women into that barn and guard them."

Anne scrambled down from the carriage, and Private Carter reached past her and scooped Rowena into his arms, running with her to the big barn.

320

Outside another shot rang out and a man screamed. Carter put Rowena down onto a pile of hay and began to load his rifle. "Stay here!" he ordered and ran towards the door.

Anne held on to Rowena's hand and listened. There was a confusion of shots and yells, the sounds of horses and the clash of steel. She could hear the clear tones of Michael's voice giving orders and then a myriad of shouts in both French and English and more shots. Finally, there was silence, and she could hear nothing more than the sound of hooves and the whinny of excited horses.

"Nan, what is happening?" Rowena said. Her voice was a whimper of terror.

"French cavalry, I think. They must be scouting further south and have moved beyond our lines. God knows we're strung out far enough up here." Anne glanced at her. "Stay still, Rowena. No point in trying to get up." She was trying desperately to remain calm although she could feel terror bubbling just below the surface. She was worried about Michael. If he were alive and unhurt, he would have run back to them.

Rowena pushed herself up onto one elbow. "Nan, you should run," she said. "Hide."

Anne looked sharply at her. "I'm not leaving you, Rowena."

"Listen to me." Rowena's voice was suddenly very calm. "I can't run. I can't even walk. Whatever they decide to do to me is going to happen. But you can get away. Please."

"Rowena, I'm not leaving you."

"Nan, for God's sake!" There was quiet desperation in Rowena's voice. "I don't want him to lose both of us. I can't get away, but you could."

Anne froze, staring down at her. There was no time to say any of the things she wanted to. She dropped to her knees and took Rowena's hand.

"Rowena, I am not leaving you, and if any one of them lays a hand on you, I swear to God I'll kill him. Not for Paul's sake, but for yours."

The other girl gave a wan smile and squeezed her hand. "I'm glad you came to Portugal," she said.

There was the sound of another shot, loud, from outside the barn and then Private Carter reappeared. He came towards them and Anne read the truth in his eyes and knew that his comrades were dead. He seemed completely calm as he reloaded his rifle then positioned himself between the two women and the barn door which was being pushed open.

"Stay behind me, ma'am," he said quietly, and Anne got up.

"Carter, no. Put it down, you can't fight them on your own."

Carter glanced at her and then back at the door and Anne saw, with a flood of relief, Michael O'Reilly backing into the barn, his hands raised. A French officer and two cavalrymen were moving towards him, and then a third followed. The officer looked over at Carter and the two women and raised his pistol.

"Put that down or I will kill your sergeant," he said in heavily accented English.

Carter paused. Anne held her breath, praying that he would not do anything rash. Finally, reluctantly, he put the rifle on the ground. The French officer waved Michael further into the barn.

"Over by that wall, both of you," he said. "Your men are dead, and no help is coming, so do not be stupid. I was wondering what an infantry patrol was doing here, but now I see. Escort duty."

"Well, you're an awful long way from the French lines yourself now, wouldn't you say, sir?" O'Reilly said, moving to stand against the wall beside Carter. His dark eyes were on Anne and Rowena. "I'm guessing you want to get back and we're no threat to you. Let the ladies go."

The French officer turned his eyes towards Anne and Rowena. "Come over here."

Anne moved forward. "My friend cannot get up," she said. "Childbirth. It is why we stopped, Captain."

The officer studied her for a long moment, his eyes moving over her in a way that made Anne feel distinctly uncomfortable. "And you are?"

"My name is Anne Carlyon, and this is Mrs van Daan. We are the wives of English officers. We're no danger to you, Captain, and neither are these men."

A fifth cavalryman came into the barn and saluted. "All dead but one, Captain Marchand, and he won't last. Chest wound."

Anne felt herself flinch but neither Carter nor Michael displayed even a flicker of emotion. Anne knew that Rowena spoke no French and it occurred to her that she was probably the only one of her party who understood what was being said. For a moment she considered speaking to Marchand in his own language, but something kept her silent. She did not trust this man.

Marchand was still studying Anne. "The villagers?"

"Dead, sir."

Anne forced herself not to react, thanking God that she had not spoken.

"Search the men, make sure they're not armed," Marchand said, in French. As the man moved to do so, Rowena made a sound. Anne ran to her side and knelt, taking her hand and smoothing the fair tangled hair back from her face as the pain built steadily.

"All right, love, just breathe. It will be all right."

Marchand walked over and stood staring down at Rowena for a moment.

"Captain, we need help," Anne said in English. "A midwife. Perhaps in the village…"

She had said it deliberately, wondering if he would admit to his massacre of the villagers but he simply shook his head.

"No midwife."

"She could die." Anne said angrily.

"Then she will die."

Anne stood up. "I expected better of a French officer."

Marchand looked her over "Madame, you should lower your expectations," he said, and Anne felt a lurch of fear at the expression in his eyes. She could remember Paul's anxiety for her safety during the retreat

322

from Talavera, his absolute conviction that she should not be allowed to fall into French hands, and she understood now why he had been afraid for her. She took a deep breath and met the Frenchman's eyes.

"We're the wives of officers, sir. I..."

"You think I give a damn who your husband is?" Marchand said flatly. "I've just watched my men enjoying themselves with half a dozen peasant women, but I am more choosy than that, Madame."

"No," Carter said furiously. "Keep your hands off her, you French bastard."

Marchand glanced over at the two men. "Kill him," he said, and one of the cavalrymen drew his sword. Anne moved fast, sick with horror, and got between Carter and the Frenchman.

"No!" she said and met Marchand's eyes. "No. Don't kill them."

Marchand studied her for a moment and then laughed. "Leave him," he said in French. "I am taking her into the farmhouse. When I've gone you can kill all of them but do it quietly. I'm curious to know just what she'll do if she thinks I'll spare them. When I've done with her, you can have her."

He moved forward to where Anne stood in front of Carter. "What will you do to save their lives?" he asked in English.

Anne met his gaze steadily. "Whatever you like," she said, and Carter swore.

"Ma'am, you do not do that to save me, not with this scum!"

"He's right, girl dear," Michael said softly. "Don't."

Anne looked at Marchand for a long silent moment. "Will you spare them?" she asked.

"I will if you make it worth my while. We're away in the morning back to Marshal Massena with intelligence. I can leave you here, no need for anybody else to die."

Anne nodded. She turned towards Michael and saw the fury in his eyes. "Lass, he'd kill me if I let you do this," he said.

"I'll be all right, Michael," Anne said softly, taking his hands. Her body was between him and Marchand. "You're not going to die here today."

She slid the knife from the sheath on her wrist and into his hand. "He's going to kill you all," she mouthed soundlessly.

Understanding dawned in the intelligent dark eyes. "Girl dear, there is nothing more you can do that will surprise me," Michael said softly.

Marchand reached for Anne's arm and Anne stepped to one side. Michael sprang forward onto the officer, faster than Anne had ever seen a man move, and the Frenchman died on a high scream with her blade buried in his throat. Blood spurted as the Irishman spun around and launched himself onto the first of the troopers. Carter leaped after him, did a forward roll and caught a second trooper around the legs, bringing him down. Anne ran over towards Rowena who lay sobbing in agony in the hay. She wanted to be out of the fight so that she did not get in the way of the two light company men. O'Reilly had taken down his third man and then Carter had dived for the pile of weapons. He stood up with a rifle in his hand, and Anne realised with

323

relief that they had not thought to take his shot belt. He loaded quickly and fired at the door of the barn where two dragoons were running towards the source of the noise. One fell dead. The other continued to run, jumping over his comrade, and Carter reloaded at speed and shot him at point blank range. He was reloading again, his eyes on the door.

Anne took Rowena's cold hand in hers. She had no idea how many dragoons there were outside. Carter took a quick glance over his shoulder.

"Sarge, get up to the hayloft, grab a rifle, it's the only other way in. Ma'am, stay where you are and keep low, you don't want to get hit by a stray shot."

He fired again and there was a cry of agony, and O'Reilly picked up a rifle from the pile, scooped up the sword of one of the fallen dragoons and scrambled up to the loft. Anne had seen the ladder going up into the loft from outside the barn and she heard yells from above and another shot as the Irishman dealt with a dragoon trying to come into the barn that way.

Rowena groaned as another pain came. They seemed to be coming more quickly and Anne cursed her lack of experience. Behind her she heard another shot and then Carter swore. Anne spun around. He was struggling with the rifle and she realised it had jammed. Two more dragoons were moving towards him and Carter took the rifle by the butt and swung it like a club.

Anne dived forward to the body of one of the dragoons and picked up his fallen sword. "Carter!" she yelled and slid the sword towards him across the floor. The rifleman dropped to the ground and reached for it then he was on his feet, advancing menacingly on the last dragoon.

Anne heard, then, noises from outside, a sudden furious volley of shots, the sounds of shouting, of men running and screams from the dying Frenchmen. Shockingly, in the still quiet of the evening, a voice cut through the sound of rifle fire and squealing horses and groaning men.

"Cooper, Dawson, six men and round the back. If it's French, shoot it, they've massacred our lads, we are not taking prisoners. I'm going in to look for the women."

Rowena's hand tightened on Anne's. "Nan," she whispered. "Was that...?"

"It's Paul." Anne could not believe it, but his voice was unmistakable. She leaned over and kissed Rowena. "We're safe, love. Stay there."

She stood up. "Paul, we're in here. Just us and Carter, Michael is in the loft."

Carter was clutching his arm, and blood was spurting bright red but the last two dragoons lay dead. Anne ran over to him. "Let me see," she ordered, and he obeyed. It was a deep cut and bleeding heavily. Anne spun around looking for a makeshift bandage.

"Here."

Anne took the length of silk, a sash from one of the dead dragoons and wound it tightly around Carter's arm. "Hold it hard, it will stop the bleeding faster."

"Are you all right, ma'am?"

Anne looked up at him. "Yes. Carter…"

"I can't believe you just did what you did, ma'am, that was the bravest thing I've ever seen, he might have gutted you on the spot."

"He wasn't going to do that straight away," Anne said and heard her voice break part way through the sentence as the reality of what had almost happened hit her.

"No, ma'am, I know bloody well what he was intending to do straight away!" Carter looked past her and Anne turned and realised that it had been Paul who had handed her the sash. Carter saluted.

"Very good to see you, sir. I was just telling Mrs Carlyon here that it's not her job to put her body between me and a French blade."

The blue eyes were surveying Anne. More than anything else she wanted to walk into his arms, but she was painfully conscious of Rowena lying in the straw. "Paul…"

"Is that what she did?" Paul asked softly.

"She did." Michael O'Reilly was coming forward. "Christ, Paul, I don't know how you came to be here but it's bloody good to see you."

"It's a long story. Are you all right, Nan?"

"Yes. Come and see Rowena, she's in labour."

"Is that why you stopped?" Paul took Anne's hand and raised it to his lips. "Thank you," he said quietly.

He went to where his wife lay and knelt. Rowena opened her eyes.

"Paul. How did you know?"

Paul reached for her hand and kissed it, then bent to kiss her white exhausted face. "I didn't know about the baby, love," he said softly. "But I knew you might be in trouble. Wellington called me in about twenty-four hours after you left, to tell me that there was a French scouting party, about fifteen light cavalry, probing the lines, taking information back to Massena. They encountered two small groups of our men. The first was a dozen KGL on their way to join Craufurd. The second was a group of the second division escorting one of Fletcher's engineers up to meet with Wellington. Only one of the KGL made it back, all the rest were slaughtered."

"Oh God, Paul."

"Wellington knew I'd sent you off. There was no way we could have expected this, a scouting party would normally have kept well out of the way of our patrols, but this bastard was on some kind of personal mission to slaughter our men. We set off within the hour, marching quick time with very few breaks. We almost didn't make it."

"Thank God you did," Anne said quietly.

"Always good to see you, sir, but especially so today," Michael said.

Paul was smoothing the fair hair back from Rowena's face. "A bit late for those poor lads outside, but you're very hard to kill, Michael."

"We'd all be dead if it weren't for Mrs Carlyon," Michael said quietly. "I'm not going to ask who taught her to carry a blade up her sleeve."

Paul looked up sharply and then met Anne's eyes across Rowena's body. "Clearly, I was wrong when I said you couldn't hold off a French scouting party with it, lass. All right Rowena, take my hand. Come on, sweetheart, we've done this before."

"Sir – Davison is still alive. Bad chest wound, though."

Anne got to her feet. "I thought they'd killed him," she said. "That's what Marchand said. He told his men to kill the three of you and..." She glanced down at Rowena without speaking and saw Paul's eyes harden. "I thought he'd done it."

"Bring him through, Cooper, it's warmer in here. Nan, can you see to him? Michael...."

"Paul, stop."

Anne turned to see Carl coming into the barn, his eyes on Paul's anxious face. He looked around, assessing the situation then looked back at Paul.

"It's under control," he said firmly. "We'll get the bodies out and find space for our men. I'll send some of them to the local villages in search of a midwife and a wet nurse. I've set sentries and I'll send a message back to Wellington. Everything else can wait. Be a husband for a while."

Paul looked down at his wife for a long moment then up again at Carl and Anne. "Thank you," he said. "You have command, Carl. I need to be with her."

***

Paul settled down into the hay beside his wife. She was very pale, her eyes enormous, and as Paul took her hand again, he felt her squeeze it. Paul studied her, his heart too full to speak for a moment. He was trying not to imagine what might have happened to her if Anne Carlyon had not been so quick-witted, or if Michael and Carter had not been such good soldiers. Most French officers would have respected the wives of their English counterparts, but there were always exceptions, and Paul could not blot out the vision of coming into the barn to find his wife and unborn child dead in the hay.

"Paul. I'm so glad you're here."

"So am I, love. I wish we could get you back to Viseu, but this child isn't going to wait for that," Paul said, smoothing the fair tangled hair back from her face. "It's all right, I'll be with you."

"Sir."

Paul glanced up. Private Carter was holding out a bottle. "French brandy, sir. Found it in the bastard's pack – begging your pardon, ma'am. Thought it might help your wife."

He passed the bottle to Paul who took it and lifted his wife slightly so that she could drink. "Try this, Rowena, it might help with the pain a little. Thank you, Carter."

Rowena drank and rested briefly, but the pains were coming more quickly now. In the background, Paul was vaguely aware of Carl taking charge, setting guards and dealing with the bodies of the French dragoons. After a while Anne returned from tending to Private Davison. He looked a question at her and she shrugged.

"I don't know, Paul. I think it's nicked the lung, but he's alive. We'll have to wait and see." Anne took her friend's hand. "I'm cross with your wife, by the way. She tried to persuade me to run and hide when the French attacked."

Paul looked sharply at her and then down at his wife and saw that Rowena was trying to smile. "You didn't listen," she whispered. "You're like Paul, you never do."

Anne lifted Rowena's hand and kissed it. "Poor Rowena. Two of us. All right, love, try and relax as much as you can. We're both here now and you're safe. You just need to concentrate on yourself and this baby."

Rowena gave a wan smile. "It is hard to do anything else at the moment," she said with a gallant attempt at humour and then her hand tightened on Anne's. "Oh. Oh dear God...."

Anne looked up into Paul's eyes. He gave her a reassuring smile and then looked down at his wife. Her whole body had tensed with agony and he reached out and smoothed the fair hair very tenderly. "Hold on to me, lass," he said softly. "I'm stronger than Nan. Now then, here we go..."

Chapter Nineteen

It was one of the longest nights of Paul's life.

He had seen death and injury on the battlefield so often and had learned to detach himself to some degree, but it was impossible to remain detached from Rowena's pain as she fought to give birth to his child. Paul had been with her the last time, as she laboured to give birth to Francis, and he could remember his horror in the small, dark cabin, remember the sheer frustration of being unable to ease her pain or speed it along. He could not tell if this was better or worse, but he felt the same sense of helplessness as he held her hand and watched her beloved face, twisted in agony.

The hours crawled by, and as full darkness came the pains came faster. With the dead and wounded dealt with, the light company lit cooking fires out in the yard and Carl appeared at the door of the barn and called softly to Paul who got up and went to join him. Private Carter was with him holding an armful of pillows and blankets.

"These are from the farmhouse, Paul," Carl said softly. "I'd suggest we move her there, but it's a mess, they killed the whole family."

"Thank you, Carl. Take them over to Mrs Carlyon, will you, Carter? I don't think we should try to move Rowena anyway, but those might help." Paul returned to Rowena and settled more comfortably on the pillows, tucking the blankets around her. Opposite him, Anne was holding his wife's hand and talking to her. Paul remembered her voice, talking to him through the agony of having the shot removed at Talavera, and recognised the soothing tones which had steadied him at the point when he had believed he was going to die. It seemed to help Rowena. She focused on Anne when each wave of pain hit her, and Anne talked her through it in steady tones.

The night wore on endlessly. After twelve hours it no longer seemed possible that the baby could be delivered alive and Rowena was growing weaker, fading before his eyes. Paul had never felt so helpless. In the face of her suffering and her courage, the battles he had fought seemed like noisy posturing. He sat beside her, talking quietly, trying to distract her from the pain with their shared memories.

During the long months of her pregnancy, Paul had refused to allow himself to think about the birth and how it might go. She had survived before, but he knew how many women did not, even in the best circumstances, and these were far from ideal. Rowena had gone into labour early, thrown about on appalling roads in a carriage, then had experienced the terror of near-death, and was having to give birth in a draughty barn on a pile of straw. Paul wanted warmth and comfort and cleanliness for her, along with the services of a midwife and a good doctor. He hated himself for bringing her here and putting her through this. The reality was that Rowena might die, and Paul was not sure that he could bear it.

"Are you all right?"

Paul looked up, startled, into Anne Carlyon's dark eyes and wondered how she knew. "Panicking a bit," he said very softly, under cover of a long groan of pain from Rowena.

"I know. Get up, stretch your legs and walk around for a minute. I'm not an expert, but I've a feeling it won't be long."

Paul nodded and rose stiffly, moved away and stretched his cramped limbs. A figure rose from by the door and he realised that Carl was there. Paul went to join him and Carl passed him a bottle.

"How's she doing?"

Paul drank the brandy gratefully. "Not good," he said. "Carl, I'm terrified. What if…"

"Don't, Paul. Don't do this to yourself. She made it last time."

"I know. But she didn't find it easy. I feel like such a selfish bastard. She shouldn't be here, she shouldn't have had to go through what she went through today. Other men leave their wives at home in safety."

"Other men's wives don't want to be with them, Paul. Rowena chose to come with you, she always wanted to be with you. And this should have been safe."

"Paul!"

Paul turned quickly at Anne's tone and ran back to drop to his knees beside his wife. Rowena clutched at his hand. "Paul, I think it's coming."

"Finally," Paul breathed. "All right, love, hold on to me. Come on, you can do this."

Rowena bore down, pushing with all that was left of her feeble strength and Paul held her, wishing fruitlessly that he could fight this battle for her. He had spent their life together trying to shield her from harm and he thought now how stupid it was when women were strong enough to endure this. Glancing across at Anne he saw her bending, reaching, her voice strong and confident although he was very sure this was her first experience of delivering a child, and he felt passionately grateful to her.

"All right, Rowena, that's the head. One more now…"

Anne eased the child out and reached for her instruments, cut and tied the cord. Paul looked at her and saw the expression on her face. For a moment he thought the baby was dead but as Anne lifted it clear he heard a feeble wail.

"It's a girl," Anne said, and his wife smiled tiredly. Then he saw her eyes widen slightly and he looked down and his stomach lurched at the spreading stain in the straw beneath her.

"Rowena…"

His wife looked at him and Paul realised with horror that she understood. Turning her head, she said:

"Nan, let me hold her."

Anne was wrapping the tiny child in a thin blanket. "All right, love," she said, and Paul was amazed at how calm she sounded. The blood was flowing too fast and there was too much of it. "Here she is. Hold her while I put some pillows under you, it might help…"

"It's not going to help, Nan," his wife said, and Paul looked at her. She met his eyes steadily, and he realised she had lost all colour from her face. Her lips had a bluish tinge.

"Rowena, no."

"You've both seen people die," his wife said, and Paul was appalled at how calm she sounded. "I might not have long and I need to say things…"

Rowena bent her head and kissed her daughter. "She's lovely." She looked up and met Anne's dark eyes which were swimming with tears.

"Look after them for me, Nan."

The tears were streaming down Anne's face. "You know that I will," she said, and Paul blessed her silently for her refusal to pretend. "But I have no idea how I am going to manage any of this without you."

Rowena smiled weakly. "You will. I've seen how well you manage." She glanced at Paul, and then squeezed his hand and looked back at Anne. "He loves you," she said, and Paul wondered how he had ever imagined that she did not know.

Anne met the fading eyes steadily. "I know," she said quietly. "But Rowena – he loves you as well."

Rowena smiled faintly. "I know," she said.

Anne bent and kissed her then got up stiffly and stepped back. Her hours of kneeling beside Rowena had cramped her whole body and she stumbled and might have fallen had Carl not been waiting to steady her. It was quiet in the barn now. Anne took the baby from Rowena's arms and moved away from them, to give Paul time to say all that he wanted to, and Paul thought despairingly that he could never have enough time. Forever would have been too short. He shifted to take Rowena into his arms.

"You'll get covered in blood."

"You think I care? Oh love…"

"I love you, Paul."

"I know. And you know, don't you, how much I love you too? My beautiful, serene swan, what in God's name am I going to do without you to keep me steady?"

She gave a weak laugh. "I'd forgotten you used to call me that."

"I've called you a lot of things, but I've never managed to tell you how much you mean to me, Rowena. I've no idea how I'll go on without you." Paul was crying, and made no attempt to hide it, she deserved his tears.

330

"You'll be a general one day, Paul, and our children will be proud of you," Rowena said tenderly. "Just remember to be happy as well, won't you?"

"That might take a while."

"Don't let it." Rowena sounded weaker. Paul could not believe how much blood soaked the ground beneath her. "You once told me you thought you'd make a devil of a husband."

"I did, love. The day I asked you to marry me."

"You were wrong, Paul. You were a very good husband."

"Not always, Rowena."

"Nobody is, always. Those things didn't matter. I've been so lucky, Paul, I've never regretted a moment."

"Nor have I."

Her eyes met his. "Not even in Yorkshire?"

"That didn't change how I felt about you, Rowena."

"I believe you. I'm glad you met her, she's been my friend. But Paul...take care of her."

"Oh, love..."

"No, listen!" Rowena whispered urgently. "Things are not right, with her and Robert. I've known it for a while, but she won't tell me. Talk to Teresa, she knows. There's something very wrong, and I'm worried about her. Promise me."

"Love, I will. Trust me, I can take an order. Don't worry about Nan, I'll look after her."

"Will you tell the children about me...?"

"I will. Rowena, I've been so lucky to have you. We've had such good times, love. I'll never stop missing you." Paul could sense that she was fading, her breathing growing slower and fainter. He was astonished at how fast it had happened, and he wanted desperately to hold onto her, to pull her back for just a little longer, but there was no more time. She seemed to weak to talk and all he could do was hold her close against him, trying to warm her chilled body against his as she slipped silently away.

Rowena stirred a little at the end and Paul bent and kissed her very tenderly on lips that were already cold. Her eyes were open again and Paul looked into them trying to convey something of his feelings since he was no longer sure she would hear him. Her body in his arms was relaxed and lifeless, but just at that last moment, her lips curved into a shadow of her lovely smile and her eyes widened, as if surprised. Then she was gone, and Paul felt, for a moment, completely numb.

Paul laid her back on the straw very gently and stood up. Realisation hit him like a physical blow, and he stood, letting grief wash over him, and wished for one insane moment, that he could have died with her.

"Paul."

Paul turned, and Carl put his arms about him and hugged him fiercely. Paul made no attempt to hold back his sobs, he could not have done so. They stood for a long time, and then he was suddenly aware of Rowena lying cold

331

and alone on the ground and he pulled back. Beyond Carl, Anne stood holding his daughter, her cheeks wet with tears. Paul looked back at his wife.

"I need to be alone with her for a while."

"Of course," Anne said immediately. "Call me if you need me, I'll be outside."

***

There were practical issues to be dealt with, which for a while Paul was completely incapable of managing. Carl took charge, sending more men out to the nearest villages in search of a wet nurse who might feed the baby. The dead would need to be buried, and men were set to digging graves. In addition to Paul's own men and Rowena, they had found the bodies of the slaughtered villagers, mostly women, children and the elderly, defenceless while their men were away at war, and Michael O'Reilly supervised their burial in the shade of an orange grove. Anne spent time with Private Davison who was clinging stubbornly to life against all expectations. Michael waited until she had finished and then went to join her in the farmyard, concerned at her white, tear-stained face.

"Are you all right, girl dear?"

"I am. Thanks to all of you."

"Ma'am, we were surprised out there and it's going to take a while before I forgive myself for that, I almost got us all killed. We lost five good men. But we're alive because of you. I'd forgotten how well you understand French. He'd no idea, had he?"

"No. I heard him tell his men to kill you and Rowena and he'd take me elsewhere and..." Anne broke off, unable to say it.

"I knew what he had in mind for you, ma'am, it was fairly obvious. The French are bastards with the local women, but I'd have expected better from an officer. He got more than he bargained for with you, and it served him right."

Anne glanced across at Paul. He had sat silently for a long time holding his wife in his arms, and then kissed her gently and moved away. "How is he?"

"I'm going to find out in a moment. Girl dear, he is going to find this awfully hard, you know."

"I know."

"For all the noblest reasons in the world. And for one or two of the less noble ones."

"Michael, this is not the time..."

"It is ma'am. It's the way the army does things. I've known a man laid in his grave one day and his wife wed to another the next. Nobody will expect Paul to live the life of a monk because he's lost his wife and there will be women enough throwing themselves at him now. But you and I both know that he isn't going to be even remotely interested in any one of them."

"He loved Rowena, Michael. And I'm still a married woman," Anne said quietly.

"Aye, to a man we all despise. I know how he felt about Rowena, girl dear. It didn't stop him falling head over heels in love with you, but it did stop him doing anything about it. But the reason you haven't been sharing a bed with Major van Daan for the past two years is about to be laid in her grave, and once he's over the shock of it and his tears have dried, he isn't going to give one single damn about the sanctity of your marriage vows, trust me. So you might want to give some thought to what you want to do about that before it happens. Just a thought."

Anne gave a small smile. "Thank you," she said. "I was raised to believe that once married, a woman stayed faithful no matter what. There were names for women who strayed, and none of them were pretty." She looked away, a flush staining her cheeks. "I know what people think," she said quietly. "Would it surprise you to know that we have never actually…?"

Michael reached out and touched her face with a kind of rueful tenderness. "I could settle a lot of outstanding bets with that piece of information," he said, and she looked up at him, startled, breaking into laughter.

"Michael!"

"I'm sorry, girl dear. But you must know that your relationship with our commander is a source of endless speculation for the entire battalion, and probably half of Wellington's army. He's not exactly been subtle."

"No. Although until Talavera, we did fairly well. After that hell, it seemed for a while not to matter too much what people thought."

"I know what I thought, you've amazed me. But lass…"

Anne shook her head. "Michael, if Paul comes knocking on my door…"

"When, lass, not if."

"I know. And I know what I ought to do. But I love him. I cared so much for Rowena that it was easy to be strong. I don't care about Robert, he doesn't deserve it."

Michael studied her. The dark eyes were still red from crying so much and she looked tired and drawn. He remembered seeing her for the first time at the barracks in Thorndale and he wondered if his commanding officer had any idea how fortunate he was. "Good," he said quietly. "Because you're the part of him that he never knew was missing until he met you, and personally I don't give a damn about a wedding ring."

Michael rose, crossed the yard and sat down beside Paul. "I don't know what to say," he said.

"I know, Michael." Paul was watching the burial party out on the hillside. "I can't believe it hurts this much. I'm worried about the baby."

"Don't be, sir. Donnelly has found a woman in one of the villages who can nurse the child for you for a day or so, she'll come back up to the lines with us. When we're back in camp I suggest you talk to Mary Phillips. She gave birth a couple of weeks ago and now that poor Ned has gone, she'll be glad of the money and a passage home."

"Thank God. As soon as I may, I'll send her back home to Patience, Mary can go with her. It's what Rowena would have wanted."

"And will you be naming her for her mother?"

Paul nodded. "I always loved her name."

"A pretty name for a pretty lass."

"Yes." Paul looked across the yard. Anne was tending to Private Carter's gashed arm. He stood shirtless as she carefully bathed the wound. "So what happened, Michael?"

"We didn't see them coming," Michael said bitterly. "Rowena's pains had started, and we were concentrating on finding somewhere to take shelter. I'd planned on sending someone back for you as soon as we'd got her comfortable. None of us expected to find a cavalry party behind our lines."

"Especially not one that was willing to slaughter an entire village including a pregnant woman. I didn't misunderstand that did I?"

"No, Mrs Carlyon heard him give the order."

"Did you kill him?"

"I did. And it was a pleasure, believe me."

"Good. Don't blame yourself, Michael, it could have happened to any of us, they shouldn't have been there. You did all the right things. Tell me what happened, would you?"

Michael glanced sideways at his commander. "You're going to get awful cross about some of this story."

"Then you'd better get it over with."

Paul listened in silence as Michael recounted the story. It was difficult to tell. Michael blamed himself and there was nothing he could do to ease that, and he knew that his commanding officer was feeling his own share of guilt at having sent the women off with such a small escort but there had been no reason to imagine that a French scouting party would be found in this area.

"They'd have killed Nan too," Paul said, when Michael had finished.

"When they'd had their fun with her. I saw the bodies of the village women, sir, and it made me sick."

"I could have lost both of them, Michael."

"Thank God you gave her that knife."

"I gave it to her on the day she told me she was coming to Spain," Paul said. "With another woman I'd have told her to stay within doors and stop putting herself at risk, but what's the point of that with Nan? So I gave her that knife and showed her how to wear it and gave her some idea of how to use it."

"I think you've been well repaid for that particular gift," Michael said. "I can't believe how calm she was. She understood everything that bastard was saying, knew what he intended to do with her, but she didn't flinch. And she literally stepped between Carter and a blade." Michael looked at him. "I'm so sorry about your wife, sir. Are you all right?"

"No. But I will be. Michael, none of this makes sense to me. I loved her. I've been with her now for six years. God knows I wasn't the most faithful husband in the world, but I loved her and she knew I did."

"She knew."

"And the worst of it is that I'm dying inside thinking that I won't see her again, and then I look at Nan…"

Michael followed his gaze to where Anne was dressing Carter's arm as he stood shirtless. "Do you think your wife ever realised?"

"Yes. She told me she did last night. I rather suspect Rowena understood me better than I ever suspected, Michael. Jesus, look at the expression on Carter's face."

"Are you surprised? She just saved his life and you never expect to owe that kind of debt to a girl."

"No. But then who would have thought I'd end up owing my life to a chance met lass I kissed in a snowstorm."

Paul stood up and walked over to where Anne was helping Carter put on his shirt and jacket, and Michael followed.

"Feeling all right, Carter?"

"Good, sir," the rifleman said, cautiously testing his arm. "Thank you, ma'am. Feels much better."

"I'm going to check on Davison," Anne said. "Paul, I think they're almost ready to bury the men. And Rowena."

"I'll get the lads together then, sir," Carter said quietly.

"Thank you, Carter. We'll wait for you, Nan."

"Thank you." She moved away towards the barn. Paul observed the expression on Carter's face and gave a faint smile. "She's spoken for, Carter," he said quietly.

"You don't have to tell me that, sir," Carter said. "All the good ones always are."

***

There was a burst of late afternoon sunlight on the row of six graves, and they laid the five soldiers in and then lowered Rowena's body, shrouded in a blanket. The men had buried the villagers early that morning while Paul and Anne were still with Rowena. Anne suspected she had been deliberately kept from seeing what the French had done to them and she was glad. She stood between Paul and Carl, her face wet with tears. All the men had buried comrades before, but this was different, and Anne could see that several of them were crying. Carl said a prayer and as was customary, the men spoke a few words about the fallen soldiers. Silence fell and Carl glanced at Paul.

"If you can't, sir…"

"No – I'll be all right." Paul's face was grave but there were no tears. Anne watched him struggle to find the words, her heart aching for him. "I met Rowena in a country church on a summer's evening. She was poor and vulnerable and very lovely, and I'm sure you all know me well enough to guess how that ended."

There was a collective gasp and then a ripple of surprised laughter through the ranks and Paul smiled slightly. "I married her, which was less predictable, and we travelled through Europe together. She gave me two children. She gave me love, she gave me stability and she gave me peace. I never appreciated her enough for any of that. But for all my shortcomings as a husband, I expected there would be time to make it up to her. When the war was over, when Boney was beaten, when I had time for her. Now I'll never get to do that. I'll never get to tell her how much I loved her. She thought she was ordinary. She wasn't. Any woman who could put up with me the way she did was something special. I'll never forget her and I'll never stop missing her."

He looked around him at the solemn rows of men. "She used to worry that she wasn't good enough at being a soldier's wife – that she wasn't brave enough. But she had the quiet courage of a woman, she just got on with things, never complained, never nagged, never whined. She was as much a part of this regiment as any of these men. They died trying to protect her. She'd have welcomed their company."

Paul looked down at Anne and she could see the sheen of tears. She squeezed his hand and he smiled and gathered her against him into the shelter of his arm while the men fired a salute. It was done, and as the graves were filled, the men filed back down to the farm. Paul stood watching the men wielding the spades.

"Paul?"

"Tomorrow I'm going to have to ride away and leave her here and I can't bear it. She should be at home. She should be raising our children in comfort and arranging flowers in the village church and helping with choir practice because it's what she loved to do. She shouldn't be here."

"She loved you more than all of that, Paul."

"I know she did. What I've only just understood is how much I loved her. I'm sorry, is this difficult...?"

"No. She was your wife and the mother of your children and you loved her. That's how it's supposed to be, Paul. She was also my friend and I loved her too."

He turned to her, tears falling silently. "I know you did. And I know how much that meant to her. I just can't stand the thought that she's lying in an unmarked grave on a hillside in Portugal. There should be a stone, a memorial - something."

His distress broke Anne's heart. She put both arms about him, not caring who saw. "We'll come back," she said fiercely. "One day, when this is over, we'll come back here, and we'll put up a memorial for her."

Paul was looking down at her. His tears had stopped, and he was studying her as though trying to read something in her face. "Yes, we will," he said. "But if anything happens to me, if I don't make it, Nan..."

"Then I will do it for you, and I'll bring her children here," Anne said.

"Thank you." Paul bent to kiss her on the forehead then he took her hand, and they followed the men back down to the farm.

The company began their march back to Viseu the following day. Anne travelled in the carriage holding tiny Rowena in her arms. Despite the desperate circumstances of her birth, she seemed to be thriving at the breast of the sturdy Portuguese widow whom Paul had persuaded to accompany them along with her own child. At the farm, Anne reluctantly handed her over to her new wet nurse and spoke a few words to Mary Phillips about the bravery of her husband, who had died in the skirmish. She was aware that she was putting off the inevitability of going back to her billet and speaking to Robert, who must be back by now, but it needed to be done.

"I'm going to find Robert," she said quietly to Paul. He regarded her steadily.

"Do you want me to come with you?"

"No, it will only annoy him more."

"I don't give a damn about annoying Robert, Nan, but I'll respect your wishes." Paul raised his voice. Corporal Carter!"

Carter looked round, confused. "Sir?"

"Over here, lad." Paul handed Carter a set of stripes. "Sew those on, will you? Or get one of the women to do it for you."

Carter's eyes lit up. "Sir – yes, sir. Thank you. I won't let you down."

"You've never let me down, Carter. Apart from refusing to get rid of that damned green coat it is completely out of place. When you make sergeant, you're getting new uniform, I don't care if I have to burn that thing. Now get going. Your first duty as corporal is to escort Mrs Carlyon back to her billet. Not too onerous."

"A pleasure, sir. Ma'am."

"Thank you," Anne said, and looked at Paul. "Will you be all right?"

"I'll cope. Although just walking into the room and seeing her things around..." Paul shook his head. "I don't know what to do with them."

"I'll come up and go through them. You'll want to keep personal things, but the clothes could be given to some of the women."

"I'd be grateful if you would."

Anne reached up and kissed him. "I'll see you tomorrow," she said.

"Nan," he called as she walked away.

"Yes?"

"Thank you. For what you did for Rowena. And for keeping Carter and Michael alive."

Anne smiled, shook her head and walked on. They made their way down through the bustling town centre, with Wellington's headquarters building looming large on the far side. At this hour of the day, it was crowded with officers on their way to and from their general's office or the mess. Anne saw Gervase Clevedon coming quickly towards her.

"Mrs Carlyon, I've just heard a rumour..."

"They spread fast. It's true, Captain. Rowena died giving birth."

"Christ, poor Paul. The baby...?"

"A little girl. She seems to be doing fine. The major is back at the farm."

"I'll go up there. I've to see Hookey first, I'll tell him what's happened. Are you all right? They said you were attacked."

"We were, and I'm fine. But the light company lost five men." Anne indicated her escort. "Carter and Sergeant-Major O'Reilly survived. Young Davison is in a bad way, they've taken him up to the hospital. And they slaughtered those poor villagers."

She glanced up, suddenly aware of being watched. Across the cobbled square her husband was standing looking at them. Anne felt a twist of fear at the expression on his face.

"Excuse me, Captain, I need to go and speak to my husband," she said quietly.

Clevedon glanced across at Carlyon and then back at Anne. He looked troubled. "Yes, of course. Ma'am, are you sure..."?

"I'll be fine, Captain." Anne summoned a weary smile. "You go on."

She took a deep breath and crossed the square to meet her husband, who appeared to have been on his way to the mess. As she got closer the expression on his face made her feel slightly sick. She had known she would have to deal with this but had not expected it to be so soon. Still, Robert could hardly cause a scene in the middle of town with half Wellington's officers watching.

Anne reached him, with Carter hovering respectfully in the background. "Robert, I was just on my way back to the house. Have you heard what happened?"

Robert gave an unpleasant laugh. "Nan, what a pleasant surprise. Has Major van Daan finished with you, then? Good of him to send you back."

Anne took a deep breath. "I wasn't with Paul," she said. "I went to be with Rowena. I told you that in my letter. Robert, something awful has happened."

"And you just happened to run into her husband along the way?" Robert said with heavy sarcasm. "Because I'm told you just drove in with him."

Anne met his furious gaze and felt her stomach lurch. It was going to be bad, she could sense it. "Robert, I'm sorry," she said. "Rowena was set on going and I couldn't let her go alone. There was no time to wait until you came back. Can we go back to our room to talk about it?"

"I don't believe you, Nan."

"Robert – she died. We were attacked by a French patrol. Paul lost five men, and then Rowena had the baby and died." Anne could scarcely say the words. Behind her she could sense Carter's solid support. "I am truly sorry if I worried you. But I'm back now."

"You didn't worry me, Nan," Robert said loudly. "If I can't find my wife, the entire army knows that Major van Daan's bed is the place to look."

It could not have been more public. Behind her Anne heard Corporal Carter catch his breath in horror. "Robert, for God's sake, you're mad!" Anne said. She was shaking with reaction. "Don't you even care that a woman died? That men were killed defending us?"

"Why would I care, Nan? Paul van Daan isn't going to give a damn, is he? With his wife out of the way he'll have a lot more time to spend fucking mine!"

Anne felt a sudden surge of complete fury. "How dare you?" she said angrily. "Get out of my way, you pathetic apology for a man, I've no patience with you! This is neither the time nor place for this! He just lost his wife and I just lost my best friend, you ought to be ashamed!"

She made to walk past him, but Robert raised his hand and smacked her hard, backhanded, across the face. Anne reeled backwards feeling her lip split open and would have fallen if a hard capable arm had not caught her. She was shocked. Robert had never hit her in public before.

"Easy, ma'am." Corporal Carter steadied her with his arm, reminding her that this time she was not alone with Robert.

"Take your hands off my wife, you scum!" Carlyon said. His tone was clearly audible and those around him had stopped to stare, openly listening. "Are you screwing the enlisted men as well now, Nan?"

Anne felt the colour drain from her face and she could hear the collective gasp of those close enough to hear him. She felt Carter's hand drop from her arm and he stepped forward. Panicked Anne threw herself on him with all the strength she had left. "Carter, no!" she screamed, and the force of her words held him. He looked down at her and she could tell it was taking all his self-control not to shake her off and hit Robert.

"Danny, no! He'll have you hanged," she said quietly, vehemently. "And then Paul will kill him. Don't. Just get me out of here."

Carter looked contemptuously over at Robert. "Good idea, ma'am," he said clearly. "Come and find a man to take care of you."

"She's staying here," Carlyon said.

"No, she's really not," drawled a familiar voice, and Anne looked up to see the blessed sight of Captain Clevedon approaching. He stepped between her and Robert and took her hand.

"Carter. Still getting yourself into trouble, I see."

"Every day, sir."

"Carry on, Carter. I'll take care of Mrs Carlyon, you have my word on it."

"Thank you, sir."

Carter walked away, and Anne leaned into Clevedon's wiry strength. Finally, she had no reserves left and he seemed to sense it. "Come on," he said gently, glancing at Robert's white, furious face. "Let's get you out of here."

"Get your hands off my wife, Captain."

Clevedon moved smoothly between Anne and Carlyon. "You just hit your wife in a public square, Captain Carlyon. I'm not leaving her here with you, and if you don't step back, you'll be sorry. Just now, if I were you, I'd take yourself somewhere you can't easily be found, because when Paul van Daan comes looking for you, and trust me he will, you do not want him to be able to track you down. Now back away."

Anne allowed Clevedon to lead her back up the hill. By the time they reached the farm, Anne felt that she could barely walk. She was trying desperately to hold back her tears. Carter was already there and she could see him speaking to Paul and Carl. At the sight of her Paul broke off and came

339

forward. He took her from Clevedon and lifted her chin gently, his eyes on her bleeding lip and bruised, exhausted face.

"Robert hit me," Anne said. Saying the words felt strange, as though she had broken some kind of taboo. She had never said them before, and the expression on Paul's face brought tears to her eyes. He was looking at her as though nothing else in the world mattered. Anne decided that nothing else did. Closing her eyes, she leaned on him and felt his arms go about her. It felt like coming home.

***

Paul felt numb. He listened to Corporal Carter's furious description of the scene he had just witnessed in the square in complete shock, but the sight of Anne's battered face made it suddenly real.

"Gervase, thank you," he said quietly.

"It was nothing. I heard about Rowena, Paul. I'm damned sorry."

"Thank you." Paul was holding Anne close and she leaned against him. "Did you see what happened?"

Clevedon nodded. "From a distance. I heard him yelling at her – Christ, Paul, half the army must have heard, it was right outside headquarters in the middle of the square. I saw him hit her and ran over there before Danny Carter killed him, which he looked likely to do."

"For that I'm grateful."

"Paul – the things he said…"

"I can guess what he said," Paul said shortly. "Nan and I have just buried my wife and five of my men, so you'll excuse me if I don't much care for the opinions of Robert Carlyon."

"You might not, but what of his wife?" Clevedon said. "How can she go back to him like this?"

"She isn't going to," Paul said. He was suddenly very certain. "We can find a room for her here. After this, I'm not letting her go anywhere near that bastard. Carl, will you go and find Teresa – she's probably at the hospital – and organise some of the lads to go down and help her to pack up everything and bring it up here. There are two rooms over my office, which are just full of stores. Carter, can you…?"

"I'll get some of the lads from the fourth to clear it out straight away, sir, and we'll find a bed for her. Mrs Ferriera will help, she likes Mrs Carlyon."

"Thanks, Danny. Is that arm all right?"

"It would have worked just fine to punch that bastard's face in, sir, but your lady wouldn't let me."

Paul saw Clevedon look sharply at Carter, and Carter looked back steadily, his eyes furious. He knew exactly what he had just said and exactly what the implications were, and he did not care. Paul felt a rush of gratitude for the Londoner's fierce loyalty.

"Paul, this is just going to fuel the gossip," Clevedon warned him.

Paul stroked Anne's head, which was still leaning against his chest. She had not looked up throughout the conversation. He had never seen her this vulnerable or this defeated, and it aroused a fierce, protective tenderness in him.

"I don't care. She isn't going anywhere near him again. I'm damned sure this is not the first time he's done this, but it is going to be the last."

When Clevedon had gone, walking back down the hill with Carl, Paul looked down at Anne. She looked completely drained, as though her husband had achieved what a company of French dragoons could not.

"Come inside," he said.

Anne followed him into the house, no longer seeming to care what anybody thought, and into his room. Paul pulled up a camp chair. "Sit down and let me look at your face."

He inspected the cut for a moment, then went for water and bathed it gently. "Not too bad. It'll probably bruise."

"I'll be all right, Paul," Anne said with a tired smile. "It's been a difficult few days for both of us. I'm sorry you have to deal with this just after Rowena…"

"Don't you dare apologise for something that isn't your fault, Nan. And don't even try to pretend it's the first time he's done this, because it isn't, is it?"

Anne shook her head miserably and Paul leaned forward and kissed her very gently. "Christ, how have I not known?"

"I didn't want anybody to know," Anne said. "What could anyone do?"

"I thought you knew me better than that, bonny lass. Don't look so worried, there's no need. It's never going to happen again. He's never going to touch you again. Come on, lie down before you fall down. We'll see to your room and your things and I'll come and wake you up later."

"On your bed, Paul?" Anne said with a tearful laugh.

"Sweetheart, you're going to find this hard to believe, but my intentions are for once genuinely honourable. Pretend to be helpless for once."

Anne sat on the edge of his bed and he knelt before her to take off her shoes. The feeling of his hand encircling her ankle was strangely natural. He looked up into her face and smiled and Anne bent forward and kissed him gently, her black hair falling about them. After a moment, his hand slid higher up her leg and Anne parted her lips under his. Then she was in his arms and they fell back onto the bed, still kissing.

"I was seriously not going to do this," Paul whispered. "What do you do to me, lass, you only have to touch me and I'm lost…"

"You know my views, Major," Anne said, and he groaned laughingly.

"Nan, I love you. Nothing is ever going to change that."

"Major!" O'Reilly's soft tones called from outside the room. "There's a lad here with a message from Lord Wellington, so if you're not decent, you need to be."

Paul raised his head. "Damn!" he said. For the first time in days, he felt better. "Here, let me help you, love."

341

"I can manage. Go outside and tell that Irishman to stop laughing."

Paul grinned, took a deep breath and emerged from the room. His sergeant-major was standing looking down into the yard where Danny Carter was supervising the clearing out of Anne's room.

"Well, this seems to be a public statement," Michael said. He glanced sideways at his commander. "Feeling better, sir?"

"Some," Paul admitted. "Am I about to behave like a fool over a woman, again, Michael?"

"She's married to another man, sir, and if you move her into your bed as openly as this, they'll be calling her a whore throughout the army."

"And what will they be calling me?" Paul asked.

"A lucky bastard," his sergeant-major said. "Just be sure. Because for you, this is not just another woman, is it?"

"You know that I'm sure," Paul said. "Are you worried about her, Michael? I know this isn't ideal, but what the hell else can I do? I can't let her go back to him, but I'm terrified of hurting her."

"She's resilient," the Irishman said.

"She is. Have you ever wondered how she got that way, Michael?"

Michael shot him a glance. "Yes," he admitted. "There's a thing she hasn't said, in all of this. Not once has she said the words 'I can't believe he would do this to me'. But Christ alive, sir, it's been two years and she's probably spent as much time around you as around him. Wouldn't you have known?"

"I should have," Paul said. "But when I'm around Nan, to be honest with you, I'm usually trying my hardest to resist picking her up and carrying her to the nearest bed. I've hated that bastard for a long time, but that was just because he had the right to do what I didn't. There are a lot of things I could have missed while I've been so wrapped up in myself."

"We're all on edge, sir, with this invasion looming. I'm not attempting to excuse him, but..."

"Sergeant-Major, I'll admit to feeling guilty about Carlyon in the past. I didn't like him. Still, there was a point when I began to think that in his own way, he might have cared about her. But as my wife lay dying, she told me to take care of Nan because there was something wrong between her and Robert. And today I am beginning to suspect she was right. Rowena often was and I didn't listen to her enough. I can't believe I didn't know this." Paul was shaking his head. "She's never going back to him. I'll help her to do whatever she wants, even if it's to go back home to her family but Carlyon is never getting his bloody hands on her again. All I can think of are the times I've kissed her and sent her back to him because I thought that was the right thing to do, and now I'm wondering what I've been sending her back to."

"Sir, don't do anything stupid, will you?" the sergeant-major said and there was genuine concern in his voice.

"Define stupid." Paul clapped his friend on the shoulder. "Take over here, I'm going to see Wellington. By now I'm guessing that somebody has told him about that scene in the square. And about Rowena."

Chapter Twenty

Paul walked down to the centre of town and across the square, conscious of covert glances from passers-by. By now, he supposed, the story of Carlyon's outburst would be going the rounds of headquarters. He thought again about Anne, kneeling in the straw beside Rowena and felt rage building up inside him. He forced it down and went up the steps, nodding to Captain Dryden in the lobby.

"He's waiting for you, Major." Dryden hesitated. "I just heard. Christ, I'm sorry."

"Thank you, Chris. As a matter of interest, which did you hear first? The death of my wife and five of my men, or the part where Robert Carlyon accused me of sleeping with his wife in front of half the army?"

Dryden flushed. "Sir, we all know Carlyon has got a mania about that black eyed wife of his. Nobody thinks…"

"That's good of you, Chris. But you and I both know that isn't true. I'd better go in to see him."

Paul knocked on the door and heard Wellington call out. His general was alone, seated behind his desk. He studied Paul for a moment. "Close the door, Major, and sit down."

Paul obeyed. The general walked over to where he always kept a tray of drinks. The scene was so familiar to Paul. He had been twenty-one the first time General Wellesley had poured him a drink with his own hands, and it had surprised him then. Wellington, like Paul, was not regularly a heavy drinker and had a discriminating palate. The brandy was French and particularly good. To his amusement Wellington set the decanter on the desk between them.

"In case one isn't enough today," he said. "Paul, I am so sorry about Rowena."

"Thank you, sir. How did you find out so quickly?"

"Captain Clevedon told me. She was a lovely woman. How is the child?"

"She seems fine so far. There is a widow in camp – her man was killed at the farm – with a young child. She is going to act as wet nurse. As soon as I can arrange a proper escort, I'll send them back to Lisbon and I'll write to my family about getting them to England. My sister-in-law already cares for my son and Grace, she'll be happy to take Rowena."

"You're naming her for her mother?"

"And Anne, for her godmother."

Wellington smiled grimly and drank. "You don't shirk difficult subjects, do you, Major?"

"It happened an hour ago outside your window, sir. Hard to avoid."

"Robert Carlyon is not a man I particularly like, Major, although I'll admit he has been useful. Every man in my army knows how he is with that wife of his. But equally, every man knows how you are with her as well."

"Do you seriously think I'd have sent my wife back to Lisbon with my mistress in tow?" Paul demanded.

"Don't lose your temper with me, Major. I'm not saying anything of the kind, but some will. Whatever you may or may not have done, you've made it obvious what you would like to do. She is in a very difficult position now. Is she all right? I'm told he hit her."

"He did. And a week ago, she was almost raped and murdered by the French. Afterwards she remained with my dying wife who was her closest friend. How do you think she is?"

"Well, most women would have taken to their bed by now, but I would be very surprised to hear that she has. Stop snapping at me, you insubordinate young fool, I'm worried about her." Wellington eyed him. "I'm also worried about you."

Paul sat quietly for a moment. "I'm sorry, sir," he said finally. "I'm not at my best. She'll be all right, but she can't go back to him. Not after this."

Wellington took a deep breath. "I try to stay out of my officers' private affairs, Major van Daan, providing they stay private and do not impact on their duty, but try to remember that at least some of the normal social rules still apply here. She is another man's wife, even if he does not deserve her." He gave a small wintery smile. "And I am genuinely fond of her, Paul. You know that."

"I know, sir. I don't yet know what she'll want to do."

"Major, I think we both have a fairly good idea what Mrs Carlyon will want to do. We just differ about whether she should be permitted to do it." Wellington looked steadily at Paul. "I did not just call you here to talk about Carlyon, I had a posting for you. But if you need to take some time out after this, I will understand. Somebody else…"

"No, sir. Sitting here missing Rowena isn't going to help me. And perhaps if I'm not around, it will give the gossip a chance to die down. Where do you want us?"

"I want you to march your battalion down to the Coa to join Craufurd and the light division. I don't want Craufurd to engage unless he has to and I'm sending orders telling him so, but Massena is on his way and I want to make sure he can't cut us off." Wellington gave Paul a severe look. "Nothing rash. Craufurd knows that, but I'm telling you as well. In the meantime, I am going to begin to organise a retreat – strategically this time. I want all our wounded

344

and supplies and non-military personnel safe behind the lines long before Massena invades and then I'm hoping to channel him the way I want him to come."

"Yes, sir."

"I'll speak to Carlyon myself about what happened today, and I intend to make it clear that his conduct was not acceptable. I will also inform him that he is to leave his wife alone unless she asks to see him. But Paul, in the meantime, for God's sake try not to do anything stupid."

"Do you know, you are the second person in an hour to say that to me, sir?"

"Which demonstrates, I think, how well we have all come to know you," the general said caustically. "Get out and get moving, Major van Daan. And I expect regular reports, especially if you are concerned that General Craufurd is about to do something stupid himself."

"Yes, sir."

Paul walked back down to the farmhouse, absently acknowledging those fellow officers who paused to offer condolences about Rowena. When he arrived, the yard was clear of boxes and junk. After a moment's hesitation Paul went up the stairs and tapped on the door of the room allocated to Anne. Teresa opened it, her hands full of bedding.

"She is not here, Major," the girl said politely. "She has walked over to the hospital with Carter. She wants to look at his wound and to see Private Davison."

"She was supposed to be resting," Paul said. "Teresa – can you come down to my office for a few minutes? I wanted to talk to you."

The Spanish girl set down the pile of bedding on a chest and followed him out of the room. Paul led her down the stairs and into his office. He perched on the edge of his cluttered desk and waved her to a chair.

"You've been with Señora Carlyon for a while now, Teresa."

"More than a year," Teresa agreed.

"I know she trusts you. You're discreet and you would never gossip about her to other people. In fact, I am beginning to suspect that is why she chose you."

The girl inclined her head without speaking.

"I am going to ask something very difficult because it involves you breaking a confidence. Please think before you decide." Paul took a deep breath. "Teresa, just before she died, my wife told me to ask you about Robert Carlyon and how he treated his wife. She seemed to think you would know."

The girl's face had paled. She did not speak or take her eyes from his face. Paul studied her and was sure. "How long has he been hitting her?"

The girl sat in silence for a long time. Paul gave her time to think about her response. He was fairly sure he knew what it would be, but he did not want to push her. She must know that if she told him the truth, everything would change.

"What are you going to do about it if I tell you?" Teresa asked finally.

345

"I am going to make very sure that he never has the opportunity to touch her again," Paul said.

"He is her husband."

"Jesus Christ, do you think I care about that?" Paul demanded savagely. "After what he's just done, he is never going near her again, but I need to know how bad this has been."

"It has been bad," Teresa said. "I think from what she has told me he hit her from the start. Twice, to my knowledge, he has beaten her with a riding crop. The last time was after Talavera."

Paul could feel the white-hot anger flooding through him. "Oh God," he said softly. "Because of me."

"Major, he did not know what happened between you. If he had, I think he would have killed her. It was just because she had been with you." Teresa shrugged. "She told me that at first he did not care what she did. But this last year it has got worse. He is jealous of every man who looks at her, but he is not stupid. He knows that it is different with you."

"Why did she not tell me?"

"She told nobody but me."

"She should have gone back to her family," Paul said. "If she'd come to me, I could have arranged it."

The Spanish girl lifted her eyes to his face. "Major, I think there were reasons why she has found it difficult to leave here."

"You mean because of me."

"She has not said so. But I have eyes, me, I am not blind."

Paul turned away, his stomach churning. "It seems that I have been," he said bitterly. "Christ, if I had known..."

"What could you have done?"

"I could have killed the bastard. I can't stand to think she's been going through this..."

"I should have told you, Major. I am sorry."

"Did she ask you not to?"

Teresa nodded. With an effort, Paul summoned a smile. "All right, Teresa. Thank you."

He waited until she had gone, and then went to the door and bellowed for Private Jenson. "Jenson, I need to call a meeting of all officers tonight, we've orders. Will you make sure they know I want them here early for dinner so that I can brief them first? We'll march tomorrow, heading for Almeida to join General Craufurd."

"That grumpy old bastard."

"He is so, but he's a damned good general, so we forgive him his temper, just as eventually you will all forgive me mine. Get a move on and when you get back, get my kit ready will you?"

"Yes, sir."

Paul watched his orderly limping across the yard, grinned, and then set off to walk up to the hospital. He found Anne in the surgery replacing the dressing on Carter's arm. He could hear them talking and laughing as he approached and it made him smile. Her resilience was astonishing.

Anne looked up as he came in and smiled. Carter moved the arm and nodded. "Much better, ma'am. Thank you." He saluted. "New orders, sir?"

"Yes. Mr Swanson will let you know, but we march tomorrow. Get your kit straight, mind, Carter, because we'll be under General Craufurd."

"Oh gawd!" Carter said, pulling a face. "Oh well, at least he's probably not going to get us killed."

"You all right to march with that?" Paul asked, nodding at his arm.

"Can hold a rifle and kill a Frenchman with it, sir."

"Good enough. Carry on, Carter."

"Yes, sir." He looked at Anne. "Thank you, ma'am. For everything."

Anne smiled and watched him go, then turned to Paul. "And what can I do for you, Major?"

"I can think of a large number of things, but I don't have time for any of them right now," Paul said, and saw the answering gleam in her eyes.

"How long does it take to kiss me?" she asked quietly, and Paul stepped forward and took her very gently into his arms, trying to be careful of her bruised mouth. She did not seem to care, and as her lips parted under his, he tightened his hold.

Finally, Paul lifted his head and looked down at her. "That will do to start with," he said softly and felt her shiver slightly under his hands.

"Paul," she whispered.

"I need to get back to brief my officers. We've to march out tomorrow to support Craufurd at Almeida where he is apparently not going to be engaging Massena, although knowing that belligerent old bugger I wouldn't bet the family fortune on that. I think Wellington expects me to be the voice of reason, which tells you just how desperate he is. I can't take you with me. Wellington is going to start preparing for a retreat back to the lines, to defend Lisbon."

"Then I'll have plenty to do here."

Paul nodded, his hands still resting lightly on her waist. "I'm going to talk to Wellington about finding Robert something to do urgently away from here. I'm not risking him coming to find you while I'm gone and I can't leave much of a guard. I don't want any of my men to come up against him anyway, he's still an officer, and although I'd very much like to shut him in a room with Danny Carter for ten minutes, I don't want Carter hanged."

"No, that worries me."

"It's a solution that will probably suit Wellington. He's not going to want Robert within a mile of you again. When I get back, when the retreat is done, and you're in Lisbon, you'll stay at the villa again and we'll talk and we'll work out what to do next. I'm not letting you go back to him. If you want to, I'll arrange for you to go home to your family. I've written to my brother and I'll be sending Rowena home. You could go with her."

"Is that what you want, Paul?"

"No. But what I want is going to bring you to social ruin."

Anne looked at him steadily. "Will your regiment still speak to me?"

"Nan, the men of my regiment would probably die for you."

"Then I'll have everything I need. Rowena has gone and there's not a female left at headquarters that I care about offending. I'm not leaving you again."

Paul regarded her steadily. The enormity of what she was prepared to give up for him both appalled him and filled him with joy. He gave a smile, which went slightly awry.

"I'm standing here trying to work out if I maybe do have time," he said. "But I'm not going to. I need a few weeks. Rowena...I need to cope with losing her before I can really be with you. And after three years of stolen moments and kisses in dark corners, and half-raping you in a snowbound barn, it's finally dawning on me that we can actually be together. I'm not going to make love to you for the first time on the grubby floor of a regimental hospital, I'm going to wait and make very sure that we both remember it for the rest of our lives."

When Paul had taken Anne back to her room, he set off to walk back down to headquarters. At this hour Wellington would probably be at dinner, which he usually took while working during the crucial part of a campaign. Paul found himself smiling as he walked through the narrow streets. He had never really thought about how well he had come to know the general and his habits over the years. Paul knew that despite their frequent disagreements, Wellington was genuinely fond of him, which given the scandal that he was about to unleash throughout the army, was probably a good thing. Poor Wellington would miss flirting with Anne at headquarters parties, but publicly at least, he was not going to be able to ignore one of his favourite officers openly taking another man's wife to his bed, although Paul suspected that privately it would make little difference to Wellington's friendship with Anne.

"Sir, are you looking for the general?"

Lost in his thoughts he had not noticed Captain Ellison from the guards hailing him from outside the headquarters mess. He paused and waited for Ellison to join him. "Yes, I need a quick word before we set off tomorrow."

Ellison laughed. "Going to join Craufurd, I hear. Rather you than me, old boy."

"I don't mind him. He's a rude old bugger, but to be honest he's mostly right so I can forgive him that. And I've the hide of an elephant so he doesn't offend me. I'll have to remind my lads to keep their mouths shut around him, mind."

"Aye, he's a disciplinarian and your light company are the most insubordinate bunch in Portugal, he'll have flogged half of them before the French arrive." Ellison said with a grin. "Hookey's not there. Walked up to the hospital to see how young Brett is doing."

"Christ yes, I heard about that. Lost a leg, didn't he?"

Ellison nodded. "Wellington's cut up about it. Friend of the family. Old Craddock got his hands on the lad and made a bit of a botch of it I hear.

Should have waited for Guthrie or Norris." He shot a sideways glance at Paul. "Or the lady who runs your hospital, who I believe did the neatest job on Davy Partridge's arm."

"Don't bait me, Tony," Paul said, shooting a glance at his friend.

"God, Paul, I'm not. Not after what you just lost. Don't forget I knew you and Rowena from Naples and Ireland before any of this started, I know how much you cared about her. She was a lovely woman, and the easiest wife in the army. Most of the men I know envied you."

"Thank you," Paul said. "She was an amazing woman and I didn't deserve her."

"Hookey will be back in an hour or so. Why don't you come and have a drink until he gets back?"

Paul glanced at the door to the mess. He was reluctant to face the barrage of consolation and sympathy, but it was probably best to get it over with. He nodded and Ellison led the way into the building and found an empty table not far from the door. He ordered wine and Paul accepted a glass. Various people stopped at his table as they passed to offer condolences, but it was surprisingly less difficult than he had expected. Several of them went on to exchange army news and ask about Paul's posting to join Craufurd, and he was beginning to relax. Loss was so common in the army that Wellington's officers were used to dealing with it. Some of these men had wives in England whom they had not seen for several years and at least one of them knew that his wife had given birth in his absence to a child, which could not possibly be his.

Paul thought again, with an ache of loss, how lucky he had been to marry a woman who had been willing to share the discomforts of army life to be with him. Somehow it did not seem real that he would not see Rowena again. For six years she had been there in the background of his life, a haven of calm and serenity. He sipped his wine feeling his throat suddenly tight again and for a moment he was appalled at the joy he had felt earlier with Anne. He remembered his wife's voice in those last terrible minutes before she had died.

"He loves you."

"I know. But Rowena he loves you too."

Pointless to try to make sense of it. He would never fully forgive himself for all his failings as a husband to Rowena but no matter how much the rest of the army condemned him, he knew that Rowena had not. She had been wiser than him, had understood more than he had, and she had told him to take care of Anne.

"What the hell is he doing in here?" a voice said, breaking into his thoughts. It was strained and slightly slurred, and Paul knew immediately that Robert Carlyon had been drinking. He had come down to see Wellington to avoid this, but it seemed after all that it could not be done. Reaching for his wine glass he took another sip. It was a good, full-bodied red and Paul thought irrelevantly that his father would have appreciated it.

"Come on, Carlyon, leave it, old man." One of the officers who had come into the room with Robert tugged at his arm. "You can't start anything here and you certainly can't start anything with a senior officer."

"Senior officer? Only because he can afford to pay for it," Robert said. Paul looked across the table and saw Anthony Ellison's appalled expression. Still Paul did not respond. He was hoping that Carlyon's companions would get him away from the table to give Paul the opportunity to leave without a confrontation. He did not trust himself to speak.

"Where's my wife, Van Daan?" Robert said. "Back in bed, waiting for you, is she?"

"Christ, Carlyon, come away," Lieutenant Sandler said, appalled. Paul set his glass down on the table and turned his head slowly towards Robert.

"And that was probably the one thing you should not have said," he remarked conversationally, and stood up, pushing his chair back from the table. Around him the room had fallen into total silence. Nobody dared speak or move. Paul looked at Carlyon. The man looked slightly dishevelled as though he had been drinking ever since that encounter with his wife in the square. Paul remembered how lovely Anne had looked in the dispensary, ignoring her cut lip, laughing with Carter. He tried not to let his imagination run wild, but it was too late and already he could visualise Carlyon hitting her; Carlyon holding her down while his crop slashed into her; Carlyon pinning her to the bed, driving into her, not caring if he hurt her.

Ellison rose and put a hand on Paul's arm. "Steady, old boy. You can't start a brawl in here, you know."

"I can. I'd rather not, but that will depend on Captain Carlyon." Paul jerked his head. "Outside."

"You can't threaten me," Carlyon said. "You're the one who should be thrown out, treating another man's wife like a whore..."

Paul took three steps forward, grasped Carlyon around the throat, lifted him up and slammed him hard down on one of the tables, pinning him there. Carlyon gave a small squawk and clutched at Paul's hands but could not release himself.

"You are a disgrace to your regiment, your family and this army, Carlyon, and you are an excrescence of a human being. Every man in this room knows what you did to your wife this morning, but what they may not know is that you've been doing it ever since you married her. You've beaten her and abused her, not for any imaginary sins she may have committed, but because you're a vicious, perverted bastard who enjoys hurting women. Well, you've swung your fist at her for the last time. I want you out of this army, and if I ever see you anywhere near her again – if I even think you might have been intending to approach her – I am going to forget all that I ever learned about army discipline and common sense and I am going to beat your fucking brains out, you piece of shit."

Carlyon could not speak. Paul released his throat and punched him twice, hard in the face. Blood spurted from Carlyon's shattered nose. He staggered forward, throwing an inaccurate punch and Paul stepped neatly aside, lifted his foot and kicked the other man's knee. Carlyon went down with a scream of pain. Paul turned away and looked across at the mess sergeant who had run forward and then stopped dead when he realised who was at the centre of the brawl.

"Clean it up and send me the bill, Ned," he said, and walked towards the door. If he did not remove himself from Carlyon's presence, he was afraid that he was going to kill the man.

"You can't get away with this," Carlyon screamed. "You'll answer for this, Van Daan. Name your friends."

Paul turned. "I really want to kill you, Rob. Are you so fucking stupid you're going to make it that easy for me?"

"Are you afraid?" Carlyon taunted.

Paul walked back and stood looking down at him. "Withdraw that challenge, Rob, and sell out. Quickly. Because pistols or swords, it'll take me less than five minutes to leave you on your knees trying to stuff what's left of your guts back inside, and after what you did to your wife, I'll enjoy it."

"Sir, for God's sake." Anthony Ellison put a restraining hand on Paul's shoulder. "You know how Wellington feels about duelling. I know you're a favourite of his, but..."

"I've challenged nobody, Tony, but if Captain Carlyon insists, I'm not going to back out. Well, Robert? What is it to be? Am I called out?"

"Yes, damn you. You think nothing can touch you, don't you?"

"I think there's very little chance of you touching me with the point of a sword, Robert, but you can withdraw from this at any time. As long as I don't see you strutting around here wearing that uniform any more, I'll let you live. Your choice."

"You wouldn't dare kill me. Nobody is going to say it out loud, because nobody has the guts to stand up to you, but you're a man who killed your wife so that you could fuck mine!"

The silence in the room was deathly. Ellison dropped his hand to his side. Quietly he said:

"I'll stand for you, Paul."

"Name your friends, Robert," Paul said inexorably. His eyes did not leave Carlyon and he was conscious of the effort needed to restrain himself from drawing his sword here and now.

"Benton, will you act for me?"

Benton nodded soberly. The room seemed frozen with shock at what Carlyon had just said. Paul did not speak, simply turned to the door. The mess sergeant approached Robert with a towel to stem the flow of blood from his nose. Robert took it and held it to his face, climbing painfully to his feet. At the door, Paul turned.

"By the way, Rob, I have a daughter. My wife is dead after fifteen hours of agonising labour in a freezing cold barn surrounded by the bodies of French dragoons. They'd have killed her anyway, and ripped that child out of her, but they didn't get the chance thanks to the bravery of your wife. She has more courage in her little finger than you could muster in your entire worthless body and you just called her a whore in front of the whole mess. I'd kill you for that alone. But for her sake, I'd like to make it clear that it's a lie. She's been faithful to you from the day she married you although God knows why, because I've tried hard enough. So challenge me if you want, over my many failed attempts to get her into my bed, because believe me you'd have cause. Or challenge me because I am calling you a coward and a bully and a liar. I don't give a shit what the pretext is as long as you end up dead in the dirt. It will need to be tomorrow morning because I have to go and kill Frenchmen, but it isn't going to take me more than ten minutes to put you in the ground, so I've time."

The door closed behind him onto silence.

***

The meeting with Paul's officers was brief and business-like and none of them mentioned any of the events of the day although Carl Swanson was sure that they must all have heard about the fight with Carlyon in the mess and the subsequent challenge. When it was finished the officers moved away to take their places for dinner. Paul walked into his office and sat down behind his desk and Carl followed him.

"Are you coming to eat?"

Paul shook his head. "I'm not hungry. Where's Nan?"

"Up at the hospital. Davison is poorly and they called her about an hour ago. I'll make sure there's food for her when she gets back."

"I'll see to it. Thank you, Carl."

Carl did not move. "Despite my conviction that you are a complete idiot, I would have acted for you, Paul," he said quietly.

"I know you would. Ellison was there and offered, and it really doesn't matter."

"So you don't require me to be around to hear your dying words?"

"I would love you to be, dear Carl, but you are more likely to get that opportunity on the battlefield than in a muddy field tomorrow with Robert Carlyon."

"You're going to kill him, aren't you?"

"Well, if I don't, he will assuredly kill me. Carl, the only alternative I have, is to back out, and that would leave Nan accused of being a whore, and me of murdering Rowena, in front of the whole army. It's so bloody stupid, isn't it? Wellington's right about duelling, but I have to go through with it for Nan's sake. The irony of it is that I was down there to see Wellington to suggest a way to avoid this, at least for a time. Trust Hookey not to be where he was supposed to be, it's the same on a battlefield, you can never find him."

"Paul, I can think of few men who need killing quite as much as Robert Carlyon. But it is going to be hard for Wellington to overlook this, especially if you then run off with the man's wife."

"Yes, it's a difficult one, isn't it? I imagine, since he is fond of me, he will allow me to resign my commission rather than dismissing me in disgrace or shooting me. And I shall take the love of my life back to England and marry her and live a happy and undistinguished life."

"You'll be bored in a month."

"In a week, probably, but I'm sure I can find something to amuse me. Certainly, life with Nan promises to be enlivening."

Carl shook his head. "Well, it might not be my job, Paul, but I'm going down to find him later and I'm going to try to talk him into withdrawing and apologising. And if I manage it, you are damned well going to accept it. You owe it to your regiment. Is that clear?"

"The honour of the regiment, Carl?"

"It's not about honour, you stiff-necked bastard, it's about the men. They'd die for you. You don't just walk away from that."

Paul's face softened into a smile. "I know. And I will accept it if I can. But he won't do it, Carl. He can't back down after what he said today. Wellington is going to hear about it and given how he feels about Nan, I wouldn't be surprised if he has him up on a charge of conduct unbecoming."

"Which will be his problem and not yours," Carl said firmly. "Do I have your word, Major?"

Paul nodded. "All right. Don't you ever get tired of clearing up after me, Carl?"

"You'd better hope I don't," Carl said.

There was the sound of voices outside in the courtyard. One of them was Anne's. With a sigh Paul got up. "I suppose I will have to tell her."

Carl peered out of the door. "Something tells me," he said cautiously, "that she might have already heard."

He moved out of the room and allowed Anne to walk past him. She did not even look at him or acknowledge him. She was holding herself very straight and her eyes were flashing with anger. Carl closed the office door carefully behind her and went to the table at the far end of the yard where Kelly was distributing plates. During the warmer weather, the officers usually ate outside.

"I wonder how thick that door is?" he said, accepting a drink from Johnny Wheeler.

"I've a feeling we might find out shortly," Johnny said. "She looked furious. Rowena, of course, would have just accepted it."

"Yes. I have a suspicion that Paul is about to discover a number of differences between Anne and Rowena," Carl said.

***

In his office, Paul studied the face of his love. "I take it you've heard, then?"

"Yes, I heard. Mrs Cartwright paid a farewell call. She is off to Lisbon in the morning, along with several other wives, but she thought that somebody should tell me that my name is officially now the talk of the officers' mess. Good of her."

353

"Nan, given that you'd just agreed to live with me openly without benefit of marriage, your name was very soon going to be the talk of the officers' mess anyway."

"So what was the point of challenging my husband to a duel about it then, Paul?"

"I didn't. We had words and he challenged me to a duel. Which I accepted."

There was a long silence. Black eyes met blue in unmistakable challenge. Paul did not speak. Eventually Anne took a long deep breath.

"I am trying to restrain myself, but what I actually want to do is hit you."

Paul felt a rush of irritation. "Very sensible. I can understand why you are anxious about such a loving husband as Robert has always been."

"What did you expect me to say, Paul? Well done and thank you? Did you think this would be a good thing? Whatever the official cause of this so-called duel, every man who knows us is going to think you are fighting him because of me."

"Your husband stood in the mess earlier today and called you a whore. I am fighting him because of you, Nan."

"I didn't ask you to do that."

"No, you didn't," Paul said angrily. "You didn't ask me to help you financially when he spent your dowry on dice and card games. You didn't ask me to help you when he beat you and raped you and humiliated you for the whole of your married life. So let us add this to the long list of things that you didn't ask me to do for you."

Anne was silent. Then she turned away. "How did you know?"

"Rowena was worried about you. She told me to ask Teresa. Extraordinary how much my wife saw that she said nothing about. I asked Teresa and she told me the rest."

"Paul, it wouldn't have helped for you to know."

"When we got back from Talavera, I kissed you and sent you back to him because I thought that was the right thing to do, and he locked you in a room and held you down and beat you with a riding crop. And I'm bloody sure that's not all he did to you that week. When I close my eyes, I'm going to see that for a while. And you ask me why I want to kill him?"

"No, Paul, I didn't ask you that, I know why you want to kill him. Did it not occur to you that I did not want you to do it? Did it not occur to you that your honour, your life, your career ought to come before the life of the creature that I married? Certainly, it didn't occur to you to ask me how I felt about it."

"Forgive me if I assumed what you would feel about it," Paul snapped. "Were you seriously intending to return to him and try to carry on as if nothing had happened?"

"Were you seriously expecting me to fall into your arms and say thank you, for risking your own future in a pointless duel which will very likely end with you being cashiered?"

"Well, it's definitely going to end with him dead, Nan, and just now that feels worth it to me. And falling into my arms isn't something you've found that difficult in the past, is it? Or have you conveniently forgotten what happened on the retreat from Talavera?"

"No. But I didn't expect you to be throwing it at me as an accusation, Paul. When I got back and looked into Rowena's eyes, I was very ashamed."

"Well, Rowena isn't here any more, sweetheart, so what exactly are we waiting for now?" Paul stepped forward, took her wrist and pulled her hard against him. He had not realised until now how angry he was. Anne pulled back and he held onto her.

"Let me go, you arrogant bastard."

"Tell me you're not planning on screaming for help, lass, you'll have me laughing in a minute. They're a chivalrous lot, my officers, but I doubt you'll find them rushing to your rescue in here. They all know what he did and I don't think they'll object to me taking what I'm owed for getting rid of the bastard for you."

Furiously Anne slapped him across the face. "And what if I say no, Paul? Do you take over where Robert left off and hold me down?"

The rage Paul had felt when faced with Carlyon earlier swept over him again.

"How dare you say that to me?"

"How do you think I would not? Don't you know me at all, Paul? Oh, I know they are all standing back and watching you destroy your career because none of them – not even Carl – has the guts to tell you the truth. What the world is going to see, is you killing Robert because you wanted to go to bed with his wife. And I love you too much to let that happen!"

"I don't need to kill Robert to get you into bed, lass. You'd have done that whenever I wanted."

"Perhaps when I was seventeen, Paul. But I grew up."

"Don't be naïve, Nan. The only thing that kept you out of my bed for so long was Rowena. Once she was gone it was just a matter of timing and opportunity. Would you like me to demonstrate? Give me fifteen minutes and this conversation will be irrelevant."

"Keep your hands off me. If this is how you spoke to Rowena, I'm surprised she put up with it."

"I never needed to speak to my wife like this, Nan. Unlike you, she was a lady."

"You bastard," Anne said, and hit him.

Her blow was no ladylike slap and delivered without restraint, it hurt enough to snap the last vestiges of Paul's self-control. She raised her hand to hit him again and he grasped her wrist tightly.

"Bitch!" he said softly, and Anne bit his hand hard.

Paul swore and yanked it away. They stood glaring at each other and he realised how badly he wanted to hit her and how badly too, he wanted to kiss her. He could not do the first, so he did the second, stepping forward and catching her to him, covering her mouth with his. Anne struggled furiously against him, and he ignored her, pinning her arms down. After a moment, Anne brought her heel down very hard onto his foot. It hurt enough to make him lift his head in surprise, and she pulled back sharply.

"Paul, no," she whispered, and he stared down at her in dawning horror, suddenly realising what he had done. The dark eyes were on him, wide and shocked, and painfully vulnerable.

"Nan – God help me, what am I doing?" he said softly.

He reached out to touch her face, and she slapped his hand away hard. "You need to leave – now!" she spat. The expression in her dark eyes gave no room for doubt. He had never seen her look so angry and his own blind fury was draining away from him.

"Oh God, lass, I'm sorry. None of that was about you. I'm still so bloody furious with Carlyon, and when I lose my temper I just lash out."

He stepped towards her and then stepped back abruptly as she lifted a heavy brass candlestick off the table next to her, pulled back her arm and threw it across the room. It hit the wall with a shuddering crash, which made Paul physically jump.

"Well, you don't just lash out at me! If you try to touch me once more, I am going to pick up the other one of those and bring it down on the back of your head. I'm going to my room, get out of my way!"

Paul stepped to one side, his eyes on her face. He thought, inconsequentially, how lovely she was and how much he loved her and he was sickened at what he had said and done. He had never behaved that way towards a woman in his life and he could not believe he had done it to Anne.

Anne walked past him and opened the door. There was not a single sound coming from the table at the far end of the courtyard and the men sitting around it were all staring at her as if they had never seen a woman before. Paul followed her out of the door. Anne stood for a moment glaring at the men and every one of them turned away and lowered his eyes to his plate. Anne gave a nod and turned to walk to the foot of the stairs which led up to her room.

"Ma'am, wait." Carl was coming through the archway into the courtyard. "You both need to hear this. It's from Wellington."

Anne turned. She did not speak. Paul came forward and carefully did not touch her. He had no idea what to say or do. He looked at Carl.

"Robert Carlyon has run." Carl said quietly. "Packed up, took his horse and a substantial purse from the headquarters pay chest and gone. Hookey is furious, he's issued a warrant for his arrest."

Paul absorbed the news. "Where can he go?"

"I've no idea, but he'd better get there fast given the mood Wellington is in, you know how he is about money. Gordon says he's frothing at the mouth. There isn't going to be a duel in the morning because your opponent just turned tail and ran like a rabbit. Thank God."

"Yes, I suppose so." Paul glanced at Anne, longing to talk to her about it, but her expression told him that she was unlikely to listen. She gave a brief nod.

"Thank you for telling me, Carl."

She turned to go and Paul reached out to take her arm. "Nan..."

"Did you hear me tell you not to touch me, Major?" Anne snapped in frosty tones.

Paul released her. "Yes, ma'am."

"Thank you. I am going to bed. I have quite unaccountably lost my appetite. And if you come anywhere near my room tonight, I will stab you."

Paul took a deep breath. "Nan, you know I didn't mean..."

"You didn't mean what exactly? To hold me still while you do what you like to me? Trust me, Paul, that feels very familiar to me, but I didn't expect it from you, and if you ever do it again, I am going to be on the next available transport home because I am not putting up with that again. Are we clear?"

"Very," Paul said. Anne turned and walked up the stairs and into her room and the door slammed with a satisfying crash. The sound of the bolt being drawn across could be heard echoing around the courtyard.

Paul went to his room as soon as he had eaten. Like Anne, he had little appetite, but he knew that he had several days of hard marching and possibly fighting ahead of him and food was a necessity not a luxury. Usually, he slept well the night before a march as if his body knew that it would need the rest, but he lay awake until the early hours, thinking about his quarrel with Anne. Pointless to replay every stupid, cruel thing he had said to her. None of it had been true or had any meaning. He had lost his temper as thoroughly with her as he had with her husband earlier in the day and he did not understand why.

Enlightenment came with the dawn and Paul got up and dressed and methodically checked his pack before going downstairs. It was too early even for his other officers. He went through to the kitchen and found George Kelly already at work. With a hot drink in his hands, he went outside and stood watching as dawn began to creep its way across the early sky. Now he could hear sounds from the other yard as his men began to get ready for their march. The smell of cooking fires filled the air.

"You're up early," a voice said, and Paul turned to see his sergeant coming through the archway.

"Couldn't sleep," he said.

"Guilty conscience?" the Irishman enquired.

Paul laughed. "Who told you, Carl?"

Michael nodded. "I came through for a drink after you'd gone to bed. He said that both your voices were nice and clear. So was the part where that candlestick embedded itself into the wall."

"I honestly think she would have killed me," Paul said. "Christ but she's got a temper."

"And you haven't?"

"Yes. And I managed to lose it twice yesterday."

"Well, it sounds as though kicking the shit out of Carlyon was a worthwhile exercise. But Nan?"

"She was furious with me for accepting his challenge. And I was furious with her for not understanding. And a lot of other things, which only really

357

occurred to me after a sleepless night. I wish we didn't have to go this morning. But perhaps it's as well. She'll have time to calm down and we can talk when I get back." Paul smiled and shook his head. "I'm not used to this," he said. "I don't think Rowena and I had a single quarrel in the whole of our married life."

"And why was that Paul?"

Paul grinned. "She never argued with me, she just put up with whatever shit I chose to throw at her, poor lass. I can see I'm going to need a different approach with Nan."

Michael nodded. "Come and eat. I know you're not hungry but halfway through the day you'll be an arsehole if you've not eaten. More of an arsehole than you're already likely to be on no sleep."

"It doesn't matter, I still won't be as much of an arsehole as Craufurd. And for God's sake, Michael, remember not to call me Paul in front of him, you know what he's like."

"I've not slipped up yet, sir. Come on."

The 110th were assembled within an hour, and Paul walked along the lines to check them, commenting freely and cheerfully on any man who did not seem to be turned out well enough to pass General Craufurd's exacting standards. His light company were lined up inside the yard and he went to them last, finding, as he had expected, that there was no criticism to be made of them. Difficult, insubordinate and foul-mouthed, they were the elite of his regiment and probably the elite of Wellington's army and they knew it. After a brief inspection he gave his orders for the march, checked that his orderly was ready with his spare mounts and that the few pack animals they were taking with them were lined up, then swung himself into the saddle and walked his horse to the head of his battalion.

"Paul."

Paul wheeled his mount, surprised. Anne was standing on the little gallery outside her room at the top of the steps, dressed in a soft flowing robe of dark blue velvet with her hair falling to her waist. He sat very still for a moment looking at her, aware of the silence around the courtyard at the sight of her. Then she moved and came down the stairs quickly, lifting her skirts to avoid tripping. Her feet were bare. Paul slid from Rufus' back, tossed the reins to Jenson, took four quick steps towards her and caught her into his arms, his mouth on hers. She kissed him back as if they had been alone in her room and he could feel the quick beat of her heart against his.

"Nan, I'm so sorry."

"You'd have been a lot sorrier if you'd ridden out that gate without saying goodbye to me," Anne said severely, but there was laughter in her eyes again. Now that she was with him, Paul could not leave without speaking to her. He glanced over at O'Reilly.

"Five minutes. Get them moving and I'll catch up."

Paul drew her into his office again which was the nearest private room and closed the door. "I'm so glad you came down. I couldn't decide what to do."

358

"For future reference, my love, when you are riding out of that door to fight, the right thing to do is always to kiss me and tell me that you'll come back, no matter how angry I've been with you."

"Love, I think yesterday is the crowning glory of the stupid things I've done." Paul smoothed her hair back from her face. "Listen to me because I don't have long. I love you. I've loved you since the day I met you, I suspect, and I'll always love you. And the reason I was so bloody furious with you, was because you didn't turn to me when you really needed help. Because you were a lass in trouble and I'd want any woman to come to me in that situation and you didn't."

"And do you know why?" Anne asked him, half-laughing.

"Oh dear love, would you believe it took me half the night to work it out? No need to state it, I think I demonstrated it very well yesterday. But in the world I've lived in, it's my job to protect you, not the other way around, so it wasn't obvious."

"If you'd been cashiered or arrested because you went after him, I could not have borne it," Anne said quietly. "I could not."

"And if he'd beaten you to death one day because he caught you with me, doing whatever it is we've been doing every time I got you alone for five minutes, how do you think I'd have felt?" Paul said quietly. He was aware of an instinct to brush aside the reasons for his resentment, but he stopped himself. This was new and he needed to learn a new way of behaving. "I've been putting you in danger, love, every time I touched you. And I didn't know it."

"Paul – I knew what you'd have done."

"Nan, I understand. But I'm not used to a lass putting herself in harm's way to protect me. It felt as though you didn't trust me."

He realised he was holding his breath, watching her face. After a long moment, Anne said:

"I do trust you, Paul, I just worry for you. I love you so much. We don't have time now, but when you get back, I'll tell you everything. Even the bits you'd rather not know."

Paul felt relief flood through him at the realisation that this time he had got it right. "Thank you. And in return, the next time I feel like I'm going to kill somebody that I'm not supposed to kill, I'll do my level best to run it past you first. I must go. That bastard O'Reilly has got them all still lined up waiting for me out there. He'll be the next one I'll murder, believe me."

Anne was laughing again. "Take care and come back to me, Paul."

"I will. I've got too much to lose now."

She was still laughing, shaking her head. "You're such a liar, Van Daan, you always had too much to lose. The first time you get in a fight and some poor Frenchman looks at you the wrong way, you'll forget all about me and take every risk you've ever taken all over again."

"Very likely. But afterwards, I will be sorry." Paul stopped took her hand and led her from the room. He stopped beside his horse, painfully aware of a hundred pairs of eyes regarding his progress with considerable interest. He swung himself into the saddle and glared down at his sergeant-major who was smiling affably. "Men at the ready, Sergeant-Major?"

"That they are, sir." Sergeant-Major O'Reilly was always at his most Irish when he was being difficult.

"Then let's get a move on. The rest of them will be halfway to the Coa by now, pissing themselves laughing about the fact that the so-called light company can't keep up with the rest of the infantry."

"I think we'll just about manage to catch them, sir." Michael shot Anne an amused glance. "We'll be seeing you soon, ma'am. Try and stay out of trouble if you can."

"You bring him back in one piece, Michael O'Reilly, or you'll know something about trouble." Anne said, and there was a ripple of laughter running through the men of the company.

"That's what they pay me for, girl dear. Although from what I've heard he's likely to be in more danger from you than from the French."

Paul had reached the archway and looked back. Anne was standing there watching him and on impulse he wheeled again and rode back past the amused eyes of his light company, scooped her up with one arm and lifted her slight form easily off her feet for one last long kiss. Then he set her down, turned and rode off to the sound of her laughter and the cheering of his men.

As the last of them went through the archway, he heard the bellow of Sergeant-Major O'Reilly. "Get your backsides to the front, lads! Double-quick march, you're the light company not the bloody guards, you're supposed to be able to move. Two columns one each side and overtake them, do you think we march at the rear?"

Chapter Twenty-One

The days passed quickly for Anne. With meticulous care she set about arranging for the removal of herself, her baggage and the remainder of the supplies and equipment of the 110th back towards Lisbon. Paul's young quartermaster appeared initially bewildered by her involvement but was quickly won over and Anne enjoyed working with Lieutenant Breakspear.

Anne was determined to ensure that the sick and wounded who were left in the hospital would not suffer the privations of a hasty and difficult journey and would have somewhere comfortable to go to when they got back to the capital. With careful nursing many of the sick who had returned from Walcheren had gone back to their regiments, but there were enough left to require several wagons to transport them. With the help of Adam Norris, who had finally been released from a French prison camp, Anne had secured the use of a large seminary on the edge of Lisbon and organised her supplies and bedding to travel along with the wounded, under the care of Dr Daniels. After the experiences of several small parties who had been surprised by marauding French skirmishers, Wellington had given instructions that nobody was to travel without a substantial escort, and most of Anne's patients set off under an escort of Portuguese militia, along with the women and children of the 110th and Paul's small daughter in the arms of her nurse. Anne remained with Teresa and a few orderlies in Viseu. There were three patients who would be difficult to move, including Private Davison. Anne knew that each extra day of rest would make a difference to them, and she was sure that Paul's battalion would come via Viseu as they moved back towards Lisbon. She could wait.

It was strange at the farm with only Teresa for company. Anne felt ambivalent about leaving Viseu. With the ebb and flow of war she might never come here again, but in this place, everything had changed for her. Her love affair with Paul, begun so impulsively in a shepherd's hut in Yorkshire and developed through the horrors and hardships of Talavera, had matured in this quiet place. Anne would always feel that shared laughter around the officers' dinner table and those long quiet afternoons in his office, learning the business of his regiment together, had cemented their bond into something real and enduring.

They had both suffered loss here too. After their passionate farewell in the courtyard, Anne had, as she had promised Paul, gone back to his room and endured the painful and difficult task of sorting through Rowena van Daan's clothes and possessions. She distributed clothing to the women of the regiment and packed up her friend's jewellery and letters and personal items. The silver backed brush and comb still held long silvery fair hairs and Anne cried unashamedly as she packed them away. She had cut, without Paul knowing, several locks of that hair in the barn, and would keep them for Rowena's children when they were older. Anne missed Paul but she was glad that they had these weeks apart. He too needed time to mourn his wife without the complicating joy of being with her. It would have been easier if he had not cared so much for Rowena. Anne had always envied them the steady, easy affection of their daily interaction, and she felt a responsibility to find a way to give him that stability herself. The passionate highs and lows of her own relationship with Paul had been born out of circumstances, but he needed something different if he were to continue to do the job that he had chosen. There were lessons she could learn from Rowena.

Against all the odds, Private Davison continued to improve. Anne walked up one morning to the almost empty hospital to change his dressing and found him awake and alert.

"Davison, you're a miracle, I would have sworn you were a dead man. What is it with the light company, don't you bleed the same as other men? By the time the major gets back you'll be marching back to Lisbon at this rate."

"Thanks to you, ma'am." Davison lay back, teeth clenched with pain as she delicately peeled back the dressing and inspected the wound.

"This is looking very good. I'm going to get Williams to sit you up more, and I think we can start you on proper food, you must be sick of broth. That'll help you to get stronger." Anne bathed the area carefully and applied a fresh dressing. "You're hard to kill."

"They had a good go, ma'am. Heard from the major?"

"I had a note delivered by one of Lord Wellington's scouts yesterday. There was a battle at the Coa, which didn't go in our favour, but they got out in one piece. I think he and General Craufurd may have had a few words." Anne carefully leaned the boy forward to bandage the dressing in place. "I can't wait to hear the full story, I've a feeling there was a good deal he couldn't say in a letter."

Anne left Teresa to tend to the other two injured men and walked back towards the farm. Wellington had already marched most of his army south-west to meet Massena's advancing troops, and the town was quiet and almost empty. The general had left instructions that the local population was to retreat with the army back behind the Lisbon defences, and many people had already left, including Señor Ferreira and his family. They were fortunate to have family to go to near Lisbon, but Anne felt sorry for those who would travel as refugees and she wondered what provision had been made for them.

362

As she passed the barn where the 110th had been billeted, Anne was surprised to see that the door was open. Curious, she went to look. It had definitely been closed the previous evening. It had been a wet and windy night and she had not wanted the banging door to keep her awake. Pulling it wider, Anne stepped into the barn and heard a stealthy movement.

"Is there somebody here?"

There was silence, but Anne had a strong sense of being watched. She stepped further in. "I can hear you. Will you come out? I'm not going to scream, if you'd been about to attack me, you'd have done it by now."

Out from behind one of the posts on the far side, a tall figure was emerging. Anne did not move. Slowly the man came forward into the light. He was young, probably no more than twenty or so, and very good looking with long dark curly hair roughly tied back and expressive hazel eyes. He wore a tattered infantry uniform, and his face was too thin and pale with dark shadows under his eyes.

"Mean you no harm, ma'am. I'll be on my way."

He bent to pick up his pack and rifle and moved towards the far door of the barn. Anne's heart settled to a normal beat. There was nothing threatening about this boy.

"Private. Did you manage to steal any food while you were sleeping in the barn?"

He turned and looked at her then shook his head. Anne gave a friendly smile. "Come into the kitchen," she said.

"Can't do that, ma'am."

"There are no soldiers here, Private. They're all marching south to meet the French. Just me."

He studied her for a long moment. Then unexpectedly he said:

"You shouldn't be telling that to a strange man in the barn, ma'am."

"Probably not, but your warning suggests I've not made a mistake. Come on, there's stew and oatcakes. You look as though you've not eaten in a week."

He followed her through into the kitchen and set down his pack and rifle. Anne wondered about that since he was not wearing a rifleman's uniform. She suspected it was stolen. "You here alone, ma'am?"

"With my maid. She's out at present. And a few medical staff at the next farm. We're waiting for an escort to go back to Lisbon." Anne went to the range and lifted the lid on the pot. "Sit down," she said, reaching for a bowl. She ladled mutton stew into it and took it to the man who was now sitting at the long wooden table. As he began to eat, she brought three oatcakes and a mug of ale. He ate with the concentration of a starving man, and Anne asked no questions. When he had finished, she refilled his tankard. "Better?"

He looked up at her with those distinctive hazel eyes and nodded. "I'm grateful, ma'am. Truly."

"Grateful enough to tell me what you're doing here?"

"You know what I'm doing here, ma'am."

"Not going to fight against Massena, I'm guessing. Desertion is a risky business; Lord Wellington has no sense of humour about it just now. Is it worth it?"

"Didn't have much choice ma'am."

Anne studied him. "I'd thought you a new recruit at first," she said. "But you're not, are you?"

"No, ma'am. Three years' service. Wounded at Talavera."

"So why now? I was at Talavera, I'd have thought that was the time you'd want to desert."

"I'm not a coward, ma'am." His accent was broad cockney, reminding her of Carter.

"No, I believe you. Why are you running?"

"Avoiding a flogging," the boy said briefly, taking another drink. "Would have been the fourth time in six months, and I'm not sure I was going to survive this one. Seemed worth taking a chance."

"What offence?" Anne asked quietly.

"Insubordination, ma'am."

Anne stood up. "May I see your back?" she asked.

After a moment, the boy nodded and stood up. He turned and lifted his coat and shirt and Anne stared in mute horror at the ruin of his back. He dropped his clothing back and sat down, reaching for his drink, not looking at her. She could sense his shame and discomfort, and she was furious.

"Which regiment?"

"87th, ma'am. First battalion, light company. Lieutenant Vane. He likes to flog, ma'am."

"That's not flogging, it's bloody butchery!" Anne said angrily, and he looked up quickly, clearly shocked at an officer's lady using bad language. "I'm sorry, but it's true. What's your name, Private?"

"Kingston, ma'am. Jamie Kingston."

"Where are you heading, Kingston?"

"Oporto, ma'am, if I can get there. Try and stow away on a wine boat." He shrugged. "They pick me up and hang me, at least I tried."

"Yes." Anne looked at him, troubled. She had no idea where Paul and his men were and had no way of reaching him. Strongly, Anne felt that if he could have sat down with this boy, he would have found a solution for him, but it was too risky to keep him here or try to take him south. He was a deserter and he would be shot or hanged without further question.

"I hope you make it, Kingston. When you leave you can take some food with you."

"That's good of you, ma'am. Is your husband with the army?"

"Yes." It was too complicated to explain and Anne did not try. "It's not likely that any troops will be passing this way soon, but best keep out of sight anyway."

"I'll be on my way, ma'am. Don't want to get you into trouble. Thank you." The boy smiled suddenly and without the careworn air, Anne was struck anew by his good looks. She regarded him with her head on one side.

"Jesus, Kingston, you must be a nightmare with the girls."

Kingston gave a slightly crooked smile. "Used to be, ma'am. Not so much recently."

"There's bread and some cheese in the pantry, and you can take a flask of ale. I'll get it for you."

Anne filled a bag and he accepted it with a smile of thanks. "Go on, get going. Try not to get yourself shot, will you?"

"Do my best, ma'am. I'm very grateful."

Anne watched him go a little sadly. It occurred to her that she was beginning to feel lonely in the quiet of the deserted farm. Perhaps after all she might have done better to go back to Lisbon with Paul's daughter and await him at the villa. Feeling somewhat aimless she went back into the kitchen, smiling at herself a little. She was used to being constantly busy, and now that there was little to do, she had too much time on her hands. Determined not to brood, she went out into the courtyard again, intending to collect one of her medical books from her room. When she was back in Lisbon, she would not have time to read, she should make the most of it.

Glancing across the courtyard Anne saw a uniformed figure coming through the archway and wondered why the boy had come back. She paused, shielding her eyes in the sunlight and the man stepped forward. Anne found herself looking into the eyes of her husband.

Robert Carlyon stopped when he saw her and they stood looking at one another. During his weeks on the run he had lost weight, and looked gaunt and hungry, his beard grown through and his hair longer than Anne had ever seen it. His clothes were dusty from days in the saddle. His eyes rested on her with an expression that chilled her.

"Who else is here?"

"Nobody," Anne said. "Wellington has taken the army to meet Massena. Paul has sent the child back to Lisbon with her nurse."

"Your maid?"

"Up at the hospital." Anne's mouth was dry with fear and her heart was hammering in her breast. "Robert..."

"Get me something to eat."

Trying not to show her fear, Anne walked through into the kitchen. Robert followed her and watched as she served more stew and oatcakes. She used the bowl she had given Kingston, so that he would not notice that somebody had eaten there recently. Robert sat down at the table, took out a pistol and set it on the table beside him.

"Get the brandy," he snapped.

Anne obeyed. His tone was indifferent, but the expression in his eyes was anything but. She could feel his eyes following her as she poured brandy into a cup and he drank, draining it and setting it down for her to refill. Anne did so.

"I thought you would be many miles away by now," she said.

"You hoped," he said mockingly. "I've passage to south America, courtesy of Wellington's pay chest. But it doesn't leave until next month, and what better way to spend my last days in Portugal than with my ever-loving wife."

"I'd have thought this a little close to the army for comfort. How were you so sure they'd all gone?"

"I've been in the area for a couple of days, watching the place. It didn't look as though the battalion was still here. Thanks to you, Nan, my life as I've known it is over. Did you think I wouldn't take the risk to make sure that you get what you deserved?"

"Thanks to me?" Despite her terror, Anne felt a rush of anger. "Jesus, Robert, you're a delusional lunatic. You started all of this the day you held me down in a stable and raped me to force me to marry you, and all you ever wanted was my father's money. And then you stole army pay. How is this my fault?"

He did not answer immediately but continued eating with the same concentration that Kingston had shown. Anne watched him, aware of the irony. She had felt completely safe alone with an unknown deserter in the kitchen, but she was terrified in the presence of her husband.

Robert drained his cup, then stood up. Picking up the pistol, he walked towards her. Anne backed up, but in a few steps her back was against the wall. He came on until he was close enough to touch her, and then he placed the muzzle of the gun against her neck and pressed hard. Anne's heart was pounding.

"That's exactly what I wanted," he said. "The money. I thought that would be enough, that I didn't give a damn what you said or did. And then you changed all that."

"I did nothing..."

"You fucking did!" he hissed furiously. "You made me want you! You made me need you! And then you flashed that smile and those pretty ankles all round headquarters and made me look a bloody fool with everybody from Lord Wellington to the barracks groom! And I wanted you so bloody badly that I put up with it. You think I didn't know how they laughed about it behind my back? But I didn't care as long as I had you. And then you did the one thing that I couldn't ignore. You came back from Talavera with Paul van Daan and it was so fucking obvious what you'd been doing with him!"

He pressed the pistol harder against her neck and the metal cut into her skin. Anne bit her lip to stop herself from screaming.

"And I notice you're not denying it now, are you?"

Anne moved her head cautiously to look at him. "You wouldn't believe me if I did," she said, trying to keep the tremor from her voice. "But you left me at Talavera, Robert. You left me without food or money in the middle of a battle because you couldn't be bothered to come and find me when you'd orders to march out. What did you think was going to happen?"

He pulled the pistol back and hit her with it sharply. Anne felt it cut into her cheek and clamped her lips together hard, so as not to cry out. "Is that what you're saying, Nan? That you slept with him to buy passage back to Lisbon? Is that what he made you do?"

"That says a lot more about you than it does about Paul van Daan, Robert. He didn't make me do anything. He took care of me. They all did. It's what decent men do."

"And you were bloody happy to do it, weren't you? You made me the laughing stock of the army with him."

"No, Robert, you did that with your jealousy. How could you have expected me to want you after what you did to me?"

"Well, you were bloody good at pretending, weren't you, Nan?" he said softly, close to her ear. "I'm wondering what you would do to keep yourself alive for another hour. And do I want you to do it? Do I want you to take your clothes off and to feel what you make me feel one more time, before I blow your pretty head off?"

Anne turned her head towards him very slowly. Her mouth was dry with fear and her heart was beating so hard that it hurt her chest. Already she knew that if she reached out to him, she could distract him. He was here not for revenge alone, she realised, but because his obsession with her was as strong as ever. For how long could she keep him occupied? It did not matter. There was no rescue party on the way, and she could not bear the thought of touching him again.

"No, Robert," she said quietly. "Not any more. Pull the trigger. Kill me. Just end it."

Carlyon released her and pushed her back hard against the wall and Anne's head slammed against the stone. While she was still dazed, he hit her hard, twice across the face. She could taste blood in her mouth. Up close to her he pushed her back against the stone and kissed her hard, bruising her already cut lip. Anne tried to keep silent, but it hurt so much she made a small sound. The noise made him stop. Suddenly he put the pistol down on the table and came back to her. He took her into his arms and kissed her again, more gently.

"I didn't want any of this," he said softly. "I just wanted you. I wanted to go back and start again, as if...as if..."

"As if what? As if our marriage didn't begin with a rape? Did you ever think that was possible, Robert?"

"If Paul van Daan hadn't come to Yorkshire you might have married me anyway," he said quietly. "Have you ever thought that Nan?"

"Or I might have got engaged to Julian Carew. What would you have done then, Robert? This is not about Paul..."

"It bloody is! You're my wife and he doesn't even try to hide what he wants from you..."

"It's nothing to do with Paul. It's nobody else's fault that you did what you did. You raped a seventeen-year-old girl for money, and I could never have fallen in love with a man who thought it was acceptable to do that to any woman."

Robert looked at her very steadily. Suddenly, unexpectedly he said:

"Did they hurt you? The French?"

"No. Sergeant-Major O'Reilly and Corporal Carter fought back."

"And Van Daan?"

"He wasn't there, Robert. I told you that."

"I thought..."

"I know what you thought. I told you the truth. You could have asked anyone in his battalion where he was. I didn't leave with him; he followed us on Wellington's orders. I went to take care of Rowena. And she died."

He was studying her and Anne thought that his expression had softened slightly. "I thought I'd come here and find you with him. And I'd made up my mind I was going to kill both of you."

"He's away fighting, Robert." Anne regarded him warily. She was not sure what was the right thing to say to keep him calm. "You were wrong, you know. About this and about Talavera. We didn't."

"I want to believe you so much. But everyone knows what he's like..."

"That doesn't change the truth. I've never shared his bed, Robert. All those beatings were for nothing."

He was looking at her with a fierce intensity. Suddenly he said:

"Come with me."

Anne's heart lurched. "What? No. I'm not going back to that again."

"You have to. I've changed, Nan. These weeks without you. It's only him. Away from him, I can make you change your mind." Robert's eyes seemed to burn into her and Anne was chilled to realise that he was not entirely sane. "I meant to leave without you but I couldn't do it. So I came here to kill you. But that isn't what I want. I want you with me. I won't hurt you again, I swear it. Come with me."

"Robert, you're mad. You can't think I'd trust you? You hit me only five minutes ago."

"Come with me. I love you. I need you."

"Love?" Despite herself Anne could not keep the scorn from her voice. "You don't beat somebody you love."

"I can't be without you. You're all I think about. That's why I came back. I need you."

"Just go, Robert. Sooner or later the army is coming back this way and you need to be somewhere else." Anne took a deep breath. "I'm not going to tell anybody I've seen you. I don't want you shot or hanged. But I need you to leave."

She saw with dread, the flare of madness in his eyes. Her face was sore where he had hit her and her head was beginning to throb where it had hit the wall.

"I'm not leaving you here alive," her husband said quietly, and his matter-of-fact tone was somehow more frightening than the times in the past when he had screamed abuse at her. "I'm not giving you to him. You've got a choice, Nan. You come with me now, to Brazil, or I'm going to kill you." Robert released her and walked to pick up the pistol from the table.

Anne's mind was working frantically. He was clearly not sane. The thought of him touching her again appalled her, but she did not want to die. She thought of Paul and the pain of loss stabbed into her heart at the thought

368

that she might never see him or touch him again. If Robert killed her, he would have to live with her loss so soon after losing Rowena. Anne wished passionately that she had gone to him during that last night before he left, to have given him that memorable night he had talked of, to keep with him down the years without her.

The thought of Paul steadied Anne. He would have told her to go, to keep herself alive, to wait for him to find her. After two years of enduring Robert, she could surely endure him a little longer. Anne took a deep breath. He was pointing the pistol at her and his hands were shaking.

"If you kill me, Robert, it will destroy you," she said quietly, making one more attempt. "You'll hear my voice in your head for the rest of your life."

He gave a short bark of laughter. "I hear your voice in my head every bloody day," he said. "I wake up every night and reach for you. I hear you laughing when I close my eyes to sleep and I dream of how you feel in my arms, so you tell me, Nan, how much worse it could be if I killed you now? Maybe I just should, because at least then I wouldn't spend my time imagining you in his arms. Maybe killing you is the only way to make it stop."

Anne stared at him in mute terror, her brain frantically trying to frame words that would stop him, but before she could speak there was an ominous click in the silence.

"I wouldn't, sir," a voice said from the back door, and both Anne and Robert jumped and turned. He was silhouetted against the light, a tall slim figure in his shabby uniform. He was pointing his rifle at Carlyon, and his hands, unlike Robert's, were rock steady.

"Who the hell are you?" Robert said.

"Just passing through, sir, like you. Best to move on and let the lady go now," Kingston said conversationally. Anne stared at him in complete astonishment. She could not believe that he had come back, or that he was calmly pointing his rifle at an officer.

Robert gave a short, harsh laugh. "You bloody fool! You're not going to shoot me. I may be a deserter, but I'm still an officer, and they'd hang you!"

"Yes, sir. So, I'd prefer not to have to do it. Just move away from the lady and go back to your horse. No reason for anybody to die here today."

Anne was watching her husband's eyes and saw them narrow in sudden determination and she knew with horrified certainty that he was going to do it. She closed her eyes and waited, her heart beating so hard that it was making her dizzy. There was a crack, deafening in the small room, and Robert gave a high scream and then made a gurgling sound. Anne opened her eyes and looked at him. He had collapsed to the ground and blood was pumping from the gaping wound left by the rifle shot in his throat. Anne stared at him uncomprehendingly and then looked past him to Kingston who was lowering the rifle. His hands were still not shaking. He looked completely calm.

"Arsehole," he said. "You all right, ma'am?"

Anne nodded. Kingston put the rifle down on the table and came to her side. Anne could feel her whole body trembling, as if she were suddenly very cold. Shock and terror, which had left her through those moments when she believed she was about to die, came flooding back and she was shivering so violently that she could not even speak. The boy looked at her with concern.

"I need to get you out of here, ma'am, you need to lie down. Christ, it looks like he's used you as a punch bag. Where's your room?"

Anne pointed, unable to speak, and he stooped and picked her up and carried her outside.

"Which way, ma'am?"

"Up the stairs, the first door." Anne's teeth were chattering.

Stripping back the covers Kingston put her into the bed and covered her, then when the shivering did not stop, he disappeared and came back with the covers from another bed, which he piled on top of her. He sat on the edge of the bed and took her hand.

Finally, after what seemed an age, the terrible shaking eased and Anne was still, an occasional tremor still running through her. "Kingston," she said, and was conscious that her voice sounded as though it was coming from a long way away. "You came back. Why?"

"Saw him ride up, ma'am. Didn't know who he was. Just wanted to check you were all right. I told you, you shouldn't be here like this on your own."

"I'm all right now," Anne said. Her head was throbbing where it had hit the wall and she could feel her face swollen and bruised from his blows. But she was alive. She was also free. Her mind shied away from that thought, unable yet to imagine how it would feel. Instead, she looked at the boy sitting beside her and realised what he had just risked for her.

"You need to leave, Kingston. Don't worry. My maid will be back soon."

"There are some soldiers up at the other farm, ma'am. I saw them as I was leaving. I can get help for you."

"No! I owe you my life; I'm not letting them hang you. Get out of here."

"No, ma'am. I'm not leaving you until I know you're safe."

"Please, Kingston. How can I stand knowing that you died because you came back for me?"

"My choice, ma'am, not yours. I'm not leaving you. You don't know how bad you look."

Anne was quiet, realising that he would not budge. He did not try to talk to her, simply sat holding her hand and Anne wondered about the man who had believed it was acceptable to thrash this boy's back raw and wanted to kill him.

Finally, after an age, there were sounds below. Anne turned her head. "Kingston. Will you do something for me?"

"Anything, ma'am."

"Just get out of sight. Go in to the next room and stay there. I don't know who this is, but once I've got help you can go down the back stairs and get out of here."

"Ma'am..."

"Look, they're not going to blame me for killing him. I don't even have a gun on the premises. As long as you're not here, I can tell them whatever story I like. Just give yourself a chance. Please."

Reluctantly Kingston stood up, lifting his rifle. "I'll be there with this loaded until I'm sure you're safe, ma'am," he said steadily.

"Jamie Kingston, you are so bloody stubborn, you should be in the 110th," Anne said. "Go."

When he had gone Anne got cautiously to her feet and went to the door. She pushed it open and looked down into the courtyard. A man was dismounting awkwardly from his horse. He stood looking around him and seeing nobody about, he took the reins and began to lead the animal towards the stables.

"Johnny," Anne said, feeling relief flooding through her body.

Captain Wheeler turned with a smile, looking up. "There you are," he said. "I was beginning to think you'd gone back to Lisbon after all. I...oh dear God!"

Anne saw his eyes widen at the sight of her bruised and battered face. He turned and led the horse to one of the iron rings set into the farmhouse wall, looped the reins, and then turned and ran to the steps as Anne made her way cautiously down into the yard. She noticed that he was limping badly.

"Nan, what the hell happened?"

"In a moment. Johnny, you're hurt. Where's Paul, is he all right?"

"He's fine, although in the worst temper...never mind that, he's on his way to join the rest of the army. I brought some of our wounded back to the hospital, I've just come from there. But ma'am, what happened?"

"Have you been into the kitchen yet?"

Johnny shook his head, his eyes on her face. "No. What am I going to find there?"

Anne took a deep breath. "Robert's body," she said steadily.

Johnny stared at her for a long moment. Then he turned and ran towards the farmhouse. Anne remained in the yard. She could not bring herself to go back into the kitchen. After a few minutes Johnny re-emerged, his face set. He came forward.

"You need to sit down, you look as though you're going to pass out," he said. "Come through into the mess room. Christ, Nan, what did he do to you? I'm guessing..."

"He came back. He wanted me to go with him to Brazil. He hit me."

"More than once, by the look of it. Who shot him?"

"I did."

Wheeler studied her. "With what?"

"A pistol. Paul left it for me. It's all right, Johnny, I need to talk to the provost marshal, I know. Perhaps you could come with me."

Wheeler looked at her for a very long time. Finally, he said:

"If I didn't know my commanding officer was thirty miles away by now, I'd be suspicious. Ma'am, I'm not sure who fired that shot but it wasn't you, even if you could present me with a pistol. That was a rifle, it was a good shot and it happened very recently. Is he still here?"

"No," Anne said.

"Don't make me go through this place, Nan."

"Johnny…"

"Don't move, sir."

She whirled and looked up. Private Kingston was descending the steps from her room steadily, his eyes and his rifle trained on Johnny. Anne shook her head.

"Private Kingston, don't. He's my friend."

"I hope so, ma'am. You need somebody to take care of you. But he isn't my friend and I just shot an officer. It's a hanging offence."

"You did it to save my life."

"They aren't going to care about that, ma'am, especially given that I'm a deserter with a charge sheet a mile long. It's all right, I'm not going to hurt anybody. I'll just carry on as I was. Once I've gone you can tell the truth, no need to get yourself into any trouble."

Anne looked over at Johnny. The grey eyes were regarding the boy with the rifle steadily. "Look, Johnny…"

Unexpectedly, Captain Wheeler smiled. "By now," he said in matter-of-fact tones, "I was hoping to be settled in the mess with a large brandy ma'am, with you fussing over this leg wound, while I told you the sorry story of the Coa. Put that gun down, Private, you're not going to shoot me. Come through into the house, this hurts and I need to sit. And for God's sake somebody tell me what the hell is going on, will you?"

There was a long silence. Then to Anne's immense relief, Jamie Kingston lowered the rifle. "You going to hand me over, sir?" he asked.

"No."

Anne felt suddenly dizzy. She closed her eyes for a moment, hoping it would pass and Private Kingston swore.

"Ma'am, you shouldn't even be out of your bed. Come and sit down for God's sake."

The descent from high drama into practicality made Anne giggle. She heard the note of hysteria in her laughter and quelled it firmly letting Kingston lead her through into the dining room. As he helped her to sit down there was a voice outside.

"You here, sir? Teresa is up at the hospital, she's getting the lads settled. I thought…"

Wheeler put his hand on the boy's arm quickly. "It's all right lad, it's just my sergeant-major. Sit next to Mrs Carlyon, you seem to be good at taking care of her. I'll go and make sure he's alone and speak to him."

***

Johnny Wheeler limped outside and saw Sergeant-Major O'Reilly coming forward. "You found her, sir?" he asked. "I thought…"

372

"Are you alone, Sergeant-Major?"

"Yes, why?"

"Because we've just walked into something. Mrs Carlyon is in the mess with a young deserter she's picked up and in the kitchen is the body of Captain Robert Carlyon with his head half blown off."

Michael froze for a long moment. "Christ in heaven, thank God the major didn't come with us," he breathed. "Is she all right?"

"She's a mess, he's given her a good beating. The lad came in and shot him. I don't know any more than that. Come through and let's find out what the hell has been going on."

Michael ran through into the dining room. Anne stood up. She looked shaky and ill and Wheeler was faintly amused at the expression of sheer fury on his sergeant-major's expressive countenance at the sight of her battered face. Michael moved forward and put his arms about her.

"Girl dear, what has that bastard done to you," he whispered. "Are you all right?"

Anne leaned into him and Johnny saw a shiver ran through her. "I thought I was going to die," she said, and Johnny could hear with helpless anger, the echo of her terror. The young deserter had risen at their entry.

"All right, Nan, we're here now," Johnny said. "You're safe. Go and sit down. I'm going to light that fire, you're shivering. Michael, get her some brandy, it's over there."

"I'll light the fire, sir, if you get down on your knees, you're not going to get up again with that leg. Why don't you get the brandy?"

Johnny nodded, went for the bottle and cups and poured. He helped Anne to drink and sat holding her hand until her shivering eased. The fire blazed into life and Michael got up and went to collect his cup. Johnny looked at Kingston who appeared completely bewildered.

"Sit down, lad and drink. If you're not in shock, you bloody ought to be."

Kingston seated himself uneasily and looked at him. "Sir, this isn't right."

"I'm not sure any of this is right, Private. Drink it anyway. What have you got there, Michael?"

"Captain Carlyon's pack, sir. Not sure what you want doing about the body." Michael studied Anne. "He beat you, didn't he?"

"Yes. He came back to kill me. He blamed me for everything. And then he wanted me to go with him, to South America. I thought I might have to go. To pretend." Anne shuddered again. "Kingston was here earlier, sleeping in the barn and I fed him. He'd seen Robert arrive and came back to make sure I was all right."

Johnny looked at the boy. "You must have known the risk," he said softly.

"Suppose so, sir. But she was good to me, I couldn't let him do it."

Michael put a hand on his shoulder. "Drink," he said, putting the cup in the boy's hand firmly. "You look like you need it."

"Johnny, what are you doing here?" Anne asked.

"We brought the wounded back. We're on our way to join up with the rest of the army, but I took a ball in the calf at the Coa. I'll let Paul tell you the full story another time, but it was a shambles. Wellington is going to feel like shooting Craufurd. A few of our lads are injured and there was the usual chaos with the wounded after the battle, so we brought ours with us and took a detour via here. The major thought you could patch them up and take any that can't fight back to Lisbon with you. I've a letter for you from him." Johnny studied the bruised face. "He wanted to come," he said gently. "But we persuaded him it wasn't the right thing to do until after he's seen Wellington. Craufurd was furious with him, it's not the time to be playing truant. Thank God he listened for once."

"Johnny, I'm so glad to see you. But we have to work out what to do. Because Kingston just saved my life, and I'm not having him hanged."

Michael O'Reilly glanced at the bewildered boy.

"Take a drink and get your thoughts in order," he said quietly.

Kingston drank. "Thank you, Sergeant-Major. But my thoughts are fine."

"Well, then you're doing better than I am, lad, because I've not the least idea what's going on. Could you help me out a bit? You see I think you got yourself lost on the way to where you're supposed to be."

"Yes, Sarge."

"Why did you run, lad?"

"Flogging, Sarge."

"How many?"

"Three in six months. Due a fourth. The first three were two hundred each but this last one I was due a thousand. It was going to kill me, I'd nothing to lose."

"A thousand?" Johnny said in astonishment. "What the bloody hell did you do, Kingston, shoot an officer?"

Kingston shook his head, and Johnny was surprised and impressed to see a gleam of genuine amusement in the boy's eyes. "No, sir, today was my first go at that."

"So you ran. How did you get here?"

"Making for Oporto. Thought I might be able to stow away. Walked for days, shot a few hares or rabbits but not much food. It was dark when I got here and I was tired. I thought I'd hide up in the barn to sleep. I was just about to leave when the lady came in and found me."

"I've a feeling I know what happened next and it doesn't involve her screaming and running for help like a normal female, does it?" Michael said, glancing at Anne. "Go on, lad, tell us the rest."

They listened to the boy's story. He was articulate for an enlisted man and Wheeler studied him and wondered what his background was. There was something astonishingly self-contained about him, given how desperate his position was. Johnny imagined him under fire and thought what a waste it would be to lose a man like this from the army.

When he was done, Wheeler got up and moved around the room. "What are you doing, sir?" Michael demanded. "Sit down for God's sake, you're limping worse than Jenson."

374

"Well, I was hoping for some medical care, but I think I'm more likely to be giving it than receiving it," Wheeler said, glancing at Anne's face. "I'm going to check Carlyon's pack." He drew out a purse, which he opened and gave a whistle. "And I see that we have the power to make Wellington's day. It's not all here, but I'd say it's more than half."

"He spent some on a passage to South America," Anne said.

"Shame he didn't bloody go," Michael said dourly. "Captain?"

Captain Wheeler studied Private Kingston's young, good-looking face. "What do you want to do?" he asked. "Carry on running? Or find a new regiment?"

"I don't see how that could work, sir."

"Would you, if you could?"

"Yes, sir. I was all right in the army until Vane started."

"Well, if you can keep your mouth shut, we'll manage it." Wheeler looked at Anne. He had been silently considering and discarding possibilities as the boy talked. It was clearly impossible to hand him over to the authorities. With Anne's testimony it might have been possible to avoid a conviction for killing an officer, but he was still a deserter and given the present state of the war and his own poor disciplinary record he was going to hang.

Johnny wondered about that record. The boy was not forthcoming about the reasons for the floggings but for a charge of insubordination they were brutal and extreme. In the 110th, which was admittedly not typical, a mouthy private was likely to get a thump from his commanding officer if the offence was severe, but Major van Daan was just as likely to give a mouthful back and send him on his way. Wheeler had a strong suspicion there was a lot that young Kingston was not saying about the 87th light company, but it was not the time to ask.

"Thank God the major didn't decide to join us," Johnny said, thinking aloud. "A few weeks ago, the entire officers' mess heard him threaten to shoot that bastard dead, nobody would have believed he'd not done it. But Sergeant-Major, you can't be here either. You're an NCO and not a particularly popular one with the establishment, given how friendly you are with the officers."

"Don't know my place, sir, that's a fact."

"You're never going to bloody learn it now, that's for sure. But they would just love to pin something like this on you. You need to get out of here and back to the rest of the regiment and you were never here. And you need to take Private Kingston with you. There'll be a spare uniform or two up at the hospital from dead men. Get him into one of those and we'll forge the paperwork in a new name. It's not hard, nobody can read the major's writing anyway. The light company, mind, because we know they'll cover for us."

"From what I've seen of him so far I suspect he'll fit right in with the light company," Michael said with a grin. "I'm with you so far, Captain. But what happened to Carlyon?"

"Honestly, Michael, the easiest thing to do would be to get rid of the body and say nothing, let them assume he ran for it. But I'm not going to do that."

"Why not?" Michael asked.

"Don't be stupid, Sergeant-Major, it's not like you. Because our commanding officer needs Captain Carlyon to be dead in order to get what he wants."

Michael glanced over at Anne who was leaning back in her chair with her eyes closed. Johnny thought that it seemed to be the first time that Michael had realised what this meant. "Mary, Mother of God," he breathed. "Carlyon is dead."

"Glad you've caught up, Sergeant-Major."

"Sorry, sir, it's been a long day. So who killed him?"

"I did. I came back here to get Mrs Carlyon to dress that wound in my calf and to look at our other injured lads and I found Carlyon about to kill her and I put him down. Neither you nor Kingston were ever here. Teresa can take care of Mrs Carlyon and I'm going to go to the provost-marshal and report what happened."

Kingston was staring at Wheeler in astonishment. "Sir – you can't take the blame for what I did."

"Yes, I can. Because I am not going to be suspected of anything untoward. I'd a valid reason for being here, I've no relationship with Mrs Carlyon and I've an excellent reputation. There will be an inquiry and I'll be exonerated and Wellington will probably stand me a drink in the mess for solving an embarrassing problem for him. Especially given that some of his money is still in Carlyon's pack. But for this to work, you two were never here. Nobody saw us arrive. I'll just tell our wounded lads at the hospital that you went straight back to the regiment, Michael, you only came with me in case I needed help, they've no reason to doubt it."

Anne opened her eyes. Johnny had not thought she was listening, but he realised she had been following his reasoning closely and was looking at him with a frown. "What if this goes wrong, Johnny?"

"It won't. You'll speak for me, and the whole army knows that he's a bastard who beat his wife. He hit you in the middle of the town square, for God's sake, and anybody looking at you now is going to know how bad this attack was. I don't have any reason to kill him other than the one I've given. Sergeant-Major, get up to the hospital and find that uniform, there's..."

"No need. There's a box in the barn, we lost three to fever. He'll only need a coat," Anne said. "There's a lot of other stuff there, I was going to take it back when we go to Lisbon. Go and make up a pack for him with what he'll need. And take some food with you, Michael. There's..."

Michael got up. "Stop talking, ma'am," he said gently. "You need to lie down. That eye is coming up badly now and don't tell me you've not a headache. I'll see to everything." He looked over at the young private. "Kingston – now that's a bloody silly name. I'm thinking we can come up with a better one before we get you back to the lines."

The boy was staring at him and Johnny could see him fighting against hoping for too much. "Yes, Sergeant-Major. But your men will know this isn't true."

"They don't need to know anything about this. All they will know is that we picked up a deserter who had changed his mind and are giving him a chance in the light company. They'll cover for you."

"Why would they do that, sir?"

"Because they're a pack of disreputable bastards and they will just love the idea of sticking two fingers up at the provost-marshals," Johnny said with a brief smile. "Welcome to the 110th, Private, you're about to get the shock of your young life. But I've a feeling you'll make it work. You've got that look about you."

"What will you do, sir?" Michael said.

"Once I'm sure you're away, I'm going to get Teresa and a couple of the orderlies down to see to Mrs Carlyon and remove the body. I'm not sure where Wellington is, but a lot of his staff are still in Viseu, there'll be a deputy provost marshal. I'll make my statement and let him deal with Carlyon and then we're going to take our wounded, along with Mrs Carlyon, back to Lisbon. She shouldn't be here. In fact, she shouldn't have bloody been left here alone in the first place, I can't believe he thought that was a good idea. Private Kingston go with the sergeant-major. Ma'am, you look as if you should be in bed."

Anne nodded. "I'm feeling terrible," she admitted. "Johnny, thank you. I'm so sorry you've been pulled into this."

Wheeler studied her then smiled and shook his head. "Nan, you think I disapprove of you, I know, but the state of your face right now convinces me that a bullet through the throat was too good for that bastard you married."

"That's not why I'm sorry. I don't like the fact that you have to lie for me."

"I'm not lying for you. I'm lying for Private Kingston." Wheeler looked at the young man and Kingston looked back steadily.

"I'm not sure why you would, sir, but thank you. You give me another chance like this, I won't let you down."

Wheeler smiled. "I believe you, Private. Just now you two need to get out of here before somebody turns up and ruins my lovely story. Come on, ma'am, upstairs. As soon as they've gone, I'll ride up and get Teresa."

When Johnny came back down the stairs, he found Michael outside the barn. "Kingston is just getting changed. There's a pile of stuff in there, he's probably going to be the best equipped man in the light company when we get there. What am I going to tell the major, sir?"

"The truth, Sergeant-Major. Tell him I'll get her back to Lisbon and then join you as soon as I can. Tell him she's safe, because she will be, I'll make sure of it."

"And she's a widow."

"Yes." Wheeler looked over towards the door leading into the kitchen. "Poor bastard," he said quietly.

"He was certainly a bastard," Michael said shortly. "Excuse me if I'm not crying over Captain Carlyon, sir."

"I know, Sergeant-Major. There's no excuse for what he just did to her. But you don't move in the same circles as I do. He's been the laughing stock of the army ever since he landed here and the gossips got a good long look at how Major van Daan was with his wife. I wonder if Paul realises what he's about to walk into with her?"

"I thought you liked her, sir."

"I do like her. Very much. But what makes you think she'll change her ways just because she's married to Paul?"

"What makes you think he'd ask her to?" Michael said. "I'm going. See you back at the lines, sir. Good luck."

"Thank you, Sergeant-Major," Wheeler said with a brief smile. "And tell that bastard he owes me, will you?"

Chapter Twenty-Two

Sergeant-Major O'Reilly found the 110th camped with the rest of Wellington's army close to the village of Nelas to the south of Viseu. The 110th had found a sheltered spot to pitch their tents alongside a working farm, and Michael arrived to find Corporal Carter sitting on a stone wall flirting with a young woman who was driving in a herd of milk cows.

"Good to see you, Corporal," Michael said genially. "Are we having a rest today?"

"Day off, Sergeant-Major. We're in Lord Wellington's good books for once, he's coming up to thank us personally apparently." Carter was studying the other man with some interest. "New recruit?"

"Yes, and I'm glad I've found you first. Corporal, this is Private Jamie Hammond who is being transferred in to the light company."

"Is he? Does the major know?"

"He's about to, I'm going up to see him. How's he doing?"

"He's calmed down a bit. Wonder if General Craufurd has?"

Michael laughed aloud. "That might take longer. I'm glad Wellington is supporting him. It took some bloody nerve to do what he did back there."

"He doesn't lack that. Thank God Wellington's in command now or it'd be Copenhagen all over again. How's Captain Wheeler, is he not with you?"

"No. I left him to take the wounded back to the farm, he'll join us later. I wanted to bring Private Hammond up here and get him settled in."

"And where did you run into Private Hammond, Sergeant-Major?" Carter asked, studying the boy.

"On the way," Michael said briefly. "Look, Carter..."

"I was deserting," Hammond said quietly. Both men turned to look at him and he gave a brief smile. "Might as well call it what it is. Captain Wheeler talked me into giving it another try."

"New recruit?" Carter asked sceptically.

"No. Wounded at Talavera, three years' service. Had a falling out with an officer and his sergeant and decided to run ahead of being flogged to death."

Carter did not speak for a moment. Michael said quietly. "Hammond, show him your back."

"Is that an order, Sergeant-Major? It's not a bloody side show."

"Just do it you obstreperous young bastard, it'll save an hour of argument that I don't have time for."

Hammond turned, his lips set in a mutinous line and lifted his coat and shirt. Michael was watching Carter's expression. The other man did not speak but his eyes widened.

"All right," Carter said. "I get the point. Bring your kit, you can come up with me. There's space in my tent."

"You've a tent?" Hammond said, startled.

"We all have tents. Welcome to the 110th laddie. You'll find the major up at the farm, Sergeant-Major, there's an informal mess in the big barn."

Michael nodded and went in search of his commander. He found the officers of the 110th taking their ease in the barn. Several of them were playing cards and Carl Swanson was writing a letter. He rose and came forward.

"You're back quickly, Sergeant-Major. Johnny all right?"

"Yes, he's taken the wounded to Viseu. It's a bit of a long story. Where's the major?"

"Bathing in the river, it's just over the back there."

Michael found Paul seated on the bank in shirt sleeves and trousers, pulling on his boots. He stood up as Michael approached and Michael saluted.

"Welcome back, Sergeant-Major. That was quick. How's my lady?"

"She's all right, sir. But I've a bit of a story to tell. Sit down and if you've brandy in your flask, get it out because mine has run out."

Paul lowered himself to the bank, his eyes on Michael's face. "What's happened?" he asked, and his sergeant-major took the silver flask he was holding out and drank deeply.

"Sir - Robert Carlyon is dead."

They sat side by side, passing the flask between them, as Michael told the story. He left nothing out, and his commander listened mostly in silence, asking the occasional question. Michael watched the expressive face and could see a range of confused emotions. When the story was told, Paul sat quietly for a while, then gave Michael a sideways glance.

"How is she, Michael? Honestly?"

"Sir, she'll be all right. Very battered, but she was walking and talking and smiling."

"You've no idea how badly I want to go after them."

"You can't. Captain Wheeler is right, out of all of us you're the one who needs to be a long way away. Thank God Lord Wellington is right here. When this story reaches him, he can't possibly suspect you of anything, you've been here with him."

"I should never have left her there. He might have killed her."

"None of us realised how mad he was, sir. He'd got the money and a way out. We all assumed he'd just take it."

380

"He was obsessed with her. And of everybody, I should have seen it. Where's the boy?"

"I left him with Carter, he'll be getting him settled and introducing him around by now. He's a good lad, I think he'll do well."

Paul got up and reached for his coat. "Thank you, Michael."

"Sir, you're not going to do anything stupid, are you?"

Paul laughed aloud. "You all have so little faith in me, Sergeant-Major, I'm not that rash."

Michael looked at him. "Copenhagen. Dublin. That woman in Naples. Sally…"

"That'll do, Sergeant-Major. I'm going to do as I'm told, although it's killing me, but I can't risk either Johnny or this lad. I'll wait. But I'm going up to speak to the boy."

"Yes, sir. Are you going to tell anybody else?"

"I'll tell Carl the truth. Nobody else, for Hammond's sake."

Paul found his latest recruit seated with Carter, Cooper and Dawson around a newly lit fire, looking surprisingly composed. As Paul approached the four men rose to salute.

"You come up to see the new lad, sir?" Carter said.

Paul studied the boy, faintly shocked at his youth. "Private Hammond?"

"Yes, sir."

"I understand you decided to give a new regiment a try?"

Hammond looked at him with steady eyes. "Not sure it was what I'd call a decision, sir."

Paul gave a choke of laughter. "Come for a walk," he said. "I want a word. Carter, stop sitting on that bottle, I bloody know it's there, no point in hiding it. And don't drink it all, save some for Hammond."

Carter grinned. "Yes, sir."

Paul led the young man up beyond the lines to where there was a view down over the river. They stood in silence looking for a while. Eventually Paul said:

"Sergeant-Major O'Reilly tells me some bastard tore your back to shreds."

"Yes, sir."

"Don't worry. I'm not going to ask to see it. I've a few of those myself, it's not pretty."

Hammond gave him a startled glance. "You, sir?"

Paul smiled faintly. "Royal Navy. I left young."

"Don't blame you, sir."

Paul laughed. "You're going to fit right in, Hammond. Look, nobody knows what you did apart from Captain Wheeler and Sergeant-Major O'Reilly. I'm going to tell Captain Swanson, he's your officer, he should know."

"Yes, sir."

Paul turned to study the younger man. "You risked your life to save a woman you knew nothing about."

"She was a girl. She needed help. What was I supposed to do, stand there and let him blow her head off? Because he was going to, sir, I'm telling you."

"That's not the point, Hammond. Most men in your position wouldn't have gone back to check on her."

"Most women in her position wouldn't have asked a deserter in for dinner, sir. She was good to me. I don't need to know anything more than that."

"You do need to know that I'm never going to stop being grateful to you for what you did for her. I know that when she sees you again, she'll tell you herself."

"Is that likely, sir?"

"Yes."

"Not my business, sir."

"It's nobody's business, but that won't stop the army gossips. She's a good person and he was a complete bastard to her for years, if you have trouble sleeping tonight, just remember that. Thank you, lad."

Paul endured the following days with unconcealed impatience. Time crawled by, as he waited to hear from Johnny. Paul was not afraid for Anne, although it was unbearable not to be able to see her, but he was anxious about his friend. Johnny's decision to take responsibility for Carlyon's death made perfect sense, and Paul thought that it was very unlikely that it would lead to a court martial, but he knew that Johnny had done this for his sake, and he was desperate to know the outcome.

His men were in high spirits, despite the near disaster at the Coa. Lord Wellington, who was furious with Craufurd for engaging the enemy at all, came personally to thank the regiment for its part in the action which had saved the lives of large numbers of retreating men.

"Thank God it wasn't worse," he said, as Paul walked him to his horse. "Craufurd is a good man but he made what could have been a catastrophic mistake."

"He did, sir, and he knows it. Thank you for coming to talk to them. It means a lot. With your approval, I'd like to have a coat pin made for each of them, commemorating the battle."

Wellington looked at him. "As long as you are not expecting the army to fund it, Major."

"No, I'm happy to do that."

"Half of them will have lost it or sold it to buy drink within six months."

"It's the other half I'm interested in, sir."

Wellington allowed himself a small smile. "Sentimental tosh, Major. You have my permission, although it will infuriate Craufurd all over again."

Paul shot his chief a glance. "Thank you for supporting me with him."

"What makes you think that I did?"

"Because I've been neither reprimanded nor arrested, and I did lose my temper with him rather badly."

"I heard," Wellington said shortly.

"I'll write to him."

"Do so. I want you to work with Craufurd in the future."

"I've been trying, sir."

"I know. You have improved." Wellington's austere face softened slightly. "Order your pins, and I will present them personally. These weeks must have been exceedingly difficult for you."

"I prefer to be busy, sir. But it's strange, I'm so used to being on campaign without Rowena, I have to keep reminding myself that she won't be there when I get back."

His chief studied him. "Will you ride up with me? I've something to tell you."

Paul summoned Jenson with Rufus. He fell in beside his commander and Wellington pulled ahead of his aides to give them privacy.

"Major, I've just received letters from Lisbon. Before I tell you this, I would like you to promise me that you will say nothing until I have finished."

"Yes, sir."

"I am told that Captain Robert Carlyon is dead. Apparently, he went back to Viseu and tried to kill his wife. He was surprised by Captain Wheeler, who had taken your wounded there, and Wheeler shot him. The provost marshal has accepted his story, there is clear evidence that the girl was beaten quite badly...."

"Is she all right?"

Wellington gave him a look. "She will recover. Captain Wheeler took her back to Lisbon. By now I imagine he is on his way back to you."

Paul said nothing. Wellington was watching him, and Paul was aware of a sense of danger, as though saying the wrong thing at this point could have far-reaching consequences. Wellington gave him plenty of time. Then he said in unemotional tones:

"Thank you for following orders, Major. You are neither a good actor or a good liar and it would have been painful to watch."

"Whatever you're thinking, sir, I didn't kill Robert Carlyon and I was nowhere close when he died, you must know that. Although if I'd walked in on him beating his wife, I would have done exactly what Johnny did, and I think you would as well. But you can't seriously think that Johnny Wheeler killed him for me."

There was a long pause. Finally, Wellington said:

"I don't. But I honestly cannot decide if you have somehow induced somebody else to do it or if you are simply the luckiest man in history, Major."

Paul turned to look at him. "Sir - I swear to God, I had absolutely nothing to do with this."

The blue-grey eyes surveyed him coolly. Finally, Wellington said:

"I have decided to believe you. Or at least to pretend that I do. Don't ever tell me anything different, Major."

"There'll be no need to, sir, I'm telling you the truth."

"Excellent. Marry the girl, for God's sake, and get back to work. I'm happy that Wheeler managed to retrieve more than half of the army's stolen money, and I'm also happy that the girl is safe, she's worth twenty of you and her husband put together, and I am extremely attached to her. Carlyon was a lunatic and there were times I wondered if he'd shoot me for flirting with his wife. But we all know that in your case he probably had cause, so get yourself married and put an end to the scandal. My chaplain is at your disposal, and I'll attend the ceremony, which will make very sure that even if people have their doubts, they'll receive her. But get on with it."

"Thank you, sir."

Paul rode back to the lines and went to find Michael, who was cleaning his rifle. Michael abandoned his task and joined Paul in the courtyard.

"Lord Wellington brought news," Paul said without preamble. "It seems Captain Wheeler is on his way back to us."

"Any trouble?"

"No, thank God, they swallowed that tale whole. I'd no idea Johnny was such a good liar. His lordship tells me I need to get myself married and stop the gossip. He's suspicious, but then he's always suspicious of me, and he's told me very specifically that he doesn't want to know any more."

"He'll be suspicious of the wrong people," Michael said. "He knows nothing about young Hammond, which was our aim. Are you going to tell anybody else?"

"Carl knows, but nobody else, for the boy's sake."

"I wonder if he really meant to kill her?"

"I agree with Hammond on this, I wouldn't have waited to find out. Carlyon was crazy enough to hit her in front of half the army and call me out in the mess. If that boy hadn't been there, I think she'd either be dead or she'd be off with him somewhere I couldn't find her. Thank God Hammond was there."

"Amen to that, sir. Have we orders?"

"Wellington is waiting for his agents to confirm which way the French are coming. He's hoping to slow Massena down while the retreat is completed and if he's right, Massena is coming via Bussaco which should be interesting, as I've seen his battle plan. After that we'll starve him out."

"Well, if we've a few days here, will you take an order from me?"

"What?"

"Will you get on your horse, ride back to Lisbon, take your lady to bed, and do us all a favour, sir?"

Paul stared at him and then began to laugh. "Am I really that bad?"

"God love you, sir, you're trying, but it's painful to watch, and you're not needed here now. Go and find her. If Wellington comes looking, we'll cover for you. He can spare you a few days, you've not had leave for years, and Captain Wheeler will be back any day."

"I should ask..."

"He'll say no, he always does. Just go."

Paul rode through the night to reach Lisbon, resting his horse often and riding in easy stages, carrying only a small pack and two saddlebags. Until he reached the narrow streets of the town he had barely thought about what he was going to say to Anne, and he rode Rufus into the stable feeling

384

ridiculously nervous. Mario met him at the door, startled at the unexpected arrival of the master of the house.

"Bom dia, Mario. Is Señora Carlyon at home?"

"Si, Major, she is in the parlour."

"Good. Will you see that we're not disturbed, please?"

Paul did not wait for Mario to reply but walked into the hallway and took the passage to the left, which led to the small cosy parlour which Anne and Rowena had always used. He pushed open the door. Anne was sitting before a small fire reading what looked like a medical book. She was clearly not dressed to receive visitors, in a dark green velvet robe with her hair unbound. She looked up in surprise as Paul entered and the sight of her soothed all Paul's uncertainties.

"Nan."

Anne made no sound. She stood up, putting the book down, and moved into his arms without hesitation. Paul's mouth found hers, and nothing else mattered. They kissed for a long time.

"I didn't know you were back yet," Anne said finally. "How are you here?"

"I'm playing truant," Paul admitted. "It will be a short visit, love, but I couldn't wait any longer."

"I feel as though I've waited forever."

Paul scooped her up into his arms. "I find it very hard to believe that we are not about to be interrupted by Sergeant-Major O'Reilly, a message from headquarters or half of Marshal Ney's first corps, but I think we're safe for a few hours at least. I've so much to say, but it can wait. Will you come to bed with me, girl of my heart?"

Anne was smiling broadly. "I could walk, Major."

"Indulge me, sweetheart."

Paul carried her up to her room, realising that he had not felt this nervous with a woman since he was fourteen. He and Anne had come so close to this, so many times, it was hard to believe that there was nothing more standing in their way.

Setting her down, Paul locked the door and turned to look at her. There was no sign of Carlyon's brutal attack apart from a faint bruising under one eye. Paul's heart was hammering in his chest.

"I'm afraid this gown buttons at the back," Anne said and Paul recognised from the tremor in her voice that she was as nervous as he was. "You'll have to..."

Her fear steadied Paul and suddenly he was assured again. "It's all right, love. This bit at least we've done before. Come here."

He turned her round and dealt quickly and easily with the buttons on her gown. Sliding it down her shoulders he lowered his mouth delicately to the soft skin of her neck and shoulders and heard her gasp in pleasure. Gently, taking his time over it, he unlaced her underclothes, and freed her, garment by garment, of the petticoats and lacy stays. With infinite patience and tenderness, he removed her stockings and then drew her gently into his arms and kissed her.

She was beautiful. Paul revelled in the scent and taste of her, absorbed the silky feel of her skin under his hands. He undressed quickly, dropping his clothes to the floor so that he could join her in the bed, and Anne reached for him, her eyes on his. Paul half expected her to flinch after the ordeal of marriage to Carlyon, but she did not and he pushed away the thought. There was no place for memories of Carlyon between them today.

Paul had never felt this way with a woman. All the years of his womanising, all the sexual encounters he had enjoyed and forgotten seemed irrelevant now. There was only Anne, arching her body into his, whispering his name, running her hands over his body until he was lost in the richness of her, his self-control and self-possession swept away in a deluge of emotion and sheer physical pleasure. He had meant to control himself, meant to concentrate on her pleasure so that this, their first lovemaking, might drive away the spectre of Carlyon's brutality, but he was caught helpless, as she was, in the intensity of their mutual need, and he realised, as he reached the shattering heights of his climax that she was there with him, sobbing his name, her nails clawing into his back. He let the sensation take over his body and felt her shudder against him until finally it was over and she was quiet in his arms.

"Nan," he whispered, and Anne moved, lifting her face for his kiss.

"Paul." She was breathless and laughing with none of the hesitation Paul had feared. If there were ghosts, they were clearly not troubling Anne.

"I love you so much, and I'm never going to forget this moment," he said very softly.

Anne turned her head and kissed the nearest part of him, which happened to be his chest. Her body felt relaxed and fluid against his. "I love you too. Two years married, and I feel as though I've just done that for the first time."

Paul realised that he could not stop smiling. "What's rather funnier, bonny lass is that I feel the same way. You've just taught me everything I've been missing all these years."

Anne laughed. "You're so damned good at this, Major, you know exactly what to say. Did you know that I've been worrying that I'd be something of a disappointment?"

"A disappointment?" Paul said incredulously.

"You've had a lot of women, love, and you've waited for me a long time. And I wanted so much for it to be good."

"Was it?"

"For me it was perfect," Anne said, and the sincerity in her voice touched him. He rolled over and looked down at her, studying the flushed face and quizzical dark eyes.

"And for me. More than perfect. Lying here like this with you is everything I've ever wanted. You're all I dreamed of and more, girl of my heart. I'm so happy."

They slept and woke hungry for each other again in the dim light of late afternoon. Outside the rain beat against the windows, and in the dimness of Anne's bedroom the only sounds to be heard were the murmur of their voices, the sounds she made which already he was beginning to know and love. Paul had imagined so many times how she might be as a lover, but after two years with Robert Carlyon he had not expected her frank enjoyment of his body to come so easily.

Anne lay wrapped in his arms finally. "It's almost dark."

"I know love. At some point we should have a conversation."

"You've said everything I need to hear," Anne said lazily and Paul laughed and kissed her.

"I'll bet I haven't. Are you hungry?"

She laughed with him. "How well you know me, I'm famished."

"I'll see if the kitchen can manage some food. Stay here, I'll send Teresa in." Paul kissed her gently and reached for his clothes.

***

Teresa appeared within a few minutes. She tidied the room, brought water to wash and dressed Anne in one of her loose velvet robes. They spoke little, the Spanish girl seeming to sense Anne's dreamy content. Eventually, when the fire was lit and the room tidy, Anne sat before her mirror for Teresa to brush her hair.

"Are you all right, Señora?"

"Yes. Never more so."

"He is a good man. I hope you will be happy with him."

"I think I will. Teresa, you'll come with me, won't you?"

"For as long as you want me."

The door opened and Paul entered. He stood watching her for a moment and then came forward with a smile and a nod to the girl and took the brush from her hand. "Thank you, Teresa," he said quietly, and the girl left. Paul ran the brush through the long dark hair, and Anne watched his face in the mirror and suddenly understood.

"Did you used to do this for Rowena?" she asked, and he nodded.

"Yes, she loved it. And so did I. I just realised how much it hurts that I'll never do it again. How mad is that, given how happy I am as well?"

"Oh, Paul." Anne sat still, and he continued to brush. She could see the glitter of tears in his eyes, and her throat felt constricted. Finally he set the brush down.

"Let's go and eat."

"Are you all right?"

Paul drew her into his arms and kissed her very gently. "You and Rowena. What in God's name did I ever do to deserve either of you?"

"It doesn't work that way, love. Unless you're about to tell me that I deserved Robert."

Paul grinned. "And what about Lord Wellington?"

387

"You are never going to let me forget that are you?"

"Nan, you have so much ammunition against me, I need to hold on to that one. Thank God you understand so well about Rowena, I couldn't bear not to be able to talk about her."

"Oh hush, I loved her too. Come on."

They walked hand in hand to the small parlour, where supper had been set out on a table before the fire. They ate mostly in silence. Paul poured glasses of rich local wine and touched his glass to hers. Anne found herself wondering how many times he had been in situations like this with a woman, and the thought made her want to laugh. It was a perfect setting for seduction, and Anne was tempted to tell him that in her case it was unnecessary, but she did not want to spoil the mood, and she was enjoying him fussing over her. When supper had finished the servants came to clear the table and Paul drew her to the sofa and settled her against him.

"Can we talk about Robert?"

Anne had known that he would want to have this conversation. She would have been happy to delay it, to luxuriate in her new-found freedom and the happiness of being in his arms without guilt or fear, but she could sense that the things that he did not know were nagging at Paul. Better to tell him and let the past go. "What do you want to know?"

"I realise that it had been going on for a long time. Was there ever a time…?"

"No, he was a brute from the start."

"Nan, why did they make you marry him? God knows I'd no idea what he was like and I don't suppose you did either, but he wasn't the man I thought you'd marry."

Anne smiled. "No. You wanted me to choose Julian, didn't you? Because you thought he cared for me."

"I thought he was very likely in love with you. And if I couldn't have you, darling girl, I wanted you to be with a man who would do his best to make you happy. Carlyon only wanted your money. I didn't think your father would force you to marry a man like that."

"He didn't. I thought I had no choice. This is hard to talk about, Paul, even now."

He bent to kiss her gently. "Take your time. There is nothing you can't tell me."

"On the morning you left Yorkshire and I came to say goodbye at the barracks, I went back to the stable where I had left my horse and I found Robert there. He raped me."

Paul did not speak or move for a moment, and Anne could feel the tension in his body as he absorbed what she had said. The laughter had gone from his eyes, and Anne wished they did not have to do this now. She leaned forward and kissed him gently. "Paul don't look so stricken. How could you have known?"

"If it hadn't been for me you wouldn't have been there."

"And then I might not be here," Anne said quietly. "I know which I'd choose, Paul. When he'd done with me, he expressed surprise that I was a virgin."

Paul looked at her sharply. "He knew?"

"He knew. He'd been watching us for months. I wonder who else knew, to be honest, we were so wrapped up in ourselves, we probably weren't as careful as we thought. He told me that I was going to marry him. He wanted my dowry and the promise of my inheritance. And he persuaded me that if I did not do it, he'd ruin me. He told my father that we'd...that we'd already..." Even now it was difficult to talk about it. "He pretended that I'd wanted to, of course, he said we got carried away by our mutual passion. It made me feel sick. My father believed him, and they insisted I had to marry quickly. I might have been pregnant."

"Why didn't you tell them the truth, Nan?"

"He said he would deny the rape and tell them about you and I and pretend that I was lying about him to protect you. He claimed we'd been seen at the barracks that morning. He painted a picture of what would happen. My sister's engagement called off, George losing his seat in Parliament over the scandal, my father the laughing stock of the Piece Hall over his daughter behaving like a whore with the major of the 110th..."

"And what did he tell you would happen to me?" Paul asked quietly.

"He suggested it would ruin your career and your marriage and your reputation. Paul – I did not want any of those things to happen to any of the people I loved. I was shocked and frightened, and I didn't know what to do, but I know how the world works. Robert painted a very convincing picture of a flighty girl who'd allowed herself to be seduced by a married rake and had willingly moved on to another lover. I think he'd have been believed, especially when I was known to be something of a hoyden. So I married him."

"And he was a brute to you."

"From the first. It went on for months, I used to worry that he would kill me. But eventually I worked out how to keep him happy and he stopped hitting me as much." Anne saw him flinch. "Paul, I told you I was going to be honest with you."

"I know. And I knew then that it changed. He went from barely noticing where you were to being completely obsessed by you, and I've a fairly good idea of how you achieved that, I just can't stand to think about it. Did he ever hit you again? Until the end?"

"After Talavera. It was always when he was jealous. He knew something had happened. He used his riding crop. Somehow, I didn't care as much then. At least I'd had that time with you."

"And when you came back with me after Rowena died it set him off again. Was it always about me?"

"He knew I flirted with other men, but I think he knew it meant nothing. Mostly it was about you."

"I want to ask why you didn't tell me, but I know, of course. And you're not wrong. If I'd known he'd laid a single hand on you I'd have killed him." Paul stroked her hair. "Why the hell didn't you tell me to stay away from you, Nan?"

"Because having you close kept me sane," Anne whispered. "It was worth the occasional beating."

Paul held her close. "I can't stop thinking about that morning. You'll never know how close I came to telling them to stop the carriage and coming back to you. God knows what I'd have said or done, but leaving you standing there was agony. If I'd done it, I might have stopped him."

"You might have walked in on it and killed him, and where would that have left you?"

Paul was studying her, his expression grave. "That's why you married him, isn't it? To protect me?"

Anne looked at him for a long time. "I could lie to you," she said eventually.

"No, you couldn't, bonny lass." Paul stood up, took her hand and pulled her up to stand against him. "Christ, Nan, if ever I wanted to know how much you love me, I think you just told me. I'm so sorry. Sorry you were so hurt and so desperate, and so unable to come to me. But I swear to God I'm going to make it up to you. I don't have the words to tell you what you mean to me."

Anne reached up and wound her arms about his neck. Paul made a small inarticulate sound, and she felt herself lifted. He carried her through the house and up into his bedroom, dropping her robe by the door. Anne lay back on the bed as he undressed, laughing both at his impatience and at the symbolic gesture of bringing her finally to his bed. When it came to herself, there was nothing subtle about Paul van Daan.

When at last, she lay still and breathless in his arms, he rolled over and lay beside her on his back, taking her hand. Suddenly he began to laugh.

"What is it?"

Paul turned his head to look at her. "I can't move. Really. If the French make it to Lisbon right now, they can shoot me in my bed, and I can't do a thing to stop them." He lifted her hand to his lips, and the blue eyes were alight with laughter. "But Christ, Nan, I'll die a happy man."

Anne gave a gurgle of laughter. "So you're not disappointed?"

"In all my experience with women I've never felt like this in my life and I'd willingly demonstrate it all over again, but I actually think I would die."

Anne giggled. "I'm sorry, Major. If I had the energy myself, I'd put that to the test, but…"

His mouth covered hers again. "You hold my heart and soul in your hands," he whispered softly in her ear. "Now get into bed and go to sleep, even you have to be tired."

They slept, shattered, through the night and into a clear blue morning the following day. Anne awoke slowly. Her body felt stiff and sore, and there was an unaccustomed weight across her legs, which she realised was Paul's

390

leg. He was heavy and she tried to move carefully so as not to wake him, but his eyes opened.

"I have a feeling I have grossly overslept," he said. "Good morning, love. How are you feeling?"

Anne gave it serious consideration. "I feel as though I should savour this moment. The first morning of actually waking up in your bed."

"And wouldn't that surprise a lot of people whose business it is not," Paul said with a grin. "Oh lass I wish I could find the words to tell you how much I love you."

"You've certainly done your best to demonstrate," Anne said, and Paul laughed, leaned over and captured her mouth. Anne had been sure that this morning he would be too tired, but she realised with a spurt of amusement that he was seriously thinking about it. Reaching up, she pulled him down to her and shifted her body under his and felt his immediate and definite response. Suddenly she no longer felt her sore body only her rising desire and as his mouth moved down her neck, she wanted him again so urgently that it shocked her. He seemed to sense it and she felt his quiver of laughter.

"Come here," he said, easing himself closer to her. "Let's not rush it this time. I'm in no hurry. In fact, I might need to take it easy today."

He took his time over her body, getting to know her, enjoying watching her responses and bringing her to the point where she was longing for him, her body trembling under his hands and mouth. Anne tried to move towards him. With a laugh he caught both her hands and pinned them very gently above her head. "Not yet, bonny lass..."

For a moment Anne froze. The memory of Robert holding her down, his hands bruising her wrists, was horribly clear. She saw by the distress in Paul's eyes, that he realised what he had done. He released her hands, but Anne shook her head.

"No. Don't stop. It's gone now. Carry on exactly as you were, I'm not letting him in here."

Paul seemed to understand, and after a moment he slid his hands back up to her wrists and then held them together with one of his hands gently but firmly and continued to tease her. When finally, he moved into her, Anne cried out, her whole body shuddering against his. She was still feeling it when his own climax came, and he murmured her name in something like a groan.

Easing his body away from hers, Paul stretched out beside her with a long sigh of content, his fair head resting on her shoulder. Anne kissed the top of his head. For some reason, she could feel laughter bubbling up, and she stopped holding it back and began to laugh for the sheer joy of him.

"Now that's not a response I've had before," Paul said.

For some reason, it struck Anne as very funny, and she laughed harder. Her mirth proved infectious, and they lay giggling like children.

"I'm sorry, Paul."

"I should hope so, you little wretch, I'll have you know a gentleman can be very sensitive about his performance in the bedroom, you'll be sorry if it turns out your ill-timed humour has put me off trying again."

"Oh, as if I could. Anyway, I should be perfectly safe since you are not a gentleman."

"We should suit very well then, girl of my heart, because I think we've successfully established that you are not a lady. You've almost killed me, I've not felt this exhausted since Talavera, and it took a French musket ball to achieve that."

Anne was still giggling, and Paul tried to kiss her, laughing too much for it to be a success. Neither of them heard sounds from below until the door opened, and Captain Swanson's voice said:

"Get up you lazy bugger and get back...oh bloody hell!"

Carl stood frozen in the doorway, and Paul reached for the long-abandoned counterpane and pulled it up to give Anne some semblance of decency. Carl backed out, holding up his hands.

"I'll see you downstairs," he said, and vanished, closing the door.

***

Paul looked at his love and saw that she was pink with embarrassment, but she was still laughing.

"I'm going to get a lock for that door," he said. "You will note that knocking simply doesn't occur to them. Every single one of the bastards uses my quarters like it's the town square on market day. Honestly, on campaign it sometimes gets so crowded in my tent there's barely space for me. Are you all right?"

"Of course I am. Poor Carl. If that had been Michael, I'd have sworn it was deliberate."

"If that had been Michael it would have been deliberate. I'd better go and see what he wants. I hope the French aren't invading, I've not got the energy to hold them off. Why don't you try and go back to sleep, love, you must be very tired?"

"But so happy."

Paul studied her and thought that it was clearly true. He kissed her very gently then slid from the bed and went in search of clothes, then left the room and went down to find Carl having breakfast in the courtyard. It was warm for the time of year and there was a heady perfume from the late flowering bougainvillea over the archway. Paul sat down and reached for the coffee pot. Wrapping his hands about the cup he said:

"I take it my presence is required elsewhere."

"I'm afraid so. Hookey is very well aware of where you are, he came up himself to speak to us. He's moving the army out, but he wishes you to know that he will be in Viseu for the next few days with his staff. And his chaplain."

Paul laughed. He could almost hear Wellington saying it, in biting tones. "He really wants us married," he said. "I'm not sure he trusts me not to create a bigger scandal than he can suppress."

"Well, he's known you for a while, Paul, so you can see why he might think you would. Are you in need of a groomsman by any chance?"

"I am."

"And the sooner the better, by the look of things," his friend said with a grin. "I am sorry about that, I just didn't think. I shall have to get used to knocking. I take it you found her fully recovered."

"As you saw," Paul said dryly. "I'll go and talk to her when I've eaten."

"Haven't you discussed this yet?"

"I'm not sure that I've actually asked her yet," Paul said with a frown. "We've been talking of other things."

"I'm not sure I'd call what you've been doing talking. But it's done you some good, that's for sure, you look five years younger."

"Just don't ask me to do anything particularly strenuous today."

When Paul had eaten, he went back upstairs and found that his love had bathed and dressed and was sitting before her mirror with Teresa pinning up her hair. He stood watching in the doorway for a moment and then came forward. She smiled and turned, lifting her face for his kiss and Paul felt a rush of pure, uncomplicated happiness at the sheer normality of the moment. "Do you have to go?"

Paul nodded. "Wellington is onto me. Still, I managed to keep out of his sights for forty-eight hours, which is fairly good going for me. But there is one particularly important matter, which we have not settled. Have I remembered to ask you to marry me?"

"I'm not sure," Anne said. "Pretend that you have."

"And what was your answer?"

"Yes, Major. It was yes."

"Good, because it's an obsession with the commander-in-chief, I think he fears for your reputation. Nan, if you want to wait, I will. Wellington is marching to Bussaco to engage Massena and I need to be there. We can be married first or we can wait until..."

"I'm not waiting, Paul, I've done enough of that. When you ride out of here, I'm coming with you, married or not."

Paul kissed her again. "I had a feeling you would say that. We can be married in Viseu, Lord Wellington is expecting us. He'll be disappointed, mind. He might have been in with a chance with Carlyon's wife, but he knows better than to go near mine. That's why I want my ring on your finger before he gets near you again. How soon can you be ready, love?"

"An hour," Anne said, and Paul began to laugh.

"You were born to be an army wife, girl of my heart, I can remember thinking that in a shepherd's hut in the snow many years ago. We'll stay another night, I think, to rest Carl's horse, but we'll leave at first light tomorrow. I'm going out, I've some shopping to do, but I'll be back. Can Teresa come with us?"

"I don't recommend you try to leave her behind, love. Where are we camped?"

393

"Between Viseu and Bussaco. Wellington is hoping to engage Massena up on the Bussaco Ridge if they march the right way. I've been there, it's a great defensive position and it will certainly give the French a headache. Fletcher's engineers have been creating an access road across the back of the lines. We'll be spread thin, but with good access...." Paul broke off and laughed. "Sorry. This is worse than my first wedding. I thought that was bad, but at least I wasn't on the battlefield forty-eight hours later."

"This is the man I'm marrying, Paul. If I wanted flowers and romance and a protracted honeymoon I could go back to England and find them. And I have work to do as well."

Paul studied her, remembering his shock the first time he had realised what she was doing in the surgeon's room. It seemed a very long time ago. "Yes, you'll be needed. I think we'd better get back love and get to work."

Anne stood up and kissed him. "Better get out of here and let me get packed, then, Major," she said, and Paul saluted, and left. There was a very good goldsmith in the lower town, and in his pocket was the gold ring he had purloined from Anne's drawer. He wanted it for size, but after that she could do what she liked with Robert's ring.

***

It had rained for three days, and the tents of the 110th had settled into the mud in sodden misery. Sergeant-Major Michael O'Reilly emerged into the first warm dry evening and looked up and down the steaming lines. At least their men had tents, small but functional, four men to a tent. There was no luxury, but it kept them warm and dry and he had often wondered how Major van Daan had managed to get the commissariat to provide them, when most regiments slept in the open, or under makeshift tents made of blankets. Presumably, he had just worn them down until it was easier to give in.

With the relief of a dry spell, Sergeant George Kelly was out chivvying the women and mess orderlies to light fires and get hot food cooked, and already there was a savoury smell of mutton stew, as the cooking pots were filled. One of the positives of this campsite was a ready supply of fresh food. As Wellington prepared to retreat behind the lines of Torres Vedras, the local Portuguese population was preparing to flee with him, leaving the land barren and scorched to starve the invading French. With the Anglo-Portuguese army encamped locally, farmers and householders came in a regular stream bringing food and wine which they either gave or sold cheaply to the troops, rather than destroy it or leave it for the French. A makeshift trestle set up near the fire was laden with fruit and bread, and several crates of local wine were piled underneath. Wellington had not yet arrived in camp, the French were not close enough to be a threat, and Michael was looking forward to dinner and a drink and a night without rain keeping him awake.

"Sergeant-Major."

Michael turned as Captain Wheeler approached. "A drink, sir?"

"Please." Johnny watched him pour and took the cup over to a camp chair. He sat down, waving to Michael to join him. Michael seated himself on an empty crate and lifted his cup.

"To victory, sir. If we ever see a battle."

"We will." Johnny studied him meditatively. "I was just thinking, Sergeant-Major, the first time I remember drinking with you was the day Rory Stewart tried to kill Major van Daan over that wife of his."

Michael laughed. "So it was. We've shared a few drinks since, sir."

"We have. But it was a bit of a landmark. Never drink with the enlisted men and keep the NCOs at a safe distance." Wheeler was shaking his head. "Paul van Daan was with us two bloody weeks and he blew every rule I ever learned right out of the water. I still don't know how he gets away with it."

"I suspect Colonel Johnstone got a few complaints. And there was Copenhagen."

"Yes, that one was close."

"A lot of the other officers don't like it," Michael said. "But he's got more discreet about it and I think Wellington chooses to ignore it. As for the 110th, most of you are as bad as he is now."

"He's corrupted us," Johnny said. "And once you get used to it...I can't really imagine going back now. I used to believe what they told me about fraternising with the men being bad for discipline but it's bollocks. Good discipline takes hard work, that's all. It's funny though, looking back. I often wonder if the major feels even the slightest awkwardness when he talks to Sally Stewart. If he does, there's no sign of it."

"None, sir. He even flirts with her, and she enjoys it. Although nobody has offered me odds on it recently."

They both sat smiling, remembering. "These days there's only one lass I'd offer odds on with him," Michael said.

"Do you think he'll be back before we engage?"

"Oh yes, Captain Swanson will have caught up with him. I'll bet he was pissed off, mind. He deserves a break, poor bastard, the last time he took proper leave was after Assaye and that was only because he was wounded. But they'll be here any day now, and I'll admit it won't distress me to know our wounded are in her care."

"I'd not thought of that. I wonder if he'll bring her with him?"

"I wouldn't fancy his chances of leaving her behind. To be fair, I doubt he'd try."

"I know. Do you think they'll be all right, Sergeant-Major? Married, I mean. Neither of them is easy."

"They're not, sir. But better together than apart."

"Yes. I couldn't be married to her. I am, I have decided, a very conventional man. But his world begins and ends with her." Johnny sipped his wine. "All the same, the scandal they've managed to create between them...it's going to be difficult."

"Sir, when he married his first wife, she could barely lift her head when she came aboard that ship, she was so embarrassed. I felt sorry for her. But that's not Anne Carlyon. She'll hold her head as high as he does, and she won't give a damn as long as she's with him."

"I suppose so. But honestly, Michael, can he keep this up? How long did it take back then, before he was in some other girl's bed?"

"It's not the same, sir. He married his first wife because it was the right thing to do. And I know how much he cared about her. But he was never like this. Besides, if she finds him in another woman's bed she will cut his balls off, I swear to God."

Johnny began to laugh. "She actually would. I'm almost looking forward to it, he's had this coming for years."

Around them, the camp came to life and the officers and men of the 110th began to congregate around the fires to eat and drink. Corporal Carter supervised the distribution of grog to the men and then returned to sit beside Michael. Beside him sat the new young private, Hammond, whom Carter seemed to have adopted. Johnny wondered if Carter knew the full story yet. Hammond looked bewildered, and Johnny did not blame him. He watched as Carter shared wine and mutton stew with the younger man and wondered what Hammond made of it. It was hard to imagine any other regiment in Wellington's army where this would feel normal.

A shout came up from further down the lines. Johnny stood up and looked along the lines of the other companies where men were shouting and cheering.

"It seems our major has made it back on time. And not alone, by the look of things."

Half a dozen horses walked up, two of them laden with baggage. Major van Daan rode at their head and beside him Johnny saw that Anne was mounted on Bella. Behind them rode Carl and Teresa.

Johnny went forward as the company dismounted and Jenson went to take the horses, calling for help to remove the baggage and take it to the tents. Carl Swanson came to greet Johnny.

"It doesn't look as though we've missed the battle."

"We waited for you." Johnny was looking at the couple. Anne was speaking to Danny Carter, her lovely face alight with happiness. Paul stood beside her, his eyes on her face. He looked, Johnny thought, like a man who had come home after a long absence.

"Sir."

Paul turned. "Johnny. It's good to be back."

"Just in time, sir. Did you have a good break?"

"It was so short I almost missed it. Bloody Wellington must have a bell attached to me somewhere."

"He'll be deaf if he has, sir, you're such a fidget," Michael said.

"He does like to know where you are and what you're doing," Johnny agreed.

"If he couldn't work out what I've been doing this week he's not fit to be in command of an army."

Johnny was very aware of the question that nobody was asking, and he looked from Paul to Anne and knew the answer. His commander had obviously noticed his look and was laughing. He glanced across at Carter. "Corporal, is there a reason we're starving and dying of thirst?" he asked plaintively, then he lifted Anne's left hand to his lips and kissed it. An intricate gold ring encircled her finger, and Johnny was fairly sure that it was not the one Robert had given her. "And will somebody find my wife a chair?"

It was perfectly timed. Around them, the lines of the light company erupted into cheers, which spread up through the other companies as the news was shouted back to them. Johnny could feel himself smiling broadly. Whatever doubts he had expressed earlier to Michael, it was impossible not to be affected by his commander's open happiness.

Paul put his arm about Anne and kissed her.

"Welcome home, bonny lass," he said.

Author's Thanks

Many thanks for reading this book and I hope you enjoyed it. If you did, I would be very grateful if you would consider leaving a short review on Amazon or Goodreads or both. One or two lines is all that's needed. Good reviews help get books in front of new readers, which in turn, encourages authors to carry on writing the books. They also make me very, very happy.

Thank you.

Lynn

Author's Note (may contain spoilers)

It is more than two years since I first published an Unconventional Officer, and a lot has happened in that time. The Peninsular War Saga has become more popular than I ever imagined, and I have a dedicated mini-army of fans from all over the world, who wait for each book to come out.

The truth about being a writer, is that we learn on the job. I have always loved this book, but six books down the line, plus two of a linked series, I feel that I have learned a lot about writing, and for a while, I've wished I could go back and revisit book one.

The decision to publish in paperback has given me the opportunity to do so. I've been delighted with how much of the book I still loved and have left unchanged, but there have been significant re-writes to some scenes. I've corrected a few minor historical errors, and I've changed some of the dialogue to better reflect my characters now that I know them better.

The plot, the characters and everything essential about this book remain the same.

An Unconventional Officer is a work of fiction firmly rooted in a time in history. As such, I've needed to take some liberties with events. If I didn't do so from time to time, my characters would be hanging about on the fringe of events with nothing to do, since the officers and men of Wellington's army were in reality managing perfectly well without them. I try to be as accurate as possible when creating my fictional regiment and when I portray actual historical figures like Wellington and Fletcher, I try to make sure that they were where I say they were, or at least they could have been. My aim is to weave fiction into fact as seamlessly as possible.

At the battle of Assaye, Colonel Maxwell of the cavalry and the men of the 78th really did play the roles I have assigned to them, although without the help of the 110th infantry.

At Oporto in 1809, a company of the 3rd under Paget were the first over the river. I have given the job to the 110th light company under Major van Daan instead, although Paget and Hill afterwards play the roles they actually did in history. Likewise, at Talavera shortly afterwards I have given the 110th some of the work which was done by Stewart's brigade, although where possible I have included the actual regiments fighting alongside the fictional ones.

The one major liberty I have taken is at the combat of the Coa in 1810 which is referred to although not actually featured in the book. On this occasion I have given the 110th under Major van Daan the task of retaking the knoll overlooking the bridge to cover the last of the retreat. This task was actually carried out by the 43rd under Macleod and the 95th under Beckwith. I apologise to them for stealing their glory on behalf of the 110th.

I always regretted not describing the Combat on the Coa in the book but including every action that Paul van Daan was involved in during the eight years covered by this book would have made it ridiculously long. In 2020 I found the opportunity to rectify this omission in a short story which I published on my website called *An Unnecessary Affray*. A lot of my regular readers follow me online as well, but I realise that those reading the paperback may not, so I've included the story as a bonus at the end of the book. For those who are interested, another missed campaign in the book is Copenhagen in 1807. Paul van Daan's role in that campaign is described in *An Unwilling Alliance*, the first book in my linked naval series, *the Manxman* and I strongly recommend you read it as it's a significant episode in Paul's life.

Regarding Anne Carlyon's somewhat unusual role in the surgeons' tents; women often helped with the wounded during this and many other wars, and accounts of the time sing the praises of their courage in helping the wounded to safety and tending their wounds. Nobody thought anything of this. A woman working as a volunteer nurse alongside the surgeons would have been accepted without question, although few officers' wives were present on all campaigns so the nurses would more likely have been wives of the NCOs or enlisted men. Nevertheless, in the later years of the war we know that Captain Harry Smith's young Spanish wife, Juana, helped with the wounded when needed and was very much admired for doing so, and there would have been others.

Anne's role is different in that she has come across a surgeon willing to teach her more than basic nursing skills. As a woman at that time, she could never have trained formally or obtained a degree, but she was formidably intelligent and proved herself more than capable as a surgeon and physician. When writing about Anne, I have always had in my mind the true story of Dr James Barry, an army surgeon in the nineteenth century who was found on his death, after a long and distinguished career, to have been a woman. Barry found his own way around the restrictions of his day; Anne was fortunate to find herself in a situation where medical staff were in such short supply that nobody was going to stop her treating the wounded, although there was considerable resentment from the more traditional surgeons. I have read a lot about the army medical service, which was frequently in chaos, although staffed by dedicated and courageous doctors, and I can understand why Dr Adam Norris welcomed Anne's help.

While researching and writing these books I am constantly amazed at how the men and women of Wellington's army were expected to live. Conditions were appalling, equipment and uniforms often lacking, pay was infrequent and violent death highly likely. Despite all this, battles were fought and won by men who showed astonishing courage and dedication to duty. This book is for my readers to enjoy but it's also dedicated to the men and women of Wellington's army who were probably more remarkable than I have made them.

An Unnecessary Affray: a bonus short story about the Combat on the Coa

It was hot on the long march from Viseu to Almeida, with the July sun beating down on the troops over a distance of some seventy miles. The pace was brisk, but not punishing, with the march beginning in the cool early dawn and stopping to rest and eat before the heat of the afternoon sun became unbearable. Ensign Evan Powell was surprised at how much progress they were able to make each day. He mentioned the steady but effective pace to his fellow ensign in the fourth company.

"The major won't push them beyond endurance unless it's an emergency, no matter what Wellington or Craufurd might say," Donahue said. "Chances are we won't see a battle. Craufurd is under orders to keep a watchful eye on the French, but not to risk the light division. By the time we get there he might already be pulling out."

"Why are we going then?"

Donahue shot him an amused glance. "The official version or my guess?"

"Both, I suppose," Evan said. He was a little in awe of Donahue who at nineteen, was two years older than him and had almost three years' experience on active service with the 110th. He had fought at Rolica, Vimeiro, Oporto and Talavera, along with several smaller skirmishes. Evan had only recently arrived in Portugal to take up a vacant commission in the fourth company of the 110th and although he had done eight weeks training with the second battalion in Melton Mowbray, and had set sail full of confidence, he found his new messmates intimidating.

"All right then. Officially, Lord Wellington is sending the 110th to reinforce General Craufurd at Almeida in case of a surprise attack by the French. It's not that strange, we're not formally designated light infantry yet, but we're all trained skirmishers and we've served with Craufurd's division out on the border for months."

"And unofficially?"

Donahue grinned. "Unofficially, old chap, you've arrived in the middle of the juiciest scandal this army has seen in a long time. Major van Daan is newly widowed, his wife recently died in childbirth, but it's very well known that for at least a year he has been enjoying an extremely passionate affair with the wife of an assistant deputy quartermaster. Last week it all blew up when Captain Carlyon smacked his wife in public right outside headquarters and accused her of making a cuckold of him with the major. Major van Daan took exception to it and challenged him, and the whole battalion held its collective breath until Carlyon did the decent thing and ran like a rabbit taking a fat purse from the army pay chest with him."

"He deserted?"

"Better that than dead, which he would have been if he'd got into a fight with our major. Anyway, Wellington took a hand. He doesn't want to lose Major van Daan over a scandal with a light skirt, so he's sent him up here to calm down, while I imagine he'll do his best to get the girl sent home."

Evan was shocked, although he tried not to show it. His family was Welsh, solid local gentry with low church leanings and the word adultery had never been heard in his mother's drawing room. His arrival in camp right in the middle of the preparations to march meant that he had barely had time for an introduction to his new commanding officer, but he had felt an instinctive liking for the tall fair officer with the ready smile who had welcomed him, apologised for the chaos, and handed him over to his company captain for further instructions. He was disappointed but also very curious. They were sitting around the camp fires, as darkness fell over the scrub covered, rocky plains and low hills of central Portugal and this was proving to be one of Evan's most interesting conversations in the midst of orders and marching and picket duty.

"Is she pretty?"

Donahue gave a faint smile. "She's beautiful. Lucky bastard. I can't say I blame him."

"Awful for his wife, though."

"Not sure she even knew, she was friendly with Mrs Carlyon, they were forever around the place together."

"Awful for him, then," Evan said, trying hard to imagine himself in such an appalling position. "He must feel so guilty."

"Not him. He can't have cared about her or he wouldn't have..."

"Mr Donahue."

The voice was quiet, and Donahue stopped mid-sentence and scrambled to his feet to salute. Evan did the same, quaking. His company captain was a completely unknown quantity and Evan's impression of Johnny Wheeler was of a pleasant, even-tempered man in his thirties who seemed well-liked by both officers and men, but there was an edge to his voice now.

"Captain Wheeler. Sir. My apologies, didn't see you..."

403

"I'd guessed that, Ensign, or you wouldn't have opened your mouth so freely on the subject of your battalion commander's personal life to a new officer."

It was impossible to see if Donahue was blushing in the firelight, but Evan knew that he was. "Sir, very sorry. I was repeating gossip, sir, should have known better."

"How the hell do you think he'd have felt if he'd heard you saying that? She was his wife of six years, she gave him two children, and he's barely holding himself together."

"Sir, I didn't think."

"There doesn't seem to be much evidence that you can think, Donahue. Get yourself out there, forward pickets, you can relieve Mr Renard. I hope it's bloody cold."

"Yes, sir."

Donahue's voice was subdued. He picked up his hat, saluted and set off into the darkness. Evan followed his example, but Wheeler stopped him.

"Not you, Mr Powell, you've done nothing wrong."

"I was part of the conversation, sir."

"I know, I heard. I also heard what you said last. Empathy is a useful quality, I hope you manage to hold onto it after a few years in the army. Stand down, lad. As you've lost your messmate, why don't you come and join us?"

Evan froze in surprise and glanced over to a group of men around an impressive fire in the centre of the camp. Donahue mockingly called it 'the golden circle' where the commanding officer of the 110th and his particular friends congregated. Wheeler was beckoning, so Evan followed, feeling gauche and awkward and painfully aware of his youth and inexperience.

"Johnny, that was the longest piss in history, I was about to send out a search party. While you're up, grab another bottle of wine, will you, there's one in my tent. In fact, bring two, since I can see you've brought a guest. Come and sit down, Mr Powell, there's a spare camp chair next to Captain Swanson. Sergeant-Major, get him a drink, will you?"

Sergeant-Major O'Reilly unfolded his long limbs from a blanket on the grass and went to collect a pewter mess cup which he filled with wine. Evan accepted with mumbled thanks and sat down, trying to look inconspicuous.

"Why did Mr Donahue disappear into the darkness, Johnny?" Paul van Daan enquired.

"He was being an arsehole and I don't much like him, so I gave him extra picket duty."

There was a general laugh. Major van Daan surveyed Wheeler thoughtfully. "Now that is something I might have said, but you, Johnny, are a model of rational behaviour. You're also prevaricating. May I ask...?"

"No, because I'm not going to answer."

The major turned blue eyes towards Evan. "Mr Powell..."

"Don't you bloody dare, Paul."

404

Evan could feel his knuckles clenching around the cup and was thankful that it was not a glass. After a long moment, the major's expression softened into a smile.

"Ensign Donahue isn't the only one being an arsehole this evening. I beg your pardon, Mr Powell, I'm not quite myself at the moment. Shift that chair over here closer to me, will you? I'm too lazy to yell, and I want to find out more about you. This must have been the worst moment to arrive, I've not had a moment to talk to you and I don't suppose Captain Wheeler has either. It feels ridiculous to ask how you're settling in, so I won't. Tell me instead, where you're from and what brought you into the army?"

The party broke up late, and Evan slept well in his shared tent and woke surprisingly refreshed. He thought about the evening as he mounted Cassie, his bay mare, and set off into the cool dawn light. It had been an evening of laughter and good conversation and for the first time since arriving, Evan had come away feeling a sense of belonging. He wondered if all regiments were like this and if other commanding officers had Paul van Daan's effective blend of authority and friendliness.

Donahue was tired and miserable the following day, with little to say. He did not ask how Evan had spent the evening and no mention was made of their conversation of the previous day. Evan privately decided that if Donahue attempted to revive the subject, he would decline to take part. Gossiping about his commanding officer no longer felt comfortable after spending an evening in his company. Evan knew nothing about Paul van Daan's private life, but he had the sense that his friends were closing ranks protectively around him and Evan understood why. Bad enough to suffer such a loss in private, but unbearable to do so under the relentless glare of army gossips.

***

The River Coa was in full flood when the 110th reached the narrow stone bridge leading on to the fortress of Almeida. Captain Johnny Wheeler surveyed the raging torrent as he rode over the bridge and thought that whatever happened, neither French nor Anglo-Portuguese troops would be able to ford the Coa which meant that possession of the bridge would be crucial in any retreat or engagement. There were pickets along the river, outposts from Picton's third division, which was quartered at Pinhal and Major van Daan halted to speak to one of the officers. Johnny watched his friend talking to the young lieutenant and thought how tired Paul looked. In the brief time since his wife's death, he had slept poorly, rising after only a few hours' sleep to sit by the dying embers of the fire with Jenson, his orderly, or walking the perimeter of the camp to chat to the sentries. Johnny was one of the few men who knew something of Paul van Daan's internal struggle between his grief and guilt for his pretty wife, and his intense longing for the dark eyed young woman who seemed to have turned his world upside down.

After about twenty minutes, Paul mounted up and joined Johnny, and Carl Swanson who commanded his light company. "I'm not happy," he said bluntly. "It doesn't sound as though Craufurd has made any attempt to withdraw across the river yet. This lad knows nothing of what's going on, but he says a lot of the officers are worried that Craufurd is lingering too long. I'm going to speed it up a bit, I want him to read Wellington's letter, it might get him moving."

Johnny saluted, wheeled his horse and trotted back to his men with the order, and the 110th set off again at a much faster pace. The area between the Coa and the Agueda rivers was a rough plateau, with low hills and rocky outcrops studded with trees and criss-crossed with low stone walls enclosing orchards, olive groves and vegetable gardens. Johnny assessed the ground and thought that it was good country for skirmishing but given the huge numerical advantage that the French had in this region, he would not choose to pit his men against Ney's tirailleurs if it could be avoided.

The 110th met the first pickets of the light division a mile on, and after a brief conversation, Paul returned to Johnny. "I'm riding up to see Craufurd, he's camped about half a mile west of here. Come with me, Johnny. Captain Swanson, get them bivouacked here until we know where he wants us."

"Yes, sir."

Brigadier-General Robert Craufurd was known as Black Bob, partly because of his dark colouring and complexion, and partly because of the violent mood swings and fierce temper which struck terror into the officers and men of his brigade and more recently his division. Paul and Johnny found him in his tent, studying what looked like a sketch map of a fortress spread out on a folding camp table. Paul saluted and Craufurd glared at him.

"What the devil are you doing here?" he demanded.

"Lord Wellington's orders, sir. I've a letter from him."

Paul held it out and Craufurd took it. "Of course you bloody have. I received a letter from him yesterday, and two days before that as well. Does he spend his entire time writing letters?"

"Pretty much, sir," Paul agreed pleasantly. Craufurd regarded him, black brows drawn together and Johnny tried not to hold his breath. Suddenly, Craufurd grinned.

"Somebody should put sand in his ink pot," he said. "Well, whatever the reason, it's bloody good to see you, boy. Sit down. You too…what's your name again?"

"Wheeler, sir," Paul said, pulling up a camp chair. "Same as last time you asked."

"Button your lip, Van Daan, and let me read this latest nonsense."

There was silence in the tent as Craufurd read. The orderly disappeared then reappeared with a tray, and Johnny took a cup of wine with a smile of thanks and waited. Finally, Craufurd looked up.

"Nothing much new there. He wants me to stay on this side of the river as long as it's safe to do so, but not take any risks. Protect Almeida, but not for too long. Use my initiative but follow orders. Listen to…"

"I get the point, sir. We all do. He's worried and he's feeling his way."

"He isn't here," Craufurd said shortly.

"I am, sir."

"And I'm supposed to consult a junior officer about my division?"

Paul said nothing and Johnny admired his silence for a while. Eventually Craufurd made an exasperated sound.

"I am about to blow up Fort Concepcion," he said. "I've left it as long as possible, but if I leave it much longer, there's a risk they'll take it. Burgoyne and his engineers are in there, making the final preparations. The rest of the division has been pulled back a mile or so, leaving only the pickets and vedettes out there. We'll withdraw when we need to."

"When will that be, sir?"

"Is that why he's sent you?" Craufurd demanded belligerently. "Has he had the bloody nerve to send a boy of your age to keep an eye on me because he can't be here himself?"

"He sent me to provide support if it's needed, sir."

"And to write back immediately if you think I'm making a balls-up."

"No, sir, if I think you're making a balls-up, I'll tell you myself. And I'm a bit worried that you might be."

"Duly noted, Van Daan. Are you sure he didn't actually send you to stop you doing something stupid in your private life?"

Johnny caught his breath and Paul went very still but did not immediately speak. After a moment, he said:

"You mean losing my wife to childbirth? Not much he can do about that really, sir."

Craufurd's expression changed. "Christ, Paul, I didn't mean that. I'm sorry. Wellington wrote to me to tell me what had happened, he thought I should know. Is the child all right?"

"She seems to be thriving. We've found a wet nurse and she'll be travelling back to England as soon as an escort can be found."

"And what of Mrs Carlyon?"

"I don't know her plans, sir."

"Liar," Craufurd said, without heat. "Wellington's worried you'll persuade her into committing social suicide with you, he has a tendre for that girl."

"So do you, sir."

"Yes, I bloody do, so take care of her. And keep that husband of hers away from her. Did he really hit her in the town square in front of half the army?"

"Yes. Don't worry about her, sir. She's safe at the farm with the medical staff and Carlyon won't come back, he's too much of a coward. Don't think I don't realise that you're using my personal troubles to distract me. Where do you want us?"

"You can stay where you are for the moment, I'll send word once Burgoyne is ready and we're on the move. Write what you like to Wellington.

I know this area and I know my men and what they can do. I'll march when I'm ready."

***

Tension mounted over the next few days. The 110th shared picket duty with several companies of the 95th and Evan listened to their grumbling and tried not to be afraid. He could see no sign of fear in either his fellow officers or his men, but this was not their first experience of war. More and more French troops seemed to be moving into position, and Evan could sense the unease of his seniors. Officers from the other battalions, the 52nd, 43rd, 95th and the Portuguese caçadores came and went, spending time with Major van Daan, and Evan suspected that the conversation centred around when the light division might withdraw and whether Craufurd was holding on for too long.

At dawn on the 21st of July, Evan woke to movement, and then the call of the bugle. During training, he had practised getting to arms at speed, and had been impressed with his men, but he was astonished at how much faster these veteran troops could manage it. Gunfire could be heard through the morning mist as Major van Daan was summoned to Craufurd's command post then returned to brief his officers.

"There's action around Concepcion. Ney's sent in the fourth corps and they're forcing in our pickets and cavalry vedettes. They're going to blow the fort, and then, please God, he'll get us over that bridge and out of here."

"We won't fight then, sir?"

"Not unless we have to, Mr Barry, we're hugely outnumbered here, and this was never meant to be more than a watching brief. The 14th dragoons are holding them off until the fort is blown. Stand to arms, I want them ready to move at a moment's notice."

The explosion was shattering, a huge boom followed by a series of lesser charges and Evan felt as though the ground was shaken beneath him. He wondered how it felt to be even closer. Around him, his men were restless, ready now for either action or retreat, and it was a relief when General Craufurd rode up to the edge of Vale de la Mula shortly afterwards and approached Major van Daan. The French were clearly visible in front of the village; three regiments of infantry and a battalion of light infantry. The major saluted.

"Orders, sir?"

"Stand to, Major."

"We've been doing that since dawn, sir. Did the explosion do its job?"

"More or less. Some casualties, though, some of the cavalry were too close. A few dead and wounded from both sides. The 14th is holding them nicely, I doubt we'll see action today."

"Are we not retreating, sir?"

"Not yet. We can wait a while longer, I believe."

Paul van Daan was frowning. "We probably can, but what's the point, sir, if we have to go. Surely…"

"You forget yourself, Van Daan. Wait for orders."

Evan watched him ride off then looked over at Major van Daan and Captain Wheeler. They were both frowning.

"You think he's got this wrong?" Wheeler asked.

"I think it has the potential to be a bloody disaster," the major said shortly. "Carl, Johnny, get the men round, I want to speak to them."

The rain began during the early evening on the 23rd and continued ceaselessly through the night. Evan was on picket duty with Donahue and a dozen men of their company, and his companion grumbled through the sleepless and rain-sodden night. Marshal Ney's 6th Corps lay close by, and for several days, the light division had manoeuvred across the plateau between the Coa and Agueda rivers, occasionally exchanging fire with French scouts.

A heavy mist hung over the ground as Evan watched his men lighting a fire to make tea. Sergeant Mackie brought a steaming cup and Evan smiled gratefully.

"Soon warm up, sir. Captain says we'll be covering some of the wagons, bringing supplies out of Almeida. If we're lucky, we can bugger off after that."

As Evan drank his tea and ate two hard biscuits, bugles sounded as the main body of the army called reveille and began the morning muster, formed in companies. Men in red, green or the brown of the Portuguese units toured the pickets with dry cartridges to replace any that had got wet in the night. After only a short time, Evan had learned the morning routine of the army and it felt soothing, familiar, almost safe.

"Mist's burning off a bit," Donahue said. "Hope they relieve us soon, I've had enough of being out here with the bloody green jackets."

Evan did not reply. Since the night Donahue had been sent out on extra picket duty, his relationship with his fellow subaltern had cooled a little. Now that he had begun to get to know some of the other officers in the battalion, he was less impressed by Donahue's stories and found his incessant complaining irritating. Their current bivouac was wet, muddy and uncomfortable but it did not help to constantly moan about it. Evan was tired of his condescending manner and was beginning to loathe some of the tales he told of his conquests among the local women. He did not know if Donahue was really such a Lothario and was painfully aware of his own complete lack of experience, but Donahue's gleeful descriptions of seduction made him cringe.

"There's movement from the French lines," Sergeant Mackie said suddenly, and something in his tone made all the men turn their heads. Suddenly they were alert, reaching for muskets and shouldering packs. Private Brown doused the fire, kicking the embers around to ensure that it could not flare up again. Evan stood staring into the mist until his eyes hurt. He could hear the sounds now, but there had been movement before and he did not know what Mackie had heard that was different although he suspected the men did. There was a sudden breeze which lifted the edge of Evan's coat and caused a mad flapping as Private Crook finished rolling up his blanket.

The mist shifted eerily, like some ghostly creature reaching out white fingers to touch the low stone wall behind which they had camped, then suddenly sunlight pushed its way through. There was a gap in the fog, then another, and Evan felt his innards turn to water at the sight before him.

"Oh shit," Donahue breathed beside him.

The broad plain was covered with French troops as far as the eye could see. They were close and fully armed, and Evan knew with utter certainty that this was not another feint in the long dance of advance and retreat that Craufurd had been playing for days. These men were ready to fight, and today he might die.

Alarm calls were sounding up and down the line of pickets, and were picked up in the rear, as the men of the light division scrambled to pack up, abandoning roll-call to line the stone walls of the orchards and vineyards where they had slept. Donahue drew his pistol and checked it methodically and Evan did the same, although his hands were shaking so much that he was not sure he would be able to aim and fire. As he thought it, there was a shot to his left and then another, and suddenly the air was filled with the crackling of musket and rifle fire as the front line of Ney's voltigeurs and the first of the rifle pickets exchanged fire.

"They're coming," Donahue said, and his voice was suddenly very calm. "Don't panic, Powell. Hear that noise?"

"Drums?"

"That's right. They're a way off yet, which means he's not brought up his main columns, these are just the skirmishers. We'll hold them off, but when I give the word, we fall back through those trees to the main force. Don't worry, they'll be waiting to give support."

"What if they're not?"

"They will be. Stick with your men, they know what they're doing. Christ, these bastards are fast."

The French skirmishers were moving forward over the rough terrain, ducking behind trees and rocks to let off a shot. They worked in pairs, covering each other skilfully, and Evan was terrified at how quickly they were approaching. He felt painfully isolated and certain that within minutes he would be dead, then the crash of a musket beside him made him jump. It was followed by another and then another and the voltigeurs began to fall. They were replaced immediately by others, and Donahue straightened, took aim with his pistol and fired.

"Fall back," he called. "We're too far out here."

Relief mingled with fear in Evan's breast, but at least he could move now. Copying Donahue, he drew his sword and ran with his men to the first line of a small copse of trees. The men found cover behind them, turning to fire again at the approaching French. Donahue reloaded his pistol and it reminded Evan that he had not yet fired his. He was a good shot, had practised for many hours with his father and brother and could bag a wood pigeon better than either, but these were not birds. Evan took aim, knowing that his shaking hands must be visible to his men, and he wondered if they thought him a

410

coward. A blue jacket came into his sight and he steadied the pistol, feeling as though he would vomit. The Frenchman roared, a meaningless sound, designed to terrorise, and it galvanised Evan into action. He fired, coping well with the recoil, and the Frenchman fell. Evan was shocked, wondering for a moment if he had somehow stumbled, then he heard Crook's voice behind him.

"Bloody hell, good shot, sir. Come on, let's get out of here."

They ran, dodging between trees as the voltigeurs came closer. Shots flew around them, most bouncing harmlessly off tree trunks. Evan did not bother to stop and reload; he could not aim in here and his men seemed intent only on escape now. There were too many Frenchmen and sounds from the right suggested that the riflemen who had formed the next picket had been overrun. A shot to Evan's left was followed by a cry of agony and he stopped, knowing that one of his own men had been hit. A hand grasped his elbow, dragging him forward.

"No time, you'll be taken. We need to get to those walls."

Emerging into sunlight on the other side of the trees, Evan could see the grey stone walls, and beyond them, red coats with the silver grey facing of the 110th. Around him, his men made no further attempt to stand, there was no cover here. Evan risked a glance over one shoulder and wished he had not, as hundreds of French skirmishers swarmed up through the rocky terrain. He had been right about the riflemen, he caught a glimpse of them surrounded by French troops, their hands in the air. Evan felt very exposed, but all he could do was run for the walls. As he did so, a shot sounded very close, so close to his ear that he ducked instinctively. There was a noise like a slap and a shout of pain, and the man running beside him went down. Evan turned his head and saw Mackie, blood spreading out over the back of his jacket, trying desperately to drag himself to his feet.

The others were ahead of Evan, scrambling over the stone wall to take refuge behind their battalions, and once they were out of the line of fire, there were shouted orders, the 110th took aim and the crackle of musketry filled the air. Only Mackie and Evan were still outside the wall and Evan saw Donahue turn and yell furiously at him. Evan looked down. The Glaswegian sergeant's eyes were dull with pain, but he was still trying to get himself up, and suddenly Evan knew that he could not leave him. He ran back, trying to keep low, shots whistling past him from both directions as the 110th and the voltigeurs engaged in a spirited exchange of fire, and bent over his sergeant.

"Come on."

Mackie grasped his arm and used it like a ladder to drag himself to his feet, his face contorted with pain. A shot grazed the top of Evan's shoulder, ripping the cloth of his coat. For a moment, terror froze him, and he wanted to drop the sergeant and run for cover, but Mackie's desperate expression stopped him. Instead, he pulled the sergeant's arm across his shoulders and began to stagger painfully towards the wall.

"Carter, keep those bastards off them!" someone bellowed, and Evan recognised his commander's voice. He took a step and then another, Mackie's

411

tall frame weighing him down, and a shot hit the ground by his feet, kicking up grass and mud. Another step. Mackie stumbled and Evan had to stop, sweat pouring down his face into his eyes. He hauled the sergeant up a little more and took another step.

"Here."

The voice from beside him startled Evan then the weight of the sergeant was eased. Two men took Mackie from him, lifting him off his feet between them. "Run, sir."

Freed from his burden, Evan covered the few feet to the wall at speed and hands reached for him, helping him over. Beyond the lines, he fell to his knees, vomiting onto the ground as his terror caught up with him. He was alive, although he had no idea how.

The two men were laying Mackie down nearby. One of them inspected the wound and the other straightened and came to where Evan knelt. Evan looked up, bitterly ashamed of his weakness, and was shocked to realise that the outstretched hand came from Captain Wheeler.

"Well done," he said. "Are you all right? I thought you'd been hit."

Evan felt the shoulder of his jacket, and realised that, through the torn cloth, there was wetness and a painful graze. He had not felt any pain at the time and the thought that he had so nearly been cut down by a bullet made him feel slightly light-headed. He looked at Wheeler then remembered he had not saluted. He scrambled to his feet and did so awkwardly. Wheeler shook his head.

"Give yourself a minute, lad, and breathe, you've had a shock. You may also have saved a man's life; we'll send him to the back with the wounded. Sit down, have a drink and then get yourself over to your men, they need you."

"They don't need me. I don't know what I'm doing," Evan said bitterly.

"You're learning," Wheeler said gently. "It's a bloody way to do it, mind. Go on."

Evan watched him go back to the wall, drank some water, and when his stomach had settled a little, went to join Donahue and the rest of his company.

***

After an hour of skirmishing and desperately holding off the French light troops, Johnny could not believe that Craufurd had not called the retreat. Even the furthest of his troops, the 43rd, were no more than two miles from the bridge, but it appeared that the general intended to make a stand. Johnny could sense Paul van Daan's anger, as the drums came ever closer and Ney's main columns marched into their battle lines, ready for the assault. Several men from the 110th had fallen, and at least three were dead. The wounded, Mackie among them, had been carried to the back of the lines, and Paul had given orders that they were to be removed to the bridge where he had already sent his orderly, Jenson, in charge of the grooms with the officers' horses.

412

Johnny wondered if they would be allowed to cross. Major Napier, Craufurd's ADC was riding between the battalion commanders, with orders to hold their ground to allow some wagons of artillery ammunition and other supplies to cross the bridge.

"They're forming up to attack," Paul said, crouching behind the wall, his eyes on the French. "Once they've got those guns ready, we're going to be fucking slaughtered here. What is wrong with him?"

Johnny was watching the cannon and the artillerymen scrambling to drag them into position, with a sick feeling in his stomach. Wellington would never have waited this long to order a retreat, but there was still no word from Craufurd.

Abruptly, Paul got to his feet. "We're pulling back," he said, and raised his voice to a bellow. "First, second, third, fifth and guards companies under Captain Clevedon, fall back to the farmyard over there, then stand. Light, fourth, sixth and eighth, under Captain Wheeler, cover them, then make a running retreat. I'm going up onto that rise to see what's going on, along the lines, I'll follow you."

"Sir, for God's sake!" Johnny yelled, exasperated, but Paul had gone, keeping low behind the lines, following a narrow goat track up the slope. Johnny watched, but decided that his commander had taken a sensible line on the reverse slope and was probably not in danger. He turned to his own company, shouting orders.

As the guns began to spit fire at the light division troops, the 110th made an untidy retreat to the farmyard, and positioned themselves around the broken walls with muskets and rifles steady in sweating palms. Johnny glanced over at his newest subaltern. He was worried about young Powell, whose white face and trembling hands made him look like a frightened child. This was an appalling first engagement for a new young officer and Powell had no idea how well he was doing, but Johnny wished he had told his lieutenants to keep an eye on the boy.

The farmyard was out of range of the cannon, but some of the rifles were coming under heavy fire, and Johnny watched anxiously as they retreated, cautiously at first and then pushed into headlong flight, racing towards the lines of the 43rd who were trying to give them cover. Craufurd's line stretched between the Almeida fortress on the left and the Coa gorge on the right, and as long as the two flanks remained steady, it could probably hold. The rifles' flight was opening up a gap to the left, and Johnny watched in dawning horror, praying that it would close before the French saw it. As he thought it, the first of the rifles reached the 43rd, and the two battalions merged, red coats mingling with green in a panicked melee.

There was a yell, and Johnny turned to see Paul running towards them, speeding over the ground with no attempt to maintain cover. He arrived, flushed and breathless, and several of his captains abandoned their men and ran to hear the news.

413

"Cavalry. French hussars on the left, our flank is turned. They're slaughtering the rifles over there, O'Hare's men are running for their lives, it's bloody chaos. We need to retreat."

"We've no orders."

"I'm giving the orders. Two halves, same formation as before, skirmishing in companies down that road towards the bridge."

"What about Craufurd?" Carl Swanson asked, and Johnny flinched internally at the expression on his commander's face.

"If he's lucky, we won't run into him," Paul said. "Get moving and get them out of here."

The retreat had disintegrated into chaos. On the left, French hussars swept through a company of riflemen and into the 43rd while to the right, the 52nd were under heavy attack from an infantry brigade. Between them, the 110th fell back, with officers and NCOs trying desperately to keep them together. It was another thirty minutes or more before Johnny, his men keeping up a steady fire behind yet another set of stone walls, saw Major Napier riding in search of Paul. Johnny glanced over his men, shouted an order to his senior lieutenant and ran to join them.

"We're sounding the retreat," Napier said. "Cavalry and guns are ordered to gallop for the bridge, the Portuguese to follow. The rest of you…"

"Give me strength!" Paul bellowed, and Johnny saw Napier jump at the volume. "We're already in full bloody retreat, did he not notice? Half the Portuguese have already run for their lives, they're probably across that bridge by now."

"They're helping to block the bloody bridge," Napier said bitterly. "There's a gun carriage or wagon or something, that's overturned, and they're panicking. We need time to clear it, Major, you can't get horses and wagons down that road quickly. The infantry is to fall back from the left, and you need to defend every inch of this ground for as long as possible and keep them off that bridge. If they get to it before we're ready to get the troops across they'll cut us off and we're all dead or prisoner. It will be a bloodbath."

Johnny understood. The road to the bridge made a sharp turn, overshooting the heights and then turning back on itself along the river bank, in order to descend the steep slope gradually. Cavalry, guns and wagons had to keep to the road because the hillside would be too steep for them, and the sharp turn would slow them down. Johnny watched Paul's face assimilating the information. After a moment, he nodded and when he spoke, he suddenly sounded very calm and very much in control.

"Understood, Napier. Where is he, is he all right?"

"No," Napier said briefly. "He's not himself, he's very agitated and I'm a bit worried he'll do something rash. He knows he's made a bad mistake, Van Daan, and he can't retrieve it, it's happened too fast."

"It's been happening for days, and he could have got it back even a couple of hours ago," Paul said quietly. "He wanted a fight, he wanted to prove something to Wellington, and he was too bloody arrogant to listen to any of us."

"I know. He knows."

"All right. Get back to him and tell him I'm forming a rear-guard and we'll keep them back as long as we can."

"The 95th..."

"The rifles took the brunt of that first cavalry charge, Charles, and they're so tangled up with the 43rd in places it'll be hard to keep order. My lads are still together. We'll all need to fight our way down there but tell him I'll hold the rear for him. Just tell him, will you?"

Napier nodded. A flurry of shots flew alarmingly close, and Paul ducked back behind the stone wall with Johnny. "And either get off that horse or get out of here before you get yourself killed," he shouted, and Napier raised a hand in acknowledgement, wheeled his horse and cantered away.

***

They had been fighting for hours, and Evan was exhausted. His fear was still there, bubbling under the surface, but there was no time to think about it. He was breathless, his voice hoarse with shouting encouragement to his men as they dragged themselves over stone walls, some of them head-height. The French were under no such disadvantage. With so many troops, they were able to send fresh men into the fray allowing those who were tiring to fall back. They hunted Craufurd's men down the slopes ruthlessly, and too many fell under heavy musket fire or lay bloody and trampled beneath the sabres of the cavalry.

Ahead of the 110th, the men of the 43rd and 95th made their way erratically towards the bridge, leaving dead, wounded and prisoners behind them. Van Daan held his men steady at the rear, pinning down sections of the French for long stretches of time to give their retreating fellows time to move on, then making a frantic dash to the next enclosure where they caught their breath behind stone walls before turning to fire again. At any moment, it seemed to Evan that the relentless tide of the approaching French would flood over them and sweep them away, but somehow, when the waves threatened to overwhelm his men, Paul van Daan was up again, shouting orders, pointing to a new shelter, a new refuge, a new yard or orchard or olive grove which he could use as a flimsy fortress. His eye for terrain was extraordinary and amid his confusion and sheer terror, Evan felt something akin to hero-worship for the tall figure who seemed to him to be keeping them alive almost single-handedly.

As they drew close to the bridge, their way was blocked by men of the 43rd and 95th, some of them wounded and being supported by their comrades. Bloody and battered, they streamed down the road towards the river, some of them scrambling down the steep slopes to reach the bridge. Above the road the two knolls which overlooked the crossing, were currently held by Craufurd's troops, but there was already fighting on the heights as the

415

advancing French sought to push the defenders off. On the route to the bridge, French fire was finding more targets as the light division men came together in a concentrated mass, and from behind every available rock, wall and bush, the enemy directed fire at the men trying desperately to reach the bridge, which was still clogged with wagons and men.

"This is a death trap," Major van Daan said. "Captain Wheeler draw them over to the left, there's some cover behind those rocks, although not much. Set up fire onto that slope, it might draw some of them off from the bridge. Who's in command up on that knoll?"

"Looks like Beckwith, sir."

"Good news, he's got a brain. Keep them low and keep them busy, Johnny, I'm going to climb up there."

"Oh, not again," Wheeler said, and Evan thought he sounded rather like an exasperated nursemaid with an over-exuberant charge. "Look, sir, if you have to commit suicide, take somebody with you. They might be able to get you out of there if you're wounded, or at least bring a message."

"What an excellent idea," Van Daan said cordially and to Evan's astonishment, smiled at him. "What do you say, Ensign Powell, do you think you can keep me out of trouble?"

Evan froze for a moment. The thought of the scramble up the slope terrified him, but he realised suddenly that there was nothing in the world that he wanted to do more.

"Paul, no! He's seventeen with no experience, and..."

"Yes, sir," Evan said loudly, and Wheeler stopped speaking and stared at him. The major was still smiling, as though musket fire was not raining down around him, and Evan felt that there was nothing that he could not do.

"Thank you. Any seventeen-year-old in his first engagement that has the guts to drag his wounded sergeant to safety is a man I'm happy to have beside me. Come on, we'll go up the reverse slope. It'll be a scramble, but we'll be out of the firing line."

They found Lieutenant-Colonel Beckwith with a telescope to his eye and Evan, who was experiencing a rush of excitement which seemed to have driven all fear from him, almost wanted to laugh at the casual way in which he greeted Major van Daan.

"I've been watching your lads, Major. Bloody good work. If only they'd clear this bridge, we might get more of them off."

"You're doing a bloody good job up here, sir. We're stuck for a bit; I'm going to hold that rocky area for as long as I can. Where's General Craufurd?"

"Down there somewhere, I don't know. Napier's conveying his orders, I've not seen him for a while."

"He's not wounded, is he?"

"I don't think so, but he's not himself today. Look, keep up your fire until they clear those wagons. The minute we can, I'll send a messenger and you can get your lads over."

"We can wait."

"Take an order, Major. You've done enough today."

"Yes, sir. Once I get them across, we'll set up the guns and we can cover your retreat."

"Good. Unless we get orders to the contrary."

"I wouldn't mind some orders," Van Daan said mildly, and Beckwith laughed and clapped him on the shoulder.

"The only orders you approve of are your own, Van Daan. Good luck."

The scramble down the slope was much quicker, and the major led the way back to the lines, keeping low and making a weaving run, which Evan followed. Behind the rocks, the men of the 110th crouched, keeping up a steady and surprisingly effective fire on the French. Most of the enemy attention was focused on the bridge, where some of Colonel Elder's Portuguese troops were finally managing to clear the tangle of wagons and guns out of the way to allow the troops to begin crossing.

***

Johnny Wheeler had lost track of time. He was beginning to worry about his men running out of ammunition and had told them to save their shots and make them count. After the first scramble to cover, the 110th remained relatively safe in their rocky fortress. A determined rush by the French would dislodge them in seconds, but Ney's men seemed wholly focused on the bridge and the detachments of the 95th and 43rd up on the knoll. Johnny guessed that, given the distance between Paul's men and the bridge, the French considered they would have plenty of time to dispose of the 110th once the other English battalions had been annihilated.

There was movement from the knoll, and Johnny watched as the English troops began to fall back, hard pressed by the French. Beside him, Paul had his folding telescope to his eye and after a long moment, he swore softly.

"What is it, sir?"

"Beckwith is pulling out. He's had orders to withdraw."

"Should we move?"

"No. Oh for God's sake, where the hell is Craufurd, he's gone mad?"

"He's desperate, sir."

"He's going to be more than desperate in a minute. Once the French have that high ground, they can pick us off at their leisure."

Paul stepped out from behind the rock and there was a yell from Ensign Powell. Instinctively, Paul dropped low, and a shot struck the rock inches from his head, breaking off shards. Paul flattened himself against the rock and yelled.

"Colonel Beckwith. Over here."

Beckwith joined him within minutes and his face was distraught. "Napier brought orders to retreat over the bridge," he gasped. "But, Major, the 52nd aren't all over. Barclay and his men are still out there fighting, nobody has given him orders to retire."

417

Johnny felt his stomach lurch and he met Paul's eyes in a moment of shared horror. "Oh no," he breathed. "The poor bastards. They're either dead or prisoners."

"No, they're not," Paul said, and stood up. "Napier! Major Napier. Over here!"

Craufurd's ADC looked around, bewildered, then trotted his horse forward. "Major van Daan."

"Barclay," Beckwith croaked. He looked to Johnny like a man driven to the edge of his endurance. "Barclay is still over there with half the 52nd, he's had no orders to retire."

"He must have," Napier said.

"He bloody hasn't, he's not having a picnic over there," Paul said furiously. "You need to get over there and tell him to pull back."

Napier hesitated and Beckwith said sharply:

"That's an order, Major."

Napier took off at a canter. A sharp volley of shots came from above and both Paul and Beckwith turned to look. Johnny followed their gaze and felt a rush of sheer despair. As the 43rd and 95th had retired from the knoll, the French had moved in. Settling down among the rocks and bushes, they were beginning to fire down onto the retreating troops who were finally making their way onto the bridge.

"Colonel Beckwith. Major van Daan. Get your men out of here and across the bridge."

General Robert Craufurd was on foot, and Johnny thought that he had never seen him so agitated. The dark hair was rumpled, as though he had been running his fingers through it, and Craufurd's face was pale, his eyes darting from side to side and his jaw clenched. Both Beckwith and Paul saluted and Johnny thought that at least one of them meant it.

"Sir, Major Napier has gone out to bring the rest of the 52nd in," Beckwith said without preamble.

"Very good. Take your men, Colonel, and lead them across the bridge. Major van Daan, fall in behind with the 110th."

Neither Beckwith nor Paul spoke. Johnny realised he was holding his breath. Eventually, Beckwith said:

"Sir, with the French up on the knoll, we're going to be cut to pieces."

"Some casualties are unavoidable, Colonel. The bridge is clear, your men will need to move quickly."

"If I could take some of the rifles back up…"

"That would be suicide, Colonel. Get moving."

Beckwith saluted. Every line of his body radiated anger, but he moved away, shouting orders to his officers and NCOs. Craufurd looked at Paul.

"Once Colonel Beckwith's men are on the move, fall in behind, Major."

Paul took a deep breath. "Sir. You're not thinking straight. Somebody needs to push the enemy back off that knoll to cover the retreat."

"It's too risky."

"It's too risky not to."

"I have given my orders, Major."

There was a long and painful pause, then Paul saluted without speaking. Craufurd turned away and made his way back down towards the bridge, his sergeant orderly at his heels. Nobody spoke for a long time. Johnny watched his friend and knew with absolute certainty what he was about to do. It was a moment of decision, a choice to follow him or to obey Craufurd's orders. Johnny knew he could probably induce some of the men to go with him across the bridge, if he told them the orders had come from the commander of the light division. He also knew that he was not going to do it. Watching Paul's expressive face, considering options and discarding them, Johnny admitted to himself that he would probably follow this man into hell and back. Finally, Paul spoke.

"First, second, third, fifth and guards. Form up under Captain Clevedon and prepare for a fast withdrawal over the bridge. On the other side, string out into an extended line and cover any troops still crossing. Grab some ammunition when you get there, the wagons are across. If any of you have any left now, share it with the rest of us, you won't be shooting going over that bridge, you'll be running."

"Yes, sir," Clevedon said soberly.

"Light, fourth, sixth and eighth, with me. We're going to take back those knolls and protect the retreat."

They took the knoll at the point of steel. Some shots were fired on the way up, with Paul's men dodging between bushes and rocks, firing where they could, but at the top there was neither space nor time to fire muskets. The French seemed shocked, having witnessed the easy withdrawal of Beckwith's troops such a short time before, and Paul's men fought with single-minded ferocity. The thought of the rest of the battalion crossing the bridge below under constant fire from the French was a spur to action and once at the top, the 110th used bayonet and sword in a brief, savage fight with no quarter given. Johnny was drenched in the blood of the men he had killed.

There was always a point in a close fight, where it felt impossible to carry on. Johnny's sword arm ached and his whole body begged for rest, so that he had to force himself onwards. A voltigeur raced towards him, bayonet raised, and Johnny side-stepped and slashed viciously, bringing the man down. There was a scarlet spurt and Johnny could smell the blood so strongly that it was almost a taste in the back of his throat.

There was a crack, then another, and Paul's men scrambled for cover as three or four Frenchmen found time to reload and fire. Johnny ran, grasping the arm of young Powell, who seemed frozen to the spot. As he rounded a tree, shoving the boy ahead, there was a sharp pain and his leg gave way. Johnny went down and rolled over, swearing. A hail of fire clattered around them and was answered immediately by the crash of rifles from Corporal Carter's men. Johnny felt his calf and his hand came away bloody. Cautiously he moved his leg, feeling all around, but the damage seemed slight. The ball had entered his calf at the fleshy part, but the bone was obviously not damaged, and Johnny thought he could still walk.

"Sir, here."

Powell was holding out a white neck cloth. Johnny shifted on his bottom to bring the damaged leg closer to the boy. "You do it, Mr Powell. Nice and tight, I'll need to walk on it in a bit."

Powell obeyed and despite their situation, Johnny almost laughed at the intense concentration on the young face. He did a good job though, and Johnny accepted his hand and got cautiously to his feet, realising that the immediate sounds of battle had died away. The French were retreating, backing away and then running in full flight, almost falling down the steep, rocky slopes, leaving dead and wounded behind, and Paul's small band stood breathless and bloody across the knoll, briefly savouring their victory.

There was no time to enjoy it. The French were regrouping at the foot of the knoll, their officers yelling orders, and the voltigeurs were strung out along the slopes where they could fire down onto the troops on the bridge. Paul shouted orders and his men settled into position, taking careful aim. Most of the companies were armed with muskets, which were not especially accurate, but his light company had rifles and they picked off individual Frenchmen with contemptuous ease. Suddenly it was the French who were under pressure and as Craufurd's light division staggered across the bridge to safety, the French cowered with gunshot whistling past their ears, ricocheting off rocks and screeching into the air. As the French fired onto the bridge, the 110th fired onto the French, and Johnny called orders as calmly as he could and tried not to think about what they would do when the ammunition ran out which it was assuredly going to.

Firing diminished as men had nothing left to fire with, and Johnny counted the shots and watched the men settling in grimly, bayonets and swords at the ready, knowing that the French could count as well as they could. Eventually, it was quiet around the knoll and Johnny looked over at Paul and saw the mobile face quirk into an attempt at a smile.

"Sorry, lad. We're going to have to fight our way out of this, and it might not be pretty. I didn't have time to ask your advice."

"I'm not an idiot, Paul, I knew what I was getting into."

"All right then. Let's not wait for them, we'll go down fast when they don't expect it. Every man for himself now, Johnny, straight to the bridge, bayonets and swords. And if I go down and any one of these bastards stops to pick me up, I'll gut him myself."

"That won't stop me trying, sir."

Johnny turned in surprise and saw Ensign Powell, his sword drawn and his young face white and set but very determined. Paul managed another smile although it lacked conviction.

"Don't you bloody dare, Ensign."

The French were coming, scrambling up the slope, and the 110th waited. There was little shooting. It was hard for the French to aim uphill, while the 110th had nothing to shoot with. Johnny stood, sword in hand, intensely aware of his men around him. He had known some of them for ten years and more and he was trying not to think of them now as individuals, with wives and children and families who would mourn their death. Below, the rest of the division was streaming over the bridge and Johnny concentrated on that thought, and on the men who would survive, as he waited for the order to attack.

The firing had been desultory, but was picking up now, and Johnny was puzzled, as he could not immediately tell where the shots were coming from. Below him, it seemed that the French advance was slowing, and Johnny peered down the slope, trying to see through the trees, wondering what was happening. His men, who had been immobile with fixed bayonets and grim faces, were stirring, uncertain now. Suddenly there was a roar, and a rush, and then the French broke and red coats, mingling with green, surged up the slope. Johnny lowered his sword and stood watching and Paul walked forward.

"Colonel Beckwith."

"Major van Daan. I've been told you disobeyed a direct order from General Craufurd."

"Did he tell you to come up here, sir?"

"No. But he didn't tell me I couldn't either." Beckwith gave a tight smile. "Barclay's men are crossing now and Macleod just made the most suicidal charge I've seen in a long time, the bloody maniac. It's time to go, Van Daan. Let's get them out of here."

***

Evan had thought that the battle was over. After the frantic scramble across the bridge, the light division lined up to defend their position, but did not occur to him that it would be necessary. Major van Daan was issuing orders, and men raced to collect ammunition and distribute it. Further back, behind the lines, the wounded were carried up to a small chapel which was being used as a temporary hospital and the surgeons tended wounds, performed amputations and in some cases, closed the eyes of men already dead. Across the bridge, the French waited for orders and Evan was sure the order would be to retreat.

He was wrong.

As the light division stood to arms, waiting, a regiment moved forward, crossing the bridge. Evan watched them come, bewildered. The caçadores, who had crossed early, were in position behind stone walls a little above the bridge, and artillery had been placed across the road to sweep it from end to end. Once Craufurd's battalions were across the river, they had placed themselves behind rocks and walls on the slope commanding the bridge. They had fresh ammunition and they were bloody and exhausted and angry, watching in disbelief as the French formed their grenadiers on the knoll and then charged at the passage, offering an irresistible target.

It was slaughter. The leading company was mown down, before it had got half way across, by musket fire from the hillside and from the right. The column broke, and the men recoiled and dispersed among the rocks and trees by the bank, firing pointlessly towards Craufurd's battalions. On the bridge, the French lay dead and dying, but more were forming up at the far end.

"Surely they're not coming again," Johnny Wheeler breathed. "It's suicide."

"What if they manage to ford the river, sir?"

"They're not fording this. A couple tried earlier and were shot down or swept away. General Craufurd has sent the cavalry out along the roads to make sure, but the river is too swollen after the rain we've had. This is their only way to cross, but they're not going to make it."

"They're going to give it a try, though," Major van Daan said. "Bloody Ney. I notice you don't see him putting his neck into this noose, he'll stay well back." He raised his voice. "Sergeant-Major O'Reilly, I want your sharpshooters to target the officers. Once they're down, I'm hoping this lot will break and run a lot sooner."

"Yes, sir."

The French made three charges, and it sickened Evan to watch the dead and wounded piling up. Wave after wave of troops flung themselves at the bridge and were cut down in appalling butchery until the bridge was blocked by the bodies. Evan could make no sense of the day and was too exhausted to try. He had thought, in his naivety, that a battle was either lost or won but he could not imagine who would claim victory or defeat on the Coa today. He only knew that he was weary and miserable and wanted it to be over.

At midnight, the order came to withdraw and General Craufurd's division slipped away through the darkness. Arriving at the edge of Pinhal, where Picton's third division lay, they received orders to stand down and rest, and Evan Powell lay on the hard, cold ground and slept the sleep of total exhaustion.

It was early when the bugles sounded, and Evan rose and went with his men to roll-call and early parade and the miserable knowledge that through the chaos of the previous day, both officers and men had died or been wounded. He listened to the names with a chill in his heart and when he was free, went to find his captain.

"What happened to Mr Donahue, sir?"

Johnny Wheeler regarded him with compassion. "I'm sorry, Ensign. He was cut down in the final retreat over the bridge. They brought his body over, we'll bury him later today."

Evan could not believe it. He stood numbly at the side of the hastily dug grave, one of many on the hillside above the Coa. Around them, the hills were a hive of activity as General Picton mobilised his third division to pull back ahead of any French advance. Evan wondered about that. Picton's men had been very close, and he was puzzled why the sound of battle had not brought the third division into the fray.

The light division formed up for the march and the 110th lined up in companies, their wounded grouped together to be loaded into wagons, Captain Johnny Wheeler among them. He was talking quietly to his battalion commander when there was an abrupt command, and the companies sprang to attention at the approach of General Robert Craufurd.

"Major van Daan. Yesterday, you disobeyed a direct order."

Paul van Daan saluted. "Yes, sir. My apologies. I was carried away in the heat of battle."

Craufurd regarded him fiercely, dark eyes glowering under beetling brows. "Bollocks," he said shortly. "You made a deliberate decision to disobey me, you arrogant young bastard, and you're going to regret it."

There was a short silence. The air was heavy with tension. As he studied Paul van Daan's face, Evan realised that he was holding his breath, silently praying that he would not respond. Craufurd looked him up and down as though he was a sloppily dressed recruit about to fail a dress inspection, but Paul remained silent. Finally, Craufurd made a snorting sound and turned his back contemptuously. Evan let out his breath slowly and he suspected he was not the only one. Craufurd took two steps.

"Actually, sir, I find that I don't regret it at all," Paul van Daan said, conversationally.

"Oh shit," Wheeler breathed, and Craufurd turned.

"How dare you?" he said softly, walking back to stand before the major. "How dare you speak to me like that?"

Van Daan's blue eyes had been looking straight ahead but now they shifted to Craufurd's face and Evan flinched at the expression in them. "Just telling the truth, sir. I don't regret taking my men up onto that knoll to stop the French slaughtering your division on the bridge, and if you were thinking clearly, you'd agree with me. You're not stupid and you're a good general, and I sincerely hope that Lord Wellington believes whatever heavily edited account of this almighty fuck-up you choose to tell him and gives you another chance. But don't ask me to play make-believe along with you. I've lost two good officers and a dozen men, with another twenty or so wounded, and I'm not in the mood."

"That's enough!" Craufurd roared. "By God, sir, you'll lose your commission for this, and when I speak to Lord Wellington, I'll make sure he knows just how his favourite conducts himself with his betters. I've made allowances for you time and again, but you're nothing but a mountebank, who thinks he can flout orders and disrespect a senior officer with impunity because he has the favour of the commander-in-chief. No, don't speak. Not another word. Since your battalion has no divisional attachment, I shall report this straight to Lord Wellington, with a strong recommendation that he send you for court martial, and I understand that it wouldn't be the first time."

Evan looked at the ground, wishing he could be somewhere else. Inexperienced he might be, but he was sure that no commander should rake down an officer of Paul's rank before his battalion, and he could sense the discomfort of both officers and men. Paul said nothing.

"You're a disgrace to your regiment, to this army and to your family. God knows, I've tried to ignore the stories about you, but I'm beginning to realise there's no smoke without fire. Six years, was it, that you led that poor woman a dance, and now that she's gone, you're sniffing after another officer's wife and driving him so mad that he…"

"That's enough!" Paul snapped. "You're entitled to say what you like about my professional conduct, sir, but if you think I'm going to stand here and allow you to drag my wife into this, you must be raving mad. She's dead. Show a little respect if you're capable of it."

Evan was holding his breath again. He found Craufurd frankly terrifying. Donahue had told stories of the man's raging temper, appalling manners and brutal discipline and at this moment it was easy to see where the rumours came from. In this mood, Craufurd appeared just as willing to shoot his own officer as the French, but Paul's words temporarily silenced him. After a moment, he said:

"I meant no disrespect to either lady, as you well know, but your cavalier attitude to army regulations is reflected in your private morals, boy, and neither has a place in my division."

"You're lucky to have a division left," Paul said. It was obvious that he was as angry as Craufurd. "We should never have been in that position, and you know it, which is why you're so bloody furious. I told you, Wellington told you, Napier told you, I think even Beckwith told you at some point, but you were too arrogant to listen to any of us, and you almost got your division slaughtered because of it. Report me to Wellington, in fact you can report me to God Almighty if you like but it won't make you feel any better. Those graves shouldn't be there. You should have retreated, but you chose to linger on in the hope of a neat little rear-guard action that would make you look good, and those men died because of it. Yes, I disobeyed a direct order, to try to save lives. I will sleep very well tonight over that decision."

"Get out of here," Craufurd hissed. "Take your battalion, while you still have one, and get out of here. You are not part of my division, and you will not march with us, sir. You are a disgrace."

He turned on his heel and stalked away. For a long moment, nobody moved or spoke. Finally, Paul van Daan stirred, as if coming out of a trance.

"If any one of you tells me I should have kept my mouth shut there, I'm going to shoot you in the fucking head," he announced. "Sergeant-Major O'Reilly, is it going to take you the rest of the morning to get my battalion on the road?"

***

After a few miles, the unsprung wagon made Johnny feel so sick that he called for his horse. The wound was painful but not agonising, and it was no worse riding. The battalion marched almost silently. Generally, Paul's officers took a relaxed attitude to the march, and there was a hum of conversation, but the 110th were too weary and too miserable after their losses and their commanding officer's altercation with General Craufurd.

After an hour, Johnny rode up the line to join Carl Swanson at the head of the light company. "Do you think he's ready to talk yet?"

"No," Carl said, his eyes on Paul's straight back. "But he probably needs to. You, me or both of us?"

"Let's both go."

Paul glanced both ways as they came up on either side of him. "Have you lost your companies, gentlemen?"

"No, it's still there," Carl said equably.

"I think mine is too," Johnny said, peering back over the heads of the marching men.

"Well, get back to them, then."

"Oh, cut line, Paul. We're worried about you. It's what friends do."

After a moment, Paul's taut expression softened a little. "I'm all right," he said. "Calming down slowly."

"Do you think he meant it?"

"Craufurd? Well, he did at that moment, but I doubt he'll follow through on it. And even if he did, I don't think Wellington will let him call a general court martial. He won't want this story bandied around in the London Gazette more than it needs to be. He'll probably tell me to apologise."

"You probably need to apologise, Paul."

"Craufurd needs to apologise, he's an arsehole. How are the wounded doing?"

"Bearing up, none of them are that serious. I'm glad you decided to bring them with us, though." Johnny shot his friend a thoughtful glance. "When we get there..."

"I'm not going to see her," Paul said. "I know what you're about to say, and you're right. Given what just happened, I need to get my battalion back to where it should be. Wellington is on the move, I'll join him. Johnny, why don't you take the wounded and a small escort and ride on to Viseu. You can get treated there and I'll send a message once I know where we are going."

"And I can check up on your lady love for you. I see through you, Van Daan. Have you heard from her?"

"Yes, she wrote to tell me that my daughter is safely on her way to Lisbon with Daniels and the bulk of the sick and wounded. Nan remained with the last of the hospital patients, but she needs to get herself out of there. I'll write a letter and you can take it for me."

"To Lisbon?"

"Yes, she can stay in the villa." Paul met Johnny's eyes and seemed to read his thoughts. "I don't know, Johnny, it's up to her. I'm going to miss Rowena to the end of my days, and I'll never stop feeling guilty about her, but you know how I feel about Nan. She's not free to marry me, and God knows when she will be. She says she'll stay with me anyway."

"That will ruin her, Paul."

"I know. Or I can send her back to England to her family and we both spend our time waiting for a man to die. I don't know what she'll do."

"Yes, you bloody do," Johnny said, torn between exasperation and affection. "She's as bad as you are."

His friend smiled, and for the first time in days it was a genuine smile. "Perhaps that's why we should be together," he said. "Cheer up, at least she's a good doctor, she can get that ball out of your leg for you. How's your new officer, Johnny?"

"I think he's doing all right," Johnny said. "What a bloody introduction to the army, though. I think it was a shock to him, losing Donahue, they'd got friendly."

"He's going to be better than Donahue," Paul said positively, and Johnny smiled.

"Yes, he is. I wonder if he realises it yet?"

"He hasn't a clue. He's in shock, he's probably still trying to remember his own name and which way to sit his horse. But when he calms down, I'd like to spend a bit of time with young Powell. He's got promise."

"If you're not cashiered, of course," Carl said cheerfully.

"Obviously. I wonder, if they kick him out, do you think they'll give the battalion to me?" Johnny speculated.

"Certainly, in the short term. Major Wheeler sounds good," Carl said. "We could club together and see if we can come up with the purchase price. Are civilians allowed to donate? I've a wealthy friend who used to be in the army, he might be good for a few guineas. Sad story, his, very promising officer but couldn't keep his mouth shut if you paid him to."

"Fuck off, both of you," Paul said.

***

Their laughter carried in the still, warm morning air, and Ensign Evan Powell heard it, and felt his spirits lifting. His company had been subdued, the loss of their officer and one of their men weighing heavily, but he was surprised to realise that, like him, their mood was lightening, and they were beginning to talk again, low voiced conversations about the weather, the road and the prospect of catching rabbits for dinner. Evan supposed that this was how it must be in the army, when men became used to burying friends and comrades, then moving on with no time for grief or extended mourning.

Evan's grief remained, but alongside it, he was aware of a strange feeling of content. He remembered sitting beside Donahue just before the battle, his mind consumed with fear, but it occurred to him now that what he had been feeling was not fear of battle, but fear of fear itself.

That at least had gone. Evan had met fear, had felt it flooding through him, and had discovered that it did not diminish him. He was still afraid of dying, of being wounded or maimed, but he no longer feared that it would freeze him. In the heat of battle, he had discovered that he could live with his terror and still function, and that once engaged, he was not aware of fear at all, only the job at hand. It was a revelation. Evan had thought for a time that this great adventure might be a mistake and that he had not the stomach or the temperament to be a soldier. Those few hours on the banks of the Coa had taught him otherwise.

426

"Powell. Got any rations left?"

Evan reached into his saddle bag and withdrew a cloth wrapped package. "Two biscuits and an apple, sir."

"Chuck the apple over, and I'll pay it back when we stop. My man bagged a couple of pigeons first thing, I'll share them with you."

It felt like a good trade, and Evan threw the apple to Lieutenant Quentin who gave a smile of thanks and beckoned to him to ride up beside him. Evan urged his horse forward and the 110th marched on over the scrub covered plains of Portugal, leaving the bridge over the Coa behind them.

By the Same Author

The Peninsular War Saga

An Unconventional Officer (Book 1)

An Irregular Regiment (Book 2)

An Uncommon Campaign (Book 3)

A Redoubtable Citadel (Book 4)

An Untrustworthy Army (Book 5)

An Unmerciful Incursion (Book 6)

The Manxman Series

An Unwilling Alliance (Book 1)

This Blighted Expedition (Book 2)

Regency Romances

A Regrettable Reputation (Book 1)

The Reluctant Debutante (Book 2)

Other Titles

A Respectable Woman (A novel of Victorian London)

A Marcher Lord (A novel of the Anglo-Scottish Border Reivers)

Printed in Great Britain
by Amazon